An Armada Three-in-One

*Three Great
Nancy Drew Stories*

ARMADA

Nancy Drew Mystery Stories® in Armada

* For contractual reasons, Armada has been obliged to publish from No. 51 onwards before publishing Nos. 47–50. These missing numbers will be published as soon as possible.

Nancy Drew® in

Carolyn Keene

ARMADA

This Armada *Nancy Drew®* *Three-in-One* was
first published in the U.K. in Armada in 1988
by William Collins Sons & Co. Ltd
This impression 1989

Armada is an imprint of
the Children's Division, part of
the Collins Publishing Group,
8 Grafton Street, London W1X 3LA

Published pursuant to agreement with
Grosset and Dunlap, Inc., New York, USA

Printed and bound in Great Britain by
William Collins Sons & Co. Ltd, Glasgow

Nancy Drew® in

The Phantom of Pine Hill

The Phantom of Pine Hill was
first published in the U.K. in a single volume
in 1973 by William Collins Sons & Co. Ltd,
and in Armada in 1981

Contents

"It's the phantom again!" exclaimed Mrs Holman

·1·

Phantom Thefts

NANCY DREW stared incredulously at the motel clerk. "But I made reservations!"

The man shrugged. "Sorry. No vacancy. We're jammed with visitors for Emerson University's June Week."

The two girls with Nancy looked despairingly at their attractive, titian-haired friend. One, George Fayne, dark-haired and boyish, declared, "The motel can't get away with this!"

Blonde, pretty Bess Marvin, George's cousin, asked in a worried tone, "What will we do, Nancy?"

"Here comes our answer—Ned Nickerson!"

A handsome, athletic young man was striding towards them, grinning broadly. He and two fraternity brothers had invited the girls for the long weekend. After greeting Ned, Nancy told him about their reservation problem.

"I'll find rooms for you," Ned assured the girls, "if Nancy wants to solve a mystery while she's here."

"Of course I do!" she exclaimed.

Ned went to a foyer phone booth and dialled a number. After a few minutes' conversation he rejoined the girls, his eyes twinkling.

"I called the uncle of one of our young professors. He lives a short distance out of town in a fine old house on Pine Hill—it's a big place with grounds that run down to the river. He's an elderly bachelor and has a housekeeper."

"Yes. Go on," Nancy urged.

"His name is John Rorick, but everyone calls him Uncle John. He likes young people and we fellows go there often."

Bess spoke up. "We're to stay at his house?"

"Yes. Uncle John was eager to have you girls as guests when I told him Nancy is an amateur detective with two fine assistants. Queer things have been happening out there lately."

Bess looked concerned. "Do you mean we may be getting into something dangerous? Dave invited me up here to have fun."

"That's why Burt asked me," said George. "But what's the mystery?"

Ned whispered, "All you have to do is catch the phantom of Pine Hill!"

"Catch the what?" Bess cried out. "A spook?"

"Uncle John will tell you all about the phantom. I'll phone Burt and Dave and tell them of the change in plans, then drive you to Pine Hill."

The girls' luggage was put back in Nancy's convertible and the group piled in, with Ned at the wheel. They drove through the pretty, tree-shaded little university town which lay at the end of a cove on a tributary of the Ohio River. Presently they turned down a side road and could see the glistening water in the distance.

"Part of the June Week entertainment will be a

pageant in the cove depicting the life of the early settlers in the Ohio Valley," Ned told the girls. "Burt and Dave and I will be in it."

"We'll get front-row seats," Bess said. With a dimpled giggle, she added, "I can't wait to see you boys in costumes. What are you going to wear?"

"That's a secret," Ned replied. "But we'll wow you!" In a few minutes he called out, "Here we are!"

He swung left into a curving driveway and pulled up at the front entrance of the Georgian Colonial house. The door was opened by a tall, white-haired man with bright blue eyes.

"Hello, Ned!" he called. "This is my lucky day. A bevy of beautiful girl detectives!"

Ned introduced them and at once the elderly man said, "Call me Uncle John. And welcome to my home." He stepped aside and his housekeeper appeared. "This is Mrs Holman, my right-hand man!"

"Thank you," the three chorused, laughing, and Nancy added, "It is very kind of you to let us come here. In return I'll try hard to capture your phantom."

She was thinking, "Mrs Holman is so much like our Hannah!" Hannah Gruen, the Drews' housekeeper, had helped Mr Drew, a busy, well-known lawyer, rear Nancy since she was three, when her mother had died. Nancy and Hannah were the closest of confidantes.

The trio's luggage was carried inside. From the moment the girls stepped over the threshold, they felt at home. The large centre hall of oak-panelled side walls and the graceful spiral stairway, all heavily carpeted, lent a welcoming atmosphere.

Nancy noticed, however, that the door to a room at

the left of the hallway had a stout padlock on it. Was this because of the phantom, she wondered.

Ned announced that he had to return to the university. Nancy offered to drive him there, but Ned said that the girls just had time to unpack and dress for the late-afternoon party at his fraternity house.

"I'll catch a bus at the next road. Be seeing you!"

After he had gone, Mrs Holman led the way upstairs to two adjoining rear bedrooms. They had been newly decorated with Colonial-style wallpaper, in keeping with the lovely old four-poster beds and hand-made rugs. Nancy put her bag in the smaller room, then joined her friends and the housekeeper.

"Isn't it charming!" Bess exclaimed.

Nancy hurried to a window and sighed in delight. Below was a garden of roses in a wide expanse of lawn. Behind this stood a large grove of pine trees with the sparkling water beyond.

"That's Settlers' Cove," Mrs Holman explained. "In the 1700's Mr Rorick's ancestors came down the river in a flatboat and landed here. They put their log cabin up on Pine Hill because of the lovely view. Later they built this house."

Crowning the hill across the cove were the sprawling buildings of Emerson University.

"What a marvellous sight!" Nancy exclaimed.

"It used to be beautiful at night, too, when the moon was out," said Mrs Holman. "But now—" As the housekeeper paused, Nancy thought she detected a frightened expression. The girls waited for Mrs Holman to finish the sentence. Finally, with fear in her voice, she burst out, "Now the phantom is seen flitting among the trees like a giant firefly."

"You've seen it?" Nancy asked, intrigued.

"No, but he's there all right. I'll have Mr Rorick tell you the rest. Come down when you're ready." She left the room.

Curious to hear more of the mystery, the girls quickly hung up their dresses and went downstairs. Uncle John Rorick met them at the foot of the stairway and escorted his guests through an open doorway to their left into the living-room. It ran the full depth of the house and was attractively furnished with fine eighteenth-century pieces.

Uncle John motioned his guests to tapestried chairs. Smiling, he said, "I dare say you want to learn about the phantom of Pine Hill. Apparently he wants something in my library. That's the locked room across the hall. The first time I noticed books out of place I made sure the windows were locked and put a padlock on the door. Despite these precautions, the intruder got in and has kept right on entering mysteriously!"

"It certainly sounds weird," George declared. "Do you have any clues?"

"Not one." Uncle John chuckled. "Mrs Holman declares he must be a phantom and come through our walls!"

Nancy asked Mr Rorick if he kept any money in his library. He nodded but said he had never missed any. "I must confess though," Uncle John went on, "I may have overlooked something. I'm pretty forgetful." He added, "It gives me a creepy feeling to know there's a ghostly visitor in my home."

"Oh goodness, yes," Bess agreed. "I hope I never see

this phantom. I'll lock my door and cover my head at night!"

The others laughed and Nancy said, "*I* hope I'll meet this apparition. I'm sure he's a real live person. What we must find out right now is how he enters the library."

"Right now," said Bess, "we'd better dress for the Omega Chi Epsilon party."

Reluctantly Nancy agreed. "But I'll start work on the mystery as soon as possible," she declared.

A short time later the three girls, wearing bright, colourful dresses, drove off to the campus. The fraternity house held a gay, chattering crowd of students and girls, sipping cool drinks and eating varied savouries. Nancy, Bess, and George knew many of the young people from previous parties. They were whisked from group to group by their dates.

Like Ned, Burt Eddleton and Dave Evans were athletic and played in the football team. Burt was husky and blond, while Dave, who had fair hair and green eyes, was rangy.

Presently a thin young man about twenty-five years old, with a slightly sagging jaw and wearing an ill-fitting waiter's coat, came towards the group. He was carrying a tray of lemonade on the palm of one hand, and grinning in a rather silly fashion at the guests. As he reached Nancy the glasses suddenly slid. The waiter tried to save them, but the next moment they showered their contents on to Nancy, then crashed to the floor.

Ned said angrily, "Why don't you watch what you're doing, Fred!"

"I'm sorry," the young man mumbled. He began to gather up the broken glass.

Nancy looked in dismay at her yellow dress, the front now stained and wet. "I'll have to go home and change," she told Ned.

At once he offered to drive her to Pine Hill. When they reached the house, Uncle John and Mrs Holman met them and were annoyed on hearing of the accident.

"Fred Jenkins did it," Ned explained. "He works for you sometimes, doesn't he?"

"Yes," the housekeeper replied. "Fred's clumsy here, too, but I've grown used to him. Can I help you, Nancy?"

"Oh no. Thank you, anyway." She hurried up the stairway, took off her dress, and quickly changed. "I think I'll wear my pearl necklace," Nancy decided, and reached into the pocket of her suitcase for the box. She opened it, then gasped.

The pearl necklace was gone!

Nancy closed her eyes for a moment, refusing to believe the truth. A thought instantly came to her. Had the phantom stolen her jewellery?

She returned the empty box, closed the bag, and slowly went downstairs. Nancy hated to tell Mr Rorick what had happened but felt it her duty to do so in view of the other mysterious happenings at the house. Uncle John, Mrs Holman, and Ned were astounded and immediately Mr Rorick said he would pay for a new necklace.

"That won't be necessary because Dad insured it," Nancy said. "But don't you think the police should be notified?"

"I suppose so. I'll attend to that. You run back to your party."

After Nancy had written out a description of the necklace, she and Ned drove away. He said sympathetically, "You've had a lot more excitement today than you bargained for!"

She smiled. "I loved it—except about my necklace."

After the fraternity party was over, Nancy's friends went to a country restaurant to have dinner and dance. It was midnight by the time the three girls reached home and tumbled into bed.

Nancy fell asleep immediately, but later a creaking sound awakened her.

"Someone's walking around downstairs," she thought, and in an instant was out of bed, thrusting her arms into a dressing-gown.

Nancy tiptoed into the dark hall and looked down the spiral stairway. At first there was only silence, then suddenly a door squeaked. In a few moments a shadow moved through the hall past the front windows. Then it disappeared.

The young sleuth pondered for several seconds on what to do. Should she wake up the others in the house? But this would alert the intruder, she knew, and he would escape.

"I'd better go alone and learn what I can!" Nancy decided, and cautiously started down the stairs.

·2·

The Shipwreck

WHEN Nancy reached the ground floor she stood motionless. There was not a sound. Was someone watching her? She felt a chill race down her spine.

Then softly a door closed. From the location of the sound she judged it to be the outside kitchen door. Her eyes completely adjusted to the dimness, Nancy tiptoed round the staircase to an open door which led into the kitchen.

Through a window Nancy had a clear view of the moonlit garden and lawn. No one was hurrying away. Was she too late to see the intruder? And where had he gone?

Just then Nancy noticed a tiny light bobbing in the grove of pine trees, and recalled Mrs Holman's remarks about the phantom. "I wonder if he's the person who was in the house," Nancy thought, "or was it someone else?"

She overcame a desire to go outside and investigate. Although brave, the young detective tried not to take unnecessary chances. Nevertheless, from her first case, *The Secret of Shadow Ranch* to her most recent, *Nancy's Mysterious Letter*, she had often met danger while sleuthing.

After making sure the intruder had not unlatched the rear and front doors or any windows, Nancy went back to bed. Despite her interrupted sleep, she was the first one awake in the morning. After bathing and dressing, she hurried downstairs to examine the house for clues to the intruder.

The padlock on the library door was still in place. "He certainly couldn't have gone in there," Nancy thought. "Since he didn't pass me near the staircase, he couldn't have doubled back into the kitchen."

Only one door remained—the open one to the left at the rear of the hall. Nancy walked through the doorway into a charming, completely pine-panelled dining-room. The big mahogany table in the centre was flanked with graceful chairs. Fine old porcelain pieces lined the plate rail.

On the wall adjoining the library was a large brick fireplace with a mantelshelf. Candles in brass holders stood at each end of it.

An open door on the opposite wall led into a butler's pantry, and from there Nancy stepped into the kitchen. "I'm sure this was the phantom's route," she thought. "Maybe I scared him off!"

At that moment Mrs Holman came into the kitchen. When she heard about the intruder, the housekeeper became upset. "It's dreadful—the goings-on here! But I can't make the police believe anything's wrong. I sometimes think they suspect me!"

"Oh, I'm sure they don't," Nancy said reassuringly.

As Mrs Holman started to prepare breakfast, Nancy said she wanted to check something, then would be right back to help. She hurried to the fireplace in the dining-room, leaned down, and tapped its sooty brick walls. Nancy hoped to detect a hollow area that might mean a secret entrance to the library, but found nothing.

Just as she and Mrs Holman had breakfast ready, Mr Rorick, Bess, and George came downstairs. The elderly man was dressed for travelling and told the girls he was leaving for a class reunion at his college several hundred miles away.

He chuckled. "I expect you to have my mystery solved by the time I get back," he said.

"I hope I can," Nancy answered.

After they sat down at the table, Nancy told the others what had happened the night before. They were astounded and Uncle John remarked, "It may have been a real burglar instead of our phantom."

"I don't think so," Mrs Holman spoke up. "None of the silver is missing. I checked when I set the table."

Bess dug a spoon into her grapefruit. "I don't know which is worse—burglars or spooks. I just hope both of them leave me alone!"

When the group finished breakfast, Mr Rorick said he would give the key to the library padlock to Mrs Holman so his "girl detective force" could investigate at any time.

"Thank you," said Nancy.

"Before I go, would you be interested in hearing a little of the Rorick family history?" he asked.

"Yes, indeed. It's just possible there might be some connection between that and your phantom," Nancy suggested.

"Hmm," said Uncle John. "I never thought of that.

You may be right. Perhaps it has something to do with the lost gifts."

The girls listened intently as he went on, "When my ancestor, George Rorick, came to this country he brought a French bride with him—a young noblewoman. She kept in close touch with her family, and when her daughter Abigail was to be married, the relatives in France sent a chest of wedding gifts. But the steamship it came on had an explosion aboard and sank in the river not far from Settlers' Cove. A short time before, a letter and a key came to Abigail from her uncle in France. I still have the key hidden away. The letter is hanging on the wall. I'll get it."

He excused himself and went to the library, but returned in a minute with a framed letter. It was dated 1835, and was written in French in an old-fashioned, precise script. Many of the words were no longer in use.

Uncle John turned the frame over. Pasted on the back was an English translation. The very gracious letter said the writer's family sent felicitations and wished the bride-to-be and her husband great happiness. A chest containing presents—a wedding dress, veil, fan, slippers, and a very special gift—was being shipped on a freighter but should reach Miss Abigail Rorick in plenty of time.

"How exciting!" said Bess.

Nancy was still reading. Abigail's uncle was at the time a member of the court of Louis Phillipe. The queen herself had selected the material for the gown and veil in Paris. The beautiful fan was a gift from her.

"They must have been lovely," Nancy said softly.

George asked, "What was the family's other gift to Abigail?"

"No one knows, but I'm sure it was valuable," Uncle John answered. "The report was that when the *Lucy Belle* sank, most of those aboard and the cargo were lost. A few of the passengers and crew were saved, but probably took only some personal possessions ashore— if any. We don't know if the gifts went down or not. And in those days no one could dive deep enough to retrieve cargo. By now the lighter pieces would have shifted and been buried in mud."

"But it is possible that in recent times scuba divers may have removed the cargo," Nancy remarked.

Mr Rorick smiled. "I doubt it. The story of the *Lucy Belle* has long since been forgotten."

Nancy asked thoughtfully, "Where did the people who were saved go, Uncle John?"

"I don't know. Maybe some of the old books in my library will tell you. There are many I've never read."

Bess asked if the *Lucy Belle* had come directly from France. Mr Rorick shook his head. "The gifts were shipped across the Atlantic to Baltimore. Then they came overland by stagecoach to Pittsburgh. There they were put on the *Lucy Belle* and came up the Ohio and into this tributary. Abigail received notice of this."

Uncle John took the old letter back to the library, then went for his suitcase. Within minutes he was in his car, waving farewell and wishing the girls luck.

But there was one more delay before Nancy could start investigating the library. A young detective arrived to take Nancy's fingerprints, since she had been out the night before when he came to investigate the case of the missing necklace.

After he had gone, Mrs Holman unfastened the padlocked door and the girls went in. Like the living-room, the library extended from the front of the house to the back.

"Oh," said Bess, "I've never seen so many books in one room. There must be thousands of them!"

Every wall was lined with shelves from floor to ceiling and filled with double rows of books. Many of the volumes looked old and fragile. A quick survey indicated a wide variety of subjects.

There were two windows on each of the outside walls, all of them securely locked. The fireplace was a duplicate of the one in the dining-room and was back to back with it.

Nancy again wondered if there were a passage between them. Then she noted the undisturbed ashes and bits of charred wood.

"If there's a secret opening," Nancy reasoned, "the phantom hasn't used it." Nevertheless, she tested the brick facing, but found no sign of a hidden entrance.

Next, Nancy studied the layout of the room. It contained a large desk which stood in the centre, several small Oriental rugs, and a safe under one front window. A long red-leather couch and matching chairs were scattered about.

"Pretty cosy place to browse," George remarked. "Well, Nancy, where do we start hunting for the phantom?"

"I suggest you begin looking through the books for a clue to why the phantom is interested in this room. Mrs

Holman, will you see if anything is missing? Bess, help me roll up these rugs. There may be a trap door underneath."

Presently the housekeeper reported that nothing was gone so far as she knew. Nancy and Bess did not discover a trap door, and relaid the rugs. Mrs Holman was about to leave the room, when George suddenly cried out:

"Wow! Guess what I've found!"

·3·

Photo Finish

As Mrs Holman, Bess, and Nancy hurried across the library, George held out an open book. In it was a sizeable heap of bills.

"My goodness!" the housekeeper exclaimed. "Did you find all that money in the book?"

George nodded. "I noticed the volume was standing upside down. When I took it out to turn it round, this is what I found."

Quickly Mrs Holman counted. "A hundred and fifty dollars!" she exclaimed.

Nancy, her eyes on the open page, noticed that the number was 150. She brought this to the attention of the others. As the money was returned and the book closed, they all read the title. It was *The Roaring Twenties*.

Nancy chuckled. "I'll bet Uncle John hides his money this way. The word *roar*—or *roaring*—may help him recall the book because of his name Rorick."

The housekeeper suggested that they check on Nancy's theory and everyone began searching. They noticed a number of books with *roar* in the title on the shelves to the left of the fireplace. "Uncle John keeps them all in this section, I'll bet," said Nancy.

"Look here!" said Bess, holding out a volume.

The title of it was *The Roaring River*, and on page 200 were ten crisp twenty-dollar bills! In a moment George came upon *The Roar of the Wilderness*. On page 50 lay a fifty-dollar bill.

There was no question now in anyone's mind but that Uncle John used this method to hide money. Had the phantom somehow found this out? And had he been removing bills?

"But," Mrs Holman said, "that still doesn't explain how he gets into this room. Well," she added, "I'll leave that to you girls and go back to my chores."

After she left, they continued their investigation and found several more books with the word *roar* in the title. The total amount of money they had uncovered was over a thousand dollars!

Bess sighed. "This is the most unique bank I've ever been in—not that I've been in many. I'm afraid my allowance and the money I've earned don't find their way to a bank account!"

"Shame on you, Cousin Bess," said George with mock severity.

A clock on Mr Rorick's desk chimed eleven. "We'd better go and dress," said Bess. "We're due at the Omega House at twelve."

"That's right," Nancy agreed. "And the crew race won't wait for us."

During the afternoon there was to be the final race of the season. Emerson would be pitted against Wellbart. Ned Nickerson was stroke for Emerson. Since each crew had already won six races, the competition was high.

Nancy padlocked the library door, returned the key, and the girls went to dress. They put on simple but attractive casual dresses, then set off in Nancy's car for the fraternity house. They found it filled with an excited crowd. Everyone was rooting for Emerson to win and the din was deafening.

Ned said to Nancy, "If I don't get out of this noise, I won't have any energy left for the race. Let's go out under the trees to eat. I'll get a couple of plates of food from the kitchen."

He led Nancy outside to a large oak some distance from the fraternity house, then went back. A few minutes later he returned with two paper plates heaped with food. Grinning, he said, "I won't dare eat much of this or I'll sink the shell!"

Nancy laughed and Ned asked, "Have you caught the spook yet?"

"I almost did," Nancy answered, and told him about the episode of the previous night.

She was about to mention the hunt in the library when a wasp landed in the midst of her food. As she jumped up to flick it away, she caught sight of Fred Jenkins standing behind the oak tree.

Ned, too, saw him. "What are you doing here?" Ned demanded.

Fred's face turned red and he stammered, "I—I was just coming to see if I could bring you anything else."

"If we want more food we'll get it," Ned told him. "You're supposed to be serving in the house. Hadn't you getter get back on the job?"

After Fred had gone, Nancy remarked, "He certainly acted guilty of eavesdropping. Since he works for Mr

Rorick, do you suppose he knows something about the mystery?"

Ned grinned. "If he didn't, he does now. Probably he heard every word you said. I only hope he won't go telling it all over town."

Glancing at his wrist watch, Ned said that it was time for him to change for the race. Then he escorted Nancy back to the fraternity house. "Remember, your seats are in the front row. I'll be listening for your cheering!"

Shortly before two o'clock the five young people found their places on the shore front below the college buildings. A band was playing a lively tune. Emerson and Wellbart banners were being waved.

Bess was chalk-white. "I'm so nervous," she said, then explained to Dave, "I always get nervous at races."

"To tell you the truth, I don't feel so calm myself," said Dave. "The Wellbart crew is mighty good."

Minutes later, the announcement of the race was made. Nancy could feel herself tensing up and held on tightly to the sides of her chair. A pistol sounded. The contestants were off!

Everyone stood up to watch the two crews. They were neck and neck as they sped across the river. Then one shell shot in front.

"Oh dear, Wellbart's ahead!" Bess said dolefully.

The words were hardly out of her mouth when the Emerson crew pulled forward. "Emerson's going to win!" cried George.

As the two shells entered the cove, the Wellbart crew caught up and rowed nearly half a boat length beyond their opponent.

"Ned! Ned! Come on!" shouted Nancy.

Emerson did catch up, and with the coxswain working his men hard, his crew pulled ahead ever so slightly. Nancy and her friends felt encouraged and screamed at the top of their voices.

Wellbart backers were equally excited. "Don't let 'em win!" cried one youth, waving a banner wildly. "Show 'em what you've got!"

The next moment the two shells were exactly even. The screaming and rooting increased.

"Oh, Ned!" Nancy cried out. "Get ahead! Get ahead!"

Both shells were nearing the finish line now. Still they looked as if they were even. The two coxswains, moving forward and backward in a frantically fast rhythm, were shouting snappy orders.

Nancy's heart was thumping madly. The excited girl was almost too choked to breathe and cry out any more. She dug her nails into the palms of her hands and never took her eyes off Ned. To herself she said, "Stroke! Stroke! You've got to win!"

Suddenly both shells slid across the finishing line. Instantly people began to call out, "Who won?"

"It's a photo finish!" Dave cried out. "We won't know for a few minutes."

A sudden hush had come over the crowd as everyone waited for the result. The heaving men in the shells sat quiet and tense, their paddles raised.

Presently the head judge stepped to the microphone. He smiled. "I know you are all eagerly awaiting the results so I will not prolong my speech except to say that personally I have never seen a better race. I congratulate every man on his good sportsmanship and fine performance. The result according to the high-speed camera shows that the winner—is Emerson University!"

"Yea! Yea!" a shout went up, then the Emerson rooters gave the college yell. The Wellbart men gave theirs, ending it with, "Emerson! EMERSON! EMERSON!"

The crew saluted with their paddles, then rowed to their boathouse.

"I've never seen anything so exciting in my life!" said Bess. "I'm exhausted!"

After a round of hugs and enthusiastic chatter, the five young people sat down to await Ned. He came in about half an hour and received excited congratulations from his friends.

"Thanks," he said. "That race sure was a tough one. To tell you the truth, I thought we had lost." He grinned. "I'm all in favour of high-speed cameras!"

After the excitement had died down, he asked Nancy if she would go out with him in a canoe. "Oh, I'd love to," she replied. "Let's visit the area where the *Lucy Belle* is supposed to have sunk."

They said goodbye to the other two couples and went to the boathouse. Nancy offered to paddle, but Ned only laughed, saying this would be an easy task after the gruelling race. He started across the large cove and then hugged the shore line on the opposite side.

"After talking with you about the *Lucy Belle* last night, Nancy, I recalled something that happened in our college library a couple of weeks ago. I noticed two men—I'm sure they didn't belong to the university—standing behind one of the stacks of books. At first I paid no attention to them, but when one of them, who had a deep, hoarse voice, mentioned 'the Rorick treasure,' I listened. Then they left."

Nancy was interested at once. "I wonder who they were. Did you see them?"

"Sorry. I didn't. But I did notice a book on the table which I'm sure they were looking at. It was a history of early Ohio River boats."

"They must have been looking up the *Lucy Belle*," said Nancy. "Ned, if you ever happen to see those men again, try to find out who they are."

Ned smiled. "At your service, Miss Detective."

She now told him about Abigail Rorick's wedding chest. "Maybe those men believe it is not lost! They might even think it was buried, and be hunting for it in the woods behind Uncle John's house! That would explain the phantom's light."

"Could be," Ned replied.

"I wish I knew more about the sinking of the *Lucy Belle*," Nancy said.

"I don't know anything about the boat, but I can tell you a few stories about the history of this area that might give you a clue. Would you like Professor Nickerson to lecture?" he asked, a twinkle in his eye.

"Please do," Nancy begged.

" 'Way back in 1807 the inhabitants of the Ohio Valley found it difficult to get cash. Silver dollars were scarce and the practice grew of dividing them into eight equal wedge-shaped pieces. These fractions got the nickname of bits and from this came the phrase "two bits," meaning one-quarter or two-eighths of a dollar!"

Nancy smiled. "I've always wondered when I hear

people mention 'two bits' where the name came from. Tell me another bit of history."

Ned said that Ohio River ports were stations for prospectors on their way to California during the Gold Rush of 1849. This was where they stocked up with provisions, including salt.

"Did you know that the first mineral product of the Ohio Valley was salt?" Ned asked. When Nancy shook her head, he went on, "As you know, salt has been an essential food for man and animal since the beginning of time. In prehistoric days salt attracted not only human inhabitants to this area, but also animals like the giant sloth, the mammoth elk, deer, and buffalo."

"That's fascinating," said Nancy. "Don't stop."

"Professor will relate one more story and that's the end of his knowledge." Nancy giggled and Ned went on, "The Indians here were frightened that the white men would take away all their territory, so they raided and burned settlements. It was not until the American Army took over that the raids were stopped, around 1794."

By this time Ned was nearing Pine Hill. Nancy happened to look up the high embankment at the woods which ran to the Rorick garden. Suddenly she caught a flash of sunlight on glass.

"Ned," she said, "somebody is watching us with binoculars! See him up there among the trees?"

Ned turned to look, resting his paddle. "You think that's your phantom?" he asked.

Nancy shrugged as they squinted into the afternoon sun, trying to see what the man looked like.

Both she and Ned had heard the sound of a motorboat

but had paid no attention. Suddenly they realized it was very close to them. The two turned and were horrified to see the craft bearing down on them.

Ned dug his paddle into the water and tried to get out of the way as Nancy shouted and waved her arms to the pilot of the motorboat. But the man, crouched low behind the wheel so that his face could not be seen, paid no attention.

A moment later he crashed into the side of the canoe. It shot out of the water and capsized, tossing Nancy and Ned overboard!

· 4 ·

Mysterious Thumbprints

SMACK! Nancy and Ned hit the water and disappeared beneath the surface for a few seconds. Then both clawed their way to the top.

"You okay?" they asked in unison.

Each nodded but declared that they certainly had had a fright.

They swam towards the overturned canoe which was badly scraped on one side. The paddle Ned had been using was smashed and the extra one that had been in the bottom of the canoe had floated away.

"What a mess!" Ned said in disgust.

Treading water, the couple talked over what to do. Since they were close to shore, they decided to swim in and tow the canoe. Then they would climb the embankment and trek through the woods to the Rorick home for dry clothes.

"Do you think that pilot hit us on purpose?" Ned asked as he beached the canoe on the gravelly shore. "You were facing him. What did he look like?"

Nancy said she had been unable to see his face. "Maybe he was just a bad pilot," she added.

Ned shook his head doubtfully as he and Nancy began to climb the bluff. Upon reaching the woods, both looked left and right for a sign of the man who had been spying on them. No one was in sight.

"That guy with the binoculars certainly took my mind off my job," Ned said ruefully. "When I first heard that motorboat I should have paddled out of the way."

Nancy said thoughtfully, "I can't figure out why that pilot didn't see us."

"Meaning that you think he meant to run us down," said Ned. "You're coming around to my point of view." He grinned.

Nancy made a wry face but did not answer. It was cool in the woods and she began to feel cold and clammy in her soaking wet clothes.

"Let's hurry!" she urged, and started off at a jog. Ned followed.

Mrs Holman answered their ring at the back door and looked at the couple aghast. "What in the world have you been doing?" she asked.

Quickly Nancy explained and the woman's face took on a worried look. At once she had a solution. "That phantom was watching in the woods and he has a confederate with a motorboat!"

"Maybe," Nancy said, shivering.

The housekeeper became solicitous. She told the young detective to go up and change. Mrs Holman herself would find some of Mr Rorick's clothes for Ned to wear. "Follow me," she directed.

As Nancy paused at her own bedroom, she said, "Mrs Holman, have you a paddle here?"

The housekeeper nodded, saying that there were several in the cellar and Ned could help himself.

"I'll walk back to the shore with you, Ned," said Nancy. "I'd like to look for clues to the person who was spying on us."

In a few minutes the two young people were ready. Nancy had put on slacks and a shirt.

She tried hard to keep from smiling as she looked at Ned. Mr Rorick certainly went in for colourful clothes! She knew that Ned would be the victim of a lot of teasing when he reached the fraternity house, so she refrained from any of her own.

The couple walked through the woods slowly, keeping their eyes alert for footprints or any other clues to the man who had been watching them, but saw none.

"If that was the phantom he has winged feet," Ned said finally, as he started down the embankment. "Be careful on your way back. I need you for the dance tonight. Burt and Dave and I will pick you girls up at seven."

After he had paddled off, Nancy studied the edge of the embankment.

"Let's see. That spy was standing over near those birches." From the water she had noticed a clump of white birch next to the pine trees which the man was using for a shield. She went to the spot and picked up his footprints. The short spaces between the small-sized shoe marks indicated that he was a slight man of medium height.

The prints led along the top of the bluff for a short distance, then went down through thick bushes to the water. Nancy guessed the man had been hiding among the brush until the couple had left the area.

"Someone must have met him in a boat, unless he

had one hidden among the bushes and Ned and I didn't see it."

The young sleuth retraced her steps up the embankment, looking for further clues. She saw nothing and with a sigh headed for the house.

The shadows were long as Nancy hurried through the woods. Suddenly she stopped short. Floating down towards her, seemingly out of nowhere, was a small white paper. As it fell almost at her feet, she looked up in the trees to see where it had come from. There was no person, bird, or animal in sight.

"I could almost believe there *is* a phantom in these woods," Nancy murmured to herself as she stooped to pick up the piece of paper.

Her eyes grew wide in astonishment. On the paper were two large, very black, well-defined thumbprints!

For several seconds Nancy did not move. There had been a few times in her life when she had been utterly confounded by some event which seemed to hold no explanation except a supernatural one. This was one of those times. But presently she shook off the mood, telling herself this was nonsense. Someone had put those prints on the paper. But where and why? And how had it come to float down to her? Were these the phantom's thumbprints?

Nancy took a handkerchief from her pocket and carefully wrapped the paper in it. Holding it in her hand, she continued to walk towards the house, hoping to find someone on the way. But there was not a sound in the grove.

When she reached the house she found Bess and George in the kitchen with Mrs Holman. The housekeeper had just finished telling them what had happened to Nancy and Ned.

George looked at Nancy. "Gosh!" she said. "We let you out of our sight for two hours and *whamo*!"

Nancy laughed. "Wait until I show you something else," she said, and opened the handkerchief.

Bess gave a little cry. "That's creepy! Where did it come from?"

Nancy told the girls and Mrs Holman. George insisted that someone was playing a trick on Nancy, but Bess and the housekeeper were worried.

"This is a bad omen, Nancy," Mrs Holman remarked. "I don't know how much more I can stand of this phantom!"

Nancy put an arm round the woman. "Please don't worry. We'll get to the bottom of this yet."

"All right," the housekeeper conceded. "I'll try to keep calm. But my dear, be careful."

After Nancy promised, George said, "Come on now, girls. Time to make ourselves beautiful!"

"This is really dress-up night," Bess remarked as they hurried to their rooms. "The dance is going to be a honey, I know. Dave was telling me about decorating the gym."

As usual, Bess had chosen a flowing dress with a full skirt, while George's choice was quite simple and fitted her boyish figure admirably. Nancy was wearing a yellow evening gown, embroidered in white with birds and flowers. It had a fitted top with an A-line skirt. She secretly hoped that Ned would like it. He had never seen it.

Nancy was a quick dresser and was ready before the

other girls. She called into their room, "See you downstairs. I'm going to a little sleuthing while I'm waiting for you."

As she came down the stairs, Fred Jenkins walked across the hall from the living-room. He stared at her in complete astonishment and admiration.

"M-Miss Nancy, you look positively—super!" As Fred spoke he let a vase of flowers he was carrying crash to the floor. He looked down in dismay. "See what you made me do! You shouldn't be so beautiful! You take my mind off my work!"

Nancy wanted to smile. Instead, she said, "I'm terribly sorry."

Just then Mrs Holman came bustling from the kitchen. She took in the scene at a glance.

"Oh, Fred," she said angrily, "that was one of Mr Rorick's favourite vases."

Fred Jenkins said, "I couldn't help it."

"Well, don't just stand there," Mrs Holman said. "Go get the dustpan and broom and a clean cloth to wipe up this mess."

Nancy came on down the stairs and Mrs Holman beckoned her to come into the dining-room. "You mustn't mind Fred," she said. "He just can't seem to hold on to things. I keep him because it's hard to get help and he's the soul of honesty."

Nancy, recalling his standing behind the tree while she and Ned were talking, asked, "Does he know about the phantom?"

"I'm sure he doesn't," Mrs Holman replied, "or he'd never work here. He'd be too scared!" She smiled broadly and winked at Nancy.

Quietly Nancy told the housekeeper she was about to do some sleuthing. Just then Fred appeared in the doorway to report that he had swept up the broken vase, picked up the flowers, and mopped the floor. Now, he said, he must leave.

After he had gone, Nancy went to look at the wall on either side of the library door. Was one of the panels a secret entrance to the room? She stepped close to tap for a hollow sound.

· 5 ·

Two Spies

As Nancy went from panel to panel of the hall, tapping each one and listening carefully, Mrs Holman came to her side. "I've never seen a sleuth at work," she said with a smile. "Show me how to do it."

Nancy illustrated by laying her head against the wood and tapping softly with her fingers. As she finished "listening" to the woodwork on either side of the fireplace, Nancy sighed. "I'm sorry not to be able to show you what I mean. These walls are solid."

Nancy glanced at her watch. There was still plenty of time for some investigating before the girls would have to leave for the Omega House.

"Mrs Holman, would you mind unlocking the door to the library? I'd like to tap the walls there."

The housekeeper went for the key and inserted it into the padlock. As the two entered the room, Mrs Holman looked around uneasily, but nothing had been disturbed.

Nancy smiled. "Now," she said, "maybe I can show you what I mean."

After a few minutes of work, she reported there were no hollow-sounding panels.

The housekeeper frowned. "Then there's only one

answer to the phantom getting in here. He *must* be a spook and come through the walls!"

Nancy knew there was no point in contradicting Mrs Holman, but she was amazed that this intelligent person could possibly believe what she had just said. On a sudden hunch Nancy went to look at the book titled *The Roaring Twenties*. As she opened it, the young detective looked grim.

There were now only one hundred and forty dollars instead of one hundred and fifty. Moreover, the bills had been moved to page 140!

A thought which had been building up in Nancy's mind now became even more disturbing. The only person with a key to the padlock was Mrs Holman herself! Was it possible that the housekeeper had invented the story of the phantom to cover up thefts of her own?

"I just don't want to believe such a thing!" Nancy told herself. "But I'm trying to solve this mystery for Mr Rorick. I mustn't get soft-hearted and miss a clue."

Hiding her feelings, she walked out of the library. After Mrs Holman had locked it, Nancy said, "Would you do me a big favour?"

The housekeeper smiled. "I'll be glad to if it's not too difficult."

Nancy had decided to put Mrs Holman to a test of honesty. "Oh, it's a very simple request. I'd like to borrow this key for tonight. After I get home from the dance, I may want to hide in the library and watch for the phantom."

Mrs Holman looked startled. "Do you think that's safe?" she asked.

"Oh, I'll keep well hidden," Nancy replied.

Mrs Holman handed over the key. "Good luck. I'd certainly like to see this house rid of that spooky creature. He makes me so nervous!"

Nancy smiled, then started back upstairs to hide the key in her bedroom. "After we return from the dance," she thought, "I'll investigate the books with the money in them. If any more has been taken—or there's other evidence that someone has been in the room during the evening—it'll make Mrs Holman's guilt unlikely. Of course," Nancy admitted to herself, "there's the possibility that she has another key—"

Just then the telephone rang. Nancy paused for a moment on the stairway to see if the call were for her. Mrs Holman answered and almost instantly said, "Oh no! Y-yes, I'll come at once."

As the housekeeper put down the phone, Nancy asked, "Is something wrong?"

"My niece—Jill Ball—was in an accident. She's in the hospital. Her husband wants me to come to his house tonight and take care of the children. Do you think you girls will be safe here alone? Oh, I hope the phantom—"

Nancy expressed her sympathy and said the girls would be all right. Mrs Holman gave Nancy the front door key. Within a few minutes a taxi came for the housekeeper and she left.

Bess and George were ready by this time and in a few minutes the boys arrived in a big car which they had hired for the evening. They drove to the Omega House, where the dinner party was being held. Finally the couples began to leave for the university gymnasium. Nancy, Bess, George, and their escorts walked over together.

As they entered the big building, Bess gasped. "What marvellous decorations!" she exclaimed. "How in the world could you boys ever think up anything so artistic?"

Their three escorts pretended to be hurt. Dave remarked, "What makes you girls think you have a corner on the artistic market?"

The apparatus in the gym had been entirely concealed with garlands of artificial roses. The centre of the floor had been left free for dancing. Tables holding six to twelve had been arranged around four sides, with each two tables screened by latticework which was also festooned with roses.

"Your decorating committee deserves a big cheer," said Nancy. "I've never been to a dance with such pretty arrangements."

The boys grinned. "Ladies," said Burt, "on behalf of Mr Nickerson, Mr Eddleton, and myself, I thank you."

"Our achievement was nothing," Ned declared. "It was only great."

Before the laughing girls could retort, there was a roll on a drum—the official announcement that the party had started. For nearly an hour, as broiled chicken, mashed potatoes, fresh peas, salad, and ice cream and cake were served, there was continuous laughter and joking.

Finally Bess remarked, "Please don't anyone else be funny. I've laughed so much I hurt all over."

"Tell you what," said Dave, who was far from ready

to be serious, "we'll take you to the infirmary and give you some laughing gas. Then it won't hurt when some-one pulls a joke."

Later, as Nancy was dancing with Ned, she told him of her early-evening sleuthing, of the missing money, and her plan to make a search when she reached home.

Ned said quickly, "I can't believe that Mrs Holman is guilty."

"I don't either," Nancy replied, "but you'll admit that I must try to find out. There is a possibility that she might even have had a confederate phone this evening to throw us off the scent."

Nancy went on to say that if the money had not been touched, she planned to spend the balance of the night hiding in the library to see if anyone entered it.

Ned looked worried. "Nancy, I don't want you to do that alone. It's too dangerous. How about letting me keep watch with you? If the phantom comes, I'll give him the old football rush!"

Nancy hesitated before answering, but finally said, "Bess and George may be hurt if I don't ask them."

"Don't worry about that," said Ned. "I'll talk to them."

The dance number ended, and as they went back to the table, Ned called Bess and George aside and explained what he proposed.

"It's a good idea," said Bess. "I'll feel safer with a man in the house. And no sleuthing for me tonight. I'm too tired."

George liked the plan, but Nancy thought she detected a gleam of mischief in her friend's eye.

"I'd better watch my step," Nancy thought. "George has some trick up her sleeve, I'm sure."

It was in the small hours of the morning that the dance ended and the six young people finally returned to the Rorick home. Bess suggested that they have a snack in the kitchen and in a short time she was scrambling eggs and making toast and a huge pot of cocoa.

When they finished eating, Dave threw out his arms and yawned. "I'm ready to call it quits. Any extra beds in this old house?"

George said quickly, "I'm afraid not, but how about the floor? That's free!"

"Gosh, but you're hospitable," said Burt. "Just for that I won't help wash the dishes."

A few minutes later Burt and Dave drove off. The others tidied the kitchen, then Bess and George went upstairs.

Nancy opened the padlock on the library door, and she and Ned went inside. Before turning on the lights, she drew the draperies close together so no one could look in to see the searchers. This done, she went for the book *The Roaring Twenties*. To her relief, the hundred and forty dollars was still on page 140.

Next, she went to the volume *The Roaring River*. A twenty-dollar bill was gone and the balance of the bills had been placed twenty pages lower. Nancy quickly picked out book after book with the word *roar* in the title. Ten dollars had been taken from each of them and the bills shifted to a page which corresponded to the remaining amount!

"The phantom has been here!" Nancy exclaimed.

Ned frowned. "I think the rest of the money should be removed from this room and put in the bank. It's certainly not safe here!"

Nancy agreed. Then Ned asked her if she had any theories as to who the phantom could be. "Surely not Mrs Holman?"

"Probably not, but to make sure she wasn't faking, I'm going to call the hospital," Nancy said.

She learned that Jill Ball was indeed a patient there. Her frantic husband was by her bedside, but the head nurse was very reassuring. Their children were being cared for by an aunt.

"That completely exonerates Mrs Holman," Nancy told Ned in relief as she came into the library and closed the door. "As far as a solution to the mystery goes, I'm right back where I started."

"Well, I guess there's no use in our staying here any longer. I'm sure the phantom won't come back again tonight."

As the couple gathered all the money and made notations on a pad of the amount taken from each book, Ned produced a theory. "Didn't it ever occur to you that Uncle John might be more than just forgetful?"

"What do you mean?" Nancy asked.

"I mean," Ned replied, "that Uncle John might be having a little fun at the expense of you girls. He probably has a duplicate key to this padlock."

The young sleuth was astounded by the remark. "Uncle John?" she said. "I can't believe it! He didn't know until you telephoned him that we were coming here. According to Mrs Holman, the mysterious happenings had been going on for a couple of weeks before that."

Ned said it was possible Uncle John was having fun at Mrs Holman's expense.

A determined look came over Nancy's face. "There's an easy way to learn if he came here tonight," she said. "Tomorrow morning I'll find a pretence for phoning Uncle John at his college reunion, and find out where he was tonight."

Nancy asked Ned to put the roll of money into his pocket. Then the lamps were turned off and the draperies opened. As Nancy pulled aside one to a rear window, she cried, "The light! See it out there in the woods!"

Ned could detect a small moving light among the trees near the river. "So that's the phantom," he remarked.

"Come on! Let's investigate!" Nancy urged.

As they hurried towards the door, they heard a low moaning sound.

"Stand back!" Ned ordered Nancy.

He whipped open the door and stepped into the hall. The next second a hood was thrown over his head and he was borne to the floor!

·6·

A Revengeful Spook

WHEN Nancy heard Ned's muffled cry, she rushed into the hall. It was dimly lighted by a lamp on the first-floor hall. She could see no one but struggling Ned. Quickly she pulled the hood off him, then snapped on the switch to the ceiling light. She found herself holding a pillowcase!

She returned to Ned, who was on his feet now. Suddenly he thought of the money. He ran his hand into his trousers' pocket. The roll of bills was still there!

He said to Nancy, "Anyway, my attacker didn't intend to rob me—unless he had no time, with you arriving on the scene so soon."

Nancy was already hunting around the floor for evidence. Suddenly the young sleuth giggled as she came across a pale-blue ribbon sash. She picked it up and walked close to Ned.

"This is from Bess's robe!" she whispered. "She and George pulled this trick!"

The couple searched and found the two culprits hiding in the dining-room.

"Okay, girls," said Ned. "You just wait! When I tackle you with a pillowcase some day, it'll be full of feathers!"

Before locking the door to the library, Nancy looked out the back window again. The light in the woods was gone.

"I was afraid of that," she said. "George Fayne, you and Bess made me miss my chance to go after the phantom."

The two girls said they were sorry and Nancy remarked that she would keep her eyes open for another opportunity. The group went upstairs and Ned was shown into Mr Rorick's bedroom.

"Thanks. And, by the way, I'll probably leave here before you girls are up. Everyone in the pageant is due for an early-morning rehearsal."

"But where will you have breakfast?" Bess asked solicitously.

"Oh, I'll grab a bite at the fraternity house." Ned took the roll of notes from his pocket. "Nancy, I'd better leave this money with you. I think you should ask Mr Rorick's or Mrs Holman's permission to remove it from the house."

Nancy agreed. The following morning Mrs Holman returned just before breakfast. She reported her niece was out of danger and that the young woman's mother had arrived to take care of the children.

"I'm glad to hear Mrs Ball is better," Nancy said. Then she told Mrs Holman about her discovery that money was missing. The woman said she would feel better if it were in safe keeping.

"Would it be possible for you to call Uncle John at his college reunion and ask him about it?" Nancy queried.

"That's a good idea," the housekeeper agreed. "I'll do it right now before he goes out."

She hurried to the telephone in the hall. When she reached her employer, she beckoned Nancy to come and talk with Mr Rorick. Laughingly, the young detective asked if he had enjoyed himself the previous evening and he went into a long explanation of the party for the old-timers at his fraternity house. Nancy was satisfied that he was really there.

She thought, "He's definitely not the phantom."

When Nancy told him that the girls had discovered the money in the books and that it was being stolen, he became alarmed. "You must catch that phantom thief!" he said.

"I'm doing my best, but it may take a while," Nancy answered. "In the meantime, may I have your permission to put the money in a safe place—your bank for instance?"

"Suppose you take it to the college bursar."

"Fine, I'll do it right away," Nancy promised.

Twenty minutes later the three girls drove up to the administration building on the campus. Nancy found the bursar to be a very understanding man and a great friend of Mr Rorick. "I'll mark this money with John's name and keep it in the safe," he said.

Nancy thanked the bursar. She got a receipt and left his office.

As she rejoined Bess and George at the car, Nancy said, "Let's walk over to the college library and see what we can find out about the *Lucy Belle*."

Having been to Emerson several times before, the girls were familiar with the campus. As they walked to the library building, Nancy told her companions about the riverboat book Ned had seen and the men he had overheard talking behind a stack of books.

The library was well-stocked and Mr Beecher, the head librarian, was a well-informed person.

When Nancy made her request, he replied, "Don't bother with the books we have here. There is a woman in Emerson named Mrs Palmer who can tell you more about the early history of this place than any book I've read." He jotted down her address, and the girls started for her home.

The house was on the river front a short distance from the campus. Mrs Palmer proved to be a delightful woman in her eighties. She was small in stature, with snow-white hair piled high, a delicate alabaster complexion, and a keen mind. Nancy introduced herself and her friends, explaining why Mr Beecher had sent them.

"Do come in," Mrs Palmer invited cordially. When the girls were comfortably seated in the old-fashioned parlour, the woman said, "I can tell you many stories that have been handed down." She asked how much they knew about the sinking of the *Lucy Belle*, and Nancy gave her what meagre information she had.

"That's all true," Mrs Palmer told her. "I always have felt bad to think of that gorgeous wedding gown and veil and the queen's gift of a fan being ruined by mud and water at the bottom of the river."

"Have you any idea what else was in the cargo?" Nancy asked.

"Well, rumour has it that there were two things aboard of particular value. One was the Rorick gifts. The other was a shipment of gold coins for the bank in Emerson. It's said that there was a great effort on the part of local citizens at the time to retrieve the box of coins, but if anyone ever found them, it was not reported. In any case, they never got to the bank."

The three girls were fascinated by this additional information about the *Lucy Belle*. George asked how much money was involved, but Mrs Palmer did not know.

"I'm sure it was considerable, however," she said. "There's another old rumour that a couple of crewmen had caused the explosion, stolen the gold coins, and taken off in a boat."

"Did the rumours mention any names?" Bess asked.

"I don't know. I never heard any names."

Mrs Palmer seemed to be tiring, so Nancy said that the girls had to leave now. She thanked Mrs Palmer for taking time to tell them the stories.

The elderly woman smiled. "It has been years since anyone has asked me about the early history of this place and I have been delighted to talk to you. Do come back sometime and let me relate what I have been told about the Indian raids. The old town of Emerson was plundered and burned several times, but the inhabitants loved it enough to rebuild it."

"Are many of the old families still here?" Nancy asked.

Mrs Palmer said sadly that she and Mr Rorick were the only two descendants left of the original settlers' stock. "But we helped to build the university," she said proudly, "and though that has changed the town considerably, we're glad to have done it."

Bess smiled. "We thank you for doing it. We're having a wonderful time during June Week. Will you be watching the pageant this afternoon?"

"Oh, yes," said Mrs Palmer. "A young friend is coming to take me."

After leaving, Nancy drove directly to the Rorick home. She asked her friends to help her search the books in the library for further information on the *Lucy Belle*.

"Not before lunch," Bess stated firmly. "I'm starved!"

"That seems to be a perpetual complaint of yours," said George. "What happened to that diet you were going to follow?"

Bess looked hurt. "You know I've lost seven pounds!"

"Which you'll put right back on if you don't stop stuffing yourself," George warned.

When the girls were ready to go into the library, Mrs Holman went along. As the door was swung back, the four gave startled cries. The room was a shambles! Books and pamphlets lay strewn on the floor and on the furniture.

"Mr Rorick's desk has been broken into!" exclaimed Mrs Holman.

The drawers were open. Nearly everything had been taken out of them and thrown on to the floor.

"It's the phantom!" the housekeeper said. "Why would he want to do it?"

George had a ready answer. "Maybe the phantom was so angry at finding that the money had been removed he decided to get revenge!"

There was silence for a few seconds, then Nancy said quietly, "There might be another reason for someone doing this."

·7·

The Perplexed Chief

STANDING in the midst of the untidy library, Mrs Holman, Bess, and George waited for Nancy to give her own theory as to why the phantom had made a shambles of the room.

"Don't you think," Nancy asked, "that if the only thing the mysterious thief wanted was money he would have taken all of it at once?"

"That sounds reasonable," the housekeeper conceded.

Nancy went on, "Since he simply helped himself to small amounts at a time, I believe he thought he was avoiding suspicion."

George nodded. "You mean that although Uncle John was hiding the money so that the amount was the same as the book page, he wouldn't be sure whether it was, say, a hundred and fifty or a hundred and forty that he had put in?"

"Exactly. And so he would not report the theft to the police."

Bess said, "But you haven't told us why the thief made a wreck out of this room."

Nancy replied that it was evident he was hunting for something important beside the money. "Perhaps he

56

knows we're working on the mystery and is getting frantic to find the thing before we do."

Bess sighed. "I almost hope he found what he was looking for and never comes back!"

"That would please me too," said Mrs Holman.

As the girls picked up the books and papers they looked at each one for a clue to the mystery. The papers gave no hint, so these were put back into the desk drawers.

Bess saw something sticking from under the desk and got down on hands and knees to look. There was another paper which she pulled out and held up.

"Oh no!" she cried.

The others turned to look. On the paper were two large thumbprints.

Instantly Nancy was excited. The prints looked like the ones on the paper which had floated to her feet in the woods!

"I'll get the other paper," she said, and hurried up the stairs.

When she returned, the black prints were compared under a magnifying glass from Uncle John's desk. They were exactly the same!

"I think I should take these papers to the police," she said.

Her friends continued to hunt for clues in the books while Nancy went to town. She found Police Chief Rankin a rather stern man. Nancy stated her errand quickly and showed him the papers with the thumbprints.

After looking at them for several seconds, the officer said, "Tell me the whole story in detail."

It took Nancy some time to give him an account of what had happened since her arrival in Emerson. When she finished, Chief Rankin said, "I'm afraid I didn't put much credence in Mrs Holman's story about a phantom. As for the missing pearls, there were no fingerprints in the room but yours and hers. Frankly," he went on with an apologetic smile, "I thought it likely you had mislaid the necklace, got excited, and reported it stolen. But now I see you're not that kind of person. I will go out to Pine Hill myself and do a little investigating," he added.

"That's what I was hoping you would do," said Nancy. "When will you come?"

"Right now. I'll follow you in my car."

Mrs Holman and the girls were astonished to see Nancy drive in with the police chief. Bess whispered to the housekeeper, "Nancy's very persuasive."

After Nancy had introduced the chief to Bess and George, he gave the library a thorough inspection. The others waited patiently while he tapped the walls, looked up the chimney, and asked if there were a trap door under any of the rugs.

Bess whispered to George, "Nancy has already done all this. Why don't we tell him so?"

"Better not," her cousin replied. She smiled. "We might be interfering with his—er—duties!"

When the officer finished, he said firmly, "There's only one possible way a thief could have entered this room. He must have a duplicate key to the padlock."

"But, Chief Rankin," Mrs Holman spoke up, "there is only one key to this padlock and the man at the lock shop assured Mr Rorick that the padlock could not be picked."

Chief Rankin frowned. He did not argue with the housekeeper, but said crisply, "Take my advice—put a new padlock on at once and don't let anyone get hold of the key to it!"

Mrs Holman was a bit hurt by his peremptory manner, but she merely said, "I will do that." Turning to Nancy, she asked, "Would you have time to run downtown and buy a new padlock?"

Nancy glanced at her wrist watch. It was just one o'clock and the girls were not due at the pageant until four. "I'll have plenty of time," she told the housekeeper.

As she went outdoors with Chief Rankin, he said that he would look round the grounds, although he did not think he would find anything helpful.

"Footprints wouldn't mean anything. There must be hundreds of them around here, with people cutting grass, gardening, and searching for clues." As he spoke the latter phrase, he looked significantly at Nancy.

She smiled in answer, then asked, "What about the bobbing light in the woods at night?"

"Have you seen it yourself?" the officer asked.

"Yes."

Chief Rankin rubbed his chin thoughtfully. "I feel sure that no thief is going to give away his position by walking round those woods with a flashlight. I'd say they're used by people who are taking shortcuts from the beach to the road."

Nancy did not comment—the police chief might be right! She said goodbye, thanked him for coming, and drove off to get the new padlock. She obtained one at Emerson's largest ironmongery. The owner assured her that the lock was the very latest model and positively could not be opened except with the proper key.

"Not even by a locksmith?" Nancy asked, her eyes twinkling.

"Well," said the shop owner, "I wouldn't go so far as to say that. But it would take a real expert to figure this one out. What are you going to use it for?"

Nancy was vague in her answer. "Put it on a certain door to keep out burglars," she said, chuckling, and the man did not ask any more questions.

She paid for the padlock and hurried home. Mrs Holman predicted that even two locks on the library door were not going to keep out the phantom. Nevertheless, she permitted Nancy and George to install the new lock to which there were two keys. She took one herself, and suggested that Nancy take the other and hide it carefully.

During her absence, Bess and George had been looking through volume after volume of Uncle John's books. But most of them had nothing to do with old boats or the history of the area.

Soon Mrs Holman announced that luncheon was ready and the girls went into the dining-room. There were cold cuts, potato salad, large, ripe tomatoes, and a delicious chocolate mousse dessert.

"You are a marvellous cook," Nancy said to Mrs Holman. "Everything is so good!"

The girls insisted upon washing the dishes. While they were working, there was a knock on the back door and

Bess opened it. Fred Jenkins walked in, grinning at the three girls.

"Hi, everybody!" he said. "I've got to work fast around here today, because I want to see that pageant, too."

Mrs Holman appeared and told him to vacuum the living-room, then the hall.

"Okay," he said, and went off to do it.

As soon as the girls had finished their dishwashing chore, they went back to the library to look at more books. Mrs Holman accompanied them, a mop and dustcloth in her hands.

Fred, coming into the hall, saw her. "Oh, you shouldn't be doing that," he said. "I'll clean the library for you."

"No, thank you," said the housekeeper. "Mr Rorick doesn't want anybody but me to work in the room."

At that moment Fred noticed the two padlocks on the door. He began to laugh. "You sure must have a gold mine in that place." The others ignored him.

As he worked in the hall, Mrs Holman kept an eye on him. Each time he came near the door to the library, she went out and found him another job which took him away from it.

"He's too nosey," she said to the girls.

Presently the telephone rang and Mrs Holman answered it. After a short conversation, she hung up and came to the library door. The housekeeper beckoned Nancy towards her and whispered:

"That was Chief Rankin. He said to tell you that the thumbprints on that paper are not on record. Whoever left them is not a known criminal."

"That makes our job even harder," Nancy commented.

By this time Fred had finished all the work which the housekeeper wanted him to do indoors that day. She told him to go outside and weed the garden.

Nancy and the housekeeper returned to the library. By this time the girls had gone through hundreds of books.

Suddenly Bess called out excitedly, "A clue! I've found a clue!"

· 8 ·

Indian Attack

Bess had been seated on top of a small ladder reading one of the very old books she had found. Now she jumped down and showed it to the others.

"There's a whole article about the *Lucy Belle*," she said. "And pasted in the back of the book is this."

She pointed to a list of names, all men. Scrawled across the bottom of the sheet was the notation, "Survivors of the *Lucy Belle*."

"Oh, Bess," Nancy cried out, "this is a wonderful find!" She began to count the names—there were nine. "Does it say in the article where the men went?"

"No, it doesn't," Bess replied. "It tells about the construction of the *Lucy Belle*, which was a combination freight and passenger steamboat."

"Then it doesn't mention the cargo?"

"No."

"Girls," said Nancy, "if we hurry, we'll have time to stop at Mrs Palmer's before we go to the pageant. Let's see if she can identify any of these names."

Bess wanted to know what good that would do. "Those men have been dead a long time."

"But they may have left families," Nancy replied. "Maybe one or more of their descendants are around here and trying to find a clue to that treasure of coins."

"You mean," said Bess, "that one of them is the phantom?"

"Possibly."

After Nancy copied the names, the three girls dressed quickly and set off for Mrs Palmer's home. She was surprised to see them so soon again, but appeared delighted. "I can tell by your eyes, Nancy, that you have more questions for me."

Nancy smiled and produced the list of *Lucy Belle* survivors.

The elderly woman eyed it in amazement. "You are real sleuths," she complimented her visitors.

Mrs Palmer settled down in an armchair to study the list. Finally she went to a bookcase, and pulled out a thin volume which she said was the genealogy of the old families of Emerson. She went through each page carefully, comparing the names on it with those which Nancy had brought.

Presently she said, "I believe I have found something!"

"Yes?" Nancy asked, leaning forward eagerly.

The elderly woman said that two names in the book were identical with two on the list, although they were several generations apart. "It's just possible that the younger ones are descendants of these survivors."

"Do they live in Emerson now?" Nancy asked.

"Well, yes and no. There are two young men at the university whose families used to reside here but moved away. Their names are Tom Akin and Ben Farmer."

The three girls exclaimed in surprise. "Why, Tom and Ben are Omegas!" George said.

Mrs Palmer smiled. "You're familiar with that fraternity?"

Nancy told her about Ned, Dave, and Burt inviting them for June Week. "Maybe the boys can give us some good leads," she added.

Unable to restrain her enthusiasm, Nancy asked if she might use Mrs Palmer's telephone. "Help yourself, my dear."

On the chance that Tom and Ben might still be at the Omega House, Nancy called it. To her delight, both of them were there. Quickly she explained why she had called.

Tom, who had answered the phone, said that indeed he was a direct descendant of the Tom Akin who was a survivor of the *Lucy Belle*. "I believe he was one of the officers."

Nancy asked that when the boys had a chance they tell her all they knew about the history of the sunken ship. "We'll be more than glad to. Say, you girls have no dates for the afternoon, have you? . . . Well, we're in the same boat. Our friends are in the pageant, too. How about sitting with us? Then Ben and I will tell you all we know."

"Marvellous!" said Nancy. "We'll be in the first row —Ned suggested that. Will you meet us there?"

"We'll go right now and save seats," Tom offered.

Before leaving Mrs Palmer, Nancy planted a kiss of thanks on the woman's cheek. "You've been a wonderful help. If I ever solve the mystery, I'll come back to tell you."

Mrs Palmer smiled. "I hope that's a promise."

When the girls arrived at the waterfront, Tom and

Ben were already there. As promised, the boys had saved three seats in the front row.

Almost at once, Tom gave an account of the sinking of the *Lucy Belle*. Both he and Ben had heard stories about it, but these did not differ from what the girls knew.

"I've heard, however," Ben said, "that my forebear survived the shipwreck, only to be massacred later with some of the other survivors near the Indian village. He had left his wife and son in Pittsburgh, but afterwards they came here to visit relatives and remained."

"Killed by Indians! How awful!" exclaimed Bess.

"The white men must have provoked them," Ben said. "Except for this one incident, they were friendly with the settlers at that time."

George remarked, "What seems strange to me is that nobody has tried to retrieve the sunken treasure."

"You mean the gold coins?" Tom asked. When George nodded, he said, "Oh, some of the college boys have tried in the past few years since scuba diving has become popular. Ben and I have been down several times."

"You didn't find any trace of them?" Nancy queried.

Tom laughed. "We couldn't even find the ship. Maybe we didn't have the right location, but everyone around here thinks the *Lucy Belle* is sunk so deep in the mud that she'll never be found. You know, the bottom of this tributary is really an underwater valley between the two shores."

There was silence for a few moments, then suddenly Nancy asked, "Is it possible to hire diving equipment in Emerson?"

Tom and Ben seemed startled by the question, but Tom answered. "Yes, it is. Don't tell me you're going to try to find the *Lucy Belle*!"

Nancy laughed. "I just might do that."

For the next few minutes Nancy and her friends studied the printed programme. There was to be a succession of floats showing how Emerson had developed from a wilderness into a university town. First came flatboats on which the earliest merchants sent their goods up into the wilderness territory.

Next came the keelboats, called barges, which ran on regular schedules as the population increased.

Presently George called out, "Here comes Burt!"

She began to giggle as she saw him playing the part of a fully bearded captain in an old-fashioned uniform and cap. He was standing on a barge with one arm outstretched in front of him, directing his crew where to take their load of iron ore.

The programme said that there had been a forge in the area where smelting was done. These forges formed little communities where the smith, his family, and his workers lived.

Suddenly Bess burst into laughter. "Oh, I can't believe it! Look at Dave!"

Her friend, wearing a bushy-haired wig, whiskers, and sideburns, was in charge of an ark filled with animals! Squealing pigs, mooing cows, and neighing horses apparently were very unhappy and Dave was having a hectic time with several helpers trying to keep the creatures quiet.

"No wonder he wouldn't tell me what part he was going to play," said Bess. "He'll never live this down!"

There were many other types of early river transportation in the parade, including one showing a shipment of salt. Other floats depicted a church and an early school building.

The last number was an elaborate one. In a disreputable shantyboat stood a crude shack. Through a large window, in a scene lighted by old-fashioned lanterns, a miser could be seen. He was seated at a table counting a large heap of coins.

Trailing the shantyboat was a large pirogue. The dugout was filled with Indians, and Ned was playing the part of their chief. As the boats neared the seated spectators, Ned and his party sneaked aboard the shantyboat, robbed the miser of his coins, and tossed the man into the water!

Quickly the Indians climbed back into their pirogue and headed for shore. It landed directly in front of Nancy's group.

Ned leaped out, and giving a war whoop rushed up to Nancy, scooped her up in his arms, and raced back to his dugout with her.

"Ned, stop it!" Nancy cried in embarrassment. "Stop it!"

She tried to struggle free, but Ned's Indian companions helped hold her and paddled off quickly. The crowd of onlookers, sure that this was part of the programme, cheered loudly.

"Ned, where are you going? What are you doing?" Nancy cried out.

Ned rose to his full height and said in a stentorian voice, "Big Chief take pretty maiden to treasure spot!"

·9·

Ancient Stump

THE pirogue was quickly paddled across the cove. Nancy asked where they were going.

Ned, with a grin, said in his natural voice, "Around the corner of Pine Hill. After you girls had left the house, Mrs Holman telephoned me. The fellows found me in the gym, where I was being made up. She said Uncle John Rorick had called and wanted to talk to you, Nancy."

"Did he give her the message?" Nancy asked.

"Yes. He wants you girls to stay longer than Sunday afternoon—in fact, he wants you to stay until you solve the mystery."

Nancy laughed. "He's taking a great chance. Who knows how long we may be in Emerson?"

"That's great with me," said Ned. "Starting from Monday we'll be studying hard because exams are the week after next, but a few dates would ease the strain on the brain!"

Nancy said she was sure Bess and George had nothing special to take them home and they would stay a few days longer, at least. Then she added, "But what does this have to do with the treasure you're going to show me?"

Ned explained that while Uncle John was talking to Mr Holman, he had suddenly remembered having heard his parents mention an old pine tree in connection with the *Lucy Belle*. He had been a young child at the time and did not understand what had been meant by the remark. Now he wondered if a pine tree might prove to be a clue.

"Ned, you mean to say you've found that pine?" Nancy said excitedly "Oh, where? How?"

Ned answered that he recalled having seen a large pine stump embedded in the embankment just round the bend of Pine Hill. "I thought that might be the one, so my friends and I brought some digging tools to find the lost treasure."

The paddlers put on speed and in a few minutes came to the spot. Everyone stepped from the pirogue and the boys began their work.

After fifteen minutes had gone by and nothing had been unearthed, one of the boys said, "I guess those old war-whoopers—or the crewmen—made away with everything worth while."

The others laughed, but Ned urged him not to give up yet. "Don't you want a share of the wampum?" he asked.

The boys widened their location of operations. They were silent for some time, during which Nancy ambled around, trying to reconstruct the scene of the sinking *Lucy Belle* and the survivors getting to shore. Was this a likely place for them to have landed, she wondered.

Suddenly one of the boys yelled and Nancy turned to see why. "Look!" he exclaimed, and held up an anchor.

The others rushed forward to examine it. The anchor was covered with rust, which the boys began to chip off with their tools.

Secretly Nancy felt that the anchor was too small to have been used on the *Lucy Belle*. Nevertheless, she watched eagerly and finally an indistinct name came to light. It was *Rover*.

The finder rubbed his perspiring brow. "All this work for nothing!"

Ned conceded defeat. He told Nancy he was sorry to have misled her, but that he had been sure he had discovered a good clue.

Nancy smiled at him. "Don't feel bad," she said. "I enjoyed being kidnapped by Indians and it has given me an idea."

"I hope it's a better one than mine," Ned said disconsolately.

He and his friends were a sorry-looking sight. They were hot, dirty, and tired. Dust and mud had spattered on their grease-painted bodies and those who had not removed their wigs were now wearing them askew. Nancy found it hard to keep from laughing.

"Let's go back to the gym," said one of them.

"Okay," Ned agreed. "Hop in, Nancy."

She shook her head. "If you don't mind, since I'm so close to the house, I think I'll walk through the woods." She took her car keys from her bag and handed them to Ned. "Would you mind giving these to Bess and George and telling them where I am?"

Ned looked at her for several seconds, then said, "You'll be safer if I go with you. That phantom may be spying on you again." He handed the keys to one of the other boys. "See that Bess and George get these, will you?"

The pirogue pushed off and the couple climbed the embankment. As they started through the pine grove, Ned said, "What is this great idea you mentioned?"

Nancy replied that she had been thinking over the historical facts she had gleaned from the pageant and concluded there were many Indians not far from Pine Hill during those days.

"That probably means they came from their village to the water. Some of their braves may have found loot washed ashore from the ship and carried it away with them."

"Maybe," said Ned. "Can't you see some Indian maiden wearing Miss Abigail Rorick's wedding dress?"

Nancy laughed. "Just the same, I'm going to try to find an antique map of this area and see if an Indian village is marked on it."

"Where are you going to look?" Ned queried.

"In Uncle John's library."

Ned said, "Suppose you tell me what you think might have happened after the sinking of the *Lucy Belle*."

"Well," Nancy began, "if the Indians stole valuable cargo, they might have buried it so that they could pretend innocence."

"That sounds logical," Ned said. "Go on."

"It's also possible that the survivors of the *Lucy Belle*, fearing they might be attacked by marauders, hid their reserve cargo underground near the Indian village. That would be an easy spot to find again."

"Well, I certainly wish you luck," Ned said. He grinned wearily. "I'm glad you're not going to ask me to do any more digging tonight. But when you find that map let me know."

He took the lead on the way to the house, but suddenly he and Nancy stood stock-still. From somewhere in the grove came an ear-piercing shriek of terror.

"Where did that come from?" Ned asked worriedly.

"Someone may have been attacked!" Nancy exclaimed.

She lay on the ground to listen for footsteps. Nancy heard them receding in the direction from which she and Ned had come. The couple ran that way but saw no one. Finally Nancy stopped and put her ear to the ground again. She could no longer hear footfalls. Swiftly she and Ned searched the grove but found no sign of a victim.

"More likely he got a glimpse of you and was terrified that he had seen an Indian warrior," Nancy teased.

"It wouldn't surprise me," Ned said, "if your phantom made that outcry just to scare us away."

"I wonder where he went," Nancy mused.

Once more the couple turned towards the house. When they reached it a few minutes later, they discovered that Mrs Holman had not yet returned from the pageant and the house was tightly locked.

"She should be along soon," said Nancy. "Let's sit down and wait."

Wearily she and Ned flopped on to the steps of the rear porch. It was not long before the housekeeper drove up in a friend's car. She smiled upon seeing Ned and suggested that he take off his disguise before going back to town.

He laughed. "If I keep this up, poor Uncle John won't have any clothes left!"

He went upstairs, took a shower, and a little while later appeared in clothes which Uncle John evidently wore when he was working in the garden.

While he had been changing, Nancy had suggested to Mrs Holman that they open both padlocks on the library door and look in. As they entered, Nancy exclaimed in horror:

"Oh no!"

All the books had been taken from the shelves and thrown helter-skelter around the room!

Mrs Holman wrung her hands. "It's the phantom again!" she exclaimed. "Every door and window in this house was tightly locked before I left!"

Ned joined them. "Wow-ee!" he exclaimed, then frowned. "Whoever did this must be desperate to find what he's looking for."

"The question is, was he successful?" Mrs Holman asked.

Nancy did not reply. She had noticed a rolled parchment on the floor beside Mr Rorick's desk. Quickly she went over, picked up the parchment, and opened it carefully. Engraved on it was a very old map showing the Emerson area in the eighteenth century. Nancy's face lighted up.

"Here's what I was going to search for!" she said excitedly.

· 10 ·

The Camouflaged Door

A CAR door slammed outside the Rorick house. Nancy, Ned, and Mrs Holman looked out to see who had arrived.

"It's Bess and George," the housekeeper said. "Why don't you wait until they come in and tell all of us what you've discovered, Nancy?"

"I will," she answered, as Mrs Holman went to open the front door.

"Is Nancy here? Is she all right?" Bess asked quickly.

The woman assured her that Nancy was fine and had enjoyed being kidnapped by the Indians. The three entered the book-strewn library.

"Gosh!" exclaimed George. "Another visit from the phantom?"

Quickly Nancy explained, then told the girls of Uncle John's request that they stay to work on the mystery.

"Okay with me," said George. Bess nodded, but she did not look happy.

"Now tell us what happened to you, Nancy," George urged.

Ned stepped forward and laid a hand on Nancy's

shoulder. "Meet Indian Princess Nonaviki," he said solemnly. "She help Chief solve heap-big Indian mystery."

Everyone laughed, but Bess said, "Oh, do be serious. What's the discovery, Nancy?"

The young sleuth pointed to the parchment. "According to this, there was once an Indian village about a mile from here. I had a hunch today that there might be one connected with our mystery."

Ned interrupted to say, "Nancy got this idea after a boo-boo I pulled." He told about the fiasco of the stump.

"Why, I think the pine tree was a very good clue," Bess said kindly. "But now you believe the gold coins may be buried in or near the old Indian village?"

"Yes, I do," Nancy replied. "The thieves probably would have buried them as soon as possible. And then, too, those crewmen might have offered some coins to friendly Indians in return for a good hiding place. The village would be a logical location."

"Tell you what," said Ned. "Suppose we go out to that old Indian village after chapel."

"That's a wonderful idea," Nancy said enthusiastically.

Ned said he would have to be excused to go back to the fraternity house. "May I borrow your car, Nancy? I'll be back for you at seven o'clock with Burt and Dave." She nodded.

Mrs Holman, Bess, and George had already started to pick up books and return them to the shelves.

After Ned had left, Nancy sat down to study the old map. She was so deeply engrossed in it that Bess and

George had to urge her three times to put it away and dress for the Omega dinner dance.

"I overheard some of the boys talking and I think there's going to be a big surprise tonight," Bess said mysteriously.

"Have you any idea what it is?" George asked.

"Not the slightest. But it's a secret they're going to spring on the guests."

When they reached their rooms, Bess and George began to conjecture what the surprise might be. Nancy, lost in thought about the Indian village and the chance that at last she might have hit upon an excellent clue, did not join in the conversation, though the connecting door was open.

Again, she was the first one dressed. This time she had chosen a turquoise gown with a slightly full skirt. It was quite plain except for an intriguing geometric design in brilliant colours embroidered on one side of the bodice. The trimming reached from the shoulders to the waistline.

Bess and George looked equally attractive—Bess in pink, George wearing a flowing black chiffon gown.

By the time the girls grabbed their wraps and came downstairs their dates had arrived. All of them whistled in admiration upon seeing the girls.

"You look super!" cried Dave. He glanced at Nancy. "Some Indian princess!"

Nancy laughed and patted Ned's arm. "The Indian Chief looks a bit dressed up too, don't you think?"

When they reached the Omega House, the teasing continued. The main topic of conversation before dinner was the kidnapping of the Indian princess. The fun did not stop until chimes sounded, announcing dinner.

The members and their guests went to the dining-room and found their chairs by place cards. Nancy and Ned were seated directly in front of the speakers' table.

The president of the fraternity, Chuck Wilson, sat down and everyone began to eat. It was nearly an hour later when he arose and signalled for attention.

"We're going to have a little business meeting now," he said with a grin. "A special one." He called on the fraternity secretary.

A serious-faced, bespectacled youth stood up and announced that two alumni members had left sizeable sums of money to the fraternity chapter.

"Now we can start building our new house," he said gleefully. Loud applause followed this exciting announcement.

"Was this the big secret?" Nancy whispered to Ned.

"I don't know. To tell the truth, I didn't hear until this afternoon that some important news would be released this evening."

When the room was quiet again, the president rose once more and said he would call on the nominating chairman to announce the officers for the following year. The Committee had felt it would be interesting for the boys' dates as well as the members to hear the results.

A husky boy, seated next to him, stood up and smiled at his audience. "I'm going to reverse the usual order," he said, "and tell you last who our new president will be." He read the name of the treasurer who would take office, then the corresponding secretary, the recording secretary, and the vice-president.

He now paused and looked over the whole room. An eager member finally called out, "Well, who is it?"

"For your next president there was only one dissenting vote. That came from himself! Modest guy! So really by unanimous vote the next president of Omega Chi Epsilon Fraternity of Emerson University is—Ned Nickerson!"

"Oh, Ned," cried Nancy, "that's simply wonderful!" She grasped his hand and kissed him.

Ned looked stunned. For a moment he seemed overwhelmed. Then as cries of "Speech! Speech!" and terrific clapping rang in his ears, he got to his feet and faced his fellow members.

"You certainly caught me off balance this time," he said. Gradually his usual composure returned and he said seriously, "Thanks, fellows. It's going to be mighty hard filling Chuck Wilson's shoes. You all know that. I'll try hard, however." He smiled. "Just don't make it too rough for me, all of you!" He sat down.

There was more applause, then the outgoing president took charge. "Ned, I'll turn the gavel over to you after the private induction ceremonies next week. In the meantime, my personal congratulations and good luck, brother."

Nancy was wondering about the private induction. This was one thing she would never learn about, she knew, but it would be a memory Ned would cherish all his life. She herself was bursting with pride as everyone in the room rushed up to shake Ned's hand and wish him well. By the time they finished, he was blushing over the compliments.

At nine o'clock a small band arrived and started

off with a lively dance number. Soon the floor, from which the tables had been cleared, was filled with swaying, happy couples.

The wonderful evening ended very late. But early the next morning Nancy was awakened by a knock on her door.

"Come in!" she called sleepily.

Mrs Holman entered and apologized for waking her guest. She extended an envelope to Nancy, saying, "I thought this might be important. I found it on the hall floor. It must have been pushed under the front door."

Nancy glanced at the crude printing of her name. Her first thought was that it might be a joke. Quickly she pulled out the sheet of paper from the envelope. When she read the note, also crudely printed, she was inclined to believe the writer meant the warning it contained. The note said:

GO HOME AT ONCE.
DANGER FROM THE PHANTOM.

Bess and George had also heard the knock on Nancy's door and now came into her room. When they read the note, Bess became worried.

"You've been all right so far, Nancy. Don't stretch your luck. I think we'd better go home after the picnic today."

Nancy shook her head. "And disappoint Mr Rorick? It's my guess that whoever wrote this note overheard some conversation about Uncle John's invitation to us to stay longer and find the phantom. The eavesdropper was hoping we would leave today."

George voted to stay. "I'd like to catch this spy. He

probably listens on the extension phones and—"

"And can go through walls!" Bess added significantly.

The girls' remarks gave Nancy a new idea. "There may be hideaways in the parts of this house we haven't searched. Mrs Holman, will you take me all over so I can hunt for them?"

"I'll be glad to, but how about you girls having some breakfast?"

This was agreed upon and the trio dressed quickly in order to do some searching before going to chapel. Nancy slipped into a pair of blue slacks and a matching polo-neck sweater, then hurried downstairs.

Since Bess and George were not ready, Nancy and Mrs Holman went to search the attic. Neither of them found any hidden rooms, secret doors, or sliding panels. Next, they looked through the first floor without success.

"The only place left is the cellar," Nancy said. "I'll dash down there myself while you get breakfast." The housekeeper nodded.

Nancy snapped on the cellar light and descended the old-fashioned stairway. The place was cool and slightly musty. Nancy found many storage nooks and cubbyholes, but none revealed a hideaway.

At the far end of the cellar Nancy saw an intriguing workshop. She pulled the chain of the old-fashioned ceiling light. The room was filled with old tools, but a heavy layer of dust and many cobwebs indicated that the place had not been used for some time.

"That proves the phantom is not interested in it," she said to herself.

Nancy began to tap the walls behind the various workbenches. There was nothing suspicious about them, but she did notice one section of another wooden wall which had nothing in front of it. Curious, she tapped it.

"This sounds hollow!" she decided excitedly.

Her deft fingers went all over the woodwork and suddenly she found a cleverly concealed latch. She tried to lift the latch, but it would not budge. To jar it loose, Nancy struck the wood next to it. A second later the door to the workshop slammed shut. Intent on what she thought she was about to discover, the young detective paid no attention to this, but tried the hidden latch again. She heard it click and gave the secret door a hard —and disastrous—yank.

The next instant the whole section of wall came towards her. It hit Nancy hard, knocking her down. She blacked out!

· 11 ·

Treasure Hunters

BREAKFAST was ready, so Mrs Holman called down to Nancy from the top of the cellar stairs. There was no answer. She called more loudly, but still there was no response. "Whatever is Nancy doing?" the housekeeper wondered.

At that moment Bess and George came into the kitchen. She asked them to try their luck getting the young sleuth to come up and eat.

"Nancy! N-A-N-C-Y!"

When they received no reply, the two girls went downstairs to find their friend. To their surprise, she was not in sight. They kept calling and investigating each storage nook. Finally they came to the closed door of the workshop.

"Nancy must be in there," said George, and gave the door a yank. It would not open.

George called loudly through the crack. Nancy did not answer, and suddenly Bess went ash white. "Oh, I'm sure something has happened to her!"

"She must be in the room behind this door," George said grimly. "The question is, did she lock it or did someone else?"

Tears began to roll down Bess's cheeks. "The phantom carried out his threat! She's a prisoner!"

George set her jaw grimly. "We must get inside!"

There was no lock on the door, so the girls assumed it must be fastened on the inside. They tried ramming their bodies against it, but the heavy wooden door would not budge.

By this time Mrs Holman had descended the steps. Upon hearing what Bess and George suspected, she instantly became alarmed.

"How can we get in here?" Bess asked.

"I don't know. That's an old workshop and there's a heavy wooden bar that locks it on the inside."

Bess said, "I'm sure Nancy didn't lock herself in. Oh, maybe she is l-lying in there injured!"

"Maybe not," said the housekeeper, trying to be calm. "Sometimes when that door swings shut, the big bar inside falls into place. If Nancy was hammering on the walls, the vibration could have made the door close. But Nancy should be able to raise the bar."

"And why doesn't she answer us?" Bess wailed.

George said, "Mrs Holman, do you have a big hammer handy?"

"There's one in the kitchen. I'll get it."

She vanished up the stairway but returned in half a minute with the hammer. George swung it heftily, trying to knock off the heavy old-time hinges. They were so deeply embedded in the wood that she could make no impression.

Bess spoke up, her voice trembling, "Mrs Holman, is there a window from the outside that opens into that workshop?"

The housekeeper shook her head. "There's no entrance to that room except from here."

"Have you a thin saw that we could put through this crack?" George asked.

"I think so. I'll look."

Five minutes elapsed before Mrs Holman came downstairs and handed a dull, rusty saw to George. The girl wedged it through the crack. She could feel the obstructing wooden bar, but though she tried hard, George could not saw through it.

Bess complained, "Oh, why can't we do something?"

"Crying won't help any," George said severely to her cousin. "Put on your thinking cap!"

Chastened, Bess thought quickly and said, "Why don't we get a hatchet or an axe and hack down the door?"

"Now you're using your head," said George. "Mrs Holman, can you produce one of those tools?"

The housekeeper was not sure but said she would look in the garage. Fortunately she found a sharp axe. George grabbed it in both hands, gave a mighty heave, and landed it on the door. There was a distinct sound of cracking wood.

Twice more she aimed at the same spot. On the third try the axe crashed all the way through. There was an opening large enough for her to put her hand through and raise the bar.

Bess pulled the door open, then gave a shriek. Across the room Nancy lay on the floor unconscious, a heavy door partly covering her body. Beyond was a gaping hole to the garden!

Mrs Holman and the two girls rushed over to Nancy.

As Bess and George lifted the door away, Mrs Holman knelt down and felt the girl's pulse. At that moment Nancy stirred.

"She's coming round!" the housekeeper said.

"Thank goodness!" Bess murmured. She crouched and ran her fingers through Nancy's hair. "Oh, Nancy, Nancy, whatever happened to you?"

Her friend did not reply. It was several minutes before she opened her eyes and looked round. She seemed to be in a daze.

"I'll get some water," Mrs Holman offered.

The soothing, cool water soon revived Nancy and in halting tones she told what had happened to her.

"Do you think the phantom did it?" Bess asked Nancy.

"No. There was no one in this room."

Mrs Holman said she thought Nancy should go upstairs and lie down. "I'm going to ask the university doctor to come in and examine you," she stated.

Nancy was sure she would be all right. "I'm just a bit bruised." But the housekeeper insisted.

She put an arm around Nancy to help her upstairs. At the housekeeper's suggestion, Bess and George stayed behind to set the hidden door in place. For the first time they noticed how unusual the outside of it was. Very thin pieces of stone had been wedged into the wood. When the door was in place, it would look as if it were part of the foundation. The two girls searched, but they found nothing to indicate that the door could be opened from the outside.

"I'll bet it was for escape in case of Indian attack," George remarked, as the girls walked to the kitchen stairway. The cousins found Nancy in the living-room, resting on the couch. After they told her about the camouflaged door, she said, "Anyway, the phantom didn't use it. That door hadn't been opened in years!"

Within fifteen minutes Dr Smith arrived and with him, Ned Nickerson, whom he had called, knowing that Ned was a special friend.

Ned rushed up to Nancy, a look of deep concern on his face. "Thank goodness you weren't killed!" he exclaimed.

Dr Smith came to the girl's side. "Oh tush! Miss Drew looks far from killed!"

He insisted that Nancy go upstairs, where he would make a thorough examination. The others waited tensely. Although Nancy had seemed all right, they knew how brave she was and that she might be hiding some really serious trouble so as not to worry her friends.

Mrs Holman asked if any of them would like to eat, but they shook their heads. Bess managed a wry smile. "For once in my life I've lost my appetite."

When Dr Smith came downstairs, Ned and the girls jumped up eagerly. "How is she?" they asked in unison.

The physician smiled. "I'm glad to give you a good report. No broken bones. A few bruises, but so far as I can determine, she suffered no serious injuries. I want Miss Drew to stay in bed at least until tomorrow morning. She didn't like it much when I told her this, because it seems she had great plans for the day."

"I'm sure they can wait," said Mrs Holman.

"May we see her and can she eat breakfast?" Bess asked quickly.

"I suggest that you give her one hour by herself. It's a shock to the system when one gets knocked out. Miss Drew will make a quick comeback, I'm sure, but sleep will help her. As for eating, only a light diet today."

Keeping as quiet as possible, they sat down and ate their own breakfast. Bess and George briefed Ned on what the young detective had been doing when the accident happened.

"Another false clue," George said with a sigh.

"We must get that secret door nailed shut," said Mrs Holman, "so that the phantom can't use it." Ned volunteered to do the job. After finishing it, he left.

At the end of the doctor's prescribed hour, the girls went to Nancy's room. She was awake and demanded something to eat.

"Coming right up!" said George, delighted that colour had returned to her friend's face and once more her eyes were sparkling.

She went downstairs to get orange juice, a soft-boiled egg, and some toast. When she returned, Nancy suggested that Bess and George go to chapel. "You don't have to stay with me. I'm perfectly all right. Take my car."

Bess and George followed her suggestion. They quickly freshened up, took off their slacks, and put on dresses. A few minutes later they were on their way to chapel.

Presently Mrs Holman came upstairs and Nancy said to her, "Early tomorrow morning I'm going to that Indian village shown on the map. I just can't wait to do a little investigating there." She was sorry that the boys

would have to study the next day and could not
accompany them.

The following morning Nancy felt fully recovered.
As soon as she and her friends could get away after
breakfast, they started for the Indian village, taking
digging tools with them. They walked to the cove, then
followed the direction indicated on the old map.
Finally they came to a clearing which Nancy figured
had once been the site of a thriving community. Here
and there on the landscape were large weed-covered
humps.

"What were they for?" Bess asked.

"It's my guess," Nancy said, "that those were the
clay ovens where the Indians baked their bread. Now
the weeds have taken over."

After hunting around for a while, the girls picked up
a few arrowheads, but apart from this evidence there
was nothing to indicate that there had ever been a tribal
settlement at this spot.

"We came to find a treasure and maybe a lost
wedding dress," Bess reminded the others. "I'm sure
we're never going to in this place."

The other girls were not so sure. George said, "If you
were an Indian, where would you hide a treasure?"

Nancy thought for a few moments, then answered,
"In a sacred place where other Indians would be too
superstitious to touch it."

"That sounds reasonable," Bess agreed. "I've read
that the sacred building or ground in an Indian village
was sometimes right in the centre."

"That's true," said Nancy. She walked around and
finally picked a spot which might once have been

the centre of the village. "Let's start digging here."

As they picked up their tools, the girls became aware of a young man walking towards them. He was Fred Jenkins.

"So you're digging for Indian relics, eh?" he asked. "I have a message for you, Miss Nancy," he said.

"For me? From whom?" she asked.

"Your father. He called up and I wrote it out. I thought I'd better get it to you right away." He handed a small sheet of paper to Nancy.

Written on it was a badly spelled message. Nancy caught her breath as she read:

"I need you at home at once. Hannah Gruen is very ill."

· 12 ·

A Frightening Message

"WHEN did this message come?" Nancy asked Fred Jenkins.

He thought a moment, then answered, " 'Bout half an hour or so ago. I was cleaning the ground floor and answered the phone—Mrs Holman was busy upstairs and didn't hear it. Your father said he wanted you to get the message right away, so I asked her where you were. She told me where this place was and I figured I'd come and tell you!"

"That was very kind of you," said Nancy. "Girls, it's too bad to leave here, but you know how I feel about Hannah. We'll have to go right home."

Fred was staring at Nancy intently. "I'm terribly sorry I brought you bad news. I hope the lady will get well soon."

As the girls gathered up their tools, Fred added, "I'll miss seeing you all around. Kind of got used to you."

As Nancy and her friends started towards the cove Fred walked ahead of them. In a few minutes he had vanished among the trees.

"I wonder what happened to Mrs Gruen," said Bess. "She seemed to be in the best of health when we left home."

"Perhaps it was an accident," George ventured.

Nancy's expression was grim and she did not comment until they had reached the garden behind the house.

"As soon as we get inside, I'm going to phone River Heights. If something did happen to Hannah, I want to know what it is."

Bess looked at Nancy, puzzled. "*If*—?"

Nancy nodded. "This whole thing could be a hoax."

"But why?" Bess queried.

"To get rid of us. The phantom could have made that phone call so we'd leave Pine Hill."

"In other words," George spoke up, "you're learning a little too much here to please this mysterious thief."

"Possibly," Nancy answered. "But there could be another reason for a fake phone call."

"What's that?" Bess asked.

Nancy said that if the phantom was hunting for the same thing the girls were—the gold coins and the Rorick wedding gifts—then he might have wanted to find out where the girls were sleuthing at the moment. Knowing the set-up of the Drew family, he had invented the story as an excuse for Fred to get information from Mrs Holman.

"And the caller may have followed Fred?" George asked.

"Yes."

By this time the girls had reached the back door. Mrs Holman admitted them. At once she expressed her sympathy over what had happened and said she hoped Mrs Gruen's illness was not serious.

"I'm going to find out at once," said Nancy, and went to the hall telephone.

She dialled the number of her home, tapping her foot impatiently as she waited for someone to answer. After several rings Hannah Gruen's voice came over the wire, clear and strong.

"Hannah!" cried Nancy. "Are you all right?"

The Drews' housekeeper chuckled. "I never felt better in my life. Why the concern, Nancy?"

The young sleuth stammered as she told the whole story.

"Well, there's not one word of truth in it," Mrs Gruen declared. "And I can't see why anyone would have made up such a wild tale."

When Nancy told her the theories she had, Mrs Gruen sighed. "I only hope you're in no danger, dear," she said worriedly. "Perhaps you ought to take the hint and come home."

"Oh, I can't do that!" Nancy replied. "No phantom is going to give me orders!"

Mrs Gruen laughed heartily. "If the whole matter weren't serious, Nancy," she said, "that would be an utterly ridiculous statement."

Suddenly Nancy realized how strange her remark must have sounded. She, too, laughed but said, "And if he's hiding somewhere near and can hear what I'm saying, I hope he knows I mean every word of it!"

Nancy learned from Hannah Gruen that Mr Drew was out of town, but that he had phoned home to learn where Nancy was and what she was doing.

"When will you be home?" Hannah asked.

"Not for a few more days," Nancy told her. "Mr Rorick wants us to stay until we solve the mystery."

Mrs Gruen said she hoped it would not take much

longer. "It's mighty lonesome around here without you."

"I miss you, too," Nancy told her. Then she described Mrs Holman and ended by saying, "She makes us feel quite at home."

After Nancy had hung up, Mrs Holman complained that Fred had not yet returned. "That's just the way he is—so unreliable. He went right off to find you and left all the cleaning materials in the middle of the living-room floor!"

The girls laughed and followed Mrs Holman round from place to place to finish Fred's work. By the time the house was tidy, it was midday and they all moved into the kitchen. As they prepared sandwiches and salad for lunch, they talked about the fake phone message.

Mrs Holman, now that her worry was over, became angry. "I think hoaxes are the lowest form of humour. I'd like to find out who played that trick."

George said, "When we solve the mystery, I'm sure we'll find out."

As soon as the group had finished eating, Nancy said she would like to go back to the site of the Indian village. The other girls agreed to go with her.

Once more the three got their digging tools and set off, taking the same route they had followed on their previous trip.

"When we come back, let's try a shortcut," George proposed. "This spade is kind of heavy."

"Good idea," Nancy agreed. "Girls, I've just had a hunch that we're going to find someone else has been digging at the village."

"You mean since we've been there?" George asked.

"Yes, I do. That was the reason for the fake phone call."

This thought spurred the other girls on. As they neared the clearing, Nancy suggested that they go forward cautiously.

"If we do find someone digging," she said, "and can capture him, we may have the phantom right in our grasp!"

"Oh, my goodness!" said Bess. "I don't like capturing criminals!"

George looked disdainful. "What kind of sleuth are you, anyway?"

Bess became silent and she stayed at the rear of the trio, which now proceeded in single file. At the edge of the clearing Nancy held up her hand and put a finger to her lips. She hid behind a tree and motioned the other girls to do so.

"Look!" she whispered.

In the centre of the Indian village were half a dozen deep holes. Nancy's hunch had been right!

Suddenly Bess and George realized that her finger was not pointing at the freshly dug pits, but at the figure of a man disappearing among the trees across from them. He was carrying a spade and running as fast as he could.

"Let's get him!" Nancy urged.

The three girls dropped their tools and took off after the man. He had a head start and ran a zigzag course which put him out of their sight most of the time. They could not see his face, but he was a rather slight man of medium height and had dark, thinning hair. Could he be the one whose footprints Nancy had followed in the woods?

After a while he failed to reappear, but the girls kept running in the direction where they had last seen him. This brought them to the shore of the cove. They looked down the embankment. He was not in sight, but suddenly Bess exclaimed, "There goes a man in a rowing-boat! Isn't he the one?"

The man was rowing hard but in reverse motion, so that his back was towards the girls—apparently to avoid identification.

"I don't see any name or number on the boat," said Nancy. "Do you?"

Neither Bess nor George did. But they felt sure that the way the man was acting proved him to be guilty of something. Was he the one who had phoned the fake message to the Rorick house?"

Nancy heaved a sigh. "If he did find the treasure— which I doubt—we know he didn't carry it with him, unless it was so small he slipped it into a pocket."

George smiled. "Maybe we'll come across a chest of gold that he dropped!"

The girls hurried back to the spot where they had left their digging tools, picked them up, and walked into the Indian village. They checked the holes made by the mysterious digger and found them empty. Then the young sleuths stopped talking and went to work with a will.

Presently George called out that she had found an arrowhead. "This place is probably full of them."

Nancy was more fortunate. About ten minutes later

she unearthed a small pottery idol. It was a bit damaged but recognizable as an Indian god.

She showed it to the others, saying, "I don't know whether I can keep this or not. One thing I never did find out was, who owns this property."

"I did," said George. "The town of Emerson."

"Then anything we dig up will be turned over to the authorities," said Nancy. "That makes it simple."

The digging went on. Bess wandered off some distance to work. After a time Nancy noticed her and was about to call when suddenly Bess gave a cry. It sounded more like fright than surprise.

· 13 ·

The Cave Clue

NANCY and George hurried over to Bess. She was standing in a pit, trembling like a leaf. They were about to ask her what the trouble was when they looked near her feet.

She had unearthed a human skull!

"Gosh!" George exclaimed. "You've dug up a grave!"

"A very old one, I'd say," Nancy put in.

Bess scrambled up out of the pit, but still cringed at the sight of the blankly staring skull. Nancy and George, however, were fascinated.

"I wonder if it's an Indian's skull or someone who died more recently," Nancy mused. "Let's dig some more and see if there's a body."

"If you don't mind," said Bess, "I'll go dig somewhere else for the treasure from the *Lucy Belle*."

The other girls smiled but told her to go ahead. Using their digging tools very carefully, they dug deeper into the pit and in a little while disinterred a whole skeleton.

"It was an Indian all right," said Nancy, as she brushed away dirt from one of its legs, disclosing a beaded anklet.

George surveyed the scene. "I wonder if this person

was buried wearing other jewellery which later was stolen from the body."

Nancy said that judging by the depth of the pit, perhaps George's second guess was right. Whoever had disinterred the Indian the first time had covered it lightly with soil and not bothered to fill in the whole deep grave.

Nancy said excitedly, "I have a feeling we have unearthed something valuable that a museum might be glad to get. I think we should notify the police and suggest that a professor from the university come and look at this skeleton."

"I think you're right," George said.

By this time Bess's courage had returned, and overcome with curiosity, she appeared at the edge of the pit. She was just in time to hear Nancy's suggestion.

"I think your idea is a good one, Nancy. Suppose I go back to the house and phone the police?"

Nancy and George grinned and told her to go ahead. They knew Bess was eager to get away from the gruesome sight.

"While she's gone," Nancy suggested, "let's dig around here a little more. Maybe we can find some of the Indian's possessions."

After ten minutes' work they uncovered a rotting bow and arrow but did not dare pick them up for fear they would disintegrate. Weary now from their digging, the girls sat down to rest and await the police.

Chief Ruskin soon arrived with two professors from the university museum and Bess. The three men stared in astonishment at the girls' find.

Professor Greentree was a newcomer to Emerson and an authority on Indian history.

"I've been planning a dig on this site," he said with a smile. "You girls have beaten me to it." He went to his car for a special stretcher. Then, very carefully, he and his colleague inserted it under the old figure. The fragile skeleton was lightly covered with a piece of gauze and carried to the professor's station wagon which was parked in a side road beyond the clearing.

"I'm glad that's over," said Bess. "And I hope we don't meet any more prehistoric men!"

"Prehistoric?" George repeated. "Why, that skeleton is probably only a couple of hundred years old. Rather handsome, too."

George's cousin ignored the remark. She turned to Nancy. "What do we do now?"

Nancy reminded the girls they had come to hunt for the long-lost wedding gifts. "Let's dig a little longer."

"I'm getting hungry," said Bess as a gentle hint that they should give up. But the others, after glancing at their wrist watches, told her it was nowhere near dinner time yet.

"Promise me we'll go in half an hour," she pleaded.

"Okay," Nancy agreed. "And instead of digging, why don't we just search this area for clues?"

Bess felt better and eagerly joined the search. Weeds were pushed aside, rocks moved out of position.

Presently Nancy said in a low voice, "Listen! I thought I heard someone."

The girls straightened up and looked all around. They could see no one.

Bess was uneasy. "Probably the phantom is spying on us. It gives me the creeps."

"Let's pretend to leave and keep turning round. Maybe we'll spot someone," Nancy suggested.

The girls picked up their tools and started walking towards the cove. Every few minutes they would stop and listen. The crackle of twigs behind them left no doubt but that they were being followed. Yet the spy kept well hidden.

Nancy purposely was taking a zigzag course, not following their usual route. Soon they rounded a low hill and stopped again to listen. There was no sound of pursuit and they walked on. Suddenly they came face to face with a shallow cave.

The girls peered inside. Its stone walls were blackened with smoke. Chest-high was a ledge, evidently man-made with crude tools.

"Do you think Indians used this cave?" Bess asked.

"Here's your answer," said George, as she picked up a tiny flint arrowhead from the mouth of the cave. "This is called a bird point and may have been used for hunting birds."

Nancy walked around, examining the rough stonework. Above the shelf she noticed an embedded rock that protruded beyond the others. Curious, she tried pulling it out. The stone gave way easily, showing a small niche behind it.

Looking inside, Nancy saw some coloured beads and a piece of ribbon, which she pulled out. The ribbon was black, about an inch wide and very old. On it in tarnished gold letters was the word *Belle*.

Nancy showed it to the others, who gasped.

"A clue!" exclaimed Bess. "This is from the cap of a sailor on the *Lucy Belle*!"

"It must be," said Nancy.

"But how did it get here?" asked Bess.

Nancy had two theories. "Either the sailor left it here, or it fell into the hands of an Indian after the sinking or the massacre. Finding the ribbon here," she added, "lends support to Ben's story." She looked thoughtful. "I wish I knew why the friendly Indians turned on the survivors."

George, who had been standing guard at the entrance to the cave, suddenly hissed, "The spy! I saw him! He looks like the man in the boat!"

"Where is he?" Nancy asked quickly.

Her friend pointed among the trees, but by now the figure had vanished.

"Did he see you?" Nancy asked.

"I don't think so."

This gave Nancy an idea. "What say we surround the spy and capture him?"

To this suggestion, Bess gave a flat veto and no amount of persuasion would make her change her mind. Nancy and George did not think they could carry out the plan alone, so it was abandoned.

Nancy put the ribbon in her pocket and the girls started off once more. This time they could hear footsteps ahead of them in the woods. Once they caught a glimpse of the slight, middle-aged man hurrying away. As the girls quickened their pace, they heard him run. Who was he? Why had he followed them?

Finally they reached the cove at a spot where the embankment was high. Nancy hastened to the edge to see if the mysterious rowboat was anywhere in sight.

As she stood on the brink, suddenly the earth gave way. Nancy struggled to save herself but plunged forward with the rocks and dirt. George tried to grab her friend but failed. She too lost her balance as the earth crumbled still more!

· 14 ·

Puzzling Characters

HORRIFIED, Bess looked down the embankment at the
rolling, tumbling girls. She managed to pull back in
time to keep from being carried down herself.

"Oh, I hope Nancy and George didn't break any
bones!" she thought worriedly.

Both girls had been able to halt their descent just
before reaching the little beach. They sat up and clawed
dirt from their faces and eyes.

"Are you all right?" Bess called down anxiously.

George looked up at her cousin. "All right, but I'm
furious. Why did that earth have to give way just when
we were on the trail of the phantom?"

Nancy smiled, despite her dishevelled condition and
several scratches. "George, you can make any awful
situation seem funny. Just the same, I'm sorry too we
lost that man."

The two girls stood up and shook dirt from their
clothes. Then, choosing a more solid section of embankment where bushes were growing, they started to climb
upward.

Suddenly Bess warned in a hoarse whisper, "Look
out there on the water! There's Fred Jenkins in a rowboat!"

Nancy and George turned, but could not see the boat very clearly through the brush. They wondered if Fred had seen them tumble. One thing was sure—he had made no effort to help them. He was far from shore and going past the spot where they were.

As the two girls reached the top of the embankment, Bess said, "The rowboat Fred was in looked just like the one we saw that mysterious man go off in!"

"The boat wasn't marked and there may be many others like it," George said. "Personally, I think Fred Jenkins is too stupid to be mixed up in this mystery."

"Well, I'm not so sure he isn't in it," Nancy declared. "Doesn't it strike you as odd that very often he is around when we are? I admit he seems stupid, but someone else may be having him spy on us. It's even possible he personally faked that telephone call about Hannah Gruen."

George was indignant. "I vote we find out at once."

Bess looked at her cousin and asked, "And how in the world are you going to do that? If Fred is guilty, you don't suppose he's going to tell us?"

George had no answer to this and the three girls walked along in silence for several minutes. Then Nancy said, "I think I have a solution. We'll ask Mrs Holman where Fred lives and quiz some of his neighbours about him."

When they reached home, the housekeeper looked in astonishment at Nancy and George. "You really meant it when you said you were going digging. Did you find anything besides the skeleton?"

Nancy showed her the ribbon with the word *Belle* on it and explained where she had found it. "That's our whole score," said George, "plus some beads and arrowheads. No wedding gifts, no gold."

The girls bathed and put on fresh clothes. They came downstairs and asked Mrs Holman for Fred Jenkins' address. She gave it to them and inquired, "Do you want to see him?"

Nancy told her what she had in mind, but pledged the housekeeper to secrecy. "I won't say a word," the woman promised.

It was late afternoon when the girls set off in the convertible with the top down. Fred lived in a section of old, small homes. The guest house where he had a room was respectable but run down.

A pleasant woman answered Nancy's ring and said that Fred was not at home. She smirked broadly. "*Three* attractive young ladies coming to visit him! And him kind of simple at times."

Bess and George were about to reveal that they were not personal friends of Fred's, but Nancy gave them a warning look. A sudden idea had come to her.

She laughed. "Fred is simple only at times?" she asked the landlady.

"That's right," the garrulous woman replied. "He's as bright as the next one when he sets his mind to it."

"I'm glad to hear that," said Nancy. "Otherwise, it would be hard for him to earn a living, I suppose."

The guest-house owner stared at Nancy. "You're a bright one yourself. You're right. Fred couldn't hold down a job if he wasn't bright sometimes."

Nancy went on quickly. "That's why we're here—to see about giving Fred a job. I want my car washed. But I'll be in touch with him."

The woman assured her that she knew Fred would be delighted to do any kind of a job for such an attractive girl. Nancy ignored the compliment. Secretly she wondered if the woman were trying to get information from her. She asked, "Oh, by the way, does Fred have a family?"

"The only one I know about is his pa. He lives here with Fred."

"I see," said Nancy. "I suppose he's employed too?"

The guest-house owner crossed her arms and leaned forward so that her face was very close to Nancy's. She spoke as if she didn't want anyone to hear her except the girls.

"Kind of funny about him. He's a strange man. Don't talk much, and as far as I know he don't work neither. But you know what? The last month or so, every single clear day he leaves here in the morning and don't come back until night."

"What makes you think he's not working?" Nancy asked.

The woman shrugged. "Oh, you can tell. I've had enough boarders in this place to know when somebody's got a regular job and when they ain't. But I just can't figure out what that man is doing with himself all day."

A silence followed which George broke by grinning and saying, "Maybe he's sitting in the park feeding the birds!"

The woman laughed, but said, "Not him. He's got a gleam in his eye, like he's got something to do. I try to talk to him sometimes, but he always cuts me off."

"Does he look like Fred?" Bess asked.

"No, he's a little fella compared to his son. Fred's

got good muscles. I think one time he did a little boxing." The woman laughed softly. "Maybe he got punched in the head and that's what makes him simple sometimes."

After thanking the landlady for the information, the girls said goodbye. Bess and George noticed that Nancy did not leave her name and address. When they had crossed the street and were back in the convertible, Bess asked her about this. "Did you really mean that about Fred washing your car?"

"You'll admit it could stand a wash and we needed an excuse for coming. The reason I didn't leave my name and address is that I'm sure Fred'll figure out who was asking for him. I'm convinced his stupidity and forgetfulness is an act. He's plenty smart enough to be working against us in this mystery."

"And what about his father?" George asked. "He sounded like a mysterious person. Do you suppose *he* could be the digger?"

Before Nancy could answer, the girls saw a short, slight man walking towards the house.

"He's the man we saw in the rowboat this afternoon!" Bess cried.

He looked at the girls for a second, then turned suddenly and hurried down the street, almost on a run.

"I'll follow him," Nancy said.

This meant turning the car round, which lost precious time. The other girls saw the man turn a corner, but by the time Nancy reached the intersection, he was out of sight.

"Why would he run away unless he's guilty?" Bess mused.

"Good question," George answered. "But guilty of what?"

If Nancy came to any conclusions, she kept them to herself. During the rest of the drive she was silent, preoccupied with her own thoughts. This had certainly been an eventful day.

"But what have I really learned from it?" she asked herself. The mystery seemed as baffling as ever, but she felt sure that the man who had eluded them was mixed up in it somehow. "And he certainly fits the description of Fred's father," she decided.

When the girls reached the Rorick home they found Ned, Burt, and Dave sprawled out in comfortable chairs in the living-room. As they rose to greet the girls, they pretended to be weak-kneed and dizzy. "Oh, all that studying today!" Dave said. "I'm only half-alive!"

The other two boys looked equally exhausted. "But you can help us," Burt said weakly.

"How?" George asked suspiciously.

"By taking pity on us," Ned said. He added, "Just go out into the country with us for dinner and some dancing. You'll be surprised how soon we'll revive."

Everyone laughed. In unison, the three girls said, "We accept."

"Chuck Wilson and his date are coming too," Ned said, "so we rented a large car."

Nancy went to tell Mrs Holman where they were going. The woman said she hoped the young people would have fun. Then Nancy went to her room to put away her car keys.

The evening was wonderful indeed, not only because of the animated conversation, good food, and excellent music, but because of plans Nancy was able to make.

She announced to the others, "Ned and I have made a date to go diving for the *Lucy Belle*!"

"That's good," said Chuck. "What do you hope to find?"

Nancy chuckled. "Treasure!"

Since the boys had to study the following morning, the girls insisted they all return home at a reasonable hour so their escorts could get up early. Ned took the wheel, and after dropping off Chuck and his date, finally turned into the Rorick driveway. The headlights shone brightly on the front of the house.

Suddenly Nancy gasped and exclaimed, "My car is gone!"

· 15 ·

Tell-tale Grass

At Nancy's announcement the six young people jumped from Ned's car and began searching for Nancy's convertible.

"Did you leave the key in the ignition or somewhere else in the car?" Ned asked.

"No, I didn't, Ned. I made a special trip to my room to put the car keys away."

He suggested that Nancy run upstairs and find out if they were still there. In a few minutes she returned, waving her keys. "Here they are. No thief took them."

Bess stated flatly, "The phantom must have stolen the car!"

"Then he's pretty clever at starting a motor without keys," Dave remarked.

"Oh, Nancy, what will you do?" Bess wailed.

Nancy said she would call the police immediately and went into the house. Mrs Holman, extremely nervous over this latest occurrence in the mystery, declared she felt responsible.

"I should have kept my ears open," she said. "But I admit I had the TV on and didn't hear a sound from outside."

"It's not your fault," Nancy said kindly, slipping an arm round the woman's shoulders.

Nancy phoned police headquarters and gave a description of her car, the licence and engine numbers. "I'll alert our men at once," the duty sergeant told her.

A few minutes later Nancy was thanking Ned for the fun-filled evening.

"I'm sorry it had to end this way," he said. "But cheer up! The Emerson police will locate your car, even if they haven't found the phantom!"

Nancy was awakened the next day by a tap on her door and called, "Come in!" Mrs Holman stood there, a broad smile on her face.

"You won't believe it, Nancy, but your car is back!"

"What!" Nancy cried. "The police found it this quickly?"

Mrs Holman said she did not know who had found it. When she had looked out of her bedroom window which faced the front of the house, there stood Nancy's car! "Come and see for yourself!"

Nancy flew into the housekeeper's bedroom and gazed down at her lovely convertible. Impulsively she hugged Mrs Holman. "Isn't this marvellous!"

"It's like a miracle," the woman said.

"I must call the police at once and ask them where they found it," said Nancy.

She hurried into Mr Rorick's bedroom and dialled the number. Chief Rankin answered the phone. As the girl bubbled over with thanks at the prompt police action, he broke in, saying, "Miss Drew, I'm as amazed as you are to learn that the car is back. My men did not pick it up."

"They didn't!" Nancy exclaimed unbelievingly.

"That's right. When the night patrol went off duty, they reported no luck. And none of the day men have called in yet."

Nancy said if she learned the answer to this puzzle, she would let the chief know. She hung up, went back to her room to dress quickly, then sped downstairs and outdoors.

Curious, she looked first at the ignition lock. There was no key in it! Nancy blinked. "If I hadn't had witnesses," she thought, "I'd think I had dreamed the whole thing!"

Now Nancy noticed that the car had been washed and polished! Instantly her mind flew to Fred Jenkins. Had the guest-house owner told him what Nancy had said? Did *he* know how to start a car without a key?

"But this is crazy! If Fred knew I wanted him to wash the car, why didn't he just come here today and do it?"

Nancy strode back into the house. By this time Bess and George were up. They were amazed to hear what had happened. Bess shook her head in complete puzzlement. "Nancy, this is the craziest mystery you've ever asked us to help you solve!"

Nancy laughed. "I guess you're right."

After breakfast Fred Jenkins arrived to cut the grass on the front lawn. She rushed outside and asked him point-blank, "Fred, did you take my car away from here last night and wash it?"

The youth, instead of being startled, grinned. "Yes, Miss Nancy, I did. Guess you were surprised."

"Surprised!" exclaimed Nancy. "I was greatly alarmed. Why did you do it?"

Fred looked at her as if he were hurt. "You wanted your car washed, didn't you?"

Nancy stared at the young man. "But how did you move it? I didn't leave the key in it!"

Fred looked blank. "Yes, you did, Miss Nancy. Otherwise, I couldn't have started it."

The two stared at each other, deadlocked on the subject. Nancy had a strong hunch Fred was lying. But what was the point of it all?

Fred looked around uneasily and said in a low voice, "You say you didn't leave the key in the lock, but still I found one. Besides, I left it there. That's kind of spooky, isn't it?"

Nancy eyed him thoughtfully. "It's gone now," she said, then asked, "How much do I owe you for washing the car?"

Fred answered loftily. "I wouldn't think of taking any money. It was a pleasure to do something for you and I'm sorry I frightened you."

"That's all right," Nancy said, smiling warmly. "Thank you so much."

Later, when she was talking to the other girls about the strange episode, George said, "Don't let him fool you, Nancy. He meant to steal the car, but somehow he heard the police had been alerted, so he washed it to have an alibi, and brought it back."

Bess was sure George was right. Nancy did not commit herself. She changed the subject and said, "Let's investigate the library and see if the phantom has been here again. Last time I was in there I switched two books with the word *roar* in them. I'll be curious to see if they're still where I left them."

Suddenly Bess giggled. "Poor Uncle John! He'll never know where to find his books again. They've been put back helter-skelter."

Nothing in the library looked as if it had been disturbed since the girls' last visit, but the two books Nancy had mentioned had been put back in their places.

"Well," said Bess, "if the phantom has been here again, he wasn't so disorderly this time."

Mrs Holman, who had followed the girls into the room, heard the remark and a look of fright came over her face.

Nancy turned to her. "Mrs Holman, have you been in this room since all of us were here together."

"No indeed. I wouldn't come in alone if I were paid to do so!"

"But somebody with bits of grass on his shoes has been," Nancy stated.

The others looked at her blankly. "How do you know?" the housekeeper asked.

The young sleuth pointed towards the safe. In front of it was a sprinkling of shrivelled-up grass clippings. There were no footprints to be seen, but Nancy rushed upstairs for her special magnifying glass and went over the carpet in front of the safe. She could find no prints. There were none anywhere else in the room except those made by Mrs Holman and the girls.

Nancy continued to stare at the bits of grass. "Fred mowed the back lawn yesterday," she said, "so the phantom must have come through it last night. These cuttings are withered."

"He got into the house through locked doors again," Mrs Holman said grimly.

Nancy decided to try once more to find an opening into the room. She would see if any of the built-in book-cases moved outwards and perhaps reveal a secret entrance to the library. She asked the others to help her and together they tugged and hunted for hidden springs. They could find nothing.

Presently Mrs Holman announced that she would have to be excused to get luncheon. She expected Mr Rorick home by one o'clock. Bess offered to help her while Nancy and George continued to search.

"How do you figure anyone can walk around here without leaving footprints?" George questioned.

Nancy shrugged. "I presume he's in stocking-feet. Let's look around outdoors and see if we can find any evidence."

Nancy locked the library door and the two girls went outside.

"Let's check the grass of the rear lawn first," Nancy suggested.

They found small mounts of withered grass clippings cut by Fred, raked up but not carried away. One pile was partly scattered.

"I guess this is our answer," Nancy said. "The phantom crossed the lawn here, and some clippings clung to the bottom of his trousers. They dropped off while he was kneeling at the safe."

Very faint depressions were visible in the pile—not clear enough to be identified as anyone's footprints. The girls could find nothing else, so now they began to scan the entire foundation carefully. There was not a single footprint near it. Finally the two searchers gave up and went into the house.

At exactly one o'clock Mr Rorick drove up and came in. He was jovial and looked rested from his vacation.

"Well, how's the mystery going?" he asked. "Have you solved it yet?"

Nancy admitted defeat, saying she really was baffled about the phantom. Uncle John praised her for what she had discovered so far and insisted she continue.

"I don't care if it takes all summer," he said. "But just don't leave me with an unsolved mystery."

"All summer!" Nancy instantly thought of all the plans she had and knew she would not be able to stay at Emerson much longer. She set her jaw in determination. Before she left, she *must* find out who the phantom was and how he entered the library!

As soon as luncheon was over, she told Mr Rorick about the pieces of grass in front of the safe. "Perhaps you'd better open the safe and see if everything is still there."

"I'll do that. But it would take a professional safe-cracker to figure out that combination."

The whole group trooped into the library. Mr Rorick knelt on the floor in front of the safe and began to dial the combination. In a few moments he grasped the handle and turned it. The door swung wide open.

Uncle John looked inside. A startled expression came over his face and he quickly began pulling out various envelopes. When they all lay on the floor, he turned to the others, his face pale.

"All the money that was in there is gone!"

· 16 ·

Stolen Coin Collection

"ALL your money's gone!" Bess exclaimed in dismay.

The other girls expressed their sympathy and George suggested calling the police at once.

The elderly man shook his head. "They wouldn't believe us about the phantom, so why should they believe me now?"

The housekeeper asked gently, "Isn't it possible that you took the money out so you'd have it for your trip to the reunion?"

Uncle John Rorick shook his head vigorously. "No," he said. Suddenly the memory of something came to him and he jumped up, his eyes staring into space and his hands clutched above his head. He began to pace the room, shaking his head from side to side as if in great pain.

"Is something else wrong?" Nancy asked.

Mr Rorick turned and faced the others. "My coin collection is gone too!"

At this announcement Mrs Holman fell into a chair. "Your coin collection! Oh no!"

There was silence for several seconds, then Bess ventured, "Was it very valuable?"

"Valuable?" Uncle John almost roared. "It was priceless!"

This statement stunned the girls.

"How were the coins kept?" Nancy asked.

"In collectors' books. They ranged all the way from pennies up to ten-dollar gold pieces in old American money. And then, there were some very rare ones from Europe. I even had some that were minted before Christ. One was a rarity among ancient coins. It contained a female head and had been minted about 350 B.C. in Carthage. The other, showing eagles attacking a hare, was made in 410 B.C. in Agrigentum."

The distraught man continued to walk up and down. Nancy asked him if he had a list of the stolen coins. Mr Rorick shook his head sadly.

"I should have. But I never made one."

"Let's write down as many of them as you can remember," Nancy suggested, "and we can give these to the police at least. You won't refuse now to tell the authorities, will you?"

"No. They should know. I want that collection back! It's worth a fortune!"

As George went to call Chief Rankin, Nancy took a pad and pencil from the desk. She wondered if the thief thought he had found part of the treasure of coins from the *Lucy Belle*.

Nancy began to write as Uncle John dictated. "One of my ten-dollar gold pieces was minted in 1798," he said. "It was in very fine condition and is worth nineteen hundred dollars."

"Nineteen hundred dollars!" Bess repeated.

"Yes," replied Uncle John. "Then there was a half eagle, minted in 1827, that had never been circulated. That's worth twenty-five hundred dollars!"

"Good grief!" George exclaimed.

After a few more minutes of dictating, Uncle John paused. Bess asked him, "What was the most valuable coin in the collection?"

Before he answered, the girls thought they detected tears in the corners of the elderly man's eyes. "It was a gold one-hundred ducat from Poland, dated 1621. On the obverse side is a picture of Sigismund III wearing armour and the collar of the Golden Fleece. On the reverse side there is a crowned shield. It is a real rarity among European coins."

"How much is that worth?" Nancy asked.

"Seventy-five hundred dollars!"

There was a great gasp from the girls and Mrs Holman. All of them came forward either to pat Mr Rorick's shoulder or put an arm round him.

"This is terrible, terrible!" said the housekeeper, who was fighting back tears.

The sad scene was interrupted by the doorbell. Mrs Holman went to answer it and reappeared bringing Chief Rankin with an officer whom he introduced as Detective Newmark.

For the first time the chief admitted that a real phantom thief was plaguing Mr Rorick. The officer expressed regret that there was not a complete list of the coins but took the paper on which Nancy had been writing. When he saw the amounts listed, his eyes widened in amazement.

Detective Newmark examined the bits of grass in front of the safe. Nancy told him how she believed they had been left there, and he thought she was right. Then he asked Mr Rorick if the combination of the safe had been written down and hidden anywhere in the house.

The elderly man shook his head. "My housekeeper and I memorized it. No one else knows the combination and there is no written copy of it."

The two officers gave Mrs Holman a searching look. Mr Rorick came to her defence at once. "Mrs Holman is like a member of my own family. I would trust her with any secret."

"Perhaps," Nancy said, "the theft was done by an expert safecracker."

"That's a possibility," the detective agreed.

"Then the thief is probably an ex-convict or a wanted criminal," the young sleuth suggested.

Chief Rankin admitted this might be the case and asked Detective Newmark to get his finger-printing materials from the car. The detective did this, and went all over the outside and inside of the safe. There was only one set of prints.

"They must be mine," Uncle John spoke up.

The detective got another kit from the car, took the old man's prints, and compared them with the ones he had lifted from the safe. "Yes, Mr Rorick is correct," he said. "Whoever the thief was, he left no finger prints."

Suddenly Mrs Holman gave a tremendous sigh. "Our phantom has no fingerprints and no footprints, and he goes right through the walls!"

Neither of the officers had an answer to the puzzles, but they promised to telephone Mr Rorick if they picked up any professional safe-crackers.

After they had gone, the girls tried once more to comfort their host. Nancy remarked, "Since we can't locate the phantom here, perhaps we can trace the coins and they, in turn, may lead us to the thief."

Mr Rorick sighed. "I'm going to lie down in my room," he said. "Don't anyone disturb me until dinnertime."

Nancy glanced at the desk clock and remarked that she had a date with Ned to go scuba diving. She excused herself and went upstairs. She put on her swimsuit and slipped a dress over it.

Bess and George came to tell her that Burt and Dave had arrived at the house. At the boys' request, they made tentative plans for the three couples to meet at dinnertime.

Ned arrived later. As he and Nancy left, Mrs Holman, on her way to the kitchen, warned the young detective to be careful.

Nancy smiled. "That's just what our housekeeper, Hannah Gruen, would have told me," she said. "Thank you. I promise."

As Ned started the convertible Nancy asked if he would first drive her to the locksmith shops in Emerson. "I want to find out if Fred Jenkins or anybody else had a key made for my car."

She told how Fred had insisted there was a key in the ignition when he had taken the convertible.

"I don't believe that," Ned stated firmly. "But we'll go to the shops and find out."

There were only two locksmiths in town and both of them told Nancy they had not made a car key for Fred Jenkins or any other person during the past two days.

"Just as I suspected!" Nancy exclaimed as Ned drove towards Settlers' Cove. "Fred lied to me and I think I know why."

"Then you're a marvel." Ned grinned.

"He took the car to make me believe that the key had been in it. Then he suggested my key had been two places at once—that there was something supernatural about the incident. He was trying to scare me."

"But why," said Ned, "unless he's mixed up with the phantom?"

"I wouldn't be surprised if he is," Nancy declared.

They discussed the handy-man until they reached the end of the dirt road that led to the riverbank.

"We'd better forget Fred and concentrate on our diving," Ned remarked. "I'm as curious as you to get a glimpse of the *Lucy Belle*."

As the couple were donning their scuba gear, Burt and Dave were talking with Bess and George in the Rorick living-room.

"Where would you like to go?" Burt asked.

George grinned. "Somewhere that won't cost you a nickel."

"Swell!" the boys said in unison.

Becoming serious, George said that she and Bess would like to do something to help Nancy with the mystery. The two couples talked for a long time but came to no conclusion.

Then suddenly Dave said, "Say, maybe that phantom goes down the chimney like Santa Claus!"

Eager for action, the four ran up to the second floor and climbed out of a window on to the roof. They turned towards the chimney which led down to the dining-room and library.

"Look!" said Burt. "There's an iron ladder built on the side of the chimney. Maybe the phantom climbs up that."

Dave offered to climb it. "I'll play Santa!" he said.

Reaching the top, he looked inside. Apparently he saw something interesting, because he leaned far down. The next instant his feet slipped off the top rung of the ladder. Dave disappeared head first down the chimney!

· 17 ·

Scuba Scare

"Oh!" Bess screamed in fright as she saw Dave fall.

She dashed across the roof and climbed the ladder. Looking into the chimney, she could see Dave's legs thrashing wildly. He was not far down.

"Are you hurt?" she called to him anxiously. His reply was a muffled, unintelligible one.

George and Burt had hurried to the foot of the chimney and wanted to know what had happened.

"Dave's stuck, but I think we can pull him out," Bess answered. "Climb up here and we'll try."

The two quickly climbed the ladder. Burt grabbed one of Dave's legs, while the two girls took the other. It was a precarious position for George and Burt, since Bess was the only one with a good foothold. In trying to yank out their friend, George and Burt might easily lose their balance.

"Be careful!" Bess warned them. "One accident is enough."

Dave seemed to be pinned in such a way that he was unable to help himself. George guessed that probably his head and shoulders were stuck in one of the flues. The imprisoned boy began to cough. No doubt he was breathing soot!

"Let's pull!" Burt urged. "One, two, three!"

He and the two girls tugged with all their might and managed to move Dave's body upwards about six inches. There were more muffled words from him, but this time Bess was sure he was saying, "Take it easy!"

Burt called down, "Hold your breath, buddy. It will make it easier for us!"

He now asked the girls to give another yank. This time Dave was able to call out clearly, "Okay," and began to help himself.

Little by little he was pulled to the top of the chimney. What a sight he was—completely blackened with soot! But Dave seemed unhurt as he perched on the edge of the chimney.

"You sure you're all right?" Bess asked solicitously.

"Sure," said Dave. "But give me first prize for being the stupidest guy in Emerson!"

Burt grinned. "And the dirtiest! You look like the black Phantom!"

Everyone laughed, then George asked if Dave had found out anything by his descent.

"Only that there are two flues that go off at angles. As a detective, I'm afraid I'm a failure. What do you say we all go into the house? I'd like to take a shower."

Bess climbed down the ladder, went across the roof, and through the attic window. The others followed in quick succession. When they reached the first floor, Bess suggested that Burt bring down Dave's sooty clothes which could be put through the washing machine and the drier.

"I'll do that," he said.

The girls found Mrs Holman in the kitchen and

explained what had happened. She shook her head and said, "I never knew people could have so many adventures in such a short time!"

Bess laughed. "This is one we can't blame on Nancy except indirectly."

George noticed a large, shopping-order pad and a pencil hanging on a hook. She removed them and began to sketch. Mrs Holman and Bess were busy talking about what had happened to Dave and did not notice the picture George was drawing.

A moment later Burt appeared with the sooty clothes and Bess asked if she might use the washer and drier.

"Yes, indeed," said Mrs Holman. "I'll go down to the basement with you and show you how they work. Afterwards, I'll press the suit for you."

While the two were gone, George continued her work. Twenty minutes later it was finished, and even she as creator had to smile at it. The sketch showed a chimney with a ladder. Diving into it head first was Santa Claus. Underneath she had printed: SANTA CLAUS GOES TO MEET THE PHANTOM.

When the whole group assembled later, she presented the picture to Dave. He roared with laughter and passed it round.

Then he said, "Santa Claus always leaves gifts. Tell you what. I'll take you all to supper if you'll pick out a place that won't empty my pockets."

George laughed. "We won't give you a chance to change your mind!"

The four young people left the house, telling Mrs Holman where they would be, in case Nancy and Ned should inquire.

At that moment the young sleuth and her companion were deep in the water. They had been swimming for some time, searching the murky bottom with the lights on their headgear. Suddenly Nancy's heart began to pound with excitement. Below them was a large hulk. The *Lucy Belle*! It was indeed sunken in a watery valley and partially covered with weeds and silt.

Nancy swam round the deck, trying to locate hatches. Not seeing any, she stood on the deck to look into the cabin.

Without warning the rotted wood below her suddenly gave way, and before Nancy could make motions to swim upwards, she fell through. Her tank hose became tangled in the broken timbers and in a moment her supply of oxygen was cut off!

Like a flash Ned was at her side. He gently pulled her upwards and straightened out the hose. She nodded her thanks. The fright had left Nancy feeling a bit weak and Ned led her away from the danger spot.

He motioned as if to say, "We'd better go up!"

But as soon as Nancy had taken a few deep breaths, she felt stronger. She pointed towards the hold of the ship and started swimming round it, hoping to find an opening.

"I want to investigate the hold," she indicated to Ned.

On the far side of the sunken vessel they found a huge hole where a hatch had evidently blown out. Apparently this was where cargo had been loaded and unloaded.

With their headgear lights turned on full, the two swimmers went inside. As they had expected, they were in the engine room where the fatal explosion had taken place. They swam through blown-out walls into the area beyond. There was no question but that this was the hold of the ship. However, there was nothing in it. They both wondered what had happened to the contents.

Ned was thinking, "Probably divers in recent years have taken whatever was here."

Nancy had the same thought, but she still had a strong hunch that the chest of gold coins and the valuable Rorick cargo had been removed from the sinking ship by one or more persons who had escaped the wreck.

The couple swam out of the hold and once more Ned pointed upwards. Again Nancy shook her head. It had occurred to her that possibly the water in the tributary was higher now than it had been back in the 1700's. There might be caves along the coast where the chests had been hidden for safe keeping.

"If something happened to the survivors before they had a chance to come back for the treasure," Nancy reasoned, "then it could still be here!"

She led the way towards the shoreline and began swimming quickly, searching for caves. There was nothing in sight. Finally Ned, indicating that their time for safety underwater was up, insisted that they surface.

In a few moments they came up at a spot not far from where they had parked the car. They removed their scuba gear and sat down in the warm, late-afternoon sun to dry off.

"I'm disgusted," said Nancy. "I didn't learn a thing."

Ned laughed. "You surprise me, Miss Detective. You've always taught me that false clues *do* prove certain things."

The young sleuth smiled. "I stand corrected. We know that the treasures we're looking for are not in the *Lucy Belle* or hidden underwater along this shore."

As soon as the couple had dried off, they walked back to the car. Nancy slipped her dress over her head and put on her sandals while Ned donned shirt and trousers.

He glanced at the car clock and reminded Nancy that it was nearly dinner-time. "Weren't we going to meet the other four?" he asked.

"Yes, if we could make it. But before we go back to the house, I'd like to drive to police headquarters and find out if they've picked up any safecrackers."

When they reached the police building, Nancy hurried inside. The chief was not there but a sergeant on duty answered her question. Two known safecrackers, now on parole, had been picked up for questioning. Both were tall men. They did not fit the description of the phantom thief.

"Thank you," Nancy said. When she reached the car, she relayed the message to Ned. "I have been suspecting a short, slight man of being the phantom. Now the question is, am I wrong or is the phantom someone who does not have a police record?"

Ned chuckled. "Nancy, you certainly can pose the most unanswerable questions. I plead ignorance."

He started the car, but had gone no farther than the next corner when Nancy said, "Please turn left."

"But why?" Ned asked. "We go the other way to Uncle John's."

Nancy explained that it was only a short distance to the guest house where Fred Jenkins lived. "I suspect he's involved in this case, not as the thief necessarily, but in some way is connected with the mystery. We might just happen to be able to learn something."

Ned turned left and Nancy directed him to the street where Fred lived. As they neared his house, Nancy suddenly exclaimed, "Here he comes out the door! And look who's with him! The man that Bess and George and I have caught glimpses of in the woods. We think *he* may be the phantom!"

"But who is he?" Ned asked.

"I believe he's Fred's father. Oh, Ned, maybe we're going to learn something really worthwhile! Let's follow them!"

· 18 ·

Secret Key Maker

FRED JENKINS and the man with him proved to be fast walkers. They apparently were in a hurry to get somewhere and did not turn once, so Nancy felt sure that they had not spotted her car following them.

After walking two blocks the men went into a garage. Ned parked some distance down the street and they waited. Soon a battered old car was driven out of the building by Fred Jenkins. The slight man sat beside him.

"Let's go!" Nancy urged. "But try to keep at least two cars behind them."

The trail led a good distance out into the country. As Ned watched the road, Nancy kept her eyes on Fred and the other man. So far as she could judge, they took no particular notice of the couple. Presently the men turned left on a narrow dirt lane which led towards the river.

"Shall I still follow?" Ned asked, stopping at the turnoff.

"Not with the car," Nancy replied. "How about parking it over there among the trees? Then we'll follow on foot."

"Okay."

After Ned had put the top up, locked the car, and pocketed the keys, the couple started down the lane. There had been no rain for several days and the roadway was extremely dusty. The tyre tracks of Fred Jenkins' car were easy to see.

Nancy walked in the grass along the side, explaining that it was less dusty and also it might be just as well if the two of them did not leave footprints.

The lane was long, and as they came near the river, there were trees on both sides. They were so close together that it was difficult to see anything beyond them.

Suddenly Nancy stopped short. "I hear a car. It sounds as if it's going from the river in the direction of the main road."

"Do you think Fred left his passenger at the river front and has taken another lane back?"

Nancy shrugged, but quickened her step. A few minutes later she and Ned could see the water. The lane turned right and ended in a small clearing where a ramshackle cabin stood. Fred's car was nowhere in sight.

"He went that way," Nancy said, pointing to a field of tall grass beyond the shack. A wide track of broken weeds showed where the car had been driven into it.

"They must have spotted us," Ned remarked, "or they'd have gone back up the lane."

"I wonder if they had business at this cabin," Nancy pondered.

As she started towards it, Ned caught her arm. "Better let me go first."

He knocked on the door. There was no answer.

After several knocks the couple concluded the cabin was vacant. Ned tried the door, which opened easily. There was only one large room and no one was in it.

"You stand guard at the door, Nancy," Ned suggested. "I'll just take a look around to see if I can pick up any clues."

Nancy looked out at the lane and the field, then turned to see what progress Ned was making. He was opening cupboards. All proved to be bare. Ned began to sing out:

> *"Snoopy Ned Nickerson went to the cupboard*
> *To find Nancy Drew a clue.*
> *But when he got there,*
> *Each cupboard was bare*
> *And so there was no clue for Drew."*

Nancy laughed heartily. She was about to remark that perhaps they had better go, when Ned slid back a panel under the sink. Forgetting that Nancy was standing guard, he cried out, "Nancy, look at this!"

She darted across the room as he began dragging out a heavy machine. Nancy stared at it in utter astonishment.

"It's a key-making machine!"

"It sure is," said Ned. He reached farther back under the sink. "And here are boxes and boxes of blanks. This is a locksmith's secret workshop!"

"And I suspect," Nancy said, "that the locksmith is Fred Jenkins' father! If I'm right, he could make keys to open many locks."

Ned looked at her. "Are you trying to say that he

opens any door he wishes to in the Rorick house? In other words, he's the phantom thief?"

"I have a strong hunch he is," Nancy replied.

"In that case," Ned said, "I think we should take this machine and the blanks to the police and you should report your suspicions to them."

"I agree about taking the machine to the police, but I haven't a shred of evidence that Fred or his father have anything to do with it." She decided not to mention their names until she had proof of their guilt.

Since the key-making machine was heavy, Ned said he would bring the car down. He asked Nancy to keep out of sight behind some trees in case the men returned. No one came, however, and in a little while the machine and the blanks were loaded into the car.

Ned drove at once to police headquarters. Chief Rankin, on duty now, was very much interested in the couple's story, and was glad they had brought in the machine. "I'll have some of my men watch the cabin to see who goes there."

As Nancy and Ned finally drove towards the Rorick house, Nancy had an idea. "Are any ironmongeries open this late?" she asked.

"One is. What's on your mind?"

"I was just thinking," said Nancy, "that if the key-making machine we found belongs to the phantom, he won't be able to make any more. So if we put a new padlock on the library door, he can't get in there!"

"That's right," Ned agreed, and turned down a side street to an ironmonger's. The new padlock was purchased, this one with an alarm on it, then the couple left.

When they reached the Rorick home, Mrs Holman told them where the other young people had gone. She and Uncle John were just about to sit down to dinner and asked the young couple to eat with them. "Then you can tell us all that has happened," the housekeeper said.

Smiling, Ned sniffed the air and said, "I smell roast beef! How could we refuse?"

The others laughed. A few minutes later the four sat down at the table. Nancy and Ned both laughed and shuddered upon hearing the story of Dave's fall into the chimney. Then they related all of their adventures and why they had bought a new padlock.

"This is a brand-new type," Ned said, showing how it worked. "The man told us they had just come in and his store is the only one in Emerson to stock them."

"It has an alarm on it," Nancy explained. "If anyone tries to pick it tonight we'll certainly know it!"

"Very good," said Mr Rorick.

Mrs Holman added, "I'm sure I'll sleep better now."

Nancy said that she had a plan to put into operation after dinner. It would prove whether or not the phantom did enter the library by way of the door.

"Uncle John, would you mind going in there as soon as it's dark and turning on all the lights? Don't draw the curtains. Take all the notes from your wallet and place them in a couple of the books with the word *roar* in them. Be sure to put them on the pages which match the amount of money."

Uncle John smiled. "You want to trap the phantom?"

Nancy laughed. "That's right. If he's watching, I'm sure he won't be able to resist the money."

Mrs Holman remarked, "It's deliberately inviting a burglar into your home. But I suppose it's worth the risk if it will trap the thief."

About ten o'clock Bess and George and their dates arrived and the whole group talked for some time. Uncle John had played his role of planting the money in the library, the old padlocks had been removed and the new one installed. Everyone felt sure the mystery was about to be solved. Ned, Burt, and Dave offered to keep watch, but Mr Rorick insisted that he could handle the situation.

The boys left at eleven o'clock. Windows and doors were securely locked, then Uncle John, Mrs Holman, and the three girls went to the first floor.

Bess and George soon fell asleep, but Nancy was restless. She kept getting out of bed and walking to the window. About twelve o'clock, as she gazed towards the woods, she saw a flickering light spring up among the trees.

"The phantom is here!" she murmured to herself.

She watched for some time, then the light went out. Was the mysterious person on his way to the house? Would he soon let himself in and find the new padlock? Nancy tensed, waiting for the alarm to sound.

The minutes crept by. All was silent. Nancy began to feel chilly and went back to bed. She listened intently but could hear nothing downstairs. Finally, in sheer exhaustion, she fell asleep.

In the morning everyone compared notes. No one had heard the alarm go off!

"But how about the money in the library?" Mrs Holman asked. "If it has been stolen, then we'll know

that the thief *is* a phantom and goes through walls!"
But the others were certain that the money would still
be in the books.

The group watched while Nancy opened the padlock, then they marched into the library. Everyone
waited excitedly while Mr Rorick went to examine the
hiding places in the books.

He picked up one and looked inside. A peculiar
expression came over his face. He did not speak. Instead, he turned the book upside down and shook it.
No money fluttered out!

· 19 ·

An Amazing Passageway

THE whole affair took an unexpected turn. Nancy went up to Mrs Holman and hugged her.

"You were right all along. The phantom literally goes 'through the walls'."

"Oh, bless you!" the housekeeper said, tears in her eyes. "I'm glad that someone believes me."

George, always practical, asked, "But which wall?"

Mr Rorick stood stupefied. He seemed completely unable to believe what had happened. Again the phantom had taken his money without any visible means of entrance and exit. The elderly man shook his head in dismay.

Finally Nancy answered George's question. "As you know, I have searched this room thoroughly, and the police have, too. There's one place left that the thief may use—a spot I thought was impossible."

"What's that?" Bess asked.

"The chimney."

"But how could the phantom get through solid brick?" Bess argued.

George snapped her fingers. "When we were up on the roof, Dave said the flues slanted towards the outside

139

of the chimney. Could that have anything to do with it?"

"It certainly could," Nancy replied. "I wish I'd known this before."

She looked up the flue in the library, then dashed out to the hall and into the dining-room. In a few moments she was back.

"The flues are far apart from left to right as you stand in front of this fireplace," she reported. "I wonder if, by any chance, there could be an opening between them which runs from here into the dining-room!"

Everyone gazed at the wooden panelling which covered the fireplace wall from ceiling to mantel. For the first time Nancy realized that the mantelshelf was very wide—wide enough for a person to stand on. Grabbing the shelf with both hands, she pulled herself up and began tapping each panel. Suddenly a broad smile lighted up her face.

"There's a small section here that sounds hollow!" she exclaimed.

Nancy hunted a long time for a hidden spring. She pushed on various sections of each panel and also tried to raise or slide them. But she failed to detect anything which might open a hidden door. The young sleuth refused to give up.

Although the panels were tightly wedged together, Nancy was sure there was some mechanism hidden between two of them.

"Bess, will you find me the thinnest nail file you can?" she requested.

In less than a minute Bess was back with an almost paper-thin one. Carefully Nancy tried inserting it between a hollow-sounding panel and the one next to it.

Suddenly her efforts were rewarded. The nail file pressed out a wafer-thin metal lever and at the same moment the whole section above the centre of the fireplace swung outwards. It swept Nancy to the floor!

"You've done it! You've found it!" Bess cried ecstatically as she helped Nancy to her feet.

The whole group gazed into a dark, narrow passageway which they felt sure opened into the dining-room.

"We'll find out in a minute!" Nancy said, running from the room. The others followed.

Nancy removed the candlesticks from the dining-room mantelshelf. Then she climbed up and inserted the nail file in the section that backed up the one above the fireplace in the library. A long, narrow door, reaching from the ceiling to the shelf, opened outwards.

Mr Rorick was flabbergasted. "This is one secret which was never passed down in the family," he declared.

"But someone else learned about it," said George. "Yippee! Nancy has solved the mystery of the phantom! He climbed through the passageway from the dining-room, did his thieving and searching, then climbed up, closed the secret door behind him, and let himself out here."

Mrs Holman, who had been speechless all this time, now found her voice. "The police should be notified at once and come here to catch that criminal!"

Before anyone else could answer her, Nancy said, "Oh, please don't do that. I want to catch him myself —not just to capture him, but to see if I can find out what else he has been searching for."

She looked pleadingly at Mr Rorick. Finally he said, "I think we owe it to Nancy Drew to let her have her way. But there must be restrictions and a time limit. Don't take any chances. And if you don't capture him by tomorrow, then I feel I ought to notify the authorities."

Nancy was ready to put a plan into action at once. "When will Fred be here again working in the house?" she asked Mrs Holman.

"I expect him early this afternoon."

Nancy smiled. "That will be perfect."

She suggested that after Fred arrived, the others were to talk about two subjects: first, that Mrs Holman and Mr Rorick would be gone for the afternoon, and that the three girls would drive out into the country and not return for several hours. The other was for Uncle John to announce loudly that he had brought some valuable jewellery back with him and would lock it in the safe before leaving.

"If Fred is helping his father or someone else, he'll immediately pass the word along. I'm sure that either he or a confederate will come into the library to take the jewellery."

She went on to say that Mrs Holman was to telephone the house at a certain time and ask Fred to carry a large amount of rubbish out to a certain place in the woods. While he was gone, the three girls would sneak back, go through the secret passageway, and hide themselves behind the sofa and chairs in the library.

Uncle John thought a few moments before giving his consent to the plan. "I suppose it won't be dangerous with three girls against one small man!"

Nancy and her friends smiled. George, to show her enthusiasm, said, "I'm going to make a trial trip through that passageway."

She pulled herself to the mantelshelf and started inside. She was forced to crouch a bit. Suddenly George gave a whoop of elation.

"Uncle John, I've found your coin collection!"

She appeared at the opening to the dining-room, carrying several large coin collectors' books. George handed them down to Mr Rorick, who kept murmuring, "I can't believe it! I can't believe it!"

George went on, "I wonder why the thief didn't take these along with him."

Nancy ventured an answer. "Probably he was afraid to carry them to his home. They're pretty large to conceal. Anyway, he wouldn't dare dispose of many coins at a time and what better hiding place could he have than this passage? By the way, Uncle John, can you tell at a quick glance how much has been taken out?"

Mr Rorick quickly turned the pages of the various books, then smiled in relief. "The thief took only a few hundred dollars' worth. The most valuable coins are still intact. I suppose I was foolish leaving them here, but I like to take the coins out once in a while and look at them."

"But shouldn't you put them in a safe-deposit box now?" Bess asked.

Nancy spoke up. "Why don't we leave them here where the thief hid them? Otherwise, he'll know that the secret passageway has been uncovered and he won't even come into the library!"

Mr Rorick agreed, and George replaced the books where she had found them.

Mrs Holman glanced nervously at her watch. "Sometimes Fred comes early. We'd better close these doors and busy ourselves with some kind of work so he won't be suspicious."

Fred arrived while the group was eating lunch. Mrs Holman asked him to dust the hall where she knew he would overhear everything that was said. The afternoon plans were discussed.

Soon afterwards, everybody in the house except Fred prepared to leave. At two o'clock all had left, and Mrs Holman telephoned Fred at two-thirty. By this time Nancy, Bess, and George had sneaked back to the Rorick home and hidden behind some shrubbery. When they saw Fred carrying the rubbish to the woods, they dashed inside the house. By three o'clock the girls had gone through the secret passageway, closing both the openings, and secreted themselves behind furniture in the library.

They never took their eyes off the chimney. At exactly three-thirty the secret door began to open. A man appeared in the opening and jumped down. He was Fred Jenkins' slightly built companion. The man wore gloves and was in his stocking-feet.

"No wonder he never left any fingerprints or foot-marks here," Nancy thought.

The intruder went directly to the safe, knelt down, and slowly turned the dial back and forth. Then he swung the door open, grabbed the velvet case containing costume jewellery which Mr Rorick had put there, closed the safe, and started for the fireplace.

"He's not going to search this time!" Nancy thought. "If we don't capture him now he may get away and take the coin collection with him!"

Quick as a panther Nancy came from behind the sofa and made a leap for the thief. "You're the phantom! Hands up!" she cried. Nancy was counting on the fact that the thief would not turn round and discover that she had no weapon.

Instead of complying, the man whipped a spray gun from his pocket and squirted it into Nancy's face. Instantly she dropped unconscious and he leaped for the mantel.

As George tried to block his way, he turned and gave her a dose of the knockout spray. She too blacked out and fell to the floor. Swiftly the man climbed on to the mantel.

Bess had looked on horrified. If she tried to stop him, no doubt he would give her the same treatment. Then she could not help her friends.

"Oh, what shall I do?" Bess thought with a panicky feeling.

· 20 ·

The Restored Treasure

BESS Marvin quickly collected her wits. She stood up and cried, "Stop!" At the same time, she picked up a heavy book-end from the desk.

As the thief turned to give her a dose from the spray gun, she hurled the book-end directly at it and knocked the weapon from his hand.

The sudden move made the man sway in his precarious position on the mantelshelf. The next instant he lost his balance completely and dropped to the floor. He hit his head hard and lay still.

Instantly Bess pulled herself up to the shelf and darted through the secret passageway. Though her legs were shaking with fright, she ran to the hall telephone.

Picking it up, she dialled the operator and exclaimed, "Send the police to Mr John Rorick's house at once! And have them bring a doctor! There's a thief here and three people have been knocked out!"

She heard a gasp on the other end of the wire but quickly hung up so that no time would be lost in having the message transferred. Bess sat still, trembling like a leaf. Would the officers and the physician come before the thief might revive and escape? She felt too weak to try overpowering him a second time.

The worried girl became aware that the kitchen door was opening. From where she sat Bess saw Fred Jenkins enter. "I must do something fast to keep him from finding out!" Bess thought.

The only thing left to her was conversation. Mustering all the courage she possessed, Bess hurried to the kitchen and smiled broadly at Fred. "I guess you're surprised to see me here," she said.

Fred looked scared. "Y-yes I am," he stuttered. "I thought you girls were going to be out for the afternoon."

Bess giggled. "You know how girls are. I got a good distance from here and then I remembered I'd forgotten something. Had to come back and get it. Then I decided to use the phone." Bess smiled. "Do you have a steady girl friend?"

"Why n-no," Fred answered. He kept glancing around and looking very uncomfortable. Finally he said, "Are you alone?"

Bess laughed. "What do you think I am—three people? Maybe I'm heavy enough to make three, but I do try to diet. Fred, how do you manage to stay so slim?"

"Me? I don't know. Did anyone come into the house after you did?"

Bess answered lightly, "Oh, I know Mr Rorick and Mrs Holman won't be back for some time. As for Nancy and George, I'll be joining them in a few minutes. As soon as I've talked to you a little longer.

"Tell me, Fred, do you like having odd jobs at different places? Wouldn't you rather have a steady job somewhere?" Before he had a chance to answer, she

went on, "You know, if you plan to get married sometime, your wife would want you to have a full-time
job."

Fred frowned. "I like what I'm doing. How soon are
you leaving?"

Bess shrugged. "You sound as if you want to get rid
of me. Don't you like talking to me?"

"Why—er—yes," Fred replied.

Bess kept listening eagerly for the sound of the police
car. She wondered how much longer she could keep
Fred in the kitchen talking about inconsequential
matters. She struggled on bravely. "Wouldn't you like a
snack?" She opened the refrigerator door. "Umm, I see
some delicious pudding. Want some?"

"No."

"How about a piece of cake?" Bess moved over to the
cakebox.

"No."

As he said this, a feeling of relief came over Bess. She
had heard a car roar up to the front of the house. "That
must be friends of mine," she told Fred. "I'll be seeing
you!"

As he stood rooted to the spot, she dashed to the front
door and opened it. Chief Rankin, two other officers,
and a physician hurried in. Quickly she said, "Go and
get that young man who's just running out the kitchen
door!"

Two of the officers raced in and captured the escapee.

As he was led back into the kitchen, Fred glared at
Bess. "You! You double-crossed me!"

"Yes, I did. Your father—or whoever that man is you
pal around with—is lying in the library unconscious."

"What!" Fred cried out. "My father is hurt!"

"So he is your father," said Bess. To the police she directed, "Follow me!"

She led the group into the dining-room and showed them the open door and the secret passage-way to the library. Having been in the house several times before, the officers stared at it, astounded.

Fred Jenkins' eyes almost popped out of his head. "You found it!"

"Nancy Drew found it," Bess answered. "She and my cousin George are lying in that room unconscious. Your father used a knockout spray gun on them!"

"You said my father was unconscious too," said Fred. "What happened to him?" When Bess told him, the young man blinked. "You're—you're that brave?"

Bess did not reply. Instead, she suggested that the group hurry through the passageway into the library. She herself would go to Nancy's room for the key to the new padlock. When she returned and opened it, the alarm sounded. Bess inquired of the physician how Nancy and George were.

"They'll come round in a few minutes," he answered. "No harmful after-effects. As to Mr Jenkins, he got a nasty bruise on his head as he fell. He'll take a while to wake up."

As the doctor finished speaking, Nancy stirred and opened her eyes. George took a few moments longer. Both girls blinked and looked from face to face. They were amazed to see the police, and stared up at Fred Jenkins, then across the floor towards his father.

Nancy sat up and asked what had happened. She and

George were assisted to chairs and then Bess told her story.

Both girls looked at her in utter astonishment. "Bess, our timid one!" said George.

Bess merely smiled. Suddenly her legs were getting rubbery. She was feeling the emotional strain and flopped on to the couch.

"I think Fred can clear up many points of the mystery," Bess said.

With a bit of braggadocio, the young man admitted that he had discovered the openings to the secret passageway. One day, while cleaning the dining-room, he had caught the faint glint of metal between two of the panels above the mantelshelf. He had picked at it with a knife, and suddenly the door had opened. The rest was easy.

"My father," he went on, "has two friends who know a lot about the sinking of the *Lucy Belle*. They think a treasure was taken from the wreck and buried somewhere around here. They went to the public library and the one at the university for some books that might tell about it but learned nothing."

Nancy said, "They must be the men Ned heard talking one day."

"They helped us trail you girls wherever you went. John Tregger and Hank More are smart. Oh, I shouldn't have mentioned their names." The police had already made notes. Nancy was sure the men would be picked up for questioning.

Fred shrugged and went on, "The four of us began to hunt and dig, but we didn't have any luck. Then after I found the secret way to get into the library, and saw all those books, my father said he would look through them. He was sure there must be some old records which would give him a hint. While he worked, I stood guard."

Nancy spoke up. "If you were trying to keep this thing so secret, why did you use light in the woods?"

Fred grinned. "That was my idea. After my father got into the locked room and disturbed the books, I heard Mrs Holman say nobody but a phantom could get into it. I thought I'd make the whole thing spooky and scare people off while we were digging. By the way, we always covered the places over with leaves, so you wouldn't find them!"

"What about the money you stole?" Nancy asked.

Fred looked blank. "I don't know anything about any money, honest. You mean money taken from this room?"

"Yes, plenty of it."

All this time the doctor had been working on Mr Jenkins and now the thief regained consciousness. When he was assisted to a chair, Chief Rankin said, "As soon as you feel able, *talk*."

The man looked sullenly from face to face, but glared at Nancy, George, and Bess. At first he was silent, but after a few prodding questions from Nancy, he admitted his guilt.

"I used to be a locksmith by trade," he said, "and also an expert on opening safes."

He admitted that the outfit at the river cabin was his. He had made keys to the various doors and padlocks in the Rorick home.

"If you could open the padlocks, why did you bother with the passageway?" George asked.

"So I wouldn't get caught. I was hiding in the passageway several times while other people were in the room."

Chief Rankin asked Jenkins why he had waited so long before robbing the safe. The man said he had found the combination a very tricky and difficult one to figure out.

"Tell me," said Nancy, "did you take only small amounts of money at a time from the books to avoid suspicion?"

Jenkins gave a wise smile. "I knew that Mr Rorick probably wouldn't notice. A tenner here and there kept me supplied with all I needed."

Fred stared at his father in shocked surprise. "What else did you take?" he asked.

Jenkins grinned at his son and confessed to the theft of the coins. He said those still missing were hidden in the guest house.

He also admitted having tried to frighten Nancy away from the Rorick home. When he found out the owner had asked her to solve the mystery, he had coaxed his two friends to help him scare her away. One had swamped Nancy and Ned's canoe, the other had shrieked in the woods when Ned was in the Indian costume, "We hoped these things would get you off our trail," he told Nancy, "but I guess you don't scare easy."

"Did you steal my pearl necklace?" she asked.

"Yes. It's hidden in the cabin. You look under the floor boards. Why do I want to give it back to you? Because I admire your grit!"

This was the first time in Nancy's life that a thief had voluntarily offered to return property because he admired her! She had to smile.

During the next fifteen minutes Fred Jenkins and his father made several other admissions. Fred's father had thought of the prank of the thumbprints. He knew a very large man with huge thumbs and for a fee got him to make marks on several papers.

"I sure had you fooled that time I dropped one of the papers." He smirked. "I was up in a tree all the time but you never spotted me."

Fred admitted to pretending that there had been a phone call for Nancy about Hannah Gruen, and pushing the threatening note under the front door. He had taken Nancy's car away to wash it. His father had helped him start the motor without a key. They had taken the car to the shack along the river. While Fred washed it, his father had made a key to the ignition to make it easier to drive back.

"We didn't leave the key in the lock, but I said it had been there to make you think the phantom had done it and you'd worry."

"What I want to know," said Nancy, "is whether or not you found any part of the treasure from the *Lucy Belle*."

Mr Jenkins shook his head. "If it's true that the treasure is still around, it's well hidden."

Chief Rankin interrupted. "If you girls have no further questions to do with the robbery, we'll take these two men in. Please ask Mr Rorick to come down to headquarters and make a formal charge against them."

The prisoners were led away. Bess said, "Won't Uncle John and Mrs Holman be amazed when they return? Just think, the mystery is solved!"

Nancy corrected her. "Only one of Uncle John's two mysteries. Don't forget we haven't found the wedding gifts."

George said she did not have one single hunch to offer Nancy. Bess declared her brain would not work any more.

"Well, I have an idea," said Nancy. "Suppose that the Indians were kind to the exhausted survivors and helped the thieving crewmen bury the treasure, thinking it belonged to everyone. In return, the crewmen promised the Indians a share of it, but did not intend to keep the promise. When they sneaked back later to dig it up, the Indians, upon discovering they had been double-crossed, became furious at all the survivors and killed them.

"The old map shows that the massacre took place near the village. I'll bet that's where we'll find the pine tree landmark Ned thought he had located on the shore."

George stood up. "It's a long chance, but let's go!"

"Now?" Bess asked.

"Right now."

Once more the girls got their digging tools and set off for the site of the Indian village. They found no old pine trees, but after a short search they located a huge, old stump.

"Let's start here," Nancy proposed.

As Bess shoved a spade into the ground, she remarked, "Nancy Drew, you'd better be right this time, because this is the last digging I'm going to do!"

Nancy and George laughed as they took positions and began to work. The ground was hard from lack of rain and the job was not easy. The girls kept on, however.

They had almost completed a deep circle around the stump, when suddenly George exclaimed that her spade had hit something. The other two girls began to help her dig away the earth. In ten minutes two iron chests were uncovered, one on top of the other. After crusted dirt had been brushed off, the words *Lucy Belle* could be seen on the lid of the top chest.

"We've found it!" George exclaimed.

The chest was locked and it took a lot of prying with a spade to lift the lid. The girls' eyes bulged at the contents—a huge heap of gold coins!

"There must be millions of them!" Bess cried out.

"What a haul!" said George.

"But not for us," Nancy reminded them. "I suppose this belongs to the town of Emerson."

At her suggestion, the three friends combined their strength to lift the heavy chest out of the hole. Then Nancy brushed the earth off the one below it. The name Rorick stood out in bold lettering cut into the metal. Eagerly the girls hauled the second chest to the surface. In it they found a small leather trunk with a curved top. On this the name Abigail Rorick had been painted.

"The gifts!" Bess said in a hushed voice.

"Uncle John has the key to it!" Nancy exclaimed.

George said practically, "How are we ever going to get these things to the Rorick house? They're too heavy to carry."

For a few minutes no one could answer her question. Nancy glanced around at the trees. "Maybe we could make a carry-all of poles like the Indians used to do."

At her direction, the three digging tools were laid a few feet apart. Next, the girls gathered blown-down saplings, which they stripped of branches and placed side by side across the metal part of the spades.

"Won't we have to tie the chests on to the poles?" Bess asked.

Nancy said she did not think so if the girls held the handles of the spades close to the ground as they dragged them along.

It was hard work, but slowly the trio pulled their precious cargo through the woods and up to the Rorick back lawn. Just as they arrived at the rose garden, Mrs Holman glanced from the kitchen window. A minute later she and Uncle John hurried out, astonished.

"What on earth—?" the housekeeper began.

For answer, Nancy slipped open the chest of coins. "And you have the key to the little trunk, Uncle John."

"I can't believe my eyes!" he cried out. "Where? How?"

The utter bewilderment on the faces of the two older people almost amused Nancy. "We'll carry these inside while you get the key, Uncle John."

He went for it and inserted the dainty key into the corroded lock, and after much difficulty, finally turned it. As the girls pushed back the lid, everyone gasped in admiration.

Neatly packed was one of the most exquisite wedding dresses they had ever seen. With it were very pointed high-heeled white satin slippers, now yellowed with age.

The lovely veil looked so fragile that the girls were afraid to touch it, but they did pick up the ivory-handled, hand-painted fan which had been the French queen's gift to Abigail Rorick.

"It's beautiful!" Nancy exclaimed.

At the bottom of the chest lay a velvet jewel case. Uncle John asked Nancy to open it. Within, pinned to the satin lining of the case, were two exquisite miniatures painted on ivory. They were framed with jewels.

"How gorgeous! They're portraits of Louis Phillipe and his queen!" she exclaimed.

Everyone continued to stare at the array of beauty for several minutes. Then finally George said, "Wait until you hear the rest of what happened while you were away."

When she finished, Uncle John and his housekeeper were open-mouthed with amazement.

"Treasures! Gifts! The phantom in jail! A secret passageway uncovered!" Mr Rorick exclaimed. He added, "I can never thank you girls enough. What can I do to show my appreciation?"

Nancy laughed. "Don't forget that you took us in when we were homeless. That was a very big favour."

Uncle John declared that the solving of the two mysteries was cause for a celebration. "We'll have it right here. I'll engage caterers to serve the food. Among the guests will be people from the university and officials of the town of Emerson."

"And Mrs Palmer," put in Nancy. "I promised to tell her the outcome of the mystery."

"Certainly," said Uncle John. "Then together you girls and I will present the chest of gold coins to the

town officials and the wedding gown and other pieces
to the university museum." Suddenly he grinned. "But
not these precious miniatures. These I will keep and
give to the first of you three girls to be married!"

Nancy, Bess, and George blushed and Nancy quickly
changed the subject by saying she wondered what her
next mystery would be. It was not long before she
became involved in *The Mystery of the Fire Dragon*.

"Perhaps the museum would like the piece of ribbon
we found in the Indian cave," Nancy suggested.

A strange look came over the old man's face. "You
—you found that place!" he exclaimed. "Why, I could
have told you all about it and the ribbon, too. I used to
play there as a boy. Why didn't you tell me?" he added.

"I thought I did," said Nancy, and was sure she had.
"But," she added politely, "I'm afraid I forgot. I'm
sorry."

The old man chuckled. "Think nothing of it, my
dear," he said. "All of us forget things now and then—
even," he added, patting her hand, "the best of young
lady detectives!"

Nancy Drew® in

The Mystery of the Fire Dragon

The Mystery of the Fire Dragon was
first published in the U.K. in a single volume
in 1973 by William Collins Sons & Co. Ltd,
and in Armada in 1982

Contents

Mr Stromberg snatched the book from Nancy's hand

·1·

Mystery in New York

"WHAT else does Ned say, Nancy?" Mr Drew asked. He was listening intently to a letter his daughter was reading.

"Ned likes being a college exchange student in Hong Kong, and he has actually learned to speak some Cantonese, Dad!"

"Excellent. That, together with his study of Chinese culture, should make him very valuable in a number of fields," Mr Drew commented.

Nancy nodded. "He'd like to go into the United States Intelligence Service." Suddenly her serious mood changed. "Dad, listen to this." She read, " 'Nancy, can't you find a mystery to solve in this far-off colony, so I might show you around?' "

Mr Drew's eyes twinkled. "Mystery or no mystery, Nancy, you just might get to Hong Kong sooner than you think!"

"What!" the attractive blue-eyed girl exclaimed. "You mean—?"

Before Nancy could finish the question, the telephone rang and she went to answer it.

"Aunt Eloise!" Nancy cried out. "How super to hear from you! Are you in New York?"

"Yes, right in my apartment. I want you to rush here. A most peculiar thing has happened. A real mystery for you to solve."

The young blonde detective was intrigued and could hardly wait to get the details from her aunt.

Miss Eloise Drew, sister of Nancy's father, lived alone and taught at a school in the city. Her large old-fashioned apartment had been converted into two separate apartments. Each had its own entrance from the hallway.

"Two wonderful Chinese people moved in next door to me a few weeks ago," Aunt Eloise began. "We've become good friends. That's why I want to help them. There's a darling old man we call Grandpa Soong and his granddaughter Chi Che, an orphan. She's eighteen, and a student at Columbia University here.

"This afternoon, when I returned from a teachers' meeting, I found a strange note on the floor. It had been shoved under the locked door between my apartment and the Soongs'."

"And what did it say?" Nancy asked eagerly.

"It was short and unfinished," Aunt Eloise went on. "I'll read it:

'Grandpa must think I am visiting student friends from Columbia. The police must not be notified I am away or Grandpa will be harmed. I am in grave danger because I have found out that—' "

"The note ends there?" Nancy asked.

"Yes, unfortunately. Well, you see why I need you here. I feel that Chi Che is depending on me to help her but I don't know where to begin. I thought you might bring Bess and her cousin George with you."

"I'd certainly like to, Aunt Eloise, but Dad has just been talking about a trip to Hong Kong. Hold the phone while I ask him about his plans," Nancy requested.

After hearing the story, the tall, distinguished-looking lawyer smiled and said, "We won't be leaving for Hong Kong for a week. In the meantime, go to New York if you wish."

Nancy hurried back to the telephone. "I'll come tomorrow, Aunt Eloise. What time will you be back from school?"

"Between four and four-thirty."

"I'll get in touch with Bess and George right away," Nancy promised. "And, in any case, I'll come."

"Good," her aunt said. "I'm really terribly worried about Chi Che. If much more time goes by, it may be too late to help her."

After saying goodbye to her aunt, Nancy dialled the number of the Marvin home. "Hi, Bess!" she said. "How about a quick trip with me to visit Aunt Eloise?"

"Sounds nice, Nancy. But why the big hurry? Don't tell me! I know—a mystery has popped up and the trail leads to New York City," guessed blonde, slightly plump, Bess.

"You're partly right," Nancy laughed. "There is a mystery, but it started in Aunt Eloise's apartment." She briefed her friend on the details.

"Oh dear, this really does sound dangerous!" Bess exclaimed. "Do you think we should—"

"Of course I think we should try to help Chi Che," Nancy declared. "We'll take the early afternoon plane tomorrow. I'll pick you up at one-fifteen."

"Okay. I'll be ready," Bess answered. "It'll be fun just to go to New York—shops, theatre—"

"Bess," said Nancy firmly, "we have a job to do. Chi Che's in danger!"

"All right, Detective Drew. Deputy Marvin signing off. See you tomorrow."

Nancy chuckled as she called George Fayne. She was Bess's cousin but as unlike her in looks and interests as two people could be. Slender, with dark, short hair, tomboyish George was always ready for adventure.

Upon hearing Nancy's invitation, George was eager to fly to New York. "The mystery sounds intriguing," she said excitedly. "And by the way, Nancy, how about talking your dad into including me in the trip to Hong Kong?"

"I'll do my best." Nancy smiled as she hung up and returned to her father. "The girls can go with me," she said. "I'll make reservations, then please tell me about Hong Kong."

Ten minutes later father and daughter were again seated in front of the log fire which felt cosy on this crisp October evening. Presently they were joined by the Drews' housekeeper, Mrs Hannah Gruen. She had lived with them for fifteen years since the death of Mrs Drew, when Nancy was only three.

"Do sit down," Mr Drew invited her. "I'd like to tell you about a case that may take Nancy and me to Hong Kong."

The pleasant-faced woman seated herself. "Oh my! This sounds so exciting!" she commented.

"I have been retained," the attorney said, "to try to locate several people named as beneficiaries in a will which is being contested here. Their last known address was Hong Kong, but they don't answer letters sent to them by the executors.

"I've decided that the best way to find out what's happening is for me to go there. Naturally I'd like my detective daughter along to help me if necessary." He smiled. "And, naturally, a certain Ned Nickerson who is studying at Chung Chi College outside Hong Kong would like—"

Hannah Gruen laughed and Nancy blushed as her father left the sentence unfinished. Then he continued, "Nancy, I'll come home from the office to lunch tomorrow and drive you and the girls to the airport. And now, if you two will excuse me, I'll say goodnight."

Promptly at one-fifteen the following afternoon, Nancy and her father were at Bess Marvin's home. A few minutes after that they picked up George Fayne.

At the airport Nancy hugged her father, who wished the three sleuths luck. "We're ready for anything," George announced. "We even have our birth certificates with us in case we have to identify ourselves!"

"Good!" Nancy applauded. "I've learned while sleuthing to be prepared for anything. I always carry mine with me."

The girls waved as they boarded the airliner, then settled down for the flight to New York. When they reached the terminal in the city, Nancy led the others to the taxi exit, where they took a cab to Miss Drew's apartment house.

"Four-twenty," Nancy announced as she pushed the vestibule bell to her aunt's apartment. The inner door clicked open. "Oh, I'm glad Aunt Eloise is home."

The tall, attractive woman met the three girls as they emerged from the third-floor stop of the self-service elevator. "You all look wonderful!" Aunt Eloise exclaimed.

Nancy kissed her aunt a second time. "That's from Dad, and Hannah sends her best wishes, too."

As soon as they had entered the apartment, and the door was closed, the young sleuth said, "Aunt Eloise, don't keep us in suspense. Tell us everything about Chi Che and what happened."

Miss Drew produced the note the Chinese girl had written. At once Nancy noticed that in the lower right-hand corner of the stationery was a small hand-painted dragon in an Oriental shade of red. She pointed this out.

"It may be a clue," the girl detective remarked.

Aunt Eloise could add little to her story, except to say that the Soongs appeared to be very fine people and very fond of each other. They rarely had guests, because Grandpa Soong was at present spending most of his time writing a book.

"Let's call on Grandpa Soong," Nancy proposed, eager to start work solving the mystery.

Her aunt agreed. As Nancy opened the apartment door, she noticed a figure running towards the stairway. The person wore dark trousers and a loose coat.

Nancy stepped into the hall. At that instant something in front of her exploded with a loud bang!

·2·

The Dragon Clue

INSTINCTIVELY Nancy put both hands over her face and stepped backwards into the doorway. Despite her quick move she was showered with a spray of paper and sandy particles.

"What happened?" Aunt Eloise asked excitedly. "Are you hurt?"

"I—I guess not," Nancy answered, as brownish black smoke spread throughout the hallway.

Bess and George dashed from the apartment to look round for the cause of the explosion. Nancy joined them and a few seconds later held up a small tube. "I believe it was a giant firecracker someone set off."

"A firecracker!" Bess repeated, thinking that mysteries for Nancy Drew had started in many unusual ways but never before with a giant firecracker.

Ever since the time Mr Drew had asked his daughter to help him unravel *The Secret of Shadow Ranch* until recently, when Nancy had solved the mystery of *The Phantom of Pine Hill*, she had been in many precarious situations. The giant firecracker might have injured the young detective badly.

Nancy was staring at the Soongs' door. Was the explosion some kind of warning to the Soongs? Or, by chance, had someone learned that Nancy was interested in the mystery and used this means to scare her off the case?

By this time all the doors along the hallway of the apartment house were being opened and curious, frightened faces looked out. When the tenants found that no damage had been done and no one had been hurt, they closed their doors again.

The last apartment to be opened was the Soongs'. An elderly man, with a long beard and wearing a black Chinese suit, looked inquiringly at the girls.

Miss Drew stepped up and said, "Hello, Grandpa Soong. I want you to meet my niece, Nancy Drew, and her friends Bess Marvin and George Fayne."

Mr Soong bowed low. "It gives me deep pleasure to meet the relative and friends of my very fine neighbour. I was on my way to answer the buzzer when I heard a loud explosion. Can you good people tell me what happened?"

"Mr Soong, we think that a giant firecracker was set off," Nancy replied. "Would you possibly know why?"

Grandpa Soong looked startled. "I know nothing about it. You think perhaps that because most firecrackers are made in Chinese territory I should know the reason?"

"Oh, no," Nancy replied quickly. Then she told about the figure she had seen running down the hall just before the explosion.

Grandpa Soong smiled. "Without a better description, I could not identify such a man or woman. But I am sure I would not know him, anyway."

The young sleuth went from door to door along the hallway, asking the various occupants if they had noticed the running figure. Each denied having seen anyone there.

When Nancy returned to the group, Aunt Eloise invited Mr Soong into her apartment so that the girls might become better acquainted with him. Under the strong light of a reading lamp, the elderly Chinese stared at George Fayne.

Suddenly he said, "Please forgive my rudeness, but you remind me very much of my Chi Che. Of course she is Chinese and you are American, but your hair, your flashing black eyes—even your dress reminds me so much of my granddaughter who is away visiting."

George was startled, not only because Grandpa Soong did not suspect that anything unusual had happened to Chi Che, but also that she herself looked so much like the missing girl. She glanced at her clothes and had to admit that her mandarin-collared top did indeed look Oriental.

Aunt Eloise and the others seated themselves and almost at once Grandpa Soong began to talk about his writing. "My book has been many years in preparation," he said. "I spent much time in the interior of China gathering very valuable archaeological data. I hope my work will be of great benefit to mankind."

"I'm sure it will be," said Aunt Eloise. "Grandpa Soong, did Chi Che give up her after-school job at Stromberg's Bookshop?"

"Oh, no," the elderly man answered. "She loves her work and her studies. They mean much to her. I presume she has asked for a leave of absence from the shop while she is away visiting."

Nancy asked, "Did Chi Che leave you a note, Mr Soong?"

"Yes." As he took one from the pocket of his jacket, he said, "I would cherish the idea if you girls would call me Grandpa Soong," and they nodded.

The note was written in Chinese characters and Grandpa Soong began to translate it. " 'Going on holiday with college friends. Home-coming indefinite.' "

Nancy had listened intently, but now her attention was drawn to a hand-painted dragon in the lower right-hand corner of the stationery. Curious, she mentioned it.

"This stationery is not the kind used by my Chi Che," Grandpa Soong exclaimed. "It must have been given to her by the friend she's with."

He laid the note on the table, then went on, "The dragon is a very old and sacred symbol of China. The ancient name of the dragon was *Lung*, and children believed in Lung just as Western children believe in Santa Claus.

"Legend tells us also that the dragon is the god of thunder. He appears in the sky as clouds which are said to be formed by his breath. Logically, then, the dragon is good because he produces rain and that, in turn, makes good rice crops, which are so necessary to the life of Chinese people."

The elderly man's audience was fascinated. Presently Nancy said, "So often when I have seen pictures of dragons they are accompanied by strings of pearls on the beasts or on the frames. Is there any significance to this?"

"Probably, but the story is lost in antiquity," Grandpa Soong replied. "The combining of pearls with dragons in decorative designs is an ancient custom, and while used principally in China, it was also used in the East Indies and Japan."

Grandpa Soong smiled. "I have heard that originally every self-respecting dragon had a pearl embedded under his chin! This gave him a special rank."

Nancy was thinking that all this information was extremely interesting, but the subject was not furthering her endeavours to glean any clue as to why Chi Che had left the note for Aunt Eloise implying she was in danger.

Finally Nancy said, "Grandpa Soong, have you a good photograph of Chi Che?"

The man's eyes twinkled. From a pocket of his coat he pulled a picture of a most attractive Chinese girl, dressed in a greenish-blue brocaded Chinese silk dress, with an inch-high tight collar.

"Chi Che *does* resemble you, George," Bess spoke up. "Of course her hair is arranged a little differently, but she certainly looks like you."

Grandpa Soong laid the picture on the table next to the note. Deep in thought, he paced up and down Aunt Eloise's living-room, his hands behind his back and his gaze on the ceiling. Finally he turned to the group. "You will excuse me, I am sure," he said. "A thought just came to me which I must put in my manuscript."

Without another word he went to the door and out to the hall. "Oh, he forgot Chi Che's picture! And the note!" said Bess. She picked them up and started after him.

Nancy took hold of Bess's arm. "Wait! I'd like to keep the picture and note for a little while," she said. "An idea just came to me."

"A brainstorm?" George asked, chuckling.

"I guess you might call it that," Nancy replied, smiling. "I think the dragon is a definite clue. But before I tell you any more of my plan, I have another suggestion. I feel sure Mr Soong as well as Chi Che may be in real danger. The person who lighted that giant firecracker rang Mr Soong's buzzer. Perhaps he planned to have the baby bomb go off in the poor man's face. It might have blinded him! Anyway, I believe we should protect him as well as try to find Chi Che."

"I agree with you a hundred per cent," Aunt Eloise declared. "What do you suggest?"

Nancy said she thought they should obtain Mr Soong's consent to keep the door between the two apartments unlocked. "We can run in every once in a while and see if he's all right. Also, being alone, he may not eat properly. How about inviting him to share meals with us?"

"I think that's a splendid idea," said Aunt Eloise. "But before I ask him, what is this other scheme you have up your sleeve, Nancy?"

The young sleuth smiled. "It's a very daring plan, I warn you."

Campus Sleuthing

"GEORGE FAYNE," Nancy said, "you are about to become Chi Che Soong!"

"What!" George cried out.

Nancy smiled. "I'm sure that with a little change in your hairstyle you could pass for Chi Che. We'll shape your eyebrows and make them heavier. We'll place a bit of rouge high on your cheekbones and change that boyish hairdo of yours into a pixie cut."

Nancy picked up the picture of Chi Che. "Look at this photograph and tell me what you think."

After the others had studied it for a moment, Bess gave Nancy a hug. "You're a genius. It wouldn't be hard to do at all, and if George puts on the dress Chi Che's wearing in the picture, I'll bet people will think she's Chi Che, at least from a distance. Nancy, what do you have in mind for George to do?"

Nancy said that first they must get Grandpa Soong's consent to keep the door between the two apartments unlocked. After George was made up, she was to leave by way of the Soongs' entrance. "Bess, you and I will follow at a distance and see if anyone is trailing her."

"You mean I'm just to walk up one street and down another and wait to be hit on the head?" George asked with a grin.

179

"Oh, do be sensible," Nancy begged. "I haven't decided yet where I'd like you to go. But please don't leave this apartment until you go out dressed as Chi Che Soong."

"I won't mind," said George. "There are some good books here to read. But you know me—I like action. So don't make it too long."

Bess now spoke up. "I was under the impression, Nancy, that you thought Chi Che was a prisoner. But if George is going to parade round the streets," she added, "this puts a different light on the mystery. You don't think Chi Che is being held after all, do you, Nancy?"

Nancy said she had not reached a conclusion as yet. "Chi Che may be a prisoner, or she may only be in hiding. But if the person from whom she's hiding thinks he sees her on the street, we may be able to find out something worth while."

Aunt Eloise and the cousins approved Nancy's idea and George said she would be willing to undertake the experiment.

"Then the next thing," said Aunt Eloise, "is for me to go next door and make the arrangements with Grandpa Soong." She left, and the girls continued to talk about the mystery until her return.

"I had no trouble at all," Miss Drew reported. "Grandpa Soong was delighted to accept our invitation, and incidentally we are to call him when dinner is ready. The door is unbolted now on his side. Come, I want to show you something exquisite."

Aunt Eloise went to the connecting door and unlocked it from her apartment. Directly behind the door hung a large silk scroll which reached to the floor.

"This is a perfect screen," Miss Drew remarked. "Anyone coming into the Soong apartment wouldn't know there is a door behind it."

Nancy and her friends squeezed past the scroll and stepped into the Soong living-room. The elderly man was not there and Aunt Eloise whispered that he was writing in his bedroom.

"What a gorgeous hand-painted scroll!" Bess remarked, gazing at the lovely, ancient Chinese garden scene with men and ladies strolling about.

Before leaving the apartment, Nancy and the other girls took a quick glance round. The room was tastefully furnished with a Chinese teakwood table, chest and chairs. There were hand-painted parchment shades on the lamps, and the floor was almost entirely covered by a heavy Oriental rug richly coloured in blue and tawny yellow and bordered with a floral design.

"There are two bedrooms and a kitchen," Aunt Eloise explained. "Grandpa Soong does all his writing in his bedroom."

Quietly the visitors went back to Miss Drew's apartment and the girls unpacked their clothes. Presently preparations for dinner were started, and when everything was ready, Miss Drew went to call Grandpa Soong.

As she brought him in, the teacher teasingly remarked that it was hard to get him away from his writing. "Perhaps we shouldn't ask," she said to him, "but if we promise not to tell, will you give us an idea of what you were adding to your manuscript this afternoon?"

The elderly Chinese smiled, put his fingers together, and looked into space. "The manuscript is finished, but I want to write a foreword. I am sure there is no harm in revealing the material I inserted. It is known to many people. In my archaeological work I dug up an ancient frieze. Until my book is printed no one will know its exact origin.

"On the frieze," he continued, "is pictured one of the early heroes of Chinese history—Fu Hsi. He lived over 4,800 years ago."

"Whew!" George cried out. "He's a prehistoric man, no less! What did he look like?"

Once more Grandpa Soong's eyes twinkled. "Fu Hsi had the head of a man and the body of a dragon!"

"Ugh!" Bess remarked. "I'm glad there aren't any such people around today. What did this man do?"

"Legend tells us that he was the king. He had six counsellors, all of them dragons. In fact, there was a line of kings, called the Man Kings, who had faces of men and bodies of dragons. This probably explains why China has often been called Dragon Land."

"Where is this frieze now?" Nancy queried.

"In a museum in China." Grandpa Soong suddenly looked pensive. "I hope to be able to go back home some time and see it."

As soon as the group had finished eating, Grandpa Soong expressed his thanks for their hospitality, then said he would like to return to his own apartment and do more writing.

By ten-thirty Miss Drew and her guests were sound asleep. All were up early the next morning. After Miss

Drew had left for school, Bess said to Nancy, "What's on our girl detective's calendar?"

"I thought you and I might go to Stromberg's Bookshop and see if we can pick up a clue about Chi Che. If we fail, then George can take over."

The two girls set out, and after walking a few blocks came to Stromberg's Bookshop. There was one woman customer inside, but no assistant. Seeing the girls, the woman, who was portly and unbecomingly dressed in a ruffled blouse and tight skirt and carrying her coat on her arm, came up to them immediately.

"This is most annoying!" she complained. "I don't know where Mr Stromberg can be and I'm in a great hurry. I come here often and it's always the same story. Nobody to wait on me!"

Nancy and Bess merely smiled, wondering why the woman bothered to come back if she were displeased with the service.

As if reading their thoughts, she said, "But Mr Stromberg has such a fine collection of foreign books that I hate to go elsewhere." She smiled in a tolerant sort of way, however, and said, "But Mrs Horace Truesdale is not one to lose her temper. No doubt Mr Stromberg has a good reason for not being here."

"Doesn't Mr Stromberg have an assistant?" Bess asked Mrs Truesdale.

"I believe so, but she's a college student and doesn't work here full-time."

The girls began to look round at the books on the shelves, trying to conceal their own impatience for the owner's return. Mrs Truesdale kept up a constant chatter.

"Have you ever been to the Orient?" she asked the girls.

When they shook their heads, the woman went on, "I'm planning to go myself with one of the tourist groups. That's why I'm here—looking for books on the Orient."

Idly she picked several volumes from a shelf and started to leaf through them. "Oh, dear, where *is* Mr Stromberg? I've been here ten minutes!" When the girls made no comment, Mrs Truesdale said, "I suppose I'm an idiot to go abroad. Air travel doesn't agree with me. Besides, I hate being away from my family for such a long time."

Nancy and Bess smiled in spite of themselves. When Mrs Truesdale moved away, Bess whispered, "I'll bet that woman's a pest. I should think her family would be glad to see her go away for a while."

Finally Mr Stromberg came in from the street.

He was about fifty years old, of medium height and build, and had piercing blue eyes, a high forehead, and a prominent nose.

He nodded to Mrs Truesdale, saying, "I have some books for you. Would you mind waiting a few minutes?"

Turning to the girls, he asked, "Can I do something for you young ladies?"

"Will Chi Che be here soon?" Nancy asked.

"I presume you mean Chi Che Soong. No," Mr Stromberg replied. "Chi Che asked for time off—wasn't certain of her return either, so I can't tell you when she'll be in."

"Well, thank you very much," said Nancy. "I'll drop by again and see if she's here."

Mr Stromberg gave a great sigh. "I wish Miss Soong would get back. We deal in foreign-language books and she was a great help to me. You know, Chi Che Soong speaks seven languages!"

"How amazing!" Bess remarked.

"Isn't there something I can do for you?" the shop-owner asked.

"Well, not in the line of books," Bess answered. "We—ah—wanted to invite Chi Che to a party."

Mr Stromberg, not interested in this subject, walked over to Mrs Truesdale, and the two girls left the shop.

"We didn't learn anything there," Bess said.

Nancy frowned and admitted that she was frankly puzzled. Chi Che's note to Aunt Eloise had indicated that it was written on the spur of the moment and under great stress. Somebody she feared must have been nearby because she was unable to finish the last part of the note. Yet Mr Stromberg said Chi Che told him she wanted time off and her return was uncertain. Nancy revealed her thoughts to Bess.

"The two things just don't make sense," she said finally.

"It's too deep for me," Bess admitted, shaking her head. "Well, where do we go from here?"

Nancy suggested that they make a trip to Columbia University and try to find out something about Chi Che. When they arrived on campus the girls went to the office of one of the deans. A young woman assistant proved to be most helpful. She suggested that the girls go to the building where foreign students often gathered.

"They may be able to tell you something about Miss Soong," the young woman said.

Nancy and Bess hurried to the designated building. It was almost lunchtime and the girls noticed everyone heading for the cafeteria in the building. Nancy and Bess stood near the door. Several Chinese young people came in. The American girls smiled at them and asked if they knew where Chi Che was. None did, and one girl added:

"Chi Che has been missing classes lately. She never did that before. I can't understand it."

Nancy said that she had heard Chi Che was visiting college friends out of town. The Chinese student looked surprised. "None of her friends here is away. If she's visiting, the person must be someone from another college."

"Would you like to come and have lunch with our group?" the Chinese girl invited.

"Why, thank you very much," said Nancy. "We'd love it. I'm Nancy Drew and this is my friend Bess Marvin."

"My name is Amy Ching," the other girl said.

The three went into the cafeteria and Amy Ching introduced Nancy and Bess to several other foreign students, but none could give any information about Chi Che Soong.

Nancy and Bess returned to the apartment early in the afternoon and brought George up to date on their findings. Nancy remarked, "Frankly I'm worried, even more than I was before. Apparently Chi Che Soong had no idea while at school on the day she disappeared that she was going to be away."

At supper that evening Nancy and the other girls, as well as Aunt Eloise, forced themselves to be gay in the presence of Grandpa Soong. The door between the two apartments was left open.

Later that night Nancy was in a deep sleep when she was suddenly awakened by a scream. As she sat up in bed she realized that the scream had come from the Soong apartment. The young detective jumped out of bed.

By this time Aunt Eloise, Bess and George were awake also. They could hear moaning from the adjoining apartment.

They grabbed their robes, rushed into Grandpa Soong's living-room, and turned on the light. No one was there.

Aunt Eloise led the way to the elderly man's bedroom. A desk lamp was on. In its rays they could see Grandpa Soong lying on the floor. He was barely conscious. As the group knelt beside him, he whispered:

"Stole—my—manuscript!"

·4·

A Disappointing Wait

"WE MUST call a doctor at once," Aunt Eloise said.
She asked Grandpa Soong who his physician was, but
the elderly man was too weak to answer. Miss Drew
turned to George and requested, "Please telephone my
physician, Dr Gordon."

Meanwhile Aunt Eloise, Bess and Nancy gently
lifted Grandpa Soong on to his bed. Then Nancy ran
back through to her aunt's apartment and out into the
hall to see if the attacker was in sight. The young
sleuth knew it was a vain hope, and as she had expected, no one was there.

Nancy realized that by the time she waited for the
self-service elevator to come up from the ground floor
and take her down again, the thief would have made his
escape.

Quickly Nancy ran down the stairs. She stopped at
each floor and looked round for any sign of the thief.
Finally, reaching the foyer without having seen anyone, she dashed to the front door and gazed up and
down the street. No one carrying papers under his arm
or a bundle or suitcase was in sight.

Nancy hurried back to Aunt Eloise's apartment, and
using the kitchen phone, immediately called police
headquarters. She was switched to Captain Gray, who

was on duty at the nearby precinct. The officer said he would send two of his men at once to investigate.

Then Nancy returned to Mr Soong's apartment to do a little investigating of her own. She found that everything had been stripped from the archaeologist's worktable except the lamp. A bottle of Chinese ink and brushes lay on the floor, and near it an exquisite, hand-painted metal vase.

Every drawer in the room was open and the contents were strewn about. Bookshelves were in disarray. Apparently the thief had made a quick but thorough search of Grandpa Soong's workshop for all papers, notes and photographs pertaining to the manuscript.

The buzzer interrupted Nancy's investigation and she went to open the door.

"I'm Dr Gordon," said the smiling young man.

Nancy led him to Mr Soong's bedroom. Aunt Eloise and the girls withdrew while the doctor made an examination of the victim. As they waited for his report, the buzzer sounded again.

Two police officers had arrived. They introduced themselves as Brady and Reed. Upon hearing that the doctor was in the bedroom, the two men said they would start in the living-room to search for a clue to the intruder.

Presently Brady said, "He didn't force an entry, so he must have had a key."

Finding nothing to help identify the thief, Officer Reed added, "Apparently the thief went immediately to the bedroom. From what you tell me, Miss Drew, Mr Soong was working at his desk when he was attacked."

Just then Dr Gordon appeared. He shook his head. "Mr Soong's condition is the result of fear as well as a hard blow. He will have to be removed to the hospital at once."

"I'll call an ambulance," Officer Brady offered, and went to the phone.

Nancy asked the doctor if it would be possible for her to talk with Grandpa Soong before he was taken away. "Yes," Dr Gordon replied. "But make it brief."

Both officers followed her inside and introduced themselves. The elderly man gave the girl a warm smile. "I am very grateful to you, my friend," he said in a whisper. "I—I do not know why my manuscript was stolen."

Officer Reed asked him for a description of his assailant.

"The man was masked," Mr Soong said, "and wore a hat pulled low, so I could tell nothing about his face or hair. He was rather small, but very strong."

At once Nancy wondered if he might be the same person she had seen running away after the firecracker explosion. That person was small too. She told this to the officers.

At that moment the door buzzer sounded. Two ambulance attendants carrying a stretcher entered the apartment. As they carried Mr Soong from the room, his friends gave him their best wishes for a quick recovery.

As soon as the attendants and their patient had left, the two police officers went towards Grandpa Soong's bedroom. One of them carried a little kit which Nancy knew was a fingerprinting outfit.

"Do you mind if I watch you work?" she asked.

"No, come along," Officer Reed replied.

As she started to follow, Nancy was detained by Bess. "Don't you think we should tell the officers about Chi Che and our suspicions that she's in danger?"

George tossed her head. "Certainly not. Chi Che asked Aunt Eloise not to."

"Just the same—"

Miss Drew spoke up. "Bess has a point, but so has George. Let's take a vote."

Nancy and Aunt Eloise sided with George. Resignedly, Bess said, "Okay. But if Chi Che is still missing by tomorrow, I'll probably ask the same question again."

Aunt Eloise smiled. "A lot can happen in twenty-four hours," she said. "You've already found that out since you came to New York."

Nancy went into Grandpa Soong's bedroom to watch the police officers. They had already opened their kit. One man was holding a camel's-hair brush and a bottle of grey powder.

"This must be one of the thief's hand marks," said Officer Brady, who was shining a flashlight on the desk-top and looking through a magnifying glass. "The finger spreads indicate a larger hand than that of Mr Soong's. And shorter fingers."

Officer Brady dusted the prints with the powder. Then, as his co-worker held the flashlight, he picked up a camera and photographed the prints.

Officer Reed turned to Nancy. "We'll get these prints two ways," he said. "Now we'll use lifting tape."

He took what looked like a large rubber patch with

a thin outer coating from the kit. First he peeled off
the coating, and Nancy noticed that the rubber under
it was very sticky. He placed this over the fingerprint,
then gently took it off.

"Very good," he said. "Come look, Miss Drew."

Nancy took a few steps forward and studied the
perfect reprint on the tape. She smiled up at the
officers. "It's fascinating," she said. "And now I'm
going to ask you a favour. If you should find that these
fingerprints are on record, will you let me know to
whom they belong?"

"I guess we can do that," Officer Reed replied.

After the two men had left, Nancy and the girls
returned to Miss Drew's apartment. "I'm going to bolt
this door," Aunt Eloise announced. "I don't want any
thieves coming in here!"

Nancy gazed into space for several seconds, then
said, "Aunt Eloise, I don't blame you for feeling the
way you do. But I think there's a good chance the thief
or some accomplice of his may come back to the Soong
apartment to try stealing something else. What I'd
like to do is spend the rest of the night there and
find out."

Miss Drew shook her head. "It's too dangerous," she
argued. "I'd never forgive myself if anything should
happen to you."

"George can stay with me," Nancy said, by way of
persuasion. "I'll place a chair under the door handle
so no one can possibly get in. If I hear anyone trying
the door, I'll call the police."

George spoke up. "Why call the police? Why don't
you and I just go out and capture the thief?"

Before Miss Drew could comment, Bess remarked, "It's just possible Chi Che herself will return and won't be able to get in."

"That's true," Aunt Eloise conceded. "Chi Che may have been held and her key to the apartment taken just so the thief could accomplish the job of taking the manuscript."

Bess's eyes sparkled. "And Chi Che will be released! Won't that be wonderful!"

"I wish I shared your optimism," said Aunt Eloise. "Just in case she should come home and try to get in, I'll permit Nancy and George to finish the night in the Soong apartment."

Bess went on, "Do you think the part of Chi Che's note 'Because I have found out that—' meant the plan to steal the manuscript?"

Nancy shook her head. "Unless Chi Che returns home tomorrow morning, my answer would be 'No.'"

Nancy and George slept fitfully for the rest of the night. By seven o'clock they were wide awake. They were just about to go back to Aunt Eloise's apartment when the Soongs' door buzzer sounded. George jumped perceptibly. Without making a sound she formed her lips into the words, "Shall we answer it?"

Nancy shook her head. Beckoning to George to follow her, she led the way to the adjoining apartment, opened the hall door, and peered out cautiously.

Mr Stromberg was standing at the Soong door!

Quickly and quietly Nancy Drew closed the door to her aunt's apartment. In hushed tones she told George about the caller. "Just as well if Mr Stromberg doesn't find out where we're staying," she whispered.

Mr Stromberg rang the buzzer again. Then, apparently deciding that no one was coming to answer it, he walked to the elevator.

"I suppose he came here to see why Chi Che hasn't returned to work," George remarked. "He sure gets round early in the morning."

Nancy frowned. "I wonder how Mr Stromberg got into the apartment house. He didn't ring the downstairs bell to the Soong apartment."

George shrugged. "Oh, well, someone was probably just going out the lobby door at the time he arrived, and that's how he got in."

Aunt Eloise and Bess were already up, and Nancy and George became conscious of the aroma of frying bacon. They went into the kitchen and reported Mr Stromberg's visit.

"You were wise not to let him know where you are, Nancy," her aunt praised her.

About an hour later the telephone rang. "Will you take it, Nancy?" Aunt Eloise requested. "I'm sorry I forgot to tell you. I must go out to an all-day teachers' meeting."

Miss Drew paused by the door long enough to learn that it was a call from police headquarters. Captain Gray was reporting that the fingerprints of the burglar had been checked with FBI records. "Whoever the thief was," he said, "he has never been arrested."

The captain went on to say that his men had checked every tenant in the apartment house with the superintendent and also the renting agent in charge of the building. "We're sure the suspect doesn't live there," he stated.

"Thank you for letting me know," said Nancy. "And I'm still very much interested in this case. If you have any further news, I'd appreciate hearing from you."

The officer chuckled. "I understand you are an amateur sleuth, Miss Drew," he said. "I heard this from Dr Gordon when he called up to give a report on Mr Soong. It seems your aunt had been telling him about you."

Nancy laughed. "I see I can't keep that a secret. Well, now that you know, I hope you won't mind if I try to solve the mystery too."

"The department would be delighted to have your help," Captain Gray replied.

After clearing away the breakfast dishes, the three girls tidied up not only Aunt Eloise's apartment but also Grandpa Soong's. Time dragged as they waited hopefully for Chi Che Soong to return home. Near noon Nancy finally said:

"I'm sure Chi Che is still either being held prisoner or is in hiding. Whichever is true, we must find her! Let's have a bite of lunch and then start our sleuthing."

She turned to George. "Are you ready to play the part of Chi Che?"

· 5 ·

A Convincing Disguise

"OF COURSE I'll play the part," said George Fayne.
"But I must admit that I'm getting butterflies in my
stomach."

The three girls decided to look through Chi Che
Soong's clothes for the dress Chi Che was wearing in
the photograph Grandpa Soong had shown them. As
much as they disliked the thought of invading the
Chinese girl's wardrobe, Nancy and her friends felt it
was quite necessary if they were to solve the mystery.

Bess opened the door of a closet in Chi Che's bedroom. "Here's the dress."

As she removed the dress from its hanger she remarked how pretty it was. "And ummm, what a sweet
sachet it's scented with—like incense."

"And now to find Chi Che's eyebrow pencil and
rouge and lipstick, if she has any here."

George opened the drawer to Chi Che's dressing-
table. "We're in luck again," she said. "And look,
here's a key. It might be a duplicate to the hall door.
I'd better carry it, so I can let myself back in."

Nancy tried the key in the lock. "This is it all right.
Well, let's go back to our own apartment now and fix
you up, George."

It was easy to apply the make-up and have George slip into the dress, but changing her hairdo proved to be a difficult task. The ends just would not turn forward and stay in position.

"What do you put on your hair, anyway?" Bess chided her cousin. "Varnish?"

"No, cement," George replied impishly. Then she said the best thing to do would be to rinse her hair with water and set it while damp.

"But that will ruin your make-up and this dress," Bess objected.

"Not necessarily," said Nancy. "Come with me, George."

She led the way to the bathroom, put a towel round George's shoulders, and told her to lean over the basin. Quickly and carefully Nancy rinsed her friend's hair and partially dried it before George raised her head. Now Nancy found it easy to arrange a hairdo very similar to Chi Che's.

When she finished, Bess exclaimed in wonder, "I can't believe it! You really do look like the girl in this picture, George." Suddenly she made a low bow. "Delighted to meet you, Chi Che Soong!"

The girls giggled for a few moments, then became serious and discussed the route George was to follow. She would leave the Soong apartment, take the elevator down, dawdle in the lobby until Nancy and Bess appeared, then stroll out into the street. She was to walk directly to the hospital, as if she were going to visit "her grandfather."

"But when you get inside the hospital, hide in the gift shop," Nancy directed. "Bess and I will really call on Grandpa Soong and find out how he is. Wait for us to come back downstairs."

"Then after that," said George, "I'm to stroll on to Columbia University and walk round the campus. If somewhere along the line a suspicious person speaks to me or follows me, you two girls will do the rest."

"That's right," Nancy replied. "Let's go!"

Almost from the moment George appeared on the street, with Nancy and Bess following at a safe distance, people began to stare at the attractive "Chinese" girl. But no one stopped to speak to her or seemed to be following.

Nancy and Bess were beginning to think that perhaps their experiment was going to be a failure when Bess suddenly grabbed her friend's arm. "Look at the man in that car!" she whispered tensely. "See how slowly he's going! And he's sure staring at George—I mean Chi Che."

The car, a dark-blue saloon, was hugging the kerb. The driver was about twenty-five years old. He was slender and dark, but not an Oriental. He drove slowly as far as the hospital, watched "Chi Che" go in, then drove off.

"Do you think he might be connected with the case?" Bess asked Nancy.

"I don't know. We can't very well follow him, but I did get his licence number."

The two girls walked into the hospital. They stopped at the desk to inquire the number of Mr Soong's room, received passes to see him, then took the elevator upstairs.

The elderly man looked better and expressed his

delight at seeing the callers. He said the doctor had told him he must remain in the hospital at least a week, maybe longer.

"Since I must stay here, I am asking you, Nancy, to bring my mail to me. And will you please answer my phone? There may be word from Chi Che. So far I have had none and do not know where to reach her."

"I'll be very happy to do that," Nancy answered.

Grandpa Soong told the girls that a nurse had brought him a message a short time before from Mr Stromberg. He had telephoned to find out how the patient was.

"I have never met him," said the archaeologist, "so I consider it very kind that he has taken an interest in me."

Nancy and Bess wondered how the bookshop owner had learned of the attack on Mr Soong. Had someone at the apartment house told him?

On the bureau in the room stood a beautiful bouquet of yellow chrysanthemums. When Bess admired them, Grandpa Soong said, "I do not know who sent them. The card of good wishes which came with the flowers has no name on it."

"How strange!" Nancy remarked. "May I see the card?"

"Certainly. It is in the top drawer of the bureau."

As Nancy took out the card, she gave an involuntary start. In the lower right-hand corner was a hand-painted dragon! Printed on the card were the words: "Best wishes for a speedy recovery."

Nancy turned to Mr Soong. "Surely you must have an idea who sent these?"

"Only a guess," he answered. "The person who gave my Chi Che the stationery may have heard of my illness and sent the flowers, but did not want me to feel obligated to write a note of thanks."

Nancy was glad that Grandpa Soong had no suspicions regarding the sender of the flowers. She herself was worried. The user of the dragon stationery obviously knew that Mr Soong was in the hospital. Did this mean that the person had something to do with the attack?

Trying not to show her true feelings, the young sleuth said lightly, "Well, Grandpa Soong, you must have an unknown admirer. Isn't that exciting!"

She slipped the card back into the drawer and closed it.

"We must go now," she told Mr Soong. "But we'll come again soon and make a longer visit."

"I shall look forward to seeing you. And I hope next time you will bring some letter or message from my Chi Che," Grandpa Soong added wistfully, handing Nancy the key to his lobby mailbox.

"Oh, something is bound to arrive," said Bess cheerfully. But as the girls walked down the hall to the elevator, she whispered to Nancy, "I wish I could have meant that. To tell the truth, I don't like the look of things at all."

"It certainly is a puzzling situation," Nancy admitted. "Well, let's see what happens from here on."

"I'll tell you what may happen," Bess said. "If some of the Chinese students we met yesterday at Columbia see us and think Chi Che is with us, and then find out she's not Chi Che, it will give the whole thing away!"

Nancy agreed, and said that she and Bess would stay far enough behind George not to arouse any suspicion. When they reached the lobby, they walked into one door of the gift shop. George, seeing them, left by another. They followed a few seconds later.

When the girls reached the Columbia campus, George smiled at various students as they came along. Suddenly she was thrilled to have someone wave to her from a distance and call out, "Good to see you back, Chi Che!"

Nancy and Bess had heard the remark. "The disguise is working!" Bess whispered excitedly.

As they went on, over a dozen young men and women students, some Orientals, others American, also waved and called to "Chi Che."

"Oh, isn't this exciting!" Bess exclaimed.

"Yes, but it doesn't seem to be leading us to the real Chi Che," Nancy replied.

The words were hardly out of her mouth when a young man, tall, red-haired, and very slender, rushed up to George. As he reached her he cried out, "How did you get away, Chi Che Soong? You little fool!"

Bess grabbed Nancy's arm. What was going to happen now?

George, though startled, played her role magnificently. She did not speak, merely shrugged her shoulders and extended the palms of both hands in a gesture of "You guess!"

The next instant the man seized George roughly by her arm and led her away. George pretended to go willingly. Nancy and Bess, with pounding hearts, kept pace with the two ahead.

· 6 ·

The Chase

WITH Nancy and Bess close on her heels, George was led by her captor from the campus and out to a side street. They were heading for a car parked at the kerb. Its engine was running.

"That's the same car which was following George on the way to the hospital!" Nancy said, recognizing the licence number.

"But there's a different driver!" Bess said.

As the masquerading "Chi Che" and her escort approached the car, the driver called out in a worried tone, "No take. While you were gone I phoned Ryle."

Startled, George's captor let go of her, jumped into the car, and it sped off.

Down the street Nancy saw an empty taxi. "Come on!" she cried to Bess, and ran to the cab. As Bess jumped in with her, Nancy called out to George, "Go home and wait for us." Then she ordered, "Driver, follow those two men who just left here!"

He started the taxi but seemed in no hurry to follow Nancy's order. Half turning in his seat, he asked, "What's going on here? You trying to date those guys?"

Nancy ignored the remark and merely said, "It's

very important that we find out where they're going. Please hurry."

The driver shrugged and put on a little more speed. The chase took them on to the West Side Highway and downtown. As they reached the exit to Canal Street, the car ahead went down the ramp. The taxi followed.

By this time the suspicious driver of the fleeing car apparently had sensed that his car was being trailed. He made several turns, evidently trying to elude the pursuers.

"Those men may be going out to the end of Long Island," the taximan grumbled.

"It doesn't make any difference where they're going. I'd like you to keep them in view," Nancy said.

Bess sensed that the taxi-driver was getting tired of the chase and probably was wondering whether he was going to get a tip large enough to warrant his trouble. Sweetly she said, "Driver, you're wonderful. I've never ridden with anyone who could handle a car so well."

The man beamed. "Thank you, miss. Not many people ever give me a compliment. They mostly complain." Now, eager to co-operate, he resumed the chase. As the taxi sped along Canal Street, suddenly the other car pulled up to the kerb and stopped. The two men in it leaped out and ran at top speed down a side street.

"Now what?" the girls' taximan asked, stopping behind the other car.

"We'll go on foot from here," Nancy said.

She glanced at the meter, gave the driver the fare

and a generous tip, then jumped from the taxi. She and Bess dashed up the street. The two men they had been following were not in sight.

"Why, we're in Chinatown, aren't we?" Bess exclaimed.

"That's right," Nancy agreed. "Those men probably don't live here, so it shouldn't be too hard to locate them. Somebody may be able to tell us where they are."

She and Bess went from shop to shop making inquiries, but no one had noticed the two running men. Finally Nancy was forced to admit defeat.

"Let's try something else," she told Bess. "We'll ask about the man called Ryle."

The girls inquired in the various stores and of people on the street if they knew anyone named Ryle. No one did.

"This is certainly disappointing," the young sleuth remarked to Bess. "Well, our only chance of finding out who those men are is through the licence plate of the car."

Nancy was determined not to give up her sleuthing completely. "But at least, Bess, we can ask about Chi Che Soong," she added. "Let's try various places on Mott and Pell streets."

The girls decided to divide the task, with Bess taking one side of the street, Nancy the other. They had been at work on this project for nearly half an hour with no results, when Nancy came to a combination stationery, art and knick-knack store. Bess joined her.

"Remember the hand-painted dragon, Bess? I wonder if the owner of this shop might help us locate the place where the stationery and card were made?"

The girls walked in. First Nancy asked the Chinese shopkeeper if he knew Chi Che Soong. The man shook his head. "I am very sorry. May I help you in any other way?"

Nancy smiled. "Perhaps you can. I see you sell stationery. Have you ever seen any with a small hand-painted dragon in the lower right-hand corner?"

The shop owner opened a drawer and took out several sheets. "Is this what you mean?" he asked.

When Nancy said yes, the man smiled and told her he was the artist.

Nancy was excited by this information. "Do you paint this stationery for some particular person?"

"No, no," the artist answered. "Many people, both Chinese and American, buy this stationery. I take no special orders. I will be glad to sell you some if you care to have any."

The young sleuth, thinking the unusual stationery might come in handy, bought a few sheets with envelopes to fit. "Do you also make cards with this design?" she asked.

Once more the man rummaged in the drawer. Presently he pulled out one exactly like the card which had been sent with Grandpa Soong's hospital flowers. Nancy said she would like to buy three or four.

"You don't make these on order either?" she asked.

The artist shook his head. Then he in turn asked, "Is there some special reason why you want to know?"

Nancy explained that a Chinese friend of hers had received a beautiful bouquet but that there was no name on the hand-painted dragon card. The recipient was most eager to find out who had sent the flowers.

"It's possible a man named Ryle is responsible," said Nancy. "Do you know anyone by that name?"

"Ryle?" the Chinese shopkeeper repeated. He looked into space for several seconds, then said, "A man named Ryle was in here several months ago with a friend. He did not buy any of this stationery or the cards. He was interested in selling me something."

"Oh, you also buy Oriental objects from people who come in here?" Nancy asked, to draw him out.

"Once in a while," the shop owner replied. "But in the case of Mr Ryle, I must admit I refrained. He had some pieces of very fine jade with him. He said he had brought them from the Orient. I was afraid the jade might have been stolen or smuggled and I did not want to get into trouble."

Nancy's heart began to beat faster. Here indeed was an interesting clue!

But the young sleuth pretended to be shocked by the possibility that Mr Ryle was a smuggler. "Then he can't be the man we have in mind," she said. "Do you know the first name of the Mr Ryle who wanted to sell you the jade?"

"No, I didn't hear it," the man answered. "The only reason I know his name is Ryle is because his companion called him that. The men haven't been in here since, so I know nothing more about them."

"This man named Ryle—was he stout?" Bess queried, hoping to get more information for Nancy.

"No. In fact, he was a small, slender man. But he looked very strong," the stationer replied. A customer came in just then, so Nancy and Bess took their leave.

Out on the street once more, the girl detective said, "I think we've hit upon a real clue. This small, slender but muscular man we keep hearing about must be named Ryle! But is Ryle his first or last name?"

"Good question," Bess remarked. "And how do you spell it?"

The girls walked back to Canal Street to hail a taxi. To their amazement the car in which the two suspects had driven to Chinatown was still standing there.

"I think I'll phone the police about this," Nancy told Bess.

She went into a booth and called Captain Gray. Without revealing anything about the mystery surrounding Chi Che, Nancy said she had picked up a clue which might lead to the man who had attacked Grandpa Soong. She mentioned the parked car and its licence number.

"I'll look into the matter at once," the officer promised.

Nancy had a hunch that the car had been abandoned, so there was little point in waiting for the two men to return. She signalled a taxi and directed the driver to take her and Bess back to Aunt Eloise's apartment.

Meanwhile, George had been having an adventure of her own. Right after Nancy and Bess had driven off in the taxi, a Chinese girl, carrying an armful of books, had rushed up to her. She had spoken excitedly in what George assumed was Cantonese, but the only words George could distinguish were "Chi Che." Did the girl think she was Chi Che or had she seen through her disguise?

Suddenly the Chinese girl, frowning, looked more

closely at George. Then she laughed and in English apologized. "Oh, I thought you were a girl I know named Chi Che Soong. My, how much you look like her! I stopped you because I heard Chi Che left her job at Stromberg's Bookshop. I wondered if I could get it."

George Fayne took an instant liking to the attractive Chinese girl. The stranger introduced herself as Lily Alys Wu. After a little more conversation, George had an idea.

"Perhaps I can get the job for you at the bookshop," she said. "Would you like to talk it over?"

"Yes. But first, please explain why you are costumed and made up the way you are. You see, I am one of Chi Che's closest friends."

George smiled but did not reply at once. Could she trust Lily Alys with confidential information about the missing Chi Che?

·7·

Strange Thefts

As GEORGE stood debating whether or not to tell Lily Alys Wu about Chi Che, an elderly gentleman carrying a briefcase came along the street. He and the Chinese girl smiled at each other.

"How are you, Professor Rankin?" Lily said.

"Very well, thank you, Miss Wu. And you?"

"Fine. I certainly enjoyed your lecture yesterday."

"I am glad," Professor Rankin said, and tipping his hat, went on his way.

The little episode helped George make up her mind. She was sure she could trust Lily Alys.

"The reason I'm masquerading as your friend Chi Che Soong," she said, "is because Chi Che seems to be missing."

"Missing!" Lily exclaimed. "I know she hasn't been to classes for the past few days. I was going to phone her this afternoon. Please tell me more."

George was guarded in her statements but did reveal that Mr Soong had not heard from his granddaughter since she left a note saying she planned to visit some college friends. "Did you know Mr Soong is in the hospital?" George asked.

"No," Lily Alys replied. "I am so sorry to hear that. What is the trouble?"

Since the story had appeared in the newspapers, George told what had happened to the elderly man.

"That is dreadful!" Lily Alys said. "I am very fond of Mr Soong. And I know Chi Che loves and respects him very much. I cannot understand why she would stay away and not communicate with him."

"That is what my friends and I cannot understand either," said George. "Would you be willing to come to the apartment where we're staying and discuss the situation? Perhaps you can give us some clue to where Chi Che might be."

Lily Alys said she would be happy to come. The two girls walked along side by side. There was no further recognition of "Chi Che" by any passers-by.

When they reached the apartment, Aunt Eloise, who had just arrived, opened the door for them. Since Nancy and Bess were not there yet, the conversation was general. Aunt Eloise served tea and biscuits.

Presently Nancy and Bess announced themselves at the front door and a few minutes later entered the apartment.

George introduced Lily Alys Wu and explained why she had brought the Chinese girl to call. Then, on a pretext that she had something in her hand-bag to give Nancy, George asked her to come into the bedroom a moment.

Quickly the two girls exchanged stories. Then George propounded the idea she had had for the past half-hour; that Lily Alys, who, like Chi Che, was a linguist, try for a position at Stromberg's Bookshop.

Nancy smiled. "I think I know what you have in mind, George. You suspect that Chi Che's message to

Aunt Eloise might have meant she had found out some secret about the bookshop, and perhaps Lily Alys can learn the same thing without being caught."

"Exactly," said George. "And I feel sure Lily Alys can be trusted."

Nancy, too, was certain of this. She and George returned to the living-room and broached the subject to the Chinese girl. "That is, if you're fortunate enough to get the position at the bookshop," George added.

Lily Alys screwed up her face and looked a little frightened at the idea. "I do not know that I am capable of such work," she said. "I have never had anything to do with solving mysteries."

"It won't be hard," George urged her. "Just do the jobs Mr Stromberg asks you to, but keep your eyes and ears open."

"And pay special attention to telephone calls," Nancy added.

The young Chinese student finally agreed and said that she hoped she would not fail in her assignment.

"I will go over to Mr Stromberg's at once," Lily promised, "and let you know later whether or not I succeed in obtaining the position."

Nancy went to the door with their new friend, and the others called, "Good luck!"

As soon as Lily Alys had left, Nancy telephoned police headquarters. There was no news about the identity of Mr Soong's attacker, the sergeant on duty reported. "The car the suspects used," he added, "was found to have been stolen."

As Nancy thanked him and hung up, she shrugged

resignedly. "Another clue has faded out," she told her friends.

George went into her bedroom to change her clothes and remove the Chinese make-up. Suddenly she called out, "Did one of you knock my clock on to the floor?"

"No," the others chorused.

"Then someone was in here while we were all away!" George exclaimed.

When they heard this, everyone rushed into the bedroom. George pointed to her travelling clock which lay on the floor by the bed.

"But how could anyone get in here?" Aunt Eloise asked.

Nancy and Bess looked at each other sheepishly. They had forgotten to lock the door between the Soong apartment and Aunt Eloise's!

"Evidently the person who has the key to the Soongs' let himself in and came through," Nancy said.

Instantly a search was begun, but twenty minutes later Aunt Eloise declared that apparently nothing had been taken.

"Then why was he in here?" George demanded.

No one could answer her question. But suddenly Bess gasped. "Maybe the intruder was hiding in the Soong apartment while Lily Alys was here and overheard our plan!"

Nancy, although concerned, pointed out that this was not necessarily true. The clock, probably knocked to the floor by the intruder, had stopped hours before. "I don't think the person would have stayed around all this time."

"I hope you're right," Bess sighed.

Nancy was quiet for a full minute, then she said, "Perhaps the intruder was hunting for Chi Che's note to Grandpa Soong. When he didn't find it in their apartment, he may have figured it was in here."

"And it was!" said Bess. "Where is it now?"

Nancy rushed to a desk and pulled open the top drawer. "Gone!" she cried. "I put it in here with Chi Che's photograph. In fact, that's gone too."

"Oh, dear, what's going to happen now?" Bess worried.

Again Nancy was silent for a while. Then she said, "It's my guess that the person who came in here wanted a sample of Chi Che's Chinese handwriting. I believe Grandpa Soong will be receiving a new note. It will be a forgery imitating Chi Che's writing."

"And what do you think it will say?" Aunt Eloise asked.

"It will beg Grandpa Soong not to notify the police of her absence."

Nancy telephoned police headquarters to report the latest theft. Two plainclothesmen arrived a short while later. After making a routine investigation, they said they had found nothing significant and went off.

A few minutes later Aunt Eloise produced a paper bag. "I stopped at an ironmongery on my way home," she said. "I decided that if one more intruder came into either apartment, I was going to put bolts on the hall doors. Who wants to help me play carpenter?"

Bess said, "I'll be glad to help. But suppose Chi Che should return and can't get in?"

Aunt Eloise said she felt certain now that Chi Che was not going to return until she was found by Detective

214 THE MYSTERY OF THE FIRE DRAGON

Nancy Drew and her friends or by the police. "However, I'll tell the caretaker I've bolted the doors. If Chi Che should come back and not be able to get in, I'm sure she'll go to him and he'll explain."

Suddenly Nancy laughed. "We can barricade the Soongs' apartment," she said, "but we'd have to use a little magic to bolt ours after we've left it!"

Aunt Eloise blinked and laughed. "Why, of course," she said. "I was certainly letting my imagination run away with me."

Nancy added that it would be a good idea to barricade the Soongs' apartment, nevertheless. "I'm positive that the intruder won't return here since he found what he wanted—the photograph and the letter."

She and her aunt attached the bolt to the Soongs' living-room hall door. Then it was shot into place and the connecting door between the two apartments also bolted.

"Anybody hungry?" the teacher asked as she and Nancy joined Bess and George.

"I'm starved!" Bess answered quickly.

The other girls smiled. It seemed that Bess, who rarely watched her weight, could eat at any time!

"I have a casserole dish in the refrigerator, ready to slip into the oven," Aunt Eloise said. "I hope you'll all like it."

The four entered the kitchen. Miss Drew turned on the automatic pilot to light the oven. Then she turned and started to walk towards the refrigerator.

Suddenly there was an explosion inside the stove. The oven door flew off, hitting Aunt Eloise squarely in the back and knocking her over!

·8·

Angry Neighbours

FEARFUL that there might possibly be a second explosion, Nancy and George lifted Aunt Eloise and rushed from the kitchen. They laid the teacher gently on her bed.

"Aunt Eloise," Nancy said, trying not to show her fright, "are you hurt?"

Her aunt smiled wanly. "I only had the wind knocked out of me, I guess," she said.

The girls were greatly relieved, but Nancy felt that she should investigate. She wondered if the explosion might have been caused by an accumulation of leaking gas. "It could've been ignited when the pilot was turned on, but we would have smelled the escaping gas when we were in the living-room," Nancy said to herself.

Puzzled, she entered the kitchen and walked to the stove. She gazed into the doorless oven. There were tiny bits of red paper and particles of sand lying about.

"Someone planted another giant firecracker! So that's what the intruder was doing in here, as well as taking Chi Che's photograph and letter."

The young sleuth went back to report to her aunt and the girls.

"How perfectly dreadful!" Bess exclaimed. "In solving a mystery it's bad enough to go after an enemy, but when he invades your home to k-kill you, maybe, it's pretty awful!"

"I'm sure he didn't mean to go that far, but he *is* trying to scare me into giving up the case," Nancy remarked.

Suddenly someone began to pound on the hall door. Nancy went to find out who it was. Several people stood there. They announced they were neighbours, on the same floor.

"What's going on here?" demanded a very stout, red-faced man.

"We—er—had a little accident with our stove," Nancy answered, thinking it best not to tell him the whole story.

"Is that all?" the man prodded.

"Come see for yourself," Nancy said. She was sure he would never guess the truth even if he noticed the bits of red paper and sand.

The whole group of neighbours crowded into the apartment and went to the kitchen. "Door blew off, eh?" the red-faced man remarked. "Well, you ought to be more careful how you use gas."

Apparently he was satisfied with Nancy's explanation. But a sharp-faced, thin woman in the group said accusingly, "Something strange is going on, and it has to do with those Soongs. And you seem to be pretty friendly with that weird old man."

"He's not weird," Nancy defended the archaeologist. "He's a very learned and fine person."

"Maybe so," the woman admitted. "Just the same,

I don't like living in a place where firecrackers are going off and people are getting knocked out by intruders."

George, who had appeared in the doorway by this time, could not refrain from commenting, "Then perhaps you should move?"

The woman glared at her. "*Me* move?" she cried out. "I think the Soongs and Miss Drew should be the ones to go. You're—you're all dangerous tenants!"

Nancy remarked icily, "Instead of you people becoming so angry and unfriendly, I think you should welcome the chance to help the police capture the person who is responsible for harming Grandpa Soong."

"What do you mean?" asked a small, shy woman.

The young sleuth told her that if any of the neighbours had seen a suspicious person in the hallway or on the elevator, he should report it now. There was dead silence for several seconds as the men and women looked at one another. Then finally the shy little woman spoke up.

"I've been so scared since that firecracker went off in the hall, I've hesitated to say anything. But I think Miss Drew's niece is right. I may have a clue. Early this afternoon I was about to go shopping. As I have been doing, I opened my door a crack and looked out to see if anyone was in the hall. I saw a short, slender man sneaking along from the stairway towards the Soongs' apartment. I was so frightened I closed my door, so I really don't know where he went."

"What time was this?" Nancy asked her.

"About three o'clock."

Nancy's thoughts began to race. The short, slender man could be the same one whom she herself had seen in the apartment hallway before the first firecracker went off. He might even have been the man driving the car which had followed George to the hospital when she played the part of Chi Che! He would have had time to change drivers, come to the Soong apartment, let himself in with the key stolen from Chi Che, and plant the firecracker in Miss Drew's stove!

The outspoken woman apologized for what she had said, and promised to be alert for any suspicious persons and report them to the superintendent or to the police. The group disbanded and Nancy closed the door.

Aunt Eloise declared she was feeling better and she and the girls discussed the affair. "One thing is sure," George spoke up. "Several people are trying to scare us off the case."

"And in *my* case," said Bess, "they're almost succeeding. Maybe we should give up the entire thing."

Aunt Eloise said she, for one, would not do this. She felt obligated to the Soongs to keep trying to solve the mystery of Chi Che's disappearance.

"And I'm certainly going to stick by you," Nancy determined. "But there is something I think we should do: take Police Captain Gray into our confidence." Her aunt agreed.

Nancy called the officer, who promised to come to the apartment that evening. After she reported this to the others, Nancy said:

"Tonight I'm going to treat everybody to dinner at a nice restaurant. I think Aunt Eloise has seen enough of her kitchen for today."

Although Miss Drew objected, she finally admitted that she would enjoy going out to eat. Bess and George accepted readily. The foursome had a delightful meal at a small French restaurant famous for its excellent cuisine.

Soon after the group had returned to the apartment, Police Captain Gray arrived. He listened intently as Nancy related the whole story from the discovery of Chi Che's note addressed to Eloise Drew to the recent explosion.

"Nancy Drew, I'm intrigued by your sleuthing ability," he said, smiling. "I couldn't have had a better report from one of my top men."

Captain Gray said that he would have the apartment house, as well as the Drew and Soong apartments, watched twenty-four hours a day. "All visitors will be checked."

The officer, as Nancy had requested, promised not to give out the story of Chi Che's disappearance, except to the particular men who would be assigned to the case. "I agree with you that it might endanger her life," he said.

Just as Captain Gray was leaving, the telephone rang. Miss Drew answered it, then called Nancy. "Please wait," she requested the captain.

"This is Lily Alys," the caller said. "Nancy, I got the job at the bookshop!"

"Good!" Nancy replied. "I'll probably see you there. But, Lily Alys, if I should come to the shop, or Bess or George, act as if you had never seen us before."

"All right," the Chinese girl promised. "And I'll try hard to do some detecting for you."

Nancy reported the conversation to the officer, then he left. Before the young sleuth retired she told the others she was going to call on Grandpa Soong the following day. "I'll take any mail that has come. And if there's one signed Chi Che, I'm sure it will be a fake. She would never stay away if she knew her grandfather were ill."

The next morning Aunt Eloise and the girls attended church. Then at about two o'clock Nancy suddenly remembered her promise to check Mr Soong's mail and went to the vestibule. There were three letters for the elderly man in the box. One was an advertisement. Another, in a man's handwriting, was postmarked Hong Kong. The third had been addressed by a woman, Nancy felt sure. It was stamped special delivery and was postmarked New Haven, Connecticut.

"This one might be from Chi Che! The writing is similar," Nancy thought excitedly, and hurried on to the hospital.

She found Grandpa Soong feeling better, but sad and puzzled about his granddaughter. "I have had no word from Chi Che," he said.

"I think I have a letter for you from her," Nancy remarked cheerfully, and handed over the mail.

"This is indeed from my Chi Che!" the elderly man exclaimed. "You will forgive me if I read it."

With trembling fingers Grandpa Soong opened the envelope and took out a sheet of stationery. From where Nancy had seated herself, she could see that the letter was written in Chinese characters. And in the lower right-hand corner was a fire dragon!

A smile came over Grandpa Soong's face. "Chi Che's

friends are taking her on a long trip. She says I am not to worry."

"Well, that is reassuring," Nancy said with a smile. But inwardly she was more worried than ever. Surely Chi Che would not of her own volition have notified her grandfather of such plans by letter instead of telephoning him. Nancy was fearful that Chi Che had been abducted, and perhaps taken out of the country!

"I wonder how long Chi Che will be gone," Grandpa Soong mused. "Well, I must be patient. I will work hard on the foreword of my book and help to pass the time," he said sadly.

The elderly man asked if the police had any clues to the person who had stolen his manuscript. Nancy had to admit that they had turned up none yet, but were working hard on the case.

"Grandpa Soong," she said, "you may think me very rude, but I should like very much to have this letter from Chi Che. If I bring it back soon, may I borrow it?"

The archaeologist did not even ask her why she wanted the note. "Take it, my dear. And there is no hurry about your bringing it back."

The next morning Nancy went directly to Columbia University and talked to the young woman assistant in the dean's office who had been so helpful before. Nancy obtained samples of Chi Che's handwriting, not only in English, but also in Chinese.

"Any news of when Chi Che may return?" the assistant asked.

"We do not know," Nancy replied. "I suppose you are curious why I want the samples of Chi Che's writing. The reason is that her grandfather received a letter from her which I suspect is a forgery. I'd like to determine if it is. But please say nothing about this to anyone."

Nancy left the young woman staring in amazement after her. She hurried directly to Captain Gray's office and showed him both the envelope and the fire-dragon stationery with its message.

"I suspect this may be a forgery," she told the officer. "Could you possibly have a handwriting expert analyse it?"

"Yes, at once," Captain Gray agreed. "This may be an invaluable clue."

Nancy also confided her fear that Chi Che might have been taken from the country. The captain frowned, and said he would notify the FBI. He then suggested that Nancy return to headquarters in about two hours. The young detective thanked him and left, but she was back soon after lunch.

"Nancy Drew, you have scored another bull's-eye," the officer told her. "The note in Chinese and the envelope in English received today by Mr Soong are definitely the work of a forger."

"Can you tell me any more?" Nancy asked.

"Yes, several things. Most important, perhaps, is that this note and envelope were written by a woman!"

·9·

Bess is Missing

"A WOMAN!" Nancy exclaimed. "I wonder who she is— probably the wife of one of the men involved in the case."

"No doubt," said Captain Gray.

"Will you show me some of the differences in the two handwritings, so that if I come across the fake one again I might be able to spot the forger?"

"Be glad to, Nancy." Captain Gray laid the envelope of the letter which had just come to Mr Soong and the sample of Chi Che's handwriting in English side by side.

"One of the hardest things to imitate in handwriting is the crossing of t's," the officer explained. "The forger is trying to be so careful that he usually goes slower and the line is slightly more wavy than the original writer would make it. Look at these two through this magnifying glass.

"The letter 'y' is another interesting one to look for," Captain Gray stated. "If it is an unfinished one with the tail going straight down, it is apt to be off centre or wobbly. If it's a completed 'y', it's even easier to spot."

Nancy studied the y's on the two different samples of writing. "It's very evident," she said. "This is fascinating." Then her brow furrowed. "Captain Gray, do you agree that Chi Che is being held against her will?"

"I would say yes," the officer answered. "Furthermore, she probably was taken away somewhere else before any members of the gang even thought of sending this note. For that reason, they had to forge it."

"Shall I take this letter back to Mr Soong?" the young detective asked. "He may become suspicious, and that's what we're trying to avoid."

The officer nodded. "We have made good photostats of it. Take the letter back, but suggest to Mr Soong that it might be accidentally thrown away in the hospital and would be safer with you. Then suppose you return it to me."

Nancy smiled understandingly and left. She found Grandpa Soong sitting up in bed, writing. He did not object to her suggestion about the letter, so she took it back to police headquarters.

"I think I'll drop in at Stromberg's Bookshop and see how Lily Alys is making out," Nancy told Captain Gray. "Perhaps she has picked up a clue already!"

Nancy hurried to the shop. There were several customers who were being assisted by both Mr Stromberg and Lily Alys. Nancy gave no sign of recognizing the Chinese girl who presently came up to her and asked:

"May I help you?"

"Yes," Nancy replied. "I'm looking for a book on the geology of New York State. Do you happen to have one in stock?"

"I think we have," Lily Alys said. "Will you come over this way, please?"

The young clerk found the volume. "Is there something else?" she asked sweetly.

"I'm not sure." Nancy looked round. "The shop is fascinating. I'd like to browse a little."

"Very well," Lily Alys said. "Let me know if you find anything else you wish to buy."

In an undertone which no one else in the shop could hear, the Chinese girl said quickly, "On the third shelf of the travel books is a volume about Asia which contains an article on Hong Kong. Inside the book I found a piece of dragon stationery."

"Was there anything written on it?" Nancy asked.

"The paper looked blank on both sides. But maybe *you* can find something."

Quickly Lily Alys went over to the desk, made out a sales slip for the book on geology, then went up to another customer. In the meantime, Nancy wandered round glancing at various volumes. Finally she came to the travel section and found the book which Lily Alys had mentioned.

She took it from the shelf, and began to look through the volume. Presently she came to a chapter on Hong Kong. But there was no piece of stationery among the leaves!

"Someone has taken it out," Nancy thought. "I wonder who. Mr Stromberg? Or someone who is using the bookshop to leave or collect secret messages? Or maybe the sheet was only a mark to indicate something in the chapter," she deduced. "I think I'll buy this book."

She walked back towards the desk with it and told Lily Alys that she would purchase the book about

Asia as well as the other. As Nancy said this, Mr Stromberg abruptly left the customer on whom he was waiting and rushed to Nancy's side.

"That book is not for sale!" he informed her in a sharp tone of voice.

Nancy looked at the man in amazement. "Not for sale?" she repeated. "It was on the shelf."

"Nevertheless, that volume is not for sale!" Mr Stromberg cried excitedly. "Give it to me!" Without waiting for her to do so, he snatched it from her hand.

Nancy pretended to be shocked by his action. "Why, is something the matter with the book?"

"Yes—uh—it's out of date. You'll have to wait until the revised edition is published."

"Oh, I don't mind if it's old," said Nancy disarmingly. "I love to read about Asia."

By this time Mr Stromberg's face was red with anger and he once more vehemently refused to sell the book. Nancy was sure now that the book held some clue to the mystery of the fire dragon. The question was how much did Mr Stromberg know about it? Was he shielding someone else? Had he been asked not to sell the volume and had it inadvertently been put on the shelf?

Nancy shrugged. "If you won't sell it, you won't sell it," she said. "Well, I'll just pay for the other book I bought."

Mr Stromberg accompanied Nancy to the desk. He wrapped the book on geology himself and took her money. There was no chance for Lily Alys to tell Nancy any more, but the young sleuth was determined to find out later that day if the Chinese girl had come across additional information.

As Nancy walked along the street towards Aunt Eloise's apartment, she decided to try another bookshop for a copy of the book on Asia. She found one without any trouble, then hurried home.

"Hello, everybody," Nancy called, entering the apartment. Seeing only Aunt Eloise and George in the living-room, she asked, "Where's Bess?"

"She went shopping for me," Miss Drew replied.

Nancy told about her experience in the bookshop and the others agreed that something strange was going on there. Next, Nancy turned to the chapter on Hong Kong in the book on Asia. First came the history of the city, then suggestions to tourists on what to see, and finally a list of shops known for fine jewellery, linen, furniture, and clothing of all kinds.

"Hong Kong is the place for expert tailoring and dressmaking," Nancy remarked. "My, and listen to these prices. Things cost about one-third of what they do in this country!"

"Me for Hong Kong," George chuckled, taking the book. Presently she said, "There doesn't seem to be anything out of the ordinary in this chapter. Maybe the contents of the book had nothing to do with the piece of dragon stationery inside."

"Then why wouldn't Mr Stromberg have sold me his copy?" Nancy argued. "I think perhaps some phrase or sentence was underlined and he didn't want anybody to see it."

George suggested that perhaps they should have the police keep a watch on Mr Stromberg. Aunt Eloise shook her head. "He might be innocent of anything underhanded. A customer may have asked him to reserve that particular volume, and not being a very diplomatic person, he practically lost his head because Nancy wanted to purchase it."

Nancy said that as soon as Lily Alys was back in her dormitory at Columbia she was going to phone her. She looked at her watch. "By the way, how long has Bess been gone?"

"Too long," Aunt Eloise replied. "She should have been back an hour ago. I can't understand it."

Nancy was concerned too. "Perhaps we should go out and try to find her."

At that moment the telephone rang. It was Lily Alys. "Oh, Nancy, I've lost my job!" the Chinese girl said worriedly.

"I'm not surprised," Nancy told her. "And I'm sure it's all my fault. Mr Stromberg became suspicious after the book episode. Isn't that it?"

"Yes, partly," Lily Alys replied. "After all the customers had gone, he called me to the desk and handed me a few dollars. He looked at me hard and said, 'Young lady, I don't know what your game is, but I want an assistant I can trust—not someone that brings customers in here to cause a scene.'"

"He meant me!" Nancy exclaimed. "I believe that Mr Stromberg must suspect you and I know each other."

"I'm afraid so," said Lily Alys.

Nancy asked if the Chinese girl had had a chance to look at the pages between which she had found the piece of fire-dragon stationery.

"Yes, I did. In the list of shops it mentioned 'mah-jongg sets.' Those two words were underlined."

"That might be a clue," Nancy said. "Did anything else happen to cause Mr Stromberg to discharge you?"

Lily Alys gave a great sigh. "Just before that happened, he went into his office in the back. I wanted to ask him a question, so walked to the door. I was just in time to hear him say on the phone, 'Don't use books again to get your message across.' "

The Chinese girl said she felt sure that Mr Stromberg knew she had heard him and this actually was the reason he had discharged her. "Oh, I am sorry I failed in my mission," Lily Alys added woefully.

"Please don't worry about it," said Nancy. "You've been a big help. Besides, I'm sure you can find a safer position somewhere else with no detective work to do."

Lily Alys agreed. "But I had hoped to do more to help find Chi Che," she said.

"You may learn something yet," Nancy told her. "If you do, be sure to let me know."

Lily Alys promised to do so, then hung up. Nancy told Aunt Eloise and George what she had just learned, then went back to the book and began to look for shops selling mah-jongg sets. There were several, and since Lily Alys had not mentioned the name of any shop, the young sleuth suggested that Lily hardly had a chance to notice the name. "She probably had to close the book in a hurry, before Mr Stromberg saw her looking through it," Nancy surmised.

"But I'll bet anything he did," George said.

Aunt Eloise, who had been gazing out of the window, said worriedly, "I'm really becoming frantic about

Bess. I can't imagine why she's staying away so long. She told me she would come straight home, since some of the groceries were needed for dinner tonight."

Nancy urged that she and George delay no longer in trying to locate Bess. They got a list from Aunt Eloise of the three stores to which Bess intended to go, then set out. At the first two stores they learned nothing, but the cashier at the third one, a large market, said she remembered pretty, blonde-haired Bess.

"That girl was loaded down with bundles," she told Nancy and George. "She and a woman behind her were laughing and talking about going in the woman's car to help the girl get all her packages home."

"Have you any idea who this woman was?" Nancy asked quickly.

"No, I haven't," the cashier answered. "I had never seen her before tonight."

George and Nancy went out to the street, trying to guess where Bess could have gone.

"Frankly, George, I'm terribly worried," Nancy said. "That woman who offered to give Bess a drive may be part of the gang that's holding Chi Che. The woman could even be the forger of the letter to Grandpa Soong!"

"Oh, Nancy, I hope you're wrong!" George said fervently. "We'd better report Bess's disappearance to Captain Gray."

But Nancy was not wrong. At that very moment Bess was seated on a chair, her eyes blindfolded and her hands tied behind her back. She had no idea where she was.

Bess's heart pounded in fright. She berated herself,

"Oh, what a fool I was to get into this awful mess!"

Her mind raced over events of the past hours. First she had encountered the pleasant woman with Eurasian features in the supermarket. The woman had said that she was a good friend of Miss Eloise Drew, and had offered to drive Bess and her many bundles to the apartment house.

Bess had accepted and the two had gone out to the car. Behind the wheel was a man who, the woman said, was her husband. Bess had noted only that he had red hair.

The moment they had climbed into the rear of the car, the woman had dropped her bag on the floor. Bess had leaned over to pick it up. The next instant she had been pushed down to the floor and warned to keep still or she would be sorry.

Now, Bess thought desperately, she was a prisoner in some unknown place. Was the red-haired man the same one who had taken George from the Columbia campus? The Eurasian woman, who was far from pleasant now, was saying harshly:

"You'd better tell us what your pal Nancy Drew is up to! And you don't leave here until you do!"

· 10 ·

Bookshop Detectives

BESS MARVIN sat in speechless amazement as her two captors continued to quiz her about Nancy's sleuthing. How had they learned she was working on the case?

"If you won't talk," the woman warned in a harsh voice, "you may never see her again!"

Bess was terrified, for she feared these people might carry out their threat. Yet she did not intend to give away any of Nancy's plans for solving the mystery.

Two rough hands gripped Bess's shoulders and shook her. She was sure they belonged to the red-haired man.

"Listen here," he said, "this silence won't do you any good. If *you* won't tell us what's going on, we'll get hold of that interfering young detective herself!"

All this time Bess had been desperately racking her brain for a likely story to allay the suspicions of her captors. Suddenly an inspiration came to her.

"Take your hands off me!" Bess ordered. "I'll tell you why Nancy Drew is in New York."

"Well, it's about time," the woman said unpleasantly. "Talk, and be sure it's the truth!"

Bess explained that Mr Drew was a lawyer and his law cases took him to many places. Nancy often did research for her father in order to save him time.

"Mr Drew is planning a trip to Hong Kong," Bess went on. "He thought if Nancy talked to some people who had been there, and read some good books on the subject, if would be of assistance to him. Mr Drew's case concerns a will."

There was a long silence, then Bess could hear the couple whispering. The imprisoned girl waited in an agony of suspense. Had her explanation been convincing enough? Would they let her go?

In a few minutes the woman spoke. "We're going to let you go. But not until after dark and not until we get you far away from this place. We don't want you to know where you've been so you can inform the police."

"Yeah," said the man. "You'd better not tell the police or anybody else *anything*, if you know what's good for you!"

A little later Bess was ordered to get up and walk. The woman held her by one arm, the man by the other. Presently she sensed that they had entered an elevator. She felt the descent, then Bess knew she was being led outdoors. She was shoved into a car and made to sit on the floor.

The motor was already running and the car started off at once. The drive was a long one, and so jolting that Bess was continually bumping her face against the hard seats. She felt that she was surely coming out of this adventure with a black-and-blue nose!

Finally, to her relief, the car was stopped. The couple helped Bess out and walked her a short distance.

"Don't move or you'll get run over," the woman warned her. "Somebody will come along and find you. And remember, don't go to the police."

"Come on! Hurry it up!" the man barked.

Bess heard the car door slam and the car roar away.

"Oh, where am I?" Bess wondered, thankful to be free, but feeling utterly helpless.

From the freshness of the air and relative lack of traffic noise she figured she was out of the city. She could hear cars not too far away, but apparently none of the drivers saw her. Though Bess had been warned not to move, she did lean over and manage to feel the ground. Dirt and grass!

"I'm at the side of some road," she thought, straightening up again.

At that instant Bess heard an oncoming car, then a screech of brakes. A moment later a car door opened and someone took off the blindfold. Her rescuer was an elderly man, and in the car sat a white-haired woman.

"Oh, thank you, sir," Bess gasped in relief. "Please untie my hands too."

The man gave a grunt. "They carry these affairs too far!" he said. "What the fraternity boys do is bad enough, but when the sorority girls get to tying new members up and leaving them by the road after dark, it's going beyond all sense!"

"It certainly is," the woman agreed.

Bess smiled wanly. She said nothing—unwittingly the elderly couple had supplied her with an explanation that satisfied them.

The man helped Bess into the rear seat of his saloon and inquired she where would like to be dropped. "At your sorority house?" he asked.

"I think not," said Bess. "I'd like to go home. Are you going into New York City?"

"Yes, we are," the man replied. "I'll be glad to take you home."

"You are most kind, but just drop me anywhere in the city."

The couple, however, insisted upon driving Bess to her home. Finally she directed them to the apartment house where Aunt Eloise lived. In Bess's bag was a small bottle of a lovely French perfume she had purchased that day. As she opened the door to step from the car, she handed the package to the woman.

"Please take this and enjoy it. You have no idea how grateful I am to you." She hurried across the pavement before the woman could comment.

When Bess rang the outer doorbell and announced she was home, she could hear shrieks of delight from the apartment. The inner door clicked open and she hurried to the elevator. Aunt Eloise and the other girls hugged her joyfully, demanding to know where she had been.

"I'm not supposed to tell you," Bess said. Now that her great fright was over, she could not help teasing the others.

"If you don't," threatened her cousin George, "*we* won't tell you what we found out this afternoon."

Bess made a face, then told her story. The others were aghast, and Aunt Eloise insisted that despite the warning of Bess's captors, they should tell Captain Gray the whole story.

"I suppose he'll want me to look through the rogues' gallery to see if I can find that woman," Bess sighed wearily. "Well, please ask him to make it tomorrow. I'm starving and I certainly will be glad to tumble into my bed."

As Aunt Eloise went to telephone the police captain, Nancy and George hurried to the kitchen. They prepared an appetizing meal for Bess and sat down with her while she ate. Then she went directly to bed and the others soon followed.

At breakfast the next morning the whole subject was discussed again. As Bess suspected, Captain Gray had requested her to come to headquarters and try to pick out the woman in the rogues' gallery. George offered to go with her.

"Maybe I can spot the red-haired man," she said. The two girls left after the meal was finished.

As Nancy helped her aunt get ready for school, she said, "I'd like to try a little sleuthing from a different angle. I am more and more convinced that Stromberg's Bookshop is a front for an underhanded scheme. Could you ask some friend of yours to go there and find out if Mr Stromberg has a new assistant?"

"I could ask my friend Mrs Becker."

"I'd like her to do something else too," said Nancy. "Do you think she would ask Mr Stromberg to come to her home and look at some foreign books she'll say she wants to sell? I'll get the volumes for her."

"Certainly," said Aunt Eloise. "I'll call her right now." She smiled. "I suppose while he's gone, you'll go to the shop to look round again." Her niece nodded.

Miss Drew dialled the number. Then, since it was getting late, she introduced her niece to Mrs Becker and told the two to continue the conversation. Nancy waved goodbye to her aunt, then explained her request to Mrs Becker.

"To avoid suspicion that I'm involved in this plan,"

Nancy said, "I'll have the books delivered to your home instead of bringing them myself."

Mrs Becker promised that as soon as the books arrived she would look them over carefully so that she would know their contents. "Then I'll go to Stromberg's Bookshop and talk to the owner. If he agrees to come to my apartment, I'll let you know what time it will be."

Nancy thanked her, then hurried off to the bookstore near the university where she had purchased her copy of the Asian book. She bought several foreign volumes in various languages. All of them were old, first editions, and rather hard to obtain, according to the bookshop owner. This was exactly what Nancy had wanted!

"Could you deliver this package immediately?" she asked the owner. The man said yes. After the books were wrapped, Nancy carefully wrote Mrs Becker's name and address on the package, paid for all the books, then left the store.

By the time Nancy returned to the apartment, Bess and George were back. "I wasn't able to identify any photograph in the rogues' gallery," Bess said.

"And I didn't find the red-haired man," George added.

"They must be new at their racket," Nancy remarked.

She told the cousins of her plan for sleuthing. "I thought you girls and I would go to Stromberg's Bookshop while Mr Stromberg's at Mrs Becker's. You stand guard in the front room, while I take a look in that back room!"

The three girls had just finished their luncheon when Mrs Becker telephoned. The woman said she had gone over to the shop during the morning but learned little. Mr Stromberg was most solicitous in helping her pick out a book she planned to buy. There was a new young woman assistant, not too efficient, attending.

"Mr Stromberg is coming to my apartment at two o'clock this afternoon," Mrs Becker told Nancy.

"Oh, that's fine," the young sleuth said. "And thank you for your help, Mrs Becker."

At exactly two o'clock Nancy, Bess and George arrived at Mr Stromberg's shop. As prearranged, the girls took up their positions. Bess at once began chatting with the assistant, and took her to a front corner of the shop where the books on fashion designing and dress-making were located. It was easy for Bess to keep the young woman intrigued by her chatter on the subject of clothes.

George wandered round the shop, trying to pick up any clues which they might have overlooked before. Nancy, meanwhile, had slipped into the back room when the shop girl was not looking. She knew that legally she must not open the drawers in the desk or the bureau in the room.

"But maybe I can detect something without doing that," Nancy told herself.

The young sleuth circled the room, looking under the desk and a table, then on the shelves hugging one side of the room. By standing on tiptoe, she could just see what was inside several open boxes on the top shelf.

Suddenly Nancy gasped. "Giant firecrackers!"

Lying on the shelf next to the telltale box were several sheets of the fire-dragon stationery!

"Oh, this is wonderful evidence!" the girl detective said to herself. "I think I had better report this to Captain Gray at once!"

As she turned to leave the room, Nancy became aware of a familiar voice in the shop. The speaker was Mrs Horace Truesdale, the woman who had been in the store the first time Nancy had come there.

"Oh, dear!" Nancy said to herself. "Now I won't dare go out there. Mrs Truesdale will be sure to see me and she's such a talker she'll certainly ask questions, and she may even tell Mr Stromberg where I've been!"

The young sleuth decided there was nothing to do but wait for the woman to leave. But when she looked at her watch, she realized Mr Stromberg might return at any minute.

Suddenly Nancy became aware of a scraping sound near her. Turning, she was just in time to see a trap door in the floor starting to lift.

"There's only one thing for me to do," Nancy thought wildly. "Hide! But where?"

A Suspect Escapes

THERE was only one possible hiding-place for Nancy Drew in the cluttered back office of the bookshop—under the kneehole desk. It had a solid front, but fortunately for Nancy it had a six-inch opening at the bottom.

Quickly the young sleuth crawled out of sight. By resting her cheek on the floor and peering out through the opening below the back panel, she could plainly see what was going on.

A moment later a man carrying a large paper bag stepped into the room. He was the driver who had trailed George to the hospital when she was masquerading as Chi Che! He was slender and rather short, but muscular-looking. Could he be the man who had attacked Grandpa Soong, and the thief who had stolen the archaeologist's manuscript?

Nancy was greatly excited. There was no question now but that the Stromberg Bookshop *was* involved in the fire-dragon mystery!

"I wonder what this man is going to do?" the young sleuth asked herself.

Quietly he moved across the room, then he crouched and moved a box away from one part of the wall. A small safe was revealed.

With deft fingers the man swung the dial left, right, left, then turned the handle. The door opened without a sound.

As the intruder scooped up a stack of papers tied with a cord, Nancy caught a quick glance at the top sheet. It was in Chinese writing.

"That may be Grandpa Soong's manuscript!" she told herself. "Do I dare try getting it away from him?"

Just then she heard Mr Stromberg's voice in the bookshop. The intruder jammed the stack of papers into the bag he was carrying and went to the trap door. Silently he descended and closed it behind him.

Nancy was thinking fast. She decided to avoid Mr Stromberg if possible and follow the man with the manuscript. "And I'll notify the police about both of them," she told herself.

Nancy wriggled from under the desk, then tiptoed across the room and cautiously raised the trap door. Lying flat on the floor, she gazed into the cellar below. A bright light in the ceiling gave her a clear view of the place. No one was in sight.

"That man must have gone out of the cellar door to the street," the young sleuth concluded. "Well, I'll do the same thing!"

Quickly she let herself down on to the narrow stairs and closed the trap door after her. Nancy descended and made her way to the front of the cellar. As she came out on the pavement, Nancy felt sure that the manuscript thief could not be far away. She looked up, then down the street just in time to see the slender man disappear round the corner. She started running after him.

"Nancy!" cried a voice behind her, and a second later Bess and George caught up to her. "You had us scared silly!" Bess scolded. "What's going on?"

Nancy stopped short. Over her friend's shoulder she caught sight of Mr Stromberg who was standing in the door of his shop looking at her angrily. Bess and George had revealed her get-away!

At once Nancy decided to give up the chase. "I can't explain now," she said. "Bess, go across the street to that phone box and telephone Captain Gray. Tell him I have pretty good evidence that Mr Stromberg is involved in some racket and ask him to send detectives here at once. Meanwhile, George and I will guard the store and cellar exits, so Mr Stromberg can't get away."

By this time the shop owner had gone back inside. Bess hurried off to do the errand, as George and Nancy took up their posts. But Mr Stromberg did not reappear. Within ten minutes two officers, Willet and Fisher, arrived. Nancy quickly explained the situation.

"We'll go in and talk to Mr Stromberg," Officer Willet said. They entered, but were back in two minutes. "Mr Stromberg isn't there," he reported.

Nancy frowned. "Did you look in the cellar? He may be hiding."

"Yes, we looked down there. Nobody around except that shop assistant. She's scared out of her wits and says she doesn't know where Mr Stromberg went."

"There's only one answer," said Nancy. "There must be a secret exit."

While Officer Fisher remained to guard the street doors of the bookshop, Officer Willet accompanied the three girls into the shop. They went at once to the back room.

"There's a wall safe behind that box," said Nancy. "Maybe there's another opening behind something else."

Against the far wall sat a very tall packing case. Nancy dashed over and peered behind it. "Here's the answer," she said. "There's a door leading outside. Mr Stromberg must have escaped this way."

The officer and the girls squeezed behind the packing case and opened the door. They found themselves in the rear yard of a department store. They ran across it and went into the service entrance. No one was there.

"Luck was with Mr Stromberg," Officer Willet said grimly.

The service entrance opened into the shipping room piled high with packages awaiting delivery. No shipping clerks seemed to be on duty. The officer and the girls rushed ahead until they came to swinging doors which opened into the ground floor of the department store.

"Mr Stromberg made an easy getaway," Willet remarked. "We may as well give up the chase and find him by some other method."

"You mean at his home?" George asked.

The officer nodded. He and the girls walked round the block until they came to the front of the bookshop. Officer Fisher was amazed to see the four arrive from this new direction. They quickly explained what had happened, then he reported that no one had come out of either entrance to the bookstore.

"Let's go back and see the assistant," Nancy proposed.

They entered the shop once more and Officer Willet asked the girl where Mr Stromberg lived.

"I—I d-don't kn-know," the girl stammered. "I don't want to stay here. I don't like it. Please let me go home!"

"Not yet," the officer told her. "But don't be frightened. We'll take care of you. We just want you to tell us everything you know about Mr Stromberg."

"N-nothing," the girl replied. "I was sent here by an employment agency that has my name. He called up for an assistant. He said another girl had worked here only a few hours."

"That's true," Nancy said.

Officer Willet looked through the desk for a clue to where Mr Stromberg lived, but found nothing. He picked up a book of customers' names and read them carefully.

"I'll phone some of these people to see if they know where Mr Stromberg lives," he said.

"I'd suggest that you try Mrs Horace Truesdale first. She was in here two different times when I was and seemed to know him well."

This attempt to locate the bookshop owner failed completely. Mrs Truesdale said she had no idea where he lived. Other customers gave the same answer.

"I'll try some of the neighbouring stores," the officer said, and went out. But he came back in a short time and reported that Mr Stromberg, who had rented the shop six months before, was known as a very uncommunicative person and no one in the other shops knew where he lived.

"We're stymied for the time being," George admitted. "But we'll get those crooks yet!"

Officer Willet smiled. "I like your enthusiasm. I hope we can live up to your hopes."

Before leaving the shop, Nancy telephoned Captain Gray to tell him the unfortunate result of her endeavours to apprehend the suspects. He sympathized with her, then remarked philosophically:

"That's a detective's life! But we never give up."

He now reported that the police still had no clue to Chi Che Soong's whereabouts. Furthermore, according to the detective guarding the entrance to Aunt Eloise's apartment house, no suspicious person had been seen there.

"But something is bound to break soon," Captain Gray said. "We have so many police working on the case they're sure to find at least one of the suspects."

As the three girls started for Aunt Eloise's apartment, all admitted to being a bit downcast. They had failed to learn anything more to help solve the mystery of Chi Che Soong's disappearance.

"Nancy," George said, "if that *was* the manuscript you saw being taken from the safe, why is Chi Che still being kept away from home?"

"I'm afraid," Nancy replied, "there's another reason for her disappearance besides someone wanting to get hold of Grandpa Soong's work. I believe Chi Che inadvertently found out about some kind of racket, and the gang involved is giving her no chance to report it to the police."

Bess sighed sadly. "Oh, dear! The poor girl!"

That evening Nancy received a telephone call from Lily Alys Wu. The Chinese girl asked what progress had been made on the case. Upon hearing the latest developments, she expressed her own great concern about Chi Che.

"What's worse," she added, "I've seen Mr Soong, and I'm afraid he senses now that something is wrong. He doesn't seem too well and he isn't doing any writing."

"How dreadful!" Nancy exclaimed. "I'll go to the hospital as soon as I can and try to cheer him up a bit."

"What do you think Mr Stromberg is going to do now?" Lily Alys asked.

Nancy thought for a few seconds, then replied, "I'm afraid he and his pals may skip the country. It's my guess they may even go to Hong Kong."

Suddenly Lily Alys broke in excitedly. "Nancy, I just thought of something that may help you solve the mystery!"

· 12 ·

Flight Plans

"WHILE I was working in the bookshop," Lily Alys told Nancy, "I walked to the back room to ask Mr Stromberg a question. Just like the other time I told you about, he was talking on the phone in a low tone.

"But I caught one thing he said that might have something to do with your case. He said to the other person, 'You have your ticket? No one will —— with all those students.' I didn't catch the one part of the sentence." Lily Alys asked Nancy what she thought the missing word might be.

"It could be any number of things," Nancy said slowly. "Of course it might be something completely innocent. But if Mr Stromberg were talking to one of the gang, the missing part might have been 'recognize you' or 'suspect you.' "

"It probably was," the Chinese girl agreed. "I wonder who the person could have been?"

"And I wonder," said Nancy, "what the ticket is for. It might be for travel, for the theatre, for some sports event—"

"That is one reason I called you," Lily Alys broke in quickly. "I said maybe I could help you. On a certain flight to Hong Kong from New York, the whole tourist section of the plane has been reserved for Chinese and American students from Columbia University."

Nancy was excited over the information. "Only I doubt that any students are mixed up in this racket of Mr Stromberg's."

Lily Alys said she was not thinking of the tourist section of the plane. "The first-class section is open to all passengers. I thought the person Mr Stromberg was talking to might possibly be among those people."

Nancy was thrilled. "Lily Alys, I believe this is a stroke of genius on your part. How soon does this plane leave?"

"In three days. It's for a ten-day vacation in Hong Kong." Lily Alys chuckled softly. "I understand that the tourist section has not been entirely filled. Perhaps, if you care to go to Hong Kong yourself, I can arrange for you to have one of the seats."

Nancy felt a surge of excitement over this possibility. She thanked Lily Alys and said she would let her know if she wanted a reservation. "As a matter of fact, my father and I were planning to go to Hong Kong sometime soon. Maybe we could take this flight!"

"But the tourist section is only for students," Lily Alys reminded the young sleuth.

"My father could go first class," Nancy told her. "He might spot the suspect without being recognized. I'll try to obtain a list of the passengers who have signed up so far."

"Do you think Mr Stromberg may be one of them?" the Chinese girl asked.

"Possibly," Nancy replied. "But if so, I'm sure he'll be travelling under an assumed name and I would have to see him to identify him. But I can alert the police, anyway, and also tell them other members of the gang may be aboard."

She thanked Lily Alys for the helpful information, then at once called Captain Gray. He too felt that perhaps Nancy had picked up an important clue. "I'll call you back and read you the list of first-class passengers," he promised, "as soon as I get them."

Hardly half an hour had gone by when he telephoned. The passengers' names were in alphabetical order and none was familiar to Nancy until he came to the T's.

"Mrs Horace Truesdale!" Nancy exclaimed.

"You know her?" the officer asked quickly.

"Well, no, not exactly. But twice I saw her in Stromberg's Bookshop. She seemed to be a regular customer."

"That doesn't prove anything, of course," Captain Gray said. "Nevertheless, I will find out more about her and let you know." He read the rest of the list of passengers but none was known to Nancy.

Within a short time the officer once more called Nancy, this time to report that there was nothing suspicious about Mrs Horace Truesdale. She was a widow who lived alone in a middle-class apartment house. "She's reputed to be a great reader and often goes on trips to visit friends."

The officer finished his conversation by telling Nancy that there was still no news of any of the suspects in the Chi Che Soong case. "But members of the force will be on hand to watch everyone boarding the plane to Hong Kong."

Later that evening Nancy telephoned her father and asked him how soon he was going to Hong Kong. The lawyer chuckled. "Confess, my dear. What's on your mind?"

His daughter laughed, then quickly related the entire story regarding recent developments in the mystery and told him of the flight to Hong Kong which some Columbia students were taking.

"I'd like to go on the flight," Nancy said. "And, Dad, I wish that you would go along in the first-class section. You could look over the passengers to see if you think any of them might be suspects."

After a pause, Mr Drew said, "I believe I could leave here in a couple of days. That would work out very nicely. I really should get to Hong Kong to interview the heirs involved in that contested will I told you about."

After further conversation, father and daughter agreed that it might be wise if the two travelled as if they were strangers.

"I'm sure," the lawyer added, "that the plan will work out to good advantage."

Nancy said she had another request to make. "I'd love to have Bess and George accompany us."

Mr Drew approved this idea at once. "The girls will not only help you, but may prove to be a safety factor. I'll phone the Marvins and Faynes and find out if they'll give permission."

"Wonderful!" Nancy exclaimed. Then she giggled, saying as she had done ever since she was a little girl, "I'll keep my fingers crossed!"

"I suppose," said Mr Drew, "that you will want to

make your own reservations through Columbia University. I'll let you know the results of my calls to Bess's and George's families. Then you can borrow money from your Aunt Eloise to purchase the tickets."

"And I'll notify Ned Nickerson of our coming," Nancy added. "He can arrange accommodation for us in Hong Kong."

"A good idea," Mr Drew approved. "But I think I had better do this, in case you're being watched. One of the gang might pick up the information."

"All right, Dad."

Within an hour Mr Drew called back to say that Bess and George had been given permission to go on the trip.

Nancy's chums were elated. "Oh, boy!" George cried. "If Chi Che is in Hong Kong, what a ball we'll have while finding her!"

"Yes," said Bess. "But we just must save some time to buy clothes there." Then she twinkled. "Do you suppose Ned will bring along a couple of dates for George and me?"

George grinned. "He probably will. But maybe you'd better go on a diet, Bess. Your huge appetite may frighten the boys away."

The other girls laughed. "Oh, *George!*" What had started out to be a wearisome evening now took a turn of merriment. Nancy used the kitchen phone to call Lily Alys, and asked her to get plane reservations for the three girls in the tourist section of the Hong Kong flight.

"This is very exciting," said the Chinese girl. "I hope you have a wonderful time and solve the mystery also.

I shall find out at once about getting seats on the plane and call you back."

For the second time that evening Nancy received good news. The three seats were available. Lily Alys told Nancy where at the university she could pay for the reservations.

"There is only one possible worry," the Chinese girl said. "If any Columbia students wish to make last-minute reservations, you will have to give up the seats."

"I understand," said Nancy. To herself, she added that she would cross her fingers!

Bess and George declared that they too fervently hoped that their trip to Hong Kong would not have to be cancelled. As the girls prepared for bed, they discussed the clothes they would need.

"I guess," Nancy decided, "the clothes we have with us will be plenty for the trip. We'll be buying more abroad, anyhow."

"Isn't it fortunate that we all had vaccinations recently?" Bess said happily.

"It certainly is," Nancy agreed. "And I've heard that it's possible to obtain passports right here in New York in case of emergency! I'm sure Captain Gray will certify to the emergency for us."

As Aunt Eloise and her three guests were preparing breakfast in the kitchen the next morning, Nancy said, "I'd like to go to Chinatown once more and see if I can pick up any further clues in the mystery."

"Suppose we go this evening and have dinner," Miss Drew suggested. "There is a delightful restaurant only two doors from that shop where you found the fire-dragon stationery, Nancy."

This plan was agreed upon. The group decided to arrive promptly at six o'clock, since Aunt Eloise said that all the food was cooked to order and there would be a long wait.

"I want to visit that stationery store again," Nancy said. "I know it's open in the evening. While we're waiting for dinner to be cooked, I can go there and talk to the proprietor. Maybe some of the gang have been in his shop again."

At exactly six o'clock Nancy and her friends entered the attractive restaurant. All the Chinese and American diners were eating their food with chopsticks.

"I'll never be able to manage that and get enough to eat!" Bess said. Her companions laughed.

Aunt Eloise and the girls ordered Peking duck and bean sprouts which were to follow birds'-nest soup.

"And now if you'll excuse me for a few minutes," said Nancy, "I'll just walk over to the stationery store."

Nancy went out to the narrow pavement and turned towards the shop. As she passed the next store, with apartments above it, an object came hurtling down towards her.

The next second it hit Nancy squarely on the back of the head. She fell to the pavement, unconscious!

· 13 ·

An Ominous Dream

As NANCY lay unconscious, people began to run from all directions to assist her. The excitement was heard in the restaurant. Aunt Eloise, Bess and George dashed outside.

"Oh, Nancy!" her aunt cried, hurrying to her side. "What happened?" she asked the bystanders.

A Chinese man pointed to a large, broken flowerpot on the pavement. "This apparently fell on the young lady. Can I be of help to you?"

"It is pretty chilly out here," Aunt Eloise said. "I think we should carry my niece into the restaurant."

By this time Nancy's eyelids were fluttering. Bess and George sighed in relief, sure she would be all right. George decided to stay outside as strong arms carried Nancy to the restaurant.

"Bess, I'm going to find out how this flowerpot happened to fall," George declared, holding her cousin back. "Maybe it toppled off a window sill accidentally, but on the other hand it might have been thrown deliberately."

Bess nodded grimly. She looked upwards above the store front and said, "There's a light in the first-floor apartment, but not in the second."

"I think we should investigate both places." George spoke with determination.

She picked up a piece of newspaper which had been dropped on the pavement and scooped up the plant and the earth. The two girls opened a door to the apartment stairway and ascended. They rang the bell to the first-floor flat. It was opened by a Chinese woman who looked at Bess and George curiously.

"Yes, please?" she asked.

"Does this plant belong to you?" George asked. "It fell from up here, somewhere."

"No, it is not mine," the woman answered.

"Do you know where it came from?" Bess queried.

"I cannot say," the Chinese answered. "But my neighbour upstairs has one like it."

"Then perhaps it fell from her window," George suggested.

"No, oh, no," the woman said. "Mrs Lin Tang is not at home. She has gone away to visit relatives."

George asked if anyone else lived in the apartment upstairs who might be at home. The woman shook her head. Then, looking intently at the girls, she said, "I *did* hear someone coming down the stairs. But when I heard the excitement on the street, I ran to look out and forgot about the footsteps until now."

"Did you see anyone leave this building?" George queried.

"No, I am sorry. I did not."

"Let's go upstairs and see if one of your neighbour's plants is missing," Bess proposed to the woman.

The three hurried up to the second floor, but the door to the apartment there was closed and locked.

"The intruder must have had a skeleton key and let himself in," George remarked. "Let's go back to the street and find out if anyone saw a person coming from the front entrance."

The Chinese woman said she would take the plant and re-pot it. The two girls thanked her and hurried down to the pavement. They began asking the people still standing around if they had noticed anyone leaving the apartment, but all said no.

Bess and George then returned to the restaurant and were delighted to see that Nancy was fully conscious. She was lying on a couch in the private office of the owner. The room contained many lovely Chinese decorations.

"Hi, girls!" she said, but the cousins noticed that she was very pale and her voice sounded weak.

"I'm so thankful the accident was no worse," Aunt Eloise said. "But we're going home. Mr Wong, the owner, has kindly consented to pack our dinner to take with us. We'll eat it in the apartment. Nancy should go right to bed."

At that moment the outer door of the restaurant suddenly burst open and a group came directly into the office. A red-haired man was being hauled in by a policeman and two Chinese men. Nancy sat up.

The officer began to speak. "These two men—" he indicated the Chinese—"say this man ran from the building after the accident. They had seen the flower-pot hurtle down and thought he might have tossed it on purpose, so they went after him. I was on the corner and took up the chase. Have any of you ever seen him before?"

"I'll say I have!" George declared. "He tried to kidnap me once!"

"And me another time!" Bess added.

"What!" the policeman exclaimed.

"You're crazy!" the prisoner shouted. "I never saw these girls before in my life!"

"Perhaps you don't recognize me," George said with a bitter smile. "The last time you saw me, you thought I was Chi Che Soong."

The man started perceptibly, but he kept up his bluster. "Officer, this is ridiculous. I admit I was in the apartment house. I went to the second floor to visit the people there but nobody was at home. I don't know anything about a flowerpot. You have no right to hold me."

"Yes, he has," Bess spoke up. "My friend Nancy Drew and I were trailing you that day you tried to kidnap my cousin. You found out from the driver of the stolen car that you had grabbed the wrong girl. Then you jumped into the car alone and raced off with the driver. We found out later you had stolen the car."

"There's not a word of truth in what she's saying," the prisoner insisted. "I'm leaving!"

"You'd better not even try," the policeman told him firmly. "Is there anything else you girls can tell me about this man?"

Nancy answered. "Everything my friends have said really happened, Officer. Also, the driver who was waiting for this man told him he had phoned to somebody named Ryle." She turned to the prisoner. "Who is he?"

"I don't know anybody by that name," the man replied defiantly.

"Suppose you tell us who *you* are," the policeman prompted.

The man refused to talk, so the officer went through his pockets. He pulled out a wallet and opened it. It contained a driver's licence issued to Ferdinand Breen.

"I think we have enough evidence to hold you, Breen," the officer stated.

"If you don't," George spoke up, "here is something else. We heard that the man named Ryle and a companion were trying to sell some jade that was thought to have been smuggled into this country."

Once more the prisoner jumped and gave George an angry look. But he said nothing.

The policeman asked to use the desk telephone. Mr Wong nodded and the officer called for a patrol car. Soon it arrived and the prisoner was led away.

"I'm sorry that you have had this unpleasant interruption in your business," Aunt Eloise apologized to Mr Wong.

"I am always glad to see law and order carried out." The restaurant owner bowed. "Please, Miss Drew, do not let the matter disturb you. The package containing your dinner is ready. I have called a taxi and it is waiting at the door."

"Thank you very much," Aunt Eloise and the girls said, as Nancy rose and they walked out. Nancy added, "I spoiled our little party, but some day I shall come back."

Mr Wong smiled and said he was glad to hear this. As soon as they reached Aunt Eloise's apartment, Nancy had some hot tea and went to bed. Soon she was sound asleep. After the others had eaten the delicious

Chinese food, George said, "It isn't too late. Bess, let's go to the hospital and see Grandpa Soong. Maybe we can cheer him up."

"You're not going to tell him what happened today?" Miss Drew asked quickly.

"Oh, no," George replied.

"All right," Aunt Eloise said. "But please take a taxi both ways for safety."

The two girls promised to do so and left. Aunt Eloise went to the telephone and called Captain Gray to relay the Chinatown incident. He told her he had just read of Breen's arrest on the police teletype. The officer inquired solicitously about Nancy's health and was relieved to hear she had not been severely injured. "I am going to talk to the prisoner right now," he said.

Bess and George reached the hospital only twenty minutes before the end of visiting hours.

The cousins were shocked when they saw Grandpa Soong. He was very listless and pale. A nurse who was in the room told them he had eaten practically nothing that day.

"I am not hungry," the Chinese said weakly. "I am greatly worried about my Chi Che."

The nurse stepped from the room and both George and Bess tried to bolster the man's lagging spirits by remarking that Chi Che probably was having a delightful time with her friends. To their amazement the elderly man shook his head.

"At first I believed that what Chi Che wrote was true," he said. "But now I am sure something has happened to her. We must have enemies—I do not know why. For a while I thought Chi Che was being held until the thief who took my manuscript could accomplish that evil deed. Then she would return. But she has not come back."

Bess and George looked at each other, at a loss for words. Grandpa Soong went on, "I had a strange dream. Chi Che was far away. She was being guarded by a fire dragon and was unable to escape. My poor Chi Che! She kept calling to me and to Miss Eloise Drew to save her."

Bess leaned forward and took the elderly man's hand in her own. "Grandpa Soong," she said, "that was a frightening dream. But you know that really there are no dragons."

The patient had been staring into space as if in a trance. Bess was sure he had not heard a word she said. Presently he asked:

"Do you girls believe in thought transference?"

They both admitted that they did. Then Grandpa Soong said, "There are men in this world who are more dangerous than fire dragons. I am sure my Chi Che is being held by one or more of them and really was calling out in her thoughts to me and to Miss Drew for help."

George felt that since Grandpa Soong was so suspicious of the truth, Nancy would agree that this was an appropriate time to reveal some of the girls' findings in connection with his granddaughter's absence. She told him about the various episodes in the bookshop where Chi Che had worked, including the fact that Nancy had seen a man open the safe in the private office and take out what appeared to be a manuscript.

"We all think it was your stolen work," George went on.

"The police have been notified?" Grandpa Soong asked excitedly.

"Yes," George replied. "One of those 'dragons' is now in jail."

"Did he reveal where my Chi Che is?" the elderly man queried.

"Unfortunately, no," George answered. "But we have several clues to the rest of the gang."

George stopped speaking, for at this moment the nurse returned. She had a delicious-looking egg-nog on a tray.

"Mr Soong, won't you please drink this?" she asked, smiling.

Without being helped, the elderly man suddenly sat up in bed. "I feel much better," he said. "My visitors have cheered me considerably. Yes, I will drink the egg-nog."

The nurse looked pleased. She set it on his night stand and again went off. As Grandpa Soong sipped the drink, he begged to hear more.

Bess and George told how Mr Stromberg seemed to be mixed up with the "dragons" and that it was just possible he and some of his friends had fled to Hong Kong.

"Nancy and George and I are flying to Hong Kong in a couple of days," Bess told him.

"Hong Kong!" Grandpa Soong repeated excitedly. "If my Chi Che has been taken there, she surely will be found. That is my twin brother's home. You must contact him as soon as you arrive."

"We will be very glad to do that," Bess said.

"My brother, Lee Soong, is retired now," Grandpa Soong went on. "But at one time he was head of the police department of Shanghai."

"Oh, this is wonderful news!" Bess exclaimed. "We will all work together. Between the New York and Hong Kong police and your brother and Nancy Drew, this mystery should be solved very quickly!"

A bell rang, indicating visiting hours were over. The girls quickly said goodbye to Mr Soong. They could hardly wait to get home and tell their news about the Shanghai ex-police chief Mr Lee Soong.

Aunt Eloise opened the apartment door. "Sh!" she said. "Nancy mustn't hear me, but I'm terribly worried!"

· 14 ·

A Hidden Microphone

"NANCY is worse?" Bess and George cried together fearfully.

"No," Aunt Eloise replied. "Come in and I'll tell you."

When the three were huddled in the living-room, the older woman whispered, "A little while ago I had a threatening phone call. The man said, 'This snooping into other people's affairs by Nancy Drew has got to stop! And if she goes on that plane, it'll be blown up!'"

"Oh, how horrible!" Bess exclaimed in an undertone.

George, equally worried, frowned. She rarely paid attention to anonymous threats, but for Nancy's sake she felt this one could not be overlooked. "That man probably means what he says!"

"It is a dreadful situation," Aunt Eloise remarked. "Perhaps, in order to save many lives, you girls should give up the trip."

Bess was inclined to agree, but George declared she was not going to let any dragon scare her off. "Anyhow, let's wait until morning and see what Nancy thinks."

The three went to bed but slept fitfully. They were concerned about the dangers which they had experienced in connection with the case.

The following morning Nancy was up, and except for a sore bruise on the back of her head, she declared she was back to normal. As the group cooked breakfast, they discussed the happenings of the evening before at great length—Nancy's accident, Grandpa Soong's story of his brother, and finally the threatening telephone message.

"The gang certainly has a good spy system," Nancy remarked, puzzled. "How in the world do they find out all our plans?"

Then suddenly she put her forefinger to her lips. The others kept quiet as she began to tiptoe around, looking behind the stove, the refrigerator, inside the cabinets, and finally behind the dainty curtains at the windows.

Presently Nancy nodded and motioned the others to come forward. She pointed out a tiny disc fastened to the window frame under the valance of the curtain. From the disc a tiny wire ran outside the window and down the side of the building.

Nancy picked up an order pad and pencil. On it she wrote:

"That disc is a microphone, and probably was hidden here the day the intruder broke in. Our enemies have been picking up all our conversations in the kitchen and recording them somewhere below. I suggest that we turn the tables. Let's all talk as if we were worried to death about the bomb scare and are going to give up the plane trip."

The others, astonished, nodded. Then Aunt Eloise began the conversation.

"Why are you girls so quiet?" she asked. "Don't tell

me. I know. You're all very brave, but this bomb threat really has you upset."

"I'm afraid you're right," said Bess, making her voice tremble. "I don't know about the rest of you, but I'd like to be counted out. I'm sure my mother and dad would never approve of my going on a plane that might be blown up!"

"You have a point there," George agreed. "If my parents knew about this, they'd put both feet down hard. But it burns me up. Here I was looking forward to a nice trip and someone we don't know steps in and ruins everything."

"Yes," said Nancy. She gave a tremendous sigh. "We were just getting some good clues and now this has to happen. Well, I suppose I'd better call my dad and tell him we're cancelling our flight tomorrow. He'll be angry, I know, but I'm sure he'll tell me to stay home."

"Do you think we could keep on with our sleuthing in New York City?" George put in.

Nancy said she wondered whether this would be worthwhile. She was sure that most of the members of the gang who were holding Chi Che had left town. "Otherwise," she added, "the police would have picked them up."

Aunt Eloise Drew remarked that she was so sorry everything had turned out the way it had. She laughed. "I suppose, Nancy, you can't expect good luck in solving every mystery you undertake."

"No," her niece agreed. "Just the same, I hate to leave Chi Che in such a dangerous situation."

"Yes," said Bess, giving a little sob. "Goodness only knows what torture they may be putting her through."

"Then we're all agreed we're giving up the trip?" Nancy asked. There was a chorus of "ayes."

The group stopped speaking. Nancy opened a cabinet drawer and took out a pair of scissors with wooden handles. Then, closing the window tight on the wire, she snipped it and wound the outer end around the curtain rod to keep it from falling to the ground when the window was opened again.

As George started to speak, the young sleuth held her finger to her lips. Once more signalling to the others to follow, she began a systematic search of the rest of the apartment to locate any other hidden microphones. But a thorough hunt revealed that the only one seemed to be in the kitchen.

Bess flopped into a chair. "Nancy Drew, you're something!"

"You sure are," George agreed. "I almost talked myself into giving up that trip during our act, but I'm not going to!"

"Nor I!" said Nancy.

Bess was a little more hesitant but finally decided that their broadcast had been convincing enough to keep any of the gang from placing a bomb on the plane.

Nancy now went to the telephone and called Captain Gray. When she had explained the whole incident, he said he would detail two men to shadow the person who came to pick up the record.

"No doubt it's in some device hidden at the ground level of the apartment house," the officer surmised. "We'll let the fellow hang himself so to speak. That is, we'll give him a chance to pass the word along that you girls have given up your sleuthing, then we'll nab him. I'll keep you posted."

After breakfast Aunt Eloise went off to school. The three girls met Captain Gray at the passport office, where he vouched for the emergency aspect of their flight. Passports were quickly issued.

"I'll call you as soon as we have any news on the tape recorder," the officer said as he dropped the girls at Aunt Eloise's apartment.

Later that afternoon when the telephone rang, Nancy ran to answer it. Captain Gray was on the line. "Good news, Nancy," he said. "We picked up the man responsible for the hidden mike and tape recorder at the apartment house. We gave him time to listen to what all of you had said and go to a phone booth.

"One of our plainclothesmen was nearby. He could tell from the spaces between the numbers what the fellow was dialling. Then our men picked him up. In the meantime, we were able to locate the party he called—a man known as Smitty. We find he was the one who accompanied Breen to Chinatown the day you chased them."

Nancy was thrilled to hear this. "And who was the man you picked up in the phone booth?"

Captain Gray chuckled. "One of the top members of the gang. His name is Reilley Moot. His nickname is Ryle."

"Oh, that's marvellous!" Nancy exclaimed. "And has he confessed to anything?"

"Not exactly," the officer answered. "But we found a giant firecracker in his pocket."

"*He* must be the one responsible for causing the explosions here!" Nancy broke in.

"Right. Looks as if things are closing in on the gang," the captain said. "You've done some fine sleuthing, Nancy. The police department can never thank you adequately."

He added that through communications received from Interpol, the police thought the men who were in jail, and their accomplices still at large, were members of a large smuggling ring.

"Just what they're smuggling we don't know," the officer went on. "But we hope to find out soon." He laughed. "If their headquarters are in Hong Kong, perhaps you will find out what they're smuggling before we do!"

"That sounds almost like an assignment." Nancy laughed too. Then she became serious. "Captain Gray, there is one thing which is being overlooked and to me that is the most important of all—finding Chi Che Soong."

She begged the officer to concentrate on that angle of the mystery, then said goodbye. Before long, Aunt Eloise came home and announced she was going to take the girls to the theatre. "I suggest that we do not mention the mystery or your future plans just in case any spies may be following us," she advised.

The girls agreed, and dressed for the festive evening. They had dinner at an uptown French restaurant, then saw a gay musical comedy.

"New York is just thrilling!" Bess exclaimed as they emerged from the theatre.

Nancy and George echoed this and Nancy added,

"Thanks a million, Aunt Eloise. This has been a terrific farewell party."

The following morning Miss Drew and the girls exchanged fond goodbyes. Aunt Eloise said it had been a wonderful visit and she hoped they would soon come again.

At three o'clock the girls set off. To keep any spies from suspecting they were headed for the International Airport, Nancy asked their taxi-driver to take them to Grand Central Station. Once there, she had him drive on and finally head for the East Side Airlines Terminal. There the girls' baggage was weighed and the travellers hurried into a limousine which took them to the airport.

Almost the first person Nancy saw in the waiting-room was her father. But as previously arranged, Mr Drew and his daughter pretended not to recognize each other.

The three girls stood a little distance from the ramp and closely watched each passenger go aboard their plane. The only one they recognized was Mrs Horace Truesdale. Finally Nancy and her companions were warned by a loudspeaker announcement to go aboard.

Quickly they got on the plane and showed their tickets to the stewardess. To the girls' annoyance, Mrs Truesdale was standing just beyond the doorway. She looked at them in amazement.

"Why, when did you decide to come on this trip?" she asked. "Are you students at the university? Or are you travelling first class?"

"Neither," Nancy replied, and started towards the rear of the plane.

"Are you going to Hong Kong?" Mrs Truesdale persisted.

"Isn't everyone on board?" Nancy countered.

"Will you be visiting friends over there?" the woman pursued.

"Yes," Nancy replied. Secretly she was thinking that this overly inquisitive woman might try to be friendly with the girls in Hong Kong and interfere with their sleuthing.

The stewardess asked Mrs Truesdale please to take her seat and motioned for the girls to go to theirs. Finally the lights went on, requesting passengers to fasten their seat belts. The door was closed and locked. The giant engines roared, and finally the plane taxied to the end of the runway.

After the great craft had stood there for over ten minutes, Bess said to Nancy and George seated alongside her, "Why don't we take off?"

At that moment the stewardess's voice came over the loudspeaker. "Your attention, please! On order of the police department, all hand luggage must be examined. Will you please co-operate?"

Nancy, Bess and George looked at one another. Were the police, perhaps, looking for a bomb after all?

The Mah-Jongg Dealer

"LET's get off the plane!" Bess urged in a tense whisper.

Nancy shook her head. "Maybe it isn't a bomb. Perhaps someone is trying to smuggle goods out of the United States."

The student group sat in strained silence. They could plainly hear a woman in the first-class section arguing loudly. Nancy recognized Mrs Truesdale's voice.

"This is an outrage!" she was shouting. "I am telling you here and now that it's a disgraceful procedure. Can't a person take a trip out of the United States without being treated like a common thief?"

Nancy and her friends had to smile in spite of the fact that there might be a bomb aboard. George remarked, "That woman is a pain!"

Presently two police officers came to the rear part of the aircraft and inspected everyone's hand luggage. As they finished their check-up, and started towards the door, Nancy asked them, "Could you tell us why you searched our bags, or is that against regulations?"

One of the officers looked at her intently, then said, "I'm sure there's no harm in telling you. Someone phoned the airport that a bomb was being carried in the hand luggage of a passenger on this plane. It must have been a crank. We did not find anything."

"Thank goodness," said Bess.

The officers left the plane, and a few minutes later the craft finally took off. It had been in the air for about an hour when Nancy saw her father walking back towards her.

"I think it's all right now for me to speak to you," he said, a twinkle in his eye.

The lawyer perched on the arm of his daughter's chair. "I've been engaging various men in conversation," he said in a low tone. "All seem to be in legitimate businesses. I'm sure there are no suspects among them."

"Did you know that the police were looking for a bomb?" Nancy asked.

Mr Drew nodded.

Nancy told him about the bomb threat the girls had received and about her own ruse to keep one from being placed in the plane.

Mr Drew frowned. "I believe your trick worked for a while, but the gang probably had you trailed to be sure. There was no time to place a bomb aboard, but they still hoped to scare you and try to keep you from going to Hong Kong."

Nancy whispered, "This must surely mean the gang has transferred its operations to Hong Kong."

Mr Drew agreed. He got up and returned to his seat.

Gradually, during the flight, Nancy made the acquaintance of the students, and in her own subtle way quizzed each one to see if by any chance there was a suspect among them. She came to the conclusion there was none.

"Members of the gang holding Chi Che must have gone by some other route," the girl detective told herself.

The great plane stopped at Anchorage, Alaska, for refuelling. Nancy and her friends were intrigued by the beautiful city. They were amazed at its size and the tall modern buildings.

"This used to be the capital," said Bess, "but now Juneau is."

Nancy remarked, "I'd love to come to Alaska in the middle of winter and ride on a dog sled!"

The travellers' next landing was Tokyo, Japan. What a bustling place the airport was! The girls were fascinated by the native people, most of whom wore Western dress, but many had on kimonos and sandals. Everyone seemed good-natured and there was lots of laughter. Men and women always bowed low to one another in greeting or when saying goodbye.

The twenty minutes during which the travellers were allowed to visit the terminal were soon up, and Nancy and her friends climbed back into the plane. It was now two o'clock on Sunday afternoon. By the time they reached their destination it was exactly eleven hours later than it was in New York.

As the plane began its Hong Kong descent, George looked at her watch and grinned. "It's one o'clock yesterday afternoon in New York," she said.

The plane set down and taxied towards the airport building. The landing and take-off strips of Kai Tak Airport fascinated Nancy. They were on a spit of man-made land and she realized how skilful a pilot had to be to use them.

"We're on the China mainland," said Bess. "Not Hong Kong Island at all."

"That's right," said George, who had studied the map. "This Kai Tak Airport actually is in the city of Kowloon."

"How do you get over to Hong Kong Island?" Bess queried.

"By ferry," George replied.

All this time Nancy, who now had a window seat, was looking intently at the crowd of people waiting behind a wire-mesh fence. She hoped to see Ned Nickerson among them!

"Oh, there he is!" A tingle of excitement rushed up and down Nancy's spine.

The plane stopped and the exit door was opened. First-class passengers disembarked. Mr Drew hurried towards the fence behind which he had spied Ned Nickerson.

"Hello, Mr Drew!" the tall, good-looking, athletic young man called. "Where are the girls?"

"They're coming." The lawyer laughed. "I travelled in style. They're in the tourist section."

At that very moment the girls were moving towards the exit. George was saying, "I hope that pesky Mrs Truesdale won't stop us and try to find out what we're going to do."

The three girls finally went down the steps and exchanged their greetings with Ned through the wire fence. Then the four travellers entered the low, white administration building. Here they went through the

immigration formalities and customs examination.
Finally they collected their baggage, then hurried to
meet Ned in the waiting-room.

"It's sure good to see you," the young man said,
giving Mr Drew a hearty handshake and kissing each
of the girls. "I have a jalopy outside. I guess we can all
crowd into it."

"Did you get us hotel accommodation?" Mr Drew
asked him.

"Yes, at the Peninsula Hotel. That's right here in
Kowloon and I'm sure you will like it." He chuckled.
"Since prices here are lower than in the States, I
asked for a three-bedroom suite with a living-room.
Nancy may want to entertain one or more villains."

"Including yourself?" Nancy teased.

"Call me anything you like," Ned responded, "but
just let me stick around."

"How much time can you spend away from Chung
Chi College?" Nancy asked him.

"A few days. Well, shall we go?"

Ned escorted the group outside the building. Two
porters stowed the luggage in Ned's small foreign car,
then everyone got in. Bess giggled. "It's a tight
squeeze!"

As the visitors approached the business section of
Kowloon, they became more and more intrigued with
the city. Most of the buildings were not more than three
storeys high, and Chinese signs hung everywhere.
There were many Western people walking about, but
the bulk of the populace was Chinese. Native men,
women and children wore trousers and loose-fitting,
straight jackets. Most of the suits were black and plain,

but here and there one would see someone wearing a beautifully embroidered garment.

Presently Ned drove to the hotel and residential area, where the streets were broad. The Peninsula Hotel was a large, attractive building. They entered the long, curving driveway and alighted at the front entrance.

"This is very charming," Mr Drew remarked as the travellers walked through the foyer to the reception desk.

The whole central section was filled with couches, lounge chairs, palms, flowers and tea tables. People, seated in groups, were sipping tea and eating small cakes.

As soon as the Drews and their friends had unpacked and freshened up a bit, they met in their living-room. Ned demanded to hear all about the mystery on which the three girls had been working. When they finished telling him, he whistled and said:

"You really picked a honey this time, Nancy. So you think Chi Che might be a prisoner here in Hong Kong?"

"I believe there's a good possibility. But even if she isn't, I'm sure this is headquarters for the smuggling ring, and that she knows their secret. If the leaders can be rounded up, Chi Che will automatically be released."

"I'm ready to help," Ned said. "Nancy, when, where and how do I start?"

The young sleuth thought for a moment, then she replied, "I want to show you something in my handbag."

Nancy obtained the bag from her bedroom and took out the two pages which she had torn from the book on

Asia. "These are the sheets which upset Mr Stromberg. Lily Alys said the words 'mah-jongg sets' had been underlined. I don't believe she noticed in which shop. Now's your chance to be a detective, Ned."

The young man took the sheets and read them carefully. Then a smile spread over his face. "I think I have a clue for you, Nancy," he said. "One of these shops is owned by a man named Lung. The word *lung* was the original Chinese name for dragon."

"Of course!" Nancy said excitedly. "I remember now! Grandpa Soong told us that. Let's go there first thing tomorrow morning."

"Fine," Ned agreed.

"George," said Bess, "this is our chance to go shopping for clothes and souvenirs."

The next morning Nancy and Ned started out directly after breakfast. They took Ned's car to the ferry, parked it, and went by boat to Hong Kong Island. As they crossed the bay, Nancy marvelled at the surrounding scenery. The harbour was filled with boats of all kinds, large and small, including junks and sampans. The island ahead of them was almost like a stone fortress which rose to a pinnacle in the centre.

"That is Victoria Peak and it's eighteen hundred and nine feet high," Ned told Nancy.

"It's amazing how they build houses right into the side of the mountain," Nancy remarked.

When she and Ned disembarked, he hailed two rickshas and the couple climbed into them. Nancy was intrigued by the man pulling her little two-wheeled vehicle. He trotted along after Ned's ricksha at a pace that a horse would trot.

Nancy found Hong Kong a fascinating combination of modern skyscrapers and quaint Oriental buildings. Presently the ricksha men turned down an alley and in a few minutes stopped. They had arrived at Mr Lung's shop.

"Like the ride?" Ned grinned.

"It was fun," Nancy replied as they alighted.

She and Ned entered the shop and gazed round at the wall decorations. Every one of them was a dragon in some form. There were painted scrolls, pictures, and a few wooden figures. Nancy shivered. "This is a creepy place," she whispered.

There was a short counter towards the rear of the small shop. As the couple approached it, a man came from behind a curtain in back of the counter.

"Mr Lung?" Ned asked.

The man nodded.

"We'd like to see some mah-jongg sets," Ned told him.

Without a word the shop owner took several from a shelf and gave the price of each. All the playing pieces were of ivory, but the less expensive sets were in plain boxes, while others were in carved teakwood chests lined with camphor wood.

"These are very beautiful," Nancy said. "Do you have any others?"

Mr Lung shook his head. "We have more that are similar, but these are samples of all the varieties I carry."

Nancy examined the boxes carefully. It occurred to her that each one contained many places in which small articles could be secreted for smuggling.

"What do you think?" Ned asked her, careful not to use Nancy's name.

"Let's decide later," the young sleuth answered. "After all, we've just started to shop." She turned to Mr Lung. "Thank you very much. We'll probably be back."

The man bowed and started to put the mah-jongg sets back on the shelf. Nancy and Ned left the shop and strolled up the alleyway. They had not gone far when Nancy heard a woman's familiar voice say loudly, "You charge too much!"

Turning, the girl saw Mrs Horace Truesdale just alighting from a ricksha. The woman, frowning, put some money in the man's hand, then walked into Mr Lung's shop.

Quickly Nancy told Ned of her encounter with Mrs Truesdale, then whispered tensely:

"Is it just a coincidence that she knows Mr Stromberg and came directly here to Mr Lung's shop? Or could Mrs Truesdale, by some chance, be part of the smuggling ring?"

· 16 ·

A Chinese Puzzle

"NANCY, that's a good hunch," Ned said. "Let's eavesdrop on Mrs Truesdale."

Quickly the couple moved up the narrow street and cautiously posted themselves, one on either side, at the door of Mr Lung's shop.

Nancy and Ned were just in time to see Mrs Truesdale take a small white paper from her bag. She held it up and turned it first on one side, then the other, for Mr Lung to see. Then, without looking, she seemingly returned it to her bag. But the paper fluttered to the floor apparently unnoticed.

"Please ship four dozen mah-jongg sets to my sister's gift shop," the woman said to the owner.

Mr Lung grinned. "Very soon," he said.

Mrs Truesdale snapped her handbag shut and started for the door, evidently unaware that the paper she had shown the man lay on the floor.

"I'd certainly like to see what's written on it," the young sleuth told herself.

"We'd better hide!" Ned warned. He took hold of Nancy's arm and hurried her into the doorway of an adjoining shop.

They saw Mrs Truesdale come out on to the street, hail a ricksha man, and climb into the cart. As soon as

280

she was out of sight, Nancy urged Ned to return to Mr Lung's shop with her.

"Suppose you buy a mah-jongg set while I try to find out what is on the paper."

"All right," he agreed.

The eager couple re-entered Mr Lung's shop. Fortunately the owner had not noticed the paper. Nancy and Ned smilingly walked up to the counter.

"We decided to come back, as you see," Ned said. "May I see your assortment again?"

The shop owner nodded briefly and turned his back. Nancy quickly leaned down and picked up the paper from the floor. One side was white. Two words were printed on it—Kam Tin.

The girl detective hastily put it in her handbag. By now Mr Lung had brought out the various sets. Nancy and Ned finally selected one in a teakwood chest.

"Shall I send this to you in the States?" Mr Lung asked.

Ned had no intention of disclosing their names. "I think we'll take it along," he said.

"I will get your set from stock," Mr Lung disappeared behind the curtain into his back room. Now was Nancy's chance to take out the paper. This time she noticed that the other side was red. Ned, too, took a glance and both of them gave a slight gasp.

The paper was definitely the cover to a package of firecrackers. On it was painted the fire dragon!

Quickly Nancy put the paper back on the floor. Mr Lung reappeared and wrapped the set. Ned paid him. Both the young people smiled and thanked the shop owner, then walked outside.

"Now then, where do we go next?" Ned asked.

"Some place where we can talk without being overheard," Nancy whispered.

"Let's go into the foyer of a small hotel near here," he suggested.

As soon as they entered the place, Ned remarked, "This firecracker business seems to prove Mrs Truesdale *is* part of the dragon gang."

Nancy nodded. "Ned, have you any idea what Kam Tin means? That was printed on the white side of the firecracker paper."

"Why, yes," he replied. "Kam Tin is an ancient Chinese walled city several miles inland in the New Territories, beyond Kowloon."

"I believe," said Nancy, "that Kam Tin is either a place where the smugglers' goods are collected, and perhaps put into the mah-jongg sets, or else it's the spot where Chi Che Soong is a prisoner."

"Oh, I hope it's not the latter!" Ned said.

"Why?"

Ned described Kam Tin as hundreds of years behind the times. "There's no plumbing in the one to two-room houses which are set close together. People and farm animals also are crowded together. The streets are extremely narrow and there's mud everywhere."

"Oh, dear! Poor Chi Che!" Nancy exclaimed.

Ned explained that the men farmed outside the walls. At night the animals were brought inside the city walls for safety.

Nancy was thoughtful for several seconds, then she suggested to Ned that they contact Grandpa Soong's brother as soon as possible. "He's Mr Lee Soong and is retired now. But at one time he was head of the police in Shanghai."

"Then he's just the one to help," said Ned. "He'll have a personal interest in this case, since Chi Che is involved."

They returned to the Peninsula Hotel foyer and Nancy immediately telephoned Mr Soong. He asked them to come to his house at once. Nancy, wondering where Mrs Truesdale was staying, consulted the desk clerk and learned to her delight that the woman was registered at the Peninsula.

"It will be easy to trail her from here," she told Ned.

The two sleuths set off for Mr Lee Soong's house. The Chinese was a very handsome man and appeared far younger than his twin brother. He was agile in his movements and spoke quickly and decisively. He was astounded and greatly concerned to hear the details of his great-niece Chi Che's disappearance. At the end of Nancy's account, he said:

"I shall get in touch with the local police at once and a search will be started for Chi Che. If she is in this crown colony, she will be found. I will work on the case personally, and I beseech you, Miss Drew, to continue your fine efforts."

Nancy promised to do so and said she was going to ask George and Bess to trail Mrs Truesdale.

Mr Soong thought this an excellent plan. "Mrs Truesdale may be the one to lead us to a real solution," he predicted. "I will also have two Chinese detectives follow all three, so no harm will come to the girls."

Nancy thanked him and said she would let him know when her friends started out. She and Ned drove back to the hotel. Mr Drew had not returned, but Bess and George came in from their shopping tour, arms filled with bundles.

"Oh, this town is fabulous!" Bess exclaimed. "Nancy, wait'll you see what we bought!"

Nancy smiled. "First, though, I want to tell you what Ned and I learned this morning. And I have a sleuthing job for you and George."

When the girls heard about Mrs Horace Truesdale they were thunderstruck. George actually fell into a chair, shocked. "And I thought that woman didn't have a brain in her head!" Bess added.

"If she does belong to the gang," said Nancy, "she might have been the one who sent the faked note and also the flowers to Grandpa Soong at the hospital. The dragon card might even have been meant for me to see so I'd be frightened off the case."

"What do you want Bess and me to do?" George asked eagerly.

"Trail Mrs Truesdale," Nancy replied. "Or better still, invite her to go shopping with you and find out everything you possibly can."

"I like that assignment," Bess spoke up quickly. "Get me into a shop and I can stand anything!" George telephoned to Mrs Truesdale's room and gave the invitation. To the cousins' delight, the woman accepted promptly and said she would be ready to go shopping at two o'clock. Nancy relayed the message to Mr Soong.

Then, turning to Ned, she asked, "How about you and I going to Kam Tin?"

The young man hesitated. "I'd rather not trust my

old car for the trip. But I'd like to go. Suppose we try to charter a helicopter."

"Perfect!" Nancy's eyes sparkled.

Ned drove to the Kai Tak Airport and went inside the building to make arrangements for the flight. Nancy, meanwhile, walked outside and along a fence. Near the control tower was a large Navy helicopter. In the distance she saw a small whirlybird.

"That must be the helicopter Ned and I will take," she figured, and walked towards it. At that moment a small car raced past her and on to the field. In it sat a Chinese man at the wheel, and a girl. She barely caught a glimpse of their faces.

Some distance farther down, the driver stopped the car. The Oriental girl alighted, hurried on to the field, and into a waiting plane. It was a small, two-engine craft. The car whizzed off.

Nancy, lost in thought about the mystery, kept on walking towards the helicopter. Presently she drew near the small craft into which the Chinese girl had hurried. Nancy noticed that there were curtains inside the plane which more than half covered the windows in the passenger compartment. The three landing steps attached to the inside of the door were down.

Suddenly a girl's voice called, "Nancy Drew?"

Nancy was startled and instinctively responded, "Yes." Instantly the Chinese girl peered through the doorway. "Come here!" she said. "I'm Chi Che. I've been a prisoner but I escaped. This pilot is going to fly me to Taipei to get away from the kidnappers. But I want to tell you my whole story first. And, please, how is my grandfather? Poor Grandpa!"

Nancy stared at the girl. She did indeed resemble the photograph of Chi Che Soong. "Hurry!" the girl urged.

Still Nancy hesitated. She wanted to be sure this *was* Chi Che. "But it's not necessary for you to go to Taipei," the young sleuth said finally. "Your uncle is here and knows all about your kidnapping. I'll take you to him and you'll be perfectly safe."

"How do I know you're telling the truth?" the Chinese girl countered. "*Please* come inside a minute. I don't want anybody to see me, but I must give you a message for my grandfather. It is very important."

Nancy turned once more to look for Ned. He was running towards her. Confident that now she would be all right, the young detective quickly went up the steps and into the plane.

Immediately the door was slammed shut. The pilot pressed the starter buttons on first one, then the other engine. The motors roared to life. At once the plane raced to the nearest runway and took off.

"I don't want to go to Taipei!" Nancy cried out. "Take me back!"

Suddenly the Chinese girl laughed. "My name is Chi Che, but it's not *Chi Che Soong*. Nancy Drew, you're a prisoner!"

· 17 ·

Pursuit of the Sea Furies

As NANCY stood temporarily stunned by her capture, a man peered from behind a curtain where baggage was usually stowed. He was tall and very thin. Nancy had never seen him before, but was sure he was an American.

"How do you do, Miss Drew?" he said triumphantly. "Sorry I didn't meet you in New York, but I've been trailing you and your boy-friend round Hong Kong. This chance to take you in our plane is a lucky break. Are you prepared for a long flight?"

Nancy recovered herself and eyed her captors unflinchingly. "You don't think you're going to get away with this, do you?" she retorted.

The Chinese girl and her companion began to laugh scornfully. Then Chi Che said, "She does not know how smart you are, Skinny Kord."

Nancy ignored the taunts. "Where is Chi Che Soong?" she demanded.

"In a place where you will never find her," Skinny Kord replied harshly.

He now took a long rope from behind the curtain and, with Chi Che's help, bound Nancy's hands behind her back. He then forced her to lie down across two seats and very securely tied her ankles together.

"You may as well have a nap," Skinny Kord sneered. "You won't be doing any detecting."

He and his girl companion walked up to the front of the plane where the Chinese pilot was accelerating the craft to top speed.

"This is a dreadful fix to be in!" Nancy groaned inwardly. "What am I going to do?"

She thought of Ned back at the airport. Had he seen her enter the plane? Would he be able to effect a rescue? "Maybe some other plane will pass us." Nancy's mind raced. "If I could only signal it!"

The young sleuth suddenly remembered the lipstick she was carrying in her skirt pocket. By wriggling and squirming, Nancy was able to pull out the metal tube. By rubbing the case of the lipstick against the rope, she managed to detach the cap. Then she twisted the end until the red stick was showing. Slowly and painfully, Nancy managed to raise herself from the seats.

Keeping her eyes on the pilot's compartment, where her captors were busily talking, Nancy backed up to the window. With the lipstick, she wrote a large SOS backwards on the pane so that it would be legible from the outside. She then drew the small curtains across the window so that the writing would not be seen from inside. Weary from her efforts, the girl detective once more lay down across the two seats.

Meanwhile, back at the airport, Ned Nickerson had arranged to charter the helicopter. He had come from the building and had been surprised to see Nancy go into the small two-engine plane. Then, the next moment, it had suddenly taken off.

"That's strange!" the young man told himself. He dashed back to the airport building and rushed to the control tower to inquire about the plane.

"We know nothing about it except that it came in from Manila last Wednesday," the Chinese controller replied. "It made an unauthorized take-off from the wrong runway before the airfield car could stop it. We tried to attract its attention by a red light from the tower, but the pilot paid no attention. No flight plan whatsoever was filed. They won't answer on the radio."

"So you have no idea of the plane's intention or destination?"

"None whatsoever."

"A friend of mine is on that plane!" Ned cried. "I'm afraid she's been kidnapped! We must do something at once!"

The official asked Ned several questions. When the youth had identified himself and told enough of the mystery to convince the man a rescue was urgent, the controller called the headquarters of the British Royal Naval Air Service stationed in Hong Kong harbour. After a lengthy and excited conversation, the official turned to Ned.

"The chase has been started. There's an aircraft carrier a few miles out at sea engaged in practice exercises. It will try to pick up the plane by radar. As soon as it does, fighters will be sent out to force its return. A Navy helicopter is standing by and is just about to leave for the carrier. Would you like to go with it?"

"I sure would!" Ned said.

In a matter of seconds he was on board. The pilot

of the helicopter introduced himself as Lieutenant-Commander Rawling, commanding officer of one of the Phantom Flights.

"Glad to have you aboard," he told Ned. "My boys will be off after that plane shortly. It should still be well within radar range."

Ned sat in the front seat beside the pilot. In a few minutes they had crossed Victoria Island and the great carrier came into view. Three Phantom planes took off from its deck, one after the other.

"We'll follow them as quickly as we can," Rawling said, "but this 'copter is much slower. I'll get the flight leader on the radio." He called and established contact. Ned could hear everything said by both men.

In a few minutes the flight leader reported, "We have the aircraft in sight."

"Close in on him and make him turn back!" Rawling commanded.

"Wilco! Closing on him rapidly now."

Ned heard the flight leader calling the aircraft on the radio, but there was no response.

"They probably hear but won't answer," Ned guessed. "Remember Nancy is on board," he said. "I hope your men won't shoot!"

"No," said Rawling. "They may try to make the pilot think they will, though."

The lieutenant-commander gave orders to the Phantoms, telling them in code the manoeuvres to follow. The flight leader called back, "There's an SOS on one of the cabin windows!"

"Nancy must have put that there!" Ned thought excitedly.

In the kidnappers' plane, Nancy was both thrilled and frightened. She watched fascinated as one plane dived in front to slow them down, another swooped below, and the third above. One second she felt she was going to be rescued, the next that she might lose her life; her captors seemed to be desperate enough to perish in the battle.

The Chinese pilot, Skinny Kord, and Chi Che were talking excitedly both in Cantonese and in English. They had heard every word the commander of the pursuing three-craft squadron had said.

"Why should we take orders from them?" Kord cried out. "We can get away. They'd never risk shooting with Nancy Drew in our plane."

"But we don't dare land in Taipei now or we would be arrested," Chi Che said. "And we may run out of fuel and crash if we keep going."

The Chinese pilot said, "If we do not go back, I am not at all sure they will not fire on us. I am not risking it. We are returning."

Since his companions could not fly a plane, they were forced to accede to his decision. In a short time, to Nancy's relief, she felt the craft bank and turn. The pilot had lowered his landing gear as a token of surrender, she later learned.

Ned was thrilled to hear a new voice calling Kai Tak and asking for landing instructions. "We've won!" he shouted.

He strained his eyes on the distant horizon. Suddenly he pointed. "There they are!"

Four dots rapidly grew in size. Soon the kidnappers' plane came into view with a fighter flying as closely as possible on either side and one just below.

"We'll follow them in," Rawling said. He radioed the airport for police to be on hand. As soon as the mystery plane had set down, the fighter leader landed, but instructed the others to return to the carrier. The helicopter was on the ground in seconds.

The police were just handcuffing the arrested trio when Ned dashed into the aircraft. "Nancy!" He unfastened her bonds.

"Oh, Ned, how can I ever thank you for rescuing me!" she cried.

"How do you feel now?" he asked solicitously.

"I feel fine—really I do."

"Thank goodness!" Ned said.

None of the prisoners would talk, so Nancy related as much of their story as she knew. Then the three captives were taken away.

The young people said goodbye to Lieutenant-Commander Rawling and thanked him profusely. Nancy and Ned then walked to the airport building, where Nancy washed her face and hands, combed her hair, and rested for a short time. Then she told Ned she was ready to go on to Kam Tin.

The young man shook his head in astonishment. "You can certainly take it!" he said admiringly.

Ned found that the Chinese helicopter pilot, Jimmy Ching, was still available. Soon Nancy and Ned were airborne, heading for Kam Tin.

It was not a long ride and soon the helicopter was hovering over the walled city. It looked like a toy city surrounded by a moat. Beyond lay a vast expanse of fields with a farmhouse here and there.

The whirlybird came down on a field and the occupants alighted. As the visitors began walking through the ancient city, the inhabitants stared at them expressionlessly.

The three proceeded up one alley and down another. They could easily look into the houses, which were all open to the roadways and had bamboo curtains. These were now raised, but the pilot said they were lowered at night. Nancy and her fellow searchers saw nothing to indicate any smuggling activities, or that Chi Che Soong was being held prisoner in Kam Tin.

Nancy observed, as they walked along, that the walled city was crowded and unsanitary. Nevertheless, she was intrigued by an artistic religious custom of the inhabitants. On walls, both inside and outside the homes, were brackets holding candles, flowers and incense. The candles were lighted and the incense gave off a fragrant aroma.

"I don't think the people of Kam Tin have anything to do with the mystery of the fire dragon," Ned whispered to Nancy presently. "The paper Mrs Truesdale showed Mr Lung might refer to some farmhouse in the area instead of a place in town."

Nancy nodded. The trio went through the city gate and set off down the main road towards the nearest farmhouse. As they approached it, the three could hear rhythmic hammering. The sound was not noisy; on the contrary, it was muffled and pleasant.

"That hammering reminds me of goldbeaters," Ned remarked.

As Nancy and her companions drew closer to the farmhouse, they suddenly noticed a car coming in the opposite direction. It turned abruptly into a lane which led to the house. "Let's hide and see if we can find out what's going on here," Nancy suggested.

They managed to conceal themselves behind a shed a few feet from the house. The driver of the car was talking to a Chinese farmer.

Ned translated, "Is the shipment ready?"

The farmer replied, "Yes."

The driver then asked, "You kept enough to pay for the work?"

The farmer replied angrily, "I cannot use this. I want Hong Kong dollars."

The argument went on. The farmer threatened to expose the caller to the authorities if he were not paid at once. Finally the driver pulled out a wad of bills and handed it to the farmer.

The farmer pocketed the money, then called to someone inside the house. Several Chinese men, carrying two heavy chests, came outside and put them in the car. The caller drove off.

"I'm sure we have a clue to the smuggling!" Nancy whispered. "We'd better get back to the airport as fast as we can!"

Her companion agreed. As soon as they reached Kai Tak, the girl detective telephoned Mr Lee Soong and told him of the Kam Tin trip, giving the car's licence number and a description of the driver.

"I will arrange to have the police find this driver and trail him," Mr Soong said. "And the farmhouse at Kam Tin will be searched."

Nancy thanked him. "I can hardly wait to find out what happens," she told Mr Soong excitedly.

A New Assignment

THE ex-police chief, Mr Lee Soong, chuckled. "Impatience," he said, "is like a goat butting its head aimlessly on the wall. All he does is mar the wall and wear himself out."

Nancy laughed. "How true that is!" she replied. "I will try to be patient, but I shall have my mind on the case every minute until I hear from you."

Mr Soong said it probably would be hours before there would be any police report on the suspicious farmer and the man who had taken away the heavy boxes.

When Nancy told this to Ned, he said, "In the meantime, how about our having some fun? We'll do a little sight-seeing with Bess and George and your father. I thought we'd go to the Chinese opera for a while, then go on to eat at a houseboat restaurant out near the little village of Aberdeen. You will be amazed at that place," he added. "I shan't tell you any more about it."

Nancy smiled. "You know the only way you could get me to stop working on one mystery is to intrigue me with another. Now I can't wait to see Aberdeen."

Mr Drew, Bess and George had not returned, so Nancy and Ned left a note explaining their plan. Then the couple set off by ferry for Hong Kong to attend the Chinese opera.

"It goes on for hours and hours," Ned told his companion. "Whole families attend, even with their small babies. It is like an indoor picnic, so far as the audience goes."

In contrast to the plain dress and noisiness of the audience, the production was most dignified and elaborate. Nancy stared in fascination at the exquisitely embroidered silk and satin costumes and the lofty headdresses worn by the players.

Each actor moved about the stage slowly and a bit woodenly. But there was grace and charm to the performance.

"It seems to me," Nancy whispered to Ned, "that the audience isn't paying too much attention. Why?"

Ned explained that the Chinese like to see the same plays over and over. Many of them practically knew the scores by heart.

"Even though they don't keep their eyes on the stage every minute, and can even converse or move about, they still know everything that is going on," Ned told her.

It was growing dark as Ned hailed a taxi to take them to Aberdeen. "It's the oldest village of the fishermen of Hong Kong Island," he explained. "Families live on the junks and even in the small sampans."

When they reached the waterfront of Aberdeen, Nancy stared in wonder. "Why, it's almost a city of boats—of all sizes!" she cried.

"Yes," Ned said, adding that the residents jumped from craft to craft when they wanted to go ashore.

"But they spend most of their time on the water," he added. "The junks go out for deep-sea fishing, but the sampans stay here. The women and children remain on them while the men are at work.

"How fascinating!" Nancy exclaimed.

"We'll hire one of the sampans," Ned said. "It's the only way to reach the floating restaurant." He pointed off in the distance where they could see a long boat brilliantly lighted.

Several women were already calling to the couple, offering to take them. Ned finally signalled a mother and daughter with whom he had ridden before. They smiled as Nancy and Ned stepped down into the sampan and walked into the arched open-front cabin at the rear.

As they left the dock, Nancy was amazed at the strength of the two women propelling their boat. Both were short and very slight, probably weighing not more than six stone. Yet they seemed to have muscles of steel as they stood so straight and rotated their heavy oars through the water.

Upon reaching the Sea Palace, Nancy and Ned climbed a stairway to the deck. They walked round to the far side where a group of people were leaning over the rail and pointing below.

"See those boats down there?" Ned asked.

Nancy had never seen anything like them. They had compartments of water in which live fish and shellfish were swimming round.

"You pick your dinner alive," the young man said, laughing.

Fishermen below were recommending the various native fish. Nancy sighed. "I wouldn't know one fish from another," she confessed. "I shall leave the entire dinner to your judgment, Ned."

"Good!" he said, and guided her inside the restaurant.

The head waiter told them there were no small tables left. "Do you mind sitting at a larger one?" he inquired. Ned said they would not, and they were escorted to one near a window.

"First we'll have bacon and cucumber soup," Ned told the waiter. "Then some stewed shrimp." He looked up at Nancy to see if she approved. When she nodded, he went on, "A little sweet-and-sour pork, beef fried in oyster sauce, bamboo shoots, rice, and almond tea."

The couple finished the delectable soup and were busy with the stewed shrimp when Nancy happened to look towards the entrance door.

"Ned!" she said tensely. "Here comes Mrs Truesdale with a Chinese escort! He's not Mr Lung, though."

Ned turned to look. The head waiter led the new-comers to a table some distance up the long room. Mrs Truesdale did not notice Nancy and her companion.

Ned suddenly grinned. "Mrs Truesdale's shadows are right behind her!"

Nancy's eyes widened. Bess and George, looking extremely weary, entered the room. As they began to follow Mrs Truesdale, Nancy quickly got out of her chair and crossed the restaurant floor to the girls.

"You!" Bess exclaimed.

"Come join us and enjoy yourselves for a while," Nancy invited. "I can see you've really been on the job."

"Have we!" George laughed. "That Truesdale woman has nine lives when it comes to energy. We've been shopping everywhere with her today, and we decided to keep trailing her this evening."

The two girls dropped exhausted into seats at the table with Nancy and Ned. They had hardly had time to put napkins in their laps when a nice-looking Chinese man hurried up to them. He paused a moment to whisper to George:

"I'll take over. Get some rest." He went on, and without waiting to be seated, pulled out a chair at the table next to Mrs Truesdale. From this vantage point, the others knew, he could overhear every word of her conversation.

"Who is he?" Ned asked George.

"I don't know, but he trailed us all afternoon."

Nancy said he must be one of the detectives whom Mr Soong had retained to follow the girls. "If he isn't, the real sleuth will doubtless be following him, so in any case I think you girls can relax."

"Thank goodness!" said Bess. "My feet hurt and I'm absolutely starved."

The others laughed. Then Ned repeated the menu he had ordered for himself and Nancy. "Would you girls like the same?"

Bess and George agreed to try the exotic dishes. As Nancy and her friends ate the delicious meal, the group exchanged stories. George reported that Mrs Truesdale had neither said nor done anything the least bit suspicious.

"Of course I have nothing to go on except what happened in Mr Lung's shop," Nancy remarked.

Bess and George were completely astounded to hear of Nancy's capture, of her rescue, of her trip to Kam Tin with Ned, and of its results.

"You had enough adventure today to do me for a lifetime," Bess complained. "And this mystery is far from solved. Goodness only knows what'll happen next."

When they finished the delicious meal, George said to Nancy, "Do you think we should stay until Mrs Truesdale leaves, so we can follow her?"

"No," Nancy replied. "I'm sure the police will trail her. We had all better get a good night's sleep."

When they reached the hotel, Nancy found a message that she was to telephone Mr Lee Soong as soon as she came in. Nancy called him at once. Mr Soong said he had several things to report to the young sleuth.

"First, the police were not able to locate the man who left the farmhouse with the heavy boxes. We think someone saw you and Mr Nickerson leaving the place and warned him to disappear.

"We did raid the farmhouse and found that the owner and his workmen have been beating gold objects of all kinds into small flat pieces. We believe that these have been smuggled out of the country inside various containers."

"Mah-jongg sets!" Nancy exclaimed.

"Possibly," Mr Soong agreed. "Every one of the

goldbeaters insisted he was innocent of any wrong-doing. They finally admitted they thought something illegal was being done with the gold, but did not know what."

Mr Soong went on to say that a police guard had been placed at the farmhouse to seize any suspicious callers. "No one has come there yet," he said, "but the police uncovered a great many gold objects which probably were stolen from shops and homes and then brought there to be beaten into small pieces."

The Chinese now changed the subject and invited Nancy and her friends to attend a big garden-party to be given by a relative of his. "The party will be held tomorrow evening. Special fireworks will be displayed and I'm sure you will enjoy them. You have probably guessed that I am about to ask you to do a little detective work while there."

"I will be glad to," said Nancy eagerly.

Mr Soong said that at his request his friend had invited several special guests. "They may or may not be involved in the mystery we are all trying to solve. You know two of them—Mrs Truesdale and Mr Lung."

Nancy could hear the ex-police chief give a sigh of hope. "Anyhow, it is just possible my twin brother's wish will be realized during the party. But the police require the help of you and your friends. Will Miss George Fayne please come looking as much like my niece as possible?"

"I am sure she will be happy to," Nancy responded.

Nancy would have liked to hear more, but Mr Soong divulged nothing further. She thanked him for the invitation and accepted it with alacrity.

· 19 ·

Symbolic Fireworks

MR DREW came in so late during the evening that Nancy did not see him until the following morning at breakfast. At her request the meal was served in the living-room of their suite. After the waiter had left, the girls brought the lawyer up to date on the happenings of the day before.

He looked at Nancy intently. "Thank goodness you're safe, my dear. I suppose there is no use asking you to give up work on this case, now that it seems so near a solution."

Nancy smiled. "Of course you know the answer would be no." Then she told him about the invitation to the party that evening and how Mr Lee Soong hoped there would be another break in the mystery. "Will you be able to go with us?" she asked.

The lawyer shook his head. "My assignment here has proved to be a tough one, and tonight I must confer with the disagreeing heirs. But I, too, hope to get a break in the case by tomorrow."

"I suppose there won't be any detective work for us today, Nancy?" Ned asked.

"I can't think of any before tonight." Nancy smiled.

302

"Then let's all do some sight-seeing. First thing I know," the young man said ruefully, "your father and you will wind up your cases and fly back to New York without having seen half of the interesting things here."

George asked Ned what he had in mind. "You most certainly should take the tramway up Victoria Peak. Then we'll drive out to Chung Chi College. I want you to meet some of the fellows. We'll have lunch with them and then go to the international volleyball game between the United States and Japan against Formosa and India."

"It sounds very exciting," Nancy answered.

Bess smiled, her dimples deep. She did not say what the others thought she was going to; that the date sounded entrancing. Instead, she asked, "Ned, I wish you could straighten me out on something. I've been so busy sleuthing since I reached this place, I haven't figured out the political set-up."

Ned laughed. "There are plenty of people who have lived here a long time and still don't understand it," he said. "But actually it is quite simple. The whole area is a British crown colony.

"Hong Kong Island was ceded to the British when the Treaty of Nanking was signed in 1842. Then, in 1860, through the Convention of Peking, a tip of Kowloon Peninsula was added, as well as small Stonecutters' Island.

"In 1898 more land was added to the colony. It was leased for ninety-nine years and became known as the New Territories. It includes the rest of Kowloon Peninsula and the hundred and ninety-eight islands in adjacent waters."

"Thank you, Professor Nickerson." Bess leaned back in her chair. "I'll try to remember all that!"

"One interesting thing I've learned," said Ned, "is that the word Kowloon means 'nine dragons.' It is named for the range of hills behind the city. In fact, it separates the city from the New Territories."

George grinned. "We can't get away from the dragons! Any more interesting stories?"

Ned laughed. "After that crack, I'm not sure I should tell you. But here is one. Out in the harbour there is an island called Lantao. On it live barking deer."

The others broke into laughter and accused Ned of teasing. But the young man insisted he was not. "If you'll stay long enough, I'll take you over there and you can hear them."

Later, the girls and Ned started their journey up Victoria Peak on the tramway. They found it an exciting experience. The cable car stopped at stations on various levels to let local residents get on or alight.

Streets stretched out in all directions on the steep mountainside, and houses nestled firmly among the rocks. The view from the top was magnificent, and the girls could take in at a glance the enormous and bustling population on both land and water.

When they descended to the foot of the peak, the sightseers returned by ferry to the Peninsula Hotel and drove to Ned's college. The girls were greatly impressed. All the buildings were new and stood on top of a hill. In a valley to one side were the very large athletic fields.

When they pulled into the parking area, two young Chinese came to meet them. Ned introduced the handsome boys as friends of his. "Charlie Tsang, and this is Philip Ming."

The two young men bowed low, then said they had arranged to eat luncheon with them in a private dining-room usually reserved for faculty members. During the meal there was a constant flow of amusing banter among the young people. The Chinese students spoke excellent English and seemed to understand American slang and humour.

But finally the conversation took a serious turn when Charlie asked, "Ned, I do not wish to pry into your private affairs, but what have you been doing in Hong Kong recently?"

Ned grinned. "Just look at my companions and see for yourself," he said.

"This is no joke," Philip Ming spoke up. "Charlie and I were called from class to the president's office yesterday afternoon. He told us two men had been here inquiring about you, Ned. They thought you should be ordered back to the college immediately because you were a menace in town."

The Americans were astonished. "A menace!" Nancy cried out. "What do they mean?"

"I cannot imagine," Charlie replied. "These same people also said that Ned's mixed up in a smuggling racket and that he's being misled by unscrupulous persons. However, the individuals do not want to prefer any charges against you, Ned, but requested that the president insist you be made to remain here at college and not go into town."

Ned and the girls were more astounded than ever. They now quickly told the two Chinese men a little about the case on which they had been working.

Nancy expressed the opinion that the two visitors to the college were part of the smuggling ring. "Naturally they'd feel Ned is becoming a 'menace' to them, and want him out of their way."

Ned suddenly laughed upon hearing this. "So I'm that important, am I?" he asked.

"I'll say you are!" George spoke up. "Nancy needs a bodyguard. In fact, I'd say she needs more than one."

At once Charlie and Philip offered to help. When Ned insisted he could do the job alone, the two boys turned to Bess and George. "Do you not need protection too?" Charlie asked. "This evening, perhaps? We would like to take you sight-seeing."

Both Bess and George said they thought it would be fun but that they had promised to meet Mr Soong. "Could we make it tomorrow evening?" George suggested.

"Tomorrow evening it is," Philip agreed, and Charlie nodded.

The young people next attended the volleyball game. They followed the contest with increasing excitement as first one side, then the other, went ahead in score. In the end the United States and Japan defeated Formosa and India.

As the visitors were ready to leave in Ned's car, Bess declared, "This has been a lucky day!"

"And we hope the luck will continue," Philip Ming said as he and Charlie bowed.

"Thank you." Bess smiled. She was thinking, "Oh, I hope we will be lucky this evening and solve the mystery of Chi Che Soong!"

When Ned dropped Nancy and her friends at the hotel, saying he would see them later, the girls went at once to one of the shops there to pick out a Chinese costume for George. As soon as dinner was over, they changed into their party clothes. Nancy and Bess helped George disguise herself as Chi Che.

She had just finished applying make-up when the telephone rang. Mr Lee Soong was calling Nancy to say that two taxis were waiting. He requested that George came downstairs alone and casually hold a scarf so that her face would be partially covered.

"Miss Drew," Mr Soong went on, "ask your friend to bow to me, and act in every way as if she were Chinese, and indeed my great-niece. She and I will take the first taxi. Will the rest of you follow in the other?"

"Certainly," said Nancy. "We will be down immediately."

"That is excellent." Mr Soong added, "It is my great hope that someone at the party tonight will be startled upon seeing Miss Fayne's disguise and reveal a clue as to where Chi Che is."

Ned joined the girls and a short time later the two taxis drew up at the gate of a beautiful estate facing the harbour. Hundreds of lighted lanterns hung from among the trees in the gardens, and haunting Chinese music was being played.

The group alighted. As Mr Soong and George walked on ahead, Bess whispered to Nancy, "George seems even more convincing as Chi Che than she did in New York." Nancy nodded in agreement.

Presently the guests heard firecrackers being set off.

"That means the celebrations are about to begin," Ned explained. "Every Chinese function starts with fire-crackers."

"Let's go and watch," Bess urged.

There were many paths and little arched bridges over ponds and brooks. One of the paths, which everyone seemed to be following, led through an attractively carved, horseshoe-shaped arch. Beyond, in the centre of a clearing, Nancy and her friends could see a series of large metal frames for the display pieces of the fireworks.

All the guests had gathered to observe the display. George was alone, having preceded Mr Soong. Among the onlookers just ahead was Mrs Truesdale! The ex-police chief spread out his arms. Nancy sensed that Mr Soong's move might be a signal for her group to separate, and suggested that she, Bess and Ned take up different positions nearby. She herself remained at the rear behind the arch.

Some of the fireworks were in the form of floral pieces, each one more beautiful than the last. Finally the centre one was set off. As one section after another of it blazed into the night sky, Nancy gasped.

It was a huge fire dragon!

"It is magnificent, but frightening!" the girl detective thought.

Nancy glanced about to see Bess's and Ned's reactions. She could not discern her friends in the crowd ahead of her. But her gaze fastened on something else that almost made her heart stop beating.

Mr Stromberg was sneaking up behind Mr Soong. Was he going to attack the Chinese?

At that very instant George stood in the full glare of the fire dragon. Mrs Truesdale turned and stared at the girl. She suddenly shrieked:

"Chi Che! You got off the junk!"

Nancy's attention had been diverted for the moment from the scene nearer her. Now she saw that Mr Stromberg was about to strike Mr Soong. At the same instant, Ned appeared from among some bushes and leaped on the bookstore owner.

Swiftly Nancy started towards Mrs Truesdale, but advanced only three feet. Someone behind her clapped a hand over the girl's mouth and, with strong arms, dragged her away.

Nancy struggled and fought, but to no avail. The man who had seized her was suddenly aided by another, who lifted up her feet.

As she was carried off, the girl detective became aware that a Eurasian woman was accompanying the two men. Her strange captors took a path which was isolated and almost dark. No one came to Nancy's rescue.

·20·

The Escape

As THE great fireworks dragon continued to crackle and emit fire and smoke, George and Bess dashed forward and grabbed Mrs Truesdale.

"Take your hands off me!" the woman ordered.

At that moment Mr Lee Soong and Ned came forward dragging Mr Stromberg. The ex-police chief told the prisoners, "As you Americans say, I think your little game is up."

"What on earth are you talking about?" Mrs Truesdale asked airily. "Just because I said something to this impostor? I don't know why she's dressed up like a Chinese. For a moment I thought she was a wash-amah I know named Chi Che. She works for a friend of mine."

By this time most of the guests had gathered. Four men pushed their way through the crowd, nodded to Mr Soong, and took charge of the two prisoners.

"These men belong to the colony police," Mr Soong explained.

All this time Mr Stromberg had been glaring at Bess and George. Finally he said, "Officer, you have made a great mistake. Mrs Truesdale and I have been friends a long time and would swear to the honesty of

310

each other. Really, this is a complete outrage"

George faced the man squarely. "If you are honest, why did you run away from your bookshop? And where are you keeping Chi Che Soong?"

"I can only guess what you're talking about," Mr Stromberg said icily. "A girl named Chi Che Soong worked in my bookshop for a short while. I understand she has disappeared, but why should I know where she is?"

"Take these people away!" Mr Soong ordered the detectives.

As the group moved off, Bess suddenly asked, "Where's Nancy?"

"She was standing by that archway back there when the trouble started," said Ned.

Mr Soong and the young people searched the estate gardens thoroughly. Nancy was not in sight.

Bess closed her eyes in terror. "I just know the gang has kidnapped Nancy again!"

The worried group held a conference. Ned said, "Mrs Truesdale mentioned that Chi Che was on a junk. Perhaps that's where members of the gang took Nancy. Have you any suggestions on how to find that junk?" he asked Mr Soong.

The Chinese thought a moment, then said, "Mr Lung recently acquired a combination sail-and-motor junk. I will try to find out where he keeps it."

Mr Soong hurried off but was back in a few minutes. He had not only obtained the information by telephone but had received permission from their hostess to use her motor launch for a chase.

"Please to follow me," the Chinese requested.

At that very moment Nancy was being pushed aboard the large, sumptuous junk. Quickly the pilot cast off and the powerful motors began to move the craft towards the sea. A handkerchief which had been stuffed into Nancy's mouth was now removed, but she was warned by her captors not to make a sound or her life would be in danger.

At that instant Nancy caught sight of a Chinese girl prisoner kneeling in the roofed-over section at the rear of the junk. From the photograph she had seen in New York, she was sure this was the real Chi Che Soong!

"Let your prisoner go at once!" Nancy demanded. "And me too."

Her captors paid no attention and shoved Nancy towards the Chinese girl. But they did untie their prisoners. In a very low tone Nancy introduced herself and told Chi Che how she herself had become involved in the mystery.

"I heard the gang talking about you," the Chinese girl whispered. "Mr Breen took my keys. He came back to the apartment house and from the hall overheard your aunt telephoning you to come and solve the mystery. He was frightened away by the arrival of the caretaker."

Chi Che now began to relate the amazing story which had led to her capture.

"One day when I was in the bookshop I overheard Mr Stromberg talking on the phone. I realized he was part of a gang smuggling gold from Hong Kong into the United States. Small pieces were hidden inside the ivories and in the chests of mah-jongg sets."

Chi Che also confirmed Nancy's other suspicions that Mrs Truesdale, Mr Stromberg and Mr Lung were the ringleaders. Because of Mr Lung's name the group had adopted the dragon as a password.

"Was the owner of the stationery-and-gift shop in Chinatown a member of the gang?" Nancy asked.

"No, he is innocent."

The Chinese girl said that after she had heard the phone conversation at the bookshop about the smuggling, she had not known what to do. "I decided to go home and talk to my grandfather about it. When I arrived, he was not there. I assumed he had gone out walking as he often did. . . . Nancy, how is my grandfather? This must have been a dreadful shock to him."

Nancy told Chi Che about the stolen manuscript but skipped lightly over the fact that Grandpa Soong was in the hospital and not very well.

Chi Che caught her breath. "I must have mentioned the manuscript to Mr Stromberg. How unfortunate!"

"Please tell me just how you were captured," Nancy requested.

"While I was in the apartment trying to decide what to do, our buzzer sounded. I opened the door, thinking Grandpa had forgotten his key. A strange man pushed his way in and warned me to keep still. The man, who I later learned was named Breen, said Mr Stromberg knew I had overheard his phone conversation about the smuggling."

"He is in jail," Nancy told her. "Also two men nicknamed Ryle and Smitty."

Chi Che went on to tell how Breen, at gun point, had made her write the letter to Grandpa Soong on stationery which he had brought with him.

"Fortunately there were two sheets," the Chinese girl explained. "While Breen was pacing around—I suppose he was looking for the manuscript—he did not notice that I was writing the note to your aunt on the second sheet. But he told me to hurry up. I handed him the note for my grandfather, and while he turned his back a moment to put it in a prominent place, I slipped the other note under the adjoining door to Miss Drew's apartment."

Chi Che said she had then been taken to Mrs Truesdale's apartment and heavily guarded. Stromberg had tried to throw suspicion away from himself by his early-morning call at the Soong apartment. If anyone had answered the door, he would have said that he had come to find out if Chi Che was going to return to her job at the bookshop.

"When you and your kind friends and the police seemed to be nearing a solution to the mystery," Chi Che continued, "my captors took me one night on a private plane going to Hong Kong. When we arrived, they brought me aboard this junk.

"We've been on the water most of the time, just putting in to shore once in a while for supplies and messages. Nancy, your capture was all planned this evening. Some of the smugglers sneaked into the party."

Nancy now told of the imminent capture of Mr Stromberg and Mrs Truesdale just as she herself was dragged away. "Chi Che, we must escape from here. Can you swim?"

"Yes, I can."

The young sleuth gave directions on how the girls would proceed. "Let's stroll out on deck. When there's a sampan not far away, I'll give the signal. We'll climb on to the side and dive in together. We'll head for the sampan."

The two girls separated, Nancy going outside first. She drew in great breaths of fresh air and stretched as if weary from her cramped position. Chi Che followed, and kept her eyes glued on the other girl. The woman and the men on board paid little attention to them.

Suddenly Nancy gave the signal. The two girls kicked off their shoes, leaped up to the top of the wooden side of the junk, and dived in. The woman on board screamed and at once the men rushed to the side.

Nancy and Chi Che were swimming towards the passing sampan as fast as they could. They reached it at the same time and pulled themselves aboard.

The women manning it cried out in astonishment. Quickly Chi Che assured them in their native tongue that they would not be harmed. She said that the girls must get to shore immediately.

"Ch'ing hao."—"Please okay," the older woman said. She and her companion began to paddle furiously, and fifteen minutes later Nancy and Chi Che were safe on land.

"I must get to a phone at once," Nancy said.

Chi Che translated this to the women and the younger one led them to a small shop which was still open. Smiling, Chi Che asked for her name and promised to pay the next day for the boat ride.

As she went off, Chi Che explained to the shop owner the reason for the girls' bedraggled appearance.

He looked startled but took them to the telephone in the back room. Nancy at once put in a call to the hotel, hoping that her father had returned.

Hearing his voice, she cried in relief, "Oh, Dad! Chi Che Soong is with me. We just swam the bay to get away from some of the smugglers. They're on Mr Lung's junk. I was captured and taken aboard. I'll be right home, but do what you can to round up those kidnappers."

"You poor child!" the lawyer exclaimed. "Get here as fast as you can. In the meantime, I'll follow through."

During this conversation, Chi Che had been talking with the shop owner about getting transportation to the hotel. He said the girls were on the Kowloon Peninsula at a small town some distance from the city. "I will see what I can do."

The helpful, excited man hurried to the street. He was gone for several minutes, then the girls saw him riding up in a dilapidated car.

A young Chinese man sat at the wheel. He smiled at the girls and said in English, "Please to pardon my old jalopy. I will be glad to take you to the hotel."

When they reached the hotel, Nancy asked the driver to wait while she went upstairs to get money to pay him for his trouble, but the young man refused to accept any payment. "I am very happy to help you. From what I hear, you have solved a great mystery and benefited our colony. I am only a humble citizen, but I thank you."

The girls smiled and hopped from the car. They waved as he went off, then hurried into the hotel and up to the Drews' suite. As they reached the door to the living-room, it opened wide. Nancy's father clasped her in his arms. Then she broke away to introduce Chi Che not only to him but to Bess, George and Ned. Mr Lee Soong greeted his great-niece in Cantonese.

The two girls changed out of their wet clothes and Chi Che was given the suit which George had worn to the party. When she put it on there was indeed a striking resemblance between her and George!

When the girls returned to the living-room, stories were quickly exchanged. Nancy and Chi Che were thrilled to learn from Mr Soong that he and Ned and some of the colony police had arrived at Mr Lung's junk soon after the girls had dived overboard.

"We caught all the men and the woman before they had a chance to get away," the ex-police chief explained. "And also the man who drove off with the chests from Kam Tin. In them were mah-jongg sets containing hidden gold. Mr Lung and several others who worked for the smugglers are also in jail."

Presently Nancy said, "All of us here are so overjoyed that Chi Che has been found, I suggest we telephone overseas to Grandpa Soong and share the good news."

The others nodded. Before Nancy could put in the call to the hospital in New York, the telephone rang. The police had a message for Mr Lee Soong—his brother's stolen manuscript had been found in Mr Lung's shop. It was now in the possession of the police.

Mr Lung had confessed that it had been stolen from the New York apartment by Reilley Moot for Mr Stromberg, Mrs Truesdale, Breen and himself as a private project outside the smuggling ring. Ryle, knowing the combination of Mr Stromberg's safe, had tried to double-cross his friends by taking the manuscript, but later had been caught by them. The others, unable to dispose of the manuscript themselves in Hong Kong, had asked Mr Lung to try selling it.

The overseas call was put through and soon Grandpa Soong was saying, "Chi Che! I can hardly believe it! You are safe?"

When Chi Che told him the stolen manuscript had been recovered, the others could hear his gasp of astonishment and delight. When he and his granddaughter finished talking, Grandpa Soong asked to speak to Nancy.

"I am such a happy man," he said. "And I must thank you for everything—you and your kind friends. If you'll permit me to do so, I will dedicate my book to you three girls."

Nancy was touched and said she could not imagine any greater reward for her efforts.

"Grandpa Soong, will you please get in touch with my aunt and tell her the good news."

"I will do that at once," Mr Soong promised.

As Nancy turned from the telephone, she felt as if she had lost something. For a second the young detective looked about her. Then she realized why she felt this way. The mystery of the fire dragon had been solved—there was nothing more for her to do! But Nancy was sure that soon another case would come along. It proved to be the *Mystery of the Moss-covered Mansion*.

Nancy's eyes sparkled. Then she said to the others, "Dad told me a few minutes ago that he, too, has won his case. So all's well that ends well!"

Nancy Drew® in

The Mystery of the Moss-Covered
Mansion

The Mystery of the Moss-Covered Mansion was
first published in the U.K. in a single volume
in 1973 by William Collins Sons & Co. Ltd,
and in Armada in 1982

© Grosset and Dunlap, Inc. 1971

Contents

*The photographer released the shutter and a stream of
tear gas shot towards them.*

·1·

The Crash

THE Drews' living-room was in semi-darkness as Nancy walked in. Only one lamp was lighted. Under its glow her father sat absorbed in a single sheet of newspaper which lay across his knees.

On the table next to him were a pad and pencil. Figures, letters, and symbols were scrawled on the top sheet.

Nancy stopped beside his chair. "Crossword puzzle?" asked the reddish-blonde-haired girl.

Mr Drew, a tall, good-looking man, glanced up at his attractive, eighteen-year-old daughter and smiled. "No, it's not a crossword puzzle. Actually it's a message in a personal column from this Florida newspaper."

"A personal advertisement?" Nancy repeated. "But why are you making all these hieroglyphics on the pad?"

"Sit down and I'll show you," her father said.

Nancy pulled up the chair from the opposite side of the table. Her father was the leading lawyer in River Heights where they lived and she was sure he was puzzling over some problem in connection with his work.

She asked, "Dad, are you busy on a normal case or one with a mystery?"

Mr Drew laughed. "A case with a mystery. I sent to Florida for newspapers of several weeks back, thinking I might pick up a clue from them."

He handed the paper to Nancy and pointed out an item in the personal column. "What does my detective daughter think?" he asked.

Nancy studied the unusual message. Finally she read the ad aloud:

" *'Son of fruit grower wishes forgiveness. Will return money.'* "

The young sleuth was silent for several seconds, then she frowned. "This could or could not be suspicious. Maybe some father and son had a difference of opinion and he ran away, taking some of his dad's money. He put this ad in the paper, expecting his father to see it and forgive him."

Mr Drew did not reply. He picked up a sheet from another newspaper dated several days later. He pointed to it and said, "Do you think this one makes as much sense as the other?"

The second ad was longer. It said, "*Natural colour oranges best antidote for grower's son's special kind of chronic asthma.*"

"This one sounds more like a code than the first," Nancy remarked.

Her father asked, "Do you see any connection between the two messages?"

"Yes, one. Both items contain the words son and grower." Nancy looked up at her father. "Dad, do you know what it means and are you teasing me to see if I can figure it out?"

Mr Drew chuckled. "Such a thing would have been

a temptation," he said, "but this time I confess I
haven't the faintest idea what these personal ads mean.
The fact that the words son and grower appear in both
makes me suspect that they're code messages."

"And you have a hunch they may relate to your
case?" Nancy inquired. Her father nodded.

Nancy picked up a sheet of paper and began to jot
down letters and numbers. Mr Drew watched her,
always intrigued by the way his daughter tackled a
code. Nancy had made a study of codes and he was sure
she would soon find the answer to this puzzle.

There was silence for a minute, then suddenly Nancy
exclaimed, "Here's a hidden message that makes
sense!"

As she leaned across the table to show it to her father,
they heard a terrific crash directly in front of the house.

"Oh!" said Nancy. "A car accident!"

She was already dashing across the room to the front
door. Mr Drew followed her through the spacious hall
and outside into the autumn night. They could vaguely
see two cars locked together. The Drews raced down
their curving driveway to the street.

Nancy and her father were appalled by what they
saw. One car had smashed through the bonnet of the
other. The lone occupant, a man, was slumped over the
steering wheel, unconscious.

Looking into the other car, Nancy exclaimed, "Bess!
George!"

Bess Marvin and George Fayne were cousins and
Nancy's closest friends. Their parents had gone away
together for a few days and Bess and George had come
to the Drews to stay.

"Girls, how dreadful!" Nancy cried out. "We'll get you into the house right away and call a doctor."

George, who had been driving, was unbuckling her seat belt. The safety belts and shoulder straps the cousins were wearing had saved them from being thrown against the windscreen.

Bess was quivering with fright, but George was angry. "That crazy driver!" she said indignantly. "He suddenly came whizzing across the street and smashed into us! I don't need a doctor! Just a new car!"

Mr Drew said, "I'm sorry about this, girls, but fortunately you seem to be all right. Nevertheless, I insist that you have your family doctor look you over. Nancy, suppose you take Bess and George inside and call Dr Clifford."

By this time the Drews' housekeeper, kindly Hannah Gruen, had come from the house to see what the commotion was.

Recognizing Bess and George, she said worriedly, "My goodness! What happened?"

Mr Drew answered. "George can explain later. Right now, will you notify the police to come at once? I'll go over and see if I can do anything for that man."

Hannah hurried into the house and called headquarters. Then she dialled Dr Clifford's number. The girls had followed her. Bess, a blonde, was naturally pink-cheeked, but now she looked like a ghost. George nervously paced the floor, though she said her legs felt like rubber.

"Please sit down, George," urged Nancy, "and try to relax."

Just then a police car arrived. Nancy ran outside to

join her father. He introduced officers Hampton and Russo.

"This young man," said Mr Drew, "lost control of his car. He seems to be in bad shape."

Officer Hampton leaned over to examine the man. He straightened up and nodded. "You're right, Mr Drew. I believe this guy is under the influence of some drug. Probably he passed out before he hit the other car."

A moment later Dr Clifford drove up. The officers asked him to give his opinion about the victim. After a quick examination, the physician agreed with Hampton's diagnosis and declared the young man should go to the hospital at once.

"We'll take him there," said Russo.

Meanwhile Hampton had been making notes and taking pictures of the two cars. He helped Russo lift the victim into the police car.

"Mr Drew," he called, "will you phone a towing company to haul these cars away at once? They're blocking the street. If you have no luck, let me know."

"I'll be glad to," the lawyer replied.

Russo said they would return as soon as possible from the hospital, and get a statement from Bess and George.

When the others entered the house, the cousins greeted Dr Clifford with hugs. He had brought them both into the world and they were very fond of him.

The doctor chuckled. "You girls don't seem very sick," he said, "but let me examine you." Mr Drew left the room. In a few minutes the physician said, "No broken bones or sprains. Nevertheless, it's bed for you, Bess and George, as soon as the police talk with you.

I'd say go now, but I suppose the law has to come first!"

Shortly after he had left, the two officers returned. Officer Hampton did the questioning while his partner took notes. The session was soon over and the men left.

Bess and George went to bed, but Nancy and her father stayed up to wait for the towing company truck. It was midnight when they turned out the lights and retired.

The evening's excitement had interrupted the discussion of Mr Drew's case and the suspicious personals in the Florida newspaper. But immediately after church the next morning it was resumed.

"Nancy, what was it you were going to tell me last night about the coded message?" he asked.

"I think I've figured out the first one you showed me. The message in it is, 'Son wishes money.' "

"It could be," her father agreed. "What method were you using?"

His daughter smiled. "Words 1, 5, 9, and 13."

The other girls were intensely interested.

Bess had picked up the second personal and tried to make sense out of it. She wrinkled her forehead. "What in the world does 'Natural antidote special asthma' mean?"

"Nothing," Nancy replied, "but how about using only the first letters of those words?"

George exclaimed, "They spell NASA!"

The others looked at Nancy in astonishment, and Bess cried out, "NASA? The National Aeronautics Space Administration?"

"Yes," the young sleuth answered. "I believe it refers to the Kennedy Space Centre in Florida!"

Mr Drew looked grim. "Now I'm convinced the personal ads relate to my case," he said. "Explosives were shipped into the base hidden inside oranges in sacks. I must get down there at once! I was wondering if—"

As her father paused, a thought raced through Nancy's mind. Was he debating if he should take her along?

·2·

Suspicious Message

NANCY watched her father's face carefully as he stared out the window. She knew he was trying to make up his mind about something important. Finally he turned towards his daughter.

"I could use some help in solving the mystery of the explosive oranges."

"And," Nancy said hopefully, "you think I might be able to help?"

The lawyer nodded. "My client, Mr Billington, was arrested for bringing explosive Hamlin oranges into the Space Centre. He is out on bail but his case is coming up soon. He's innocent. Mr Billington owns a grove on Merritt Island, which produces only Pineapple oranges. Someone secretly borrowed a truck of his and delivered several sacks of Hamlin oranges to the Centre. The person presented an official card bearing Mr Billington's name, and signed a slip with his signature. Of course it was a forgery."

Mr Drew went on, "Unfortunately I can't represent him in Florida because I have no licence to practise in that state. My main reason for going down is to engage the services of a Florida lawyer. He and I will work together on the legal angle. I can't stay long this time because I have other urgent matters coming up. But the mysterious culprit must be found before the trial."

Nancy could not refrain from saying, "Dad, if you can't remain on Merritt Island, how about Bess and George and Hannah and I making the trip and staying there?"

"Just what I was thinking," her father replied. "Mr Billington received special permission from the authorities to leave Florida and come north to sign for the purchase of some property. The buyer is going to Europe, so the transaction had to be made at once.

"Mr Billington has offered me the use of his house and car and invited anyone else I would like to bring along. He and Mrs Billington are on their way now but they have a caretaker and his wife who live in the residence. They're Antin and Tina Resardo. She takes care of the house and does the cooking. Antin is foreman of the grove and the sorting and packing house."

Bess and George said they would love to go but would have to obtain permission from their parents. George made the long-distance call. First she told her father about the accident and the wrecked car. "But Bess and I are okay."

"It's too bad about the car, but I'm glad you and Bess weren't hurt," he replied. "George, report the damage immediately to our insurance agent, Mr Dowley."

"All right, Dad." George now told him about the proposed trip.

"That sounds great!" Mr Fayne said. "I'll ask the Marvins." He came back to the phone, saying, "It's okay. Have a good time."

George spoke to her mother and Bess talked to her parents. When she finished, George phoned the insurance man and within fifteen minutes he was at the Drew house. She gave Mr Dowley all the details and he promised to take charge of the matter.

"You go on to Florida and have fun," he said. "When do you leave?"

George went to find Mr Drew and asked him. He smiled. "I'd like to catch a plane this afternoon," he said. "Do you think you could be ready?"

George looked at her watch. "It will take me about twenty minutes to pack some lightweight clothes and my swimsuit."

It was decided that the group would have an early lunch at the Drews' and leave immediately afterwards. While they were eating, the telephone rang. Nancy answered it.

The others heard her exclaim, "Ned! How good to hear from you. Where are you?"

From there on Ned did most of the talking. He was an attractive Emerson College football player who was Nancy's steady boyfriend.

When she came back to the table, her eyes were sparkling. "Great news!" she announced. "You know Ned's parents have had a house on Merritt Island for some time. Mr and Mrs Nickerson are there right now and they're going to have a house party. Bess and George, you're invited, as well as myself, and Ned will bring Burt and Dave along."

Burt Eddleton and Dave Evans were George's and Bess's favourite dates. They, too, went to Emerson College.

"Fabulous!" Bess exclaimed.

"Super!" George added.

Nancy remarked, "We'll have time to work on the mystery before the house party starts."

Mr Drew chuckled. "Well, we'd better leave. I'll load your luggage in the car, while you girls tidy up the kitchen. Hannah, will you see that all the doors and windows are locked and the burglar alarm set?"

The housekeeper hurried off to do this. Then the travellers grabbed their coats and left the house. On the way to the local airport, Mr Drew said they had a choice of flying either to Orlando or Melbourne, Florida. "Melbourne is a little closer to Merritt Island so I've chosen that one. We land at Kennedy Airport there. I phoned the Billington house and asked Tina if she and Antin would meet us. She agreed."

Hours later, when the Drews and their friends reached Melbourne, they looked everywhere for the couple. No one fitting their description was around. Finally only one elderly woman and a naval officer were left in the passenger waiting room.

"I think I'll telephone the house and see what happened," Mr Drew said.

He closed himself into a phone booth and tried for ten minutes to get an answer. At last he came outside.

"No one was there, so maybe the Resardos are on the way. I guess we'll just have to wait."

An hour passed and still Antin and Tina had not arrived. Mr Drew was annoyed. "We'll have to take a taxi," he said. "It'll be an expensive trip. I wonder what happened to the Resardos."

The group enjoyed the drive past the many beautiful

homes and glimmering lakes and inlets, some small, others large. When they reached Cocoa the driver went across the bridge to Merritt Island, then along various winding roads. Finally the taxi pulled up in front of a large Spanish-type house on the Indian River. The ground floor had a patio across the front and on one side. There were several chairs under a small grove of shady trees.

While Mr Drew was paying the taximan, Nancy went to the front door and rapped with the knocker. The visitors stood waiting but no one came to let them in.

George walked to the rear of the dwelling and pressed a buzzer at the back door. No response. She rejoined the others.

"Nobody home," she announced, and dropped into a garden chair. Her companions also seated themselves and waited. About twenty minutes later a car pulled into the driveway and a couple got out.

As they approached the visitors, the man said, "We are the Resardos. Where have you been?"

Mr Drew looked directly at Tina. "Exactly where I asked you to meet us."

The woman rolled her eyes towards her husband but did not speak. He said angrily, "You told my wife we were to meet you at Orlando but you weren't there."

"I told her Melbourne," Mr Drew replied, "but never mind. Just let us into the house, please. How much time do we have to unpack before dinner?"

Antin glared at the newcomers. "My wife has a bad headache and must lie down. You people will have to get your own dinner."

He unlocked the front door, ushered Tina in, and followed her.

"Warm reception," Bess whispered to the other girls.

"I can foresee trouble with that couple," George replied.

Tina went upstairs, but Antin stalked to the back door and went out. He walked off to the right into a large orange grove.

The newcomers climbed the stairs and chose bedrooms. They found that one was closed and locked and assumed this must lead to the Resardos' quarters.

After unpacking, Hannah and the girls located the kitchen and examined the contents of the refrigerator. There was plenty of food for a good meal and Hannah chose a big pot of chicken cooked with rice and gravy. The girls set the table in the flower-papered dining room, which had a large glass-top table and white wicker chairs.

When the meal was ready, Antin walked in. Without saying a word, he took one of the plates warming on the stove and helped himself to a very generous portion of everything. He then filled a second plate with food.

He said to Hannah, "I'm taking this up to my wife. We'll eat in our room."

The others assembled in the dining room and after grace had been said by Mr Drew, they began to eat the delicious dinner. Before they had reached the dessert course, Antin came down the stairs carrying the empty plates, which he put into the sink.

The others heard him open a cabinet door and knew he was getting plates for the dessert, which was an apple pie. The visitors were aghast to see Antin going through

340 THE MOSS-COVERED MANSION

the hall with at least half the pie on two plates!

After he had gone upstairs, George burst out, "What's eating him?"

Bess giggled. "Nothing. He's eating everything."

Nancy jumped up and went out to look at the pie. The portion that was left, if cut into five slices, would give each person a piece one-inch wide!

"That man is the limit," she complained to Hannah, who had followed her.

"He certainly is," the housekeeper agreed, "and I suppose he expects me to wash his dirty dishes."

A little later Antin returned and left two empty plates. Nancy stopped him. Eager to start work on the mystery at once, she asked him what he knew about Mr Billington's case.

The caretaker scowled. "Nothing that you don't know," he replied and went outdoors.

From the window Nancy saw him go into the orange grove. Dusk had fallen and she could not see which direction he had taken.

After the dishes had been put into the washer and the dining room vacuumed for crumbs, George said that she and Bess had promised to let their parents know of the girls' safe arrival.

"I'll do it," Bess offered and went to the rear of the hall. As she picked up the phone, the unfamiliar voice of a man was saying. "You know what to do next. Keep your eye on all visitors."

Bess hung up and came back to the living room to report the conversation. "Are the Billingtons on a party line?" she asked.

"No," Mr Drew answered. He frowned. "I don't like

this. There must be an extension phone and somebody in this place is talking on it."

"I'll check!" Nancy offered.

She knew there was no other phone on the ground floor, so she started to climb up to the top. Halfway up the stairs, she heard a door close softly. She ran the rest of the way and walked along the hall. There was an extension in Mr Billington's bedroom but nobody was there. The Resardos' door was closed.

"Perhaps Tina was using the phone up here," Nancy thought.

What had the message meant? she wondered. And were she and her father and her friends the "visitors" that the man had referred to? Nancy went downstairs and told the others her suspicions.

"There's probably another extension outside somewhere," Nancy said. "Perhaps in the orange packing house! Let's see if anyone's there!"

·3·

Spooky Grounds

WHEN Nancy rushed from the rear entrance of the Billington home, she headed for the orange grove. A distance beyond she could see a wavering light and assumed that someone with a flashlight was walking among the trees.

"I wonder who the person is?" she asked herself. "Antin?"

When George and Mr Drew caught up to Nancy, they said Bess had remained with Hannah. Nancy mentioned the light. They had not noticed it and now the beam had vanished.

The three had left in such a hurry they had neglected to bring flashlights. As they progressed deeper into the grove, the searchers could see practically nothing under the trees.

"We'll never be able to find the orange packing house," George remarked.

They went on for several seconds, then Nancy stopped. "I guess you're right. We'll come back in the morning and find out if there is an extension in the packing house. I'm inclined to believe it was Antin calling from there. What do you two think?"

Mr Drew agreed, but George said, "It might have

been Tina. Don't forget, Nancy, that you heard a door close softly."

Nancy made no reply. She had turned to go back to the house but suddenly realized she did not know which direction to take. She consulted her companions.

Mr Drew laughed. "I should think a detective like you could find her way in the dark," he teased.

"Just for that," said his daughter, "I'll lead you right back to the Billingtons'."

She began to feel the tree trunks, saying to herself, "We came north and that would be the roughest side of the tree." Presently she found the south side and then said, "Follow me!"

The trees, though planted in straight rows, were not in lines parallel to the compass. Nancy felt the bark of each tree she came to and kept veering slightly eastward. In a little while the lights of the Billington house came into view.

"You did it!" George praised her friend.

Nancy laughed. "I played leader this time but either of you could have found the way."

When the three came into the kitchen they were greeted by Hannah and Bess. "Mission accomplished?" Mrs Gruen asked.

"I'm afraid not," Nancy replied. Then she whispered, "Has Antin come in?"

Bess replied, "Yes. He rushed past the two of us without saying a word and went upstairs. He sure is a weirdo."

In low voices the group discussed the Resardos. While they had no proof the couple was dishonest, each of them had a feeling of mistrust. Hannah suggested that

as a safety precaution the visitors lock their bedroom
doors. Everyone looked at Mr Drew. Would he agree
to lock his?

To their surprise he did. He said no more, but the
others were sure Nancy's father was taking no chances
with the caretaker and his wife in the house. The night
passed peacefully, however.

When the Drews and their friends assembled for
breakfast, Antin and Tina had not yet come downstairs.
Just as the group finished eating, the couple appeared.
They said good morning but carried on no conversation.
They helped themselves to the food Hannah had left on
the stove and ate in the kitchen.

Presently Antin went out the rear door. Tina
announced she was going shopping and did not offer to
help with the housework. She hurried away.

Hannah Gruen was exasperated. "How long does
that woman expect me to wash her dirty dishes and
prepare meals?"

"I'll speak to them later," Mr Drew promised. "I'm
leaving now in Mr Billington's car to see Mr Datsun,
the lawyer I engaged to help me on the case."

Tina had already left in the Resardos' car. Was she
going grocery shopping or on some errands of her own?

"I don't know whether to buy any supplies or not,"
said Hannah. "What do you think, girls?"

Bess, who was hungry most of the time, answered,
"I vote we buy some food and not depend on that awful
creature."

"But how are we going to get it?" George spoke up.
"We have no car."

Mrs Gruen sighed. "I guess we can make out until

your father returns and you can borrow the car."

As soon as the necessary housework was finished, the girls set off through the orange grove to find the packing house. It was a good distance ahead. On the way Nancy and her friends saw many men picking oranges and putting them into baskets. A small truck would pick them up.

The packing house at the far end of the grove was a long, rectangular building. It contained machinery for sorting oranges by size, cartons for mailing fruit, and net sacks for local delivery. Men and women were busy picking out defective fruit.

There was a glass-partitioned office in one corner. On the desk stood a telephone!

Nancy walked up to one of the men and inquired if Antin was around. She learned he had not been there all morning.

"I can't say when he'll be back," the workman continued. "He stays away from here a good deal nowadays. But that's all right. We get along without him."

The girls looked questioningly at one another but made no comment. Nancy asked the man, "Is the telephone here on a separate line or is it an extension of the one at the house?"

"It's an intercom system with four extensions on this one number. Two of them are in the house. A third is at the side of this building. Would you like to make a call?" he asked.

"Yes, I would," Nancy replied, glad of the chance to let her eyes roam around the office desk for a clue to the mysterious phone conversation.

She was disappointed not to find any, but Hannah Gruen had a message for her.

"Mrs Nickerson called. She said something of interest has come up and she wants you to stop over as soon as possible."

"She didn't say what it was?" Nancy queried.

"No," Hannah replied.

Nancy said the girls would visit Mrs Nickerson when they could use Mr Billington's car. "We'll see you in a little while, Hannah."

She and her friends watched the sorting and packing operation. Nancy spoke to several of the workers. Not one of them could give any information about the identity of the man who had delivered the oranges with the explosives in them. All the men declared they knew nothing about it except what had been in the newspapers. One thing they were sure of—Mr Billington was innocent. They hoped he would soon be exonerated.

The girls heard a truck arriving and went outside to watch it being unloaded. Baskets of oranges were lifted on to a belt which carried them to a chute where the fruit was dumped into the washing and sorting machine.

Nancy stood near the truck, gazing at the man who was lifting out the baskets. Suddenly one slipped from his hands and came tumbling directly towards Nancy's head!

"Look out!" cried Bess behind her.

Fortunately Nancy had seen the basket and leaped out of the way. The fruit smashed to the ground. Her first thought was that the man had dropped it on purpose, then she rationalized what possible purpose could he have in harming her? He did not apologize.

Nancy asked a workman for the other man's name.

"It's Jackson," he replied. "We call him Old Clumsy Fingers." Nancy smiled and said that explained why she had almost been hit with a basket of oranges.

Nancy, Bess, and George walked back through the grove, disappointed that they had learned nothing to advance their sleuthing.

As they approached the house, Nancy told the girls about Mrs Nickerson's call. "But we can't go there without a car. It's too far. I hope Dad will be back soon."

When he had not returned by late morning, Nancy became restless. She was on the verge of telephoning Mrs Nickerson, when George, who had been exploring the grounds, dashed into the house.

"Guess what I saw!" she explained. "The Billingtons' boat. It's great! Why don't we go to the Nickersons in that?"

"Great idea!" Bess spoke up. "Let's see if it will run."

Nancy told Hannah where the girls were going, then the three hurried through the Billingtons' lovely garden to the waterfront. Only a few motor-boats were purring along the shores of the Indian River.

The end of the garden was several feet above the water level and had a bulkhead to keep the soil from washing away. A boathouse extended into the river. Inside it was a sleek speedboat, the *Starbeam*. The key was in the ignition.

"What a beauty!" Bess cried out. "But it looks powerful. Nancy, would you dare take it out?"

The young detective smiled. "Of course."

She made sure there was sufficient fuel and familiarized herself with the various gadgets. Her eyes twinkling, she said, "Here goes!"

In a few seconds the motor was throbbing quietly and she steered the craft into the river. Twenty minutes later she pulled alongside a dock which bore the name Nickerson. The girls tied the boat securely and went up to the house.

Ned's mother was a very attractive woman. When greeting Nancy she showed the deep affection she held for the girl.

"What I wanted to tell you," Mrs Nickerson said as they all sipped glasses of cola, "is that friends of ours who have gone North to live have put their house on the market. It's listed with Mr Gilbert Scarlett, a local estate agent. I was thinking how wonderful it would be, Nancy, if your father would buy the place."

"I'd love to see it," Nancy replied. "Is it far from here?"

"No, we can walk there easily."

Mrs Nickerson led the girls to a charming place about a quarter of a mile away. The house stood halfway between the river and the road. It was a two-storey building with attractive, well-kept grounds.

"How lovely!" Nancy exclaimed.

"The owner, Mr Webster," said Mrs Nickerson, "has all kinds of unusual trees and shrubs on the place besides an orange grove. He even has a sausage tree. It is rarely seen in this country."

The visitors were intrigued by the wide variety of trees and shrubs. Each had a plaque attached that gave its Latin botanical name and the English equivalent. Finally they came to the sausage tree.

It was about thirty feet tall with a profusion of leaves. From the branches hung greenish sausage-shaped fruit that resembled rough-textured melons. These were nearly six inches wide and twelve inches long.

George felt one. "Wow! This would make a really swinging weapon!" The others laughed.

Mrs Nickerson said the fruit was not edible and the pollen was carried in the spring from one flower to another by bats.

"Ugh!" Bess exclaimed.

The tree was near a high wire-mesh fence which looked strong enough to stop a large, fast-moving truck.

Bess remarked, "That place next door sure is spooky with all those old oak trees dripping with Spanish moss. Who lives there?"

"I don't know," Mrs Nickerson replied.

At that moment a chilling scream came from inside the grounds!

· 4 ·

Newspaper Clue

THE piercing scream was not repeated. Nancy and her friends peered through the wire-mesh fence for a glimpse of a house. The jungle of trees with their long streamers of Spanish moss concealed whatever buildings might be on the property.

Nancy turned to Mrs Nickerson. "Have you ever been in there?"

"No," Ned's mother replied. "The place is so forbidding I never tried to get acquainted with the occupants. Besides, I suspect whoever lives there owns some wild animals!"

George said she was curious to find out what she could. "If this fence doesn't go round the whole property, let's look for an opening and go in."

Bess objected at once. "Not me!"

Nancy settled the matter. "Actually we don't have time," she said. "Dad will be home, I'm sure, and I want to see if he has any news for us. But we'll come here the first chance we have."

Mrs Nickerson teased, "Now I understand how you girls become involved in mysteries."

Nancy smiled. "Sometimes we do stumble upon them."

The group walked back to the Nickerson home, said goodbye, and hurried to their boat. When they reached the Billington house, Mr Drew was there. He was smiling and Nancy was sure he had had a successful morning.

"I like Mr Datsun very much. It didn't take long to talk over the case," the lawyer said.

Mr Drew delved into a breast pocket of his sports jacket and pulled out an envelope. "Surprise for you girls," he announced.

He handed the envelope to Nancy. She opened it and took out six badges on which the word PRESS was printed.

Mr Drew explained, "As an accredited writer I was given badges at the news centre for you and the boys to watch the moon shoot next week."

Bess and George stared at Mr Drew. "You are an accredited writer?" Bess asked.

He chuckled and nodded. "I have a number of publications to my credit. Of course they're all on legal matters."

"How exciting!" said George. "Now we can see the lift-off and be as close as anyone is allowed."

"Right." Mr Drew asked Hannah and the girls if they would like to make a tour of the Kennedy Space Centre that afternoon. All were enthusiastic and Nancy said, "It will give me a chance to get acquainted with the place where the explosive oranges were taken. I might pick up a clue."

As soon as luncheon was over they set off for the vast, well-kept government grounds that stretched along the ocean for miles. Mr Drew parked the car near a sprawling building with a large, roofed-over patio area.

Under it were benches. Nancy and the others sat down to wait for a bus while her father bought tickets.

"This is the Visitor Information Centre," Mr Drew remarked when he came back.

Nancy was impressed by the large number of European and Asiatic tourists who were there.

"The Kennedy Space Centre means a lot to the whole world," she thought, then walked up to the adjoining building to peer inside. There was a room with illuminated wall pictures of the various types of missiles. Here visitors could purchase books, postcards and souvenirs. Nancy saw an intriguing miniature model rocket. "I must come back and buy that," she decided.

"All aboard!" called George, and Nancy hurried to join the others.

The two-hour tour began, and the driver announced that they would cover fifty miles. Nancy and her friends were fascinated by the mock-ups of missiles and rockets stretching ahead of them in long rows. Most of them were in the familiar cone shape.

The guide said that the very first missile sent up from the Cape was a two-stage Bumper.

"The first stage was a captured German V-2 missile and the second an army WAC Corporal rocket. It was launched in July 1950."

Mr Drew whispered to his daughter, "Our country has certainly come a long way in rocket building since then."

As the guide indicated gantries and rockets, Nancy recognized the names Thor, an early anti-ballistic missile, Titan, Minuteman and Saturn.

Next, the guide talked about the artificial satellites orbiting in space. He explained that the man-made moons are classified according to the jobs they do: (1) communication satellites, (2) weather satellites, (3) navigation satellites, (4) scientific satellites, and (5) military satellites.

"You, no doubt, are familiar with the Tiros and other satellites that take weather pictures and track hurricanes. Communication satellites, like Early Bird and Telstar, make it possible to send radio messages, telephone calls, and television programmes from one continent to another in a matter of seconds."

The tour continued on to the moon rocket, which stood majestically next to its gantry. The onlookers craned their necks to see the top where the astronauts would live and work.

"It's all so overwhelming!" Hannah Gruen exclaimed.

The next stop on the tour was at the mammoth Vehicle Assembly Building. George remarked, "This is a real skyscraper."

"And it covers eight acres," the driver said. "The ceilings in the wings of this building are twenty storeys high. That's where the smaller rockets are put together. The centre section is fifty-two storeys high. The big Saturns for trips to the moon and other planets are assembled in this area. Each booster for them is brought here on a very long covered barge which resembles an aluminium Quonset hut, painted white. The capsules come by truck or air."

When the sightseers walked inside to the Vehicle Assembly section they gasped. The centre section was

tall enough to accommodate a 360-foot rocket standing
upright. Around the walls of the huge structure were
metal scaffolds on which men had worked to complete
the latest rocket assembly. From the ground floor those
who were busy high above the visitors looked no larger
than small boys.

"This is absolutely fascinating and unbelievable,"
Nancy said.

Suddenly she realized that Hannah Gruen was not
with them. She looked at all the visitors but did not see
the Drews' housekeeper.

"Maybe she stayed in the bus," Nancy thought, and
went outside to look. Hannah was not there.

"Where could she have gone?" Nancy asked herself,
then told her father and the girls.

All of them searched but could not find Hannah. The
guide was already calling to his passengers to board
the bus.

"I don't want to leave without Hannah," Nancy said
to her father. "This building is so huge if she started to
walk around it, she couldn't possibly be back by this
time."

Mr Drew said he had an appointment with Commander Nichol at the Base in connection with the case.
"Suppose I go ahead," he suggested, "and you girls
keep on searching for Hannah. You can catch the
next bus."

He spoke to the driver, who agreed that this would
be all right.

Nancy, Bess, and George went back inside the big
building and began looking again for Hannah. Moments
later the door to an office opened. Hannah Gruen

walked out, followed by a young man. They came directly to the three girls.

"This is Herb Baylor," Hannah said. "He's a distant relative of mine but I didn't know he was here. I happened to see him walk into an office and followed."

After the pleasant young man had acknowledged the introductions, Hannah went on, "Herb's an engineer and works on the assembling of rockets."

Nancy asked him, "Of course you know about the oranges containing the explosives that were sent into the Base."

"Yes, and I hear you're on Merritt Island to solve the mystery and clear Mr Billington." He smiled boyishly. "I'll tell you a possible clue that I gave to Security."

"Wonderful!" Nancy replied. "What is it?"

Herb said he happened to be near the truck when it was leaving. "Part of a newspaper blew out. I picked it up and noticed a pencil-ringed personal ad. It was a garble of words that made no sense."

"What did it say?"

Herb replied, " '*Son on board ship ready to be sailor for peaceful kind of action.*' "

Nancy took a pad and pencil from her handbag and asked Herb to repeat the message. Quickly she read words numbered 1, 5, 9, and 13. The hidden message was, "Son ready for action."

She thanked Herb, telling him that the girls would work on it.

"I wish you luck," he said, smiling. "Now I must go back."

When the next bus came Nancy and her friends climbed aboard. The tour continued, and Nancy listened attentively to the driver's descriptions.

"On a long flight, like to the moon," the guide said, "an astronaut gets about twenty-eight hundred calories of food a day. Seventeen percent of this is protein, thirty-two percent fat, and fifty-one percent carbohydrates."

Bess gave a low giggle. "That's the place for me!"

The guide went on to say that the men eat four meals a day and a series of menus are rotated every four days. "All the food is in bars, cubes, and powders sealed in plastic pouches, or pastes which are kept in tubes."

Bess called out to the guide, "Could you tell us what some of the menus are?"

The man smiled. "Yes. How would you like this for breakfast? Strawberry cereal cubes, bacon squares, peanut-butter sandwiches, and orange juice."

"That's great," said Bess.

"Here's a typical dinner menu," the guide told her. "Beef with vegetables, spaghetti with meat sauce, toast squares, fruit cake made with dates, and tea."

"That would suit me," Bess commented. "It sounds yummy."

When the bus returned to the Visitor Information Centre, Mr Drew was waiting for them and they walked to the parking area.

As soon as they were seated in their car, George said, "Nancy, don't keep us in suspense any longer. What did you figure out of that newspaper clue?"

Nancy told her and the conversation turned to a series of guesses as to what it meant. They could only surmise that someone, somewhere, was ready to strike a blow. But who and at what?

When the group reached the house the Resardos were not there. Hannah remarked, "I suppose they won't show up until dinner is ready."

The girls offered to help her prepare dinner. When Nancy went into the dining room to set the table she noticed that a photograph of her father which he had sent Mr Billington was gone from the buffet. She asked the others if any of them had placed it elsewhere. No one had.

"How strange!" said Hannah. She hurried into the living room and called out, "A picture of Mr and Mrs Billington is gone too."

On a hunch Nancy rushed upstairs to her father's room. A photograph of her with Bess and George, which he always took with him when he travelled, had been removed from the bureau. Next the young detective went to her own room and pulled out one of the drawers. She had left a wallet in it containing a snapshot of her father and one of Ned Nickerson. They were missing. But none of the other contents had been taken.

Nancy dashed down the stairs. "Every photograph has been taken!" she exclaimed. "I'm sure they were stolen to use as identification of us because we're trying to solve the mystery of the explosive oranges!"

· 5 ·

Alligator Attack

WHEN Bess heard about the missing photograph of
Mr Drew, she ran from the living room and up the
stairs. Deep in her suitcase she had left a snapshot of
herself with Nancy, George, Ned, Burt, and Dave. Bess
riffled through the clothes still in the bag but could not
find the picture.

"That was stolen too!" she told herself and hurried
back downstairs to tell the others.

George said angrily, "Nobody has been in this house.
We locked all the doors and windows before we left and
they were still locked when we came home. I'm sure the
Resardos took those pictures!"

Everyone agreed but Mr Drew warned them that
they had no evidence to prove this.

"Why don't we search their room?" George asked.

Before anybody could stop her, she bounded up the
stairway to the couple's quarters. But the Resardos'
door was locked and continuous knocking on it brought
no response. Dejected, George returned downstairs.

"Now what do we do?" she asked Nancy.

"Suppose I phone the orange sorting and packing
house. Antin may be there."

The worker who answered said that Antin had not

358

been in all day. "He didn't tell us he wasn't coming, so we have no idea where he is."

Nancy thanked him and hung up. The Resardos returned just as the group was about to eat dinner.

"Where have you been all day?" George burst out.

Tina and Antin scowled but replied they had received word a relative in a distant city was ill and had gone to visit him. The couple turned towards the stove and picked up two dinner plates which were warmiug. As they helped themselves from each of the pots, Mr Drew approached them.

"One minute," he said. "What can you tell us abont all the photographs missing from the house?"

The Resardos looked at each other, then Antin said, "What are you talking about?"

When Mr Drew explained, Antin declared he knew nothing about the pictures.

Tina spoke up. "I don't either. Are you accusing us of taking them?" She began to laugh raucously. "What would we want with photographs of you people?"

Mr Drew turned on his heel and walked into the dining room. The Resardos filled two plates, got out some silver, and sat down at the kitchen table to eat.

The others were surprised that they had not gone upstairs. Nancy, however, figured the couple wanted to hear the conversation in the dining room. In a whisper she warned the rest not to discuss the Billington case. If the Resardos had hoped to pick up any information, they were disappointed. The talk was general, mostly about the fascinating trip through the Space Centre.

When everyone finished eating, the Resardos piled

their dirty dishes in the sink as usual, and went up to their room.

"I won't wash them!" Hannah Gruen said firmly.

Nancy smiled. "Tonight you're not washing anybody's dishes. You go into the living room and watch TV. Bess and George and I will take care of everything."

While the girls were doing this, Mr Drew telephoned the police to report the theft of the photographs. Two officers came to the house. They agreed that it appeared to be an inside job and asked to talk with the Resardos. The couple vehemently declared their innocence. As the police were leaving, they told Mr Drew that without any clues there was little hope of apprehending the thief.

Tina and Antin cast black looks at the others, then went upstairs without saying goodnight.

In the morning, when Nancy and her friends came downstairs, she found that the Resardos had already eaten breakfast and left the house. Their dirty dishes were piled up in the sink!

Hannah Gruen stared at the dried egg on the plates and the stained coffee cups in disgust. But she said nothing and started getting breakfast for the others.

When Mr Drew came down, Nancy said, "Dad, I haven't had a chance to tell you about a darling house that's for sale." She described the Webster property.

He smiled at her enthusiasm. "I'll look at it," he said. "I can see you've fallen in love with the place."

While they were eating, a telephone call came for Mr Drew. After a few minutes' conversation, he returned to the table and said he must leave for River Heights. "Something important has come up and I'll

have to return home at once. Will you girls drive me to
the airport?"

"Of course," Nancy replied. "Do you want me to call
and see about planes?"

"If you will, please."

Nancy found out that if they left the house within ten
minutes, her father could catch a non-stop flight to
New York from Melbourne and get another plane to
River Heights soon afterwards. She hurried upstairs to
tell her father and help him pack.

When Mr Drew and the girls were ready to leave, he
said to Hannah, "Take care. Better lock yourself in."
The housekeeper nodded.

Two hours later the girls were ready to return from
the Melbourne airport. Bess spoke up, "Let's take a
scenic route home."

"All right," Nancy agreed. She consulted a road map
and figured out what direction to take.

As they neared the area of the Cape, Bess spotted a
long, wide ditch of water choked with water hyacinths,
with bluish-violet lily-type blossoms.

"Oh I want to get some of those!" she said. "Please
stop."

"They are pretty," Nancy agreed and pulled up to
the side of the road.

Bess jumped from the car and went over to pick some
of the blooms. After plucking several, she laid them at
the edge of the water.

"Don't lean over so far or you'll fall in," George
warned her cousin.

Bess rested on her heels and reached for another
beautiful flower. Just as her hand touched it, something

rustled among the leaves. The next moment an alligator thrust its snout from among the leaves and opened its jaws wide!

Bess screamed, jerked back, and sat down hard on the muddy bank. The alligator moved towards her! Terrified, Bess scrambled up and ran to the car. The alligator disappeared under the water hyacinths. Nancy and George had hopped from the car to help her in. Bess was trembling and now began to sob.

"He—he was going to bite me!" the frightened girl exclaimed.

Nancy and George tried to calm her. In a few minutes Bess was all right but her white slacks were wet and muddy.

To take her mind off the unpleasant incident, Nancy said, "As soon as you change your clothes, Bess, let's go to see the estate agent who is handling the sale of the Webster house. I want to look at the inside. After that we'll work on the explosive orange mystery."

"Good idea," said George. "Who is the agent?"

"Mr Scarlett."

When they reached the Billingtons', it did not take Bess long to change into dark-blue slacks and a clean shirt. After a quick lunch the girls set off again. They drove directly to Mr Scarlett's office. Nancy parked and they walked up to the one-storey building, then stopped short. A sign tacked to the door read:

CLOSED FOR VACATION
WILL OPEN IN TWO WEEKS

"We can't stay that long!" said Bess.

"I know," Nancy agreed. "Wait here, girls."

She went to a nearby shop and asked where Mr
Scarlett lived. She hoped the agent was not out of town.

"He didn't tell me his plans," said the shopkeeper,
and gave her the address of Mr and Mrs Scarlett.

When the girls rang his doorbell, there was no
answer. Windows were closed and blinds were down.

"Maybe they're only away for the day," George said
optimistically.

Nancy was determined to see the inside of the
Webster house and told herself, "I'll find a way!"

George remarked, "Normally an estate agent
wouldn't go away without making provisions for
prospective buyers to see properties he has listed."

On the way back to the Billington house, Bess gave
a tremendous sigh. "Can't we relax and play some
tennis?" she asked. "Then we'll go sleuthing."

"Great idea!" said George. "I'll take on both of you."

Bess giggled. "How we hate ourselves," she teased.
"Just for that, I accept. Nancy and I will whitewash
you! Three love sets in a row!"

Bess came near being right. She and Nancy won the
first two games. By the time the girls had finished three
sets, the scores stood two sets for Nancy and Bess and
one for George.

"I'll get even another time!" George vowed with a
wide grin.

As they walked from the court, the cousins asked
Nancy what was next on the schedule.

"You're so good at keeping your mind on two things
at once," said Bess, "that half your brain was playing
tennis and the other half conjuring up something."

Nancy laughed. "I was just thinking that if I call

Dad's friend Commander Nichol at the Base he'll give me the name of the guard who admitted the driver with the explosive oranges."

"And after that—" George prodded her.

"After that," Nancy replied, "we'll try to talk to that man."

Commander Nichol said that the guard's name was Patrick Croft.

"He has been dismissed," the commander went on, "but hasn't left town. He's at home," and gave Nancy the address.

After she had said goodbye, Nancy turned to the girls. "Let's go! Maybe by talking to Mr Croft we can get a clue to the man who impersonated Mr Billington and drove into the Base."

·6·

Exciting Evening

PATRICK Croft lived alone in a small house. When Nancy explained why the girls had come, he invited them inside. Before he sat down the sad-looking man offered them some toffee he had made. They learned he was a bachelor and liked to cook. Nancy surmised that Mr Croft was reserved and not apt to defend himself when any trouble arose.

"That's too bad," the young detective told herself. "Maybe if Croft had been more aggressive, he wouldn't have been dismissed from NASA."

When Nancy queried him about the driver of the truck with the explosive oranges, Croft described him minutely.

At once Nancy thought, "It is true then that this man could have passed as Mr Billington!"

Croft went on, "The driver said he was Mr Billington, whom I don't know. He had all the proper credentials with him, so of course I let him in. The last I saw of him he was turning towards the food supply depot and I assumed that was where he went."

"And he didn't?" George asked.

Mr Croft smiled. "A guard got aboard and took him there. Fortunately the explosive oranges were discovered before any damage was done. But it's my opinion he intended to blow up part of the rocket while it was still in the Vehicle Assembly Building.

"I'm mighty sorry about the whole thing, but I don't think I should have been dismissed. The explosives had been put in the oranges very cleverly and they looked innocent enough in the sacks.

"I hope someday I'll be reinstated." Mr Croft heaved a great sigh. "By the way, I was taken to identify Mr Billington. He and the impostor look enough alike to be twins."

The girls felt sorry for Croft. They realized his dismissal had been necessary. After the saboteur was caught, perhaps Croft would be exonerated.

Nancy told him that her father was the lawyer who had been retained to defend Mr Billington, but that he in turn had engaged the services of Johnson Datsun.

Croft said he had heard of Mr Datsun. "He's a very fine lawyer. If anybody can straighten out this case, I'm sure he can."

"But it's not just a legal matter," Bess spoke up. "It's a mystery too. Nancy's an amateur detective and—"

Nancy smiled. "And with the help of my two good friends here, I have solved some mysteries."

Mr Croft's eyes opened wide. "That's wonderful," he said. "I always wanted to be a detective, but I wasn't cut out for that kind of work. The nearest I came to it was checking people's credentials when they entered the Space Centre." He sighed again.

Nancy stood up. Bess and George took the cue from her and did the same.

"Mr Croft," said Nancy, "if you should hear or recall anything that might help us solve this mystery, will you telephone me?"

"I'll be glad to," the man replied. Nancy gave him the Billingtons' address and telephone number, then the girls left.

Upon reaching home, they found Hannah Gruen quite excited. George asked, "Have the Resardos pulled another fast one?"

"No," the housekeeper replied. "I haven't seen them all day. But I think I've picked up a clue for you. If I'm right, it may spell trouble or danger for you, Nancy, and your father."

"What do you mean?" Nancy queried.

Hannah produced the day's newspaper. She pointed out a personal ad. It read:

"Dorothy's son has just released trunk. It is empty. Advise at once where to find contents."

Immediately the three girls read words numbered 1, 5, 9, 13. These said, "Dorothy's released empty where."

Bess said, "They don't make sense."

Hannah was eager to tell her clue. "But put the first letters of those words together," she said. "They spell Drew."

"Wow!" George exclaimed. "What could this possibly mean?"

Nancy did not answer. She had not yet figured out the meaning of the personal but one thing was certain—someone was sending a message which could have dire consequences for her and her father and possibly her friends. She was worried but did not speak her thoughts aloud.

Bess admitted that she was scared. "I think we'd better give up our sleuthing and leave here," she declared.

George said, "Bess, you know as well as I do that the thrust of a Saturn rocket couldn't force Nancy to give up this case."

Nancy smiled. "A wild thought just occurred to me. Suppose this reference to Drew has something to do with our interest in the Webster house. We already know that Mr Scarlett has gone on vacation. For some reason unknown to us, the people who use the code may not want us here and encouraged Scarlett to go away. What we must do is find out that reason."

Hannah Gruen reminded the girls that their dinner was ready. "The meal will be spoiled if you don't eat it now."

Nancy, Bess, and George washed their hands and combed their hair, then sat down at the table with Hannah. All had good appetites and thoroughly enjoyed the delicious roast beef. They were tidying up the kitchen when Bess remarked, "The Resardos missed a good dinner, but we certainly didn't miss them."

"Maybe they're not coming back at all!" George said with a grin. "It would please me if I never saw that couple again."

"I agree with you," said Mrs Gruen.

That evening the phone was kept busy. First Nancy called her father and told him all she had learned that day.

After hearing the whole story, he observed, "It's

evident that someone or a group is keeping an eye on us. The situation could become dangerous."

"But you're not going to let them scare us away, are you?" Nancy asked.

She was sure her father was going to say no and he did not disappoint her. He warned Nancy, however, to keep alert for trouble.

"I'll get back there as quickly as I can," he added.

Nancy had just put down the phone when it rang. The voice at the other end said, "Well, I'm glad I got you at last. I've been trying for hours to get hold of you."

"Hi, Ned!" Nancy said. "We can hardly wait for the house party to start, but we haven't been idle. There'll be lots to tell when you boys arrive."

"No doubt," Ned said. "I've never known a time when you weren't doing as much as three people. I have just one favour to ask—that you have this mystery solved before Burt and Dave and I arrive. We want to have fun."

"Why, Ned," said Nancy, a teasing tone in her voice, "I thought you adored solving mysteries and tracking down villains."

Ned laughed. "You're right. Okay, Nancy," he added, "I'll help bring this mystery to a quick termination!"

"Actually there are two mysteries," said Nancy. "The explosive oranges and the spooky-looking grounds of an estate on this island. When I get a chance I'm going to investigate the place."

"I'll take the spooky one," Ned answered.

Nancy laughed. "I hope to have at least one of them solved before you arrive."

Ned chuckled, then became serious. "Watch your step. I don't want anything to happen to you."

After he and Nancy had said good night, she joined the other girls. Within seconds there was another call.

"Maybe it's Burt," George spoke up.

"And maybe you're both wrong," Hannah remarked. "The call might be for me—from Herb. He said he'd phone and make a date to call on us. I think he was very much impressed with you three girls."

As Hannah had predicted, the caller was Herb, who told her he had been put on special assignment. "I won't be able to come over to the Billington house until after the lift-off."

"By that time we'll probably be gone," Hannah said, "but give us a ring anyway."

The girls were giggling when Hannah returned. Bess teased her. "Did Herb want to make a date to take you up in a rocket?"

The housekeeper flushed slightly but joined in the banter. "Don't think I didn't catch on. He wanted to see you girls!"

Just then the phone rang again. Burt and Dave were calling. Both boys were eagerly looking forward to the house party at the Nickersons' and sent their best wishes to Hannah and Nancy.

By bedtime the Resardos still had not returned and everyone wondered if the couple would put in an appearance.

As the group was about to go upstairs the telephone rang again. Nancy, nearest the instrument, answered.

"Is this Nancy Drew?" a man asked.

"Yes."

"This is Patrick Croft. I've been trying to call you but your line has been busy. A man phoned me around eight o'clock. He sounded like the driver I let into the Base with the oranges. He told me I was to have nothing more to do with Nancy Drew or I'd be harmed."

"That's dreadful!" Nancy said.

The words were barely out of her mouth when Patrick Croft gave a cry of panic. "Someone's breaking in!" he shouted. "Help! Help!"

·7·

False Information

THE phone connection remained on but there were no
voices. Evidently Patrick Croft had run away from the
instrument without hanging it up. Nancy could hear
banging and shouting, then a crash, as if the intruder
had broken open the door.

Nancy hung up, waited a few minutes for the connection to be broken, then called police headquarters. She
told the sergeant on duty what had happened at
Croft's house. He assured her that two officers would be
sent there immediately.

Nancy rushed upstairs to tell Hannah and the girls of
Croft's predicament. "I'm going over to see what
happened!"

"Not by yourself," Hannah spoke up firmly. "We'll
all go. This is shocking. Poor Mr Croft!"

With Nancy at the wheel, they covered the distance
to his house in a short time. A police car and an
ambulance stood in front and sympathetic neighbours
had begun to gather.

"Oh, he's been hurt!" Bess exclaimed.

Nancy pulled up to the kerb and jumped out.

Patrick Croft was just being brought out on a
stretcher. He was unconscious and his face the colour of
pale alabaster.

372

Two policemen followed. After the ambulance pulled away, Nancy spoke to the taller officer, telling him she was the person who had phoned headquarters.

"I'd like to explain to you in more detail what I know about the attack tonight."

"Come with me, miss," said the officer, and added, "My name is Regan."

He led the way back into the house, then took a notebook and pencil from a pocket. "Tell me everything you can," he said. "Sometimes a small detail that the average person considers unimportant can prove to be a valuable clue."

Nancy knew this very well from her own sleuthing experiences. She introduced herself and told where she was from, then said, "Mr Croft was a security guard at NASA. He's the one responsible for allowing the truck with explosive oranges to come on to the Base."

"Oh you know about that," the officer replied.

Nancy nodded, then related Patrick Croft's telephone conversation verbatim.

"So Croft thought the caller might have been the truck driver," Officer Regan observed. "If he wasn't Mr Billington, have you any idea who he is? And why did the person who phoned not want Croft to contact you?"

"I don't know the man's name," Nancy answered. "That's what I'm in Florida to find out. My father and a local lawyer are trying to solve this case and prove Mr Billington innocent."

"I see," the policeman said. "Poor Croft was beaten into unconsciousness so it will be some time before he'll be able to answer any of our questions."

Regan told her that there was only one set of clear footprints but this was not a help in identification because the intruder had worn flippers.

"Also, the man must have had on gloves," the officer said, "because he left no fingerprints."

The word "flippers" caught Nancy's attention and she remarked, "The man you'll be looking for could be a scuba diver."

"You're right," Regan admitted. Then he asked, "By the way, have you and your friends visited the Real Eight Museum of Sunken Treasure yet?"

"No, we haven't."

"Do by all means. It's most interesting, even though a little terrifying if you visualize what happened during one of the worst hurricanes on record. Well," the officer said, "I must go. Thank you for your information."

He escorted Nancy outside. His fellow officer produced a padlock for the broken front door and pocketed the key. The police car pulled away. A curious group of neighbours who had gathered finally dispersed.

Hannah and the girls started home. On the way Nancy said she felt largely responsible for what had happened to Croft.

Hannah asked, "How could you possibly be responsible?"

Nancy replied, "We know there are people who don't want us working on Mr Billington's case. They're probably watching all our movements. They found out I went to Croft's house today and figured he had told me all he knew about the case. That's why he was beaten up!"

"How terrible!" Bess said angrily.

"Here's another possibility," said George. "Suppose Croft is actually one of the gang? He might have been the inside man."

Hannah spoke up. "If Croft is one of the gang, why would they beat him up?"

"Because," George replied, "he was given a job to do at the Base and he bungled it."

Nancy remarked, "That's good reasoning, George. I don't happen to agree with it, though. I think Croft was given the beating to keep him from saying any more. He may suspect other people whom he didn't tell us about."

When she turned into the Billingtons' driveway, George said, "The Resardos' car is here."

"That Antin is a cheat!" Hannah burst out. "Mr Billington pays him for working in the grove and taking care of these grounds. He hasn't touched the lawn or garden since we came. The grass is getting so brown I put on the sprinkler today."

The housekeeper unlocked the rear door and turned on the light. "How about a little ice cream before we go to bed?" She went to the refrigerator to take some out.

Nancy glanced at her watch. It was after eleven o'clock. "I wonder if it's too late to call Mr Datsun," she said to the others. "I think I should tell him what happened tonight."

Hannah, Bess, and George agreed, so Nancy went to the phone and picked it up. Someone was using it!

As the young detective listened, a man said, "Got it straight? R-day."

George had followed Nancy to the hall. Nancy made

motions indicating that her friend was to run upstairs and see who was on the extension phone.

As George took steps two at a time, Nancy heard a man's muffled reply, "Okay." The connection was cut off.

George came down the stairs to report that she had found no one using the extension phone up there.

"The call must have been made from the orange packing house," Nancy declared.

Hannah had come to see what was troubling Nancy. After hearing about the conversation, she said firmly. "Nancy, you're not going to that place to find out. It's too dangerous. Anyway, the person who used the phone has probably left by this time."

Nancy agreed. "But I think Antin should investigate," she said. "I'm going upstairs to tell him."

George gave a sardonic laugh. "He won't thank you for waking him up."

"I don't care," Nancy replied, and mounted the stairway. She knocked on the Resardos' door. There was no response, but after a second knock, a woman's sleepy voice said, "Who's there?"

"It's Nancy Drew, Tina. I'd like to speak to Antin. It's very important."

There was a long pause, then finally Tina came to the door. "Antin can't see you now. He's taking a bath."

"Please tell him that some prowler is in the packing house. He'd better go find out about him."

"Okay, I'll tell him."

Nancy went down the stairs again. She and the others ate their ice cream, but Antin Resardo did not appear.

THE MOSS-COVERED MANSION 377

"Some more of his indifference," George remarked. "He's a surly person."

"Yes," Bess spoke up. "He's no help at all around here. I certainly think Mr Billington should be told."

"You can bet he will be," Hannah informed her.

When they finished the ice cream, the girls washed and dried the dishes and spoons. Then they put out the lights and followed Hannah up the stairway. Suddenly Nancy turned back.

"What is it?" Bess asked her.

"Listen!" said Nancy. "I think someone is using a key to open the kitchen door."

Led by Nancy, the group tiptoed down the stairway and went towards the kitchen. The rear door opened just as Nancy clicked on the overhead light. They were astounded to see Antin Resardo coming in.

"You weren't taking a bath at all as Tina said!" George cried out. "You were in the orange packing house phoning!"

Nancy walked up to him. "What does R-day mean?" she demanded.

Antin gave a start, then suddenly his face flushed with anger and he glared at the young detective.

"You little sneak!" he yelled.

The next second he grabbed her by the shoulders and shook her so hard Nancy felt as if her head would snap off.

Doubting Workmen

"STOP that!" George yelled at Antin.

She grabbed his arm and as Nancy staggered away, George buckled the man's knees and flipped him over her shoulder. He fell to the floor with a crash.

"Good for you, George!" exclaimed Bess in glee.

Antin had been taken completely by surprise and had had the wind knocked out of him. Slowly he stood up.

Meanwhile Hannah had rushed to Nancy s side and asked, "Are you all right? That was a contemptible thing to do to you!" she said. "Antin, hereafter don't you ever dare lay a finger on Nancy or any of the rest of us!"

Nancy assured Hannah she would be her normal self in a few minutes and flopped into a chair. Antin looked at her, then said grudgingly, "I didn't mean to hurt you. I'm sorry if I did. You make me see red when you act suspicious of me. You mentioned my taking a bath. By the time I finished, Tina was asleep.

"It worried me that since I'd been away all day the machinery might not have been switched off in the packing house. I went to investigate.

"While there, I decided to put in a phone call to a friend of mine who is giving a surprise birthday party for his wife. Her name is Ruth. We are calling it R-day."

The commotion had brought Tina downstairs in her robe and slippers. She looked at the group questioningly. Antin repeated his story about R-day to her and she nodded affirmation.

Hannah spoke up. "There may have been misunderstanding on all sides. Why don't we talk this whole thing out?"

"Good idea," said Antin.

Mrs Gruen went on, "In the first place, I may as well tell you I resent your not helping in the house. You eat the food I cook and even leave your dirty dishes for me to wash."

Tina retorted, "Mr Billington didn't tell me I had to wait on these extra people. He just told me Mr Drew and his daughter might be down. I'm not strong and I'm not too well," she went on, "and I won't wait on so many people! That's final!"

"She's right," Antin burst out. "Between all the extra work and you people practically accusing us of being crooks, I think Tina and I will move to a motel until after you go home."

Hannah and the girls looked at one another. It would be a great relief to have the unpleasant Resardos out of the house. But if the couple stayed, they could be kept under surveillance.

Antin went on, "You think I had something to do with those explosive oranges. Well I didn't, and I gave the FBI an airtight alibi about where I was the day it happened."

Nancy did not like the man's defensive attitude. She knew that guilty people often play the part of aggrieved persons, trying to cover up the truth. Was this the case with the Resardos?

Again Hannah spoke up. "I'm glad we had this talk," she said. "Tina and Antin, I'm sure Mr Billington would be very hurt if you leave and he might even decide not to let you come back."

This thought startled the couple. They looked at each other and finally Tina said, "All right, we'll stay. I'll help with the cooking whenever Antin and I are here. I guess all of us can keep the house clean."

Nancy sensed the Resardos were annoyed because Hannah had won her point. The couple wished the others goodnight and went to their room. George looked after them. Did she imagine it, or was Antin limping a little because of her judo trick?

The atmosphere the next morning was a bit strained, but Tina did help prepare breakfast. She did not serve the food, however. Instead she and Antin sat down in the kitchen to eat, while the others carried their plates of eggs and bacon to the dining room.

Immediately after breakfast Nancy and Bess went upstairs to make their beds. George was about to follow a few minutes later when she saw Antin leave the house. On a hunch she trailed him, keeping well out of sight.

The foreman went directly to the packing house and George started back through the grove. Suddenly it occurred to her that she might get a clue to the orange mystery from some of the pickers. Seeing two of them a little distance away, she walked towards the men.

When George came near, she heard one man say, "I wouldn't trust that guy any place."

His companion replied, "Me neither."

The other man said laughingly, "I'll bet you the boss is making a killing for himself!" Were they talking about Antin or Mr Billington?

Puzzled but suspicious, George hurried back to the house. By the time she arrived Tina had gone upstairs and Bess and Nancy had come down. George told them what she had heard in the grove.

"Which boss do you think the men were talking about?" she asked.

Nancy smiled. "I'll try to find out."

She went to the phone and called the packing house. When a man answered, she said, "I'd like to speak to the boss."

"Okay. I'll call him," the worker replied. He yelled. "Antin, you're wanted on the phone."

Noiselessly Nancy put down the receiver and reported to the other girls.

"Shall we go tackle him?" George asked. "I'm sure he's doublecrossing Mr Billington."

Nancy agreed but said, "I have a feeling that today Antin will be on his best behaviour. In the meantime let's try once more to get into the Webster house. I can't wait to see the inside."

"How are you going to accomplish that without a key?" Bess queried.

Nancy said she would start by going back to Mr Scarlett's office. She might be able to learn something from nearby store owners.

When the girls reached the agent's office, they were surprised to see the door open. Lovely, low singing was coming from within. Wondering what was going on, the three callers walked inside. A stout, pretty woman was singing a lullaby as she dusted the furniture.

Upon seeing the girls she smiled broadly and said, "You want Mr Scarlett?"

"Yes we do," Nancy replied.

The pleasant woman jerked her thumb towards a closed door. "He's in there."

Nancy was surprised and delighted. Now she could get the key!

She knocked on the closed door. A voice said, "Come in!"

As Nancy walked in, she said, "Good morning. I'm Nancy Drew."

"Oh yes. Mrs Nickerson left a note you might come. Why did you?"

"To have you show me the interior of the Webster house," she answered.

The real estate agent scowled. "Don't you know I'm on vacation?"

"Your sign said so, but you seem to be right here," the young detective replied with a smile.

"Well, I am on vacation. There were certain papers in my files I had to pick up."

Nancy pretended not to notice he was trying to evade her. She said pleasantly, "I'm lucky to have found you. If you can't show me and my friends the Webster house, then, since you know the Nickersons, will you please lend me the key? I'll return it through your letter box, unless my father decides he wants to buy the place. In that case I'll keep the key."

"You'll do nothing of the sort," Mr Scarlett said unpleasantly. "The house is not for you. You wouldn't like it and there are lots of things the matter with the place."

"Like what?" Nancy asked.

Mr Scarlett frowned. "It's not necessary for me to go into that."

Nancy was not ready to give up yet. She smiled. "Why are you so anxious to keep us away from the Webster property? If I were a suspicious person, I would think something wrong was going on there."

Mr Scarlett's eyes narrowed angrily. "Nonsense."

"Then why are you refusing to let me see it?"

Mr Scarlett bit his lip. "Oh, all right," he said. "I don't have time to show you the place myself." He opened the drawer and took out a key with the letter W cut into it. A tag marked Webster was attached. "Here you are," he said icily. "But if anything is missing or disturbed, you'll be held responsible."

"I understand," Nancy said.

She took the key and joined Bess and George. They said goodbye to the cleaning woman and went out to the car. Nancy drove directly to the lovely house on the Indian River and the three girls went in.

"How wonderful!" Bess exclaimed, after looking around. "It's even nicer inside than outside."

Nancy too was charmed by the place, which was attractively furnished. The walls of the modern Spanish-type rooms were artistically decorated. In this warm climate the whole place had an air of coolness and true hospitality.

"I don't see anything the matter with this house," said George. "Mr Scarlett's opinion is for the birds."

The others agreed and all of them wondered why the agent had tried to discourage them.

Suddenly they were startled by the same chilling scream they had heard when looking over the grounds with Mrs Nickerson.

"There it is again!" Bess murmured. "Ugh! I wouldn't want to live here with that gross thing next door."

"Let's find out what it is!" Nancy urged.

"Not me," Bess said firmly.

"Don't be chicken," George chided her cousin.

Reluctantly Bess went outside and Nancy locked the door. The girls hurried towards the heavy wire-mesh fence. There was another scream, followed by a snarl.

"It's a wild animal!" Bess whispered. "We'd better run!"

·9·

Jungle Threat

"No, Bess," said Nancy. "If Dad decides to buy this place, we must know what's going on next door. And I plan to find out right now. Let's walk along the shore and investigate."

Though Bess was fearful, she followed the others along the fence. It ran on to a peninsula beyond the Webster property. At the riverfront the fence turned left abruptly.

There was no bulkhead along the water and the earth was muddy and slippery. After a few steps Nancy, Bess, and George decided to take off their shoes and carry them. They rolled up their slacks knee-length and started across the swampy ground.

"Watch your step!" Bess warned. "No telling what we might step on—a lizard, snake or—Oh!"

She lost her balance but managed after a few gyrations with her arms to right herself. "I knew I shouldn't have come," she complained.

Moments later the girls reached the corner of the steel-mesh fence near the far side of the peninsula. It turned left again. The three trekked alongside through the mass of trees and bushes. They found it helpful to use the steel wire for support.

The girls had not gone far before they realized this

was a real jungle. Going barelegged and barefoot did not seem safe, so the three friends put their shoes back on and rolled down their slacks.

"When will we get to the end of this?" Bess asked impatiently. Nancy said she judged it could not be much farther to the street.

The next moment the girls stood stock-still. From inside the grounds had come a loud roar.

"That's a lion!" George exclaimed. "Maybe this is a zoo."

Nancy said it was certainly not a public one.

"If it were," she surmised, "I'm sure Mrs Nickerson would have known about it and told us. Besides, we'd have seen signs posted."

She and George pushed ahead, with Bess at their heels, terror-stricken. She suddenly gave a cry and pointed inside the fence.

A group of large wild animals was galloping among the trees towards the girls. Roars, growls, and hisses filled the air. The big beasts, having scented the newcomers, pawed and clamoured at the fence to get at them. A huge black panther eyed the intruders, then began to climb the steel mesh.

Bess screamed and cried, "Look out, George!" Her cousin stood by the fence, fascinated, as Bess ran.

Nancy backed away quickly, but through the moss-draped oaks she could see a powerful-looking man running towards them, snapping a long whip.

The cracking of it finally had an effect on the animals. All of them slunk back except the panther. He had almost reached the top of the fence and might spring over at any second!

"Get down!" the man thundered at him.

He wore a khaki suit and helmet like those used on African safaris. Now he swung the whip against the fence. It made a ringing sound and vibrated the wire mesh.

The panther looked at his keeper balefully, then slowly climbed down. The man kept cracking the whip in the air and against the ground until all the animals loped off among the trees.

Their master turned his attention to the girls. He asked angrily, "What are you doing here?"

"Just looking," Nancy replied.

The man stared hard at each one of them before speaking again. "I guess I don't have to tell you this is a dangerous place. Stay away!"

From a little distance Bess called back, "You bet we will."

George said nothing, but Nancy asked, "Why do you have such dangerous animals here?"

"I train them and sell them to a circus."

The young detective was surprised to hear this. She knew that few circuses own the animals which are shown. They belong to the trainers who perform with them.

"What circus do you sell them to?" she queried.

Once more the big man stared at the girl until his eyes were only slits. Finally he opened them wide and said, "Tripp Brothers."

"Thank you," said Nancy. "How do we get to the main road from here? Follow this fence?"

The trainer replied shortly, "Go back the way you came."

Nancy would have preferred walking alongside the enclosure all the way to the street, but the man stood watching.

After they had traversed the full distance to where the fence turned, Nancy looked over her shoulder. The trainer was gone. She said eagerly, "Let's turn round and follow this side to find out what we can."

"Oh please don't!" Bess begged. "Those animals may come after us again and the panther may jump over the fence!"

"I'm willing to take the chance. George, are you?" Nancy asked.

"Sure thing."

Nancy took the key to the Webster house from her pocket. "Bess," she said, "if you don't want to come with us, why don't you go on and wait in the house?"

Bess could see that there was no talking Nancy and George out of learning more about the jungle-like property. With a great sigh she said, "Oh, all right. I'll tag along. But if anything happens, don't say I didn't warn you."

The girls began their trek up the peninsula through the woods, following the fence. A distance ahead it suddenly turned to the left.

"The fence ends at a house!" Nancy whispered.

She and the others approached carefully and stared at the building. It was a very old mansion but large and well preserved. The walls were covered almost entirely with clinging vines and green moss. Great oak trees with long streamers of Spanish moss surrounded it, giving a weird and forbidding effect.

"A real spook house!" Bess said in a low voice. "Well, Nancy, have you seen enough? Let's go!"

Nancy inched closer to the wire fence and peered through. She could see several large cages attached to the rear of the house. The animals that had tried to attack the girls were now in them and sleeping. At the moment the breeze was blowing towards the girls, and the animals could not pick up their scent.

Bess tugged at Nancy's arm. "Let's not tempt fate," she begged. "Please come on."

Nancy could feel Bess trembling and nodded in agreement.

Nancy wondered how far it was to the street. There seemed to be no road leading out, but she concluded there must be some way for cars and people to get in and out of the grounds.

Presently she spotted a truck off to one side. There was no name on it but she jotted down the licence number.

"Here's what I've been looking for," she whispered, and pointed to a narrow road which zigzagged among the moss-covered trees.

As the girls walked along it silently, they listened for sounds of anyone approaching and watched the ground to avoid any holes. George, however, sank down in a soft spot. Her feet were sucked in so quickly she could not pull them out.

After trying for several moments she called out, "Girls, come and help me! I'm stuck!"

It took the combined efforts of Nancy and Bess to pull George out of the oozy mass. She looked down at her shoes which had changed from white to brown.

"I'm sure a mess!" she said. "The sooner I can get into a tub the better I'll like it." She thanked her rescuers who could not help laughing at George's appearance. Mud was splattered over her clothes, hair, and face.

A few feet farther on, the ground was harder and the girls quickened their pace. As they zigzagged along the curving road, the three grew careless about being watchful.

Nancy suddenly pulled back and bumped against George. The others looked to see what had startled her. A snake had begun to unwind itself from a tree branch and was trying to reach Nancy with its forked tongue!

She recovered her wits quickly and said, "He won't harm us if we don't bother him."

"I hope you're right," said Bess, and took a circuitous route to avoid the reptile.

In a few moments the girls came to a small orange grove. As they hurried through it, Bess picked one of the luscious-looking fruit and put it into her pocket.

"In case I get hungry," she explained to the others.

A few minutes later the girls reached another bit of jungle-like area. If it had not been for the roadway, they would have found it hard going through stout reeds and brier bushes. At last the street came into sight.

Nancy, in the lead, suddenly called back in a whisper, "Hide!"

·10·

Disastrous Fire

"QUICK!" said Nancy, ducking behind a brier bush "Mr Scarlett is just outside in a car!"

Bess and George squatted down too. The three remained very still, not making a sound.

Mr Scarlett got out of his car and walked up and down, looking and listening. The girls were puzzled by his actions. Perhaps someone had seen them going towards the moss-covered mansion and had reported this to him.

In a few minutes the estate agent seemed to be satisfied about something. He got back into his car. Then, to the girls' amazement, he drove towards them along the winding path. They crouched lower behind the tall bushes. His car soon disappeared but they could hear the motor. Seconds later it was shut off approximately where the house would be.

"He must know the animal trainer," Nancy thought.

She and her friends came from hiding. Nancy wanted to go back to the moss-covered mansion but Bess objected. "I think we've had enough adventures for one day. Besides, George is a mess. Please, let's return to the Billingtons'."

As they walked down the street towards the Webster

391

house to get their car, the girls discussed Scarlett's furtive behaviour. Why had he come to the mansion with the wild-animal enclosure?

"He's hiding something, that's sure," George declared. "Nancy, if you see him again, are you going to ask him why he was here?"

"No, George. I believe we can find out more by having him think we didn't see him."

When they reached home Hannah Gruen met them at the kitchen door. "My word, George, where have you been?" she cried out. "Did you fall in the water?"

"I wish I had," said George. "I'd have been better off." Quickly she explained about their sleuthing trip to the moss-covered mansion.

The housekeeper was aghast. "The place sounds dreadful. You had better not go there again."

Bess said, "You can bet I'm not going to."

She pulled the orange from her pocket, and told Hannah she had taken it from a tree at the strange house.

"This isn't the same kind as Mr Billington's," Bess said. "Do you suppose it's a Hamlin, the same as the oranges that were delivered to the Space Centre?"

The thought intrigued Nancy. On a bookshelf she had noticed a volume marked *Oranges* and went to get it. The book was filled with colour pictures and one by one she compared Bess's orange with those in the book.

"This is not a Valencia," she said, "because it's the wrong time of year for that kind of tree to be bearing. The fruit's ripe in the spring. Mr Billington's, as you know, are Pineapple oranges. Remember their bright-orange skin and pineapple shape?" Nancy turned the page and exclaimed, "Here it is! The oranges at the moss-covered mansion are not Hamlins but Parson Browns. Hamlins have a smooth skin while the Parson Browns are pebbly-skinned."

George sighed. "I guess we'll have to ride around looking for Hamlin groves to see if we can pick up any clue to the ones that were brought into the Space Centre."

The girls decided to start their search directly after luncheon. They hurried upstairs to take baths and put on fresh clothes.

By the time they came down again, Tina was in the kitchen helping Hannah. The three girls winked at one another and began to set the table.

The menu called for baked chicken with a special kind of cream sauce. Tina said she had never heard of it and did not know how to make the sauce.

"Nancy does it very well," Hannah said proudly, and called, "Nancy dear, will you come and make cream sauce for the chicken?"

Smiling, Nancy hurried to the kitchen and prepared it.

When everything was ready, Hannah and the girls went to the dining room. They invited Tina to eat with them, but the woman refused, saying she was not hungry. Perhaps by the time Antin came in, she would be ready for her lunch.

Instinct told Nancy not to talk about the moss-covered mansion within Tina's hearing. The group were relieved when she went outdoors and walked into the grove.

The telephone rang. Nancy answered it. Mr Datsun,

the lawyer, was calling. He wanted to know if Nancy had anything to report. She gave a quick account of her sleuthing but admitted she had learned little about the explosive oranges.

"No one has been able to track down any clue except to Mr Billington," the lawyer said.

On a hunch Nancy told him about the old mansion. "Do you know who lives there?"

"No," the lawyer replied. "Why?"

Nancy explained about the possibility of her father buying the Webster place and the strange behaviour of Mr Scarlett. "Are you acquainted with him?"

"I know there is an estate agent of that name," said Mr Datsun, "but I can't tell you anything about him. I'm afraid I'm no help to you, but I'm hoping you can help me.

"Nancy, a very odd note was left under my office door. Maybe you can figure it out. This is what it says:

" *'Can a mouse with a brain of jelly capture a lion with nerves of steel?'* "

"How strange!" Nancy remarked. "Would you mind repeating it?"

Mr Datsun read it again and Nancy quickly wrote down the words and read those numbered 1, 5, 9, 13. Neither the words nor the first letters of them made any sense.

"Are you still there?" Mr Datsun asked.

"I'm sorry," said Nancy. "I was trying to see if there might be a code in this message. I think not. But it occurs to me that it could have been written by some sarcastic person interested in the case of the explosive oranges. The message might imply that you and my father are as helpless as a mouse against a lion."

"That's a very good guess," the lawyer remarked.

Nancy went on, "Whoever the lion is, we'll catch him!"

"Indeed we will!" Mr Datsun agreed.

After the conversation ended, Nancy continued to think about the message. She suddenly remembered the lion at the moss-covered mansion. Suppose that by some chance this was the beast referred to in the mysterious note! It could mean that the strange set up of the animal enclosure and the odd behaviour of Mr Scarlett were connected with the explosive oranges!

"It would explain why the girls and I aren't wanted at the Webster house," Nancy told herself.

At this moment Bess came to warn her that Antin and Tina had come in. The caretaker was taciturn. Not only did he not speak to anyone but did not wait to eat lunch. Instead, the couple went up to their room.

"What's the matter with him?" George asked.

Before anyone could hazard a guess, an alarm bell began to ring.

"What's that for?" George asked.

There was pounding on the stairway and Antin came rushing down. "Fire!" he shouted, and rushed out the rear door.

Everyone followed. He sped through the grove to the packing house.

Suddenly Nancy stopped. "I wonder if anyone notified the fire department," she said. "I'd better go back and phone them anyway."

"I'll go with you," said Bess. "This might have been

a ruse to get all of us out of the house." They had left the doors and windows open.

"We'll soon find out," said Nancy.

Hurrying inside, she dashed to the telephone and called the fire department. They had not been notified but said they would come at once.

Quickly Nancy and Bess locked all the doors and windows, and took the kitchen door key with them. As they ran through the grove towards the packing house, the girls noticed that blazes had sprung up here and there among the trees.

"This fire has been deliberately set!" Nancy declared. "Someone started it while the workers were at lunch." Immediately she wondered where Antin had been. Could he possibly be the arsonist and if so why?

When they caught up to George and Hannah, Nancy told them that the firemen were coming. She rushed up to a burly picker and asked how she could help.

"You're a girl," he said. "What can you do?"

Nancy was angry. She turned away. There was nothing she could do to save the orange packing house which was now a mass of flames, but she might be able to do something to preserve the trees. She ran over to Tina, who was sobbing, and asked her.

The woman pointed towards the river. "There's a hose and a pump down there," she replied.

Nancy did not wait to hear more. She quickly told Bess and George, and the three rushed off towards the river. It seemed as if trees were burning everywhere. They found the pump and hose, quickly unwound it, and turned on the nozzle. Within minutes they were able to put out the fire in the nearby trees.

"Let's try another section," George suggested, and began lugging the hose forward.

Just then they heard the fire engines arriving. The girls, however, kept on with their own work.

In a short while two of the firemen came into the grove dragging a large hose. Suddenly they realized that the trees were already being hosed, and were astounded to see the job being done by three girls.

"Good work!" said one.

With the two steady streams of water, the rest of the fires in the grove were soon extinguished.

"Who's in charge here?" one of the firemen asked Nancy.

"The foreman, Antin Resardo. I think he's at the packing house."

"Let's get out of here," Bess suggested. "This place smells horrible."

The scent of scorched oranges mixed with burning wood was bad enough, but added to this was rank-smelling steam. The girls' eyes were smarting and they were covered with soot.

"We'll take care of your hose," said one of the firemen. "You'd better go to the house and bathe your eyes."

"We will," Nancy replied.

On the way back they met Hannah, who reported that the packing house was a complete wreck.

"It's a shame," she said. "The fire chief is convinced this was the work of a firebug."

Nancy said she thought the arsonist might be the enemy of Mr Billington who had used his name to deliver the explosive oranges. "Whoever the person is he knows he's being pursued. He hopes to intimidate Mr Billington into dropping the hunt by ruining his orange business."

The others agreed. Hannah said a neighbour had offered to let Mr Billington use his packing house until he could build a new one. "Only I'm afraid there aren't many good oranges left."

When they reached the house Nancy said she must telephone her father at once. "I'll tell him what has happened so he can pass the word along to Mr Billington."

Fortunately he was in his office and she quickly told the story. Mr Drew was astounded.

"I'll get in touch with Mr and Mrs Billington immediately about coming down. Please stay there. I'll call you back."

Within half an hour Mr Drew phoned. He and the Billingtons were leaving River Heights at once in order to make a quick plane connection in New York.

"We'll get to Melbourne about ten tonight," he said. "Please meet us, Nancy."

"Bess and George and I will be there," she promised.

Nancy reported the conversation to Hannah and the girls, then said, "I'd like to go back to the packing house and look through the ruins if they're cool enough. Maybe we'll find a clue to the arsonist."

Bess and George were eager to join her.

"Setting those fires was a wicked thing to do," Bess declared.

When the girls arrived at the water-soaked ruin, they walked around it, their eyes alert for any clue. Suddenly, in a heap of half-burned papers, Nancy spotted some-

thing that could be a clue. She bent down and picked
up a scrap of paper.

"Look at this!" she exclaimed excitedly.

Off the Market

THE partially burned newspaper which Nancy showed to Bess and George was a copy of the edition which held the name *Drew* in the code message.

"It's ringed with red crayon!" Bess burst out. "What does that mean?"

George made a guess. "I think the person who set the fire is a member of some gang out to ruin Mr Billington's reputation and business. He's worried because Mr Drew and Nancy have been brought in to solve the mystery."

Nancy agreed. "We have very few clues," she said, "and everything seems to be so disconnected. What we must do is find a motive for the whole thing."

Bess suddenly caught her breath. The other girls looked at her and asked, "What's the matter?"

Bess's reply was upsetting. "Suppose that firebug takes it into his head to burn down the house we're staying in!"

There was silence for a few moments. Finally Nancy said, "Perhaps we'd better go back and talk this over with Hannah."

When they reached the house, Tina and Antin were with Mrs Gruen. Hannah became alarmed at the thought of another fire.

"I wish we had a good watchdog here," she said.

Tina was fearful of the house being set on fire, but Antin shrugged off the idea.

"What reason would anyone have for doing such a thing?" he asked Nancy.

She replied, "What reason would anyone have for burning down the packing house and setting fires in the grove?"

As she spoke, Nancy watched the caretaker's face intently. He showed no change of expression.

Nancy thought, "He certainly is a strange person." Aloud she asked, "What do you think is going to happen to Mr Billington's orange business?"

Antin set his jaw. "That's up to Mr Billington. I know what I'd do if it belonged to me—forget the whole thing. But of course I'll follow whatever orders he gives me." The foreman stalked from the house.

As it neared time for the girls to leave for the Melbourne airport to pick up Mr Drew, Hannah confessed that she felt uneasy about staying alone. The Resardos had already left, saying they were going to Ruth's birthday party.

When George suggested that she come with the girls, Mrs Gruen said, "I don't think I should go along and leave this house unprotected."

"You're absolutely right," said Bess. "Nancy, I'll stay here with Hannah."

Nancy and George set off. On the way George remarked, "Wouldn't you think after what happened here today Antin and Tina would have stayed home and waited for the Billingtons? They didn't even offer to pick them up at the airport!"

Back at the Billington house, Hannah and Bess were startled by loud knocking on the front door. Hannah went to answer it.

"Don't let anybody in!" Bess called out.

Hannah asked, "Who's calling?"

"Mr Scarlett."

Mrs Gruen opened the door and the man stepped inside.

"Where's Nancy Drew?" he asked abruptly.

"She's not here."

"Where did she go?"

Bess started to tell him, but Hannah gave the girl a warning look and answered for her.

"Nancy has gone on an errand. Do you have a message for her?"

Mr Scarlett said indeed he did—a very important one. "Mr Webster has taken his house off the market. It's no longer for sale. I must have the key of the house at once. Get it for me."

Hannah said she had no idea where it was. He would have to wait until Nancy returned.

"I can't wait," the agent snapped. "I must have the key now." He turned to Bess. "She probably told you where it is. Bring it to me!"

"I don't know," the girl replied firmly. "When Nancy returns, I'll tell her you want the key. She can bring it to you in the morning."

Mr Scarlett seemed nonplussed as well as angry. Before he had a chance to make any further demands, Hannah said to him, "That's all. Goodnight, Mr Scarlett."

She held the door for him and reluctantly he went out.

Immediately Bess said, "Nancy's going to be dreadfully disappointed about the Webster house being taken off the market. I wonder what the reason was. I gathered from Mrs Nickerson that Mr Webster was eager to sell the place."

As they continued to discuss the strange turn of events, Nancy and George were bowling along the road towards Melbourne. When they were about halfway there, George remarked that a car was racing up behind them.

"That driver certainly is in a hurry," Nancy remarked, glancing into the rear-view mirror.

Instead of whizzing by, the car suddenly drove up alongside and the driver yelled, "Stop!"

Nancy suddenly recognized the driver and stopped her car.

"Mr Scarlett!" she exclaimed. "What do you want?"

"The key to the Webster house," he replied. "Hand it over."

Nancy said she did not have it with her. She changed the subject abruptly and asked Mr Scarlett who lived in the moss-covered mansion next to the Webster home.

"I don't know," he replied. "I've never been in there."

Nancy and George looked at each other but said nothing. Why had Scarlett lied?

The agent came back to the subject of the key. "Give it to me!"

"I told you I don't have it with me," Nancy replied. "But tell me why you want the key. My father is coming down tonight and I need it to show him the house tomorrow morning. I'm sure he'll buy the place."

"It's no longer for sale," Mr Scarlett snapped. "Mr Webster has taken it off the market."

"What!" George exclaimed. "I understood he wanted to sell it as soon as possible."

"Not any more. Tell me where the key is and I'll go back to the house and get it from your friends."

Nancy had no intention of doing this. It had occurred to her that this whole story might be false. She would ask her father to get in touch with Mr Webster direct and learn the truth.

"Hurry up!" Mr Scarlett shouted.

Before Nancy had a chance to answer, a trooper on a motorcycle whizzed up and stopped. He pulled out a pad and pencil and said to Mr Scarlett, "You were going way beyond the speed limit."

"I was in a hurry," the agent replied.

George nudged Nancy and whispered, "Now's your chance to get away."

Nancy thought so too. Putting the car into gear, she drove off down the road.

George glanced back several times to see if Mr Scarlett was following them. There was no sign of his car.

As they neared the airport, George said, "It seems strange he knew where to find us. Do you suppose he was at the house and Hannah or Bess told him?"

"Even if he were there, I'm sure they wouldn't tell him. Besides, they could truthfully say they didn't know where the key is because I hid it and forgot to tell you all the place."

Nancy parked and glanced at her watch. Ten minutes to ten.

"Dad should be in soon," Nancy said, a smile crossing her face. "It will be so good to see him again."

As the girls walked into the terminal building, they noticed that people waiting to meet relatives or friends looked tense and worried. One woman was pacing the floor nervously, wiping perspiration from her face, though the night was cool.

As she came close to the girls, she said, "The New York plane is in trouble."

"What's wrong?" Nancy asked her.

The woman looked at the girl, terror in her eyes. "The landing gear jammed. The wheels won't come down. This means a crash landing!"

·12·

Frustrated Thief

THE girls gasped and rushed outside to watch the plane carrying Mr Drew and the Billingtons. It was circling the field. The runway had been sprayed with foam. A fire truck and an ambulance stood nearby. Soon the great airliner began to descend.

"But the landing wheels aren't down!" murmured the woman who had followed the girls outdoors.

With Nancy and George she watched breathlessly. Upon landing the plane might spin round.

Fortunately the pilot made a skilful belly landing and all the waiting friends and relatives gave sighs of relief. Mr Drew and the Billingtons were among the first to get off. The pilot had already come out and the two men hurried to catch up to him.

"Congratulations on your fine work!" Mr Drew called. Mr Billington also complimented the pilot.

"It's all in a day's work," the young captain answered with a smile, then disappeared into the offices of the airline.

Mr Drew introduced the Billingtons, who said they had been looking forward to meeting Nancy and her friends. As soon as they were seated in the car, Mr Billington requested that the girls tell him about the fire.

Nancy reported on it in detail and told him the arsonist had not been caught. "Mr Billington, we have found Tina and Antin a complete mystery. Do you think it possible that he had anything to do with the fire?"

"Not Antin," Mr Billington said quickly. "I always thought he loved my orange grove and would be heartbroken if something happened to it."

Nancy and George made no comment. Antin had certainly not shown this kind of regret about the burned trees and packing house.

George told about the girls' experience on the way to the airport. "Mr Scarlett was positively contemptible, and he said that the Webster house had been taken off the market."

"Dad," said Nancy, "could you find out if it is really true?"

When he nodded, she added, "The girls and I have wondered if Scarlett is acting in collusion with the owner of the moss-covered mansion." She told the men about the wild animals they had seen. "The trainer was very hostile to us. I suspect he doesn't want any new neighbours."

Mr Drew asked, "Have you talked to the police about the place?"

"No, I haven't," Nancy replied, "but I'll do so first thing in the morning."

When the Drews and their friends arrived at the Billington house, they were amazed to hear of Mr Scarlett's rude behaviour towards Hannah and Bess.

Mr Drew scowled. "I don't like his actions. I doubt that he is to be trusted. You say he went into the grounds of the moss-covered mansion furtively?"

"Yes," Nancy replied. "Suppose I call the police right now and ask if they can tell us anything about who lives there."

She phoned at once but was told she would have to wait until morning when the office with the local records was open.

The next day Nancy lost no time in getting the information. The old house had been purchased by a man named Fortin. He had been a trainer of wild animals for a circus. Fortin had received a permit to have the beasts there as long as they were properly caged. Nancy thanked the clerk and hung up.

"I wonder if Fortin was that tall heavy-set man with the whip," she said to Bess and George.

Nancy was more convinced than ever that Fortin was behind the move to keep the Drews from buying the Webster house. He might have found out she was an amateur detective and did not want her so close. She might report that he allowed the dangerous animals out of their cages.

"I wish I could get inside that mansion," Nancy said. "I have a strong hunch there's something going on between Scarlett and Fortin which has a direct bearing on the Webster property."

Bess spoke up. "You'd better forget it, Nancy. We came down here to solve the mystery of the explosive oranges. Why don't we forget that place with the wild animals and go hunting for Hamlin orange groves as George suggested?"

"I'm ready to start," Nancy said.

The girls set off in the Billingtons' car. Nancy drove

up one road and down another. Many people had small groves, others large ones, but none had Hamlin oranges. Most were apparently Valencias.

At last the girls spotted a big grove of smooth-skinned Hamlins. Nancy turned into the long driveway and went to the packing house. She introduced herself and her friends to the foreman, saying they were from River Heights and were interested in solving the case of the explosive oranges.

"My father is the lawyer for Mr Billington," she said. "I'm eager to find out which grove those particular oranges came from. Can you help me?"

The foreman, who told them his name was Tom Seever, smiled. He looked up at the darkening sky and said, "We'd better run into the packing house. I'll tell you what I know. Looks like a heavy shower coming any second."

The girls hurried after him and went into the shelter. Pickers from the grove and a visitor who had just driven in began rushing inside too. By the time the rain came down hard, the place was so crowded that moving around was impossible.

Suddenly the lights went out. A few seconds later Nancy felt a rough hand against her arm. She realized that someone was trying to cut the strap of her handbag.

Quickly she clutched the bag in one hand and with the other grabbed the man's wrist. Finding it, she pinched the flesh so hard that the bag snatcher cried out in pain. Instantly she could feel him moving away.

A few seconds later the lights went on. Nancy craned her neck to look at all the people who had taken shelter in the packing house. It was hopeless to try identifying the suspect, but she saw the visitor dash to a car and drive off. Was he guilty and had he followed her here?

The rain had stopped and the man had begun to file outside. Nancy and her friends were the last to leave the building. After talking to Mr Seever for a few minutes about the mystery, she was convinced that there was nothing he could tell them which would cast any light on the case. All his oranges were sold to trustworthy buyers he knew well, and no fruit had been stolen.

The young sleuth asked if he would give them directions to another Hamlin grove.

He told her of one about a mile away and the three girls headed for Owen's Grove.

It was a large grove and there were many pickers at work. Nancy was directed to the office of the owner, Mr Owen. It was in a small building that stood a short distance from the packing house.

She went to the door and asked, "May I come in?"

The owner rose, smiling, and said, "Yes, indeed. Won't you sit down?"

Bess and George had stayed outside to look over the packing house.

The young detective introduced herself. "My father is working on Mr Billington's case. Since the explosive oranges that were brought into the Base were Hamlins, I wondered if you might possibly have a clue to help solve the mystery."

Mr Owen said he did. "The FBI were here, of course, and I told them a suspicion of mine. One of my workers never showed up here after the affair. He was a strange, uncommunicative person by the name of Max Ivanson.

We tried to get in touch with him where he boarded but were told that he had disappeared."

"Did he take anything from here with him?" Nancy asked.

Mr Owen nodded. "Several sacks of oranges were missing. We think he took them. I've forgotten the number now but it corresponded with the count which the NASA authorities had listed in their report about the delivery."

Nancy was intrigued by this information. "What did Max Ivanson look like?"

Mr Owen opened a desk drawer and pulled out a photograph. "This is the man. I just came across it."

Nancy tried not to show her surprise. Ivanson looked enough like Mr Billington to be a brother!

"Can you tell me anything more about him?" Nancy queried.

"A little. Ivanson's a bachelor. He was a good picker but would never stay to work overtime."

Nancy got up. "You have been most kind and helpful," she said, putting out her hand.

Mr Owen shook it warmly and wished her luck in solving the mystery. "I'm glad if I've been of help," he said.

Bess and George were excited when Nancy told them what she had found out, and discussed the clue as they started for home. A shortcut led them past the Nickersons' house.

"Let's go in," Nancy suggested, and turned into their driveway.

Both of Ned's parents were home and were amazed at all Nancy had accomplished, particularly her last clue. Then the conversation turned towards the Webster house and the moss-covered mansion.

"I certainly wish I could get inside that weird-looking place with the wild animals," said Nancy.

Mr Nickerson grinned. All three girls thought how much Ned looked like his father when he smiled broadly.

"I think I just might arrange such a visit," Mr Nickerson said. "I know a man who is an animal control officer in the Public Health Service. Perhaps he could make a routine inspection of the moss-covered mansion and"—he winked at Nancy—"perhaps he could take a secretary with him!"

·13·

Eerie Inspection

"WHAT an exciting suggestion!" Nancy exclaimed. "Think of going inside the moss-covered mansion!"

All the others agreed it was a good idea except Bess, who looked worried.

"Nancy, please think this over. You know the trouble we almost got into with those wild animals on the outside of the house. No telling what may happen if you go indoors."

Nancy turned to Mr Nickerson. "Surely it can't be dangerous if the Health Department goes there regularly to inspect the place."

Ned's father nodded. "I can soon solve this," he said. "My friend Mr Wilcox, the animal control officer, will know whether or not it's possible and also safe for you to go into the moss-covered mansion."

He went to make the call. While waiting, George said she was envious of Nancy's visit to the place. Bess remarked timidly, "Well I'm not. I don't mind telling you those animals frightened me half to death."

Mr Nickerson soon returned, a wide smile on his face. "Everything is arranged. Mr Wilcox will be here tomorrow morning at ten to pick you up."

"That's wonderful!" the young detective exclaimed.

"I think we'd better dash home now. I'll see you at ten o'clock tomorrow morning. By the way, Mr Nickerson, will you request Mr Wilcox not to introduce me at the moss-covered mansion?"

"That's a good idea," he agreed. "If they know your name, you might not get a friendly greeting! Anyway, since you are not a regular member of the Public Health Service staff, let the people at the mansion think of you as Wilcox's Girl Friday."

This reference to the Robinson Crusoe story struck Bess as funny and she began to laugh. "You'll be Mrs Robinson Crusoe," she remarked. On the way home, however, Bess sobered again. "I just hope nothing happens to you!"

"I promise to keep my eyes open," Nancy told her friend.

She could hardly wait for the following morning to come, but during the remainder of the afternoon, Bess kept referring to the possible dangers Nancy might encounter.

Once she said, "Suppose that leopard mauls you!"

George looked at her cousin severely. "Will you be quiet? Nancy is determined to go and I don't blame her. There's no point in trying to scare her away."

Bess said no more but Hannah Gruen did. She was inclined to agree with Bess. "I know Mr Wilcox will be with you, but what protection would he be against an angry lion?"

When Mr Drew and Mr Billington heard what the plan was, they took a different attitude. Both were sure Nancy could not be harmed if Wilcox was with her.

The lawyer added, "I know you will keep alert,

Nancy, and look in all directions at the same time."

Nancy bent to kiss her father and patted him on the cheek. "Are you trying to make me into some kind of a wonder of science?" she teased. "I've never learned to swivel my head!"

He chuckled, then said that he and Mr Billington were going out to have dinner with Mr Datsun.

"See you in the morning," he told the others and the two men set off.

The three girls went up to Nancy's room to help her pick the outfit she would wear the following morning. The choice was a white dress and shoes. Nancy would arrange her hair in a bun so that she would look older.

Bess announced she was suffering with hunger pangs so the trio went downstairs to have dinner with Mrs Billington and Hannah. Once more the Resardos were not there. The rest of the evening was spent reading the latest reports of the forthcoming flight to the moon.

"I see that there are going to be many celebrities here," Mrs Gruen remarked. "Even the president may come down!"

The newspaper carried pictures of well-known press correspondents who had arrived to report on the launch. There were photographers by the hundreds and a sprinkling of visitors from other countries.

"It's going to be fabulous!" Bess exclaimed. "Aren't those astronauts who are on the mission handsome?"

"Yes, and remarkably brave and intelligent," George added.

Finally it was time for the group to retire. Nancy was too excited to drop off to sleep but eventually she did and woke up refreshed and ready for the day's adventure. After breakfast the girls drove to the Nickerson home. A few minutes later Mr Wilcox arrived and was introduced to them. He wore a khaki over-all.

"So this is the young lady who will accompany me," he said, smiling at Nancy, "and act as secretary for the trip." He handed her a stenographer's pad and a pencil. "Take lots of notes," he added with a wink.

Nancy laughed. "I understand. Some for you and some for me."

The two went to the car. Nancy noticed a pair of asbestos gloves on the seat.

"I wear those whenever I have to go inside a cage," he explained.

When they arrived at the moss-covered mansion, Wilcox turned into the narrow path that wound through the orange grove and the jungle to the house. He parked and they walked up the steps of the old-fashioned house.

The Public Health officer rang the bell. He and Nancy stood waiting but there was no answer.

"Maybe the bell doesn't work," Nancy suggested.

Her companion pounded loudly on the door. After a long while it was opened a crack. Nancy's heart began to beat a little faster. Would the huge man with the whip open the door?

Wilcox called into the crack, "Mr Fortin?"

"Yes," came the answer. "No visitors allowed!"

"I'm Wilcox from Animal Control of the Public Health Service," he told him. "I have an order to inspect your place again. Here are my credentials."

All this time two dogs had been yelping and barking

in the background. Mr Fortin certainly had protection, Nancy thought.

"Wait until I tie up these animals," the owner said.

He closed the door and was gone so long that Nancy thought perhaps he was not going to let them in. Finally the door opened.

Fortin was a slender man about fifty years old with a reddish complexion. It flashed across Nancy's mind that he did not give the appearance of an animal trainer. His hands were rather soft-looking, not like those of a person used to heavy work. He escorted the callers through the centre hall and out to the kitchen. He opened a rear door which gave a view of the many cages backed up against the house just beyond the kitchen door. Nancy got her notebook ready.

"These cages look very clean and the animals well-kept," Wilcox remarked, and Nancy wrote this down.

She followed him outdoors and round the three sides of the cages which seemed to be well-constructed. Each had a sheltered area.

"Very good," said Wilcox.

All this time Nancy's eyes had been roaming around the jungle. She could not detect anything suspicious.

Fortin led the way back inside the house and headed for the front door. At once Wilcox spoke up. "I have orders to look over the whole mansion."

The owner frowned and said, "Why is this necessary? A licence issued to me to keep the animals certainly doesn't permit the Public Health Service to pry into my private life!"

Wilcox replied, "Those are my orders. There could be vermin in the house from those wild animals." Before

Fortin could object, Wilcox started up the stairway. Nancy followed, then Fortin.

After a quick inspection of the first-floor rooms, Wilcox said, "Everything seems to be all right." He turned to Fortin. "I thought maybe you had some small animals up here."

"Well I don't!" Fortin snapped.

He started down the stairway, but Nancy held the health officer back. She whispered, "See that door over there? It probably leads to the second floor."

Her companion nodded. "I want to take a look upstairs, Mr Fortin," he called and walked over to the door.

As Wilcox opened it, the owner's face turned red with anger, but all he said was, "You'll find nothing up there. It's an old tower."

Nevertheless, Wilcox climbed the stairs, with Nancy at his heels and Fortin behind her. The tower had windows which looked out on the ocean. In front of one stood a powerful telescope.

"That came with the house," Fortin explained. "It's so old I guess it was put in soon after the people built the place. They probably watched the ships at sea."

Nancy had walked over and looked through the telescope. She could plainly see the Space Centre and the rocket that would take the astronauts to the moon.

"Everything okay?" Fortin asked in a sarcastic tone.

"Everything's okay," the Public Health officer replied, and Nancy wrote this down, along with her observations relating to the telescope.

As the visitors were coming down from the second floor, Nancy noticed a man in the lower hall. He was the big fellow with the whip! Instinctively she held the notebook partly across her face so that she would not be recognized.

When they reached the foot of the stairs Fortin ignored her. He introduced his associate to Wilcox as Joss Longman, saying he was the best animal trainer in the world.

Wilcox nodded, then checked through the ground floor with Nancy. They found nothing suspicious. Back in the hall the two men were waiting for them sullenly.

"That's all now," Fortin said sharply and walked towards the front door, but Wilcox did not move.

"We haven't seen your basement yet," he said.

Hearing this, Longman turned quickly and hurried towards the kitchen. Nancy saw him open a door at the back of the hall and disappear.

Once more Fortin began to argue that the Public Health Service had no right to intrude on his privacy.

"Orders are orders," Wilcox said firmly. "Take me to your basement."

Fortin glared at the visitors, then he slowly walked to the kitchen. When they came to the door at the rear of the hall through which Nancy had seen Longman disappear, she put out her hand towards the knob.

"Don't go in there!" Fortin shouted at her. "That's a clothes cupboard."

Nancy doubted this but she followed him into the kitchen. Fortin began to talk about how old-fashioned the room was.

"That's only a coal stove," he remarked. "It's pretty hard learning to cook on it. As soon as I get more money, I intend to replace it with a modern range."

Nancy suspected that the man was stalling for time. He went on talking about the outmoded plumbing and what trouble they had with it. She was convinced that Longman had gone ahead to conceal something in the basement.

"What is it," she wondered, "that they don't want us to see?"

Finally Fortin opened a door in the kitchen and clicked on a light in the basement. He led the way down a steep flight of wooden steps. Longman was not in sight. Nancy was sure he had used a secret entrance to the place.

Wilcox had already started walking around the basement which contained nothing but old furniture and piles of rubbish thrown against the walls. This seemed odd to Nancy. The Public Health officer did not act as if he suspected anything.

Fortin asked, "Well, are you satisfied now with your inspection?"

Wilcox looked stern. "I don't think much of your housekeeping," he replied. "Please see that the trash is cleaned out of here."

"Okay," Fortin growled.

The two men started up the stairway. Nancy, pretending that she was writing down what Wilcox had said, purposely leaned against a pile of old furniture. Presently the load shifted. Nancy grabbed a child's desk for support.

The next moment the whole conglomeration of furniture came tumbling down on her!

·14·

Outsmarting a Liar

THE racket caused by the falling furniture sent Wilcox and Fortin running back to the basement.

The animal trainer, instead of asking if Nancy had been hurt, said to her angrily, "What were you trying to do? You have no right touching anything around here! You were snooping, that's what. Talk!"

Wilcox said icily, "I'm sure she meant no harm. Are you hurt?"

By this time Nancy had picked herself up and though her clothes were dusty from the furniture, she had not been injured.

"I'm sorry, Mr Fortin," she said, "I used to have a desk very much like this one. When I touched it, the whole pile came tumbling down."

Fortin's face was grim. Nancy thought he was going to say he did not believe a word of her story. Quickly she asked, "Is this desk for sale?"

"No!" the animal trainer almost shouted at her. "And I'd appreciate your leaving. I have work to do."

Mr Wilcox spoke up. "We'll go at once and I'll give the Health Service an excellent report about your animal operation here."

While Nancy brushed dust from her clothes, she took

in every detail of the wall behind the pile of furniture. She had spotted a steel door. Evidently Longman had rushed downstairs to try hiding it with the pile of furniture. Something secret must be inside!

Nancy had also noticed heavy cables in the basement. One of them ran through the wall next to the half-hidden door.

Fortin said sarcastically, "Listen, miss, you're delaying my work. Please go at once."

"Oh I'm sorry," Nancy apologized and scooted up the stairway.

She was puzzled by what she had seen. The young detective had a strong hunch that something besides the training of wild animals for a circus was going on at the moss-covered mansion.

Mr Wilcox and his "secretary" left the house and drove off. Nancy told him what she had seen in the cellar. "Why do you think Fortin was trying to conceal that door?"

Wilcox smiled. "I'm no detective, but I suspect he had something hidden behind it. Since I insisted upon seeing everything, he was probably afraid I might want to look in there. I'm sure no wild animal was inside. Otherwise it would have picked up our scent and made some kind of noise."

Nancy said no more and in a short time she and the health inspector reached the Billington house. She thanked him for his help and jumped out of the car.

Bess and George met her at the front door. "Thank goodness you're here in one piece," said Bess.

George asked, "Did you learn anything exciting?"

Nancy related her experience to the girls, Mrs

Billington, and Hannah Gruen. All of them tried guessing what might be beyond the steel door where the furniture had been piled up.

"Even though Mr Wilcox doesn't think so," Bess put in, "I'll bet there's some kind of an animal behind that door."

"You could be right," Mrs Billington said, frowning.

George had a different theory. "I'm sure Fortin only keeps those wild animals to scare people away and isn't training those beasts to perform. There's some other reason he and Longman are living at the moss-covered mansion."

"Like what?" Bess asked.

"There could be all kinds of secret rooms," her cousin replied.

Nancy was intrigued by this idea. "They might even be storing explosives!"

Bess stared at her friend. "Are you hinting that Mr Fortin might have been responsible for the explosive oranges that were shipped into the Space Centre?"

George answered. "I wouldn't put it past him."

Mrs Billington looked worried. "If you're right and anything should go wrong, the whole of Merritt Island could be blown up!"

Nancy turned to Hannah. "You haven't said a word. What do you think?"

Looking worried, the housekeeper replied that their suspicions about the moss-covered mansion should be reported to the FBI.

Nancy pointed out, "But it's mostly speculation—we haven't any constructive evidence."

She also reminded the others that the FBI had a good

lead about the person responsible for stealing the
oranges and delivering them to the Space Centre. He
was Max Ivanson. The man had disappeared and not
been found yet.

When Mr Drew and Mr Billington came in, the
results of Nancy's visit to the moss-covered mansion
were reported to them. The men were as interested in
the story as the others had been. They had no solutions
to offer.

Mr Drew said that he had obtained a postponement
of Mr Billington's trial. "I have some other news, too,"
he added. "I found out there's no Tripp Brothers Circus
listed. Of course that doesn't mean there isn't one. It
may be too small and unimportant to be in the police
information files."

"I'm sure," Nancy said, "that the whole thing is a
cover-up for something sinister."

Bess sighed and changed the subject. "While you
were out, Nancy, we had a call from Mrs Nickerson.
Ned and Dave and Burt will be down tomorrow."

Nancy's face broke into a smile. How glad she would
be to see Ned! "And it will be great to have him help
on the mystery," she thought.

Bess told Nancy that she and George had been busy
laundering the girls' clothes, including Nancy's. "So
we're all ready for the Nickersons' house party," she
told her.

"You were sweet to do that," said Nancy. "Thanks."

She learned that Tina and Antin had the day off, so
all the work had fallen on the others.

"Would you mind doing the shopping?" Mrs
Billington asked Nancy. "We need a number of things.

Perhaps you three girls could go and divide the shopping list."

"I'd like to," Nancy replied. "By the way, do you have the Websters' new address?"

"No, I'm sorry I don't."

Nancy decided to stop at the post office on the chance she could get it. She said, "Mrs Billington, I don't trust Mr Scarlett and I'd like to check his story with the owner."

The girls drove to town and each went in a different direction to buy meat, vegetables, fruits, paper napkins and various other items.

As soon as Nancy finished her shopping, she walked to the post office. There she asked if she might have Mr Webster's other address, and told why she wanted it.

The postal clerk smiled but said he was not allowed to give out such information. "If you wish to write a letter and mail it, I'll be glad to forward it."

"I'll think about that," Nancy replied and turned away.

A woman who stood nearby had heard the girl's request. Now she came up to her and said, "I'm a friend of Mr and Mrs Webster. I know their city address. Would you mind telling me in more detail why you want it?"

Nancy explained the complication about the couple's Merritt Island home and that she wanted to speak directly to Mr Webster about its being taken off the market.

The woman smiled. She took an address book from her handbag and flipped the pages to W. Then she wrote down the address of her friends, the Websters, and handed it to Nancy.

"Thank you very much," Nancy said. "As soon as I get home, I'll phone them."

As the young detective was about to leave the post office, she saw something that made her step back quickly. Walking along the street and carrying on an animated conversation were Mr Scarlett and Mr Fortin!

"They *are* friends," she decided. "I wish I could hear what they're talking about."

This was not feasible because Scarlett would identify her and tell Fortin. Perhaps Fortin had already described her to Scarlett and he in turn had told who she was!

Nancy waited until the men were out of sight, then went to the Billingtons' car where the girls had arranged to meet. When Bess and George heard about the men, they agreed with Nancy that no doubt she had been identified.

"This means more trouble!" Bess prophesied.

As soon as Nancy reached home she telephoned Mr Webster long-distance. He answered immediately. Nancy introduced herself and told why she was calling.

"I'm certainly glad you got in touch with me," Mr Webster said. "I can't understand Mr Scarlett's actions. He has had no instructions from me to take my Merritt Island house off the market. I'll call him at once and set him straight."

"You may have a hard time finding him," Nancy remarked. "He says he's on vacation, and no one answers the doorbell at his house. However, I've seen him several times. Mr Scarlett even chased me in his car while I was on my way to the airport to meet my father. He demanded that I return the key which he had lent me."

"You have the key?" Mr Webster asked. "In that case, you keep it and go into the house as often as you please."

Nancy told him about her experiences at the moss-covered mansion. "Didn't the wild animals bother you?" she asked.

"No. In fact, I doubt if they were there then."

Nancy mentioned the friendship between Fortin and Scarlett. Mr Webster was amazed.

"It certainly sounds as if something phony is going on. I'll give your father a long option on the house and notify Mr Scarlett he no longer has it on his list."

"That's very generous of you," said Nancy. "My father will be in touch with you."

Mr Drew and Mr Billington had gone out again. They did not return until dinnertime that evening.

"I have nothing new to report, Nancy," her father said. "How about you?"

Nancy told him of her telephone talk with Mr Webster. The lawyer was delighted to hear of the long option on the Webster house. "I know that if the mystery of the moss-covered mansion can be cleared up, you'd like me to buy the place."

His daughter laughed. "I guess I'd like it anyhow, but I admit we'd certainly have strange neighbours."

"Who could be very dangerous," Bess put in.

Suddenly Hannah Gruen said, "Oh, I forgot!"

All eyes turned in her direction. She went on, "There was a personal advertisement in today's paper that caught my eye. Using the code words 1, 5, 9, and 13 the message read, 'Beam ready for action.' "

Each one at the table pondered the words. "What do they mean?" George asked. "This message is the hardest one yet."

The others agreed but no one had an interpretation to offer. After dinner Nancy sat down in a big chair in the living room and stared straight ahead of her.

Mr Drew said, "That brain of yours is cooking up something. How about telling us what it is?"

Nancy told them she had come up with a daring idea to help solve the mystery. "Using the numbered words code, I'll run a personal advertisement in Sunday's paper. It will arrange a meeting for the people who are communicating through the personal column."

"That's a clever idea!" her father said. "I wish you luck."

Nancy found a notebook and pencil. She drafted message after message but was not satisfied with any of the combination of words. The whole sentence must make sense as well as the code words. Finally the others said goodnight and went upstairs. An hour later Nancy heard the Resardos' car pull into the driveway.

"Oh dear! I don't want them to see these papers," she thought and quickly gathered them up.

When she reached her room, the young detective sat down to continue her work. Just as sleep was overtaking Nancy, a new idea for the wording of the personal advertisement came to her.

"I have it!" she told herself.

·15·

Stolen Car

NEXT morning nothing was said about the personal advertisement which Nancy wanted to put in the newspaper. The Resardos hung around, so the others kept their conversation to inconsequential matters.

Finally Antin went off to the grove, presumably to see what fruit might still be saleable. Tina was unusually talkative. She assisted with all the work and even offered to help make the beds.

"Thank you but that won't be necessary," Hannah Gruen told her.

She was as eager as the girls to hear what Nancy had worked out on the code message. She kept Mrs Resardo on the ground floor, however, so the rest could go upstairs and talk out of earshot.

They gathered in Nancy's bedroom. Bess, bursting with curiosity, asked, "Nancy, did you finish the coded message?"

"Yes," she replied, and took a sheet of paper from her handbag. The others crowded around to see it.

"Does that sound innocent enough?" she asked her father.

"Very good, my dear," he replied. "I see you have underlined the vital words." He read it aloud:

" '*Meet round ship museum Monday twelve.*' "

"Where is that?" Mr Drew asked.

Nancy explained it was in Cocoa Beach. "The museum has a replica of one of the Spanish Plate Fleet vessels which went down in 1715 off the coast of Cape Kennedy, then known as Cape Canaveral.

"One of the worst hurricanes on record drove the ships on to the rocks. Nearly everyone on board was drowned. Only one ship escaped and returned to Spain to tell the story."

Mr Drew nodded. "At that time the Spaniards had conquered the Aztecs in Mexico and were robbing them of all their exquisite gold objects. These in turn were made into Spanish coins and packed in boxes and shipped to Spain."

Mr Billington added, "Some of this treasure has been salvaged. The museum contains many gold coins and pieces of eight as well as other treasures. You'll be intrigued when you see them."

"Sounds great!" George said. "Nancy, I take it that you hope the coded message will be seen by the men involved in the explosive oranges mystery, and they'll gather outside the museum."

Nancy nodded. "Once we see who they are, we can report them to the authorities."

"That's right," Mr Drew said. "Don't try capturing them yourself!"

Nancy laughed and said she would like to put the ad in the paper at once. "May I borrow your car?" she asked Mr Billington.

"Yes indeed."

Mr Drew smiled. "I have a surprise for you girls.

Yesterday I rented a car for you to use during the rest of your stay here. It had to be serviced, so I said you'd pick it up this morning." He took the receipt from his pocket and handed it to Nancy.

"Wonderful, Dad!" she exclaimed, and kissed him. "Thank you loads. George and Bess can bring your car back, Mr Billington."

"No hurry, Nancy. Your father and I have some work to do here on the case. We'll be around until after lunch."

The three girls left the house and drove directly to the newspaper office. Nancy handed in her coded message for the personal column and paid for it. She was assured it would appear the following day.

As Nancy and the other girls strolled outside, Bess asked, "What's next?"

Nancy said she wanted to tell Mr Scarlett that she had Mr Webster's permission to keep the key, in case the agent had not already been informed.

"We're not far from his office. Let's see if he's there."

She drove to it but found the door locked. She went to his home. No one answered the doorbell.

A woman in a neighbouring yard called out, "The Scarletts aren't here. They drove off early this morning."

"Thank you," Nancy said. "I'll leave a note for Mr Scarlett."

She took a sheet of paper from her bag and wrote down the message. Then she slipped it through the slot in the front door.

"When do we get our car?" George queried.

"Right now."

Nancy headed for the centre of Cocoa Beach and

drove to the rental agency. Bess and George waited for her while she went into the office. Nancy showed the receipt and the clerk led her to a car park at the back of the building. He pointed out an attractive tan estate car.

"It looks new," Nancy said, delighted.

"It's practically new," the man told her. "I don't know why the owner wanted to sell it. Normally we don't buy private cars but this was such a good bargain we couldn't pass it up."

Nancy eagerly got behind the wheel and waved to the girls. George started the Billington car and headed for home. Nancy chose a different route. She was making good time along the highway when suddenly a motorcycle roared up behind her. Riding it was a policeman.

"Pull over!" he ordered. "Let me see your licence."

Nancy was sure she had done nothing wrong but did not question the officer. She showed him her licence.

"Where did you get this car?" he asked.

Nancy gave the name of the rental agency and showed the receipt. The officer looked at her sharply, then said, "Are you aware you're driving a stolen car?"

The young detective gasped. "I certainly wasn't."

"Follow me!" the motorcycle policeman said. "We'll go back to that agency and see what it's all about."

The man in charge was shocked when he learned about the theft. He assured the policeman he was innocent, and explained that his company had purchased the car from an individual.

"What was his name?" Nancy asked.

"Rimmer," the clerk said. "Robert Rimmer."

The policeman said, "I suggest that you give this young lady another car and a new receipt."

The exchange was made and Nancy went on her way. When she reached home and told about the incident, Hannah Gruen began to laugh. "Nancy Drew," she said, "it seems as if you can't go anywhere without having an adventure."

"But I just love it," Nancy replied with a broad grin. "Dad, have you any news?"

"No, I've been checking to find out if there has been any word on Max Ivanson. It certainly looks as if he's the one who carried the explosive oranges into the Base."

Mr Billington spoke up. "And there's no clue to who set fire to the packing house and started the blazes in the grove. Ivanson might have done that too."

He added, "I'm well-covered by insurance, but a lot of time will be lost in building up a grove. You can construct a packing house fairly quickly, but you can't make an orange tree grow overnight!"

All this time Tina had been buzzing around, setting the table and going up and down the hall. Nancy suspected that the woman was not missing a word of the conversation.

Presently the Drews and their friends sat down to luncheon. Mrs Billington asked, "Nancy, what time are the boys arriving?"

"We're to meet them at the airport at four o'clock," she replied. "By the way, we're not officially starting the house party until tomorrow. We girls thought it would be nice to give Ned a chance to visit with his parents before we all move in there. And Mrs Nickerson agreed."

Soon afterwards the girls began their long drive to the Melbourne airport. The plane was on time. Ned was the first of the boys to alight. Seeing Nancy, he rushed up to her.

"How's my little sleuth?" he asked, kissing her.

"I'm fine and have a million things to tell you."

Bess and George had found Dave and Burt. On the way to the Nickersons' the boys plied the girls with questions.

"We're going to start you working on the mystery Monday," Nancy told them. "At noon we're to station ourselves at the Real Eight Treasure Museum and see if we can spot a few criminals."

"You mean it?" Dave asked.

Nancy explained her plan and the boys were eager to help.

Ned remarked, "Thinking up that coded message was pretty clever, Nancy."

"I only hope it works," she answered.

The boys were dropped off at the Nickerson home. They said they would come over to see the girls after dinner. "Is there some place we could all go and have fun?" Burt asked.

"I have an idea," said Nancy. "The Billingtons have a lovely motorboat. Why don't we make use of it?"

"Good idea," Dave remarked. "I'll bring my guitar."

The three boys arrived at eight o'clock. Nearly an hour was spent talking with Mr Drew and the Billingtons. Since the Resardos were out, the mystery could be discussed freely.

"It sounds complicated to me," Dave remarked. "I'd like to have some time free from mystery. May we borrow your boat?" Mr Billington nodded.

"I'll get the *Starbeam*'s key," Nancy said. She had noticed it on top of the TV set.

The young people excused themselves and walked down to the dock. Nancy turned on the boathouse lights, then she and her friends climbed into the motorboat.

"Which way?" asked Ned, who had taken the wheel.

Nancy suggested that he turn right and cruise around for a while, then come back and go past the Webster property.

Half an hour later they pulled up to the Webster dock. "The house!" Bess exclaimed. "It's all lighted up!"

Everyone was puzzled. Had Mr Drew stopped in? Or was an intruder there?

"We'd better investigate," Nancy said quickly. "Ned, let's tie up at the dock."

He pulled alongside and the group scrambled out. While the boys secured the boat, the girls ran ahead. They had not gone far into the small orange grove when the lights in the house were extinguished one by one. When the visitors reached the back door, the place was in total darkness.

"Watch to see who comes out," Nancy called to Bess and George. She herself ran round to the front entrance. No one emerged from the house. By this time the boys had caught up.

"Do you suppose someone's hiding in there?" Bess asked Dave.

"Could be," he replied.

Nancy turned to Ned, who had found her. "Will you go back and use the phone in the boat? See if Dad is there and whether he has been here."

Ned hurried off. The others continued to watch the house, but nobody appeared.

Finally Ned returned. "Your father hasn't been here, Nancy," he reported. "But Mr Drew said he'll be right over."

In a short time the lawyer arrived with Mr Billington. "Did you bring the Websters' house key, Dad?" Nancy asked.

"No. None of us knew where you had hidden it," he answered.

"In my raincoat pocket," she said. "It's in my wardrobe."

Mr Drew had brought several flashlights which he distributed among the three couples.

"Let's look through the windows," Nancy suggested, and beamed hers through a front window.

"Oh!" she exclaimed. "The place is flooded with water!"

Misfit Shoes

"A PIPE must have burst!" Nancy cried out. "Oh dear! I wish I'd brought the key. We must do something fast!"

Mr Drew decided to break a windowpane and crawl inside the house. Ned offered to do it and Nancy's father nodded his agreement.

"But go around to the back where the break won't show," Mr Drew suggested.

Ned dashed off with the rest of the group following. As if about to kick a football, Ned made a run of several feet, lifted his right foot, and aimed it at a kitchen window.

Crash!

Ned reached inside, opened the latch, and raised the window frame. He pulled himself through the opening and unlocked the rear door. The others trooped inside. Nancy, making sure she was standing in a dry spot, clicked on the kitchen light.

Less than two feet away water was slowly flowing towards her! The taps in the sink had been turned on full and water was pouring out. It was spilling over the edge and cascading on to the floor. George jumped forward and turned off the taps.

At once a search for the intruder began. Mr Drew

called out, "Don't touch any switches if you are standing in water!"

"I won't," Bess assured him. "I don't want to be electrocuted."

Water had already flowed into the other ground floor rooms. It was also spilling down the stairway. Burt and Dave rushed up to shut off taps in the bathrooms.

"Ned, let's look for the main valve and turn off the water," Nancy suggested. "I think it may be in the laundry room."

The two dashed into the room adjoining the kitchen. They found that the taps in a sink and a laundry tub had also been opened. Ned closed them, while Nancy looked for the main valve. She located it and turned off the flow.

When everyone assembled in the living room to compare notes, each declared he had seen no sign of the intruder.

"I guess he escaped by the front door before you got there, Nancy," Burt stated.

Bess gave a great sigh. "I'd say we have an all-night mopping job ahead of us!"

Dave grinned at her. "You forget I'm mop-up man for the Emerson football team. It won't take long. Let's go!"

Every broom, mop, and rag in the house was put to use. George and Burt found a couple of electric fans and plugged them in.

"Operation Dry-out is in good hands," Mr Drew said with a grin.

He and Mr Billington returned home ahead of the young people. The front light was on. As the two men walked up to the door, Mr Drew bent down and picked up a shiny object.

"What is it?" Mr Billington asked.

"A key. Someone must have dropped it."

Mr Billington took the key. "This isn't ours," he said. "Why, look, it has the letter W cut into it."

"W?" Mr Drew repeated. "Do you suppose it could stand for Webster? Maybe this is the key Nancy hid. Someone may have stolen it, then had no opportunity to replace the key, so he left it here."

When the men entered the house, Mr Drew told Hannah Gruen about the find.

"That's strange," she said. "Nobody has come here this evening except the Resardos and they've been in their room all the time."

"Nancy hid the Webster key in her raincoat pocket," Mr Drew remarked.

"I'll get it," Hannah offered.

Mrs Gruen was gone only a couple of minutes, then returned holding the key. They compared it with the one Mr Drew had found. It matched exactly.

"Queer things happen every day," Hannah remarked. "I wonder what will be next."

Mr Drew did not answer. He went to the telephone and spoke to the police captain about the flooded house and the key he had found on the doorstep. The officer promised to send a couple of men to the Webster house immediately.

Over at the soaking wet home the mopping-up operation was almost finished.

Nancy and Ned searched the house but found no clues to the intruder. While they were still hunting, the police car came in. Nancy spoke to the two men.

"The intruder must have had a key to this house," she said.

The police identified themselves as Needham and Welsh. They told of Mr Drew's having found a key with a W on it near the Billingtons' front steps. Nancy and Ned looked at each other. Had Scarlett dropped it—or perhaps Antin?

As she and Ned walked to the rear of the house with the two officers, Nancy beamed her flashlight towards the river.

Suddenly she exclaimed, "I see some large shoe prints!"

They stepped forward to examine them. "The guy sure has big feet," Needham commented. "I think we should take plaster impressions of these." He requested his partner to drive back to headquarters for the equipment.

Nancy knelt on the ground and examined the prints, which went towards the water. Did she imagine it or were they wobbly looking, as if the person was unsteady on his feet?

"Or," Nancy thought, "did the intruder deliberately put on shoes much bigger than his feet to disguise his size? He even took long strides and that too could account for the wobbliness."

She and Ned and Officer Needham followed the prints. Possibly the vandal had hidden a small boat among the bushes along the shore. The three made a thorough search but the only boat around was the Billingtons'.

The officer stopped to look at it. "She's a beauty!"

he said. "It's a good thing that intruder didn't help himself to it!"

"It's locked," Ned said, "and I have the key in my pocket. Apparently the vandal escaped in his own boat."

By the time the searchers had returned to the house, Officer Welsh had come back with the plaster cast kit. While he was working, Nancy and Ned took his partner through the house, pointing out the damage.

The officer made a lot of notes and said the case would be put on the police blotter at once and a search started for a tall man with long feet. Nancy mentioned her own theory about his wearing oversize shoes and Needham was impressed.

"That's an idea," he said. "I'll jot it down."

Just then Officer Welsh came in. He said he had completed his work and if Needham was ready they might as well leave. The lights were turned off and the front door slammed shut.

As Nancy and her friends trudged through the orange grove and down to the river, Burt remarked, "We boys didn't have to wait long after our arrival for some excitement."

"It always happens," Bess added. "I vote that for the rest of the evening we forget about detective work."

She had hardly said this when George and Burt, who had started ahead, cried out in dismay.

"Our boat's gone!" George exclaimed.

The others ran to the dock. They could not believe their eyes. Mr Billington's motorboat had been securely tied and Ned had locked the motor.

"There's only one way it could have been taken," Nancy spoke up. "It was towed away!"

"By whom?" Dave asked.

No one had an answer. A few seconds later Bess gave one of her great sighs. "It's a long trek from here to the Billingtons' house."

"It sure is," George agreed, "but let's get started."

Nancy said, "You all go and ask Mr Billington to call the police about the stolen boat. Ned and I will stay here a while. I want to hunt for clues to the thief."

The other four hurried off. With her flashlight Nancy searched for footprints.

"Here they are!" she cried gleefully. "The thief was the same person who was up at the house!"

Ned looked at her, puzzled. "But how could he have been? We were down here after he'd gone and our boat was still at the dock."

Nancy pointed out that the man could have towed the boat away when the police and everyone else were in the house.

"Or he might have been hiding up the shore a distance and a pal came to pick him up. Together they tied Mr Billington's craft to a motorboat and went off."

Just then they heard a motorboat in midstream. "Let's hail it!" she said. "Maybe the pilot passed our boat."

Ned shouted lustily. The pilot heard him and slowed his motor. He steered for the Webster dock and called out, "Somebody need help?"

Quickly Ned explained. The pilot said he had not seen the stolen craft, but added, "How about hopping in here and we'll look for it?"

Nancy and Ned did not need a second invitation. As soon as the motorboat pulled up to the dock, they climbed in.

·17·

Tear Gas

NED introduced Nancy and himself. Their teenage pilot said his name was Bud Musgrove. As his small motor-boat sped along, they looked into every cove and indentation of the river, going up one side, then starting down the other. So far there had been no sign of the Billingtons' craft.

"I'm sorry," Bud said. "You say you have the key to the motor, Ned. Then the person who took your boat might have known about it and has a duplicate. Have you any idea who he is?"

Instantly Nancy thought of Antin, but said nothing. Was he accustomed to borrowing the craft whenever he pleased?

She asked herself, But why should he have gone to the Webster home? As Nancy was trying to puzzle this out, Ned suddenly exclaimed, "I think I see our boat! Over there at that rickety old dock."

Bud headed for the spot. A house on the property had burned down. The area was secluded.

"It's a good place for someone to hide a stolen boat," Nancy thought. "And for a thief to hide too!" Aloud she said, "Cut the motor! Quick!"

Bud obeyed. In the sudden silence Nancy spoke softly. "The thief may be hiding there, too. Let's go quietly and take him by surprise!"

The momentum of the craft carried it along quietly as Bud steered towards the dock. He pulled alongside the stolen boat.

"No one's in it," Ned announced. He looked around. "I guess this has been abandoned." He pulled the key from his pocket and jumped in.

Nancy was about to follow, but Bud held her back. "Better wait and see if the *Starbeam* starts."

Ned turned on the motor but there was not a sound. He tried again and again without result.

"That thief probably tampered with the boat and now it won't run," Nancy remarked. "Is the motor warm?"

"No," Ned replied, "so the *Starbeam* must have been towed here."

Bud jumped into the craft and together he and Ned examined the engine while Nancy beamed a searchlight on it.

Finally Bud said, "Several parts are missing. You won't be able to run this boat until they're replaced. I'll tell you what. Let's tie it to the back of my motorboat and I'll tow you home."

"Great! Thanks," Ned replied.

When they arrived at the Billingtons' dock Nancy invited Bud to come in.

The young man smiled. "Sorry, but I'm supposed to be on my way to a party. My date will think I've jilted her."

The group at the house was amazed when they heard

Nancy and Ned's story. Mr Billington called the police to report that the boat had been found.

He said to the others, "I'm certainly burdening the authorities lately. We make at least one call a day to the police!"

Everyone smiled and Nancy thought, "We've come up with a few clues for them, too!"

Bess told Ned that his mother had phoned and was preparing a midnight snack for the young people. She was hoping the girls would move over there at once to start the house party officially.

"I'm all for that," Bess added, "Tonight's adventures have given me a tremendous appetite."

George teased her cousin. "You'd have had an appetite without any adventures."

The three girls hurried upstairs and packed the clothes they would need for the next few days. When they were ready to leave, Nancy promised her father she would keep in touch with him and the Billingtons to exchange news about the case. Mr Drew said he would contact Mr Webster and tell him of the vandalism.

"I'll ask him if he wants to have someone in town take care of it or if he'd like me to."

As he kissed his daughter goodnight, Mr Drew wished her luck in getting results on Monday to her personal advertisement.

"Maybe you'll find out who the members of the gang are. Anyway, my dear, watch your step."

Nancy and Ned rode in the rented car, while the others took the Nickersons'. Despite the fact that the official opening of the house party lasted until almost two o'clock, none of the young people slept late the next morning.

After they had attended church services, Dave suggested that the whole group take a tour of the Space Centre that afternoon. The others agreed.

Nancy was just as intrigued by her second visit to the Base as she had been before. The boys were especially fascinated by the rocket soon to lift off for the moon.

George, who had been silent for several minutes, said, "I'd like to be an astronaut. What do you think my chances are?"

"Oh no!" Bess exclaimed. "Suppose you went to the moon and got stranded there!"

Smiling, Nancy remarked that she too would like to become an astronaut.

Ned grinned and said, "How about letting us boys go first? We'll tell you how it is."

The bus driver, who had overheard the conversation, seemed to be amused. He turned slightly and said, "You boys had better get started on your training. While you're here, why not go for a physical check up and briefing?"

"Great!" Burt replied with a wink.

George leaned forward in her seat. "What about me? Could I get the same treatment?"

"I think so," the driver answered, grinning broadly.

The others looked at Nancy. "How about you?" Ned asked.

"Perhaps," she replied, knowing they were kidding her. "After this case is over."

In a short time the bus reached the Vehicle Assembly

Building. The tourists went inside. They were told about the immense structure and what took place there.

Then the guide said, "The space vehicle that will lift-off for the moon on Tuesday was transported from here to its launch pad several weeks ago."

Nancy and her friends were the first to leave the building. They wanted to get a better view of the huge spaceship.

As they were coming out the door, two men, heavily bearded, came up to them. "Pardon me," said one. "We're doing an article on the moon flight for a science magazine. Would you mind if we take your picture, and quote what we overheard you say on the bus about wanting to be astronauts?"

The six young people looked at one another but did not answer.

"Over here," said the second man who had a large camera. "We won't use your names."

He led the way round the corner to the side of the building away from the tourists.

"I guess there's no harm in it," Ned whispered to Nancy.

She nodded and followed the two men down the far side of the building. While one arranged the group against the wall with the girls in front, the other man focused his camera.

"All ready," he said.

His companion dashed out of the way and the photographer pressed the shutter. Instantly a stream of tear gas shot towards them. Nancy and her friends tried to run, but their eyes began to smart and they could not see.

In the distance the guide was calling out, "All aboard!"

Nancy heard running footsteps and assumed their attackers had fled. As the fog of tear gas dissipated, Nancy was able to see dimly, but not well enough to move very fast for fear of bumping into something. She realized, however, that a man was coming towards her.

He proved to be one of the guards from the Vehicle Assembly Building. Rushing up, he asked, "What happened?"

Nancy choked out the answer. "Tear gas! Two men with beards. One man had a camera that shot the stuff at us."

"Follow me!" the guard said. "We'll give you something to soothe your eyes."

"My friends too!" Nancy told him.

She could vaguely make out the rest of her group. Nancy called to them to follow her.

By the time they reached the front door of the Vehicle Assembly Building, the bus had gone. Nancy said there was a chance the attackers were on it.

"Hadn't you better phone the Visitors Centre and have the bus checked?" she asked the guard.

"I'll do that at once—that is, as soon as I find someone to take care of your eyes."

Suddenly Nancy remembered the young engineer who was a relative of Hannah Gruen's. She asked, "Is Herb Baylor around? I know him."

"I'll get him," the man promised, and hurried off.

When Herb Baylor saw Nancy and the rest of the group and heard what had happened, he instantly took them to the infirmary where a young doctor gave them first aid. He put a few drops of a soothing solution in their eyes which soon relieved the burning sensation.

There was a knock on the door and the same guard walked in. He was holding two wigs with beards attached and a camera. "I found these at the side of the building," he said.

Nancy gasped. "The men who used the tear gas must have been wearing them!"

Ned added, "Now we can't describe those villains and they'll get away easily!"

"Too bad," Herb remarked. "What was their motive?"

George answered, "To scare us into dropping our detective work. But they can't do it!"

·18·

A Ruse Works

HERB Baylor thought Nancy and her friends should return to the Nickersons at once. "Take it easy," he advised.

The young people were glad to, and went to bed early. By morning everyone felt fine. A few hours later they set off for the Real Eight Museum of Sunken Treasure, reaching Cocoa Beach by five to twelve. Quickly Ned parked out of sight of the front entrance. Nancy and her friends took up positions behind posts on the covered patio of the octagonal-shaped building.

Exactly at twelve o'clock a car pulled in near the entrance. A few moments later a second one drew up behind it. Then a third and a fourth automobile stopped. A man got out of each car and the four assembled on the broad walk leading to the building.

Nancy's heart was pounding. One of the men was Scarlett, another was Antin!

"So Antin *is* one of the gang," she thought.

There was a heavy-set stranger. "That must be Max Ivanson!" Nancy decided. "He looks very much like that photograph I saw."

The last person to come towards the building was a young man.

Nancy thought, "Could he be the 'son' in the personal advertisements? His face looks familiar. Why do I think I know him?" Then it suddenly dawned on her. He strongly resembled Mr Fortin, the owner of the moss-covered mansion.

The men came closer and then stopped to talk. Nancy could hear them plainly. Each inquired about who had written the personal advertisement in Sunday's paper. When all of them denied having done it, looks of fright spread over the men's faces.

"I'll bet the FBI found out about our code," said the heavy-set man. "I'm leaving!"

He ran to his car and the others fled to theirs. Moments later they roared off.

"Shall I chase any of them?" Ned asked.

Nancy replied, "Try Ivanson."

Ned and Burt rushed off and soon were out of sight.

Meanwhile Nancy had raced inside the museum to telephone her father. She paid the admission fee and dashed into a booth. Mr Drew was astounded at what Nancy had discovered.

"I'll inform the police of this development," he told her. "They will certainly question Antin and search his room. I'll also clue the authorities in on who the other men are that may be responsible for the explosive oranges."

Nancy had remembered to jot down the licence numbers of the men's cars and now gave these to her father. "Good work!" he said.

When Nancy emerged from the phone booth, Dave and the other girls stood waiting and demanded to know what was going on. In whispers she told them.

"Oh, Nancy," said Bess, "you've all but solved the case!"

Nancy did not think so. George was eager to go to the Billington house to learn the climax.

"But we have no car," Nancy replied. "We don't know when the boys will be back. Meanwhile, since we've all paid our admission, let's look at the exhibits."

A young woman came up to them and said, "You forgot to take your tapes and earphones. The tapes tell you all about the exhibits. Start on the left."

They went back to a counter where she handed each of them one of the little boxes to hold. They plugged in the tiny earphones. The tour began.

In the centre of the room stood a replica of one of the ships dashed to pieces on the Florida coast in 1715. The old-time vessel had sailed entirely under canvas and for this reason was no match for a violent tropical storm.

Around the circular wall was a panorama of the history of the cargo carried aboard these Spanish vessels that sailed between the homeland and the New World. The treasures on display were from ten of the eleven vessels in the ill-fated Plate Fleet.

As Nancy listened to the tape she learned that the Spaniards had subdued the Aztec Indians and made slaves of many of them. They were forced to work their gold and silver mines and fashion the metal into Spanish coins, jewellery, and other objects. Overseers were often cruel and the slaves worked long hours.

Other scenes showed gold ingots being packed into boxes, and gold and silver coins in others. Moving on, Nancy and her friends listened carefully to the running account on their tape recorders. Many of the objects on exhibit, such as sabres and sword handles, dishes and bracelets, were encrusted with coral.

Nancy found Bess rooted to one of the glass cases. "Isn't that touching?" she asked, pointing to a small wedding ring imbedded in coral. "It's so little, a tiny woman must have worn it. Maybe she was the wife of one of the captains."

George walked up. She had heard Bess's remark and said, "I can't find much sympathy for those people. They were just plain thieves."

Nancy commented, "They certainly ruined the Aztec civilization, which in many respects was far above that of their conquerors."

Before leaving the museum, Nancy and her friends went into the gift shop. The articles for sale fascinated them. Everyone bought pieces of jewellery made from gold or silver dug from the bottom of the ocean.

Nancy purchased a lovely necklace of pieces-of-eight coins for her Aunt Eloise in New York. She decided on a bracelet made of silver coins for Mrs Billington, and a large piece-of-eight brooch for Hannah Gruen.

After the young people had looked at everything in the shop, they left the building. Ned and Burt were just returning.

"Any luck?" George asked.

"No," Ned answered. "All the men disappeared in the next town. We couldn't find them or their cars."

"Let's go home," Nancy urged.

Bess insisted that they eat lunch before going to the Billingtons'. The boys found a lunch stand. Everybody was ravenously hungry except Nancy. She tried to hide the fact that her curiosity was getting the better of her but her friends sensed it.

"I'll eat this hamburger as fast as I can," Bess told her.

Nancy laughed. "Don't get indigestion!"

She ordered a lobster-salad sandwich and declared it was the best she had ever eaten.

"No dessert!" Ned spoke up. "I know Nancy's itching to leave and I am too!"

When they pulled into the driveway of the Billington home, a police car was there. Nancy and her friends hurried into the house.

There was wild confusion in the living room. Tina was screaming at a policeman that her husband was innocent of any wrongdoing. Antin was shouting that he was the victim of a frame-up.

At that moment a policeman and an FBI agent came down the stairs. The FBI man was carrying a bomb which he said had not yet been activated. The officer held supplies used in constructing homemade bombs. Nancy and her friends were told that Tina and Antin were attempting to move their possessions out when the officers arrived.

After advising the couple of their constitutional rights, the agent asked, "Mr and Mrs Resardo, if you're innocent, how do you account for these things?"

Instead of replying, the couple tried to make a dash for the front door. They were quickly stopped and brought back, but refused to admit anything.

Nancy whispered to the detective, "May I ask the prisoners a question?"

"Yes, go ahead. But of course they don't have to

answer without having their own lawyer present."

The young detective looked directly at the Resardos. "Who set the fire in Mr Billington's grove?" There was no response.

She tried another approach. "Is Max Ivanson a pal of yours?"

This question startled the Resardos, but they remained silent. Seconds later the prisoners were taken to jail.

Hannah Gruen gave a great sigh. "I'm glad they're gone," she said. "Imagine their making bombs right in this house!"

"Please don't talk about it!" Bess begged. "It makes chills go up and down my spine."

She wandered outdoors, more upset than she wished to admit. Dave had followed her and suggested that they all do something pleasant and get away from the mystery for a while.

"Like what?" she asked.

Dave thought for a moment, then said, "How about going to the Webster house to see if it has dried out yet?"

Bess liked this idea and so did the others. They climbed into the rented car and Ned slid into the driver's seat.

When they reached the Webster place, Burt said, "We couldn't see much of the grounds in the dark last night. Let's walk around now."

The boys were intrigued by the unusual trees in the garden, particularly the sausage tree. Everyone went over to it.

Suddenly they heard snarling in the jungle on the

other side of the fence. The young people shrank back just as the panther came running from the direction of the cages.

"He's loose again!" Bess cried out.

Directly behind the animal was Longman with his whip. He kept snapping it against the ground and shouting to the beast. The panther paid no attention. Snarling and hissing, the agile beast climbed the fence.

The next moment he made a flying leap across it and landed in the sausage tree next to the young people.

19

The Mansion's Secret

BRANCHES of the sausage tree broke under the panther's weight. They crashed to the ground, together with several of the hard, twelve-inch melon-like fruit.

Screaming, Bess dashed towards the Webster house. She kept urging the others to follow her.

"Run! Run!"

Longman, on the other side of the high fence, seemed stunned for a couple of seconds. Then he cried out, "Catch this and slash that beast!" He tossed the whip to the boys.

Nancy, to avoid being recognized by the animal trainer, turned and ran to the house. In the meantime Burt and Dave had each grabbed a broken branch with the heavy sausage-shaped fruit and were ready to ward off the animal if he should attack.

As Ned caught the whip, he yelled to Nancy and George, "Open the garage door! We'll chase the panther in there!"

This was easier said than done. At first the panther refused to come down from the tree. Then, responding to Longman's commands, he made a great leap towards the fence, but missed it and dropped to the ground.

Ned cracked the whip in the air and on the ground.

The beast started to make another leap, then stopped. Lowering his head, he looked balefully at Burt and Dave and crouched as if about to spring at them. The two boys waved their tree-branch clubs in the air. By now the panther was thoroughly confused.

With Ned working the whip and his friends flourishing their fruit-laden branches, the frightened beast was finally driven into the garage. Quickly George and Nancy yanked down the door.

Inside, the panther set up a fearful racket. Above the loud snarls, the young people heard Longman call, "Keep him there! I'll get my van!"

While they were waiting for the trainer to come, an idea suddenly came to Nancy. She said to Ned, "This is our chance to get into the basement of the moss-covered mansion and find out what's behind the steel door. Will you go with me?"

Ned's eyes opened wide in amazement. "You mean ride in the van with the panther?"

"Of course not," Nancy answered. "After the animal is inside and Longman is in the driver's seat, you and I can quickly climb up to the roof of the van and lie flat. He won't know we're there and we can get off before he opens the van door."

Ned replied, "You know you're taking a terrible chance, Nancy. But I'm game to go with you."

To the surprise of everyone, Bess came speeding up the driveway in their car. They had assumed she was in the house.

She jumped out and said excitedly, "I brought some meat with a tranquillizer in it."

"You what?" George asked.

Bess explained that she had noticed a doctor's sign on a house in the next block. She had driven over there and explained to him what had happened. He could not come himself but had given her the chunk of raw meat with a tranquillizer pill imbedded in it.

The others stared at her in amazement. Finally Nancy said, "That's wonderful, Bess. It was quick thinking."

Dave took the chunk of meat. As the others carefully lifted the garage door a couple of inches, he poked the food inside. Then the door was shut tight again.

The enraged animal apparently sniffed at the meat, then ate it, because for a few minutes there was silence. Again he began to howl objections, but this time they did not last long.

"Bess, you're the heroine of the occasion!" George told her cousin. She grinned. "And you know I don't say that often."

The others laughed, heaving sighs of relief. When they saw Longman's van coming, Nancy and Ned moved to another side of the house, so she would not be seen by the animal trainer. Bess and George followed.

As he jumped down, Burt told him that they had tranquillized his panther. He looked at the boy disbelievingly. "How?" he asked.

Burt explained what Bess had done. "That tranqulilizer should keep your animal quiet for a while."

"Very good." Longman looked around and asked, "Where are your friends?"

No one answered his question. But Dave said quickly, "Let's get to work. You'd better move the panther to your place before the tranquillizer wears off."

"That's right," said Longman, and opened the rear door of his van.

The young people saw that a cage had been fitted inside. Longman opened the gate to it.

Burt and Dave rolled up the garage door gradually, in case the panther was not asleep as they thought. This precaution was unnecessary, for the beast lay peacefully on the floor. It took the combined strength of Longman and the two boys to lift the panther into the van. Then the cage gate and the van door were locked. The animal trainer murmured something that sounded like "thanks," and swung himself up into the driver's seat.

Instantly Nancy and Ned came from hiding. In a jiffy they had climbed to the van's roof and lay face down. By holding on to each other with one hand and grabbing bars along the sides with the other, the couple felt reasonably secure. Silently their friends watched them leave, hoping for safety and success.

Fortunately there was no one on the road to observe the two stowaways. The van turned into the grounds of the moss-covered mansion. When it reached the fence at the house, Longman got down and unlocked a gate. Then he drove through. The gate swung shut and locked itself.

Nancy saw a clump of bushes which would make a good hiding place. She whispered to Ned, "Here's where we get off."

The van was going so slowly towards the animal cages that the couple accomplished this easily without being injured. Instantly they dodged behind some bushes.

After Longman had unloaded the panther, he

secured the beast's cage with a double lock. Then he drove off.

"Now what?" Ned asked Nancy.

"I'm sure there's an outside entrance to the basement," she said. "Let's see if we can get in."

Luck was with them. They found a narrow door on the opposite side of the house. It was unlocked!

"Someone may be in there!" Ned cautioned in a whisper. "Let me go first."

Carefully he pushed the door open. It made no sound. The couple stepped inside. They were in the large basement room where Nancy had come with Inspector Wilcox.

The first thing she noticed was that all the debris had been moved away from the walls. Several doors were revealed. On tiptoe she and Ned walked towards the first one and Ned opened it. The place was well lighted and before them was a swimming pool filled with steaming, boiling water!

Nancy and Ned looked questioningly at each other. What was the pool used for, they wondered. Ned quickly closed the door. They moved to the steel door where the load of furniture had fallen on Nancy two days earlier.

In the room beyond, also well lighted, was an amazing laboratory. A complicated-looking machine with a dish-shaped parabolic reflector stood in the centre of the floor. It faced the outside wall, which was made of glass building blocks.

"What is it?" Nancy whispered.

Ned walked around the machine, squinting at the various parts. He came back to Nancy and said, "Unless

I'm all wrong, it's a very powerful transmitting antenna—a beamer."

"You mean some kind of signal is sent out from down here?" Nancy asked.

"Yes," Ned replied. "The telescope you told me about that's in the tower may act as a sighting device. It could locate the exact bearing and elevation of an object to be destroyed by the beamer."

Nancy was horrified. The telescope was aimed directly at the rocket scheduled for lift-off the next morning. She also thought about Antin's phone message regarding R-day. Instead of meaning Ruth, it could have referred to Rocket day.

"Ned," she said quickly, "would you know how to deactivate this machine?"

"I can try," he said. "But Fortin would have time to fix it before the launch."

"Meanwhile we could send the police here," Nancy told him.

Ned found some tools on a workbench near a series of wall cabinets. He worked with the tools for several minutes.

Presently she and Ned heard voices. To their amazement they were coming through a loudspeaker in the ceiling.

While listening, Nancy felt that no doubt Fortin, if it was necessary, could barricade himself in the laboratory and listen to conversations taking place upstairs. It would be a means of finding out how trustworthy his fellow conspirators were.

The couple recognized two voices as those of the tear-gas assailants at the Space Centre. Nancy and Ned learned that Fortin was a clever and well-known scientist who had once been connected with NASA. He had become imbued with the ideology of a foreign power and was now using an assumed name.

He had entered into a conspiracy to undermine the U.S. space programme and had agreed to cause great damage at the Centre and to wreck the moon rocket. To accomplish this he had a spy working with the men in top-secret procedures. From this traitor Fortin had obtained the secret signals for the exact frequency and modulation for lift-off. In this way he could set his beamer to destroy the rocket.

Nancy whispered tensely to Ned, "He'll be murdering the astronauts!"

Just then Fortin spoke up. "Scarlett," he said, "I'm paying you off but not so much as I promised if you had done a good job."

Scarlett whined, "I did the best I could. I discouraged people from looking at the Webster house, but when Nancy Drew arrived, she was determined to see it. I pretended to go on vacation but she found me. I flooded the place to keep the Drews away, but she discovered it in time to avert any great damage."

"That's enough," said Fortin. "Ivanson, you certainly bungled that explosive orange deal. You were supposed to put those oranges around in strategic spots, so the lift-off would be delayed until my beamer was perfected. Luckily I have it ready in time."

Ivanson said belligerently, "You don't know what it feels like passing yourself off as somebody else even if I look like him. Fortunately they didn't examine the oranges while I was there. I guess Billington delivers lots of oranges to the Base, and since I had his truck, they must have thought the delivery was all right. I had no chance to drive around, though. A guard got aboard and directed me to the Space Centre food supply depot and made me leave the sacks there."

"Here's your money," said Fortin. "Get out of here and never let me see you again."

A younger voice spoke. "Dad, I want to leave and go far away. I'm through!"

Fortin laughed. "You couldn't take care of yourself, son. You haven't been able to hold a job. I kept you away from here and even forbade phone calls so you wouldn't be involved if anything went wrong. You did think up that great father-son code but that backfired. We don't know yet who figured it out. But you came here to hide in case it was the FBI."

Young Fortin was not to be put down so easily. "If you expect me to stay, you've got to get rid of every one of those wild animals. You know they scare me to death."

Longman shot back, "We need those wild animals here to protect us."

"What's the latest news on Antin?" Fortin asked.

His son replied that a newscast had reported both the Resardos were in jail.

"What!" the scientist shouted. "There's no telling what they'll say to the authorities!"

"I can assure you," said one of the tear-gas attackers, "they won't talk. I made it pretty plain that if they ever did, their lives wouldn't be worth a nickel. And don't forget, boss, the Resardos did some good work. They stole those photographs and passed them over to us so we'd recognize Mr Drew and the girls and their boy friends.

"Antin found out where they were going so we could watch them. Stevie here and I fooled them completely at the Vehicle Assembly Building and knocked them out with tear gas."

During the ensuing conversation Nancy and Ned learned that it was Max Ivanson who had started the fires in the Billington grove.

"Another stupid idea," complained Fortin.

Ivanson defended his actions. "I thought Drew would get scared and send his daughter and her friends home, but nothing shakes that bunch loose."

Scarlett grumbled, "Until Nancy Drew came along, we had the charge of the explosive oranges pinned neatly on Billington."

Nancy whispered to Ned, "I think we'd better go before some of those men come down here. Besides, we should notify the authorities at once!"

The two tiptoed to the door through which they had entered. They were taken aback when the huge form of Longman appeared in the opening.

"You!" he cried and reached up to push a button on the wall. An alarm sounded upstairs.

"Let us out!" Ned demanded.

The towering Longman looked at the couple in amusement. "We have a special treatment for snoopers."

Nancy and Ned tried to break past him, but his huge, powerful body blocked the doorway like a stone wall.

Within seconds footsteps pounded down the stairway from the kitchen. Fortin appeared, leading the rest of his gang.

He glared at Nancy. "So you finally found out my secret. But you won't have a chance to tell anyone else. Ivanson, you and Stevie take these young detectives,"— he sneered—"and put them in the room with the steaming pool!"

·20·

Countdown

EXERTING every bit of resistance they could, Nancy and Ned tried to escape from their captors. But their efforts were futile. They were shoved towards the room with the boiling pool and put inside.

"That's what happens to snoopers!" Fortin shouted excitedly. "I won't be thwarted in what I intend to do!"

The heavy door was swung shut and locked. The captured couple was forced to hug the wall since the ledge round the water was only six inches wide.

"Oh, Ned, I'm so sorry," Nancy said. "It's all my fault. I never should have asked you to come to this place with me."

"I certainly wouldn't have let you come alone," he replied. "Let's not give up hope of rescue."

Nancy nodded. Surely as soon as their friends realized Nancy and Ned had been gone too long, they would make a search.

"Only I hope they won't be captured as we were!" she worried.

Nancy and Ned tried changing their positions but almost tumbled into the water. To keep their balance they stood as straight and immobile as wooden soldiers.

"Something's got to break soon!" Ned remarked. "Maybe some of our captors will be afraid of a worse charge if they're arrested and the authorities find us in this pool. One of them may open the door."

No one did, however. Nancy and Ned assumed the men had left the basement. As the couple shifted their gaze, they noticed two tiny barred openings in the walls near the ceiling. One evidently admitted fresh air from the outside, the other from the basement.

Meanwhile, back at the Webster house the other young people were becoming more and more alarmed about their missing friends. Burt and Dave paced up and down the front yard. Bess nervously rumpled her hair, then smoothed it out and in a few seconds repeated the operation.

Finally George burst out, "We've got to do something! I just know Nancy and Ned were caught in a trap!"

The rest agreed. "We've waited long enough," said Burt.

Bess offered to drop the others off at the moss-covered mansion. "I'll drive over to the Nickersons and get help."

When they reached the entrance, George and the two boys got out of the car and set off along the winding road that led through the jungle. They listened and watched carefully.

"Do we dare pound on the door?" George asked.

Both boys vetoed this idea. "We'd surely be captured," Dave replied.

By this time Bess had reached the Nickersons. When Ned's father heard her story, he immediately rushed to the telephone. First he called Mr Drew and Mr Billington, who notified NASA headquarters. He reported the group's suspicions regarding the activities of the occupants in the moss-covered mansion, and the disappearance of Nancy and Ned.

"We'll send men at once," the man at NASA promised.

Mr Billington telephoned the local police, who also said they would rush to the suspected house immediately.

Twenty minutes later, just as Nancy and Ned felt completely discouraged, they heard a loud commotion outside.

"Open up!" came a shout.

The couple heard no reply, but moments later there was a stampede of footsteps on the stairway to the basement. Fortin's voice rang out, "Police! NASA agents! FBI! Open the secret lock, Longman! Let the animals loose!"

The pounding on the front door became more insistent and a voice cried out, "Open in the name of the law!" Inside the house the two dogs were barking madly.

The noise, coupled with Fortin's orders to release the wild animals, made chills go up and down the spines of Nancy and Ned.

"This is horrible!" she wailed.

Her remark was followed by screams from outside the house. Then came a roar. Had the animals attacked the law-enforcement men?

Suddenly there was silence in the basement. Moments later a voice called out, "Nancy! Ned! Where are you?"

Mr Drew!

"Oh, Dad," Nancy cried out, "open the door that's below the vent near the ceiling."

Within seconds the heavy door was unlocked and opened. Nancy and Ned had inched along the ledge of the steaming pool and now literally fell into the arms of their waiting friends.

Bess gave a scream of horror. "Oh, you might have fallen into the boiling water!"

Nancy and Ned were pretty shaken by their experience, but recovered in a few minutes.

"Who's with you?" Nancy asked.

"FBI and NASA men and the police," George replied.

Quickly the couple reported what they had overheard before being captured. "I think I've deactivated the machine in the laboratory, but a NASA expert had better check," Ned said.

He walked over to open the heavy steel door to the laboratory. It would not budge. They all looked for a way to unlock it but could not find any.

"Let's go upstairs," Mr Billington suggested. "I want to see what's happening."

They hurried to the kitchen and watched from a window. There was a great deal of excitement on the grounds of the moss-covered mansion. Tranquillizer guns were being used on the escaping animals. Finally all of them were quietened.

Longman came from the house with a policeman and one by one they dragged the beasts into their cages, then locked the gates. Looking around furtively, Longman tried to escape but was caught and taken indoors.

The Drews and their friends found that the suspects, handcuffed, had been herded into the living room. Nancy and Ned were asked to come forward and tell the officers what they knew.

Before beginning, Nancy looked over the assembled crowd. Fortin was missing!

"The ringleader—the scientist—isn't here!" she exclaimed.

Nancy was assured that the man could not have left the house because it had been surrounded.

"Then I believe he's hiding in his laboratory," she stated.

Nancy led the NASA and FBI men downstairs, while the police stayed to guard the other prisoners. Engineers from the Space Centre tried to unlock the steel door but concluded it must be fastened inside.

Nancy and Ned pleaded with them to break in. "I tried to deactivate the beamer that's going to destroy the rocket," he said, "but I can't be sure I was successful."

One FBI man suggested that they use a steel drill, but a NASA engineer said, "No. Vibrations might set off the beamer."

Nancy caught her breath. Suppose Fortin had decided not to wait until the next day to use his nefarious machine! He might blow up the rocket at any minute!

Quickly she told about the telescope in the tower which she and Ned believed was part of Fortin's set up.

Ned added, "Perhaps it's a sighting device to locate the exact bearing and elevation so Fortin can aim the parabolic reflector antenna in his workshop."

"We'll go right up there," one engineer stated. He and the two FBI men hurried to the second floor.

Meanwhile, the other NASA man put a radiation detector against the steel door. The results were negative.

Nancy and Ned returned to the living room. The saboteurs waived their constitutional rights to have a lawyer present and confessed their guilt. All were taken to jail except Longman.

"He will remain here with two detectives until the authorities can make arrangements for the wild animals to be moved," said one of the policemen.

The trainer told them he had become involved in Fortin's sabotage plan after forging the scientist's name on some bank cheques. To avoid arrest, he had acceded to Fortin's demands that he care for the animals and keep intruders away.

"Fortin is a brilliant man," Longman went on as the other prisoners were led off. "But he became obsessed with some dangerous political ideas and joined a radical group. I'm glad he's going to be prevented from doing the terrible thing he planned."

George asked Longman about the boiling pool. "Did Fortin build it?"

"Yes. It was one of his cruel ideas to dispose of intruders in case his animals didn't get them."

The trainer was questioned about how the authorities could get into the laboratory but he declared he did not know. They also asked him if Fortin could destroy the rocket from his basement laboratory. Again Longman insisted he did not know.

Guards were left at the moss-covered mansion inside

and out. Two FBI agents had been stationed in the basement. Periodically they tried to persuade Fortin to give himself up but there was no response from inside the laboratory.

The Drews and their friends had mixed feelings about the mystery. It had been solved, but the instigator of the dreadful plot might still be able to destroy the rocket and possibly the three astronauts as well.

When they reached the Nickerson home, the young people were bombarded with questions by Ned's mother. She took a sensible view of the whole matter.

"I'm sure that if there is the slightest bit of doubt about the safety of those astronauts, NASA will not allow them to climb into the rocket."

Harbouring this comforting thought, everyone went to bed feeling a little better. They were up and dressed by six the next morning. During breakfast they watched the television news. According to the report the moon launch was planned for nine o'clock and at the moment all systems were go.

When the young people reached the building where the news media offices were located, they signed in. Together they walked out to get into buses and were taken to the Press Site.

"What a huge place!" Bess remarked.

The structure was really a large covered stadium. On each tier were long counters containing telephones. Behind them were rows of chairs, each one numbered. Nancy's group climbed the steps and found seats which had been assigned to them.

Men were bustling about, many with cameras, some

with tape recorders, others with portable typewriters. Nearly everyone had binoculars.

In front of the Press Box was a long open lawn beyond which the Banana River gleamed in the sunlight. Near the shore, television and newspaper cameras had been set up by photographers. Across the river on Merritt Island stood the rocket, about three miles away, with condensed moisture, caused by the liquid oxygen, pouring from the base of it.

Every few minutes there would be an announcement and the young people would hold their breath. Was the countdown still on and would the rocket take off?

"Oh I hope Fortin was captured and had no chance to use a secret device to hurt the astronauts!" said Bess.

"I hope so too," Nancy replied.

There was a long wait before lift-off time. Nancy asked Ned if he would go with her to inspect the various trailers she had noticed off to one side of the Press Box. They went down and were told that these contained the broadcasting stations. Stepping across numerous cables, the couple walked along the row, then turned back. Behind the Press Box they found a snack bar.

"Let's grab a bite," Ned suggested.

While he bought hamburgers and milk, Nancy tried to phone the Billington house, but all the circuits were busy. When she and Ned returned to their seats, they learned that their friends had also been down to get a second breakfast.

As the countdown drew nearer zero, everyone who had been wandering around came to take their seats. Typewriters were clicking everywhere and cameras with telephoto lenses were busy.

Nancy wondered if ever again she would be so excited. Some time later she encountered another mystery, *The Hidden Staircase*, which also brought her some harrowing adventures.

It was five minutes to nine. The countdown for the moon shoot proceeded. Finally the announcer called out the final seconds:

"*Three . . . two . . . one . . . zero!*"

There was a burst of orange, green, and yellow gases from the base of the rocket. As it zoomed upwards, enveloped in a multi-coloured cloud, the noise was ear-splitting and the grandstand shook as if a giant hand were shaking it violently.

"It's off!" someone shouted.

Nancy and her friends were holding hands, their nails pressing into one another's palms.

"Nothing is wrong so far!" Nancy thought, as a white vapour trail formed behind the spaceship. "Oh, I hope —I hope—"

The rocket curved slightly and in a few moments disappeared among the clouds. Bess said shakily, "Ev-everything's A-OK!"

Seconds before this, a shout of triumph had gone up from the onlookers. Nancy and her friends did not cry out. Instead they were silently saying prayers of thankfulness.

When Nancy was breathing normally again she picked up the telephone in front of her. The main switchboard connected her with the Billington house.

Mr Drew answered. "I knew it was you," he said. "Everything's A-OK here too. Fortin finally gave himself up, and his spy was caught. The transmitting antenna was ruined. The news was immediately telephoned to the Cape. This is why the astronauts were allowed to climb into the rocket and it was able to lift-off on time."

"Oh, Dad, that's wonderful!"

The lawyer chuckled. "You'll be interested to know that Fortin blames his failure on your detective work. But I'm terribly proud of you!"

Have you seen
NANCY DREW
lately?

Nancy Drew has become a girl of the 80s! There is hardly a girl from seven to seventeen who doesn't know her name.

Now you can continue to enjoy Nancy Drew in a new series, written for older readers – THE NANCY DREW FILES. Each book has more romance, fashion, mystery and adventure.

In THE NANCY DREW FILES, Nancy pursues one thrilling adventure after another. With her boundless energy and intelligence, Nancy finds herself enrolling at a crime-ridden high school, attending rock concerts and locating the missing star, skiing in Vermont with friends Bess and George and faithful boyfriend Ned, and temping at a teenage magazine based in wildly exciting New York.

COMING IN SPRING 1988

The Nancy Drew Files

No. 1 Secrets Can Kill
No. 2 Deadly Intent
No. 3 Murder on Ice
No. 4 Smile and Say Murder

ARMADA

STEVIE DAY SUPERSLEUTH
(that's me!)

I'm on my way to being the first female Commissioner of the Metropolitan Police. It's true I have a
few personal problems: for a start I'm small and
skinny and people are always mistaking me for a
boy. I'm 14 – though you wouldn't think so – and
my younger sister, Carla, not only looks older than
me but she's much prettier too. Not that that really
matters. You see, she doesn't have my brains.

If you want to see my razor-sharp mind in action or
have proof of my brilliant powers of deduction then
read about my triumphant successes in:

STEVIE DAY: Supersleuth
STEVIE DAY: Lonely Hearts
STEVIE DAY: Rat Race

Forthcoming teenage fiction
published in Armada

Class of 88 1–4
Linda A. Cooney

In A Spin
Mark Daniel

Nightmare Park
Linda Hoy

Sin Bin 1–4
Keith Miles

Run With the Hare
Linda Newbery

ARMADA

'Furst's ⟨...⟩ ⟨...⟩ ⟨...⟩ears of humanity under pressure ... It is a thri⟨...⟩ ⟨...⟩ith real people and real history. I cannot wait fo⟨...⟩ ⟨...⟩xt Furst'
    Denis MacShane MP, Minister fo⟨...⟩ ⟨...⟩is 2001–05,
                                                                        Independent

'Intensely cinematic ... the ⟨...⟩ure is rich and the Furst-world closes around ⟨...⟩with an agreeable chill from the outset' *Times Lite⟨...⟩ Supplement*

'The literary style belies a deftly paced plot in an old-fashioned spy thriller more reminiscent of John Le Carré and Graham Greene than Ian Fleming. Highly recommended' *Irish Times*

'Alan Furst ... has set standards that none of his feted contemporaries can match' *Sunday Telegraph*

'Complex, intelligent and highly intriguing – Alan Furst is in a class of his own' William Boyd

'Furst's research is such that one gets the impression he hasn't just travelled, he has time-travelled. He evokes beautifully the haunted precarious existence of Europeans caught up in the march of war' *Financial Times*

'Furst's tales ... are infused with the melancholy romanticism of Casablanca, and also a touch of Arthur Koestler's *Darkness at Noon*' *Scotsman*

'Mr Furst excels at period atmosphere ... His characters are wonderfully human: complex and ambiguous, fearful and determined ... Mr Furst is a subtle, economical writer who knows precisely when to stop a sentence' *Economist*

'Furst [is] so pleasurable and rewarding to read' *Spectator*

Alan Furst is the author of eleven highly acclaimed espionage novels, including *The Foreign Correspondent*, *Red Gold* and *The World at Night*. He has lived for long periods in France, especially in Paris, and has travelled as a journalist in Eastern Europe and Russia. He has written extensively for *Esquire* and the *International Herald Tribune*. Visit his website at www.alanfurst.co.uk

By Alan Furst

Night Soldiers
Dark Star
The Polish Officer
The World at Night
Red Gold
Kingdom of Shadows
Blood of Victory
Dark Voyage
The Foreign Correspondent
The Spies of Warsaw
Spies of the Balkans

SPIES OF THE BALKANS

Alan Furst

PHOENIX

A PHOENIX PAPERBACK

First published in Great Britain in 2010
by Weidenfeld & Nicolson
This paperback edition published in 2011
by Phoenix,
an imprint of Orion Books Ltd,
Orion House, 5 Upper St Martin's Lane,
London WC2H 9EA

An Hachette UK company

1 3 5 7 9 10 8 6 4 2

A CIP catalogue record for this book
is available from the British Library.

ISBN 978-0-7538-2726-0

Typeset by Input Data Services Ltd, Bridgwater, Somerset

Printed and Bound in Great Britain by Clays Ltd, St Ives plc

The Orion Publishing Group's policy is to use papers
that are natural, renewable and recyclable products and
made from wood grown in sustainable forests. The logging
and manufacturing processes are expected to conform to
the environmental regulations of the country of origin.

www.orionbooks.co.uk

In August of 1939, General Ioannis Metaxas, the prime minister of Greece, told a Roumanian diplomat 'that the old Europe would end when the swastika flew over the Acropolis.'

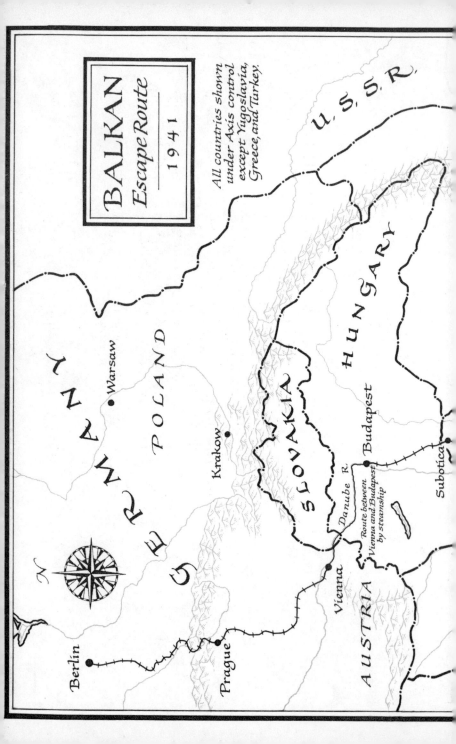

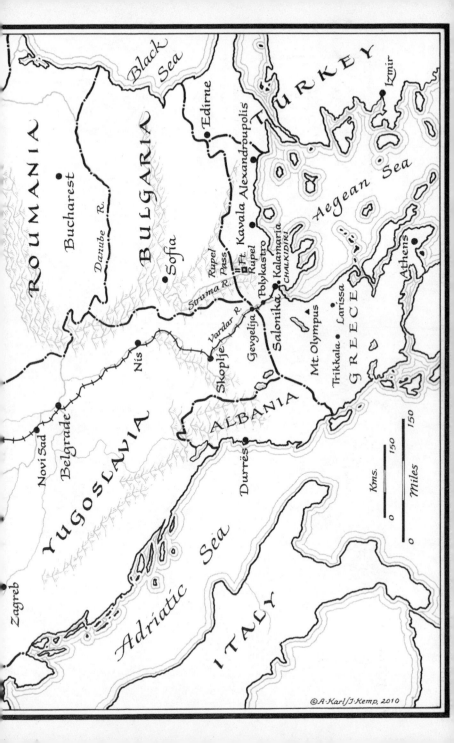

DYING IN
BYZANTIUM

In autumn, the rains came to Macedonia.

The storm began in the north – on the fifth day of October in the year 1940 – where sullen cloud lay over the mountain villages on the border of Bulgaria and Greece. By midday it had drifted south, heavier now, rolling down the valley of the Vardar River until, at dusk, it reached the heights of the city of Salonika and, by the time the streetlamps came on, rain dripped from the roof tiles in the ancient alleyways of the port and dappled the surface of the flat, dark sea.

Just after six in the evening, Costa Zannis, known to the city as *a senior police official* – whatever that meant, perhaps no more than a suit instead of a uniform – left his office on the top floor of an anonymous building on the Via Egnatia, walked down five flights of creaky wooden stairs, stepped out into the street and snapped his umbrella aloft. Earlier that day he'd had a telephone call from the port captain, something to do with the arrival of the Turkish tramp freighter *Bakir* – 'an irregularity' was the phrase the captain used, adding that he preferred to pursue the matter in person. 'You understand me, Costa,' he'd said. Oh yes, Zannis understood all too well. At that moment, Greece had been ruled by the Metaxas dictatorship since 1936 – the length of women's skirts was regulated; it was forbidden to read aloud the funeral oration of Pericles – and people were cautious about what they said on the telephone. And, with much of Europe occupied by Nazi Germany, and Mussolini's armies in Albania, on the Greek frontier, one wasn't sure what came next. So, *don't trust the telephone.* Or the newspapers. Or the radio. Or tomorrow.

Entering the vast street market on Aristotle Square, Zannis furled his umbrella and worked his way through the narrow aisles. Rain pattered on the tin roofing above the stalls, fishmongers shouted to the crowd, and, as Zannis passed by, the merchants smiled or nodded or avoided his eyes, depending on where they thought they stood with the Salonika police that evening. A skeletal old woman from the countryside, black dress, black head scarf, offered him a dried fig. He smiled politely and declined, but she thrust it towards him, the mock ferocity of her expression meaning that he had no choice. He tore the stem off, flicked it into the gutter, then ate the fig, which was fat and sweet, raised his eyebrows in appreciation, said, 'It's very good, thank you,' and went on his way. At the far end of the market, a sponge peddler, a huge sack slung over his shoulder, peered anxiously out at the rain. Marooned, he could only wait, for if his sponges got wet he'd have to carry the weight for the rest of the night.

The customs house stood at the centre of the city's two main piers, its function stated on a broad sign above the main entry, first in Greek, then with the word *Douane.* On the upper floor, the port captain occupied a corner office, the sort of office that had over the years become a home; warm in the chilly weather, the still air scented with wood smoke and cigarettes, one of the port cats asleep by the wood-stove. On the wall behind the desk hung a brightly coloured oleograph of Archbishop Alexandros, in long black beard and hair flowing to his shoulders, hands clasped piously across his ample stomach. By his side, formal photographs of a stern General Metaxas and a succession of port officials of the past, two of them, in fading sepia prints, wearing the Turkish fez. On the adjoining wall, handsomely framed, were the wife and children of the present occupant, well fed, dressed to the hilt and looking very dignified.

4

The present occupant was in no hurry; a brief call on the telephone produced, in a few minutes, a waiter from a nearby *kafeneion* – coffee house – with two tiny cups of Turkish coffee on a brass tray. After a sip, the captain lit a cigarette and said, 'I hope I didn't get you down here for nothing, Costa. In such miserable fucking weather.'

Zannis didn't mind. 'It's always good to see you,' he said. 'The *Bakir*, I think you said. Where's she berthed?'

'Number eight, on the left-hand side. Just behind a Dutch grain freighter – a German grain freighter now, I guess.'

'For the time being,' Zannis said.

They paused briefly to savour the good things the future might hold, then the captain said, '*Bakir* docked this morning. I waited an hour, the captain never showed up, so I went to find him. Nothing unusual, gangplank down, nobody about, so I went on board and headed for the captain's office, which is pretty much always in the same place, just by the bridge. A few sailors at work, but it was quiet on board, and going down the passageway towards the bridge I passed the wardroom. Two officers, gossiping in Turkish and drinking coffee, and a little man in a suit, with shiny shoes, reading a newspaper. German newspaper. Oh, I thought, a passenger.'

'See his face?'

'Actually I didn't. He was behind his newspaper – *Völkischer Beobachter*? I believe it was. Anyhow, I didn't think much about it. People get around these days any way they can, and they don't go anywhere at all unless they have to.'

'Submarines.'

The captain nodded. 'You may just have to swim. Eventually I found the captain up on the bridge – a man I've known for years, by the way – and we went back to his office so I could have a look at the manifest. But – no passenger. So, I asked. "Who's the gent in the wardroom?" The captain just looked at me. What a look!'

'Meaning . . .?'

5

'Meaning *Don't ask me that*. Life's hard enough these days without this sort of nonsense.'

Zannis's smile was ironic. 'Oh dear,' he said.

The captain laughed, relieved. 'Don't be concerned, you mean.'

From Zannis, a small sigh. 'No, but it's me who has to be concerned. On the other hand, as long as he stays where he is . . . What's she carrying?'

'In ballast. She's here to load baled tobacco, then heading up to Hamburg.'

'You didn't happen to see the passenger come this way, did you?'

'No, he hasn't left the ship.'

Zannis raised an eyebrow 'You're sure?'

'I've had a taxi waiting out there all afternoon. If he tries to enter the city, two beeps on the horn.'

This time the sigh was deeper, because Zannis's plans for the evening had vanished into the night. 'I'll use your telephone,' he said. 'And then I'll take a little walk.'

Zannis walked past the taxi on the pier – the driver awake, to his surprise – then continued until he could see the *Bakir*. Nothing unusual; a rust-streaked grey hull, a cook tossing a pail of kitchen waste into the bay. He'd thought about ordering up a pair of detectives, then decided not to get them out in the rain. But now the rain had stopped, leaving in its place a heavy mist that made halos around the streetlamps. Zannis stood there, the city behind him quiet, a foghorn moaning somewhere out in the darkness.

He'd turned forty that summer, not a welcome event but what could you do. He was of average height, with a thick muscular body and only an inch of belly above his belt. Skin a pale olive colour, not bad-looking at all though more boxer than movie star, a tough guy, in the way he moved, in the way he held himself. Until you looked at his face, which suggested quite a different sort of person. Wide generous mouth and, behind steel-framed spectacles, very blue eyes: lively eyes. He had dry black hair which, despite being combed with water in the morning, was tousled by the time he reached the office and fell down on his forehead and made him look younger, and softer, than he was. All in all, an expressive face, rarely still – when you spoke to him you could always see what he thought about whatever you said, amusement or sympathy or curiosity, but always something. So, maybe a tough guy, but your friend the tough guy. The policeman. And, in his black suit and soft grey shirt, tie knot always pulled down and the collar button of the shirt open, a rather gentle version of the breed. On purpose, of course.

He'd certainly never meant to be a cop. And – once he fell into being a cop – never a detective, and – once promoted to that position – never what he was now. He'd never even known such a job existed. Neither of his parents had been educated beyond the first six years; his grandmother could neither read nor write, his mother doing so only with difficulty. His father had worked his way into half-ownership of a florist shop in the good part of Salonika, so the family was never poor; they managed, pretty much like everyone else he knew. Zannis wasn't much of a student, which didn't matter because in time he'd work in the shop. And, until 1912, Salonika had remained a part of the Ottoman Empire – Athens and the western part of the nation having fought free of the Turks in 1832 – so to be Greek was to know your place and the sort of ambition that drew attention wasn't such a good idea.

By the age of twelve, as the Greek army marched in to end the Second Balkan War, Zannis's private dreams had mostly involved escape; foreign places called to him, so maybe work on a ship or a train. Not unusual. His mother's brother had emigrated to America, to a mysterious place called Altoona, in the state of Pennsylvania, from whence postal cards arrived showing the main street or the railway station. Until 1912, at times when the money ran out, the Zannis family considered joining him, working in his diner, a silvery building with rounded corners. Yes, maybe they should go there; they'd have to talk about it. Soon.

And, six years later, they did leave, but they didn't go to Altoona. In 1917, as Anglo-French and Greek forces fought the Bulgarians in Macedonia, a sideshow to the war in France, Salonika burned, in what came to be known as the Great Fire. The Zannis house, up in the heights by the ancient battlements, survived, but the florist shop did not, and there was no money to rebuild. Now what?

It was his father's brother who saved the day. He had, as a young man, involved himself in fighting the Turks, with a pistol, and the day came when, threatened with life in a Turkish prison, he had to run away. He ran to Paris, mostly walking or riding trains without a ticket until they threw him off, but in time he got there.

And, with luck and determination, with playing cards for money, and with the advent of a jolly French widow of a certain age, he had managed to buy a stall in the flea market in Clignancourt, in the well-visited section known as Serpette. 'Forget Altoona,' he wrote in a letter to his brother. 'I need you here.' A little money was sent and the Zannis family, parents and grandmother, Costa and his younger brother – an older sister had earlier married an electrician and emigrated to Argentina – got on a fruit ship and worked their way to Le Havre. And there, waving up at them from the wharf, was the benevolent uncle and his jolly wife. On the train, Zannis's heart rose with every beat of the rails.

Two hours later, he'd found his destiny: Paris. The girls adored him – soon enough he fell in love – and he had a lot of money for a seventeen-year-old boy from Greece. He worked for his uncle as an *antiquaire*, an antiques dealer, selling massive armoires and all sorts of junk to tourists and the very occasional Parisian. They had a magnificent old rogue with a great white beard who

8

turned out Monets and Rubenses by the yard. 'Well, I can't say, because it isn't signed, maybe you should have somebody look at it, but if the nice lady comes back in twenty minutes, as she swore she would, we'll have to sell it, so if I were you . . .'

The happiest time of his life, those twelve years.

At least, he thought later, it lasted that long. In 1929, as the markets crashed, Zannis's father went to bed with what seemed like a bad cold then died a day later of influenza, while they were still waiting for the doctor. Bravely, Zannis's mother insisted they stay where they were – Costa was doing so well. By then he spoke good French – the lingua franca of Salonika – and he'd taken courses in German and learned to speak it well: some day the stall would be his, he'd met a woman, Laurette, a few years older than he and raising two children, and he was enchanted with her. A year earlier they'd started living together in Saint-Ouen, home to the Clignancourt market. But, as winter turned to spring, his mother's grief did not subside and she wanted to go home. Back to where she could see her family and gossip with friends.

She never said it aloud but Zannis, now head of the household, knew what she felt and so they went home. Laurette could not, or would not, leave with him, would not take her children to a foreign place, so her heart was broken. As was his. But family was family.

Back in Salonika, and urgently needing to make a living, he took a job as a policeman. He didn't much care for it, but he worked hard and did well. In a city where the quarter known as the Bara held the largest red-light district in eastern Europe, in a city of waterfront dives and sailors of every nation, there was always plenty of work for a policeman. Especially the tolerant sort of policeman who settled matters before they got out of hand and never took money.

By 1934 he was promoted to detective and, three years later, to, technically, the rank of sub-commander, though nobody ever used that title. This advancement did not just happen by itself.

An old and honoured expression, from the time of the Turkish occupation, said that it was most fortunate to have a *barba sto palati*, an uncle in the palace, and it turned out, to Zannis's surprise, that he had that very thing. His particular talent, a kind of rough diplomacy, getting people to do what he wanted without hitting them, had been observed from on high by the head of the Salonika police, a near mystic presence in the city. Vangelis was at least eighty years old, some said older, with the smile of a saint – thus St Vangelis, at least to those who could appreciate irony and veneration in the same phrase. For fifty years, nothing had gone on in Salonika that the old man didn't know about, and he'd watched Zannis's career with interest. So in 1937, when Zannis decided to resign his position, Vangelis offered him a new one. His own office, a detective, a clerk and a greatly improved salary. 'I need someone to handle these matters,' Vangelis told him, and went on to describe what he needed. Zannis understood right away and in time became known to the world at large as *a senior police official*, but to those with knowledge of the subterranean intricacies of the city's life, and soon enough to the Salonika street, he was simply 'Zannis'.

Was the Belgian consul being blackmailed by a prostitute? Call Zannis.

Had the son of an Athenian politician taken a diamond ring from a jeweller and refused to pay for it? Call Zannis.

Did a German civilian arrive 'unofficially' in Salonika on the freighter of a neutral nation?

When Zannis walked back to the foot of the pier he found his assistant, Gabriel – Gabi – Saltiel, waiting for him, smoking a cigarette, leaning back in the driver's seat. Saltiel loved his car, a hard-sprung black Skoda 420, built by the Czechs for Balkan roads. 'Pull over behind the wall, Gabi,' Zannis said. 'Out of sight, where we can just see the pier.'

Saltiel pushed the ignition button, the engine rumbled to life and he swung the car around and headed for the customs house. A grey fifty-five, Saltiel, tall and shambling, slump-shouldered and myopic, who viewed the world, with a mixture of patience and cynicism, through thick-framed glasses. A Sephardic Jew, from the large community in Salonika, he'd somehow become a policeman and prospered at the job because he was intelligent, sharp, very smart about people – who they really were. And persistent – a courteous, diffident bulldog. On the day that Vangelis offered Zannis the new job, saying, 'And find somebody you can work with,' he had telephoned Gabi Saltiel, explained what he'd be doing and asked Saltiel to join him. 'What's it called, this department?' Saltiel said. 'It doesn't need a name,' Zannis answered. Ten seconds passed, a long time on the telephone. Finally, Saltiel said, 'When do I start?'

Now Zannis headed for the taxi, gave the driver some money, thanked him and sent him home. When Zannis slid into the passenger seat of the Skoda, Saltiel said, 'So, what's going on?'

Zannis repeated the port captain's story, then said, 'As long as he doesn't enter the city, we leave him alone. We'll give him a few hours to do something, then, if he's still holed up in the ship, I'll get some detectives to replace us.'

'What if he waits until morning, strolls down here and shows a passport to the control officer?'

'Follow him,' Zannis said. 'I don't want him running loose in the city.'

'German, you said.'

'Reads a German newspaper, who knows what he is.'

'A spy, you think?'

'Could be. The Turkish captain more or less said he was. With a look.'

Saltiel laughed. 'The Levant,' he said. 'A look indeed – I wouldn't live anywhere else.' After a moment he added, 'What's a spy after in Salonika? Any idea?'

'Who knows. Maybe just the war, coming south.'

'Don't say such things, Costa. Down here, at the arse-end of the Balkans, who cares?'

'Not Hitler. Not according to the newspapers. And he has to know what goes on here, up in the mountains, when we're occupied.'

Saltiel looked thoughtful. 'Still,' he said.

'What?'

'Well, I have a nephew who teaches at the technical school. Geography, among other things. A smart boy, Manni, he says that as long as Hitler stays allied with the Russians, we're safe. But, if he attacks them, we could be in for it. On the map of Europe we're the right flank – if somebody's heading east, the right flank that goes to the Caucasus, for the oil. Anyhow, that's Manni's theory.'

'Believe it?'

Saltiel shrugged. 'Hitler's cunning, I wouldn't say intelligent, but cunning. Jews he attacks, Russians he leaves alone.'

Zannis nodded, it sounded reasonable. 'Before I forget,' he said, 'did you bring what I asked for?'

'In the glovebox.'

Zannis opened the glovebox and took out a Walther PPK automatic, the German weapon preferred by Balkan detectives. There were bright metal scratches on the base of the grip. 'What have you been doing with this?'

'Hanging pictures,' Saltiel said. 'The last time I saw my hammer, one of the grandkids was playing with it.'

'Kids,' Zannis said, with a smile.

'I'm blessed,' Saltiel said. 'You ought to get busy, Costa, you're not getting any younger.'

Zannis's smile widened. 'With Roxanne?' he said, naming his English girlfriend.

'Well . . .' Saltiel said. 'I guess not.'

8.20 p.m. It had started to rain again, a few lightning flashes out in the Aegean. 'You awake?' Zannis said.

'Just barely.'

'You want a nap, go ahead.'

'No thanks. Maybe later.'

10.30 p.m. 'By the way,' Zannis said, 'did you telephone Madam Pappas?'

'This morning, about eleven.'

'And she said?'

'That she hated her husband and she's glad he's dead.'

'That's honest.'

'I thought so.'

'Anything else?'

'No, she was getting ready to scream at me, so I got off the phone – you said to go easy.'

Zannis nodded. 'Let the detectives deal with her.'

'She kill him?'

'She did.'

'Naughty girl.'

1.15 a.m. Quiet, in the city behind them. Only faint music from the tavernas on the seafront corniche and the creaking of the pier as the tide worked at the pilings. The sound was hypnotic and Zannis fought to stay awake. He took a cigarette from the flat box in his pocket – a Papastratos No. 1, top of the line in Greece – and struck a wooden match alight with his thumbnail. Expensive, these things, so a luxury for him. He made good money now, Vangelis had seen to that, but good money for a cop, which wasn't very much, not with four people to feed. His younger brother Ari, for Aristotle, sometimes made a few drachmas by carrying messages in the city. Poor soul, he did the best he could but he wasn't quite right, had always been 'different', and the family had long ago accepted him for who he was.

It was getting smoky in the car and Saltiel rolled down the window. 'Do you think there are men on the moon?' he said.

'I don't know. I suppose anything's possible.'

'They were arguing about it, yesterday, in the barbershop.'

'Little green men? With one eye? Like in Buck Rogers?'

'I guess so.'

'Somebody in your barbershop thinks those movies are true?'

'That's what it sounded like.'

'I'd change barbers, if I were you.'

3.30 a.m. 'Wake up, Gabi.'

'I wasn't sleeping. Not really.'

'Here he comes.'

Of medium height, the man wore a raincoat and carried a briefcase. He had a hard, bony, chinless face beneath a hat with the brim tilted over his eyes. As he neared the end of the pier, Zannis and Saltiel ducked down below the windscreen. By now they could hear footsteps, determined and in a hurry, that approached, then faded away from them, heading around the east side of the customs house, towards the city – to the west lay the warehouse district and the railway station. Zannis made sure of the Walther in the pocket of his jacket, slid out of the passenger seat and was careful not to slam the door, leaving it ajar. 'Give me thirty seconds, Gabi,' he said. 'Then follow along, nice and slow, headlights off, and keep your distance.'

Zannis walked quickly to the east side of the customs house, paused at the corner and had a quick look around it. Nobody. Where the hell had he gone? There was only one street he could have taken, which served the warehouses. Zannis, moving at a fast trot, reached the street, turned the corner and there he was – there somebody was – about two blocks away. Now Zannis realized he was getting wet, put up his umbrella and moved into the shelter of the high brick wall of the first warehouse. Up ahead the German sped on, with long strides, as though, Zannis thought, he was taking his evening constitutional on a path in some Deutschland forest. A few seconds later the Skoda turned the corner behind him and Zannis signalled, waving his hand backwards, for Saltiel to stay where he was. Zannis could hear the engine idling as the Skoda rolled to a stop. Could the German hear it? Doubtful, especially in the rain, but Zannis couldn't be sure – the street was dead silent.

Then the German glanced over his shoulder and turned right, down a narrow alley. He'd likely seen Zannis, but so what? Just a man with an umbrella, trudging along, shoulders hunched, on a miserable night. Zannis walked past the alley, ignoring it, eyes on the ground ahead of him, until he passed the far corner and moved out of sight. He didn't stop there but went farther down the street – if he could hear the German, the German could hear him – then looked for a place to hide. He saw a loading dock across from him and moved quickly, soaking one foot in a puddle between broken cobblestones, hurried up the steps and stood in the angle of the shuttered entryway and the wall, which was blind from the street – as far as the alley, anyhow. The German wasn't going anywhere, Zannis realized, not from this alley, where, a few years earlier, a porter had stabbed Hamid the moneylender in an argument over a few lepta – not even a drachma – and it was blocked by a high stone wall covered with a wisteria vine. Hamid had staggered as far as the wall and pulled at the wisteria, thinking to climb over, but the vine came away from the crumbling stone and he died right there. The porter covered him up with the vine but in a few hours – it was summertime – Hamid had made his presence well-known and the crime was discovered. A sad business, Zannis thought, the moneylenders preyed on the waterfront labourers like hawks on pigeons. Was this a law of nature? Perhaps it was. A real hawk had once tried to get at one of his little brother's canaries, in a cage on the windowsill, and bent the hell out of the wire frame.

Zannis looked at his watch, 3.39, and settled down to wait. This was a meeting, of course, and somebody was going to show up, sooner or later. If he was dumb enough to walk past the idling Skoda, they'd get both of them. If not, just the German, though Saltiel would probably take off after the second man. Woman? Maybe, anything was possible.

3.48 a.m. *Hurry up, you bastards, have your fucking meeting and let me go home to bed.* After arrest, and a trip to the police station, where they'd get what they could, then run him back to the ship. After all, he hadn't done much – entered Salonika without having his passport stamped. No point in keeping him. The German consul would squawk, Vangelis would be irritated, the hell with it.

4.00 a.m. What was the German doing down there? Was there a way through to another street that Zannis didn't know about? Oh, a fine thing that would be! *I stood there in the rain until dawn but I never saw him again.* Zannis sighed, shifted from his wet foot to his dry one and thought about Roxanne, about making love, which was what they did. Sure, a restaurant now and ... Suddenly, his mind snapped back to full attention.

From the other end of the street, at the corner of a distant alley, headlights – no car yet, just beams probing the mist. What? Could you get through down there? Zannis didn't know, but obviously somebody did because the lights swung left into the street and now pointed directly at him. He scurried along the iron shutter to the opposite corner and wound up facing the Skoda. What would Saltiel do? Nothing. The lights stayed off. *Good, Gabi, that's the way.*

And next, he thought, addressing the unseen driver of the car, *you'll turn into the alley.* It was a Renault sedan that muttered past him, going very slowly, but his prediction was off. The Renault paused at the alley, moved forward a few feet and backed in. *Clever,* Zannis thought, ready for a fast getaway. What was this? Another murder in the alley? Was it cursed? Was this long, boring, stupid night going to end in melodrama?

Whatever happened down there didn't take long. It happened in the alley and it happened quickly and it happened where Zannis couldn't see it. A car door slammed, an engine roared and the Renault reappeared, taking a fast left turn into the street and speeding off. Zannis squinted into the rain, trying to see through the cloudy rear window – someone in the passenger seat? No, he didn't think so. As he hurried down the steps from the loading dock, he watched the Renault as it flew past the Skoda. *Count: one, two, three, four*; then the Skoda's lights came on and Saltiel made a nice easy turn and followed the Renault, which had turned east up the deserted corniche.

As Zannis approached the alley, the German came out. They stopped dead, facing each other, maybe thirty feet apart, then the German, like Hamid the moneylender, went scuttling back down the alley. Heading for the wisteria vine? No, he had a better idea, because by the time Zannis entered the alley, he'd disappeared. The magic German. Where? Zannis trotted along the sheer wall, very tense about some sort of unseen cover at his back, very certain that he was about to be shot. But then, just at the foot of the alley, a door. A door that, he guessed, would lead into the office of the warehouse. Had he forgotten it? Had it even been there, back then?

Walther. Yes, the time had come, work the slide, arm it, assume Gabi kept it loaded, assume he'd put the bullets back in the clip when he'd finished hanging up his picture. For he'd surely *un*loaded it, knowing full well that banging loaded weapons on hard surfaces wasn't such a good idea – the very least you could hope for was embarrassment and it got quickly worse from there. Grandpa! The cat! No, Gabi had done the right thing because Gabi always did the right thing. No?

Zannis closed the umbrella and set it by the wall, freed the Walther's clip, found it fully loaded and locked it back in place. Then he stood to one side of the door and, making sure of his balance, raised his foot and kicked at the knob, intending to make it rattle on the other side. No bullets from inside, so he reached over, turned the knob and opened the door. Unlocked. Always unlocked? Unlocked at the moment. Keeping to the cover of the wall as much as he could, he swung the door wide, waited a beat, then rushed in low, Walther pointed ahead of him.

17

He'd expected an office, and hoped for a telephone. Right, then wrong. It was an office, open to the warehouse floor – filing cabinets, two desks and an old-fashioned telephone, no dial, on the wall. But the line had been cut a few inches below the wooden box. Cut years ago? Or thirty seconds ago? He didn't know. But he did know where he was – the Albala spice warehouse. The air was thick with scent; a dense compound of fennel, opium poppies, foul silk cocoons and Mediterranean herbs; sage and thyme and the rest. Stacked in burlap-covered bales and wooden crates out in the darkness, ready to be shipped.

He listened for a time, but heard only silence. Then waited, hoping his eyes would adjust to the darkness but the only light in the warehouse seeped through closed louvres, set high on the walls. One hand ahead of him, he moved forward, but he knew it was hopeless, he wasn't going to find the German crouched behind a bale of fennel. So he returned to the office, took hold of the door handle and slammed it shut, then walked out into the darkness, making no attempt to move quietly.

Something moved, something much bigger than a rat. The sound, weight shifting on boards, came from somewhere above him. He waited, changed gun hands and wiped his sweaty palm on his trousers. Again he heard it, almost directly above his head. So, the second floor. How did one get up there? No idea. He reached in his pocket, lit a match, discovered he was in an aisle with stacked bales on both sides. Lighting a second match, he saw what looked like a stairway on the far wall.

It wasn't a stairway but a wooden ramp and, when he got there, he found what he was looking for. At the foot of the ramp was a metal cabinet with a lever affixed to one side. He pulled the lever down and the lights went on. Not a lot of light, a few bare bulbs in outlets screwed to the boards of the ceiling, and only on the first floor, but enough. Whatever was up there moved again, fast, running, then stopped.

Zannis was finding it hard to breathe – how the hell did people work in here? – the air was so charged, so chemically

18

sharp, his eyes were watering and he had to take his glasses off and wipe away the tears. Then, in a crouch, he scurried up the ramp and dived flat at the top, his head just below floor level. Quickly, he raised up to get a look but, even with some ambient light from the first floor, the gloom at the top of the ramp quickly faded into darkness. He sniffed – this place was really reaching him – then spoke, not loud and not angry, in German. 'Sir, please come out from wherever you're hiding, and let me see your hands. Please. You won't be harmed.'

That did it.

Running footsteps on the far side of the second floor, then a series of thumps punctuated by a cry of panic and, after a few beats of silence, a moan. Using two matches to reach the opposite wall, Zannis realized what had happened. There was another ramp over there but, if you didn't want to use it, there was an alternative; a square cut in the floor with a narrow and very steep set of stairs, almost a ladder, that descended to the floor below. The German's descent had clearly taken him by surprise and he was lying face down with his head on the boards and his feet on the steps above – Zannis saw that he was wearing green socks – briefcase still clutched in one hand. Carefully, Walther still held ready for use, Zannis walked down the stairs. The German said something – it sounded as though he was pleading but his voice was muffled and Zannis couldn't make out the words. He checked for weapons, found none, then took the German under the arms, turned him over, hauled him upright and managed to get him seated on a step. For a moment he just sat there, eyes shut, nose bleeding, then he pressed a hand to the centre of his chest and said, 'Hospital. Hospital.'

Well, Zannis thought later, I tried. He'd put one arm around the man, held him up and walked him along a step at a time, meanwhile carrying the briefcase in his other hand. It was awkward and slow; by the time they reached the street that led to the customs house, dawn had turned the sky a dark grey.

There they were lucky – a taxi was cruising slowly along the corniche, looking for the last revellers of the night. Zannis waved it down and settled the German in the back seat and the driver sped off, reaching the hospital only a few minutes later. And when they pulled up to the emergency entrance a doctor showed up right away and climbed into the back of the taxi. But then the doctor shook his head and said, 'Can't help him here. You might as well take him to the morgue, or maybe you want us to use the ambulance.'

'You're sure?'

The doctor nodded and said, 'I'm sorry.'

By ten the next morning he was on the phone with Vangelis, who said, after hearing a brief version of the story, 'And what was in the briefcase?'

'Photographs. Seventy photographs. And a sketch, in sharp pencil, a freehand map of the area around Fort Rupel.'

'How do you know it was Fort Rupel?'

'It's labelled. Printed in Roman letters. The pictures were taken from a distance: roads, barbed wire, the fort itself.' The line hissed, finally Zannis said, 'Hello?'

'Yes. I'm here.' A conventional answer, but the tone was sad and grim.

Zannis repeated what he'd said to Saltiel in the car. 'Maybe just the war, coming south.' Fort Rupel protected the Rupel Pass on the Bulgarian border, directly north of Salonika. The invasion route from there, down the Struma valley, was more than two thousand years old. Farmers' ploughs turned up spearheads, broken swords, bayonets and bones.

'Not yet,' Vangelis said. 'The Nazis don't care about us. Yet. What are you doing about the Renault?'

'Saltiel didn't manage to catch him, but he did get the registration number. Local car, so all I have to do is call the clerk.'

'All right, Costa, just proceed as you think best.'

'I called some friends at the newspapers – German tourist

20

found dead on the pavement near his hotel. Heart attack the apparent cause. I gave them the information on the passport: Albert Heinrich, domiciled in Essen, fifty-three years old.' He paused, then said, 'You wouldn't prefer a spy scandal, would you?'

Vangelis snorted and said, 'Oh fine! Good idea!' then added a version of a local Albanian expression. 'Let's fart up Hitler's nose. We'll have them down here in no time at all.'

'I thought you would see it that way. As for the photographs, what's your pleasure?'

'Drop them off here, I'll send them over to the army.'

'And Spiraki?'

'I was afraid you'd ask that. Tell him what happened; write him a report – he'll like that; have your clerk type it up, on Salonika police stationery. And Costa? Make damn sure you get rid of the passport before you contact Spiraki – those people love passports.'

'It should go to the German consulate.'

'It must. Tell me, was it really a heart attack? You didn't, ah, do anything to him, did you? Not that I'd blame you if you did.'

'No, sir, he did it to himself. He was scared – afraid of being caught, afraid of failure – he was running around up there like a rat. Falling down the stairs didn't help, but if I had to have a theory I'd say he frightened himself to death.'

Vangelis's voice was disgusted. 'Miserable business,' he said. Then, 'Oh well, keep me informed.'

When he'd hung up, Zannis took a piece of paper from his drawer and began to write the first draft of a report to Spiraki. Formerly an Athenian lawyer, Spiraki ran the local office of the Geniki Asphalia, the State Security Bureau. It had changed names several times, becoming the Defence Intelligence Bureau in 1936; then, a few months later, as the Metaxas dictatorship took hold, the General Directorate of Foreign Citizens, but most people still called it 'state security'.

Zannis found Spiraki himself not so easy to deal with. Tall, heavy, balding, sombre, with a thick moustache, he was given to light-blue suits, formal language and cold-eyed stares. He never responded immediately to anything you said, there was always a dead moment before he spoke. On the other hand, he could've been worse. His office was supposed to ensure obedience to the dictatorship's morality laws, forbidding hashish and prostitution, the traditional targets, and they'd tried to go beyond that, prohibiting lewd music, the *rembetika* – filthy, criminal, passionate, and very dear to Salonika's heart. But Spiraki didn't insist, and the police were tolerant. You couldn't stop these things, not in this city. And, after four hundred years of Turkish occupation, it was unwise to press Greeks too hard.

The grey sky wouldn't go away, seagulls circled above the port, their cries doing nothing to disperse the melancholy. Saltiel showed up at eleven, tired and slumped, and he and Zannis tried to finish up the investigation. The clerk at the city hall found the registration number, to her great delight. It belonged to a Renault registered by one K. L. Stacho. Zannis knew who he was, a Bulgarian undertaker, third-generation proprietor of a funeral home that buried Bulgarians, Albanians, Serbs and Vlachs, who died with sufficient regularity to provide Stacho with a handsome villa in Salonika's wealthy neighbourhood, by the sea east of the city.

Zannis telephoned and Saltiel drove them out there ten minutes later. Poor Madam Stacho, red-eyed, a balled-up handkerchief clenched in her fist, Zannis felt sorry for her. Her husband had left the house, to take care of some unspecified business, long after midnight. And he never returned. She'd been frantic of course but, at eight in the morning, a neighbour had come knocking at her door to say that Stacho had telephoned and asked her to relay a message: he would not be coming home. Not for a long time. He was well, she was not to worry. Beyond that, Madam Stacho didn't know a thing.

So, did Mr Stacho have German friends?

Not as far as she knew

A camera?

Well, yes, he did have one, photography was a hobby of his.

For how long, a hobby. Years?

No, only a few months.

And, please Madam Stacho, excuse us, we're only doing our job, may we take a look around the house?

No answer, a wave of the hand, *Do what you like, I don't care any more.*

They did take a look. Rooms crowded with heavy furniture, thick curtains, tiled floors, a frightened maid, but no undertaker in a wardrobe or beneath a bed.

When they returned to the parlour, Madam Stacho wondered what her husband had done to provoke the interest of the police.

They couldn't tell her, but he might have information they needed for an investigation that was currently under way.

'And that's all?' she said, obviously brightening.

'Is that not enough?'

'When he left, when I learned he wasn't coming home . . .'

'Yes?'

'I thought it was a woman.'

'Nothing like that.'

Now she was very close to beaming, held Zannis's hand warmly at the door. 'Thank you, gentlemen,' she said. 'Thank you.'

'Perhaps you would notify us, if he returns; he can clear his name by answering a few questions.'

Oh definitely; surely, absolutely, no doubt about it.

In the Skoda, Zannis had Saltiel drive him back to the alley behind the Albala spice warehouse.

But the umbrella was gone.

That night, he was supposed to take Roxanne to the movies, a Turkish western – *Slade Visits Wyoming* was his attempt at translation – but by the time he reached the Pension Bastasini, the hotel where she lived, he was in another kind of mood. His love affair with Roxanne Brown had gone on for more than a year and had reached that pleasantly intimate plateau where plans were casually made and just as easily changed. 'Perhaps the Balthazar,' he suggested. The name of a taverna but it meant much more than that.

'Then we shan't be visiting Wyoming? With Effendi Slade?' This in English, but for the Turkish title. Her Greek was close to perfect but she knew how her English voice affected him. Prim, upper-class, clipped and chilly, a voice perfectly suited to her firm horsewoman's body, weathered face, mouth barely touched with lipstick.

'Perhaps we could go later. Or now, if you prefer.'

'No,' she said. 'I prefer depravity.'

Balthazar, tucked away in a cellar beneath lowlife Vardar Square, wasn't far away so they walked, protected by her umbrella, a hideous thing with pink polka dots on a green field. Very much a couple; his arm reached around her shoulders – they were just about the same height – hers around his waist. 'Is the world being good to you, this week?' he said.

'Not too bad. The school has a recital coming up this weekend but I refuse to worry about it.' Arriving in Salonika in 1938, by way of expatriate years spent first in southern France, then in Capri, she had purchased the Mount Olympus School of Ballet and, once every eight weeks, the daughters of the city's bourgeoisie, *all* shapes and sizes, twirled around the stage to Tchaikovsky. As rendered by a Victrola that ran, in its old age, not as fast as it once did, so the dance was perhaps a little on the stately side, which frankly suited some of the statelier daughters.

'Am I invited to the recital?' he asked.

She pressed her cheek against his. 'Many things I might ask of you, my dear, but . . .'

'Do you perform?'

'In tights? I think not.'

'Don't tell *me* you can't wear tights.'

'*That* is for you to look at, not the butcher and his wife.'

Balthazar was delighted to see them and offered a solemn bow 'So pleased,' he said, 'it's been too long,' and led them to a very small, very private room. Filled with ottomans, wool carpets and low brass tables, the soft, shadowy darkness barely disturbed by a spirit lamp flickering in one corner. Balthazar lit some incense, then prepared two narghilehs, each with a generous lump of ochre-coloured hashish. 'You will eat later?' he said. 'A nice meze?' Small appetizers – aubergine, feta, hummus.

'Perhaps we will.'

He well knew they would but didn't make a point of it, saying only, 'As you wish,' and closing the door carefully – their privacy his personal responsibility.

Music would have been nice and, as it turned out, music there was. If not from Balthazar itself, from the taverna next door, a bouzouki band and a woman singer, muffled by the wall, so just the right volume. They sat on a love seat, shoulders and hips touching, and leaned over a worked-brass table. When Zannis inhaled, the water in the narghileh bubbled and took the harsh edge off the hashish so he could hold the smoke in for a long time.

They were silent for a while, but eventually she said, 'Quite nice tonight. The smoke tastes good, like ... what? Lemon and lime?'

'Have you ever eaten it?'

'No.'

'Best not.'

'Oh?'

'Very powerful. It will take you, ah, far away. Far, far away'

'I'm rather far away as it is.' After a moment she said, 'You see that little lamp in the corner? It reminds me of Aladdin, I believe it might have been in a book I had, as a child.' She stared into the distance, then said, 'Do you suppose, if I rubbed it ...?'

'You'd burn your fingers, the genie keeps it hot.'

'Doesn't want to come out?'

'Not in this weather.'

She giggled. 'Not in this weather.' She tossed the tube of the narghileh on the table, turned sideways, rested her head on his shoulder and began to unbutton his shirt. That done, she spread it apart and laid her cheek on his chest – hairless and smooth, with broad, flat plates. Putting her lips against his skin, she said, 'You *smell* good.'

'I do? I took a bath, maybe it's the soap.'

'No, it isn't soap, it's something about you, something sweet.'

For a time they drifted, then, returning from wherever he'd been, he said, 'Would you like to sit on my lap?'

'I always like that.' She stood, hiked up her dress, settled herself on his thighs, leaned her weight against him, and raised her knees, so that, as if by magic, his hand covered her bottom. On the other side of the wall, the singer's voice grew plaintive. That made them both laugh, as though she could see through the wall. 'Can you understand the lyric?' he said.

She shook her head.

'She's singing about her flower.'

'In her garden?'

He moved her top knee a little and said, 'No, this one.' The tips of his index and middle fingers rested on tight cotton. She was, he thought, so very clever, wearing white cotton panties, just right for a proper Englishwoman, but they were cut to provide a snug fit, and the cotton felt very fine, very soft, to his fingers. After a few moments, a breath escaped her; he could feel it and he could almost, but not quite, hear it. Delicately, he moved his fingers, not ambitious, simply savouring the warm reception, and much more pleased than proud.

On. And on. Until she raised her head and spoke quietly by his ear, in the King's English: 'Let's have those off, shall we?'

Later, after Zannis had gone out into the public room and Balthazar had brought them – now famished – the meze, she scooped up some hummus with a triangle of pitta bread and said, 'Strange, but it just now occurs to me that the ottoman is an extraordinary piece of furniture, ingenious.'

'Yes?'

'Oh yes. Because you can, you know, also sit on it.'

After such a night, going back to work the next day was something like a punishment. Sibylla, the office clerk, always starched and taut, was wound especially tight that morning – neither Saltiel nor Zannis would admit it but they were both afraid of her. She stood straight as a stick, with fair hair set every Wednesday in a warrior's helmet. And *warrior* was, at the moment, the very word, for she had come to work in a bad mood and was taking it out on the files.

Of these, there were two distinct sets. The first lived in a row of wooden filing cabinets in what was called *the other room* – there were two, with a bathroom in the hall – and included all the various paper that flowed through a government bloodstream: directions from on high, carbons of correspondence, letters from the citizenry, and various oddments, like newspaper clippings, that got themselves into the files and stayed there. Though sometimes – as witness Sibylla's *attack du jour* – not forever.

'Gabi,' she said, holding a paper so that Saltiel could read it, 'is this important?'

Saltiel didn't want to read it. 'Probably not.'

'A memorandum, from Station Six. It seems to concern the cemetery.'

'Which one?'

'The old Turkish one. The subject is "Copulation at Night".'

'By the living?'

'If not, keep it,' Zannis said, looking up from his desk. They couldn't really get Sibylla to laugh, but they never stopped trying.

Instead, a sigh. What bad boys they were. 'Dated 10 September 1938.'

'By now, they're likely done copulating,' Saltiel said. 'Get rid of it.'

27

The other file was maintained by Zannis, on five-by-eight cards in shoeboxes, and, taken altogether, was a working map of the power centres – and there were many – of Salonika. Thus it included cards for shipowners and bankers, Greek Orthodox prelates, consuls, spies, resident foreigners, journalists, politicians, high-class criminals and courtesans – anybody who mattered. For an official whose job was to work behind the scenes, it was crucial to keep track of the cast of characters.

The files, both sets, played a central role in the unnamed office on the Via Egnatia, with support from three typewriters, three telephones and one more device which, from time to time, would remind them of its presence by ringing a little bell. As it did at that moment, producing a mumbled '*Skata*' from Zannis – the Greek equivalent of the French *merde* – by which he meant *now what*. The device, on its own private table in the corner, was a Model 15 Siemens teleprinter, and now, all by itself, it began to type, fast and furious, a page rising slowly from a slot above its keyboard. Zannis stood by the table and read the text as it appeared.

AS PER YOUR QUERY 6 OCTOBER 1940 STOP MAIN
BORDER STATIONS REPORT NO RECALL RENAULT MODEL
UNKNOWN LICENCE SK 549 ENTERING BULGARIA LAST
48 HOURS STOP NO RECORD GREEK NATIONAL K L
STACHO THIS OFFICE STOP SIGNED LAZAREFF END

The teleprinter waited, making its *thucka-thucka-thucka* sound, for thirty seconds, then shut down. Well, Zannis thought, I gave it a try. On a hunch that Stacho had fled up to Bulgaria, he'd had Sibylla send a teletype to his old friend, Ivan Lazareff, in Sofia. If he'd thought that Stacho was spying for Bulgaria – a perfectly reasonable assumption – he wouldn't have done it, but the undertaker, a Greek citizen of Bulgarian descent, was spying for Germany, or at least for a man carrying German documents, so he'd taken a chance. And why not? He'd known Lazareff for years; they'd had plenty of good times in Greek and Bulgarian bars back when they'd both been detectives. At one time they'd talked on the telephone – mostly in German – but now that Zannis was a police official and Lazareff a chief of detectives, they communicated back and forth by teletype.

Logically, the purchase of the Siemens equipment should have been animated by some urge for progress, but it wasn't so. As German power surged in Europe, German corporations drove deep into the Balkans, buying up raw materials at preferential prices and selling – often trading – technology in return. Roumanian wheat moved east; back the other way came Leica cameras, aspirin, harmonicas and, in some of the police stations in the cities and towns of southern Europe, teletype systems. In many cases, the purchase wasn't optional, was instead dictated by a very apprehensive foreign policy – *we must appease these people, buy the damn machine!* And yes, there were stories of hens nesting atop teleprinters in Serbian villages, and no, you really weren't going to hunt down the goat thief sought by a Roumanian police officer, but the system did work and, soon enough, some Balkan policemen found that it had its uses.

10 October. Hotel Lux Palace, Salonika.

Maybe just the war, moving south.

The end of her cigarette was marked with lipstick, dark red, a colour that emphasized her black hair and pale skin. *Stunning*, Zannis thought, was the word for her. And seductive, future delights suggested in the depths of her glance. And a liar, because she had no intention of going to bed with him or anybody else. She was important, this woman; she would never do such things. She was, however, scared, and not used to it, so she flirted a little with the handsome policeman, because she needed help.

He was here, in the best suite the best hotel in the city had to offer, at Saltiel's suggestion. No, request, though put mildly enough. This was a Jewish matter, originating with some pillar of the Sephardic community who knew to reach Zannis by way of Saltiel.

She ordered coffee, sat Zannis in a brown velvet armchair, turned the chair that went with the escritoire halfway and perched on its edge, facing him. Heels together, posture erect. 'Frau Krebs is terribly formal,' she said, her voice in cultured and well-modulated German. 'Everybody calls me Emmi, for Emilia.'

'And I'm Costa, for Constantine. My last name is Zannis. And they are?'

He referred to two children, the boy seven, he guessed, the girl perhaps nine, in a staged tableau beyond the open bedroom door. They were perfectly dressed, Jewish by their looks, the girl reading a book, the boy colouring with crayons.

'Nathanial and Paula.' The girl looked up from her book, smiled at Zannis, then went back to reading – or pretending to read.

'Attractive children, no doubt you're proud of them.'

Silence. She hesitated, a shall-I-lie hesitation that Zannis had seen many times before. She inhaled her cigarette, tapped it above the ashtray and finally said, 'No.'

'Not proud?' He smiled, of course she meant no such thing.

'They're not my children.' Then, regret. 'Does it matter?' She was worried that she'd made a mistake.

'It doesn't matter, but it is interesting. I'm sure you'll explain.'

The waiter arrived, bringing croissants, butter, jam, Greek pastry and coffee. In ordering, she'd covered all the possibilities. 'I thought you might like something to eat.'

'Maybe later.'

The tray was set on a table and she tipped the waiter.

'Two days ago, I arrived at the Turkish border on what used to be called the Orient Express. But we were turned back by a customs officer, so here we are, in Salonika.'

'A Turkish customs officer?' he said. Then made the classic

baksheesh gesture, thumb rubbed across the first two fingers, and raised his eyebrows.

She appreciated the theatre. 'Oh, I tried, but I somehow managed to find the only honest official in the Middle East.'

'For what reason, Emmi, turned back?'

'Some question about papers.'

'Are they legitimate?'

'I thought they were. I was told they were.'

'By . . .?'

'A lawyer in Berlin. I paid him to obtain the right papers, Turkish entry visas, but what I got were – um, cooked up. False papers. That's what the officer said.'

'And then you offered a bribe.'

'I started to but, oh, you should have seen his face. I think he might have put us in prison.'

Sympathetic, Zannis nodded. 'Always best, we think here, to avoid time in Turkish prisons. Emmi, if they're not your children, whose are they?'

'A friend's. An old school friend. A Jewish friend. She can't get out of Germany; she asked for help, I volunteered to take the children out. To Istanbul – where there are people who will take care of them.'

'And where you will live.'

Slowly, she shook her head, then put her cigarette out, pressing the end against the glass. 'No, I will go back.'

'Forgive me, I assumed you were Jewish.'

'I am.'

Zannis didn't answer. It was properly hushed on the top floor of the Lux Palace; from the corridor outside the room he could hear the whir of a vacuum cleaner. He stood up, walked over to the window and looked out to sea, at a steamship and its column of smoke against the sky. As he returned to the chair she met his eyes. Stunning, he thought again, and hard, much harder than he'd first thought. *What have I stumbled on?* Back in the chair, he leaned forward and

31

spoke quietly. 'You don't *have* to say anything, if you don't want to. I'll still help you.'

She nodded, grateful for his understanding. In the bedroom, the boy said, his voice just above a whisper, 'Should this be green?'

'No, blue,' the girl said.

Emilia Krebs bent towards him and lowered her voice. 'It was very hard for them. They couldn't go to school, they couldn't really go outdoors – Berlin is brutal now. Do you understand?'

His expression said that he understood perfectly.

'So, my friend asked me to get them out, somewhere safe. Because she knew I could go in and out of Germany. *Krebs* is Colonel Hugo Krebs, my husband, and a very powerful man.'

'In the party?' He meant the Nazi party, and kept his voice light and neutral.

'Never.' She was offended that he could even suggest such a thing, and her voice knew how to be offended. 'No, he isn't like that. He's a career officer; he serves on the General Staff of the Wehrmacht, a manager of logistics – trains getting where they're needed on time, enough socks – it's not glamorous, but it is quite important.'

'I know what it is,' Zannis said. 'Is there a *J* stamped in your passport?' That was now a legal requirement in Germany, a *J* for Juden, Jew.

'Oh no, not mine; they wouldn't dare.'

'No, likely they wouldn't, not with you married to a man in his position, and he's probably not Jewish – he couldn't be, the way things are in Germany.'

'A Lutheran, from a solid old family, though nothing special. We met, we fell in love and we married – he's a wonderful man. We were never able to have children, but we lived a good life, then Hitler came to power. Hugo would have resigned his commission but he realized that, with a Jewish wife, it was better for us if he stayed where he was.'

Zannis nodded, acknowledging an unfortunate truth. *And,*

32

he thought, *logistics is the word*. How to get this woman and the two children to Turkey? 'Could you tell me how, once you reached Istanbul, you planned to return to Berlin?'

'I didn't see it as a problem,' she said, hesitant, not sure what he had in mind.

'By steamship?'

'Heavens no. It's faster to fly. From Istanbul to Bucharest, then on to Berlin. Lufthansa has routes to all the neutral countries.'

'But you didn't fly to Istanbul. I imagine, with two children, it would have been expensive.'

'It wasn't that, I don't care about money. Hugo and I thought the three of us might be a little too noticeable at Tempelhof – Gestapo everywhere, at the airport – so better to go on the train. By stages, you see, first to Vienna, then Budapest, Belgrade, Sofia and on to Istanbul. We got as far as the border control at Edirne, in Turkey.'

'But you came back to Salonika.'

'Because I knew there were Jews in Salonika – "the Jerusalem of the Balkans", all that.'

'Yes, at one time a majority here, and still a large community.'

'I couldn't think what else to do. Going back to Berlin was out of the question, of course.'

'Why?'

'Because' – she paused, then said – 'that would have been, well, failure.'

'And you don't fail.'

'How could I?' With a shift of her eyes, she referred to the children in the bedroom.

Zannis thought for a moment; then he said, 'There *is* one thing I wondered about.'

'Anything.' She encouraged him with a smile; certainly they had become, almost friends, she hoped.

'You said, "I don't care about money," and I don't mean to pry, but I suspect you weren't talking about the pay of an army colonel.'

'You don't mean to pry?' Arch and amused.

Zannis's turn to smile.

'I have money of my own. I am Emilia Krebs but I used to be, I suppose I still am, Emilia Adler. A name you might recognize, if you were German. Emilia Adler, of the Frankfurt Adlers, private bankers since the Middle Ages and very, very rich. There, it's out.'

Zannis was puzzled and showed it. 'Now? Under the Nazis? My impression was that they'd stolen all the Jewish money in Germany, forced the sale of Jewish businesses, prevented funds from leaving the country. Not true?'

'Not quite. Because once the Nazis got hold of the money they had to do something with it. Much of it went to Switzerland, but a substantial amount was deposited with my grandfather, at the Adler Bank in Frankfurt. That's because he pays interest of twelve percent – which the Swiss, believe me, don't.'

Zannis was impressed. 'Twelve per cent.'

'There's no way he can invest at that level, of course, though the Nazis think he can – the cunning Jew, working in secret . . . But, in fact, the money is coming from his own resources, it is a rather elegant form of bribery.'

After a moment, Zannis said, 'Forever?'

'No. But for a time, maybe a year, maybe more. He knew they would come after him, in 1936, he knew, so he went after them. Gently. He is on the surface a very gentle man, though he's not really like that.'

'Nor are you.'

'Nor am I.'

'And your father, works for the bank?'

'My father died ten years ago.'

'I'm sorry.'

'In Persia, where we held bonds for the building of water systems.'

'Of . . . an illness?'

'Of passion. A heart attack in a bordello. We like to believe

34

he died happy. So there, Herr Zannis, now you have it all.'

'Almost. I'd like to know how you managed to secure exit papers for the children.'

'The lawyer *did* do that – at least he got something right.'

'How was it done? Do you know?'

'With a bribe, according to the lawyer. Fifty thousand reichsmarks. Anyway, that's what I paid him, besides his fee, but all I have is his word.' She shrugged. 'It might have been less.'

Zannis raised his eyebrows – a *lot* of money. 'What, in dollars: twenty-five thousand? People could live on that for years.'

'Closer to twenty, I believe. Still, a substantial sum; this kind of transaction has become very expensive in the Reich. The Nazis are vicious and criminal but, thank God, they are also venal. The ideology, for many of them, is only skin-deep – they like power, and they *love* money.'

'Well, I'll need the exit papers, for a day or two, maybe longer.'

As she went for her handbag, Zannis rose to his feet and said, 'Now I think I will have a coffee – may I pour one for you?'

'Please.'

'Nathanial?' Zannis said. 'Paula? Would you like a pastry?'

12 October. The Club de Salonique.

It was *the* place in the city, so much so that even the mighty Vangelis had had a difficult time getting Zannis a membership. 'Not only did I have to put my thumb in a certain place,' the old man told him, 'but I had to press hard.' Nonetheless, it was crucial for Zannis to belong, because some of the most important business in Salonika was done there, in the club's own building at the fancy end of the corniche. The atmosphere in the dark mahogany dining room, with its view over the sea and its hushed luncheon ritual – subdued conversation, just the barest music of china and silverware – was privilege transcendent.

Just the setting for Celebi, the Turkish consul. Easily a film version of the diplomat, Celebi – silver hair, serene smile, ivory cigarette holder; Roxanne had once described him as *debonair*.

35

The waiter arrived, they ordered indifferently – the food was too polite to be good – and Zannis was properly grateful for Celebi's seeing him at such short notice. Aperitifs were served, Zannis said he needed a favour, Celebi's expression changed only slightly – *oh*? So it was to be a sophisticated sort of a luncheon, based on the most sophisticated sort of understanding about life and politics, though somewhat less sophisticated was the view out of the window, where a merchant freighter, torpedoed that morning, burned while they dined. Mostly black smoke but, if one of your sideways glances came at just the right moment, you might catch a bright dot of fire.

'She's a very cultivated woman,' Zannis said. 'Jewish, and a person of some standing in the social world of Berlin.'

'Really?'

'So it seems.'

'She must be terribly rich, then. I'm afraid the rest of them . . .'

'I know.'

'She's in difficulties?'

'In a way. She's trying to get a friend's children out of Berlin.'

'And into Turkey?'

'Yes. Will you have another one?'

'Oh, I don't know . . .'

'Waiter?'

'Sir?'

'Two more, please.'

'I shouldn't . . .'

'Let's go to hell a little, no? A nap this afternoon . . .'

'Maybe *you* can . . .'

'You're busy?'

'It's frightful. Half the world trying to get in the door. I'm over *January's* limit now, for entry visas, and my superiors in Istanbul are becoming tiresome.'

Zannis shook his head. 'Damned war.'

'We could've done without, that's certain. Why don't you just smuggle them in? Everyone else does.'

'They're kids, Ahmet. Sweet kids. I don't want them to pee their pants every time some cop looks at them in the street.'

'Oh, yes, well, you're right then. They'll need real documents.'

'Can you reason with Istanbul?'

'Umm, yes and no. But, truth is, I may have to sweeten somebody.'

'Well, *that* won't be a problem.'

'No?'

'No, I don't think so.'

Celebi took a cigarette from a silver case and twisted it into his cigarette holder.

Zannis flicked a lighter and, as Celebi bent towards the flame, said, 'What do you think, four hundred?'

'I assume you don't mean drachmas.'

'Dollars.'

'Apiece?'

'Yes. An adult and two children.'

'Can she get dollars?'

'In Salonika?'

Celebi nodded, amused, to himself: *of course.* 'I'll send Madam Urglu along, say, tomorrow afternoon?'

'I'll expect her. I have an envelope with me – German exit visas, you can get the information from them.'

'On the way out,' Celebi said.

Zannis nodded in agreement. So elegant, the dining room of the Club de Salonique, not a place to be passing envelopes across the table.

Blue sky, that afternoon, sparkling air after the rain, the snow-capped Mount Olympus visible across the bay. Zannis walked back to the office along the busy Via Egnatia, taking his time, pausing to look at the windows of the shops. He made a mental

37

note to contact Emilia Krebs when he reached the office, giving her time to arrange the money for the bribe – he doubted any of it would ever reach Istanbul – so that by the following afternoon he could give an envelope to Madam Urglu.

He didn't much care for Madam Urglu, said to be Celebi's chief spy. In her fifties, pigeon-breasted and stout, with glasses on a chain around her neck and a sharp tongue. Spiraki at state security claimed she served as a spymaster for various secret agents – 'coded wireless transmission Monday and Thursday nights,' he'd said, 'from the top floor of the consulate.' Probably he was right, Zannis thought, staring at a display of tennis rackets and a poster of a blonde woman in mid-backhand, but he wondered what intelligence, secret intelligence, the Turks wanted in Salonika. Whatever it might be, he was hardly shocked.

After all, they'd been fighting the Turks forever – famously in Troy, in Homeric days, but that surely wasn't the first time. The last time it started was in 1919, when the Greek armies had gone into Turkey and occupied the coastal city of Smyrna. There was even talk in those days about getting Constantinople – Byzantium – back, the great capital of the Byzantine Empire, taken by Moslem Turks in 1453. They'd had it long enough, no?

Well they still had it, now Istanbul. And the Turkish armies had retaken Smyrna in 1922: burned the town, slaughtered the Greek population and changed the name to Izmir. In the following year a treaty was signed: three hundred and fifty thousand Turks left Greece, and a million and a half Greeks came to Greece from Turkey, came back home, where they hadn't lived for a thousand years. Thus, in the autumn of 1940, there was still a taverna called Smyrna Betrayed, located on what had once been known as Basil-the-Slayer-of-Bulgars Street. Renamed the Street of the Franks, in memory of yet another conquest. Easy enough to find new names in a city where the wars outnumbered the streets.

★

38

Back at the office, he telephoned Emilia Krebs at the Lux Palace. She was very emotional, close to tears – as close as she ever came, he thought, and these would've been tears of relief. Yes, she had the money, and the minute she got off the phone she'd go out and buy dollars. Victory. He supposed you had to call it that: two kids off to grow up in a foreign country, perhaps never to see their parents again, but at least alive.

And late in the afternoon on 16 October, he rode in a taxi to the railway station so Emilia and the children could board the 17.20 express to Istanbul. In the waiting room, Nathanial and Paula sat quietly – too quietly, too much had happened to them – and Emilia Krebs gave him a sheet of Lux Palace notepaper with her address and telephone number in Berlin. 'There may come a time,' she said, 'when I can return the favour.'

'Maybe,' he said, meaning *likely never.*

'The way the world is going now, you can't tell about the future.' The approaching train sounded its whistle and she put a hand on his arm. 'I can never thank you enough,' she said. 'For helping me.'

'You don't have to thank me,' he said. 'Who could say no?'

He left the office early that day and headed back to his apartment – two small rooms on a cobbled lane called Santaroza, between the railway station and the port. Not the best part of town, on the border of what had been the Jewish district before the Great Fire. He would play with his big mountain sheepdog, Melissa – honeybee – who would be waiting for him in the doorway after a hard day's work in the neighbourhood. This was a night, one of two or three every week, when he would go to his mother's house for dinner. Melissa always accompanied him and would stay until he returned for the next visit.

She was a big girl, eighty pounds, with a thick soft black-and-white coat and a smooth face, long muzzle, and beautiful eyes – not unlike the Pyrenean mountain dog. Queen of the street, she started her morning by walking him a few blocks towards the office, to a point where, instinct told her, he was no longer in danger of being attacked by wolves. Next, she returned home to protect the local kids on their way to school, then accompanied the postman on his rounds. That done, she would guard the chicken coop in a neighbour's courtyard, head resting on massive paws. If a marauding fox didn't show up, she'd wait until it was time to trot off to the school and see the kids safely home.

Nobody taught her any of this, it was all in her bloodline, coming from the mountains where her ancestors – perhaps descendants of Turkish Akbash dogs – guarded flocks but didn't herd them. Thus she would never trot in front of or behind her charges, but stayed always to one side. Watchful. And independent; when Zannis had tried putting her on a leash she'd responded by lying down and refusing to move. Nonetheless, a splendid girl, from a mountain village where these dogs were highly valued. Zannis counted himself lucky to have been able to buy a puppy from a good litter.

She stood when he appeared, gave a single low bark of greeting, then had her pretty ears smoothed back, her muzzle flapped and her ruff given a few affectionate tugs. Across the lane, two old ladies sitting on kitchen chairs – always brought out in good weather – beamed at the spectacle. Then he took her up to his apartment. There were two floors in the narrow building; he had the second. 'We're going to see Grandma tonight,' he told her. Melissa's ears shot up. At the house in the old Turkish quarter by the battlements, Zannis's grandmother always brought home the most succulent butcher's scraps on the nights when Melissa came for dinner.

But the shopping didn't end there. Accompanied by Zannis's mother and his brother, Ari, his grandmother campaigned through the markets, coming home with fresh creamy feta, baby red mullet, calamari, or a chicken with yellow skin – the best kind of chicken, the *only* kind of chicken – making sure that she got extra feet for the soup pot. Oh they spoiled him rotten, begged him to stay over, which he often did, then sent him off with two of his shirts, boiled white and perfectly ironed.

17 October. Life back to normal, thank heaven. A few cases referred to the office – not much to be done with most of them. A local politician's wife had gone missing; they could work on that, probably to discover she'd run off with her lover. Otherwise it was quiet. Strange – with half the continent occupied by Germany, and Great Britain standing alone in opposition and fighting for its life – but quiet. At one time, Zannis had received letters from Laurette, in Paris, but now, with the occupation, the letters came only once in a great while. He answered them, carefully, carefully, because they would be read by the German censor. So Laurette would know he was well, that he often thought of her, and something of the Salonika weather.

On the evening, of the seventeenth, a party. At the house of a young lecturer in the literature department at the university, more Roxanne's friend than his, but he was happy enough to go. Roxanne had a huge appetite for parties; Zannis went along, smiled, talked, looked covertly at his watch. This particular party was nothing new – Salonika's high bohemian caste gathered for wine and retsina, seductions physical and social – but it was apparently one of the more important parties that autumn, because Elias showed up. Elias, the king of the city's poets, and of sufficient stature and self-esteem to call himself by one name only, perhaps his first, perhaps his last, perhaps neither – maybe chosen for mellifluous sonority, who knew. Elias certainly looked like the king of the poets, with snow-white prophet's beard and Einstein hair. 'He doesn't own a comb,' went the local witticism. 'He just unscrews the bulb and sticks his finger in a lamp.' Discovering Zannis – they'd met several times – hiding in a corner, Elias rocked back on his heels and squinted his eyes, like a zoologist encountering an interesting animal. 'Ah Zannis, you're here.'

'Nice to see you, Elias.'

'So, how goes life with the bullyboys?'

'Myself, I avoid them.'

'Really? So do I.'

'Are you hard at work, these days?'

'I am, yes I am. Perhaps a new book next year.'

'I look forward to reading it.'

'Do you have the others?'

'I've given a couple of them as gifts, and I have one of my own. *Dawn* – um . . .'

'*Dawn of the Goddess.*'

'That's it.'

'Maybe not my best. Early work.'

'I liked it,' Zannis said. 'The one about the owl.'

Elias thought for a time. '"Night in the Field?"'

'Could be. I don't exactly remember.'

'"In the late night, the huntress wakes to hunts"? That one?'

'Right. That one.'

'Zannis, it isn't about an owl. It's about – well, a woman, a woman I knew.'

You knew a woman who ate mice? Skata! 'Elias,' he said, 'I'm just a policeman.' He didn't say, 'just a *simple* policeman,' but even so Elias heard the *simple*, which meant that Zannis had pushed the proper button, because the word made him a *worker*, a *worker of the world* who would, in some misty future, *unite*.

'Well, maybe you have a point,' Elias said, his voice not unkind. 'If you take it literally'

Zannis sensed that Elias was preparing to escape, but Zannis wasn't ready to let him go. 'Tell me, Elias, do you ever go up into the mountains? See old friends?' It was said of Elias, and Zannis believed it to be true, that as a young man he'd gone to the mountains and fought alongside the klephts. This was the name given to the men from the mountain villages who'd fought the Turks – essentially resistance fighters – and who were sometimes shepherds and sometimes bandits, as well as guerrillas.

Elias changed; his party-guest hauteur vanished. 'No,' he said ruefully, now the Elias of a former life. 'No, I don't. I don't see them. I do go up there, especially in the spring, because it is so beautiful, but what you're talking about, no, that was a long time ago.'

'True, many years ago. But I'd guess your old friends are still around. The ones who survived.'

Elias had the last sip of his wine. 'Are you asking as a policeman?'

Zannis didn't care for the question. 'No, not at all. Those days are long gone, and people in my family did the same thing, against the Turks. I was only curious and, if you really want to know, I was wondering if you'd ever write about it.'

Elias shook his head. 'Not me, not ever. Up there, secrecy is a religion, and even though it was long ago you keep faith with it. Not that I'd mind seeing them again; when you fight alongside people, their life is in your hands, yours in theirs; it's beyond anything else – family, love, anything. And they aren't like people down here. To them, freedom is everything. You know how they refer to themselves, as *adespotoi*. Masterless.'

'Yes, I know the word. They aren't the only ones.'

'Well, maybe not, we'll see.'

'We'll see?'

'The war.'

'You think it will come here?'

'The Four Horsemen of the Apocalypse, yes, all of it, and there will be cowardice and bravery.' Elias paused for a moment, then said, 'Of course I hope I'm wrong. The Turkish gendarmerie was bad enough, believe me, but these people ...' He looked down at his glass and said, 'It appears I'm going to need some more of this.'

'I'm glad we had a chance to talk,' Zannis said.

Maybe Elias wasn't so glad. His expression, as he nodded a brusque farewell and went off to refill his glass, was vaguely troubled. But not for long. As he reached the middle of the

43

room, he cried out, 'Helena! My heart's desire! Where've you been hiding?'

People arrived, nobody left, the room grew warmer, the party got louder, somebody put on a *rembetika* record, a woman closed her eyes and danced without moving her feet. Zannis talked to a lawyer's wife, to an actor – 'It's like Sophocles, only modern' – to the lecturer host, to the cultural attaché from the German embassy in Athens – 'We are madly Hellenophile; you know, we have a great passion for Greece' – and was happily engaged with a woman painter when Roxanne appeared and towed him away. 'Somebody you must meet,' she said.

A tall fellow leaning against a doorframe smiled expectantly as Roxanne led Zannis towards him. Zannis knew immediately that he was English: sand-coloured hair swept across a handsome forehead, lines of early middle age graven in a youthful face that made him look like an old boy.

'This is Francis Escovil,' Roxanne said. She gave the name some extra flavour, as though Zannis was expected to know who he was. 'The travel writer,' she added.

'Hello,' Escovil said, smiling as he shook hands. He wore his shirt with collar open and one button undone, had an old tweed jacket draped over his shoulders, and was drinking beer from a bottle.

'Please, to meet you,' Zannis said, in his shaky English.

'I hope you'll be patient with my Greek,' Escovil said, in Greek.

'Francis did Classics at Cambridge,' Roxanne said.

'Ancient Greek,' Escovil said, apologetic. 'I'm trying to learn the demotic. You'll have to forgive me if I say odd things.'

'We all say odd things. In all sorts of languages.'

Escovil found the remark amusing. 'I see why Roxanne likes you.'

'You're writing about Salonika?'

'I believe I will. Will try.'

44

Zannis was puzzled. 'You didn't come here from *Britain*, did you?'

Escovil laughed. 'Now there's an idea! "Despite the war"' – with a dramatic shading of his voice he implied quotation marks – '"I was off to old Salonika. On the merry battleship – umm, *Valorious!*" No, no, when we declared war in 'thirty-nine I happened to be in Alexandria, so I took a job with the local English newspaper. Not much of a job – it barely pays, you know – but they allow me to do the occasional travel piece.'

Out of the corner of his eye, Zannis could see that Roxanne had the glow of a woman whose two attractive male friends are getting along well. He nodded, *now I understand*, then said, 'Still, it must be hard to find places to write about, with a war going on.'

'Only the neutrals. "On Skis in Frosty Switzerland!" "A Visit to Sunny Spain!" And, truth to tell, it's hard to reach even those countries.'

'At least there is Salonika,' Zannis said. 'Or anywhere in Greece, or Turkey.'

'And so I'm here. Not for the old come-and-see-it travel writing, but more wishful thinking, these days, a reminder of better times.'

'Just for readers in Alexandria?'

'Oh, I expect the pieces will appear in the British papers. In the *Daily Express* anyhow, they've always run my stories.'

'Well, if I can be of help . . . Where are you staying?'

'I've been lucky, Roxanne helped me find a place in a fishing village down on the peninsula. It's all whitewashed houses, little alleys with stone steps, cypress trees – you know.'

'Picturesque,' Roxanne said, in English.

'Gawd, Roxy, don't say that word.'

'It means . . .?' Zannis said.

'Cute.' Now she was tormenting Escovil. Then, to Zannis, 'Beautiful in an old-fashioned way.'

'They *are* beautiful, these villages,' Zannis said. 'And you can buy wonderful food from the fishermen. By the way, I meant what I said, about help. Having your own place, it sounds like you'll be here for a while.'

'Maybe a month – it's a kind of working vacation. And, frankly, I'm glad to get away. Alexandria's impossible now – soldiers and sailors everywhere, a lot of the old families have left for the countryside.' He paused, reflectively, then answered a question Zannis hadn't asked. 'I *did* try to join up, in 'thirty-nine, but . . .' He tapped his heart, then shook his head at the idiocy of it all. 'Hard to believe they turned me down – I've climbed mountains, run for trains, ridden camels – but they say my heart's no good.'

Liar, Zannis thought, with a sympathetic smile.

Roxanne put a hand on Escovil's arm. 'You have a perfectly fine heart, my dear.'

'*I* think so. Anyway, we're fighting the Italians now, out in the Libyan desert. Pretty much a stalemate, but if things go wrong I expect they might reconsider.'

'Until then,' Zannis said, 'I hope you'll enjoy your stay in Salonika, Mr Escovil.'

'Please, call me Francis.'

It was very late, not long until dawn, in Roxanne's saggy bed at the Pension Bastasini. Tired – from too many people – and groggy – from too much wine – Zannis had intended to drop Roxanne off and go back to his apartment, but she'd insisted he come up for a drink, and one thing had led to another. Parties always aroused her, so she'd been avid, and that had had a powerful effect on him. Which led in turn to her present condition: content, feline and sleepy, her damp middle clamped to his thigh as they lay facing each other on their sides. Intimate, and warm, but temporary. In time he knew she would move a little, and then a little more. But not quite yet, so Zannis gazed idly at the red glow at the end of his cigarette.

'What went on with you and Elias?' she said.

'Nothing much.'

'It looked like more than gossip.'

'Oh, his misspent youth.'

'Misspent youth? Misspent entire life, you mean, the old satyr.'

'He's tried to make love to you?'

'Of course. To every woman he meets.'

'Well, it wasn't about that. He fought with the guerrillas, the klephts, a long time ago, and we talked about it. Briefly.'

'Hardly misspent, from the Greek point of view.'

Oh let's talk politics. Instead of answering, Zannis yawned.

'You're not going to sleep, are you?'

'Not yet.'

'What did you think of Francis?'

'Pleasant fellow. And a spy, of course.'

'He *is*? *Francis?*'

'Yes, can't you tell?'

'No. How do you know?'

'Silly story, about a working vacation in the middle of a war.'

'Really.' She thought it over. 'A British spy.'

'Or a secret agent. This, that, the other thing, call it whatever you like, but he's working for one of the intelligence services, and maybe for a long time. Is he really a travel writer?'

'Oh yes, and top class. Up there with Robert Byron and Peter Fleming and Waugh. Are they all spies?'

'It's possible. More likely they were recruited, one, two, or all of them, after 'thirty-eight, when it was pretty damn clear to everyone but Chamberlain that Britain was going to have to go to war.'

'Will you, I don't know, will you *watch* him?'

'I doubt it. The British are our friends. In fact, the British are just about our *only* friends. I don't know what he wants here, but I don't think he, I should say *they*, mean us harm.' Tired of the conversation, he lowered his head and brushed her nipple with his lips. 'Anyhow, *you're* British, and you're my friend.'

She didn't answer.

47

Instead, a luxuriant stretch and then, down below, she moved. Ran her hand beneath his arm and pressed it against his backside, drawing him closer and resetting her legs around his thigh. Said a barely audible 'Mm,' and again moved, slid.

27 October. Late in the afternoon, a call from one of the detectives – detective-inspector in rank – at the CID, Salonika's Criminal Investigation Division. One of Salonika's most prominent citizens, a banker, had not shown up at his bank for three days. His second-in-command had telephoned, no answer, then gone out to the house and knocked on the door. Again, no answer. Back at the bank, it was discovered that a great deal of cash – large-denomination drachma notes, Swiss francs, British pounds – was missing.

Zannis knew the detective, who was young for the job, ambitious and vain, and wore a vain little moustache and a very expensive fawn-coloured hat. He picked Zannis up at the office and drove him out to the city's fanciest quarter where, in front of a splendid villa – portico, columns – a locksmith was waiting. 'Thought I'd better call him,' the detective said; this was not a neighbourhood where one kicked in doors. Likely they couldn't have kicked it in even if they'd wanted to. The villa, built by some Turkish bey around the turn of the century, was massive and well-secured.

Even better inside: dark, silent, perfectly maintained and, Zannis's sense of smell told him, not host to a corpse. *Thank God for that*. Only a note for the maids, in the kitchen. Here were two thousand drachmas for each of them – a lot of money, almost two hundred dollars – thank you for being such good girls, we'll be back some day. The money itself was gone, the house was clean, sheets covered the furniture.

They searched the rooms, finding wardrobe trunks but no hand luggage. 'Do you have a theory, sir?' the detective asked. 'Been stealing for years, perhaps?'

'Always possible,' Zannis said. But he knew better; he knew

48

what this meant and the more he thought about it, the more he knew. Suddenly, he didn't feel so good, tightness in the chest. He went to the kitchen cabinet, found a glass, filled it with cold water and drank most of it. Then he lit a cigarette. The detective went to the parlour and returned with an ashtray.

When he was done with the cigarette, they continued the search. No passports, no bankbooks, a dog's rubber ball with a bell inside it but no dog and no dog leash. On a desk, family photographs and three empty frames. In the wife's dresser, expensive scarves but no underwear. Fashionable dresses in the wardrobe, and three empty hangers. 'Very nice,' the detective said. 'Quilted hangers.' A diary in the desk drawer. Pages from 15 October to 5 November cut, not ripped, out.

'Carefully done,' Zannis said. 'Probably reservations, a ship maybe, or hotels somewhere.'

'I suspect you're right, sir,' the detective said. 'They just took off. Left town. Because of the missing money.'

'No. I expect that when we look at his accounts we'll find they've been cleaned out. The day before he left, but normal before that. I think this is somebody who decided to take his family out of Europe, now, before anything else happens. And he might have figured that this money would vanish, so why not take it for himself? One thing about flight: the more money you have, the easier it's going to be.'

'Where do you think they went?'

'I'd say you'll find him listed on the manifest of some ship, out of some Greek port, maybe not here, maybe Athens, or Istanbul. As to where he went, it's anybody's guess. Argentina? America? Mexico?'

'Anywhere safe from the guns,' the detective said. 'Are you feeling better, sir?'

'I am, thanks.'

'Maybe you need a day off.' Then, 'What became of the dog?'

'With the maids. You might look for a car, though if they parked it at a dock somewhere it's probably stolen by now.'

The detective began turning off the lights. 'I'll write this up as a theft from the bank. And issue a fugitive warrant.'

'Not much else you can do,' Zannis said.

They locked up the house and walked towards the detective's car. *This banker knew it was coming*, Zannis thought. Knew somebody who knew somebody, and they told him, 'get out, while you still can.' And maybe he, or she, whoever it was, nameless, faceless, wasn't wrong. *Enough*, Zannis told himself. *Forget it, at least for today.*

But it didn't forget him, and he wasn't done for the day. Because when he returned to the office, Sibylla told him that the telephone operator at a hotel in Basel was trying to reach him.

So Zannis couldn't go home. He waited at the office, Sibylla left at five-thirty and Saltiel went home an hour later. The phone didn't ring until after nine. On the other end of the line, 'Hello? Hello?' It was a bad connection, charged with crackling and static, the woman's voice faint. Zannis put a hand to his other ear and said, 'Yes? Can you hear me?'

'Hotel Mont Blanc operator, sir. I have to send a porter to find your caller. *Please* hold the line.'

'Yes, fine,' Zannis said.

Three minutes later, another distant voice. 'Hello? Herr Zannis?' The woman was almost shouting.

'Yes?'

'This is Emilia Krebs.'

'Hello. Are you all right?'

'I'm in Basel. I came here in order to call you.'

'Oh?'

'It's about the two sisters. Called Rosenblum.'

'Who?'

'Two sisters, in their forties. They were librarians, in Berlin. Have they . . .'

The line went dead. Zannis said, 'Hello? Hello?'

Then the static returned. ' . . . to Salonika. Hello?'

'Hello. Yes, I'm here. What did you say?'

'I gave them your name.'

You did? 'Of course, I see.'

'Have they called?' Her voice was tense, barely under control.

'No, I'm sorry, they ...' Again, the line went dead, and this time it stayed dead. Zannis wasn't sure what to do. Wait for the connection to return? Or hang up so the operator could make a new call? He looked at his watch, let two minutes go by, then placed the receiver back on the cradle. What had she done? Clearly she'd sent fugitives, two Jewish women from Berlin, to Salonika. Where he was to help them. *She could have asked, at least*. But maybe she couldn't, he thought. He sat there, his mind working, staring out of the window at a streetlamp on the Via Egnatia. Then the phone rang and he snatched the receiver.

'Hotel Operator, Mont Blanc. Your call is reconnected, one mo—...'

The static was worse on the new connection. Emilia Krebs shouted, 'Hello? Herr Zannis?'

'Listen to me.' Zannis's voice was loud and urgent and he spoke quickly. 'I don't know where these people are, they haven't contacted me, but if they do, I'll send you a postal card. It won't say anything special, simply a greeting from abroad.'

'Meaning they've arrived safely.'

'That's it. Now, if you want to write to me, just buy Panadon tablets, the aspirin. Are they available in Berlin?'

'Yes.'

'Melt them in cold water, then write with the water between the lines of a letter and, if you get a letter from Greece, iron it, not too hot, the writing will appear.'

'How ma—...' Again, the line went dead.

It came back a few seconds later. Zannis said 'Hello?' and started to speak, but, after a click, a new connection. Now the voice of a woman, some operator in some country, spoke angrily in a language Zannis couldn't identify, and then, with another click, the connection was cut off. He waited at the desk until ten-thirty, staring at the telephone, but it was silent.

He would never hear from the sisters, he was almost certain of that. Evidently they'd set out from Berlin, some days earlier, trying to make their way to Salonika, where Zannis could help them get to Turkey, or Palestine, or wherever they could manage to slip over a border. Slip over, or bribe their way over, because as Jews in flight they were welcome nowhere in the world. Nowhere. Not one single country. And now, not as adept and forceful as their friend in Berlin, they had vanished. Well, lately people did. And they were never heard of again.

Back in his apartment, Zannis couldn't sleep. He was exhausted, had expected to be dead to the world the instant his head hit the pillow, but he'd been wrong. He tossed and turned, his mind racing. What had happened to him at the banker's villa – that tight band across the chest? He'd always been healthy, he had to be, there was no choice. Now what? Or maybe it was just nerves, which was, he thought, maybe even worse. But it had *reached* him, he had to admit that, the almost certain knowledge that invasion was imminent. This banker was a certain type of man, a type Zannis knew well. He had friends who knew things, and you couldn't plan an invasion – recall soldiers from leave, resupply your army with ammunition, medical stores and everything else – without people finding out about it. So the banker fled, and fled in a hurry – grabbed all the money he could and ran. *Sauve qui peut!* Run for your life! Write a note to the maids, do something about the dog, lock up the house and go. Poor dog. They were, the dogs, considered special spirits in Greece: faithful friends, fearless guardians. *I'm sure I was right about the dog*, Zannis thought, flipping his pillow over. The maids, the 'good girls', would take care of it.

And they were special spirits, faithful guardians.

Thus it was Melissa who figured it out, sensed it, before he did. Zannis must have dozed because, just after dawn, she growled, a subdued, speculative sort of growl – *what's this?* And Zannis woke up.

'Melissa? What goes on?'

She stood at the window, *out there*, turned her head and stared at him as he unwound himself from the snarled bedding. What had caught her attention, he realized, were voices, coming from below, on Santaroza Lane. Agitated, fearful voices. Somebody across the street had a window open and a radio on. It wasn't music – Zannis couldn't make out the words but he could hear the tone of voice, pitched low and grim.

He opened the window. One of the ladies who sat in a kitchen chair on sunny days was standing in the street, her black shawl pulled tight around her head and shoulders, gesticulating with her hands as she talked to a neighbour.

Zannis leaned out of the window, called her by name and said, 'What's going on?'

She looked up at him. 'The Italians,' she said. 'They've invaded us.'

Poor Mussolini.

Such a puffed-up, strutting horse's arse. Not a man to be ignored, the way he saw it. And surely he had been ignored. Left standing there, shouting slogans from the balcony, thrusting his chubby fist in the air, while that sneaky Hitler conquered the world. Took Austria, Czechoslovakia, Poland, France, Belgium, the Netherlands, Norway and Denmark. Now *that* was an empire!

And Mussolini? And his new Roman Empire? What glory had it won? Not much. Occupied Albania, publicly scorned as 'a handful of rocks'. And Ethiopia. What would you call that, a handful of mud? And Libya, a handful of sand? And oh yes, not to forget that when Hitler invaded France, Mussolini rushed in ten days later and took … Nice! So now the doorman at the Negresco would have to bow down to the might of Rome.

Ha-ha!

Said the world. But the worst thing you can do to a dictator is laugh at him – that's contempt, not awe, and it made Mussolini mad. Well, he'd show the world, he'd take Greece. So there, still laughing? And he didn't tell Hitler about it, he didn't ask permission, he just went ahead and did it. And when Hitler heard the news, as dawn broke on the twenty-eighth of October, he was reportedly enraged. Known to be a *tepik fresser*, a carpet chewer, he'd likely gone down on his knees, once he was alone, and given his favourite rug a good thorough grinding.

Zannis got the details on his way to work, from headlines on the newspaper kiosks, from the newspaper he bought – which he read while walking – and from people in the street. Greece was at war, everybody was talking to everybody, there were no strangers that day. Least of all the soldiers, reservists called to duty, hundreds of them, many accompanied by wives and children so they could say goodbye at the railway station. And not a soul abroad that morning didn't stop to wish them well.

'Be careful, my child.'

'Remember, keep your head down!'

'You give them a good kick in the arse for me, and don't forget!'

'So maybe you need a little extra money? A few drachmas?'

'Here, have a cigarette. I *see* you're smoking, take it anyhow, for later.'

'Good luck, take care of yourself.'

This from Zannis, looking up from his newspaper. He might well be joining them, he thought, before the day was done. In 1934, when he'd become a detective, he had automatically been assigned to a General Staff reserve unit in Salonika. If Greece went to war, the army could call up however many detective-grade officers it required because, in a small country, every male below the age of sixty had to be available to serve.

According to the paper, there had been a grand dinner party

the night before, in Athens. Count Grazzi, the Italian ambassador, had invited the most important people in the city, including General Metaxas. Seated beneath the crossed flags of Italy and Greece, the guests drank 'to our eternal friendship for Greece', Count Grazzi himself having stood to propose the toast. Eventually, they all went home. But then, at three in the morning, Grazzi was driven to the home of General Metaxas, who came to the door in his dressing gown. Grazzi presented an ultimatum: Let our army march into your country and occupy the cities. Metaxas's answer wasn't complicated; it could be seen at the top of every front page of every newspaper.

'No.'

When Zannis opened the office door, he saw that Sibylla was knitting. She worked feverishly; hands moving quickly, needles clicking, a ball of grey wool in her lap. 'By the time I got to the shop,' she said, 'and they had it open at six-thirty, all the khaki was gone. Imagine that! Not yet seven-thirty when I got there, and all the khaki wool bought up.'

'What will it be?'

'A sweater. One has a choice, sweater or socks, but I'm good at it, so I decided to make sweaters.'

All over the country, women were knitting warm clothes for the Greek boys who would be fighting in the cold mountains. A poor country, less than eight million in population, they had to improvise. So Sibylla's fingers flew and, when the phone rang, she propped the receiver between chin and shoulder and never dropped a stitch. Producing, Zannis thought, a rather curious juxtaposition. 'And what time did you say he was murdered?' Click, click.

Zannis tried to telephone Vangelis but the line was busy, so he looked over at Saltiel and said, 'What about you, Gabi? Are you leaving today?'

'Too old to fight. Officially. For the time being, I'm to take the place of an ambulance driver who's going up to the border with the medical corps. So I get to drive around the city at night with a siren on. So what's new.'

'And days?'

'I'll be here. What about you?'

'I'm waiting for orders,' Zannis said. 'I'm in a reserve group, we're a communications unit, and I'm liaison with an officer of the Yugoslav General Staff. Not really sure what that means, but I guess I'll find out.'

It was late in the morning when he finally got through to Vangelis. 'I'm waiting,' Zannis explained, 'for a call or a telegram. But I could be ordered to report. Maybe even today, or tomorrow.'

'Have you given any thought to what you might do if they occupy the city?'

'No, but I suppose I should.'

'We wouldn't want them to have the files,' Vangelis said. 'After that, it will be up to you. Just remember, if you decide to work underground, be careful with your address book. Just in case.' He paused, then said, 'For the moment, who will run the office?'

'Saltiel and Sibylla. They'll do fine.'

Vangelis didn't answer immediately, his way of saying that it wasn't true. 'I'm not sure what lies ahead, Costa, but if I need you, I may have you brought back. We'll just have to see how it goes.'

'We may surprise them,' Zannis said.

'Yes, I think we will,' Vangelis said. 'If we don't run out of bullets.'

Late in the afternoon, a telephone call for Zannis. Not the General Staff, but Roxanne. She sounded rattled, almost desperate. This was something new – she'd been cool and composed from the first day he'd met her. 'I didn't want to call you,' she said, 'but I didn't know what else to do.'

'What's wrong?'

'I have to get to the airport. But there isn't a taxi to be found in the whole city, and my friends with cars don't answer their phones, or they're driving somebody to Athens, or – or *something!*'

'Roxanne . . .'

'What?'

'Calm down.'

'Sorry, I've just had—'

'There's no point in going to the airport, all commercial flights are cancelled; we're at *war* – the military has taken over out there. Now, tell me where you need to go and I'll see what I can do.'

'I need to go to the airport. Please.'

'Are we going to fight about this? You think I didn't tell you the truth?'

'Costa, can you borrow a car? Or get one from the police?'

After a moment, he said, in a different tone of voice, 'What is this?'

'A favour. I have never asked you for a favour, not ever, but I'm asking now. And part of the favour is not trying to make me explain on the telephone, because I have to be there right away.'

'Hold on.' He turned to Saltiel and said, 'Gabi, may I use your car for an hour?'

Saltiel stared at him. *I don't let anyone drive my car.* 'Well, I suppose you can, if you need it.' He was clearly not happy.

'Did you hear that?' Zannis said, on the phone.

'Yes.'

'I'll pick you up in ten minutes.'

It was a rough ride to the airport, some fifteen miles east of the city. Convoys of army trucks were rolling west, towards them, heading for the roads that went up to the Albanian border. And, being army convoys on the first day of a war, saw no reason, in the national interest, not to use both lanes. So more than once Zannis had to swerve off the road, the Skoda bumping over a rocky field. Teeth clamped together, he waited for the blown-out tyre or the broken spring, though it happened, over and over again, only in his imagination. But that was bad enough.

Meanwhile, from Roxanne, stony silence, broken occasionally by English oaths, *bloody* this and *bloody* that, delivered under her breath every time the trucks came at them. Finally, answering the unasked question, she said, 'If you must know, it's just some friends who want me *out* of here.'

'Powerful friends,' Zannis said. 'Friends with aeroplanes.'

'Yes, powerful friends. I know you have them; well, so do I.'

'Then I'm happy for you.'

'*Bloody* ... ' A muttered syllable followed.

'What?'

'Never mind. Just drive.'

Coming around a bend, they were suddenly confronted by a pair of petrol tankers, side by side, horns blaring. Zannis swung the wheel over, the back end broke free and they went skidding sideways into a field. The car stalled, Zannis pressed the ignition button, the Skoda coughed, then started. But the army wasn't done with them. Just before they reached the airport, a long convoy came speeding right at them – and this time they almost didn't make it. The car idled by the side of the road, pebbles hit the windscreen, soldiers waved, Roxanne swore, Zannis fumed.

The airport was deserted. The Royal Hellenic Air Force – about a hundred planes: a few PZL-24s, Polish-built fighters, and whatever else they'd managed to buy over the years – was operating from airbases in the west. A sign on the door of the terminal building said ALL FLIGHTS CANCELLED, and the only signs of life were a small group of soldiers on guard duty and a crew gathered beside its anti-aircraft gun. They'd built a fire and were roasting somebody's chicken on a bayonet.

Roxanne had only a small valise – Zannis offered to carry it but she wouldn't let him. They walked around the terminal building and there, parked in a weedy field by the single paved runway, was a small monoplane, a Lysander, with a British RAF roundel on the fuselage. The pilot, sitting with his back against the wheel, was smoking a cigarette and reading a Donald Duck comic book. He stood when he saw them coming and flicked his cigarette away. Very short, and very small, he looked, to Zannis's eyes, no more than seventeen.

'Sorry I'm late,' Roxanne said.

The pilot peered up at the gathering darkness and strolled back towards the observer's cockpit, directly behind the pilot's – both were open, no canopies to be seen. 'Getting dark,' he said. 'We'd better be going.'

Roxanne turned to Zannis and said, 'Thank you.'

He stared at her and finally said, 'You're not going to England, are you.'

'No, only to Alexandria. I may well be back; it's simply a precaution.'

'Of course, I understand.' His voice was flat and dead because he was heartsick. '*Now,*' he added, 'I understand.' *And how could I have been so stupid I never saw it?* The British government didn't send Lysanders to rescue the expatriate owners of ballet schools, they sent them to rescue secret service operatives.

Her eyes flashed; she moved towards him and spoke, intensely but privately, so the pilot wouldn't hear. 'It wasn't to do with you,' she said. 'It wasn't to do with you.'

'No, of course not.'

Suddenly she grabbed a handful of his shirt, just below the collar, and twisted it, her knuckles sharp where they pressed against his chest. It surprised him, how strong she was, and the violence was a shock – this hand, in the past, had been very nice to him. 'Wasn't,' she said. Her eyes were dry, but he could see she was as close to tears as she ever came. And then he realized that the hand clutching his shirt wasn't there in anger, it was furiously, almost unconsciously, trying to hold on to something it had lost.

The pilot cleared his throat. 'Getting dark,' he said. He knotted his fingers, making a cup out of his hands, nodded up at the observer cockpit and said, 'Up we go, luv.'

Zannis walked with Roxanne the few feet to the plane. She turned and looked at him, then rested her foot on the waiting hands and was hoisted upward, floundered for a moment, skirt rising to reveal the backs of her thighs, then swung her legs over into the cockpit. The pilot smiled at Zannis, a boyish grin which made him look even younger than seventeen, and said, 'Don't worry, mate, I'm good at this.' He handed Roxanne her valise, jumped up on the wheel housing and climbed into the pilot's cockpit. A moment later, the engine roared to life and the propeller spun. Zannis watched the Lysander as it taxied, then lifted into the air and turned south, heading out over the Aegean towards Egypt.

Back in the office, a yellow sheet of teletype paper lay on his desk. From Lazareff in Sofia.

COSTA: DO US ALL A FAVOUR AND CHASE THESE
BASTARDS BACK WHERE THEY CAME FROM

The message was in Bulgarian, but Zannis had grown up in Salonika, 'a city where even the bootblacks speak seven languages,' and was able to figure it out. Normally, he would have enjoyed Lazareff's gesture, but now he just sat there, his mood dark and melancholy, and stared at the wall.

He came to believe, after going back over their time together, that Roxanne hadn't lied, that he'd not been the target of a British spy operation. He could not recall a single time when she'd asked him anything that might touch on the sort of information that spies sought. So, in fact, it wasn't to do with him. He'd had a love affair with a woman who'd been sent to Salonika as part of an intelligence operation. Then, when war came, when occupation by an Axis force was more than possible, they'd snatched her away. Or maybe she simply did have friends in high places, friends with the power to organize an RAF Lysander flight to Greece. No, she'd actually confessed. 'It wasn't to do with you.' The *it*. To do with somebody else. The Germans, the Italians, the Vichy French consul; there were many possibilities.

Should he tell somebody? What, exactly, would he tell? And to who? Spiraki? Never. Vangelis? Why? His job was discretion; his job was to keep things quiet. Well, he would. And if she returned? It might be easier if she didn't. At the least, they'd have to come to some sort of understanding. Or pretend it had never happened? Slowly, he shook his head. *This war — look what it does.* In truth, he missed her already. Maybe they weren't in love but they'd been passionate lovers — she'd been his warm place in a cold world. And now he had to go up north and kill Italians, so maybe he was the one who wouldn't be coming back.

The telephone rang and Saltiel answered it, said 'I see' and 'very well' a few times, made notes and hung up.

'What was that?' Zannis said.

'The mayor's chief assistant.' He rubbed his hands back through his hair and sighed. 'Sometimes I don't know whether to laugh or cry.'

Sibylla looked up from her sweater.

'It seems the mayor has a niece, a favourite niece, recently married; she lives out by Queen Olga Street.'

'I know who she is,' Zannis said. 'Pretty girl.'

'Well, maybe she was distracted by the war, maybe, I don't know, something else. Anyhow, this afternoon she went to feed her pet bird, a parakeet. And, unfortunately, she left the door of the cage open, and it flew away.'

Zannis waited a moment, then said, 'And that's it?'

'Yes.'

Sibylla turned away, and, as she started to knit, made a small noise — not a laugh, but a snort.

'It's true? You're not just saying this to be funny?'

'No. It's true.'

Now it was Zannis's turn to sigh. 'Well, I guess you'll have to call her,' he said. 'And tell her ... what? Put an advertisement in the newspaper? We can't go out and look for it.'

'Tell her to leave the window open,' Sibylla said, 'and the door of the cage, and have her put some of its food in there.'

Saltiel made the call, his voice soothing and sympathetic, and he was on for a long time. Then, ten minutes later, the telephone rang again and, this time, it *was* the General Staff.

8.35 p.m. It began to rain, softly, no downpour, just enough to make the road surface shine beneath the streetlamps. Still, it meant that it would be snowing in the mountains. Zannis waited on the corner of the Via Egnatia closest to Santaroza Lane, a canvas knapsack slung on his shoulder. The Vardari, the wind that blew down the Vardar valley, was sharp and Zannis turned away from it, faced the port and watched the lightning as it lit the clouds above the sea. Moments later the thunder followed, distant rumblings, far to the south.

He'd had a hectic time of it since he left the office. Had taken a taxi back to Santaroza Lane, packed some underwear, socks and a sweater, then threw in his old detective's sidearm, the same detective's version of the Walther PPK that Saltiel had, and a box of bullets. Then he changed into his reservist's uniform, a close cousin to what British officers wore, with a Sam Browne belt that looped over one shoulder. He searched for, and eventually found inside a valise, his officer's cap, and, Melissa by his side, hurried out of the door to find another taxi.

Up at his mother's house in the heights, the mood was quiet and determined – basically acceptance. They fussed over Melissa, fed her and set out her water bowl and blanket, and gave Zannis a heavy parcel wrapped in newspaper – sandwiches of roast lamb in pitta bread – which he stowed in his knapsack on top of the gun and the underwear. For some reason, this brought to mind a scene in Homer, dimly remembered from school, where one of the heroes prepares to go to war. Probably, Zannis thought,

62

given some version of the lamb and pitta, though that didn't get into the story. After he buckled the knapsack, his brother, mother and grandmother each embraced him; then his grandmother pressed an Orthodox medal into his hand. 'It saved your grandfather's life,' she said. 'Keep it with you always. You promise, Constantine?' He promised. Melissa sat by his side as he was saying a final goodbye, and, last thing before he went out of the door, he bent over and she gave him one lick on the ear. She knew.

On the corner, Zannis looked at his watch and shifted his feet. Well, he thought, if you had to go to war you might as well leave from the Via Egnatia. An ancient street, built first in the second century B.C. as a military road for the Roman Empire. It began as the Via Appia, the Appian Way, in Rome, went over to Brindisi, where one crossed the Adriatic to Albanian Durrës and the road took the name Via Egnatia. Then it ran down to Salonika and went east, eventually reaching Byzantium – Constantinople. Thus it linked the two halves of the Byzantine Empire, Roman Catholic and Italian in the west, Eastern Orthodox and Greek in the east. Sixteen hundred years of it, until the Turks won a war.

Zannis lit a cigarette and looked at his watch again, then saw a pair of headlights coming towards him down the street. A French-built staff car, old and boxy, a relic, with a blue-and-white Greek pennant flown from the whippy radio aerial. When it drew up in front of him, a General Staff captain in the passenger seat opened the back door from inside. 'Lieutenant Zannis,' he said. Zannis saluted and climbed in; two other men in the back seat moved over and made room for him. It was smoky in the car, and rain dripped through a tear in the canvas top.

The driver worked hard, winding up into the mountains on dark roads, the wiper brushing across the windscreen. He was employed, he said, by the telephone company in Salonika, as a maintenance supervisor, 'but I spent years working on the lines, relay stations, the whole system.' The other two men simply gave their names and, still civilians, shook hands, though they were sergeants, and Zannis, who'd signed up for the reserves when he became an officer, a lieutenant. The captain was a real serving captain, very smart-looking in his uniform, with a small moustache and glasses. 'I'm in signals,' he said, 'communications of all sorts,' and let it go at that.

For a time, the mountain roads were deserted; then, climbing a steep grade that curved sharply to the right, they came up behind an army truck. The headlights revealed soldiers, rifles between their knees, sitting on two benches that ran the length of the truck bed. One of them waved.

'*Evzones*,' the captain said. The word meant sharpshooters. Their ceremonial uniforms – white kilt and hat with tassel – were derived from the klephts who'd fought the Turks. In fact, once the ceremonial uniforms were changed for traditional battlefield dress, the Evzones were the elite combat units of the army. 'I don't think,' the captain said, 'the Italians will be glad to see them coming.'

'Well, I am,' said the man next to Zannis. In his late forties, he'd served in the army as a wireless/telegraph operator. 'But that was years ago' he said. 'Now I work in a pharmacy.'

The bend in the road seemed to go on forever, jagged walls of stone rising above them in silhouette against the night sky. When at last the road straightened out, the driver swung over into the left lane and tried to pass the crawling truck. A foot at a time, the staff car gained ground.

'Can we do this?' the captain said.

'*Skata*,' the driver said. 'My foot is on the floor.'

As they drew level with the cab of the truck, its driver rolled down his window, turned and grinned at them, stuck his hand out and, waved it forward with comic impatience: *faster, faster*. Zannis watched the horizon for headlights coming towards them but there was nothing out there. 'A snail race,' said the man next to Zannis. The driver of the army truck leaned out of the window and shouted.

The captain said, 'What did he say?'

'Move your arse,' Zannis said.

The captain laughed. 'Poor old thing, she fought in France.'

They were rounding another bend before they finally got back into the right lane. 'Can you tell us where we're going?' Zannis asked.

'Can't be sure,' the captain said. 'Right now, we're supposed to be based in Trikkala, but that might change. As of five this afternoon, the Italians – the Alpini division, the mountain troops – have advanced ten miles into Greece. They are going for Janina, supported by a tank column, the centre of a three-pronged attack which will cut the only rail line and the two main roads – that would mean no reinforcements from Macedonia. It's the plan you draw up in military school, however—' He paused as the staff car skidded and the driver swore and fought the wheel. When the car steadied he said, 'However, I doubt they'll reach Janina, and likely not Trikkala.'

'Why not?' the wireless operator said.

'Oh ... let's just say we knew they were coming. Not when, but we knew where and how. So we prepared ... a few things.'

The silence following that admission was appreciative. The wireless operator said, 'Hunh,' which meant something like *that's the way.* Then he said, 'Fucking *makaronades*.' Greek for macaronis, the national insult name for the Italians. There was contempt in the expression, as though their ancient enemies, Bulgarians, Albanians and Turks, were at least serious opponents, whereas the attack by Italy was somehow worthy of contempt. In August, off the island of Tenos, an Italian submarine had torpedoed the cruiser *Helle*, in harbour, in full view of the people on the island, and on a religious holiday. This was seen more as cowardice than aggression, a Roman Catholic attack on an Eastern Orthodox religious festival, thus especially dishonourable. Not that they hadn't disliked the Italians before that. They had, for centuries.

A few minutes later, the driver stopped the car – there was nowhere to pull over – and, shoulder to shoulder, they all peed off the side of the mountain. It was a long way down, Zannis saw, a long, long way. As he rebuttoned his fly, the truck carrying the Evzones came chugging up the road, its engine labouring hard. When the driver saw the staff car, he swung around it and, passing close to the men standing at the edge of the mountain, and observing what occupied them, he blew a mighty blast on his klaxon horn, which echoed off the mountainside. Then it was the turn of the soldiers who, as their truck rumbled away, called out a variety of suggestions and insults, all of them obscene.

The driver, standing next to Zannis, swore and said, 'Now I'll have to pass them all over again.'

'Oh well,' the captain said, giving himself a couple of shakes, 'the fortunes of war.'

THE BACK
DOOR TO HELL

Poor Mussolini.

He, like everybody else in Europe who went to the movies, had seen the Pathé newsreels. First a title, in the local language, flashed on a black screen: GERMANY INVADES POLAND! Followed by combat footage, the Panzer tanks of the Wehrmacht charging across the Polish steppe, accompanied by dire and dramatic music. Loud music. And the words of a narrator with a rich, deep, theatrical voice. The effect was powerful – here was *history* being made, right before your eyes.

Mussolini hated it, couldn't get the image out of his mind. For he sensed that whatever made Hitler look powerful made him look meagre, but, fifteen months later, here came a chance to put things right – he'd had more than enough of being mocked as the conqueror of . . . Nice! Now he'd show the world who was who and what was what. Because he had tanks of his own, an armoured formation known as the Centauri Division, named after the mythic Greek figure, half man, half horse. Shown always as the top of the man and the back of the horse, though there were those who suggested that, in the case of Mussolini's army, it should be the other way round.

Mussolini paced the rooms of his palace in Rome and brooded. Was the lightning attack known as Blitzkrieg the private property of Adolf Hitler? Oh no it wasn't! He would storm into Greece just as Hitler's Panzers had done in Poland. And his generals, whose politics carefully conformed with his own, encouraged him. The Centauri would smash through the vineyards and olive groves of southern Greece; nothing could stop them, because the Greek army hadn't a single tank, not one. Hah! He'd crush them!

Alas, it was not to be. The problem was the geography of *northern* Greece, massive ranges of steep jagged mountains – after all, this was the Balkans, and 'balkan' literally meant 'mountain' in Turkish. So Mussolini's Blitzkrieg would have to attack down the narrow valleys, protected by Alpini troops occupying the heights above them. Which might have worked out but for the Evzones, one regiment of them opposing the Alpini division.

The Greeks, contrary to Italian expectations, fought to the death.

Took terrible casualties, but defeated the Alpini, who broke and fled back towards the Albanian border. Now the Greeks held the mountains and when the Centauri came roaring down the valleys two things happened. First, many of the tanks plunged into a massive ditch that had been dug in their path, often winding up on their backs, and second, those that escaped the ditch were subject to shelling from above, by short-barrelled, high-wheeled mountain guns. These guns, accompanied by ammunition, had been hauled over the mountains by mules and then, when the mules collapsed and died of exhaustion, by men.

As the first week in November drew to a close, it was clear that the Italian invasion had stalled. Mussolini raged, Mussolini fired generals, Greek reinforcements reached the mountain villages, and it began to snow. The unstoppable Axis had, for the first time, been stopped. And of this the world press took notice: headlines in boldface, everywhere in Europe. Which included Berlin, where these developments were viewed with, to put it mildly, considerable irritation. Meanwhile, poor Mussolini had once again been humiliated, and now the Greek army was poised to enter Albania.

In Trikkala, an ancient town divided by a river, the snow-capped peaks of the Pindus Mountains were visible when the sun came out. Which, fortunately, the first week in November, it did not do. The sky stayed overcast, a solid mass of grey cloud that showered down an icy rain. The Italian bomber pilots, at the airfields up in Albania, played cards in their barracks.

The Salonika communications unit was at least indoors, having bivouacked in the local school along with other reservists. They'd stacked the chairs against the wall and slept on the floor. Dry, but bored. Each member of the unit had been armed for war by the issue of a blanket, a helmet and a French Lebel rifle made in 1917. The captain took Zannis aside and said, 'Ever fire one of these?'

'No, never.'

'Too bad. It would be good for you to practise, but we can't spare the ammunition.' He chambered a bullet, closed the bolt and handed the weapon to Zannis. 'It has a three-round tube. You work the bolt, look through the sight, find an Italian and pull the trigger. It isn't complicated.'

There was, that first week, little enough to do. The General Staff was based in Athens, with a forward position in Janina. But if things went wrong at Janina they would have to serve as a relay station, take information coming in over the telephone – the lines ended at Trikkala – and transmit it to front-line officers by wireless/telegraph. 'We are,' the captain said, 'simply a reserve unit. And let's hope it stays that way.'

As for Zannis, his liaison counterpart from the Yugoslav General Staff was apparently still trying to reach Trikkala. Where he, if and when he ever showed up, could join the unit in waiting around. Yugoslavia had not entered the war. In the past, Greeks and Serbs had been allies in the First Balkan War in 1912, and again in the Balkan campaigns against Germany, Bulgaria and Turkey in the 1914 war, and greatly respected each other's abilities on the battlefield. But now, if Yugoslavia attacked Mussolini, it was well understood that Hitler would attack Yugoslavia, so Belgrade remained *on alert*, but the army had not mobilized.

Meanwhile, they waited. Early one morning, Spyro, the pharmacist-turned-wireless-operator, sat at a teacher's desk and tapped out a message. He had been ordered to do this, to practise daily, and send one message every morning, to make sure the system worked. As Zannis watched, he sent and received, back and forth, while keeping a record on a scrap of paper. When he took off the headset, he smiled.

'What's going on?' Zannis said.

'This guy up in Metsovon . . .' He handed Zannis the paper. 'Here, take a look for yourself.'

TRIKKALA REPORTING 9 NOVEMBER.
WHY DO YOU SEND ME MESSAGES?
I AM ORDERED TO SEND ONCE A DAY.
DON'T YOU KNOW WE'RE BUSY UP HERE?
I HAVE TO FOLLOW ORDERS.
WHAT SORT OF MAN ARE YOU?
A SOLDIER.
THEN COME UP HERE AND FIGHT.
THAT WOULD BE FINE WITH ME.
LOOKING FORWARD TO SEEING YOU.

Every day it rained, and every day long lines of Italian prisoners moved through Trikkala, on their way to a POW camp somewhere south of the town. Zannis couldn't help feeling sorry for them, cold and wet and miserable, eyes down as they trudged past the school. When the columns appeared, the reservists would bring out food or cigarettes, whatever they could spare, for the exhausted Greek soldiers guarding the prisoners.

Late one afternoon, Zannis walked along with one of the soldiers and gave him a chocolate bar he'd bought at the market. 'How is it up there?' he said.

'We try not to freeze,' the soldier said. 'It's got to a point where fighting's a relief.'

'A lot of fighting?'

'Depends. Sometimes we advance, and they retreat. Every now and then they decide to fight, but, as you can see, much of the time they just surrender. Throw away their rifles and call out, "*Bella Grecia! Bella Grecia!*"' When he said this, one of the prisoners turned to look at him.

'Beautiful Greece?'

The soldier shrugged and adjusted the rifle strap on his shoulder. 'That's what they say.'

'What do they mean? That Greece is beautiful and they like it and they never wanted to fight us?'

'Maybe so. But then, what the fuck are they doing down here?'

'Mussolini sent them.'

The soldier nodded and said, 'Then fuck him too.' He marched on, tearing the paper off his chocolate bar and eating it slowly. When he was done he turned and waved to Zannis and called out, 'Thank you!'

By the second week in November, Greek forces had crossed the Albanian border and taken the important town of Koritsa, several small villages and the port of Santi Quaranta, which meant that Greece's British ally could resupply the advance more efficiently. At the beginning of the war, they'd had to bring their ships into the port of Piraeus. Also, on Tuesday of that week, Zannis's Yugoslav counterpart showed up. He was accompanied by a corporal who carried, along with his knapsack, a metal suitcase of the sort used to transport a wireless/telegraph. The two of them stood there, dripping on the tiles just inside the doorway of the school.

'Let's go and find a taverna,' Zannis said to the officer. 'Your corporal can get himself settled in upstairs.'

Zannis led the way towards the main square, a waterproof groundsheet draped over his head and shoulders. The reservists had discovered that their overcoats, once soaked, never dried out, so they used what was available and walked around Trikkala looking like monks in green cowls.

'I'm called Pavlic,' the officer said. 'Captain Pavlic. Reserve captain, anyhow.'

'Costa Zannis. Lieutenant Zannis, officially.'

They shook hands awkwardly as they walked. Zannis thought Pavlic was a few years older than he was, with a weather-beaten face, sand-coloured hair and narrow eyes with deep crow's-feet at the corners, as though he'd spent his life at sea, perpetually on watch.

'Your Greek is very good,' Zannis said.

'It should be. I grew up down here, in Volos; my mother was half Greek and my father worked for her family. I guess that's why I got this job.' They walked for a time, then Pavlic said, 'Sorry I'm so late, by the way. I was on a British freighter and we broke down – had to go into port for repairs.'

'You didn't miss anything, not too much happens around here.'

'Still, I'm supposed to report in, every day. We have another officer in Janina, and there's a big hat, a colonel, at your General Staff headquarters in Athens. It's all a formality, of course, unless we mobilize. And, believe me, we won't do any such thing.'

In the taverna, rough plank tables were crowded with local men and reservists, the air was dense with cigarette smoke and the smell of spilled retsina, and a fire of damp grapevine prunings crackled and sputtered on a clay hearth. It didn't provide much heat but it was a very loud fire, and comforting in its way. The boy who served drinks saw them standing there, rushed over and said, 'Find a place to sit,' but there was no table available so they stood at the bar. Zannis ordered two retsinas. 'The retsina is good here,' he said. 'Local.' When the drinks came, Zannis raised his glass. 'To your health.'

'And to yours.' When he'd had a sip, Pavlic said, 'You're right, it is good. Where are you from?'

'Salonika. I'm a policeman there.'

74

'No!'

'Don't like the police?'

'Hell, it isn't that, I'm one also.'

'You are? Really? Where?'

'Zagreb.'

'*Skata!* A coincidence?'

'Maybe your General Staff did it on purpose.'

'Oh, yes, of course you're right. You can trust a policeman.'

From Pavlic, a wry smile. 'Most of the time,' he said.

Zannis laughed. 'We do what we have to, it's true,' he said. 'Are you a detective, in Zagreb?'

'I was, for twenty years, and I expect you know all about that. But now, the last year or so, I'm in charge of the cars, the motor pool.'

'Your preference?'

'Not at all. It was a, how should I put this, it was a *political* transfer. The people who run the department, the commissioner and his friends at city hall, got at.'

'Got at.' Such things happened all the time, but Zannis couldn't stop himself from being shocked when he heard about it. 'Bribed?'

'No, not bribed. Intimidated? Persuaded? Who knows, I don't. What happened was that I didn't hold back, in fact worked extra hard, investigating certain crimes. Crimes committed by the Ustashi – Croatian fascists, and great friends with Mussolini; they take money from him. Maybe you're aware of that.'

'I'm not. But it's no surprise.'

'Of course they consider themselves *patriots*, fighters in the struggle for Croatian independence – they sing about it, in the bars – but in fact they're terrorists, Balkan Nazis. And when it was reported that they'd beaten somebody up, or burned his house down, or murdered him in front of his family – their favoured method, by the way – I went after them. I hunted them down. Not that they stayed in jail, they didn't, but it was a matter of honour for me. And not just me. There were plenty of us.'

Zannis's face showed what he felt: disgust. 'Still,' he said, after a moment, 'it could have been worse.'

'That's true. I'm lucky to be alive. But you know how it goes – you can't take that into account, not when you do what we do.'

'No, you can't. At least I can't. I'm a fatalist, I guess.' Zannis drank the last of his retsina, caught the eye of the woman behind the bar, raised his empty glass and wiggled it. The woman quickly brought two more. Pavlic started to pay but Zannis beat him to it, tossing coins on the bar. 'I'm the host,' he said. 'Here in scenic Trikkala.'

'All right. My turn next time.' Pavlic raised his glass to Zannis, drank some retsina, reached into the inside pocket of his uniform tunic and brought out a packet of cigarettes. 'Do you smoke? Try one of these.'

On the packet, a bearded sailor looked out through a lifebelt. 'Player's,' Zannis said. 'English?'

'Yes. I got them on the freighter.' Pavlic lit their cigarettes with a steel lighter. 'What do you do, in Salonika?'

'I run a small office where we take care of ... special cases. We deal with the rich and powerful, foreigners, diplomats – whatever's a little too sensitive for the regular detectives. I report to the commissioner, who's been a good friend to me, for a long time.'

'Lucky.'

'Yes.'

'But you have something similar to the Ustashi: the IMRO – they used to work together, if I have my history right. What is it, Internal Macedonian Revolutionary Organization?'

'It is. And founded in Salonika, back in the last century. They're slavic Macedonians, Bulgarians mostly, who think they're going to have a separate Macedonia. But, thank heaven, they've been quiet for a few years.'

'More luck – especially for your Salonika Jews. Because our

Jews, in Zagreb, are right at the top of the Ustashi *list*. They'd like to get rid of the Serbs, and the Croat politicians who oppose them, but they really have it in for the Jews. If the Ustashi ever took control of the city, well . . .'

Zannis heard the words *our Jews* as though Pavlic had emphasized them. For some reason, a fleeting image of Emilia Krebs crossed his mind. 'That won't happen in Salonika,' he said. 'Not with IMRO, not with anybody.'

'It's a damn shame, what's being done to them, up in Germany. And the police just stand there and watch.' Pavlic's face showed anger, his policeman's heart offended by the idea of criminals allowed to do whatever they wanted. 'Politics,' he said, as though the word were an oath.

For a time they stood in silence, sipping their retsinas, and smoked their English cigarettes. Then Pavlic nodded towards the window and said, 'Here's *some* good news, anyhow.'

Through the cloudy glass, past the dead flies on the window-sill, Zannis saw that the wet street in front of the tavern was steaming. 'At last,' he said. 'It's been raining for days.'

Pavlic stubbed out his cigarette, making ready to leave the taverna. 'Once my corporal gets his wireless running, I'll let them know up in Belgrade: "Pavlic reporting. The sun's come out."'

Zannis smiled as he followed Pavlic through the door. The captain stopped for a moment and closed his eyes as he raised his face to the sun. 'By the way,' he said, 'I'm called Marko.'

'Costa,' Zannis said. And they headed back to the school.

The officers did their best to keep the reservists busy – callisthenics, marching drills, whatever they could think up – but the soldiers were there to wait until they were needed, waiting was their job, and so time passed very slowly. At night, as the chill of the schoolroom floor rose through his blanket, Zannis found it hard to sleep. He thought about Roxanne, reliving some of their warmer moments together: the way her face looked at climax;

times when she'd thought something up that particularly, spontaneously, excited her. Or maybe such ideas came to her when she was by herself, lost in fantasy, and she tried them out when she got the chance. That was true of him, likely true of her as well. A lot of love got made when lovers were apart, he thought.

But, with snoring men on either side of him, fantasy of this sort led nowhere. Instead, his mind drifted back to recent life in Salonika, which now seemed remote and distant. He sometimes recalled the German agent; more often Emilia Krebs and the two children. But, most often, the Rosenblum sisters he'd heard about during the frantic, disrupted telephone call from Switzerland. Unmarried sisters, he guessed: older, librarians. Helpless, vulnerable, trying to make their way through some dark night in Budapest, or wherever they'd been caught. No ability whatever to deal with clandestine life, with border patrols, police raids, informers, or conscientious fascist citizens who knew a Jew when they saw one, no matter the quality of their false papers.

Could he have helped them? How? He was absolutely sure that Emilia Krebs would not stop what she was doing – Germany was now the very essence of hell; continuous torment, no escape. And so her fugitives would be taken by the machine built to hunt them down. Again and again. This thought reached a very sore place inside him, and he could not stop thinking it.

The military population of Trikkala began to thin out as reservists were sent up to the fighting to replace the dead and wounded. Pavlic and Zannis worked together, Zannis receiving situation reports from the captain and handing them on to Pavlic for translation and transmission to the Yugoslav General Staff. Now and then Pavlic wanted to know more, and now and then Zannis went to the captain and requested more, and now and then clarification or expansion was provided. Mostly the reports included the daily numbers – enemy dead, wounded and captured – and names – villages, rivers and positions, taken or abandoned – as the Greek infantry laboured over the snow-covered mountains of Albania. The Yugoslavs read the reports, but their support wasn't needed, and so they did nothing. What help the Greeks had came from their British ally.

A senior officer, for example, who appeared with a truck one morning, a truck stacked with wooden crates. Almost a stage presence, this officer, who stood ramrod straight, had a splendid cavalry moustache and lacked only the monocle. Some forty reservists, Zannis among them, were organized to move the truck's cargo up to a village a few miles behind the front lines. The reservists stood in front of the school while the British officer addressed them in classical Greek – as though Shakespeare were making a speech to a platoon of East London sappers. But nobody smiled.

'Men,' the officer said, at a volume meant for the parade ground, 'these crates are important. They hold anti-tank rifles, fifty-five-calibre weapons with tripods that are fired by a single soldier, like Bren guns. The square crates contain anti-tank rounds, and you will take turns carrying them, because the ammunition is heavy'

There were two trucks for the reservists, and they managed to drive some way north on the rutted dirt roads, but with altitude the snow deepened and soon enough they were spending more time pushing their vehicles than driving them. So, unload the crates, and start walking. Which was hard work, in the snow. Zannis sweated, then shivered as the sweat dried in the icy chill of the mountain air. One reservist sprained an ankle, another had pains in the chest; none of them were really in fighting shape.

When darkness fell, Zannis rolled up in his blanket and groundsheet and slept in the snow. The wind sighed through the trees all night long and when the cold woke him he heard wolves in the distance. In the morning he was exhausted and needed force of will to keep going. Spyro, the former pharmacist, said, 'I don't know how much longer I can do this'; then he regripped the rope handle at his end of the crate and the two of them plodded forward. High above them, an eagle circled in the grey sky.

They reached the village late in the afternoon, where men from the forward positions would take the anti-tank rifles the rest of the way. When the small cluster of houses came into view, the dogs appeared – Melissa's *cousins*, Zannis thought – barking and threatening until a piercing whistle sent them trotting back home. When the column reached the centre of the village, the reservists went silent. The village well, which might have been there for a thousand years, was no more – some of the stonework remained, shattered and blackened, but that was all. And the houses on either side of the well were in ruins. 'A bomb,' the villagers said. They'd seen the planes above them; one of them descended towards the village and dropped a bomb. They'd watched it as it tumbled from the plane. It had killed two women, a child and a goat, and blown up their well. 'Why?' the villagers asked. 'Why did they do this to us?'

At the end of October, when war came to Trikkala, Behar saw it as an opportunity. He was Albanian, his family had lived in Trikkala since the time of the Ottoman Turks, but he was no less Albanian for that. Aged twenty-five when the war began, Behar had been a thief since the age of fourteen. Not that he was very good at it, he wasn't. As a teenager he'd spent a few months in the local jail for stealing a radio and, later on, a year in prison for trying to sell stolen tyres, on behalf of a man called Pappou. The name meant grandpa, a nickname, not so much because he was old and grey, but because he'd been a criminal for a long time and people were afraid of him, so he could call himself whatever he liked. Sometimes Pappou, just like a grandpa, would help out his little Trikkala 'family': give them something to sell and let them keep some of the money. Thus, for Behar, better to stay on the good side of Pappou.

With the war, and the soldiers crowding into Trikkala, Behar thought he would prosper. These people came from cities in the south; to Behar they looked rich, and rich people spent lavishly – perhaps they'd like a nice girl to keep them warm, or maybe a little hashish. They were, it was said, going to free Albania from the Italians, but Behar had never been to Albania and couldn't have cared less who ruled there. No, what mattered to Behar was that these people might want things or, if they didn't, could be separated from what they had: wristwatches, for example, or rifles. One way or the other, Behar knew they were meant to put money in his empty pockets.

But the soldiers weren't such easy targets, they were always together, they didn't pass out drunk in an alley – at least not in the alleys where he searched for them – and they went to the brothel for their girls. After a few days, Behar began to despair, war was not going to turn out to be much of an opportunity at all.

But then, in the second week of the war, Pappou came to his rescue. Behar lived in a shack at the edge of the city, with his mother and two sisters. They never had enough wood for the stove, so they froze during the winter and waited anxiously for spring. He was lying on his cot one afternoon when a boy came with a message: he was to go and see Pappou the following day. Two o'clock, the boy said, at the barbershop Pappou owned, where he did business in the back room.

Behar was excited. He walked to the edge of Trikkala to find his eldest brother, who owned a razor, and there scraped his face. Painful, using the icy water, because his brother was not so prosperous as to own soap. Behar made sure he got to the barbershop on time. He wore his grimy old suit, the only clothing he had, but he'd combed his hair and settled his short-brimmed cap at just the proper angle, down over his left eye. It was the best he could do. On the way to the shop he looked at himself in the glass of a display window; scrawny and hunched, hands in pockets, not such a bad face, he thought, though they'd broken his nose when he'd tried to steal food in the prison.

To Behar, the barbershop was a land of enchantment, where polished mirrors reflected white tile, where the air was warmed – by a nickel-plated drum that heated towels with steam, and scented – by the luxurious, sugary smell of rosewater, used to perfume the customers when they were done being barbered. There were two men in the chairs when Behar arrived, one with his face swathed in a towel, apparently asleep, though the cigar in his dangling hand was still smoking, the other in the midst of a haircut. The barber, as he snipped, spoke to his customer in a low, soothing voice. The weather might change, or maybe not.

When Behar entered the back room, Pappou, sitting at a table, spread his arms in welcome. 'Behar! Here you are, right on time! Good boy.' Sitting across from Pappou was a man who simply smiled and nodded. His friend here, Pappou explained, was not from Trikkala and needed a reliable fellow for a simple little job. Which he would explain in a minute. Again, the man nodded. 'It will pay you very well,' Pappou said, 'if you are careful and do exactly as you're told. Can you do that, my boy?' With great enthusiasm, Behar said he could. Then, to his considerable surprise, Pappou stood up, left the room and closed the door behind him. Outside, Pappou could be heard as he joked with the barbers, so he wasn't listening at the door.

The man leaned forward and asked Behar a few questions. He was, from the way he spoke, a foreigner. Clean-shaven, thick-lipped and prosperously jowly, he had a tight smile that Behar found, for no reason he could think of, rather chilling, and eyes that did not smile at all. The questions were not complicated. Where did he live? Did he like Trikkala? Was he treated well here? Behar answered with monosyllables, accompanied by what he hoped was an endearing smile. And did he, the foreigner wanted to know, wish to make a thousand drachmas? Behar gasped. The foreigner's smile broadened – that was a good answer.

The foreigner leaned closer and spoke in a confidential voice.

Here were all these soldiers who had come to Trikkala; did Behar know where they lived? Well, they seemed to be everywhere. They'd taken over the two hotels, some of them stayed at the school, others in vacant houses – wherever they could find a roof to keep them out of the rain. Very well, now for the first part of the job. The foreigner could see that Behar was a smart lad, didn't need to write anything down, and so shouldn't. Mustn't. Behar promised not to do that. An easy promise, he couldn't have written anything down even if he'd wanted to, for he could neither read nor write. 'Now then,' the foreigner said, 'all you have to do is . . .' When he was done, he explained again, then had Behar repeat the instructions. Clearly, Behar thought, a very careful foreigner.

He went to work that very afternoon, three hundred drachmas already in his pocket. A fortune. At one time he'd tried his hand – disastrously – at changing money for tourists, and he knew that a thousand drachmas was equal to ninety American dollars. To Behar, that was *more* than a thousand drachmas, that was like something in a dream, or a movie.

But then, delight was replaced by misery. As the light faded from the November afternoon, he walked the streets of Trikkala, his eyes searching the rooftops. He knew where the reservists lived, or thought he did, and went from one to the next, crisscrossing the town, but no luck. In time, he became desperate. What if the foreigner was *wrong*? What if the accursed object didn't exist? What then? Give back the three hundred drachmas? Well, he no longer had the three hundred drachmas. Because, immediately after leaving the foreigner he had, maddened by good fortune, visited a pastry shop where he'd bought a cream-filled slice of *bougatsa* with powdered sugar on top. So good! And then – he was rich, why not? – another, this one with cheese, even more expensive. Now what? Make good what he'd spent? How?

Thirty minutes later, fate intervened. In, for a change,

Behar's favour, as, for the third time in an hour, he paced the street in front of the school. A building that held, for Behar, nothing but terrible memories. The reservist soldiers went in and out, busy, occupied with important military matters. Up above, the sky had grown dark as it prepared to shower down some nice cold rain. Then, just for a moment, a thick cloud drifted aside and a few rays of sun, now low on the horizon, struck the school's chimney at just the proper angle. And Behar caught a single silver glint. Finally! There it was! Just as the foreigner had described it. A wire, run up from somewhere in the building and fixed in place by a rock atop the cement surround that topped the stuccoed plaster. Immediately, he looked away.

The rain held off. Fortunately, for Behar, it went away and found somewhere else to fall, because, for the second part of the job, he required sunshine. Which, the following morning, poured through the window of the shack and sent him off whistling to the better part of town, that part of town where people were used to certain luxuries. But this too turned out to be a difficult search, since the little gardens behind these houses were walled, so that Behar had to find a deserted street, check for broken glass cemented to the top of the wall – he'd learned about that years ago, the hard way – get a good grip and hoist himself up. His first few attempts were unproductive. Then, at the very end of a quiet street, he found what he was looking for: a garden with two fig trees, a clothes line strung between them, laundry out to dry. Underpants, panties, two towels, two pillow-cases and two big white sheets.

He hauled himself the rest of the way and lay on the wall. Anyone home? Should he go and knock on the front door? *Does Panos live here?* No. He stared at the house; shutters closed over the windows, all silent and still. He took a deep breath, counted to three and was over the wall. *Steal the underwear.* But he resisted the urge, snatched one of the sheets off the line and sprinted back to the wall. He hauled himself up, made sure the street was still deserted and sprang down. He folded the sheet, held it inside the front of his jacket and walked away.

Back home, he experimented. Working with concentration – the remaining seven hundred drachmas shimmered in his mind – he found he could wrap the sheet around his bare upper body and then button his shirt almost to the top, as long as he didn't tuck it into his trousers.

Now for the hard part. He stayed at home through the early evening, going out only after the bell in the town hall rang midnight. When he reached the school, the street was empty, though there were lights shining in the windows on both floors. But he had no intention of going in there, there wasn't a bluff in the world that would get him past all those soldiers. No, for the Behars of the world there was only the drainpipe, at a corner towards the back of the building. He knew these pipes, fixed together in flanged sections, the flanges extending from the curve every three feet or so, he'd climbed them many times in his stealthy life. First, shoes off – the soles worn so thin and smooth he'd get no traction at all. He had no socks, so he climbed barefoot, his toes pressed against the flange, his fingers pulling him up to the next level.

In a few minutes he was on the roof. He crouched down, keeping his silhouette below the sight line from the street, and crawled over to the chimney. Yes, here was the wire. He wanted to touch it, this ribbon of metal worth a thousand drachmas, but he had no idea what it might be for; perhaps it was charged with some mysterious form of electrical current and would burn his fingers with its magic. It was certainly a secret wire – that much he'd sensed in the voice of the foreigner – so, *leave it alone.* He took off his jacket and shirt, unwound the sheet and laid it flat on the roof.

What if the wind . . .? He searched the dark rooftop, looking for weight, but found only some loose stucco where a crack ran along one corner. He prised up a few pieces, not very heavy, and distributed them at the corners of the sheet. They would have to do. Below him, on the second floor of the school, he could hear voices, a laugh, another voice, another laugh. He scuttled back to the drainpipe, descended to the ground, put on his shoes and, feeling better than he'd felt in a long time, walked home. What did it mean, the sheet on the roof? He didn't know, he didn't care, he knew only what it meant to him.

The following morning he hurried off to the barbershop. In the back room, Pappou was cold and frightening. 'Is it done? Whatever it is – done properly?' Behar said yes. Pappou sat still, his eyes boring into Behar's soul, then he picked up the telephone and made a brief call. Asked for somebody with a Greek name, waited, finally said, 'You can have your hair cut any time you want, the barber is waiting for you.' That was all. The foreigner appeared ten minutes later, and Pappou went out into the shop.

The foreigner asked where he'd found the wire; Behar told him. 'Maybe I'll go up to the roof myself,' he said. 'What will I see?'

'A big white sheet, sir.'

'Flat?'

'Yes, sir.'

'Behar.' A pause. 'If you ever, *ever*, tell anybody about this, we will *know*. Understand?' With a slow, meticulous grace he drew an index finger across his throat, a gesture so eloquently performed that Behar thought he could actually see the knife. 'Understand?' the foreigner said again, raising his eyebrows.

A frightened Behar nodded emphatically. He understood all too well. The foreigner held his eyes for a time, then reached into his pocket and counted out seven one-hundred-drachma notes.

28 November. For Costa Zannis, it began as a normal day, but then it changed. He was standing next to the captain in the school's narrow cloakroom, which, with the addition of a teacher's desk, had been turned into what passed for a liaison office. Pavlic was just about to join them, it was the most

common moment imaginable; pleasant morning, daily chore, quiet talk. Zannis and the captain were looking down at a hand-drawn map, with elevations noted on lines indicating terrain, of some hilltop in Albania.

Then the captain grabbed his upper arm. A grip like a vice – sudden, instinctive.

Zannis started to speak – 'What . . .' – but the captain waved him into silence and stood frozen and alert, his head cocked like a listening dog. In the distance, Zannis heard a drone, aircraft engines, coming towards them. Coming low, not like the usual sound, high above. The captain let him go and ran out of the door, Zannis followed. From the north, two planes were approaching, one slightly above the other. The captain hurried back into the school and grabbed the Bren gun that stood, resting on its stock, in one corner of the entrance hall. The windows rattled as the planes roared over the rooftop and the captain took off towards the street, Zannis right behind him. But the captain shouted for him to stay inside, Zannis followed orders, and stopped in the doorway, so lived.

In front of the school, the captain searched the sky, swinging the Bren left and right. The sound of the planes' engines faded – going somewhere else. But that was a false hope, because the volume rose sharply as they circled back towards the school. The captain faced them and raised the Bren, the muzzle flashed, a few spent shells tumbled to the ground, then machine guns fired in the distance, the captain staggered, fought for his balance and sank to his knees.

What happened next was unclear. Zannis never heard an explosion, the world went black, and when his senses returned he found he was lying on his stomach and struggling to breathe. He forced his eyes open, saw nothing but grey dust cut by a bar of sunlight, tried to move, couldn't and reached behind him to discover that he was pinned to the floor by a beam that had fallen across the backs of his legs. In panic, he fought free of a terrible weight. Then he smelled fire, his heart hammered and he somehow stood up. *Get out.* He tried, but his first step – it was then he discovered his shoe was gone – landed on something soft. Covered with grey dust, a body lying face down. Somebody ran past him, Zannis could see he was shouting but heard nothing. He turned back to the body. Let it burn? He couldn't. He grabbed the feet and, as he pulled, the body gave a violent spasm. Now he saw that one of the legs was bleeding, so he took the other leg which, as he hauled, turned the body over and he saw it was Pavlic.

As he pulled Pavlic's body towards the entrance, there was a grinding roar and the rear section of the second storey came crashing down onto the first floor. Zannis heaved again, Pavlic's body moved. He could see an orange flicker now and then, and could feel heat on the skin of his face. Was Pavlic alive? He peered down, found his vision blurred, realized his glasses weren't there and was suddenly infuriated. He almost wanted – for an instant a scared ten-year-old – to look for them, almost, then understood he was in shock and his mind wasn't quite working. He took a deep breath, which burned in his chest and made him cough, steadied himself and dragged the body out of the building, the back of Pavlic's head bouncing down the steps that led to the doorway. Immediately there was someone by his side, a woman he recognized, who worked in the post office across from the school. 'Easy with him,' she said. 'Easy, easy, I think he's still alive.' She circled Zannis and took Pavlic under the arms and slid him across the road surface.

With one bare foot, and unable to see very much of anything, he headed back towards the school. As he entered the building, a reservist came crawling out of the doorway, and Zannis realized there were still people alive inside. But the smoke blinded him completely and the heat physically forced him backwards. In the street, he sat down and held his head in his hands. Not far from him, he saw what he thought were the captain's boots, heels apart, toes pointing in. Zannis looked away, tried to rub his ankle and discovered his hand was wet. Blood was running from beneath his trousers across the top of his foot and into the grey powder that covered the street. Very well, he would go to the hospital but, when he tried to stand, he couldn't, so he sat there, holding his head, in front of the burning school.

He wasn't hurt so much. They told him that later, in a dentist's office where the lightly wounded had been taken because the town clinic – there was no hospital in Trikkala – was reserved for the badly injured. The reservists lay on the floor of the reception area, the dentist had tried to make them comfortable by putting the pillows of his waiting room couch under their heads. Zannis could hear out of one ear now, a wound in his leg had been stitched up and there was something wrong with his left wrist. He kept opening and closing his hand, trying to make it better, but motion only made the pain worse.

As dusk fell, he realized he was tired of being wounded and decided to seek out whatever remained of his unit. In the street, people noticed him, probably because a nurse had cut off the leg of his trousers. Zannis met their eyes and smiled – *oh well* – but the people looked sorrowful and shook their heads. Not so much at a soldier with a bare leg and one shoe. At the bombing of their school and the men who'd been killed, at how war had come to their town.

And it wasn't done with them. And they knew it.

Two days later, Zannis went to the clinic to see Pavlic. Some of the wounded lay on mattresses on the floor, but Pavlic had one of the beds, a wad of gauze bandage taped to one side of his face. He brightened when he saw Zannis, now fully dressed. After they shook hands he thanked Zannis for coming. 'It is very boring here,' he said, then thanked him also, as he put it, 'for everything else.'

Zannis simply made a dismissive gesture: *we don't have to talk about it.*

'I know,' Pavlic said. 'But even so, thanks.'

'Here,' Zannis said. He handed Pavlic three packets of cig-arettes, a box of matches, the morning newspaper from Athens and two magazines. German magazines. Pavlic held one of them up to admire it; Brunhilde, naked, full-breasted and thickly bushed, had been photographed in the act of serving a volleyball. Pavlic said, '*Modern Nudist*. Thanks, I'll share these.'

'You should see what we have in Salonika.'

'I can imagine. What becomes of you now?'

'Back home, so they tell me. I've lost the hearing in one ear. And they say I might get a little medal if there are any left. And you?'

'Concussion, cuts and bruises.' He shrugged. 'I have to stay for a few days, then I'm ordered back to Zagreb. I suspect they don't think what I was doing was so important. They'd rather I keep the police cars running.'

'Marko,' Zannis said. Something in his voice made Pavlic attentive. 'I want to ask you to do something.'

'Go ahead.'

Zannis paused, then said, 'We have Jews coming into Salonika now. Fugitives from Germany, in flight. At least some of them have disappeared on the way. Where I don't know.'

'I thought they went to the port of Constanta.'

'Some of them do,' Zannis said.

'But the way things are going in Roumania these days, it may be easier for them to get away if they try from Greece.'

'As long as I'm there, it will be. And we have more ships, and more smugglers. For Europe, it's like slipping out of the back door.' After a moment, he said, 'What do you think about it, this flight?'

Pavlic said, 'I don't know,' then hesitated, finally adding, 'God help them. I guess that's the way I'd put it.'

'Would *you* help them?'

For a time, Pavlic didn't answer. He was still holding the nudist magazine. 'Costa, the truth is I've never thought about – about something like that. I don't know if I . . ., no, that's not

90

true, I could, of course I could. Not by myself, maybe, but I, I have friends.'

Zannis said, 'Because—' Pavlic cut him off. 'I don't know about you, but I saw this coming. Not what you're talking about, exactly, but something like it. That was in 'thirty-eight, September. When Chamberlain made a separate peace with Hitler. I remember very well, I thought, So much for Czechoslovakia, who's next? It's going to be our turn, sooner or later. So, what do I do if we're occupied? Nothing?' The word produced, from Pavlic, the thin smile of a man who's been told a bad joke.

'Well,' he went on, '"nothing" doesn't exist, not for the police. When somebody takes your country, you help them or you fight them. Because they will come after you; they'll ask, they'll *order*: 'Find this man, this house, this organization. You're from Zagreb – or Budapest, or Salonika – you know your way around; give us a hand." And if you *obey* them, or if you obey them during the day and don't do something else at night, then—'

'Then?'

For a moment, Pavlic was silent. Finally he said, 'How to put it? You're ruined. Dishonoured. You won't ever be the same again.'

'Not everybody thinks that way, Marko. There are some who will be eager to work for them.'

'I know, you can't change human nature. But there are those who will resist. It goes back in time forever, how conquerors and the conquered deal with each other. So everyone – well, maybe not everyone, but everyone like you and me – will have to take sides.'

'I guess I have,' Zannis said, as though he almost wished he hadn't.

'How would you do it, Berlin to Vienna? Cross into Hungary, then down through Yugoslavia into Greece? That's by rail, of course. If you went city to city you'd have to transit Roumania,

I mean Budapest to Bucharest, and if you did *that* you'd better have some dependable contacts, Costa, or a lot – and I mean a *lot* – of money. And even then it's not a sure thing, you know; the way life goes these days, if you buy somebody they're just liable to turn around and sell you to somebody else.'

'Better to stay west of Roumania,' Zannis said. 'The rail line goes down through Nis and into Salonika. Or even go from Nis into Bulgaria. I have a friend in Sofia I think I can count on.'

'You don't know?'

'You never know.'

'How do we communicate? *Telephone?*' He meant that it was beneath consideration.

'Does your office have a teletype machine?'

'Oh yes, accursed fucking thing. The Germans wished it on us – never shuts up, awful.'

'That's how. Something like, "We're looking for Mr X, we think he's coming into Zagreb railway station on the eleven-thirty from Budapest." Then a description. And if somebody taps into the line, so what? We're looking for a criminal.'

Pavlic's expression was speculative: *could this work?* Then, slowly, he nodded, more to himself than to Zannis. 'Not bad,' he said. 'Pretty good.'

'But, I have to say this, dangerous.'

'Of course it is, but so is crossing the street.'

'Do you know your teletype number?'

Pavlic stared, then said, 'No idea. So much for conspiracy.' Then he added, 'Actually, a typist works the thing.'

'I know mine,' Zannis said. 'Could I borrow that for a moment?'

Pavlic handed over the *Modern Nudist*. Zannis took a pencil from the pocket of his tunic and flipped to the last page, where a group of naked men and women, arms around one another's shoulders, were smiling into the camera below the legend SUN-SHINE CHUMS, DÜSSELDORF. Zannis wrote 811305 SAGR. 'The letters are for Salonika, Greece. You use the rotary dial on

92

the machine. After it connects, the machine will type the initials for "who are you" and you type the "answer-back", your number.' He returned the magazine to Pavlic. 'Perhaps you shouldn't share this.'

'Does the message move on a telephone line?'

'Telegraph. Through the post office in Athens.'

'I think I'd better have the typist teach me how to do it.'

'Someone you trust?'

Pavlic thought it over and said, 'No.'

Pushing a cart with a squeaky wheel, a nurse was moving down the aisle between the beds. 'Here's lunch,' Pavlic said.

Zannis rose to leave. 'We ought to talk about this some more, while we have the chance.'

'Come back tonight,' Pavlic said. 'I'm not going anywhere.'

7 December, Salonika. Zannis wasn't sorry to be home, but he wasn't all that happy about it either. This he kept hidden; why ruin the family pleasure? His mother was very tender with him, his grandmother cooked everything she thought he liked and, wherever he went that first week, room to room or outdoors, Melissa stayed by his side – she wasn't going to let him escape again. As for his brother, Ari, he had exciting news, which he saved during the first joyous minutes of homecoming, only to be upstaged by his mother. 'And Ari has a job!' she said. With so many men away at the fighting, there was work for anybody who wanted to work, and Ari had been hired as a conductor on the tram line.

And, he insisted, this was something his big brother had to see for himself. So Zannis had ridden the Number 4 tram out to Ano Toumba and let his pride show – sidelong glances from Ari made certain Zannis's smile was still in place – as Ari collected tickets and punched them with a silver-coloured device. He was extremely conscientious and took his time, making sure to get it right. Inevitably, some of the passengers were rushed and irritable, but they sensed that Ari was one of those delicate souls

93

who require a bit of compassion – was this a national trait? Zannis suspected it might be – and hardly anybody barked at him.

So Zannis returned to daily life, but a certain restless discomfort would not leave him. Able to hear out of only one ear, he was occasionally startled by sudden sounds, and he found that to be humiliating. A feeling in no way ameliorated by the fact that, just before he returned to Salonika, the Greek army *had* managed to find him a little medal, which he refused to wear, being disinclined to answer questions about how he came to have it. And, worst of all, he felt the absence of a love affair, felt it in the lack of commonplace affection, felt it while eating alone in restaurants, but felt it most keenly in bed, or out of bed but thinking about bed, or, in truth, all the time. In the chaos that followed the bombing of the Trikkala school, whatever goddess had charge of his mortality had brushed her lips across his cheek and this had, he guessed, affected that part of him where desire lived. Or maybe it was just the war.

On the evening of the seventh, Vangelis threw him a welcome-home party. Almost all were people Zannis knew, if, in some cases, only distantly. Gabi Saltiel, greyer and wearier than ever, was still driving an ambulance at night but traded shifts with another driver and brought his wife to the party. Sibylla, her helmet of hair perfectly lacquered for the occasion, was accompanied by her husband, who worked as a bookkeeper at one of the hotels. There were a couple of detectives, a shipping broker, a criminal lawyer, a prosecutor, two ballet teachers he'd met through Roxanne, an economics professor from the university, even a former girlfriend, Tasia Loukas, who worked at the Salonika city hall.

Tasia – for Anastasia – showed up late and held both his hands while he got a good strong whiff of some very sultry perfume. She was small and lively, dressed exclusively in black, had thick black hair, strong black eyebrows and dark eyes – fierce dark eyes – that challenged the world from behind spectacles with grey-tinted lenses. Did Vangelis have something in mind for him when he invited Tasia? Zannis wondered. He'd had two brief, fiery love affairs with her, the first six years earlier, the second a few months before he'd met Roxanne. Very free, Tasia, and determined to remain so. 'I'll never marry,' she'd once told him. 'For the truth is, I like to go with a woman from time to time – I get something from a woman I can never get with a man.' She'd meant that to be provocative, he thought, but he wasn't especially provoked and had let her know that he didn't particularly care. And he truly didn't. 'It's exciting,' she'd said. 'Especially when it must be kept a secret.' A flicker of remembrance had lit her face as she spoke, accompanied by a most deliciously wicked smile, as though she were smiling, once again, at the first moment of the remembered conquest.

Vangelis gave famously good parties – excellent red wine, bottles and bottles of it – and had stacks of Duke Ellington records. As the party swirled around them, Zannis and Tasia had two conversations. The spoken one was nothing special – how was he, fine, how was she – the unspoken one much more interesting. 'I better go and say hello to Vangelis,' she said, and reluctantly, he could tell, let go of his hands.

'Don't leave without telling me, Tasia.'

'I won't.'

She was replaced by the economics professor and his lady friend, who Zannis recollected was a niece or cousin to the poet Elias. They'd been hovering, waiting their turn to greet the returning hero. Asked about his war, Zannis offered a brief and highly edited version of the weeks in Trikkala, which ended, 'Anyhow, at least we're winning.'

The professor looked up from his wine glass. 'Do you really believe that?'

'I saw it,' Zannis said. 'And the newspapers aren't telling lies.'

From the professor, a low grumbling sound that meant *yes,*

but. 'On the battlefield, it's true, we are winning. And if we don't chase them back into Italy, we'll have a stalemate, which is just as good. But *winning*, maybe not.'

'Such a cynic,' his lady friend said gently. She had a long intelligent face. Turning to the table at her side, she speared a dolma, an oily, stuffed grape leaf, put it on a plate and worked at cutting it with the side of her fork.

'How do you mean?' Zannis said.

'The longer this goes on,' the professor said, 'the more Hitler has to stop it. The Axis can't be seen to be weak.'

'I've heard that,' Zannis said. 'It's one theory. There are others.'

The professor sipped his wine; his friend chewed away at her dolma.

Zannis felt dismissed from the conversation. 'Maybe you're right. Well then, what can we do about it?' he said. 'Retreat?'

'Can't do that either.'

'So, damned if we do, damned if we don't.'

'Yes,' the professor said.

'Don't listen to him,' the professor's friend said. 'He always finds the gloomy side.'

The warrior in Zannis wanted to argue – *what about the British army*? Because if Germany attacked them, their British ally would arrive in full force from across the Mediterranean. To date, Britain and Germany were bombing each other's cities, but their armies, after the debacle that ended in Dunkirk, had not engaged. Hitler, the theory went, had been taught a lesson the previous autumn, when his plans to invade Britain had been thwarted by the RAF.

But the professor was bored with politics and addressed the buffet – 'The aubergine spread is very tasty,' he said, by way of a parting shot. Then gave way to one of Zannis's former colleagues from his days as a detective – insider jokes and nostalgic anecdotes – who in turn was replaced by a woman who taught at the Mount Olympus School of Ballet. Had Zannis heard anything from Roxanne? No, had she? Not a word, very troubling, she hoped Roxanne wasn't in difficulties.

Minutes later, Zannis knew she wasn't. Francis Escovil, the English travel writer and, Zannis suspected, British spy, appeared magically at his side. 'Oh, she's perfectly all right,' Escovil said. 'I had a postal card, two weeks ago. Back in Blighty, she is. Dodging bombs but happy to be home.'

'I'm glad to hear it.'

'Yes, no doubt busy as a bee. That's probably why you haven't heard from her.'

'Of course,' Zannis said. He started to say *give her my best* but thought better of it. That could, in a certain *context*, be taken the wrong way. Instead, he asked, 'How do you come to know Vangelis?'

'Never met him. I'm here with Sophia, who teaches at the school.'

'Oh.' That raised more questions than it answered, but Zannis knew he'd never hear anything useful from the infinitely deflective Englishman. In fact, Zannis didn't like Escovil, and Escovil knew it.

'I wonder, could we have lunch sometime?' Escovil said, trying to be casual, not succeeding.

What do you want? 'We might, I'm pretty busy myself. Try me at the office – you have the number?'

'I think I might . . .'

I'll bet you do.

'. . . somewhere. Roxanne put it on a scrap of paper.'

Escovil stood there, smiling at him, not going away.

'Are you writing articles?' Zannis asked, seeking safe ground.

'Trying to. I've been to all sorts of monasteries, got monks coming out of my ears. Went to one where they haul you up the side of a cliff; that's the only way to get there. Just a basket and a frayed old rope. I asked the priest, "When do you replace the rope?" Know what he said?'

'What?'

'When it breaks!' Escovil laughed, a loud *haw-haw* with teeth showing.

'Well, that's a good story,' Zannis said, 'as long as you're not the one in the basket.' Out of the corner of his eye, he saw that Tasia was heading towards him. 'We'll talk later,' he said to Escovil, and turned to meet her.

'I'm going home,' she said.

'Could you stay a while?'

'I guess I could. Why?'

'I'm the guest of honour, I can't leave yet.'

'True,' she said. She met his eyes, no smile to be seen but it was playing with the corners of her mouth. 'Then I'll stay. But not too long, Costa. I don't really know these people.'

He touched her arm, lightly, with two fingers. 'Just a little while,' he said.

She had a large apartment, near the city hall and obviously expensive. One always wondered about Tasia and money but she never said anything about it. Maybe her family, he thought. Once inside, she fed her cats, poured two small glasses of ouzo and sat Zannis on a white couch. Settling herself at the other end, she curled into the corner, kicked off her shoes, rested her legs on the cushions, said '*Salute*' and raised her glass.

After they drank she said, 'Mmm. I wanted that all night – I hate drinking wine. Take your shoes off, put your feet up. That's better, right? Parties hurt your feet? They do mine – high heels, you know? I'm such a peasant. Oh yes, rub harder, good ... good ... don't stop, yes, there ... ahh, that's perfect, now the other one, wouldn't want it to feel neglected ... yes, just like that, a little higher, maybe ... no, I meant higher, keep going, keep going ... ... no, don't take them all the way off, just down, just below my arse ... there, perfect, you'll like that later. Remember?'

★

He was tired the following day and nothing seemed all that important. It had been a long while between lovers for Tasia, as it had for Zannis, they were both intent on making up for lost time, and did. But then, a little after eleven, on what seemed like just another morning at work, he got something else he'd wanted. Wanted much more than he'd realized.

A letter. Carried by the postman, who appeared at the door of the office. Not his usual practice, the mail was typically delivered to a letter box in the building's vestibule, but not that day, that day the postman hauled his leather bag up five flights of stairs, came to Zannis's desk, took a moment to catch his breath, held up an envelope and said, 'Is this for you?'

Obviously a business letter, the return address printed in the upper left corner:

Hofbau und Sohn Maschinenfabrik GmbH
28, Helgenstrasse
Brandenburg
DEUTSCHLAND

With a typewritten address:

Herr C. N. Zannis
Behilfliches Generaldirektor
Das Royale Kleidersteller
122, via Egnatia
Salonika
HELLAS

'Yes,' Zannis said. 'That's for me.' The letter was from, apparently, a manufacturer of industrial knitting machines in Brandenburg – not far from Berlin – to the assistant general manager of the Royale Garment Company in Salonika. *Well done*, he thought.

The postman leaned towards Zannis and spoke in a confidential voice, as though Saltiel and Sibylla might not be in on the game. 'I don't care if you want to do this kind of thing. These days ... well, you know what I mean. But I almost took this back to the post office, so in future leave me a note in the letter box, all right?'

'I will,' Zannis said. 'But if you'd keep an eye out for, for this sort of *arrangement*, I'd appreciate it.'

The postman winked. 'Count on me,' he said.

As the postman left, Zannis slit the envelope with a letter opener, carefully, and slid out a single sheet of folded commercial stationery; the address printed at the top of the page, the text typewritten below.

30 November 1940

Dear Sir:

I refer to your letter of 17 November.

We are in receipt of your postal money order for RM 232.

I am pleased to inform you that 4 replacement motors, 11 replacement spindles and 14 replacement bobbins for our model 25-C knitting machine have been shipped to you by rail as of this date.

Thank you for your order. Hofbau and Sohn trusts you will continue to be satisfied with its products.

Yours truly,

S. Weickel

'Sibylla?' Zannis said. He was about to ask her about an iron. Then he stopped cold. She said, 'Yes?' but he told her it was nothing, he'd take care of it himself.

Because he saw the future.

Because there was some possibility that the darkest theories of the war's evolution were correct: Germany would rescue the dignity of her Italian partner and invade Greece. Yes, the British would send an expeditionary force, would honour her treaty with an ally. But Zannis well knew what had happened in

Belgium and France – the chaotic retreat from Dunkirk. So it hadn't worked then, and it might not work this time. The Greek army would fight hard, but it would be overwhelmed; they had no answer to German armour and aircraft. Salonika would be occupied, and its people would resist. *He* would resist. And that meant, what? It meant clandestine leaflets and radio, it meant sabotage, it meant killing Germans. Which would bring reprisal, and investigation, and interrogation. Saltiel and Sibylla might be questioned, so he could not, would not, compromise them, endanger them, with information they should not have. If they knew, they were guilty.

So Zannis left the office at noon, walked down to the market, found a stall with used irons in every state of age and decay, and bought the best electric model they had. 'It works good,' the stall owner said.

'How do you know?'

'I can tell,' the man said. 'I understand them. This one was left in the Hotel *Lux Palace*, and the settings are in *English*.'

Zannis walked back to his apartment, left the iron in his kitchen, returned to the office, couldn't bear to wait all afternoon and went home early.

First, he practised, scorched a few pieces of paper, finally set the dial on WARM. Then he laid the letter flat on a sheet of newspaper on the wooden table in the kitchen and pressed the iron down on the letter's salutation. Nothing. He moved to the text in the middle – 'I am pleased to inform you that 4 replacement motors' – but, again, nothing. No! A faint mark had appeared above the *p* of 'pleased'. *More heat.* He turned the dial to LOW, waited as the iron warmed, pressed for a count of five and produced parts of three letters. He tried once more, counting slowly to ten, and there it was: '... ress KALCHER UND DRO ...'

Ten minutes later he had the whole message, in tiny sepia-coloured block letters between the lines of the commercial text:

Reply to address KALCHER UND KROHN, lawyers, 17, Arbenstrasse, Berlin. Write as H. H. STRAUB. 26 December man and wife travelling under name HARTMANN arrive Budapest from Vienna via 3-day excursion steamer LEVER-KUSEN. He 55 years old, wears green tie, she 52 years old, wears green slouch hat. Can you assist Budapest to Belgrade? Believe last shipment lost there to Gestapo agents. Can you find boat out your port? Please help.

Last shipment meant the Rosenblum sisters, he thought, unless there had been others he didn't know about. Also lost. Budapest? How the hell could he help in *Budapest*? He didn't know a soul in Hungary; why would he? Why would Emilia Krebs think he did? What was wrong with this woman? *No, calm down*, he told himself. It isn't arrogance. It is desperation. And, on second thoughts, there might be one possibility. Anyhow, he would try.

He never really slept, that night. Staring at the ceiling gave way to fitful dozing and awful dreams which woke him, to once again stare at the ceiling, his mind racing. Finally he gave up and was at the office by seven-thirty. December weather had reached them: the clammy chill of the Mediterranean winter, the same grisaille, grey days, grey city, that he'd come to know in Paris. He turned on the lights in the office and set out his box of five-by-eight cards. Yes, his memory had not betrayed him: *Sami Pal*. His real – as far as anybody knew – Hungarian name, *Pal* not an uncommon surname in Hungary. Or, perhaps, a permanent alias.

Szamuel 'Sami' Pal. Born Budapest 1904. Hungarian pass-port B91–427 issued 3 January 1922, possibly counterfeit or altered. Also uses Nansen passport HK33156. Resident in Salonika since 4 May 1931 (renewable visa) at various rooming houses. Operates business at 14 Vardar Square, cellar room rented from tenant above, Madame Zizi,

Fortune Teller and Astrologer. Business known as World-wide Agency – Confidential Inquiries. Telephone Salonika 0891.

According to Salonika police records: investigated (not charged) for removal of documents from office of French consul, May '33. Arrested, September '34, accused by British oil executive R. J. Wilson of espionage approach to valet. Released, valet refused to testify, likely bribed. Arrested June '38, accused of selling stolen passport. Released when witness could not be found. Investigated by State Security Bureau (Spiraki) November '39. (Salonika police consulted.) No conclusion reported to this office.

Previous to arrival in Salonika, Sami Pal is thought to have escaped from prison, city unknown, country said to be Switzerland by local informant, who claims Pal deals in merchandise stolen from port storage, also in stolen passports and papers.

9 December. For this interview, Zannis borrowed an interrogation room at the police station in the Second District – his last headquarters when he'd worked as a detective. His old friends were pleased to see him. 'Hey Costa, you fancy sonofabitch, come back to join the slaves?'

Sami Pal was waiting on a bench in the reception area – had been waiting for a long time, Zannis had made sure of that – amid the miserable crowd of victims and thugs always to be found in the police stations. For the occasion, Zannis had chosen two props: a shoulder holster bearing Saltiel's automatic – his own weapon having disappeared in the collapse of the Trikkala school – and a badge, clipped to his belt near the buckle, where Sami Pal was sure to see it.

Summoned by telephone the previous afternoon, Sami was looking his best. But he always was. A few years earlier, he'd been pointed out by a fellow detective in a taverna amid the bordellos of the Bara and, as the saying went, Zannis had seen him around. Natty, he was, in the sharpest cheap suit he could buy, a metallic grey, with florid tie, trench coat folded in his lap, boutonnière – a white carnation that afternoon – worn in the buttonhole of his jacket, a big expensive-looking watch that might have been gold, a ring with what surely wasn't a diamond, and a nervous but very brave smile. As Zannis got close to him – 'Hello, Sami, we'll talk in a little while' – he realized from the near-dizzying aroma of cloves that Sami had visited the barber. To Zannis, and to the world at large, Sami Pal, with the face of a vicious imp, was the perfection of that old saying, 'After he left, we counted the spoons.'

The interrogation room had a high window with a wire grille, a battered desk and two hard chairs. Zannis introduced himself by saying, 'I'm Captain Zannis,' lowering his rank for the interview.

'Yes, sir. I know who you are, sir.'

'Oh? Who am I, Sami?'

Sami's prominent Adam's apple went up, then down. 'You're important, sir.'

'Important to you, Sami. That's the truth.'

'Yes, sir. I know, sir.'

'You like it here, in Salonika?'

'Um, yes. Yes, sir. A fine city.'

'You plan on staying here?'

After a pause, Sami said, 'I'd like to, sir.'

Zannis nodded. Who wouldn't want to stay in such a fine city? 'Well, I think it's possible. Yes, definitely possible. Do you have enough work?'

'Yes, sir. I keep busy. Always husbands and wives, suspecting the worst, it's the way of love, sir.'

'And passports, Sami? Doing any business there?'

Once again, the Adam's apple rose and fell. 'No, sir. Never. I never did that.'

'Don't lie to me, you—' Zannis let Sami Pal find his own word.

'Not now, sir. Maybe in the past, when I needed the money, I might've, but not now, I swear it.'

'All right, let's say I believe you.'

'Thank you, sir. You can believe Sami.'

'Now, what if I needed a favour?'

Sami Pal's face flooded with relief, this wasn't about what he'd feared, and he'd had twenty-four hours to consider his recent sins. He fingered his carnation and said, 'Anything. Anything at all. Name it, sir.'

Zannis lit a cigarette, taking his time. 'Care for one of these?' He could see that Sami did want one but was afraid to take it.

'No, sir. Many thanks, though.'

'Sami, tell me, do you have any connections in Budapest?'

Sami Pal was stunned; that was the very last thing he'd thought he might hear, but he rallied quickly. 'I do,' he said. 'I travel up there two or three times a year, see a few friends, guys I grew up with. And my family. I see them too.'

'These friends, they work at jobs? Five days a week? Take the pay home to the wife? Is that what they do?'

'Some of them ... do that. They're just, regular people.'

'But not all.'

'Well ...' Sami's mouth stayed open, but no words came out.

'Sami, please don't fuck with me, all right?'

'I wasn't, I mean, no, yes, not all of them, do that. One or two of them, um, make their own way.'

'Criminals.'

'Some would say that.'

'This *is* the favour, Sami. This *is* what will keep you in this fine city. This *is* what may stop me from putting your sorry arse on a train up to Geneva. And I can do that, because you were right, I am important, and, just now, *very* important to you.'

'They are criminals, Captain Zannis. It's how life goes in that city, if you aren't born to a good family, if you don't bow down to the bosses, you have to find a way to stay alive. So maybe you do a little of this and a little of that, and the day comes when you can't go back, your life is what it is, and your friends, the people who protect you, who help you out, are just like you, outside the law Well, too bad. Because you wind up with the cops chasing you, or, lately, some other guy, from another part of town, putting a bullet in your belly. Then, time to go, it's been great, goodbye world. That's how it is, up there. That's how it's always been.'

'These friends, they're not what you'd call "lone wolves".'

'Oh no, not up there. You won't last long by yourself.'

'So then, gangs? That the word? Like the Sicilians?'

'Yes, sir.'

'With names?'

Sami Pal thought it over, either preparing to lie or honestly uncertain, Zannis wasn't sure which. Finally he said, 'Sometimes we use the – um, that is, sometimes *they* use the name of a leader.'

This errant pronoun *we* interested Zannis. One end of a string, perhaps, that could be carefully pulled until it led somewhere, maybe stolen merchandise or prostitutes travelling between the two cities. And not years ago, this week. But the clue was of interest only to Zannis the detective, not to Zannis the operator of a clandestine network. So he said, 'And which one did you belong to, Sami? Back in the days when you lived up there?'

Sami Pal looked down at the desk. Whatever he was, he wasn't a rat, an informer. Zannis's first instinct was to show anger, but he suppressed it. 'He won't be investigated if you tell me his name, Sami. You have my word on that.'

Sami Pal took a breath, looked up, and said, 'Gypsy Gus.'

'Who?'

'Gypsy Gus. You don't know Gypsy Gus?'

'Why would I? He's a Gypsy?'

Sami Pal laughed. 'No, no. He left Hungary, when he was young, and became a wrestler, a famous wrestler, in *America*, Captain, in *Chicago*. I thought maybe you would know who he was, he was famous.'

'Then what's his real name?'

After a moment Sami Pal said, 'Gustav Husar.'

Zannis repeated the name, silently, until he felt he'd memorized it. He was not going to write anything down in front of Sami Pal, not yet. 'Tell me, what do they do, Husar and his friends.'

'The usual things. Loan money, protect the neighbourhood merchants, help somebody to sell something they don't need.'

Zannis had a hard time not laughing at the way Sami Pal thought about crime. *Boy scouts.*

'That's the way it used to be, anyhow.' *In the good old days.*

'And now?'

'There's bad blood now. Didn't use to be like that, everybody kept to their own part of town, everybody minded their own business. But then, about three years ago, some of the, well, what you call gangs got friendly with a few individuals on the police force, maybe money changed hands, and the idea was to help certain people and maybe hurt some other people. It was after Hitler took over in Germany, sir, we had the same thing in Budapest, guys in uniforms, marching in the streets. There were some people in the city who liked what Hitler said, who thought that was the way life should go in Hungary. But not my crowd, Captain, not my crowd.'

'Why not, Sami? Why not your crowd?'

'Well, we were always over in Pest, across the river from the snobs in Buda. Pest is for the working class, see? And when the politics came in, that's the way we had to go. We're not reds, never, like the Russians, but we couldn't let these other guys get away with it. That meant fighting. Because if the workers were just having a drink somewhere, and here came some guys with iron bars, looking to cause trouble, we helped out. Maybe one of our guys had a gun, and he knew how to use it, understand?'

Gold! But Zannis merely nodded. 'What about the Jews, in Budapest?'

Sami shrugged. 'What about them?'

'What does ... your crowd, think about them?'

'Who cares? There was one who used to work with us, he's in jail now, but it didn't matter to anybody, what he was.' After a pause, Sami Pal said, 'We knew he was a Jew, but he didn't have sidelocks or a beard or anything, he didn't wear a hat.'

Zannis drummed his fingers on the desk. Would it work? 'This Gypsy Gus, Gustav Husar,' he said. 'He looks like a Gypsy?'

'No, sir.' Sami Pal grinned at the idea. 'They made him a Gypsy because he came from Hungary, he's got the photographs. Big moustache, like an organ-grinder, a gold hoop in his ear, and he wore a fancy sort of a shirt, and that little hat. You know, captain, *Gypsy Gus*.'

'And where would I find him, if I went to Budapest?'

Sami Pal froze. In his mind's eye, he saw his old boss taken by the police – guns drawn, handcuffs out – and all because it was Sami Pal who'd sold him to the cops in Salonika.

Zannis read him perfectly. With hand flat, palm turned towards the desk, he made the gesture that meant *calm down*. And softened his voice. 'Remember my promise, Sami? I meant it. Nobody's going to do anything to your friend, I only want to talk to him. Not about a crime, I don't care what he's done, I need his help, nothing more. You know the sign on your door, in Vardar Square? It says CONFIDENTIAL INQUIRIES? Well, now you've had one.' He paused to let that sink in, then continued. 'And I mean *confidential*, Sami, secret, forever, between you and me. You don't go blabbing to your girlfriends, you don't go playing the big shot about your friend on the police force. Understand?'

'Yes, sir. I have your promise.' He sounded like a schoolboy.

'And ...?'

'It's called Ilka's Bar. When Gypsy Gus was a strong man in the circus, in Esztergom, before he went to Chicago, Ilka was his, um, assistant, on the stage, with a little skirt.'

Now Zannis set pad and pencil on the desk in front of Sami Pal. 'Write it down for me, Sami, so I don't forget. The name of the bar and the address.'

'I can only write in Hungarian, Captain.'

'Then do that.'

Zannis waited patiently while Sami Pal carved the letters, one at a time, onto the paper. 'Takes me a minute,' Sami said. 'I don't know the address, I only know it's under the Szechenyi Bridge, the chain bridge, on the Pest side, in an alley off Zrinyi Street. There's no sign, but everybody knows Ilka's Bar.'

'And how does it work? You leave a message at the bar?'

'No, the bar is his ... office, I guess you'd call it. But don't show up until the afternoon, Captain. Gypsy Gus likes to sleep late.'

11 December. *Now for the hard part.* He had to tell Vangelis. He could do what he meant to do behind the back of the entire world – all but Vangelis. Zannis telephoned, then walked up to the office in the central police headquarters on the same square as the municipal building. Vangelis was as always: shaggy white hair, shaggy white moustache stained yellow by nicotine because he'd smoked his way through a long and eventful life, and more and more mischief in his face, in his eyes and in the set of his mouth, as time went by – *I know the world, what a joke.* Vangelis had coffee brought from a *kafeneion*, and they both lit Papastratos No. 1 cigarettes.

They spent a few minutes on health and family. 'Your brother makes a wonderful tram conductor, doesn't he?' Vangelis said, his pleasure in this change of fortune producing a particularly beatific, St Vangelis smile. Which vanished when he said, 'The mayor is still telephoning me about his niece, Costa. The lost parakeet? I know you can't do anything about it, can you?'

'I can't think of anything,' Zannis said. 'Write another report? That we're still looking?'

'*Anything*, please, to get that idiot off my back.'

Zannis said he would write the report, then told Vangelis what he was going to do. No names, no specifics, just that he intended to help some of the fugitives moving through the

Balkans, and to that end he might be spending a day or two in Budapest.

Vangelis didn't react. Or perhaps his reaction was that he didn't react. He took a sip of coffee, put the cup down and said, 'A long time, the train to Budapest. If it's better for you not to be away from your work for so long, perhaps you ought to fly. The planes are flying again, for the moment.'

'I don't think I have the money for aeroplanes.'

'Oh. Well. If that's all it is.' He reached into the bottom drawer of his desk and brought out a chequebook. As he wrote, he said, 'It's drawn on the Bank of Commerce and Deposit, on Victoros Hougo Street, near the Spanish legation.' Carefully, Vangelis separated the cheque from the stub and handed it to Zannis. The signature read *Alexandros Manos*, and the amount was for one thousand Swiss francs. 'Don't present this at the cashier's window, Costa. Take it to Mr Pereira, the manager.'

Zannis looked up from the cheque and raised his eyebrows.

'Did you know Mr Manos? A fine fellow, owned an umbrella shop in Monastir. Been dead for a long time, sorry to say.'

'No, I didn't know him,' Zannis said, echoing the irony in Vangelis's voice.

'One must have such resources, Costa, in a job like mine. They've been useful, over the years. Crucial.'

Zannis nodded.

'And, Costa? Gun and badge for your trip to Hungary, my boy, servant of the law, official business.'

'Thank you, Commissioner,' Zannis said.

'Oh, you're welcome. Come to think of it, maybe the time has come for you to have one of these accounts for yourself, considering ... your, intentions. Now, let, me, see ...' Vangelis thought for a time, leaning back in his chair. Then he sat upright. 'Do you know Nikolas Vasilou?'

'I know who he is, of course, but I've never met him.' Vasilou was one of the richest men in Salonika, likely in all Greece. He was said to buy and sell ships, particularly oil tankers, like penny candy.

'You should meet him. Let me know when you return and I'll arrange something.'

Zannis started to say thank you once more but Vangelis cut him off. 'You will need money, Costa.'

Zannis sensed it was time to go and stood up. Vangelis rose halfway from his chair and extended his hand. Zannis took it – frail and weightless in his grasp. This reached him; he never thought of the commissioner as an old man, but he was.

Vangelis smiled and flipped the backs of his fingers towards the door, shooing Zannis from his office. *Now go and do what you have to*, it meant, a brusque gesture, affectionate beyond words.

He was busy the following day. For one thing, because of absent personnel – the war, the fucking war, how it *manifested* itself – the office had to handle a few commonplace criminal investigations. So now they'd been assigned a murder in Ano Toumba, a dockworker found stabbed to death in his bed. Nobody had any idea who'd done this, or why. By noon, Zannis and Saltiel had talked to the stevedores on the wharf, then to some of the man's relatives. He wasn't married, couldn't afford it, didn't gamble or patronize the girls up in the Bara, gave no offence to anybody. He worked hard, played dominoes in the taverna, such was life. So, why? Nobody knew, nobody even offered the usual dumb theories.

After lunch he cashed Vangelis's cheque, visited the Hungarian legation and was given a visa, then bought a ticket at the TAE office: up to Sofia, then Lufthansa to Budapest. The ticket in his hand was not unexciting – he'd never flown in an aeroplane. Well, now he would. He wasn't afraid, not at all.

It was after six by the time he got to his front door, greeted the waiting Melissa, trudged up the stairs and found his door unlocked and Tasia Loukas naked in his bed. 'I remembered your key,' she said. 'Above the door.' She was propped on one elbow, wearing her tinted glasses and reading the Greek version of one of Zannis's French spy novels, *The Man from Damascus*. 'You aren't sorry to see me, are you?'

He drew the sheet down to her waist and kissed her softly, twice, by way of answer. Then he went into the kitchen, gave Melissa a mutton bone, a hunk of bread and two eggs. 'I have to take a shower,' he said as he returned to the bedroom. 'Really I have to, it's been that kind of day.'

'I have a surprise for you,' Tasia said.

'Oh?'

'But not until later. At eleven we have to go back out.'

'What is it?'

'You'll see. It's a nice surprise.'

He began to unbutton his shirt, she watched attentively as he undressed.

'I see you're ironing your own clothes now,' she said.

The iron was still sitting on the table in the kitchen. 'Yes,' he said. 'A small economy.'

'I'd like to watch you do it,' she said, amused at the idea. 'Can you?'

'I'm learning,' he said. He stepped out of his underpants and bent over to pick them up.

'Come and sit with me for a little,' she said. 'I don't care if you smell.'

How to say no?

He sat on the edge of the bed, she began to stroke him, observing the result like an artist. 'I daydreamed all day, at work,' she said, voice tender. 'A little voice in my head. It kept saying, "Tasia, you need a good fucking," so here I am. Did you think you were too tired?'

'I did wonder.'

'But you are not, as we can see.'

He woke up suddenly and looked at his watch. 9.33. He could hear rain pattering down on Santaroza Lane, a gentle snore from

Melissa, which now stopped abruptly because she'd also woken up, the instant after he had. She always knew. How? A dog mystery. Tasia was asleep on her stomach, arm beneath the pillow, mouth open, face delicately troubled by a dream. Her lips moved, who was she talking to? As he watched, one eye opened. 'You're awake,' she said.

'It's raining.' The first attack of a campaign to stay at home.

She sat up, sniffed, then got out of bed and, haunches shifting, walked to the bathroom, closed the door almost all the way and called out, 'What time is it?'

'Nine-thirty.'

'Hmm.'

When she emerged, she began to sort through her clothes, which lay folded on a chair. 'I have a funny story for you,' she said, stepping into her panties.

Oh no, she still wants to go out. They had eaten nothing, so he'd have to take her somewhere, though, for him, making love was a substitute for food. 'You do?'

'I forgot to tell you,' she said.

He waited as she put on her bra, hooking it in front then twisting it around.

'I have a little nephew. A cute kid, maybe four years old. And you know what he did? You won't believe it when I tell you.'

'What?'

'He tried to kill Hitler.'

'He *what*?'

'Tried to kill Hitler. Really. They have one of those shortwave radios, and they were listening to some music programme. Eventually the news came on and there was Hitler, shouting and screaming, the crowd cheering. You know what it sounds like. Anyhow, the kid listens for a while, then he picks up a pencil and shoves it into the speaker.'

Tasia laughed. Zannis laughed along with her and said, 'That's funny. It really happened?'

'It did,' she said. She put on a black sweater, combing her hair back in place with her fingers once she had it on. 'Aren't you hungry?' she said.

The surprise was, in truth, a surprise. They left the apartment, then stopped at a taverna for fried calamari and a glass of wine, and Tasia told him what she'd planned. A friend of hers owned the cinema in what had been, until the population exchange of 1923, a Turkish mosque, and he had got hold, somehow, of a print of Charlie Chaplin's *The Great Dictator*. 'It won't have subtitles,' she said, 'but you understand English, don't you?'

'Some. Not much.'

'Never mind, you'll manage. He's showing it for friends, so we'll at least have a chance to see it. Otherwise, we'd have to wait a long time, for the official release.'

The film was accompanied by considerable whispering, as people asked their neighbours to explain the dialogue, but that didn't matter. Hitler was called Adenoid Hynkel, Mussolini appeared as Benzino Napaloni, which Zannis supposed was amusing if you spoke English. Mussolini teased and tormented and manipulated his fellow dictator – that didn't need translation either. Still, even though it was Chaplin's first talking picture, the physical comedy was the best part. Everybody laughed at the food fight and applauded Hitler's dance with an inflated globe, literally kicking the world around. The political speech at the end was spoken out in Greek by the cinema owner, who stood to one side of the screen and read from notes.

Zannis didn't find it all that funny, the way Mussolini provoked Hitler. The movie was banned in Germany, but Hitler would no doubt be treated to a private screening – trust that little snake Goebbels to make sure he saw it. Hitler wouldn't like it. So, some comedian thought the Axis partners were comic? Perhaps he'd show him otherwise. When the movie was over, and the crowd dispersed in front of the mosque, Zannis wasn't smiling. And in that, he saw, he wasn't alone.

'So!' said a triumphant Tasia. 'What will Adolf think of *this*?'

'I wouldn't know,' Zannis said. 'I'll ask him when he gets here.'

14 December. The Bréguet aeroplane bumped and quivered as it fought the turbulence above the mountains. Zannis was alarmed at first, then relaxed and enjoyed the view. Too soon they descended above Sofia airport, then zoomed towards the runway – *too fast, too fast* – and then, just as the wheels bounced on the tarmac and Zannis held a death grip on the arms of his seat, something popped in his left ear and the sound of the engines got suddenly louder. He could hear in both ears! He was overjoyed, smiling grandly at a dour Bulgarian customs official, which made the officer more suspicious than usual.

It was dusk when they landed in Budapest. Zannis took a taxi to the railway station and checked into one of the travellers' hotels across the square. In his room, he looked out of the window. Looked, as big wind-blown snowflakes danced across his vision, at the people hurrying to and from their trains, holding on to their hats in the wind. Looked for surveillance, looked for men watching the station. What happened to the fugitives who came here? Who was hunting them? How was it managed?

The following day, he waited until one in the afternoon, rode a taxi across the Szechenyi bridge, and made his way to Ilka's Bar. Which was small and dark and almost deserted – only one other customer, a tall attractive woman wearing a hat with a veil. She was not a casual patron but sat nervously upright, staring straight ahead, a handkerchief twisted in her hands.

As for Gustav Husar, he was nowhere to be seen. Except on the walls: a glossy publicity photograph of a menacing Gypsy Gus applying a headlock to a bald fellow in white spangled tights, and framed clippings from newspapers: Gypsy Gus with his arm around a blonde actress, a cigarette holder posed at an angle in her gloved hand; Gypsy Gus flanked by four men who could only have been Chicago gangsters; Gypsy Gus sitting on another wrestler as the referee raised his hand to slap the canvas, signalling a pinfall.

Zannis had a cup of coffee, and another. Then, some forty-five minutes after he'd arrived, two men strolled into the bar, one with a slight bulge beneath the left-hand shoulder of his overcoat. He nodded to the barman, glanced at the woman and had a long look at Zannis, who stared into his coffee cup. As the other man left, the barman took an orange, cut it in half and began squeezing it in a juicer. Very quiet at Ilka's, the sound of juice splashing into a glass seemed quite loud to Zannis.

The barman's timing was exquisite – so that Gustav Husar, entering the bar, could take his glass of orange juice to a table in the corner. Zannis started to rise, but the tall woman was already hurrying towards the table. There was not much to be seen of the wrestling Gypsy, Zannis realized, only the rounded shoulders and thick body of a man born to natural strength, now dressed in a cashmere overcoat and a stylish silk scarf. On his huge head, where only a fringe of greying hair remained, a black beret. He had blunt features and, flesh thickened at the edges, cauliflower ears. His eyes were close-set and sharp. *Cunning* was the word that came to Zannis.

As Husar and the woman spoke in hushed tones, she reached beneath her veil and dabbed at her eyes with the handkerchief. Husar patted her arm, she opened her handbag, and took out an envelope. This she handed to Husar, who slid it in the pocket of his overcoat. Then she hurried out of the door, head held high but still dabbing at her eyes. The man with the bulging overcoat was suddenly at Zannis's table and said something in Hungarian. Zannis indicated he didn't understand. 'I can speak German,' he said in that language. 'Or maybe English.' Foreseeing the difficulties of a Greek needing to speak with a Hungarian, he had studied his English phrasebook, working particularly on words he knew he'd require.

The man turned, walked over to Husar and spoke to him briefly. Husar stared at Zannis for a time, then beckoned to him.

As Zannis seated himself, Husar said, 'You speak English?'

'Some.'

'Where you from? Ilka's in the office, she speaks everything.'

'Greek?'

'Greek!' Husar gazed at him as though he were a novelty, produced for Husar's amusement. 'A cop,' he said. 'All the way from Greece.'

'How do you know I'm a cop?' Zannis said, one careful word at a time.

Husar shrugged. 'I know,' he said. 'I always know. What the hell you doing up here?'

'A favour. I need a favour. Sami Pal gave me your name.'

Husar didn't like it. 'Oh?' was all he said, but it was more than enough.

'Sami gave me the name, Mr Husar, nothing else.'

'Okay. So?'

'A favour. And I will pay for it.'

Husar visibly relaxed. A *corrupt* cop. This he understood. 'Yeah? How much you pay?'

'Two thousand dollars.'

Husar swore in Hungarian and his eyes widened. 'Some favour! I don't kill politicians, mister—'

'Zannis. My first name is Costa.'

'Your right name? I don't care, but—'

'It is.'

'Okay. What you want from me?' *I'm going to say no, but I want to hear it.*

'You know people escape from Germany?'

'Some, yeah. The lucky ones.'

'I help them.'

Husar gave him a long and troubled look. Finally he said, 'You are, maybe, Gestapo?'

'No. Ask Sami.'

'Okay, maybe I believe you. Say I let you give me two thousand dollars, then what?'

'People come off the . . .' For a moment, Zannis's memory failed him; then it worked. 'People come off the excursion steamer from Vienna and get on the train to Yugoslavia. Zagreb, maybe Belgrade. You hide them, help them safe on the train.'

Husar puffed his cheeks and blew out a sound, *pouf*, then looked uncertain. 'Not what I do, mister. I run business, here in Budapest.'

'This is business.'

'It ain't business, don't bullshit *me*, it's politics.'

Zannis waited. Husar drank some of his juice. 'Want some orange juice?'

'No, thank you.'

'Why I said Gestapo is, they're *around*, you understand? And they play tricks, these guys. *Smart* tricks.' He leaned forward and said, 'The Germans try to take over here. And there's Hungarians want to help them. But not me. Not *us*, see? You got this problem? In Greece?'

'No.'

'We got it here.' He drank more juice, and made a decision. 'How I find out what you want? What people? When? Where?'

'You own a cop here, Mr Husar?'

'Gus.'

'Gus.'

'Yeah, sure, I do. I own a few.'

'We send him . . . It's like a telegram, a police telegram.'

'Yeah? Like a "wanted" notice?'

'Yes. It must be a detective.'

'I got that. It's easy.'

'Just give me a name.'

'First the dollars, mister.'

'In a week.'

'You don't have with you?'

Zannis shook his head.

Husar almost laughed. 'Only a cop—'

'You will have the money.'

118

'Okay. Come back here tonight. Then, maybe.'

Zannis stood up. Husar also rose and they shook hands. Husar said, 'It's not for me, the money. Me, I might just do it for the hell of it, because I don't like the Germans, and they don't like me. So, let's see about you, I'll call Sami today.'

'I'll be back tonight,' Zannis said.

It snowed again that evening, big slow flakes drifting past the streetlamps, but Ilka's Bar was warm and bright and crowded with people. A thieves' den, plain to be seen, but the sense of family was heavy in the air. Gustav Husar laughed and joked, rested a big arm across Zannis's shoulders, marking him as *okay* in here, among Husar's boys. Thugs of all sorts, at least two of them with knife scars on the face, their women wearing plenty of make-up. There was even a kid-size mascot, likely still a teenager, with dark skin and quick dark eyes, who told Zannis his name was Akos. He spoke a little German, did Akos, and explained that his name meant 'white falcon'. He was proud of that. And, Zannis sensed, dangerous. Cops knew. *Very* dangerous. But, that night, friendly as could be. Zannis also met Ilka, once beautiful, still sexy, and it was she who gave him a piece of paper with the name of a detective, a teletype number, and a way to send the money – by wire – to a certain person at a certain bank.

Very organized, Zannis thought, Sami Pal's crowd.

19 December. Vangelis might have waited weeks to connect Zannis with secret money, and Zannis wouldn't have said a word, but there were newspaper headlines every morning, and speeches on the radio, and talk in the tavernas, so nobody waited weeks for anything, not any more they didn't.

Thus Vangelis telephoned on the morning of the nineteenth; come to lunch, he said, at the Club de Salonique at one-thirty, yes? Oh yes. The twenty-sixth of December, when the 'Hartmanns' would be leaving Berlin, was closing in fast, and

Zannis knew he had to get the two thousand dollars into the account Husar controlled in Budapest.

Zannis was prompt to the minute, but he'd got it wrong – his first thought, anyhow. From the glasses on the table and the ashtray, he could see that Vangelis and Nikolas Vasilou had been there for a while. Then, as both men rose to greet him, Zannis realized this was simply St Vangelis at work, making time to say things to Vasilou about him that couldn't be said once he'd arrived. 'Am I late?' Zannis said.

'*Skata!* My memory!' Vangelis said. Then, 'It's all my fault, Costa. But no matter, here we are.'

Vasilou was taller than Zannis, lean and straight-backed, with a prominent beak of a nose, sharp cheekbones, ripples of oiled silver hair combed back from his forehead, and a thin line for a mouth. 'Very pleased to meet you,' he said, his eyes measuring Zannis. Friend? Foe? Prey?

They ordered a second bottle of retsina, with lamb and potatoes to follow, and they talked. The war, the local politics, the city, the weather, the war. Eventually the main course showed up and they talked some more. Zannis contributed little, his status well below that of his partners at luncheon. Smiled at their quips, nodded at their insights, tried not to get food on his tie. Finally, as triangles of tired-looking baklava arrived on the club's French china, Vangelis excused himself to go to the lavatory.

The businessman Vasilou wasted no time. 'The commissioner tells me that you need, how shall we say . . . private money? A secret fund?'

'That's true,' Zannis said. He sensed that Vasilou had not made up his mind, so the instinct to persuade, to say more, to say too much, was strong inside him but, with difficulty, he fought it off.

'Money that cannot, he tells me, come from the city treasury.'

Zannis nodded. After a moment he said, 'Would you like me to explain?'

'No, not the details,' Vasilou said, protecting himself. 'How much are we talking about?'

Zannis gave the number in drachmas, two hundred and fifty thousand, his tone neutral, and not dramatic. 'It will have to be paid out in dollars,' he said, 'the way life works in Europe these days.'

'A lot of money, my friend. Something short of twenty-five thousand dollars.'

'I know,' Zannis said, looking gloomy 'Perhaps too much?'

Vasilou did not take the bait and play the tycoon. He looked, instead, thoughtful – *what am I getting myself into*? The silence grew, Zannis became aware of low conversation at other tables, the discreet music of lunch in a private dining room. Vasilou looked away, towards the window, then met Zannis's eyes and held them. 'Can you confirm,' he said, 'that this money will be spent for the benefit of our country?'

'Of course it will be.' That was a lie.

And Vasilou almost knew it, but not quite. 'You're sure?' was the best he could do.

'You have my word,' Zannis said.

Vasilou paused, then said, 'Very well.' Not in his voice, it wasn't *very well*, but he'd been trapped and had no way out.

Vangelis returned to the table but did not sit down. 'I've got to forgo the baklava,' he said, glancing at his watch.

'They will wrap it up for you,' Vasilou said, looking for the waiter.

'No, no. Another time. And I really shouldn't.' Vangelis shook hands with both of them and made his way out of the dining room.

'A valued friend,' Vasilou said. 'He speaks well of you, you know"

'I owe him a great deal. Everything. And he believes in ... what I'm doing.'

'Yes, I know he does, he said he did.' Vasilou paused, then

said, 'He also told me you might some day become commissioner of police, here in Salonika.'

'Far in the future,' Zannis said. 'So I don't think about things like that.' *But you'd better.*

Vasilou reached inside his jacket – revealing a swathe of white silk lining – and took out a chequebook and a silver pen. 'Made out to you? In your name?' he said, 'You can convert this to dollars at the bank.' Vasilou wrote out the cheque, signed it and handed it to Zannis.

They spoke briefly, after that, a reprise of the lunch conversation, then left the club together. Walked down the stairs and out of the front door, where a white Rolls-Royce was idling at the kerb. As they said goodbye, Zannis looked over Vasilou's shoulder. The face of the woman, staring out of the window of the back seat, was the most beautiful thing he'd ever seen. Olive skin, golden hair – truly gold, not blonde – pulled straight back, eyes just barely suggesting an almond shape, as though wrought by a Byzantine painter.

Vasilou turned to see what Zannis was looking at and waved to the woman. For an instant her face was still, then it came alive, like an actress before the camera: the corners of the full lips turned up, but the rest of the perfect face remained perfectly composed. Flawless.

'Can we drop you somewhere?' Vasilou said. He didn't mean it; Zannis had had from him all he was going to get for one day.

'No, thanks. I'll walk.'

Slowly, the window of the Rolls was lowered. She was wearing a bronze-coloured silk shirt and a pearl necklace just below her throat. 'Can you get in front, darling?' she said. 'I've got packages in the back.'

Vasilou gave Zannis a certain look: *women, they shop.* A chauffeur slid from behind the wheel, circled the car and opened the front door.

'Again, thank you,' Zannis said.

Vasilou nodded, brusque and dismissive, as though Zannis, by taking his money, had become a servant. Then walked quickly to his car.

26 December. Berlin.

Only the wealthy could afford to live in the Dahlem district of Berlin, a neighbourhood of private homes with gardens. The houses were powerfully built, of sober stone or brick, often three storeys high, sometimes with a corner tower, while the lawns and plantings were kept with the sort of precision achieved only by the employment of gardeners. However, in the last month of 1940, hidden here and there – one didn't want to be seen to acknowledge shortage – were the winter remains of vegetable gardens. Behind a fieldstone wall, a rabbit hutch. And the rising of the weak sun revealed the presence of two or three cockerels. In Dahlem! But the war at sea was, in Berlin and all of Germany, having its effect.

At five-thirty, on a morning that seemed to her cruelly cold, wet and dark, Emilia Krebs rang the chime on the door of the Gruen household. She too lived in Dahlem, not far away, but she might have driven had not petrol become so severely rationed. When the door was answered, by a tall distinguished-looking gentleman, Emilia said, 'Good morning, Herr Hartmann.' That was Herr Gruen's new name, his alias for the journey to Salonika.

He nodded, *yes, I know,* and said, 'Hello, Emmi.'

Emilia carried a thermos of real coffee, hard to find these days, and a bag of freshly baked rolls, made with white flour. Stepping inside, she found the Gruen living room almost barren, what with much of the furniture sold. On the walls, posters had been pinned up to cover the spaces where expensive paintings had once hung. The telephone sat on the floor, its cord unplugged from the wall – the Gestapo could listen to your conversation if the phone was plugged in. She greeted Frau Gruen, as pale and exhausted as her husband, then went to the cupboard in the hall and opened the door. The Gruens' winter coats, recently bought from a used-clothing stall, were heavily worn but acceptable. They mustn't, she knew, look like distressed aristocracy.

Emilia Krebs tried, at least, to be cheerful. The Gruens – he'd been a prominent business lawyer – were old friends, faithful friends, but today they would be leaving Germany. Their money was almost all gone, their car was gone, soon the house would be gone, and word had reached them from within the Nazi administration – from Herr Gruen's former law clerk – that by the end of January they would be gone as well. They were on a list, it was simply a matter of time.

Frau Gruen poured coffee into chipped mugs but refused a roll. 'I can't eat,' she said, apology in her voice. She was short and plump and had, in better times, been the merriest sort of woman – anyone could make her laugh. Now she followed Emilia's eyes to a corner of the living room where a green fedora-like slouch hat rested on a garden chair. 'Let me show you, Emmi,' she said, retrieving the hat and setting it on her head, tilting the brim over one eye. 'So?' she said. 'How do I look?'

Like a middle-aged Jewish woman. 'You look perfect,' Emilia said. 'Very Marlene Dietrich.'

The hat was meant to provide a kind of shadow, obscuring her friend's face, but if the Gruens, travelling as the Hartmanns, ran into difficulties, it would be because of the way Frau Gruen looked. Their papers, passports and exit visas, were excellent forgeries, because resistance friends of Emilia's had managed to link up with a communist cell – they left anti-Nazi leaflets in public buildings – and with this very dangerous connection had come one of the most desirable people to know these days in Berlin: a commercial printer.

Emilia and the Gruens drank their mugs of coffee in silence, there was nothing more to say. When they were done, Emilia said, 'Would you care for company on the way to the tram?'

'Thank you, Emmi,' Herr Gruen said, 'but we'll go by ourselves, and say farewell to you now.'

And so they did.

They left early, seeking the most crowded trains, and they were not disappointed. During the run to Dresden, two and a half hours, they stood in the corridor, packed in with people of all sorts, many with bulky parcels and suitcases. Their own luggage was a simple leather valise, packed for the eyes of customs officers. On this leg of the journey they were ignored, and the passport control on the German side of the Czech border was perfunctory. They were on their way to Vienna, part of the Reich, and so were most of the other passengers. Not quite so smooth was the entry control on the other side of the border – by then it was two-thirty. The officers here were Sudeten Germans, newly empowered, and so conscientious. One of them had a good long look at Frau Gruen, but was not quite so discourteous as to mention that he thought she looked like a Jew. He stared, but that was it, and so failed to notice the thin line of perspiration at her husband's hairline – on a frigid afternoon. But their papers were in order and the officer stamped their visas.

Vienna was a long way from Prague, some eight hours on the express train. Here the Hartmanns were in a first-class compartment, where passengers were rarely subject to unscheduled security checks by Gestapo detectives. One didn't want to annoy powerful people. The Gruens, in preparatory conversation with Emilia and her friends, had determined that friendly chit-chat was dangerous, better to remain silent and aloof. But certain travellers, especially the newly prosperous, felt that first-class status was an opportunity to converse with interesting people and were not so easily turned aside. Thus a woman in the seat across from Frau Gruen, who said, 'What takes you to Vienna?'

'Unfortunately, my wife's mother has passed away,' Herr Gruen said. 'We're going for the funeral.' After that they were left alone.

A useful lie, they thought. How were they to know that this woman and her mouse of a husband would be on the *Leverkusen*, the excursion steamer to Budapest?

In the war of 1914, the German and Austro-Hungarian empires had fought as allies. After surrender in 1918, Hungary became a separate state but Germany, with a new war on the horizon in the late 1930s, sought to rekindle the alliance, courting the Hungarians in the hope they would join up with Hitler in the planned conquest of Europe. *We must be friends*, said German diplomacy, accent on the *must*, so commercial links of all sorts became important. For example, the round-trip excursion steamer that sailed up and down the Danube between Vienna and Budapest. True, it crossed the border of the Reich, but not the border of national amity. It was *fun*. A band played on the dock in Vienna, another on the dock in Budapest. The food aboard the *Leverkusen*, even in time of rationing, was plentiful – as much potato as you liked. Not that there wasn't a passport control, there was, beneath great swastika banners, but the Austrian SS men kept their Alsatians muzzled and at a distance, and the officers, on the border with a new ally, were under orders to be genial. 'The ice on the river is not too bad, not yet,' one of them said to Herr Gruen, who for the occasion wore a Nazi party pin in his lapel.

'One can be glad of that,' Herr Gruen said, with his best smile.

'You'll have a jolly time in Budapest, Herr Hartmann.'

'We expect to. Then, back to work.'

'In Berlin, I see.'

'Yes, we love it there, but, always good to get away for a bit.'

The officer agreed, stamped the exit visa, raised his right arm and said, amiably, 'Heil Hitler.'

'*Sieg Heil,*' said the Gruens, a duet. Then, relieved, they climbed the gangway.

Standing at the rail of the steamer, watching the passengers as they filed past the border control, was the woman from the train and her husband. 'Isn't that . . .?' she said. She had to raise her voice, because the oompah of the tuba in the dockside ensemble was particularly emphatic.

'It is, my dear.'

'Very curious, Hansi. He said they were going to a funeral. In Vienna.'

'Perhaps you didn't hear properly.'

'No, no. I'm sure I did.' Now she began to suspect that the pleasure of her company had been contemptuously brushed aside, and she started to get angry.

Poor Hansi. This could go on for days. 'Oh, who knows,' he said.

'No, Hansi,' she said sharply. 'They must explain themselves.'

But, where were they?

The Gruens had taken a first-class cabin for the overnight trip to Budapest and planned to hide there. Hunger, however, finally drove Herr Gruen to the dining room, where he ate quickly and ordered a cheese sandwich to take back to the cabin. As he left the dining room, here was the woman from the train. Her husband was nowhere to be seen, but she was sitting on a lounge chair just outside the door and rose when she saw him. 'Sir,' she said.

'Yes?'

'Excuse me, but did you not say on the train that you were attending the funeral of your wife's mother, in Vienna?'

Herr Gruen flinched. Why had this terrifying woman, cheeks flushed, arms folded across her chest, suddenly attacked him? He did not answer, looking like a schoolboy caught out by a teacher, said, 'Well,' to gain time, then 'I did, *meine Frau,* say that. I'm afraid I did not tell the truth.'

'Oh?' This was a threat.

'I did not mean to trouble you, *meine Frau*, but I felt I could not honourably respond to your question.'

'And why not?' The admission had not appeased her; the prospect of a really nasty confrontation apparently provoking her to a sort of sexual excitement.

'Because we *are* married, but not to each other.'

The woman's mouth opened, but no words came out.

'We are in love, *meine Frau*, so much in love, we are.' He paused, then said, 'Tragically.'

Now she went scarlet, and stuttered an apology.

For her, he thought, just as good as a fight. *Humiliation.* Possibly better. It wasn't until he was back inside the cabin that he realized his shirt was soaked with sweat.

27 December. In the sunless light of a winter morning, the Gypsy musicians on the Danube dock seemed oddly out of place, as though they'd become lost on their way to a nightclub. Still, they sawed away on their violins and strummed their guitars as the passengers disembarked from the *Leverkusen*. Holding hands as they walked down the gangplank, the Gruens were as close to peace of mind as they'd been for a long, long time. True, their train to Belgrade didn't leave until the morning of the twenty-ninth, so they would have to spend two nights in a hotel. This didn't bother them at all – they were no longer on German soil, and the hotel would be luxurious. A Hungarian officer stamped their passports in the ship's dining room, and they'd begun to feel like normal travellers as they headed for the line of taxis waiting at the pier.

But they were, just then, intercepted.

By a strange creature, small and dark and vaguely threatening, who wore a narrow-brim brown hat with a card stuck in the hatband that said *Hotel Astoria*. Not a bad hotel, but not where they were going. 'Hello, hello,' said the creature.

'Good morning,' said Herr Gruen. 'We're not at the Astoria, we're booked at the Danube Palace.'

The Gruens started to walk away, but the creature held up a hand, *stop*. 'No,' he said, 'you can't go there.' His German was rough but functional.

'Excuse us, please,' Herr Gruen said, perhaps less courteous now.

The creature seemed puzzled. 'You're the Hartmanns, right? Green tie, green hat?'

Herr Gruen's eyes widened. Frau Gruen said, 'Yes, we are. And?'

'I'm called Akos, it means "white falcon"'. I'm sent by your friend in Salonika, and I'm here to tell you that if you set foot in the Palace, well, that's the end of you.'

Herr Gruen said, 'It is?'

'A big fancy hotel, Herr Hartmann, so Germans all over the place, and they've bribed every waiter, every porter, every maid. You won't last an hour because they *know*, they know fugitives when they see them.'

'So it will be the Astoria?'

'What? Oh, I forgot.' Akos took off his hat, slipped the card from the hatband and put it in his pocket. 'No, I got this just for the dock. It's not so nice where I'm taking you, but you'll be safe.' He glanced sideways, at something that had caught his attention, something he didn't like. 'Let's go,' he said. 'And let's make it look good,' he added, taking the valise from Herr Gruen. They walked to the line of taxis, then past it, to a taxi parked in a side street just off the waterfront. Akos opened the door for the Gruens, then stared towards the dock as they settled themselves in the back seat.

The taxi sped away, cornering through side streets as Akos, from time to time, turned the rear-view mirror so he could see out of the back window. The driver said something in Hungarian, Akos answered him briefly. They crossed a bridge, then drove for a few minutes more, entering a narrow street with dead neon signs over nightclub doors. 'It gets busy here at night,' Akos explained. Midway down the block they stopped in front of a hotel – an old building two windows wide, brick stained black with a century of soot. 'Here we are,' Akos said. The Gruens peered out of the window – *here*? 'Don't worry,' Akos said. 'You'll survive. Wait till you get to Serbia!'

The smell inside was strong: smoke, drains, garlic, God only knew what else. There was no receptionist – a bell on the desk, a limp curtain over a doorway – and Akos led them upstairs, up three flights past silent corridors. The room was narrow, so was the bed, with a blanket over a mattress, and the paint had been peeling off the walls for years. 'If you want food,' Akos said, 'just go downstairs and ring the bell, somebody will get you something, but you don't leave the hotel.' He stood to one side of the window, moved the curtain an inch with his index finger and muttered to himself in Hungarian. It sounded like an oath. To the Gruens he said, 'I'll be back. Something I have to take care of.'

Gus wanted these people kept safe, and Akos was proud that he'd been chosen for the job. But now he had a problem. A man he'd spotted at the dock stared at every passenger leaving the *Leverkusen*, then a taxi followed his own through a maze of back streets and now the hotel was being watched by the same man. Not young, with the sort of head that looks as if it's been squeezed flat, a brush moustache and waxy complexion, he wore a grimy pearl-grey overcoat. Who was he? A policeman? Akos didn't think so. The guy definitely didn't act like a detective; he was furtive, and he was alone. He was, more likely, some miserable little sneak who sold fugitives for cash – cash from the Budapest cops, or even from the Germans.

These people he'd hidden in the hotel were on the run, surely using false papers. And how did the sneak know that? Because when people ran from the Nazis they ran through Budapest, and when you see something often enough you learn to recognize it; you can smell it. And if the guy was wrong, so what? He was still some cop's lapdog, next time he'd get it right. Cops lived off informers; that was how they did their work. They'd tried it with Akos, but only once: he shrugged, he didn't know anything, I'm the dumbest guy in town. In the gang Gus ran, no rats allowed, there were *stories*, bad stories, better to be loyal. Akos left the hotel, made a sharp turn away from the man in the doorway of an abandoned shop, then, head down, in a hurry, he walked around the block, coming up on the man from behind.

Akos carried a little knife, simple thing, a cheap wooden handle and a three-inch blade. But that was all you needed, if you knew what you were doing. Only a three-inch blade but he kept it sharp as a razor, so it had to be protected by a leather sheath. As he neared the man, he took the knife out of its sheath and held it behind his leg. What to do? Slide it in and out? That would be that. Put it in the right place and the victim never made a sound, just fell down, as though the air had been let out of him. But now you had a corpse, now you had a murder, so there would be cops on the street, sniffing around. They would search the hotel.

Akos dropped his hand on the man's left shoulder and, as he turned in that direction, circled around on his blind side. Startled, the man opened his mouth, ready to tell some tale but he never got it out. *What an ugly tie*, Akos thought. Maroon, with a grey knight-on-horseback in the middle. Who would wear such a thing? He took the bottom of the tie between thumb and forefinger as though to study it, then the knife flashed, so fast the guy never saw it, just below the knot. Ah, but maybe Akos wasn't as deft as he thought, because the blade not only sliced off the tie but took a shirt button as well, which flew up in the air; landed with a click on the pavement and rolled away. Still holding the bottom of the tie, Akos folded it in half and stuck it in the pocket of the man's shirt. The man whinnied with fear.

'Could've been an ear,' Akos said. 'I think maybe you should go back wherever you came from. And forget what happened.

Because if you don't . . .' Akos put the knife away.

The man said, 'Yes, sir. Yes, sir,' turned, and hurried off.

29 December. The train was classified as an express, but it never speeded up, just chugged slowly south across the Hungarian plain, past snow-covered fields where crows waited on the bare branches of the trees, through mist and fog, like a countryside in a poem or a dream. The Gruens were nine hours from Belgrade, in the neutral nation of Yugoslavia, as Germany faded away with every beat of the rails.

And so, slowly, they began to believe that they had escaped. The wretched hotel in Budapest had been frightening; neither of them had ever been in such a place. But with the appearance of the little gangster Akos — what a character! — a hand had reached out to protect them. Now all they had to do was watch the scenery and talk about the unknown future, a life different from anything they'd ever contemplated, but at least a life. This optimism, however, proved to be unfounded.

They passed easily through Hungarian customs; then the train stopped in Subotica, the first town in Serbian Yugoslavia, for border control. Ten officers boarded the train and took the Gruens, and many other passengers, into the station. The officers were ferocious — *why? Why? What had they done?* One or two of the officers spoke some German but they didn't explain; that was the ancient prerogative of border guards. They gestured violently, shoved the passengers, swore in Serbian and took all documents away for examination behind the closed doors of the stationmaster's office. The passengers were forced to stand facing a wall. For more than an hour.

When the officers returned, they took Frau Gruen and two other women into the office and made them undress, down to their slips, while two men in suits and ties ran their hands over every seam and hem in their clothing, then slit the shoulder pads in their dresses and jackets. But, Frau Gruen realized, Emilia Krebs had saved her, had told them both not to *think*, even, of sewing jewels or coins or papers or *anything* in their clothing. And, apparently, the clothing of the other women also hid nothing. As the search proceeded, the women's eyes met: why are they doing this to us? Later, Frau Gruen learned that her husband and several other men had been subjected to the same treatment. And one man, the passengers thought, had been taken away.

They weren't sure. When they were permitted to reboard the train, they gathered in the corridor of the first-class car and, as the engine jerked forward and the station fell away, they argued. Had there not been a fat man with red hair? Perhaps he had simply left the train, perhaps he lived in Subotica. No, one of the passengers didn't think so; she had spoken with this man, and he'd said he was Polish. Well, yes, perhaps he was, but did that mean he didn't live in Subotica? As the train made slow progress through a frozen valley, the dispute went on and on. No one claimed to have actually seen him being led away, but somebody said, 'That's the way it's done!' and again they could not agree. Mysterious disappearance? Public arrest? The passengers had stories to tell, had seen arrests, had heard of disappearances. In time, they returned to their compartments, in accord on only one point: the man was gone.

Twenty minutes later, a woman came to see the Gruens. She had been taken into the office alone, an afterthought. While she was there, a senior officer, speaking halting German, had attempted to telephone an office in Berlin. In his hand, she said, was a piece of paper with the name *Hartmann*, and what she thought were passport numbers. 'I don't know your name,' she said, 'but I am telling everybody who was searched.' The Gruens were silent; could do no more than stare at her. 'Don't worry,' she said. 'He never got through. Something wrong with the line, maybe a storm in the north. He shouted and carried on, then the operator got tired of him and cut him off.' After a moment, Herr Gruen, his heart pounding, admitted they were the Hartmanns, and thanked her. Later he wondered, *Was that safe?* It was surely the decent thing to do but, perhaps, a mistake.

When the train stopped in Novi Sad, the station before Belgrade, a uniformed police lieutenant opened the door of the Gruens' compartment, as though searching for an empty seat. When Herr Gruen looked up, the lieutenant made eye contact with him and gestured, a subtle nod of the head, towards the corridor. He waited there until Herr Gruen joined him; then they walked along the carriage together. He had a friend in Zagreb, he explained, who'd asked him to see 'the Hartmanns' safely through the police control in the Belgrade railway station. He knew they would be changing trains there, for the line that ran south to Nis, not far from the Greek border.

So when they left the train at Belgrade station, the lieutenant accompanied them, spoke briefly to the officers and the Gruens were waved past. In the station waiting room, he bought a newspaper and sat nearby, keeping an eye on them. When the train for Nis was announced, he followed them along the platform and, once they found seats, paused at the window and gave them a farewell nod.

The train to Nis was slow and dirty and crowded. There was no first-class carriage. Across the aisle from the Gruens, a woman was travelling with two rabbits in a crate, and at the far end of the carriage, a group of soldiers got drunk, sang for a time, then went looking for a fight. To the Gruens, none of this mattered at all – they had travelled deep into the Balkans, now far from central Europe, thus the rabbits, the soldiers, the women in black head scarves, meant safety, meant refuge.

In Skopje, capital of Yugoslavian Macedonia, they sat in the waiting room all night and, in a slow rain that came with the dawn, boarded the train that followed the Vardar River down to the customs station at Gevgelija, then across the border to Greece, at Polykastro. At last on Greek soil, in sight of the blue and white flag, Frau Gruen broke down and wept. Herr Gruen comforted her as best he could while Greek soldiers, manning machine guns and an anti-aircraft cannon, stared at them. Greece was at war, and the border guards were courteous but thorough. As they walked towards the waiting train, a man in civilian clothes was suddenly by their side. 'My name is Costa Zannis,' he said, adding that he was an officer of the Salonika police, would escort them into Salonika and arrange for their passage to Turkey. Frau Gruen took his hand in both of hers, again close to tears. 'I know,' he said gently. 'A long journey.' He took his hand back and smiled, saying, 'We'd better get on the train.'

A very old train, that ran to Salonika. Each compartment spanned the width of the carriage and had its own door to the exterior, where a narrow boardwalk allowed the conductor to move between compartments as he collected tickets. Brass oil lamps flanked the doors and the seats were made of wood, with high curved backs. As the train rattled along, Zannis took a pad and pencil from the pocket of his trench coat. 'Forgive me,' he said. 'I can see you are exhausted, but I must ask you questions, and you must try to be as accurate as possible.' He turned to a fresh page on the pad. 'It is for the others,' he said. 'The others who will make this journey.'

In Berlin, at the Gestapo headquarters on Prinz-Albrechtstrasse, Hauptsturmführer Albert Hauser kept a photograph of his father on his desk. It had been taken in a portrait studio during the Great War, but it looked older than that, like a portrait from the previous century: a rotund, solemn man, sitting at attention on the regal chair provided by the studio. The subject wore a white handlebar moustache, a Prussian-style helmet and a uniform, for he had been, like Hauser himself, a police officer in the city of Dusseldorf. A good policeman, the elder Hauser, stern and unrelenting and, in much the same way, a good father. Whose son had followed him into the profession.

Hauser, on a frosty day in mid-January, looked nothing like the photograph. He was heavily, powerfully built, with blunt features, hair worn Prussian-army style: near-shaved on the sides, an inch long on top. Hauser smoked cigars, an old habit from his days as a detective in Düsseldorf, an antidote to the smell of death, sweetish and sickening, that nobody ever got used to. But a policeman's lot was murder, suicide and week-old corpses who'd died alone, so Hauser smoked cigars.

He'd been very good at his job in Dusseldorf, but as his family grew in the mid-1930s he needed more money. 'You should come and work for us,' a former colleague told him. 'Join the SS, then work for the Gestapo, we are always keen to hire talented men.' Hauser didn't much care for politics, he liked a quiet life, but membership in the SS seemed to entail quite a bit of marching and singing, attendance at Nazi rallies and riotous drinking in beer halls. Though none of this appealed to Hauser, he applied to the SS, was welcomed and discovered that they didn't insist on marching and singing, they simply wanted his skills: his ability to discover crime, to investigate and to hunt down criminals and arrest them. Working for the Gestapo, of course, the criminals were different from those he'd pursued in Düsseldorf. No longer burglars, or thieves, or murderers, they were instead Jews and communists who broke the political laws of the new Nazi state. Laws that concerned flight and false documents, non-payment of special taxes levied on Jews, and, in the case of the communists, agitation and propaganda intended to undermine the state. To Hauser, it didn't matter; laws were laws – you simply had to learn how they worked – and those who broke them were criminals. Nothing could be simpler. By January of 1941 he'd risen quickly to the rank of Hauptsturmführer, captain, and by his standards was paid very well indeed.

At nine-thirty that morning he stubbed out his cigar – an expensive cigar, for now he could afford such things – and slipped his arms into the sleeves of his overcoat, an expensive overcoat, so nice and warm. From his office on the third floor, he walked down to the Prinz-Albrechtstrasse, where his partner, a thin, rather bitter fellow called Matzig, waited behind the wheel of a Mercedes motorcar. He had to work with Matzig, formerly a detective in Ulm, but didn't much care for him, a man who took his membership in the Nazi party quite seriously, reading, in fact studying, certain books and going endlessly to meetings. Oh well, to each his own, and he didn't see all that much of Matzig, working mostly by himself. But today they were going to make an arrest, a couple called Gruen, a lawyer and his wife, Jews, suspected of affiliation with communists. His department in the Gestapo had a long list of such people, wealthy Berlin intellectuals for the most part, and was, at a steady pace, arresting and jailing them for interrogation, so that they might be persuaded to confess to their crimes, provide names of others, be tried and imprisoned.

Matzig drove cautiously, much too slowly for Hauser's taste – the little shrimp was irritating in so many little ways – but soon enough they were in the garden district of Dahlem, one of Berlin's finest neighbourhoods, where many on Hauser's list were resident. Matzig parked the car and, as they walked up the path to the Gruen doorway, Hauser instinctively made sure of his side-arm, a Walther PPK, the smaller version of the standard police pistol. Not that he'd need it. These arrests were easy, you had only to open the back door of the car and the criminals climbed in. Not like the old days; much calmer and, important to a family man like Hauser, much safer.

Matzig pressed the button by the door and they heard, from within the house, the sound of a chime.

A FRENCH KING

Storms, in January. Snow covered the mountain villages. Down in Salonika, windswept rain came sheeting across the corniche, where the locals staggered along, struggling with their umbrellas and scowling harder each time a gust hit them. When, after work, Zannis returned to Santaroza Lane, a welcoming Melissa shook off a great spray that decorated the wall of the vestibule and the apartment was filled with the musky aroma of wet dog. Lately, Zannis was often alone there – Tasia Loukas didn't visit very often. She sensed in him a certain distraction and she was right. For, again and again, his imagination replayed the scene on the street in front of the Club de Salonique. Behind the window of a white Rolls-Royce, a vision, olive skin and golden hair, then, from perfect composure, the smile of an actress.

Idiot, he called himself. For indulging in such fantasies. *But nothing new,* he thought. Down through the endless halls of time, forever, there wasn't a man in the world who hadn't wanted what he'd never have. 'Do you know Vasilou?' he asked Tasia. 'And his wife, what's-her-name?'

'Demetria, you mean? The goddess?'

'Yes.'

'I know him by sight, he doesn't mix with people like me. What do you want with him?'

'I was just wondering.'

'Not about *her.* Were you, little boy?'

'No.'

'Better not.'

So, he thought, *Demetria*.

And schemed. Absurdly – *Oh no, the house is on fire, I'll have to carry you out.* Or, not so absurdly – *A cocktail party? I'd love to.*

Meanwhile, much realer schemes absorbed his day, schemes involving the Balkan railways and Turkish documents. As the Gruens left for Istanbul, six new refugees – a couple, a single man, a family of three – appeared at Salonika railway station. For reasons of economy, and because the management was sympathetic, Zannis housed them in the Tobacco Hotel, a weary but functional relic of the nineteenth century. There, grey and exhausted, they tried to recover from long days and nights on the escape route. Tried to recover from the slow brutal succession of torments experienced as Jews living in Nazi Germany. Seven years of it.

As for the final link in the chain, Ahmet Celebi had had his fill of the indifferent food at the Club de Salonique, and now Zannis dealt exclusively with Madam Urglu, nominally a deputy to the commercial attaché, in fact the Turkish legation's intelligence officer. An intimidating presence, Madam Urglu, with her opaque, puffy face, her glasses on a chain, and her – well, *inquisitive* nature. They met at a taverna owned by Greek refugees who'd come to Salonika in the great population exchange, thus called Smyrna Betrayed, where, in the winter damp, Madam Urglu was partial to the fish stew.

'So,' she said, 'this turns out to be an ongoing um, project. One might as well call it an "operation" no?'

'It is,' Zannis said. 'Someone has to help these people.'

'Can they not remain in Salonika?'

'They would be welcome, this city has always taken in refugees.' Zannis tore a piece of bread in half. 'But the Wehrmacht is in Roumania – maybe it won't stop there.'

'We hope they don't go into Bulgaria. That puts them on our border.'

'Only tourists, right now,' Zannis said. 'Very fit young men, in pairs, with expensive cameras. Tourists with a passion for the ancient Bulgar culture, like airfields, and port facilities.'

Madam Urglu smiled. 'Such finesse,' she said. 'Our Teutonic friends.' She retrieved a mussel from her stew, open perhaps a third of the way, stared at it for a moment, then set it beside her bowl. 'But at least they're not in Greece. And the English are doing what they can.' There were now sixty thousand British Commonwealth troops, divisions from Australia and New Zealand, on the island of Crete.

'We're grateful,' Zannis said. 'But we can't be sure how Hitler sees it. Provocation? Deterrent? And Mussolini must be screaming at him, because the RAF is bombing the Italians in Albania.'

'Which we applaud. Unofficially, of course. And it isn't just a feint, I see they've put shore artillery in Salonika.' She gestured with her head towards the waterfront, where long cannon were now facing the Aegean.

'They have.'

'One wonders if more is coming.'

'It's possible,' Zannis said, preparing for the attack.

'Perhaps more guns. Or, even, an RAF squadron.'

'We'd be happy to have them,' Zannis said.

'You haven't heard?'

'I'm not told such things Madam Urglu. I'm only a policeman.'

'Oh, please. Don't get coy, not with me.'

'Truly, I don't know.'

'But I'm sure you could find out. If you cared to.'

'Not even that. I expect the military would be informed, but they're known to be secretive.'

For just a bare instant, a look of irritation, compressed lips, darkened Madam Urglu's face. Then she said, 'Naturally,' and with some resignation added, 'they are. Still, it would be something of an achievement, for me, to learn of such plans. One always wants to do well in one's job.'

'And who doesn't?' Zannis said, meaning *no offence taken*.

'You *would* like to see me do well, wouldn't you?'

'You know I would.'

'Then, maybe sometime, if you should discover . . .'

'Understood,' Zannis said. 'It's not impossible.'

'Ah me,' Madam Urglu said, gently rueful, *how the world goes around.*

Zannis smiled, *yes, it does.* Then he said, 'I'll need six visas, this time.'

'*Six!*'

'Yes, it's more desperate every day, up north.'

'My, my. Would five help you?'

'Madam Urglu, please.'

'All right then, six. It's five hundred dollars each. I trust you have the money with you.'

'It was four apiece, the last time.'

'I know, but our friend in Istanbul ...'

'Why don't I give you two thousand, four hundred today, and I'll make up the remainder at our next meeting.'

'Oh very well,' she said, 'if I must. I'll send the papers over when they're ready.'

'Thank you, Madam Urglu,' Zannis said, meaning it.

'Of course they *could* be free,' she said. 'It wouldn't take much. Really. It wouldn't.'

Her face softened. She was – Zannis saw it – almost pleading. He nodded, sympathy in his eyes. 'Yes,' he said. 'I know.'

As to what exactly he knew, he didn't say. Perhaps that it was a hard machine, national interest, which would in time destroy both of them. She was, without doubt, perfectly aware that he would never spy on his British ally, no? Not that he couldn't – and Madam Urglu understood precisely his standing in the politics of Salonika – because he could. He'd seen, of all things, a memorandum from the traffic office of the police department. 'Interruption of traffic planned to begin on 2 February, for important waterfront construction.' A new municipal garden, perhaps? But he would not, could not, reveal such things, no matter how little it would mean for the Turks to know in advance about the additional armament. They'd *see* it, eventually. But

144

eventually was the active word. Until then, well, one didn't spy on a faithful friend, it just wasn't done.

All that much.

The commissionaire – doorman, porter, messenger – at the Tobacco Hotel was a straight-backed old fellow who'd fought valiantly, in his day, against the Turkish gendarmerie. Very solemn and courtly, in the old-world manner. The assistant manager had found for him somewhere, probably in the markets, a doorman's overcoat from some bygone hotel. The epaulettes were ragged – more than a few gold braids missing – three of the gold buttons had been replaced, and the original owner had obviously been taller and heavier than the present one. Still, it was the uniform he had, and he wore it with pride.

He was more than aware of the new guests, who spoke German, and who'd clearly had a hard time of it. One in particular touched his heart – she was thin as a rail, with iron-grey hair cut quite short. Likely an aristocrat, in the past, who never failed to give him a gratuity, a pitiful coin or two, when he went out to get her something to eat. Yes, pitiful, but the best she could do, and she never failed him.

Going to work one morning, he took a detour through the market, and there was his young nephew, a sweet boy, working at a flower stall. They gossiped for a few minutes and then, as they parted, his nephew handed him a small bouquet and said, 'Here, Uncle, take this. Brighten up your room.' He said thank you and then, later, on a sudden impulse, took the bouquet up to the nice lady's room. 'Please,' he said, fixing the bouquet in a water glass. 'To brighten up your room.' Oh how she was moved, by this generous act. And he would not accept the coin she offered him.

Instead, they talked. Or at least she did. He would not sit down, but stood by the door as she told him her story. She came from Berlin, from a prominent family, at one time, but then the odious Hitler had risen to power and their circumstances declined quickly. Most of them had left, years earlier, and she finally had to follow them. But it had been a dreadful trip, into Hungary and down through the Balkans: unheated railway carriages, almost nothing to eat, and police controls every day. Fortunately, some people had helped them, and for this she was grateful. She was no more explicit than that. He said he would hope for, on her behalf, a better future, and left with a nod of the head that suggested a bow. And the flowers did, indeed, brighten up the room.

Two days later, he had his weekly meeting with the British travel writer, not long resident in the city, called Escovil. They met, as usual, in one of the old Byzantine churches, almost always deserted, and there the commissionaire passed along bits of gossip about the city and various doings at the hotel – Escovil was always curious about foreign guests. For this the commissionaire was paid a small stipend, money which, given his meagre salary, made all the difference in the way he lived.

Was it wrong? He didn't find it so. He would never have given information to a German, or even a Frenchman, but the British: that was another story. They had been good friends to Greece, as far back as the nineteenth century when the great English poet, Lordos Vyronos himself, Lord Byron, had come to fight in their wars of independence; and the British had fought and died in the hills of Macedonia, in 1917, where they'd faced the Bulgarian army.

That afternoon, the commissionaire told the travel writer about the aristocratic German lady and her difficult passage to Salonika. Was she, Escovil wanted to know, the only one? No, there were a few others, and, he'd heard, more were expected. And a good thing too. In these times of war, people didn't travel so often, and there were too many empty rooms at the hotel. And these rooms were paid for in full, promptly, by the well-regarded police official himself, Constantine Zannis, from an old Salonika family.

★

Escape line!

Francis Escovil hurried back to the room he kept at the Pension Bastasini, where his predecessor in Salonika, Roxanne Brown, had stayed. There he wrote a report of his contact with the commissionaire, then drove his car out to a house on the Chalkidiki peninsula, where his assistant encrypted the message and sent it on to London by wireless/telegraph.

The following night, the Secret Intelligence Service wired back. And very excited they were! Could he get at least one name? One true name? There had been, for some years, contact with anti-Nazi Germans in Berlin: intellectuals, lawyers, communist workers and aristocrats; some Jewish, some not. Were the people using the escape line from that group? Or another, that they didn't know about? Were 'the friends' – operatives of the Jewish agencies in Palestine – involved? Could this policeman Zannis be recruited? Bribed? Coerced? Intimidated? Find out more! Most urgent!

Escovil was, despite himself, almost amused. *Hit a tender spot, have I?* It reminded him of something he'd heard about Churchill, who, excited by some new discovery, would head his minutes, memoranda, with the phrase *Action this day.* Escovil's assistant was less amused; the five-digit groups of numbers took a long time to decrypt. 'The hell have you done?' he grumbled. To the fishing village outside the cottage, he was known as Plato, a deaf-mute taken to be Escovil's intimate companion. In fact his name was Geary, formerly a corporal in the Irish Guards and a famous pub brawler. Once, to emphasize the nature of the companionship, Escovil had taken his hand as they walked through the village. This was a practice common enough between any and all Greek men, but Geary didn't like it and said, in an undertone, 'Let go me fookin' hand, you damned poofter.' To Escovil, a Greek woman radio operator would have been a more credible arrangement, but there weren't any such to be found, so 'Plato' had to serve.

In any event, the message radioed back to London wasn't so

long. He would try to learn a name. Zannis could be asked to help, but any sort of pressure wouldn't work.

On 18 January, a hand-carried envelope reached Zannis at his office. The message within was typewritten: Colonel Simonides, of the Royal Hellenic Army General Staff, requested his presence at a meeting of 'certain residents of Salonika' at a house in the officers' quarters of the army base, east of the city. The meeting was to take place the following day, at six in the evening, and this invitation was, Zannis realized as he reread it, very close to an order. He took a taxi to the base, where he had to show his identity papers to a lieutenant, list in hand, at the guardhouse by the gate. He was then escorted to the residence of, apparently, a senior officer, with fine though well-worn furnishings. On entering a large parlour, Zannis saw that many of the guests had preceded him, to what looked like a social gathering: a number of Salonika's rich and powerful, some with their wives; the city's chief rabbi was there, as was Spiraki, head of the local State Security Bureau; and Vangelis, who waved to him from across the room. In one corner, a professor at the university was talking to a well-regarded journalist. There were, Zannis estimated, close to fifty people in the crowded room, sitting, standing and drinking coffee, available at a table to one side of the doorway.

A uniformed officer – harsh, slightly reddened face, black moustache – tapped a spoon on a coffee cup to get their attention. As Zannis looked over the crowd he saw, obscured by two large guests, a flash of golden hair. Was Vasilou there? Of course he would be. So then, was that who he thought it was? Could it be? His heart raced, and he started to move to a position where he could get a better view.

But then, the officer cleared his throat and said, 'Citizens of Salonika, allow me to introduce myself, I am Colonel Simonides, and the first thing I would ask, is that you will please consider this a private meeting, not a subject for gossip – not with friends, not with associates. We – that is, the General Staff of the army –

148

have chosen you carefully. You are crucial to the way our city works; you are crucial, in our opinion, to Greece itself.

'Two further things I would ask: please do not question me when I've finished speaking. For reasons ranging from the unknown future to state security, I won't be able to answer. And, second, please don't seek us out later and ask for our assistance. If this information seems useful and you wish to act on it, you'll do so as you see fit. And if you must share this information, do it carefully, and *don't* say where it came from. Do I have your agreement?' He looked around the room, all were silent, their faces deadly serious. Zannis watched as the golden hair moved slightly, then was still.

'Very well,' the colonel said, finality in his voice. 'Our war with Italy continues, we are certainly winning, though for the moment we've reached stalemate in central Albania, and we anticipate an Italian counter-offensive in the spring. No matter, we'll drive them back. And I know you will agree that the very last word that can describe the Greek armed services, or indeed almost any Greek, is *defeatist*.' Again he looked around the room, as though to challenge anyone who might, even privately, contradict this assertion. Then, after a pause, a muscle ticked in his cheek and he said, 'However . . .'

What followed was known, in military terminology, as a 'strategic appreciation', though phrased for a civilian audience and stripped of any reference that might reveal secret information. Much of what Simonides said was known to the people in the room. Or, rather, it was believed to be true. Roumania and Hungary had signed treaties with Germany; Yugoslavia and Bulgaria had so far refused to do so. So far. The Greek General Staff had undertaken studies – a nice word for it, Zannis thought – indicating that, with the April thaw in the Balkans, this situation would change and, once the Wehrmacht moved across the Yugoslav and Bulgarian borders, Greece would be next. Metaxas, as premier of Greece, would not give way under pressure, so there would be war with Germany. 'We,' the colonel said, 'will fight hard, and the British will fight by our side, but, when a nation of seventy-five million goes to war with a nation of eight million, the outcome will not long be in question. And what we are suggesting tonight is that you prepare yourselves for that eventuality.'

Simonides paused and let that sink in. 'In time, Hitler will be defeated, after, we calculate, a long and difficult war. Here there will be occupation, resistance and insurgency, and then, when the war is over, Greece will have to, once again, as we did after we drove out the Turks, restore itself as a state. On that day, we judge that the people in this room will be of significant help, will play an important role in the recovery. So we want you alive. And, by the way, you might give some thought to the fact that the Germans will soon learn who you are. People just like yourselves have been murdered in Poland – an attempt to behead potential resistance – and we don't want you to share that fate.'

After a moment, he went on. 'As to *what* you may do, and *how* you do it, that's clearly up to you. We invite you here tonight to tell you only that it is not too soon to begin preparation. That is, I fear, the only way you can secure the safety of yourselves and your immediate families.' He paused, then said, 'Thank you for attending this meeting,' turned on his heel and left the room.

For a time, nobody said a word. Then the man standing next to Zannis turned to him and introduced himself. Mid-fifties, spectacles, balding, nobody who would stand out in a crowd. 'You're Costa Zannis, aren't you?' he said. 'From the police department.'

'I am. And what is it that you do in Salonika?'

'I'm the traffic manager for the railways. What do you make of all this?'

'I'm not sure. "Get out while you can?" Something like that.'

'And will you?'

'No, I'll stay. And you?'

'I hadn't really thought about it. Where would I go?' He

shrugged, said he thought he'd get himself a coffee and headed for the table by the door.

Zannis again searched the room. Now he was rewarded! Demetria Vasilou was standing behind a sofa, in conversation with an older woman. She was listening with apparent interest but then, just for a moment, she turned towards him, and smiled. Not the smile of an actress, just the briefest acknowledgment that she was aware of him, that she knew who he was, that she remembered him. Then she returned to the conversation. She wore, that night, an ice-blue blouse, again with a pearl necklace, and a soft, grey wool skirt, not exactly snug, but tight enough to reveal her shape. Now she began to talk to the woman opposite her, not frivolous but making some kind of point. She folded her arms above her waist and leaned backwards, so that the top edge of the sofa pressed into the curve of her ample derrière, for one second, then another. As she straightened up, and the woman in front of her began to speak, she glanced at him again and, just for an instant, their eyes met.

His mind raced. Had he seen what he thought he'd seen? Did it mean what he thought it meant? *I want* you. No, no, impossible. Tired of standing, she'd simply taken a moment to lean on a sofa, and desire had led him to believe it was a gesture of seduction. But a voice from within knew better. A *signal*. Not overt, but not subtle either. *That's the way women do things.* Don't they? Perhaps? He stared at her; he couldn't stop. Her profile was like, like ... Now he remembered that Tasia had called her 'the goddess', as though people spoke of her in that way. An irony? Not to him. Well, enough, just go over there and talk to her. *Be brave!*

His foot never moved. The traffic manager materialized in front of him with two cups of coffee. Extending one of the cups, he said, 'I thought you might like a coffee.'

Zannis couldn't escape. Heartsick, he watched as Vasilou appeared, took Demetria's arm and led his prize away.

★

22 January. His letter confirming yet another arrival in Salonika crossed Emilia Krebs's letter to the Royale Garment Company. Two men would be setting out from Berlin on the twenty-ninth, papers in the names of Brandt and Wald; both were university lecturers. This time, for a recognition signal, Brandt, who wore a trimmed beard, would carry a pair of gloves in his left hand. After Zannis had informed her of the difficulty at the Subotica border station, the refugees now went west, from Budapest to Zagreb, then back east to Novi Sad, and Belgrade. This deviation added another day to the journey, and Zannis could only hope they were making the right choice. Dipping his pen in the Panadon solution, he confirmed that day's arrival and the departure of three refugees to Turkey. The following day, in the office, he sent teletype messages to Pavlic in Zagreb and Gustav Husar's detective in Budapest. Wanted for questioning by the Salonika police: one WALD, one BRANDT, who wears a trimmed beard and has been known to carry a pair of gloves in his left hand. Believed to be arriving – then the dates – 'by excursion steamer' to Budapest, 'by express rail' to Zagreb. When the teletype messages had been confirmed, he returned to his desk. On a pad he printed *Belgrade/Skopje*? Based on his questioning of the refugees at the Tobacco Hotel, he'd discovered that Emilia Krebs had an operative riding that train. He drew a box around what he'd written and went back over it, darkening the line. Only eye contact, from what the refugees said, but more than once – two or three times. 'He was just making sure we were safe.' Only some of the refugees said it, and not the Gruens. Still, the ones who did report the man also said that he'd appeared on the platform at Skopje. Once more, Zannis's pencil traced the box. He would write again, to the Kalcher and Krohn lawyers that night. He had to ask her. Who was it? Why hadn't she told him? Because, God forbid, she might not know.

Later that morning he invited Gabi Saltiel to lunch. They left early – Smyrna Betrayed was always crowded – and took the most private table, in the corner. That day the taverna had a freshly caught octopus. A tentacle was hung from a hook in the kitchen ceiling, the customer would proceed to the kitchen, indicate the desired width of the portion and one of the cooks would slice it off with a fearsomely sharp fish knife. Zannis didn't much care for the knife, he'd too often seen what it could do as a weapon, back when he'd been a detective.

While they waited for their lunch – the slice, grilled over coals, turned sweet and was something like lobster – they lit cigarettes and drank ouzo.

'How are things at home?' Zannis said.

'As usual, nothing too exciting.' Saltiel paused, then said, 'Thank heaven.' He stopped there and waited; he sensed Zannis had something he wanted to discuss.

'Gabi,' Zannis said. 'I think it wouldn't be such a bad idea to talk about the future.'

Saltiel waited, *what now?*

'I've begun to hear things about the Germans. Maybe going into Bulgaria.'

'Real things? Or just . . . talk?'

'Real things.'

Saltiel's face tightened. 'Bad news for us, chief, if that's true, because it's our turn next.'

Zannis agreed. 'What would *you* want to do, if that happened? Because – well, if the Germans take the city, they'll be interested in our office.'

'They know about us?'

'I think we'd better assume they do. And, if they do, once things quiet down they'll come calling. Polite at first, then not.'

'Costa?' Saltiel leaned back in his chair. 'What are you saying?'

'Make plans, Gabi. Then get out.' After a moment he added, 'Even if you didn't work for the office you ought to think about it. Because, for the Jews—'

'I know,' Saltiel said. 'We're all talking about it. Talking and talking.' They were silent for a time, then Saltiel forced his attention back to the conversation. 'So, get out. When, next week?'

'If the Wehrmacht moves across the Danube, from Roumania to Bulgaria . . .'

'It's very hard to think about this, Costa,' Saltiel said, his tone faintly irritated. 'To leave the place where you've always lived because something may happen later.' He shook his head. 'Have you talked to Sibylla?'

'Not yet. I will.'

Saltiel thought for a time, then said, 'How long will it take, this, this *potential* German advance? Not a lot of bridges over the Danube, you know; those countries don't like each other.'

'I don't know,' Zannis said. 'Days. Not weeks.'

'Will they use the railway bridge, at Vidin?'

'They could use pontoon bridges.'

'Here comes the waiter,' Saltiel said, stubbing out his cigarette emphatically.

They ate for a time, dutifully, Zannis telling himself that if he didn't eat something he'd be hungry later. Then Saltiel said, 'Oh, by the way, did you hear about the man in the synagogue—'

Zannis looked up, knife and fork suspended above his plate. Was this a joke?

'—photographing books?'

'What?'

'You know that the synagogues in Salonika are famous for their sacred texts: ancient books, Talmuds, Torahs, five, six hundred years old. Very valuable, if anybody ever sold anything like that. So last week, the rabbi at the synagogue on Athonos Street left his glasses in his office, then late that night he went back to get them and discovered some guy, using a desk lamp, had some of the books out and was taking photographs.'

'Did the man taking photographs say anything?'

'He ran. The rabbi is eighty years old, he couldn't chase him. Maybe he yelled at him, I don't know. Then he talked to two or three rabbis at other synagogues, and one of them said he'd found his books in the wrong order, though he didn't think anything of it at the time.'

Zannis put his knife and fork down on his plate, so much for lunch. 'Nothing stolen,' he said.

'No. Photographed.'

'Which means,' Zannis said slowly, 'somebody is taking an inventory, in order to know what to steal.' He paused, then added, 'At some time in the future.'

The waiter noticed that Zannis wasn't eating his lunch and walked over to the table. 'Everything all right, gentlemen?'

Zannis stared at him. *I've had enough of tentacles for one day.* 'It's just,' Zannis said, 'I'm not hungry.'

As they walked back towards the Via Egnatia, they passed Sami Pal, sharp as ever, a red carnation boutonnière in the buttonhole of his jacket, standing in the doorway of a tobacco shop. 'Good afternoon, Captain,' he said.

'Sami,' Zannis said.

As they went around the corner, Saltiel said, 'Ah, the slick Sami Pal. You're a captain, now?'

'He thinks so.'

'There are things you don't tell me, chief.'

'There are. And I may have to, one of these days. In the meantime, Turkish visas. What will you need?'

Saltiel turned his head towards Zannis and raised an eyebrow 'What have you been doing, Costa?'

'Private business. How many?'

It took Saltiel a while. 'Strange, you never count your family,' he said. 'There are, with the grandkids, ten of us. Is it possible that you have a way of getting ten Turkish visas?'

'Yes.'

'What will this cost?'

'I'll worry about that.'

Almost to himself, Saltiel said, 'How in God's name would I ever make a living in Turkey?'

'When the Wehrmacht reaches the Macedonian border, something will occur to you.'

Saltiel thought for a time. 'Don't do anything right away, I have to talk this out with the family. Is there a time limit?'

Zannis thought about that, then said, 'Not right now.'

Back in the office, Zannis grabbed the telephone and called Vangelis, repeating Saltiel's story, asking what could be done. 'Not much,' Vangelis said. 'I assume they lock the synagogue doors. Beyond that, I don't know.'

'This could be coming out of the German legation.'

'I suppose,' Vangelis said. 'It's possible.'

'You understand what it means?'

'Of course I do.' Vangelis's voice was sharp. 'The Nazis have some kind of commission for the study of Jewish culture and religion, maybe it's them. They steal everywhere else, why not here?'

'What if I interviewed the consul? Asked him about it?'

'Von Kragen? He'd just tell you, politely, to go to hell.'

'What about Spiraki?'

'No, he wouldn't be interested.'

'Then what?'

'Leave it alone, Costa. Go break your balls on something else.'

Zannis, looking out of the office window, found himself going back over his conversation with Saltiel. *Ten visas*. He knew that the more visas he requested, the harder Madam Urglu would press him: *tell me something*. And then, how much money did he have left? Enough, he thought, though if Emilia Krebs's operation went on for months, the bribes and the payments to Gustav Husar would deplete his secret bank account. Then he'd have to contact Vasilou. Did he have the telephone number? He thumbed through his card index, yes, there it was, the office on the waterfront, the number at home. The number at home.

The number at home.

★

There were reasons he shouldn't. One reason: if Vasilou found out ... *But he won't find out.* And, if he did, there were other wealthy men in the city, including wealthy Jews, who might be the best people to approach. One hand resting on the phone, Zannis fought it out with himself but the outcome was never really in doubt. In his imagination, Demetria once again pressed herself against the back of the sofa. *Look what I have for you.* That's what she meant. And then? Then this: Soon enough the world was going to end, the world he knew, and his life – he wasn't going to run away – would end with it. *So, to love one last time before that day comes ...*

He dialled the number.

Made a mistake? A man answered and said, 'Plakos here.'

Tried again. Now, a woman's voice: 'The Vasilou residence.'

'Is Madam Vasilou there?'

'Just a minute, please.'

He could hear a vacuum cleaner, a voice gave instructions, then the telephone was picked up and the voice said, 'This is Demetria.'

'Hello,' he said. 'It's Costa Zannis.' He waited, ready to turn the call towards some meaningless enquiry, everything depended on what she said next.

Silence. Only the vacuum cleaner. Then: 'Oh, Mr Ionides, please forgive me, I won't be able to come to the office this afternoon. Unfortunately, I must attend a funeral, at the Evangelista cemetery, at four. It will have to be another time.'

'I'll be there,' Zannis said.

More silence, then the phone was hung up. As he replaced the receiver, he realized that his hand was trembling.

He made a great effort not to leave the office too early, then he did precisely that. *I can't just sit here.* It had drizzled all day, on and off, from a leaden winter sky, so he took an umbrella. By twenty minutes to four he'd reached the cemetery, decided to walk down to the waterfront, circled the White Tower, a former Turkish prison now pictured on postal cards, then went back up the hill.

As he passed through the entry gates, a group of mourners, led by an Orthodox priest, was on its way out, all dressed in black and wiping their eyes with handkerchiefs. Forcing himself to a slow pace, he walked down the central pathway until he reached the older part of the cemetery, past long rows of graves – headstones askew, clusters of cypress trees, and monuments with pillars and rusted iron doors. He searched as he walked, peering into the misting rain and fading light, but found no living soul, only the dead. Then, with a view from the top of a crumbling stairway, he saw, by the high wall that bordered the cemetery, a figure in a brown raincoat. Head covered by a black kerchief, a bouquet of anemones in clasped hands.

She saw him, as he approached, and stood still, heels properly together, posture erect, waiting. When they were a foot apart, he stopped and they stared at each other, as though uncertain what to do next. At last he said, 'Demetria.' Then very slowly raised his hand and touched her lips with two fingers. When he did this she closed her eyes, dropped the bouquet, and with her hand pressed his fingers against her. After a moment she let him go and, when he withdrew his hand, said, very quietly, 'My God.' *I cannot believe that this has happened.* As he leaned forward, as though to kiss her, she said, 'Please,' her face close to tears. 'It isn't safe here.'

'Can we go . . . somewhere else?'

Sorrowfully, she shook her head.

'I . . . ' he said. She gazed at him, closer yet to tears. 'I have fallen—'

'Don't! I know.' She was pleading with him. 'You will make me cry.'

He didn't understand.

She saw that he didn't, said, 'I mustn't. I must not.' She stared into his eyes, in love with him, her lips quivered and she turned them inward and pressed them together. But, he saw, she couldn't hold it in.

'Quick! Think of a monkey!'

A great bark of laughter escaped her and she clapped her hand over her mouth. Then, her composure regained, she moved closer, almost touching him. She was, he thought, beautiful beyond belief; above her brown eyes, the smooth olive skin of her forehead met golden hair at the edge of her kerchief. 'You don't,' she said, 'remember me, do you.'

'Remember you?'

'From a long time ago.'

He had no idea what to say.

'You don't,' she said. 'How could you? I was twelve, you must have been, sixteen? Our schools were side by side.'

'We *knew* each other?'

'I knew who you were, I looked at you often, we never spoke. I was just a skinny little girl, just a kid. I had long hair, little gold earrings . . .'

He tried, but he had no memory of her whatsoever. 'It's all right now?' he said. 'No tears?'

'Thank God. They'd *see* it, they'd know I'd been crying – my eyes would be red. They *watch* me.'

'The servants?'

'Yes. He pays them extravagantly, he buys their loyalty.'

Not far from them, halfway down a row of graves, a woman was on her knees, despite the wet ground, and was placing flowers at the foot of a headstone. Demetria followed his eyes, then stepped back. 'Too many people know me,' she said.

'I have an apartment,' he said. 'On Santaroza Lane.'

She didn't answer, and looked down at the ground, her eyes hidden from him. Finally, her voice barely audible, she said, 'I am not so brave.' The top of her kerchief was turning dark with rain and he extended his umbrella, attempting to cover them both, at least covering her. Then, on the side away from the woman at the grave, he took her hand. Which was cold and damp and, for a moment, lifeless. But it tightened, slowly, until she held him hard and said, 'Near the railway station.'

Zannis took his hand back and brought out a slip of paper on which he'd written the telephone number at his office. As he held it out to her it moved in the wind. When she'd put it away he said, 'If you don't call me, I will call you. In the afternoon.'

'Yes,' she said. 'I know about "the afternoon".' Her smile, as she said this, was sad, rueful, *what secret lovers must do*. She thrust both hands deep in the pockets of her raincoat. 'I suppose I'd better go home now.'

'May I kiss you goodbye?'

Slowly, she shook her head. It meant *no*, but it was – the way she did it, the expression on her face – the most seductive gesture that Zannis had ever seen. Hands still in pockets, she turned and walked away, looked back at him once, then, at the end of the path, descended the stairway, and was gone.

The two men from the Secret Intelligence Service came to see Francis Escovil in Salonika. Well, almost in Salonika: out in the bay. They arrived on a small yacht, from Alexandria, anchored beyond the harbour, and sent the captain to the Pension Bastasini with an envelope. Escovil wasn't there, so the captain waited in the lobby, the residents glancing at him, at his uniform – of no country, of the land of yachts – as they came and went. When Escovil returned, the captain let him go upstairs, then followed. In the room, the captain gave Escovil the envelope and then they left together, walking down to the wharf where two sailors in a rowing boat awaited them.

Once on board the yacht, he was taken to the salon: grand twenty years earlier, now fallen into gentle decay, the fabrics faded, the brasswork tarnished, mildew in the air. It was, Escovil had noted as the rowing boat approached, called the *Amenhotep II*, so, an Egyptian yacht.

Escovil had never before seen these men. Jones and Wilkins, they called themselves and perhaps they were, Jones and Wilkins, or perhaps not. It didn't matter to Escovil who they said they were, he knew what they were. Jones was tall and bony and mournful –

Escovil's interior description, adding *though mournful about what God only knows*, while Wilkins was military: stiff, moustached, hostile and potentially dangerous. To the enemy, to his wife, to his dog. *Maybe not the dog*, Escovil thought. More sentimental, probably. *Only you love me, Fido.* That was very possibly true, Escovil sensed, so was relieved to find Jones in charge. It seemed, anyway. Perhaps Wilkins had been brought along merely to frighten him, or was eager to have a ride on the yacht.

They gave him a big whisky and soda from the bar and treated themselves to one as well. Settled in the smelly chairs, and smiled. Both of them. It was utterly horrible.

'We have a bit of a nightmare,' Jones said. 'So you'll have to help us out.' He had a high insinuating whine of a voice. 'Really, this is somebody else's mess, but we're the ones who have to clean it up.'

'Somebody with a name?' Escovil said.

'Oh, we can't tell you *that.*' Jones said. He stared at Escovil. *Are you mad?*

'I see,' Escovil said, faintly amused.

Which wasn't at all the proper response. 'Do you,' Wilkins said.

Only in England, Escovil thought, could 'Do you' be spoken in such a way that it meant *So now I shall cut your throat.* In full retreat, he took a sip of whisky and tried to look compliant. This was war, and he'd signed up to fight a filthy enemy, but he would never be one of them, the Joneses and the Wilkinses – they didn't like him and they never would.

'Once upon a time,' Jones said – glass in hand, he settled back against the chair and crossed his legs – 'there was a little man called Henry Byer. You wouldn't know the name, but if you'd been one of the chaps hanging about in the science labs of Cambridge in the nineteen-twenties, you most certainly would. A physicist, Harry, as he's called, and brilliant. Studied sound waves and radio beams, very theoretical back then, nobody had the faintest idea such things could be used in war, nobody had ever heard of radio navigation. It helps bombers flying at night, who can find their targets only by use of radio beams, locator beams we'd call them now. Who could have known that a radio beam would become a crucial weapon, could win or lose a war? Now the Germans have their own radio beams but, using the methods that Harry Byer discovered, we can alter them. And the Luftwaffe may know we're doing it, but they don't know how Harry Byer knows how.'

Jones stopped for a drink, then went on. 'Anyway life went well for Harry; a lectureship at Cambridge, where he worked in the physics lab, he married his sweetheart, a pretty girl—'

'Smashing girl,' Wilkins said. 'Big bosoms.' He indicated the magnitude of the bosoms with his cupped hands.

'Mmm,' Escovil offered, raising his eyebrows in appreciation, one of the boys.

Jones cleared his throat and said, 'Yes, well.' Then, 'But, in the summer of nineteen thirty-nine, life went sour for the Byer family, because la wife found somebody she liked better. Harry was, how shall I say, unprepossessing physically, you see, very smart certainly, but came the day when very smart just didn't . . . *compete.*

'And, well, still, who cared? But Harry took it badly, oh, very badly indeed. And just about then the first of September comes rolling around and Adolf sends his tanks into Poland. So Harry Byer, in a terrible huff, marches himself down to London and enlists in the RAF. He'll show the wife what's what, he'll go and get himself killed! Hah! There! Take *that!'*

Something rumbled inside Wilkins which, Escovil figured out a moment later, was laughter.

'Oh, but you know, Escovil, somebody *should* have cared about this fellow who's crucial to the war effort. Because Hitler's got legions of goose-stepping SS goons, but Britain has *scientists.* And scientists win. You see?'

'I do see,' Escovil said.

'But the *aristocrat,* who's supposed to be watching, a very *titled* aristocrat I might add, who goes to country houses with *divinely* important people, slips up. Not that he does anything right away, when there's still time to do something about it, no, either he isn't told or he ignores it.'

'The latter, I'd say,' Wilkins offered.

'And Arthur's got it right. Because that class of individual doesn't make mistakes. They simply go on. No balls-up here, everything is tickety-boo. But, as you might have guessed, everything really isn't tickety-boo. Now the RAF isn't going to allow Harry Byer to actually fly an aircraft, good heavens no, but he is something of a gnome, a little runt, and that qualifies him as a tail gunner because he fits in the turret. So off he goes, in his Wellington bomber, dropping incendiaries on Germany, and good for him.'

'Amen,' Escovil said.

'Well, it damn near *is* amen, as you say, because early in January, Harry's Wellington is hit by flak over the Ruhr. The pilot makes a valiant effort but it's no good and the crew bails out over France. Now, luck intervenes. Some of the crew are caught straight away, but Harry lands in just the right farmer's field and the French, perhaps a resistance group, or simply French, take charge of him and smuggle him up to Paris. And there he sits, as they try to make arrangements to get him out of the country.

'Now, just about here, the aristocrat is told what's become of Harry and gives forth a mighty British roar. And who do you suppose he roars at? To clean up this God-awful mess? He roars at us, who else?'

Jones waited. Escovil knew he had been called on to recite, and what came to him was, 'And now you're roaring at me.'

Impertinent. Wilkins said, 'We're not roaring, Francis. Yet.'

'So then, what shall I do?'

'Why, get him out. What else?' Jones said. There was a folder on the table by Jones's chair. Jones opened it, withdrew a photograph and held it out to Escovil, who had to go and retrieve it. When he'd returned to his chair, Jones said, 'There he is. Taken when he reached Paris, just to make sure they have who they say they have.'

In the photograph, Harry Byer looked like an owl who'd flown into the side of a barn. Owlish he had always been – hooked beak of a nose, small eyes, pursy little mouth – while the barn wall had left livid bruises by his right eye and the right-hand corner of his mouth. Injured in the aeroplane? Beaten up? 'When was this taken?' he said. He started to rise, intending to return the photograph.

But Jones waved him back down and said, 'A week or so after he landed.'

'And how did, um, we come to hear about it?'

'Whoever these people are, they were in contact with an underground cell operating a clandestine radio.'

'Back to London.'

'Back to the French in London.'

'Oh.'

'Quite.'

'You don't suppose the Germans are in control of them, do you? Waiting to see who shows up?'

'Haven't a clue.'

Silence. Wilkins had now assumed the same posture, drink in hand, legs crossed, as his colleague. They were, Escovil thought, rather good at waiting. Finally he said, 'So you'll want me to go up there.'

Jones cackled. 'Are you daft? Of course not, you'll send your agent, what's-his-name, the policeman.'

'Constantine Zannis? He's not my agent. Who told you *that?*'

Wilkins leaned forward and said, 'Oh damn-it-all of *course* he is.' He glanced at his watch. 'Has been for a while – ten minutes, I'd say, more or less.'

I'd like to be in the room when you tell Zannis that. But Escovil knew there was no point in starting an argument he couldn't win. 'Paris is a long way from here. Why wouldn't you take Byer out by fishing boat, from the French coast?'

'Option closed,' Jones said. 'For the time being. Somebody got himself caught up there and the Germans shut it down. We'll get it back, in time, but right now you'll have to use your escape line.'

'It isn't mine.'

'Now it is.'

Oh piss off. 'And why does *Zannis* have to go?'

'Because Byer will never make it by himself, speaks not a word of any continental language. He can read a scientific journal in German, but he can't order lunch. And, more important, if he's caught, we have to be able to show we did everything we could. We have to show we *care*.'

Escovil suppressed a sigh. 'Very well, I'll ask him.'

'No,' Wilkins said, now quite irritated, 'you'll *tell* him. "Ask him" indeed.'

Jones said, 'Do it any way you like, but keep in mind, Francis, we don't take no for an answer.' He stood, collected Wilkins's glass, then Escovil's, and poured fresh drinks. When he'd re-settled himself, he said, 'Now,' in a tone of voice that was new to Escovil, and went on to explain how they thought the thing might actually be done. Bastards they were, to the very bone, Escovil thought, but at least, and thank heaven, smart bastards.

27 January. A telephone call from Escovil, early that afternoon. Could they meet? Privately? Zannis's instinctive reaction was to refuse, courteously or not so courteously, because the word 'privately' told the tale: the spies wanted something. And it wasn't such a good day to ask Zannis *anything*, because he was miserable. He had waited for a call from Demetria, waited and waited, but it hadn't come. Five long days had crept by, his heart soaring every time the telephone rang: It's her! But it never was. Now, he would either have to assume she'd thought better of the whole thing, or was waiting for him – as he'd promised, very nearly threatened – to call her. Meanwhile, the spies were after him. Back in the autumn, in his time with Roxanne, he would have laughed. But the world had changed, the war *was* coming south, and only the British alliance might save the country.

And didn't they know it.

'It's really rather important,' Escovil said. Is there some-where . . . ?'

Skata. 'You can come to the office after six,' Zannis said, a sharp edge to his voice. 'Do you know where it is?'

'I don't.'

Oh yes you do. Zannis gave him directions, then said, 'It's very private here, once everyone's gone home, you needn't be con-cerned.' *And the hell with your damn bookstores and empty churches.*

And so, at five minutes past six, there he was. 'Hello.'

He'd been drinking, Zannis could smell it on him. And there were shadows beneath his eyes, which made him seem, with his sand-coloured hair swept across his forehead, more than ever a boy grown old. Beneath a soiled raincoat, the battered tweed jacket.

Once he was seated on the other side of the desk, Zannis said, 'So then, what do you want?'

Such directness caused Escovil to clear his throat. 'We must ask a favour of you.'

We. Well, now that was out of the way, what next? Not that he wanted to hear it.

'It has to do with your ability to bring refugees, bring them secretly, from northern Europe to Salonika.'

'You know about this?'

'We do.' Escovil's tone was apologetic – the secret service was what it was and sometimes, regretfully, it worked.

'And so?'

'We need to make use of it, for a fugitive of our own. An important fugitive – that is, important to the British war effort.'

Zannis lit a cigarette. That done, he said, 'No.' Lighting the cigarette had given him an opportunity to amend his first answer, which had been, *Get out of my office.*

Escovil looked sorrowful. 'Of course. That's the proper response, for you. It's what I would say, in your place.'

166

Then goodbye.

'You fear,' Escovil went on, 'that it might jeopardize your operation and the people who run it.'

'It could very well destroy it, Escovil. Then what becomes of the men and women trying to get out of Germany? I'll tell you what: they're trapped, they're arrested, and then they are at the mercy of the SS. Want more?'

'No need,' Escovil said, very quietly. 'I know' He was silent for a time, then he said, 'Which might still happen, even if you refuse to help us.'

'Which *will* happen.'

'Then . . .'

'It's a question of time. The longer we go on, the more lives saved. And if some of our fugitives are caught, we can try to fix the problem, and we can continue. People run away all the time, and the organization designed to catch them adjusts, gets what information it can and goes to work the next day. But if they discover an *important* fugitive, perhaps a secret agent, it suggests the existence of others, and then the organization starts to multiply – more money, more men, more pressure from above. And that's the end of us.'

'He's not a secret agent.'

'No?'

'No. He's a downed airman. Who, it turns out, is a scientist, and shouldn't have been allowed to join the RAF, and certainly shouldn't have been allowed to fly bomber missions. But he escaped the attention of the department which – umm, *attends* to such individuals. And now they want him back.'

'And you can't get him back on your own? *You?*'

'I don't like saying this, but that's what we're doing.'

'And I don't like saying *this*, but you're endangering many lives.'

'Well, frankly,' Escovil said, 'we do nothing else. We don't *want* to, we'd rather *not*, but it seems to work out that way.'

Zannis thought for a time. 'You have no alternative?'

'Not today.'

'I'll tell you something, Escovil, if I find out you're lying to me, you'll be on the next boat out of here.'

'I take your point, but that won't happen. Don't you see? It's gone beyond that now. The war, everything.' He paused, then said, 'And I'm not lying.'

'Oh, well, in that case . . .'

'I'm not. And you can assure yourself that the individual is precisely who I say he is.'

'Really? And how exactly would I do that?'

'Ask him.'

Zannis didn't go directly home. He stopped at the neighbourhood taverna, had an ouzo, then another, and considered a third but, nagged by guilt over putting off Melissa's dinner, hurried back to Santaroza Lane. Then too, the third ouzo wouldn't, he realized, have much more effect than the first two, which had had no effect whatsoever. His mind was too engaged, too embroiled, to be soothed by alcohol. It lifted briefly, then went back to work. *Sorry!*

He simply could not persuade himself that Escovil was lying. Years of police work had sharpened his instincts in this area, and he trusted them more than ever. After Escovil's little surprise – 'Ask him' – he'd gone on to explain the proposed operation, which was artfully conceived and made sense. Made the most perfect sense, as long as Zannis was willing to accept a certain level of danger. And who – given the time and circumstance – wouldn't? Not him. He *had* to go to Paris. *He* had to go to Paris. And do what had to be done. And that was that.

Lying on the bed in his underwear, he reached towards the night table and had a look, yet again, at the photograph he'd been given. Yes, Byer was exactly who Escovil had said he was, bruises and all. And how had Escovil's organization managed to get the photograph out of France? Escovil had claimed not to know and, as before, Zannis believed him. Next he studied the second photograph of Byer, the one in the Sardakis passport, a real passport photo, it seemed, and a real Greek passport. Perhaps for them not so difficult but, even so, impressive. So, was this a man who would murder his wife and her lover in a fit of jealousy? Well, it surely was – the owlish, seemingly harmless intellectual. *Skata!* He'd *seen* such murderers, that was exactly what they looked like!

He returned the passport and the photograph to the night table and turned his mind towards what he had to do in the morning. The gun. Why had he not replaced his Walther, lost in the Trikkala bombing? Why was he so . . .

The telephone. Who would call him here, his mother? She had no telephone, but, in an emergency . . . 'Hello?'

'Hello, it's me.'

Her! 'Demetria. Did . . . did I give you this number?'

'Are you angry with me?'

'Good God no!'

'Vasilou had it, in a card index in his study.'

'Is everything . . . all right?'

'Better now. But it's been a terrible week, Vasilou is suddenly *affectionate*, back early from the office, wanting, you know. But poor Demetria has eaten a bad fish. He is enraged, shouting. He will buy the restaurant and fire the cook! Meanwhile, I hide in the bathroom.' A memory of that moment drew from her a kind of amused snort. 'Anyhow, at last I'm free to telephone. It is the servants' night out but they dawdled before they left and I realized you wouldn't be at work.'

'Can you come here now? Even for a little while? Just to see you . . . .'

'Oh Costa I can't.' But with her voice she let him know how much she wanted to, and, almost better, she had never said his name before and hearing it thrilled him.

'Tomorrow?'

'The day after. He is off to Athens, the maids are going to a christening, and I told everyone I was invited to a mah-

169

jong party. So I can see you at five, and we will have two hours, unless . . .'

'Unless what?'

'I must warn you, Costa, he is a dangerous enemy, a very dangerous enemy. Some of the people who work for him, they will do . . . anything.'

He wondered why she thought Vasilou would discover them so quickly, then he knew. 'Demetria, do you want to tell him? Now? Leave him and stay with me?'

The line whispered. Finally she said, 'Not now. Not yet.'

She was, he thought, testing him. *I know you will lie in bed by me, but will you stand by me?* 'I am not afraid of him, Demetria.'

'You are not afraid of anybody, are you.'

'No. And the day, the hour, you want to leave, it's done.' When she didn't speak he said, 'Do you still love him?'

'No, I never did, not really. I thought I might, at one time, yes, I suppose I did think that.' After a moment, she continued. 'I am, you know, his third wife – he simply wanted something different, a new possession, but even so, I hoped. He was forceful, masculine, rich – who was I to refuse him as a husband? And I had been married – and all that that means in this country – so I was grateful, and he was honourable; he went to my father and asked for my hand. Very old-fashioned, very traditional, and it *affected* me. I was alone, and getting older, and here was, at least, a luxurious life.'

'That can happen, I think, to anyone.'

'Yes, I guess it might. And I *am* "anyone", Costa, inside . . . all this.'

'I'm afraid you're not just "anyone", not to me.'

'I know. I saw that. From the car when you and Vasilou came out of the club.' She hesitated, then sighed. 'I want to tell you everything, but not on the telephone.' A pause, then, 'You haven't told me where you live.'

'There are no numbers on Santaroza Lane, but it's the fourth house up from the corner towards the bay, the door is old wood, unpainted. I have the upper floor.'

She waited, said, 'So,' then, 'I have to go now. But it's only two days. One day, and part of another.'

'At five,' he said.

'Yes, at five,' she said, her voice lovely, and hung up the phone.

Salonika's best gun shop was at the western end of the Via Egnatia, in what had been, before the Great Fire, the city's Jewish district. The owner, called Moises, the Sephardic version of the name, had been there forever, more than thirty years. Still, his sidelocks were not quite grey. He always wore a black homburg, a formal hat, with a waistcoat and a colourful tie, his shirtsleeves buttoned decorously at the wrists. The shop smelled of gun oil, not far from bananas. Policemen had always received a discount from Moises, so Zannis showed his badge.

Moises said, 'You are Costa Zannis, no?'

'That's right.'

'What can I do for you?'

'I need a Walther, the PPK detective's model, and a holster. Also a box of ammunition.'

Grimly, Moises shook his head. 'I thought maybe you wanted something repaired.'

'No, a new side-arm.'

'Ach, forgive me, but I haven't got one.'

'Well then, used. Maybe even better.'

'All gone, I'm afraid. New, used, everything.'

'What do you mean, all gone?'

'I'm down to practically nothing – everything's been bought up: hunting rifles, shotguns, all the handguns.' He shrugged. 'I wish I could help you. I write to the Walther company, they say next month.'

Zannis thought it over. 'Moises, I have to ask you, as a special favour to me, to try and buy one back. I'll pay whatever it costs.'

Moises scratched the back of his head and looked doubtful.

'I don't know, I've never done such a thing. Once the customer buys, it's his, that's that.'

'Of course, but, this time, I must have one. A PPK.'

'Well, I had one customer who bought twenty model PPKs, I suppose he might make do with nineteen. I wonder, maybe it's better if you ask him yourself.'

'Would he mind, that you gave me his name?'

Moises considered it. 'Not you. Anybody in this city can tell you anything. And, come to think of it, I'd imagine you're acquainted with him.'

'Who is it?'

'Elias, the man with one name. You know, the poet.'

'Twenty handguns?'

'Not so strange. Who can see into the future?'

'Maybe Elias can. I'll get in touch with him.'

'Tell him, tell him I was reluctant, to give you his name.'

'He won't care.'

'Poets buying Walthers,' Moises said. 'I don't remember anything like that, and I've been here forever.'

Zannis walked back to the office. *Fucking war*, he thought. Salonika was preparing for resistance, people buying weapons and hiding them. But Elias, one step ahead of the game, meant to go – bearing gifts – up into the mountain villages where, once the Germans came, the bandits would once again become *andartes*, guerrilla fighters, as they had during the Turkish occupation.

Zannis telephoned, then met with Elias at a *kafeneion* an hour later. He'd come away from the gun shop with a belt holster and ammunition, now, ceremoniously, Elias handed over a box containing a Walther. When Zannis reached into his pocket, Elias held up a hand. 'Not a drachma shall I take from you, Officer Costa. This is my pleasure. My gift, my gesture. For it's my job, as a Greek poet, to be oracular, to see into the future, so I know what this weapon will do, and to who. As I said, my pleasure.'

★

29 January. An excited Costa Zannis left his office at three to pick up the sheets he'd taken to be washed 'and *ironed*, Elena.' Then, once back at the apartment, he made the bed and started to sweep the floor, but stopped, realizing that this chore had to be preceded by another, and began to brush Melissa. Probably she liked food more than a brushing, but it was surely a close second. She rolled over on her back, paws up, tongue lolling out of the side of her mouth, so Zannis could brush her chest. 'Yes, Melissa, we are going to have a guest. An important guest.' Melissa's tail gave a single thump against the floor.

He was humming some song, the words forgotten, when there was a sharp knock at the door. Zannis looked at his watch. *She's early!* It was not much after four but, who cared; they would have more time together. He opened the door and there stood a detective – Tellos? Yes, he thought so, a few years earlier they'd served in the same squad. What the hell was he doing here?

'Come in,' Zannis said.

'Vangelis sent me to find you,' Tellos said, apologetically. 'I went to the office, but you weren't there. I have a car downstairs.'

'What's wrong?'

'You haven't heard?'

'No.'

'General Metaxas has died. In a hospital in Athens.'

'Assassinated?'

'No, though people are saying all sorts of things – poisoned by the Italians, you name it, conspiracies of every sort.'

'But not true.'

'No. Vangelis talked to people in Athens. The general had a tonsillectomy and died of toxaemia. Anyhow, we may have to deal with demonstrations, riots, who knows what, so there's a meeting at the mayor's house, east of the port, and Commissioner Vangelis wants you there.'

Zannis was enraged. He feared Tellos would see it and covered his face with his hands. *What evil fate contrived to take from him the thing he wanted most in the world?*

Tellos rested a sympathetic hand on his shoulder. 'I know,' he said. 'This man saved Greece, and now he's gone.'

30 January. There were no riots. The Metaxas government had never been popular; surely half the population would have preferred a republic, long championed by the noble voice of Greek democracy, Venizelos. But Venizelos had died in exile in 1936, while Metaxas, dictator though he was, had led the country well in war. Now King George II had named one Alexandros Koryzis, a former governor of the Bank of Greece, as the new prime minister. Hardly anyone had ever heard of him. Therefore, no marching in the streets. Instead, melancholy and silence. Poor Greece, no luck at all, why did fate treat them so badly?

Zannis might have had similar feelings, but there was barely room in his wretched heart for emotion about the national politics, for he had to go to Paris the following day and, if the operation went wrong, he would never again see Demetria. It tore at him, this loss. If only they'd been able to meet, if only they'd made love. Two stolen hours, was that too much to ask? So it seemed – their hours together stolen in turn by a bizarre twist of destiny: a man got tonsillitis. Zannis couldn't stop brooding, angry and sad at the same moment.

But then he had to, because he had difficulties beyond this, and these he'd brought on himself. He knew he would be away for at least ten days, and during that time it was more than likely that a letter from Emilia Krebs would arrive at the office. And so he had no choice but to designate Gabi Saltiel – and Sibylla, she could no longer be excluded – as his deputies in running the Salonika end of the escape line. Saltiel never said a harsh word, but Zannis could tell his feelings were hurt – why hadn't he been trusted from the beginning? As for Sibylla, feelings didn't enter into it, she was simply intent on getting everything right.

Not all that easy. 'You melt six Panadon in a glass of water and use a clean pen with a sharp point.' And the rest of it: the iron, the lawyer's address in Berlin, the teletype numbers for the detectives in Zagreb and Budapest. 'You can depend on us, chief,' Sibylla said. And, Zannis realized, she meant it.

That done, Zannis's eye inevitably fell on the telephone. He didn't *dare*. Umm, maybe he did. Oh no he didn't! Oh but yes, he did. Vasilou would still be in Athens, and Zannis just could not bear to leave the woman he loved, perhaps forever, with no more than an unanswered knock on a door.

Very slowly, tempting fate but unable to stop, he worked the dial with his index finger, running each number around to the end. But then, at last, good fortune: it was Demetria who picked up the receiver. He spoke quickly, in case she had to hang up. 'I'm sorry, I was taken away to a meeting. Because of Metaxas.'

'I see,' she said, voice breathy and tentative; the call had frightened her. 'Perhaps ... I could try ... next week?' Then, her mind now working quickly, she added, 'For another fitting.'

From the background: 'Now who the hell is that?'

Skata, Vasilou!

'It's the seamstress, dear.'

'Well, make it snappy. I'm expecting a call.'

'Yes, dear, just a minute.'

'Oh Lord,' Zannis said, 'I didn't realize ...'

'The hem is just too long, so—'

'I'll be away, for ten days. I'll call you.'

The sound of approaching footsteps. 'Can't hang up?' Vasilou shouted. 'Then let me show you how it's done!' The footsteps grew louder.

'I have to say goodbye.' Her voice wobbled. 'But, please—'

The receiver was slammed down.

At Gestapo headquarters, on the Prinz-Albrechtstrasse in Berlin, Hauptsturmführer Albert Hauser studied a long list of names typed on yellow paper. When a name caught his attention, he riffled through a metal tray of five-by-eight cards, where, in alphabetical order, information about each of the names was recorded. If that was insufficient, he had dossiers for most of the names, dossiers filled with pages of information obtained from surveillance, paid informants, denunciations and interrogation. The yellow list was a sort of Who's Who of dissidents in Berlin, all suspected – some more than suspected – of activity against the interests of the Reich. Rather loosely defined, those interests; thus it wasn't difficult to say the wrong thing, to know the wrong person, to own the wrong book. *Welcome to the list!*

So then, A to Z, six and a half pages long. Some of the names had a mark next to them, Hauser's symbolic note to himself: question mark, exclamation point – you didn't want that! – asterisk, and others, even an x – the last, for instance, beside a couple whose names appeared early in the D section. This couple was believed, after coming under pressure from the Gestapo, to have committed suicide, but, Hauser thought, committed suicide in an irritating way, so that their bodies would not be identified when found. Spiteful, wasn't it. To go to some distant city and manage the business in some little hotel room, having first burned one's identity papers. Defiant even in death and, really, very annoying.

He turned the page. Beside the name GRUEN, two entries for man and wife, two question marks. On what had been meant to be their final day of freedom, missing. Fled? Fled where? One word used by these people – Jews, communists, even aristocrats – was *submerge*. It meant hiding in an apartment, sharing a friend's food obtained with ration coupons, rarely if ever going outside, and then only with borrowed or false identification.

Others, like the couple D, killed themselves. Still others contrived to flee the country – into Switzerland, if they were lucky. Or, sometimes, to the unoccupied zone of France, where the Vichy police agencies were dedicated to catching them, but not always. The trouble with the unoccupied zone, the southern part of the country, was that fugitives might make their way to Marseille. And, once in Marseille, with some money to spend, one could do just about anything. *That's how it is*, Hauser thought, *with port cities*, like Naples. Or Odessa – even under the rule of the ruthless NKVD, for so Hauser thought of them. Where else? Hauser's inner eye wandered over an imaginary map of Europe. Constanta, in Roumania? A long way to go, for a fugitive. Equally Varna, on Bulgaria's Black Sea coast.

Go to work, lazybones, Hauser told himself, stop woolgathering. Where were these Gruens? He rose and walked over to the wall, where large sheets of brown paper showed diagrams of relations between the dissidents. Solid lines, dotted lines, some in red pencil: who met with who, who worked with who, who telephoned who, and on and on. Hauser located the circle containing the name GRUEN and traced the radiating lines with his index finger. Popular, weren't they. Here was, for example, the circled name of KREBS. And who was that?

He returned to his list and flipped over to the Ks: KREBS, EMILIA, and KREBS, HUGO. The latter was marked with a triangle, which meant, in Hauser's system, something like *uh-oh*. Now to the three-by-five cards. Yes, there it was, definitely worth a triangle; this Krebs was a colonel on the Oberkommando Wehrmacht, the General Staff, and *not* to be pestered. *Scheiss!* You had to be careful in this work. You had to be on your toes! Or you'd wind up in Warsaw, God forbid. Still, he wondered, and had a look at KREBS, EMILIA. Close and long-time friend of the Gruens, neighbour in Dahlem, Jew. Hunh, look at that. This Colonel Krebs must be powerful indeed to have a Jewish wife and get away with it.

He was distracted from this line of thinking by two taps on the door and the entry of the department's chief clerk: tall, fading blond and middle-aged. Something of a dragon, Traudl, with her stiff hair and stiff manner, but smart, and relentless in her commitment to the job. No surprise there; at one time she'd worked for some of the better – mostly Jewish, alas – law firms in the city. Then, with Hitler's ascension, she'd seen the light and come to work for the Gestapo. 'Hauptsturmführer Hauser?' she said. 'Pardon the intrusion, but I have brought your morning coffee.'

'Thank you, Traudl.' He set the steaming cup on his desk.

'Will there be anything else, sir?'

'No, thank you,' Hauser said. 'I'll be going out for a bit.'

He took a sip of the coffee. Real coffee, and strong – oh, the little pleasures of this job. He returned to his paperwork, drumming his fingers on the yellow list. *So, who wants to see the Gestapo today?* But he already knew that, some tiny clicker in his brain had decided to go out to Emilia Krebs's house. That wasn't pestering the husband, was it? No, certainly not, he would never know about it, because she would never know about it. Just a little spur-of-the-moment surveillance. Just a look-see.

Hauser picked up his phone and dialled a two-digit number, which connected him with the office of Untersturmführer, Lieutenant, Matzig, his partner. 'Matzi?'

'Yes, Albert?'

'Let's go for a little ride, I need some air.'

'I'll bring the car around,' Matzig said.

So, yet another ride out to Dahlem. Lord, this neighbourhood was a dissident *nest*! But, in the end, there wasn't much to see. Hauser and Matzig sat in the front seat, talking idly from time to time, waiting, the principal activity of the investigative life. The winter darkness came early, a light snow began to fall, and eventually the colonel came home from work, dropped off at his door by a Wehrmacht car. The colonel disappeared into his house and, though the two officers waited another hour, that was it for the day.

They tried earlier the following day, waited longer, and were rewarded with a view of the Krebses going out for dinner. Thus Hauser and Matzig got to wait outside Horcher's while the couple dined. No fun at all, visiting the best restaurants in Berlin, but not a morsel of food. After dinner, the couple went home. Matzig drove the Mercedes to their chosen vantage point, Hauser lit a cigar and said, 'Let's go home, Matzi. We'll give it one more day, tomorrow.' All he could afford, really, because like any job you had to show your bosses some success, some production, and there was nothing yet to warrant even the most diffident interview.

But then there was. Patience paid off, at least sometimes, because just after five on the third day, the lovely Emilia Krebs, in sober grey coat and wide-brim grey hat, briefcase in hand, left her house, walked quickly down the path that led to the pavement, and turned left, towards the centre of the city. As she passed the low hedge that bordered her property, here came a fellow in a dark overcoat: half-bald, heavy, wearing glasses – some sort of intellectual, from the look of him. For the length of a block, he matched her pace. Hauser and Matzig exchanged a look; then, no discussion required, Matzig turned on the ignition, put the car in gear and drove past Emilia Krebs to a side street with a view of the nearest tram stop.

She arrived soon after, followed by the man in the dark overcoat. They stood at a distance from each other, mixed in with a few other people, all waiting for the tram. Five minutes later it appeared, bell ringing, and rolled to a stop. Emilia Krebs and the others climbed on, but the man in the overcoat stayed where he was and, once the tram moved away, he turned and walked back the way he'd come.

'Did you see what I saw?' Hauser said.

'A trailer, you think?' The function of a trailer, in clandestine practice, was to make sure the person ahead wasn't being followed.

'What else?'

6 February. Paris. Occupied Paris: triste and broken, cold and damp, the swastika everywhere. Following the operational plan, Zannis played the role of a Greek detective in Paris, come to escort a prisoner back to Salonika. In trench coat and well-worn blue suit, heavy shapeless black shoes and holstered pistol on his belt, he took a taxi to the commercial hotel Escovil had named – on a little street near the Gare du Nord – and slept all afternoon,

recovering from days of train travel. Then, around eight in the evening, he ventured forth, found a taxi and went off in search of Parisian food and Parisian sex. So, if anybody was watching, that's what they saw.

He left the taxi at the Place de la Bastille, found the proper café on the second try, and the woman right away. She was, according to plan, reading *Le Soir*, the evening tabloid, and marking the classified ads with a pencil.

'Excuse me,' Zannis said, 'are you waiting for Émile?' He hadn't been in France since the time he'd worked as a Parisian *antiquaire*, more than ten years earlier, but the language, though halting and awkward, was still there.

'I'm waiting for my grandfather,' she said, completing the identification protocol. Then, looking at her watch, added, 'We'd better be on our way. You shall call me Didi.'

Didi! Good God. For whoever she was – and she'd given *Didi* her best effort: neckline much too low, 'diamond' earrings, scarlet lipstick – this woman had never been picked up in a café, she'd never *met* a woman who'd been picked up in a café. What was she, a baroness? Possible, Zannis thought: narrow head, small ears, thin nostrils, aristocratic tilt to the chin. Didi? *Oh fuck, these people are going to get me killed.*

'Off we go, honey,' Zannis said, with a coarse grin, a nod towards the door and a proffered arm.

The aristocrat almost flinched. Then she recovered, stood, took his arm, pressed it to her champagne cup of a noble breast and off they went – circling the Place Bastille, heading for a brasserie down a side street. Zannis took a deep breath. These people were brave, were resisting the occupation, were putting their lives in jeopardy. They were, he told himself, doing the best they could.

So the Greek detective, in case anybody was watching – and there was no way to know whether they were or not – had found a girl for the evening and would now take her out for dinner. The restaurant was called the Brasserie Heininger, a man in an apron and a fisherman's waterproof hat was shucking oysters on a bed of shaved ice by the entryway.

When Zannis opened the door, the interior hit him hard – much fancier than any place he'd been to when he'd lived in Paris. The brasserie was fiercely Belle Epoque: red plush banquettes, polished brass and vast gold-framed mirrors lining the walls, the waiters in mutton-chop whiskers, the conversation loud and manic, the smoky air scented by perfume and grilled sausage. And, as the maître d' led them to a table – that sexy slut Didi had reserved ahead – Zannis saw what looked to him like half the officer class of occupied Paris, much of it in Wehrmacht grey, with, just to set off the visual composition, a sprinkling of SS black. As they weaved their way among the tables, the aristocrat crushed Zannis's arm against her breast so hard he wondered why it didn't hurt her, or maybe she was so scared she didn't notice. At last they were seated, side by side on a banquette at a table where the number *14* was written on a card supported by a little brass stand. The aristocrat settled close to him, then took a deep breath.

'You're all right?' Zannis said.

She nodded, gratitude in her eyes.

'Good girl,' he said. 'Didi.'

She gave him a conspiratorial smile; the waiter brought menus in golden script. 'Here one takes the *choucroute garnie*,' she said. 'And order champagne.'

Sauerkraut? Oh no, not with the way his stomach felt. On the surface, Zannis showed a certain insouciant confidence, but every muscle in his body was strung tight; he was ready to shoot his way out of this restaurant but not at all prepared for sauerkraut. 'Maybe they have a fish,' he said.

'Nobody orders *that*.'

He searched the menu. 'Shellfish,' he said.

'If you like.'

He looked up for a moment, then said, 'What the hell is that? Behind your shoulder, in the mirror.'

'It's very famous,' she said. 'A memorial to a Bulgarian waiter, slain here a few years ago.'

'It's a *bullet* hole.'

'Yes, it is.'

'They don't fix it? Back where I come from, they have them fixed the next day.'

'Not here.'

The waiter returned. "*Sieur et 'dame?*'

Zannis ordered the seafood platter, which he would try to eat, followed by the *choucroute*, which he would not, and a bottle of champagne. As the waiter hurried off, Zannis discovered his neighbours in the adjacent booth: two SS officers with French girlfriends: puffy and blonde, green eyeshadow, pouty lips. One of the SS men looked like a precocious child, with baby skin, a low forehead and glasses in tortoiseshell frames. The other – Zannis understood immediately who he was, what he was – turned to face him, rested an elbow on the plush divider and said, '*Bonsoir, mon ami.*' The set of his face and the sparkle in his eyes suggested a view of the world best described by the word *droll*, but, Zannis saw, he was a certain kind of smart and sophisticated German who'd found, in the black uniform and death's-head insignia, a way to indulge a taste for evil.

'*Bonsoir,*' Zannis said.

'Your girl's a real looker.' He moved his head to get a better view of Didi, said, 'Hello, gorgeous,' with a sly smile and waggled his fingers by way of a waved greeting. The aristocrat glanced at him, then looked down. The SS officer, at that stage of inebriation where he loved the world, said, 'Aww, don't be shy, gorgeous.'

Zannis turned back and began to make conversation. 'Had much snow this winter?'

From behind him. 'Hey! I was talking to you!'

Zannis faced him and said, 'Yes?'

'You Frenchmen can be very rude, you know.'

'I'm not French,' Zannis said. Maybe the SS officer wouldn't figure it out but the girlfriends certainly would.

'No? What are you?'

'I'm from Greece.'

The officer spoke to his friends. 'Say, here's a Greek!' Then, to Zannis, 'What brings you to Paris, Nick?'

Zannis couldn't stop it: a hard stare that said *Shut your fucking mouth before I shut it for you.* Then, making sure his voice was soft, he said, 'I'm a detective, I'm here to bring back a murderer.'

'Oh,' the officer said. 'I see. Well, we're friendly types, you know, and we were wondering what you were doing after dinner.'

'Going home,' Zannis said.

'Because I have this very grand apartment up on the avenue Foch, and you and Gorgeous are invited, for, well, some ... champagne.'

The aristocrat sank her clawed fingernails into Zannis's thigh; he almost yelped. 'Thanks, but the lady is tired, I'll take her home; after dinner.'

The officer glared at him, his head weaving back and forth.

The woman beside him said, 'Klaus? Are you ignoring us?'

Thank God for Frenchwomen, puffy blonde or not! 'Enjoy your evening, my friend,' Zannis said, employing a particular tone of voice – sympathetic, soothing – he'd used, all his years with the police, for difficult drunks.

And it almost worked; the officer couldn't decide whether he wanted to end this battle or not. Then he lurched, and his face lit up. What went on? Maybe his girlfriend's hand had done something under the table, something more enticing than the aristocrat's. Whatever it was it worked, and the officer turned away and whispered in girlfriend's ear.

'*Plat de la mer!*' the waiter cried out, wheeling to a stop at the table, a gigantic platter of crustaceans held high, balanced on his fingertips.

★

A taxi was waiting in front of the brasserie, and Zannis directed the driver back to his hotel. A much-relieved aristocrat sank back against the seat and said, voice confidential, 'Thank God that's over. I was afraid you were going to shoot him.'

'Not likely,' he said. *This thing in the holster is just for show.* And so he'd believed, until his third and final meeting with Escovil. Who'd said, just before they parted, 'Finally, I must say something a bit ... *sticky.* Which is, you mustn't allow Byer to be taken by the Germans, we *cannot* have him interrogated. So, if it looks as if the game is up, you'll have to, to, to do whatever you must.' Zannis hadn't answered: at first he couldn't believe what he'd heard, then he had to, but such madness, murder, was far beyond what he was willing to do.

At war, the city was blacked out; every window opaque, the occasional lighted streetlamp painted blue, car headlights taped down to slits, so the taxi moved cautiously through the silent, ghostly streets. When they reached the hotel and were alone as they approached the doorway, his companion said, 'Not long now. Your friend has been brought to the hotel, and you're meant to catch the early train.'

'The five-thirty-five.'

'Yes, the first train to Berlin. You have all the papers?'

'Stamped and signed: release from the Santé prison, exit visas, everything.'

The night clerk was asleep in a chair behind the reception desk, a newspaper open across his lap. They made sure they didn't wake him, climbing the stairs quietly as he snored gently down below. When they reached the third floor, Zannis stood by his door and said, 'Where is he?'

The aristocrat made an upward motion with her head. 'Forty-three.'

In his room, Zannis shed his trench coat and had a look at his valise, which appeared to be undisturbed, but, he well knew, an experienced professional search would leave no evidence. The aristocrat, waiting at the door, said, 'Ready to go?' In her voice, as much impatience as, true to her breeding, she ever permitted herself to reveal. These people were amateurs, Zannis thought, and they'd had all they wanted of secrecy and danger.

They climbed another flight, the aristocrat tapped twice on the door, then twice again, which was opened to reveal a darkened room. The man who'd opened the door had a sharp handsome face, dark hair combed straight back, and stood as though at attention: A military posture; he was perhaps, Zannis thought, a senior officer. The aristocrat and the officer touched each other's cheeks with their lips, Paris style, murmuring something that Zannis couldn't hear but certainly an endearment. So these two were husband and wife. The officer then said, to Zannis, 'I can't tell you my name,' as though it were an apology. 'You are Zannis?'

'I am.'

They shook hands, the officer's grip powerful and steady. 'Your problem now,' he said, nodding towards the interior of the room.

In the shadows, the silhouette of a small man sat slumped on the edge of the bed. Zannis said, 'Harry Byer?'

A white face turned towards him. 'Yes,' the man said in English. 'More or less.'

Zannis went downstairs to his room and collected his trench coat and valise. When he returned to Room 43, the officer said, 'We've arranged a car. At oh-four-forty hours. A police car, actually. So your arrival at the Gare du Nord, which is closely guarded, will look authentic.'

'Stolen?'

'Borrowed.'

'Better.'

'And driven by a policeman. Well, at least somebody wearing the uniform.'

The aristocrat laughed, silver chimes, at the idea of whatever old friend this was, playing the role of a policeman. As she started to remove her earrings, Zannis noticed a bare ring finger. Now he realized that these two were probably not married but were, instead, lovers. This sent his mind back to Salonika and a fleeting image of Demetria, by his side, in an occupied city.

Zannis crossed the room, the bare boards creaking beneath his weight, and shifted the room's single chair so that he sat facing Byer. Then, very laboriously, in his primitive English, he explained how the operation would work. When he showed Byer his photograph in the Greek passport, he was rewarded with at least a flicker of hope in the man's eyes. 'It might even work,' Byer said. He took the passport and studied it. 'I do speak a little French, you know. I did it at school.'

'He does,' the officer said. 'If you speak slowly.'

Zannis was relieved and switched to a mix of the two languages, making sure at the end of every phrase that Byer understood what he'd been told. 'At the borders, Harry, and on the trains – at least as far as Yugoslavia – you can't say anything at all, because you're supposed to be Greek. And nobody will speak to *you*, once you're wearing these.' He took a pair of handcuffs from his pocket. Byer stared at them. Zannis said, 'Better than a POW camp, right?'

Byer nodded. 'What did I do, to be in the Santé?'

'You murdered your wife and her lover, in Salonika.'

After a moment, Byer said, 'Not the worst idea.'

Zannis ignored the irony. 'It had to be a murder of some kind, for the Germans to believe that we'd got the French police to arrest you, after you'd fled to Paris.' He paused, then said, 'The only plausible crime would be a crime of passion. You don't much look like a gangster.'

Zannis stood, took a cigarette from his packet, then offered it around. Only the officer accepted, inhaling with pleasure as Zannis extinguished the match. He started to speak, but something caught his attention and he looked at his watch and said, almost to himself, 'It's too early for the police car.' Then, to Zannis, 'Can't you hear it?'

In the silence of the room, Zannis listened intently and discovered the low beat of an idling engine. The officer went to the window and, using one finger, carefully moved the blackout curtain aside, no more than an inch. 'Come and have a look,' he said.

Zannis joined him at the window. Across the street from the hotel, a glossy black Citroën, the luxury model with a long bonnet and square passenger compartment, was parked at the kerb. The air was sufficiently cold to make the exhaust a white plume at the exhaust.

The officer kept his voice low, his words meant for Zannis and nobody else. 'The only people who drive these things in Paris are the Gestapo and the SS. It's the official German car.'

Zannis understood immediately, though he found it hard to believe. 'We had a problem at the restaurant,' he said, 'with an SS officer. It seems he followed us back here.'

'Why would he do that?'

'He wanted your woman friend. He was very drunk.'

'Then let's hope it's him.'

'Why?'

'Because if it isn't, we've been betrayed.'

'Is that possible?'

'I'm afraid it is.'

The aristocrat joined them at the window. 'What's going on?'

'There's a car out there. See it? Zannis thinks some SS man followed you home from the restaurant.'

The aristocrat peered past the curtain. She swore, then said, 'Now what?'

'We'll have to think of something.'

'Will they search the hotel?' she said.

Byer said, 'What's going on?' His voice rose to a whine. 'What is it?'

The officer said, 'Keep quiet, Harry.' Then, 'They might search the hotel. Maybe he's waiting down there for a squad to show up.'

'Is there a back door?' Zannis said.

'There is, but it's padlocked. And, even if we got out that way, what happens when our friend shows up with the police car?'

They were silent for a moment. The officer again moved the curtain and said, 'He's just sitting there.'

'There were two of them, and their girlfriends,' the aristocrat said. 'Maybe they'll just go away. They have to assume I'm in this hotel for the night.'

'Maybe they will. Or maybe they'll wait until morning,' the officer said.

'Could anybody be . . . that crazy?'

Nobody answered. Finally Zannis said, 'Can you somehow contact your friend and warn him off?'

The officer looked at his watch. 'No, he's left his hotel by now. The police car is up at Levallois, in a garage. The owner helps us.'

Again, silence.

Zannis's mind was racing. He had seen, when he'd first entered the hotel, a metal shutter pulled down over a broad entryway. Not a shop, he guessed, because the pavement ended at either side of the shutter and a cobblestone strip led to the street. 'If Byer and I aren't here,' he said, 'would it matter if a Gestapo squad searched the hotel?'

The officer thought it over. 'No, it would just be the two of us in a room. And, when our friend arrives, he'll see the Gestapo vehicles and drive away.'

'I think we'd better do something now,' Zannis said. He put on his trench coat and grabbed the handle of his small valise.

'Good luck,' the officer said. He shook Zannis's hand, and the aristocrat kissed him on both cheeks and said, 'Be careful.'

'Let's go, Harry,' Zannis said.

In the dark lobby at the foot of the staircase, the night clerk snored on, dead to the world. Zannis shook him by the shoulder and he woke with a start and said, 'What . . . what do you want?' His breath smelled of sour wine.

'Is there a garage in this hotel?'

'Yes.'

'What's in there?'

'A car, belongs to the guy who owns the hotel. He can't drive it – the Bosch tried to confiscate private cars, so some people hid them.'

'Is the car locked?'

The clerk sat up straight. 'Say, what do you think—' Zannis drew the Walther and showed it to the clerk, who said, 'Oh,' then, 'The key's in the office, in the desk.'

Zannis gestured with the Walther and the clerk stood up, went into the office behind the reception desk and searched in the bottom drawer until he found car keys on a ring.

'And next,' Zannis said, 'I'll want the key for the back door.'

'On a nail, just next to you.'

'Harry?'

Byer came around the desk; Zannis gave him the key. 'Run this upstairs. Tell them to open the back door and get out right away.'

Byer hurried off and Zannis turned back to the clerk. 'The shutter over the garage doorway, it's locked?'

'Of course.'

'From inside? Is there an entry from the hotel?'

'No, it has a lock at the bottom, you have to go out to the pavement.'

'Get the key.'

Muttering under his breath, the clerk searched the middle drawer, threw pens, a rubber stamp, an ink pad and miscellaneous papers on the desk. At last he found the key, and started to hand it to Zannis, who waved him off. 'Is there petrol in the car?' Zannis said.

'Yes.'

'Battery connected? Tyres still on?'

'I charge the battery twice a week, late at night. The boss wants it ready to drive.'

'He does? Why?'

'The hell would I know? Maybe he wants to go somewhere.'

Zannis heard Byer, running down the stairs, likely waking every guest in the hotel. *This will not work*, Zannis thought. There was no way he could get this man back to Salonika. A moment later, Byer, breathing hard, arrived at the reception. 'They said thank you.'

'Now it's time,' Zannis said to the clerk, 'for you to go outside, unlock the shutter and roll it up.'

'*Me?*'

'You see anybody else?'

'Why can't your pal do it?'

Zannis rapped him on the shoulder blade with the barrel of the Walther, just hard enough.

The clerk mumbled something Zannis was not meant to hear and said, 'All right, whatever you want.'

Keeping Byer behind him in the darkened lobby, Zannis unlocked the hotel door and watched as the clerk went out of the door and turned left, towards the shuttered garage. Across the street, the Citroën idled, but Zannis could see only dim shapes behind the steamed-up windows.

The clerk came quickly through the door. 'Done,' he said. 'That Citroën out there, are they ...?'

'Go back to sleep,' Zannis said.

'What about the boss's car?'

'Send me a bill,' Zannis said. 'After the war.' He turned to Byer. 'Ready, Harry? We're not going to run, we're going to walk quickly. You get in the back and lie on the floor.'

'Why?' Byer's eyes were wide.

'Just in case,' Zannis said.

Keeping Byer on his left – the side away from the Citroën – and the gun in his hand in his coat pocket, Zannis walked through the hotel door. The shutter was rolled up to reveal an old Peugeot sedan, the metal rims around the headlights spotted with rust. He thought he might get away with it: the SS officer hadn't seen him in his trench coat, the seductive Didi wasn't with him, and the people in the Citroën wouldn't be able to see much of anything through the cloudy windows.

On the first try, wrong key – boot key, of course – then the driver's door opened, Zannis unlocked the back door and Byer, as ordered, lay flat on the floor. As Zannis settled behind the wheel, the driver's door of the Citroën swung open and the baby-faced SS he'd seen at the brasserie started to get out, then turned his head as though somebody in the back seat had spoken to him. Zannis searched for the starter button, found it and pressed it with his thumb. Nothing. *Betrayed.* By night-clerk malice, or by an old car on a damp night, it came to the same thing.

'What's going on?' Byer said.

Zannis pressed again.

Now the other SS officer climbed out of the Citroën. From the Peugeot's engine, a single, rather discreet, cough. The SS man heading for the garage wasn't in a hurry. A little unsteady on his feet, he kept one hand out of sight behind his leg. Zannis held the button down, which produced a second cough, another, and one more. Then the engine grumbled and came to life. Zannis shoved the clutch pedal to the floor and put the car in what he thought was first gear. It wasn't. As the clutch pedal came up, the Peugeot stalled. The SS man, now ten feet away, was amused and shook his head – a world populated by fools, what was one to do?

The starter worked once again and this time Zannis found first gear and gave the engine as much gas as he dared. The SS man's hand came out from behind his leg, Luger pistol held casually, barrel facing down. He changed direction in order to block the Peugeot and held up his other hand – the amiable traffic cop. Zannis slammed on the brake, the Peugeot lurched to a stop and then, looking sheepish and embarrassed, he cranked the window down. He had almost hit a German officer, what was *wrong* with him?

The SS man smiled, *that's better*, and, obviously very drunk from the way he walked, approached the driver's side of the car. He was just starting to bend over so he could have a word with the driver when Zannis shot him in the face. He staggered backwards his hat fell off, blood ran from his nostrils, and Zannis fired twice more; the first clipping off the top of his ear, the second in the right eyebrow. That did it, and he collapsed.

Zannis hit the accelerator, first gear howling. As he swung into the street, the baby-faced SS scrambled out of the Citroën. *Idiot*. Zannis snapped off two shots but the car was moving and he didn't think he'd hit him. Or maybe he had, because the last Zannis saw of him he was limping back to his car. Just as, in the rear-view mirror, Zannis saw the two puffy blondes take off like rabbits, high-heeled shoes in hand, running for their lives down the dark street. *Go fuck Germans and see where it gets you*, Zannis said to himself.

From the back, Byer said, 'What happened? What happened?'

Zannis didn't answer. Finally put the Peugeot into second gear – he could smell burning clutch – then third, and turned hard right into a side street, then right again, so that he was now heading north, towards the Porte de Clignancourt.

Slowly, Zannis worked his way through the back streets, which angled off the main boulevards, so, a series of diagonals. But Zannis couldn't have gone much faster if he'd had to – the untaped headlights were turned off, and it was hard to see in the blacked-out city. After ten minutes of driving, he stopped the Peugeot so Byer could move to the passenger seat and Zannis told him the details. Byer took it well enough; after everything he'd been through since the Wellington went down, this was but one more nightmare. As Zannis again drove north, he heard the high-low sirens in the distance, converging on the hotel, but he was well away from it. A few blocks on he passed a pair of French policemen, in their long winter capes, pedalling easily on their bicycles. One of them gave him a sour look, and Zannis wondered if Paris was under curfew, often the case in occupied cities. He didn't know but, if it was, it was a German curfew, and the policemen couldn't be bothered to stop him.

Of course that would change, violently, in the morning. The Gestapo and the French Sûreté would turn Paris upside down, looking for him – they'd have a good description – and for the Peugeot. Maybe, he thought, he should have tied the clerk to a chair, evidence that the man wasn't complicit in the crime, but he hadn't thought of it and he'd been intent on escaping from the hotel. In any event, the escape south by railway was no longer possible, he'd have to find another way to get out of the country.

He reached Saint-Ouen soon enough, wondering if Laurette, his lover when he'd lived here, was still in the apartment they'd shared. It didn't matter if she was; he couldn't go anywhere near her. Moments later, at the edge of Saint-Ouen, he entered the vast flea market, a labyrinth, endless twisting lanes lined by shuttered stalls. Clignancourt didn't precisely have borders, it faded away to the north in a maze of alleys and storage sheds, and here Zannis found an open courtyard behind a workshop with boarded-up windows. He parked the car and lit a cigarette. Dawn was still hours away, and ten in the morning farther yet. He was very tired, nothing more than that, and, in time, both he and Byer dozed, woke up and dozed again.

10.15 a.m. Zannis left Byer in the Peugeot and made his way to stall number fifty-five of the section known as Serpette. The market was nearly deserted, many of the stalls unopened, only a few shoppers wandering listlessly among the aisles, past old chinaware, old clothes, old maps and books, antlers for the wall above the fireplace, a collapsible opera hat. You had to be clever here, to find that priceless object, its value unknown to the owner of the booth, then you had to bargain hard to get the meagre price lower, so the *antiquaire* never suspected you were cheating him out of a fortune. Day in, day out, year in, year out, the devious customers carried off their treasures, displayed them in their parlours and boasted to their friends.

Zannis was relieved to find his uncle, seeing him from behind as he sat with two friends, playing cards on a mahogany tabletop held up by three upended fruit crates. Zannis's heart lifted – that bald pate, freckled and scarred, with its fringe of wiry grey hair, could belong to no one else. 'Anastas?'

His uncle turned, his eyes widened with disbelief, then he shouted, 'Constantine!' rose to his feet and embraced his nephew. Strong as an ox, Uncle Anastas, who held him tight while Zannis felt, on his cheek, tears from his uncle's eyes. 'Oh my God, I thought I'd never see you again,' Anastas said. Then took him by the arms, stepped back, stared at him lovingly and said, 'Constantine, my own nephew, what the fuck are you doing *here?*'

'A long story, Uncle.'

'My brother's son,' Anastas said to his friends. '*Look* at him.'

'A handsome boy,' one of them said, in Greek.

'Are you still playing, Anastas?' said the other.

'I fold my cards,' Anastas said, wiping his eyes.

Uncle Anastas wanted to show him off at the *antiquaires'* café but Zannis told him, as gently as he could, that they should close the booth and speak inside, so Anastas shooed his friends off, lowered the shutter over the front of the stall, then went to the café and returned carrying coffees spiked with Calvados. Zannis had meanwhile discovered – lying on a demi-lune table artfully coated with dust – a copy of that morning's *Le Matin*. On the front page a headline: SS MAJOR SHOT BY JEWISH GANGSTERS!

His uncle, having had time to think things over on his walk to the café, was good and worried by the time he returned. He waited one sip of coffee, then said, 'You better tell me the story, Constantine.'

Zannis held up the newspaper.

'*Skata!* You're not a Jew.'

'Not a gangster either.'

Anastas switched on a lamp with a coloured-glass shade, read the first few sentences of the article, then said, 'Well, it's in the Zannis blood. I got my first Turk when I was sixteen. A gendarme, but only a corporal, not a *major*.'

'I remember the story,' Zannis said.

Anastas put the paper down and looked puzzled. 'But tell me something, why did you have to come all the way to Paris to do this thing? You could've waited, you know, they'll be in Greece soon enough.'

'I came up here to rescue an Englishman, Uncle Anastas.'

'Oh, I see. You're involved in ... secret work?'

'Yes.'

'Bad business, dear nephew, they kill people who do that.'

'I know. But what happened last night was accidental – we were supposed to leave here quietly. Now we're stuck.'

'You wouldn't be the only one. All sorts of people in hiding here, waiting for the war to end, waiting for the Americans to stop sitting on their arses and do something.'

'I can't wait, Uncle. I have to get out, and I have to get my Englishman out.'

Anastas thought it over, finally said, 'Not easy.'

'No, it isn't.'

'But not impossible. Do you have any money?'

'Plenty. Grandma sewed it in the lining of my jacket.'

'Because that's what it takes. And if you don't have enough—'

'No, Uncle, I have a lot. In dollars.'

'Dollars! *Skata*, I haven't seen dollars in a long time. How much, hundreds?'

'Thousands.'

'Constantine!'

'It's the war, Uncle. Everything's expensive.'

'Still, you must be very important. I mean, *thousands*.'

'The English do *not* want this man captured.'

From outside the stall, a low two-note whistle. Zannis could see, in the space between the bottom of the shutter and the ground, a pair of shoes, which then moved away. 'What goes on?' he said.

'Police.' He tugged the little chain on the lamp, darkening the stall, then rested an elbow on his knee and rubbed the corners of his mouth with thumb and index finger. 'What to do with you,' he said. 'Where have you hidden your Englishman?'

Zannis described the building and the courtyard.

'He'll be safe there, but not for long. When these clowns go away, you'll bring him to my apartment.'

'Thank you, Anastas,' Zannis said.

'What the hell, you're family. And maybe I have one idea.'

'Which is?'

'I know somebody.'

'Always good, to know somebody.'

'You'd better,' Anastas said. 'Otherwise ...'

In the apartment, Zannis and Byer settled down to wait. Byer would sleep on a chaise longue, Zannis on a tasselled couch. And, later that morning, one of Anastas's card-playing friends took a can of blue paint and a number plate over to the courtyard where they'd hidden the Peugeot. He then drove the newly painted car to a nearby village, parked it on a mud flat by the river and took a train back to Paris. 'I suspect it was gone before I got on the train,' he told Anastas. 'Into a barn until the war ends.'

'Harder than I thought,' Anastas said at dinner. His French wife had prepared steaks, with spinach and onions sautéed in oil, and they drank a *very* good red wine in unlabelled bottles. 'The man I know ... ?' Anastas paused to chew his steak, then took a sip of the wine. 'Well, he had to go to a man *he* knows.' Anastas met his nephew's eyes, making sure he understood the magnitude of such an event. 'So prepare to pay, nephew.'

'When do I meet him?' Zannis said.

'After midnight, two-thirty. A car will come for you.'

Byer looked up from his plate and said, 'Thank you, madame, for this wonderful dinner.'

'You are welcome,' she said. 'It is in your honour, monsieur, and Constantine's. To wish you safe journey.' She smiled, warm and affectionate. If the occupation had affected her, there was no evidence that Zannis could see.

'We drink to that,' Anastas said. And they did.

2:30 a.m. The glossy black motorcar was surely worth a fortune. Zannis had never seen one like it and had no idea what it was. It rolled to a stop in front of Anastas's apartment building in Saint-Ouen, the back door swung open and Zannis climbed in. The interior smelled like expensive leather. The driver turned to face him, holding him with his eyes for a long moment, probably making sure Zannis knew who he was dealing with. He knew. He recognized the breed: confident young men to whom killing came easily and smart enough to profit from it. Then the driver rested his hands on the wheel but the car never moved, simply sat there, the huge engine purring softly.

Zannis had known corrupt men of every sort, high and low, over the years he'd been with the police, but the friend of the friend, sitting next to him, was something new. He looked, Zannis thought, like a French king; prosperously stout, with fair, wavy hair parted to one side, creamy skin, a prominent nose, and a pouch that sagged beneath his chin. 'I'm told you wish to leave France,' he said, his voice deep and used to command.

'That's right.'

'The price, for two individuals, is two thousand dollars. Have you the money with you?'

'Yes.'

'I believe you are the man who shot a German officer. Did you do this because you have a hatred of Germans?'

'No. My friend was lying on the floor of the car, the officer would have seen him, so I had to do it. Why do you want to know?'

'To inform certain people – the people who need to know things. They don't care what is done, they simply require information.'

'Germans?'

The man was amused. 'Please,' he said, not unkindly. Then, 'It doesn't matter, does it?' It was as though he enjoyed innocence, found Zannis so, and instinctively liked him. 'Now,' he said, 'there are two ways for you to leave France. The first choice is a freight train controlled by communist railway workers. Travelling in this way you may go to Germany, Italy or Spain. However, once you've crossed the border – there will be no inspection of papers – you are on your own. Hopefully, you've made arrangements that will allow you to proceed from one of those countries.'

'I haven't.'

'I see. In that case, you may wish to travel by aeroplane.'

'By aeroplane?' Zannis was incredulous.

'Yes, why not? Are you reluctant to fly?'

'Just . . . surprised.'

The man's shrug was barely detectable. 'If you wish to leave tomorrow, and for you that might not be a bad idea, the plane is going to . . .' He leaned forward, towards the driver, and said, 'Leon?'

'Sofia.'

'Yes, Sofia.'

'That would be best,' Zannis said.

'Very well.' He held out a hand, creamy and fat, palm up, and said, 'So then . . .'

Zannis had removed the money from his jacket lining and put

the thick wad of notes in the pocket of his coat; now he counted out two thousand dollars in fifty-dollar notes. The man next to him, the French king, stowed the money in a leather briefcase, probing first to make room for it. Then he gave Zannis directions: the name of a village, how to identify the road that led to an airstrip, and a time. 'All memorized?' he asked Zannis.

'Yes, I won't forget.'

'When you describe your adventures in France, as no doubt you will have to, I would take it as a personal favour that you remain silent about this particular chapter, about me. Do I have your word?'

'You have it.'

'Do you keep your word?'

'I do.'

'Then good evening.'

Uncle Anastas had a friend – also an émigré Greek, it turned out – who owned an ancient truck, and he picked them up at dawn. A few minutes later he joined a long line of produce trucks, coming back empty after delivery to the Paris produce markets, and the soldiers waved them through the control at the Porte Maillot. Then he headed north-west from Paris on the road that followed the Seine, with signs for DIRECTION ROUEN. A wet, steady snow that morning, from a low sky packed with grey cloud. 'We won't fly today,' Byer said, staring anxiously out of the window.

'We may have to wait,' Zannis said. 'But I expect we'll take off.'

'Not in this.' After he spoke, Byer swallowed.

Zannis studied him. What went on? 'Everything all right?' he said.

Byer nodded emphatically. Nothing wrong with *me*.

It was hard to see, the windscreen wiper smeared snow and road grime across the window, not much more than that, and the driver leaned forward and squinted, cursing eloquently in

Greek. Finally he found the *route départementale* for La Roche-Guyon, the truck skidding as he made the last-minute turn. The narrow road wound past winter farmland for a long time, then it was Zannis who spotted the stone marker with a number chiselled into it, and the truck drove, in low gear, up a muddy, deeply rutted path. Finally, when they knew they'd taken the wrong turn, they saw an aeroplane in a ploughed field. A compact twin-engine aircraft, a workhorse used for a few passengers or a small load of freight, with a white cross in a red circle in a red insignia behind the cockpit. *Swiss markings*, Zannis thought. *What a clever king.* Two men were loading crates into the plane, through a cargo hatch on the underside of the fuselage. 'You can walk from here,' the driver said. As he worked at getting the truck turned around, Zannis and Byer trudged across a field, wind-driven snow in their faces. When they neared the plane, one of the men saw them, stopped loading and waited until they reached him. 'You are the passengers?'

'Yes.'

'Bad morning.'

'Will we be able to fly?' Byer said.

'Me?' The man grinned. He had high, sharp cheekbones, hair sheared off close to the scalp and, Zannis could hear it, a hard Slavic edge to his French. A Russian? A Serb? He wore a leather jacket and a dirty white scarf spotted with oil – a cinema aviator – with a holstered revolver on his hip. 'You give us a hand,' he said. 'We'll take off sooner.'

The crates were heavy, MAS 38 stencilled on the rough wooden boards. Zannis wasn't certain, but he had a pretty good hunch he was loading French machine guns. When they were done, the pilot's helper headed towards a farmhouse on the horizon. The pilot rubbed his hands and looked up at the sky. 'One of you can sit on the crates, the other can use the co-pilot seat.' He led them around the plane, to a door behind the cockpit with a short steel-frame ladder propped against the bottom of the doorway.

Standing at the foot of the ladder, Zannis waited for Byer to climb up. When he didn't, Zannis said, 'Time to go.' He sounded cheerful, but he knew he had trouble.

Byer stood there. He was in a trance, face dead white, eyes closed.

'Harry?'

No answer.

'Let's go,' Zannis said sharply. *No nonsense, please.* The pilot was staring at them through the cockpit window.

But Byer was rooted to the earth. Zannis guessed that something had happened to him when the Wellington went down, and now he couldn't get on the plane.

The pilot's patience was gone, the engines roared to life and the propellers spun. Zannis tried once more, raising his voice over the noise. 'One foot in front of the other, Harry, your way back to England. Think about England, going home.'

Byer never moved. So Zannis took him by the back of the collar and the belt, hauled him up the ladder and shoved him into the plane. Then he sat him down on a pile of crates. From the cockpit, the pilot called out, 'I have a bottle of vodka up here, will that help?'

'No, it's all right now,' Zannis yelled back, closing the door, pulling a bar down to secure it.

The plane began to bump across the field, gathering speed, then, heavily loaded, it wobbled aloft and climbed into the grey cloud.

Melissa stood on her hind legs, tail wagging furiously, set her great paws on his chest and licked his face. 'Yes, yes girl, I'm back, hello, yes.' The welcome from his family was no less enthusiastic – they knew he'd been up to something dangerous and were relieved that he'd returned. A demand that he stay for dinner was gently turned aside; he wanted to go back to his apartment, to his bed, because he wanted to sleep more than he wanted to eat. So he promised he would return the following night and, by the time he let Melissa out of the door, his grandmother was already at her sewing machine, working the pedals, restitching the lining of his jacket. As he walked down the hill towards the waterfront, Melissa ran ahead of him, turning from time to time to make sure he hadn't again vanished, a sickle slice of moon stood low in the night sky, the streets were quiet, it was good to be home.

The flight to Bulgaria had been uneventful. At one point – was it Germany down there? Austria? – a pair of patrolling Messerschmitts came up to have a look at them, then banked and slid away. Perhaps the French king had permission to fly his crates over Germany – from some office, in some building. Perhaps more than one office, perhaps more than one building, perhaps more than one country. Perhaps the French king could do whatever he wanted; it had not been easy for him to find room in his briefcase for the two thousand dollars. Zannis had, in time, accepted the pilot's invitation to sit in the co-pilot's seat. From there he watched the passage of the nameless winter land below, the hills and the rivers, and wondered what to do about the crates. Machine guns to Bulgaria? For who? To shoot who? So, say something to Lazareff? Who worked for the Sofia police department? Tell Bulgaria – the historic enemy of Greece? He'd given his word to the French king, he would keep it. Did that include the crates?

In the end, it didn't matter.

Because the pilot landed at a military airfield north of Sofia, and a squad of Bulgarian soldiers was waiting to unload the shipment. The officer in charge at the airfield had no idea what to do with unexpected, and unexplained, passengers, and had pretty much decided to hold them at the base and await orders from above. But then, at Zannis's insistence, he'd made a telephone call to Captain Lazareff, which produced a police car and a driver, who dropped them off at a restaurant in Sofia.

There, over plates of lamb and pilaf, accompanied by a bottle of mastika, Lazareff and Zannis conversed in German, which excluded Byer, who, now back on solid ground, hardly cared. Lazareff enquired politely about the flight, Zannis responded politely that it had been smooth and easy. Lazareff suggested – still polite, though with a certain tightness at the corners of the mouth – that it would be better if Zannis were to forget he'd seen the plane's cargo.

'What cargo?'

'You'll tell your friend there? Whoever he is?'

'What friend?'

'Ha–ha–ha!'

More mastika, tasting like anise, and lethal.

'By the way,' Lazareff said, 'the situation in Roumania is a little worse than the newspapers are letting on. We calculate six hundred and eighty thousand troops, maybe sixty Wehrmacht divisions, artillery, tanks, all of it. They have to be fed, it isn't cheap, so they're obviously there for a reason. Probably they're meant to intimidate us or, if it comes to that, invade. Or maybe they're there to threaten the Serbs, or maybe Greece. Our response, so far, has been to tell Hitler that we're not quite ready to sign his pact.'

'Not quite ready?'

'Not quite. We've destroyed the bridges over the Danube.'

'That would be a message, I'd think.'

'A tantrum. We've seen the materiel, struts and floats, that can be assembled into pontoon bridges.'

'I appreciate your telling me,' Zannis said.

'I expect your generals know all about it,' Lazareff said. 'But I think you should know also, Costa, so you can make your own, personal . . . arrangements. If you see what I mean.'

From there, they'd moved to lunchtime conversation. And by mid-afternoon, after Zannis had telephoned Escovil, and with exit visas provided by Lazareff, Zannis and Byer were on the train to Salonika. At six-thirty in the evening, Byer was delivered to Escovil at the Pension Bastasini. 'How did you get here so quickly?' Escovil said, accusation in his voice.

'It's a long story,' Zannis said. 'For another time.'

'You didn't travel on the trains,' Escovil said. It wasn't a question.

'You were watching, weren't you.'

'Of course. So we'll want you to explain.'

'Later,' Zannis said. 'I'm going to see my family.' He was exhausted, at the last available edge of patience. Escovil knew what came next, so left it there and, a brief taxi ride later, Melissa came to the door to greet the returning hero.

Back at his apartment, the hero was exhausted – threw the mail on the kitchen table, washed his hands and flopped down on the bed. But then, his mind charged with the images of the past few days, he realized he was not going to be able to sleep any time soon, so took off his shoes and socks and covered himself with a blanket. He tried to return to Inspector Maigret, waiting on his night table, but memories of the real Paris intruded and the book lay open on his chest while he brooded about them. Uncle Anastas was a shining example of survival, even prosperity, in an occupied city, but that was Anastas, who could deal with anything. So could he, come to that, but his family couldn't. According to Lazareff, time was growing short, the Balkans would be overrun and Zannis had to make plans to save his family. Where could they go? How, once he became involved in resistance and likely in hiding, would he support them? The Germans would eventually figure out who had shot their SS officer, would they dare to come after him in Greece? Maybe not, but they would be looking for him the day they entered the city.

For these problems he had no solutions, so tried Maigret again but couldn't concentrate – Madame *Canard was who*? Time *was* running short – so why was he alone on this bed? What was Demetria doing? In bed herself? In bed with Vasilou? What a bastard, the bully he'd heard on the telephone. So, there was also Demetria to save. *What if he telephoned . . . ?*

He woke with a start, then turned off the lamp. While he'd slept, Maigret had disappeared. No, there he was, under the blanket.

ESCAPE FROM
SALONIKA

10 February 1941. Well before dawn, Costa Zannis woke from a night of bizarre and frightening dreams. He lay there with his eyes open, supremely grateful that none of it was real and so, fearing that further horrors awaited him if he went back to sleep, forced himself to get out of bed. He washed, dressed for work, let Melissa out of the door and walked down to the waterfront corniche, to a *kafeneion* that stayed open all night for the stevedores and sailors of the port. There he drank coffee, smoked cigarettes and stared out of the window, where the sky was streaked with red cloud as the sun, coming up over the Aegean, lit the whitecaps in the bay and the snow on Mount Olympus in the distance. The fishing caiques were heading out to sea, attended by flocks of seagulls, their cries sharp in the morning silence.

The *kafeneion* was quiet, only the sleepy waiter, a fiftyish prostitute with dyed-red hair and a man dressed in merchant seaman's sweater and wool watch cap. Zannis took a morning paper from the counter and looked at the headlines: somebody had taken a potshot at the mayor, the bullet punching a hole in his briefcase and coming to rest in the sheaves of official paper packed inside.

The prostitute was watching Zannis as he read and said, 'Terrible thing.'

Zannis mumbled an assent – it was too early in the morning to talk, and, once he went to work, a full day's talking lay ahead of him.

Turning to the seaman, she said, 'Don't you think? Shooting at a mayor?'

The man raised his hands and shrugged; he did not understand Greek.

'Always something here,' the waiter said. 'They never catch them, people like that.'

But, Zannis found when he reached the office, they already had. Sort of. 'What they say in the papers' – Saltiel had his feet up on the desk, his jacket over the back of the chair – 'is that he was shot at, yesterday morning, while getting into his car. True, as far as it goes. But the detective who questioned the mayor told me that he was getting into the back seat, because he has a driver, and his left foot was up on the floorboard as he bent over to go through the door, with his briefcase in his left hand, swung slightly behind him. Try it, Costa, and you'll see what went on.'

'What?'

'The way the detective sees it, somebody tried to shoot him in the backside.'

'A warning?'

'More like a lesson. I talked to some people, especially the mayor's secretary, who knows all, and what happened is that the mayor's wife caught him in bed with his girlfriend and made him cut her loose. Girlfriend doesn't like it – she thought she was the one and only – so she goes out and hires somebody to pop him one in the arse. Or maybe she did it herself. She's nobody to fool with, according to the secretary.'

'The mayor never turned around? Never saw anybody?'

'At the time they thought, the mayor and the driver, they'd heard a car backfire. Or at least that's what they told the detectives.' Saltiel raised his eyebrows. 'According to the mayor, he didn't realize he'd been shot at until he got to his desk and opened the briefcase. The bullet stopped right in the middle of *Papadopoulos v. City of Salonika.*'

'So, case closed,' Zannis said.

'Not around here, it isn't. The mayor can't have *that* in the newspapers, so the investigation is transferred to this office and we're supposed to question a few communists, or Macedonian terrorists, or whatever we can think up. At least tell the press we're doing it.'

'Maybe a disappointed office-seeker,' Zannis said.

'Yes, that's good. Or a lunatic.'

'Well, we're not going hunting for lunatics, but somebody better talk to the girlfriend and tell her not to try *that* again.'

'Somebody?' Saltiel said.

'All right, Gabi, get me a telephone number.'

There was more that had gone on in his absence. Saltiel opened his desk drawer and handed Zannis a message from Emilia Krebs. In ochre letters above the lines of the typed commercial paragraphs she said that three men and two women would be leaving Berlin on the eleventh of February, adding that she had no knowledge of the man seen on the platform of the Zagreb railway station. The secret writing was far more legible than what Zannis had been able to produce. 'Who heated the letter?' he asked Saltiel.

'Sibylla. I've never used an iron in my life.'

'Well done, Sibylla,' Zannis said. 'Did you send the teletypes?'

'I did,' Sibylla said. 'They were confirmed, and I made copies for you.'

'Thank you,' Zannis said. 'And I mean it.'

'Oh, you're welcome,' she said, both surprised and pleased that Zannis was so grateful. 'I'll do the next one too, if you like.'

As Saltiel returned to his desk, Zannis prepared to telephone Demetria's house. He'd almost done it the night before, because the time he'd spent in Paris – the Germans, the shooting, the escape – had had its effect on him. On the flight to Sofia he'd thought, in fact told himself, *your time is running out*, and more than once. Now he was going to reach for her, any way he could, and to hell with the consequences. But, as his hand moved towards the telephone, it rang.

'Yes? Hello?'

'Hello. I'm calling from the Bastasini.'

Escovil. 'And?'

'I understand you were tired last night, but I would like to talk to you, as soon as possible.' Escovil was trying to sound casual, but his voice was strained and tense.

'I can't, right now,' Zannis said, cold as ice. 'I'm busy.'

The line hissed. 'Some people I know are very, *concerned.*'

And you're so scared of them? 'Why? They got what they wanted.'

'They'd like to know – the details.'

'Ask *him.*'

'Um, he isn't sure how it worked. So they're, well, anxious to hear your story. And this would be better in person, not on the telephone.'

Instead of attacking Escovil, because the urge to do that was very powerful, Zannis took a deep breath. 'You know the address here?'

'Yes.'

'I'll see you downstairs, in the vestibule, in ten minutes. There's something I have to do first, so you may have to wait for me.'

When Escovil answered, it sounded as though he were reading a sentence he'd written out beforehand. 'Actually, my friends would like to meet you. To thank you. In person.'

'Come over here in ten minutes, and come alone. Understood?'

Escovil hesitated, then said, 'I'm on my way.'

Zannis hung up, but didn't leave the receiver on the cradle long enough for a dial tone, so had to do it again.

A maid answered.

'Is Madam Vasilou there?'

'Gone away.' This was a different maid; she barely spoke Greek.

'What do you mean, "gone away"?'

She tried harder, raising her voice. '*They gone.*'

'Where did they go?'

'Gone away,' the maid said, and hung up.

Zannis made himself wait ten minutes, then walked down the stairs. He couldn't believe what had happened; where were they? Had they left the country? He wanted to break something. And here, on top of it all, was Escovil. Who hadn't put on a coat, had instead looped a woollen scarf around his neck, stuffed the ends inside his buttoned jacket and turned the collar up. With the addition of brown leather gloves, he looked like a country squire going up to London on an autumn day.

If Escovil was already anxious about the meeting, the expression on Zannis's face did nothing to reassure him. 'I hurried straight over,' he said.

'What do you want from me?' Zannis said.

'Byer told us you flew from Paris to Sofia. How did you manage that?' After a moment he added, 'The people I work for would like to know how you did it.' *It isn't me.*

'I was helped by some friends in Paris, people I met when I lived there.'

'And they are ... ?'

'Friends in Paris. And now, let me ask *you* something. Who had the idea that I should go to a *restaurant*? Because I'm sure Byer told you what happened.'

Escovil hesitated. 'A senior person, in London, felt you should act like a visitor. The original idea was the Eiffel Tower, but the time didn't work. So, a brasserie.'

'Very clever,' Zannis said. 'Except that it wasn't.'

'We need to know about the aeroplane,' Escovil said, desperation in his voice. 'It could be very important, *very* important.'

'Well, you know as much as I'm going to tell you. I understand what your people want, they want to be able to use what I used, any spy service would, but they'll have to find their own way.'

'Would you at least meet them?'

Zannis stared at Escovil. 'No,' he said.

A muscle ticked in Escovil's cheek. He half-turned towards the door, then turned back to face Zannis. 'I'm serving in a war, Zannis. And so are you, no matter whether you like it or not.' He reached the door in two strides and, over his shoulder, said, 'I'd think about that if I were you.'

It was just after six when Zannis got back to Santaroza Lane. As he took Melissa's butcher's scraps from his tiny refrigerator, he saw the mail he'd tossed on the table when he'd come home the night before. He fed Melissa, then, looking for anything commonplace to make him feel, if not better, at least occupied, he began to look through the pile of envelopes. A few bills, an invitation to a formal party, a letter. No return address. Inside, a single sheet of paper:

5 February

C.

We have left Salonika and gone to Athens. I have said my mother is ill and I had to come here, to Kalamaria, to take care of her. She has a telephone, 65–245. I don't know how long I can stay here, and I don't know where you are. I hope you read this in time.

D.

He called immediately and was out of the door minutes later. Kalamaria wasn't far away, maybe ten miles south, down the peninsula. Out on the corniche he found a taxi and paid the driver extravagantly to take him to the village, where, Demetria had told him, there was only one hotel, the Hotel Angelina. He arrived at seven-ten and took a room. The hotel was barely open, in February, but a boy led him up to Room 3 – probably their finest, since Zannis was their only guest – and lit a small oil heater in the corner. It produced a loud pop and a flash, and the boy swore as he jumped aside, but the thing worked and, ten minutes later, the room began to warm up.

The Hotel Angelina was on the bay and the room had one large window that faced west, over the sea. Not so bad, the room. Whitewashed stucco walls, a narrow bed with a winter blanket, a lamp on a night table, a wooden chair and an armoire with two hangers. Zannis hung his trench coat and jacket on one, and left the other for his guest. He tried sitting in the chair, then lay on the bed, set his glasses on the night table and waited. There were rain squalls on the bay that night, accompanied by a gusting wind that sighed and moaned and rattled the window. Eight o'clock came and went. Eight-fifteen. Where was she? Eight-twenty.

Two light knocks on the door.

When he opened it, there she was. Beautiful, yes, but unsmiling and, he sensed, maybe a little scared. He'd planned to embrace her – *finally, at last!* – but something told him not to, so he rested a light hand on her shoulder and guided her into the room. 'Hello, Demetria,' said the passionate lover. 'May I take your coat?' She nodded. He could smell her perfume on the coat as as he hung it up in the armoire.

Sitting on the edge of the bed, she wore a heavy slate-coloured wool sweater and skirt, with thick black cotton stockings and lace-up shoes. 'Oh lord,' she said.

'Yes, I know.'

'You can sit down,' she said.

He was standing there, hesitant, and as tense as she was. 'I can go downstairs. Maybe there's some retsina, or wine.'

She brightened. 'Whatever they have. It's *cold* in here.'

He went downstairs. The hotel didn't exactly have a bar; a shelf with bottles stood above a square plank table. The door by the table was ajar, Zannis could hear a radio. 'Hello?' he said. When the woman who had rented him the room came out, he bought a bottle of retsina and she gave him two cloudy glasses, then said, 'Good night, sir.'

Demetria was sitting exactly where he'd left her, rubbing her hands.

'What a night,' Zannis said. He poured retsina into the glasses and gave her one. When he sat by her side, the bed sagged beneath them.

Demetria laughed. 'Ah, Kalamaria.'

'Did you live here? As a child?'

'No, my mother came here after my father died. Returned. It was her home village.'

'Is she actually ill?'

'Oh no, not her. Never. Not that I can remember.'

'You told her, ah, what you're doing?'

From Demetria, a tight smile. 'She knows, Mama does. Knows her daughter.'

They clinked their glasses together and drank. The retsina was strong.

'Not so bad,' Zannis said.

'No, not bad at all. A good idea.' She put her glass on the floor and rubbed her hands, trying to get warm.

'Shall we get drunk and forget our woes?'

'Not *that* drunk.'

When she again picked up her glass, Zannis saw that she wasn't wearing her wedding ring. And she'd pulled her hair back with an elaborate silver clip.

'I called your house, this morning,' he said. 'I came home last night but I didn't see your letter until just before I called you.'

'I knew . . . I knew you would call. I mean, I knew you would call the house in Salonika, so I telephoned, from Athens. Nobody answered . . .' She put her glass on the floor, rubbed her hands and said, 'My hands are so cold.' *You dumb ox.*

'Give them to me.' He held her hands, which weren't all that cold, and said, 'You're right. They need to be warmed up.' He took her left hand in both of his and rubbed the back, then the palm.

After a time she said, just the faintest trace of a hitch in her voice, 'That's better.' With her free hand, she drank some retsina, then put her glass on the floor.

'Now the other. You were saying?'

'That I called, from Athens . . . .'

He worked on her hand, his skin stroking hers. 'And?'

She leaned towards him a little. 'And you . . . weren't home.'

'No.' He noticed that the dark shade of lipstick she wore flattered her olive skin. 'No . . . I wasn't.'

'So I wrote it.' She was closer now.

He took both her hands, meaning to move her towards him but she was, somehow, already there. 'I did get it.'

'I know.' Her face was very close to his, so she spoke very softly. 'You said.'

He pressed his lips against hers, which moved. After a time he said, 'So . . .' They kissed again, he put a hand on her back, she put a hand on his. With his lips an inch away from her mouth he whispered, '. . . I telephoned.' The wool of her sweater was rough against his hand as it went up and down.

It was awkward, sitting side by side, but they managed, until he could feel her breasts against him. When she tilted her head, her lips lay across his, and she spread them apart, so that his tongue could touch hers. Involuntarily, he shivered.

He knelt on the floor and began to untie the laces of her shoes. As he worked at one of the knots, she ran her fingers through his hair, then down the side of his face. 'Can you do it?'

The knot came undone.

They had set the hard pillows against the iron railing at the foot of the bed in order to see out of the window, where, across the bay, a lightning storm raged over Mount Olympus. The mountain was famous for that. Almost always, in bad weather, forked white bolts lit the clouds above the summit – which meant that Zeus was angry, according to the ancient Greeks. Zannis was anything but. Demetria lay sideways against him, the silver clip cold where it rested on his shoulder.

When he'd finished with her shoes, he had returned to her side and taken the hem of her sweater in his hands but she held them still and said, her voice low and warm, 'Let me do this for you.' Then she stood, turned off the lamp and undressed. It wasn't overly theatrical; she might have been alone, before a mirror, and took her time because she always did. Nonetheless, it was a *kind* of performance, for she clearly liked being watched. Carefully, she folded her clothing and laid each piece on the chair, using it as – a prop? She wore very fancy silk panties over a garter belt and, after she'd slid them down, she turned partly away from him and braced her foot on the chair in order to remove her stocking. From this perspective, her bottom was fuller, as it curved, than promised when she'd leaned against the back of a sofa. And the angled form of a woman in that position suggested a seductive painting, though it was a natural, a logical, way to go about removing a stocking.

Was it not?

When she'd laid the garter belt on top of her clothes, she stood there a moment, head canted to one side. *So, here is what you shall have.* Was it what he'd hoped for? She was heavier, sturdier, than the naked Demetria of his imagination, with small breasts, small areolae, erect nipples.

Demetria may have taken time to undress, Zannis most certainly did not. He shed his clothes, took her in his arms and drew her close, savouring the feel of skin on skin. And here, pressed between them, was an emphatic answer to her silent question. Until that evening, Zannis had been in a way ambivalent; for in his heart a tender passion, which he thought of as *love*, had warred with the most base desire. But tender passion, as it turned out, would have to wait. And he was only half to blame. Maybe less.

And so?

Lightning flickered in the distance and, when a squall passed over the Hotel Angelina, wind-blown rain surged against the window. 'You could, you know' – Zannis spoke the words slowly – 'never go back to Athens.'

She didn't answer, and he couldn't see her face, but she nestled against him, which meant *no* and he knew it.

'No?' he said, making sure.

'It is . . .' she said, suppressing the *too soon*, then started over. 'It would be very sudden.'

'You have to go back?'

'Don't,' she said.

He didn't. But, even so, she rolled away from him and lay on her stomach with her chin on her hands. He stroked her back, a deep cleft in the centre. 'Can you stay until the morning?'

'Well, I'm certainly not going anywhere now.'

'Is it a long walk? To your mother's house?'

'Not far. It's on the water, just around the bay. One of those stucco villas.'

'Oh?'

'"Oh?"' she said, imitating him. 'Yes, my love, now you know.'

'Know what?'

'That she could never afford such a thing. Nor could I. And you should see where my sister lives, in Monastir.'

'Oh.'

'You think I'm paid for, like . . . I won't say the word.'

'That isn't true.'

She shrugged.

'So he's rich, so what?'

'That barely describes it. He buys French paintings, and Byzantine manuscripts, and carved emeralds. He spends money like water, on anything that takes his fancy. Have you noticed a small white ship, practically new, that stays docked in Salonika? I think it was an English ship, one of those that carried mail and pasengers to the Orient. Anyhow, it sits there, with a full crew on board, ready to go at an hour's notice. "In case," as he puts it, "things go badly here." Then we will all sail away to safety.'

'Not a yacht?'

'The yacht is in Athens, in Piraeus. Not meant for an ocean in winter.'

'You will leave with him, if "things go badly"?'

'I don't know Maybe. Maybe not.' She thought for a time. 'Perhaps I won't be invited, when the day comes. He has a girlfriend lately, seventeen years old, and he hasn't been ... *interested* in me for a while. So, when I return, I don't want you to think that I ...' She left it there.

Zannis sighed and settled down next to her, in time laying his leg across the backs of her knees and stroking her in a different way. She turned her head so that their faces were close together. 'I get the feeling you're not ready to go to sleep.'

'Not yet.'

11 February. The rains continued. Hanging from a clothes tree in the corner of the office, three coats dripped water onto the floor. When Zannis reached his desk, a note from Saltiel – a name, a telephone number – awaited him. 'This would be the mayor's girlfriend?'

'It would.' Saltiel was not only amused, he was anticipating the performance.

'Hello? Madam Karras?'

'Yes?'

'My name is Zannis, I'm with the Salonika police department.'

'Yes?' The way she said it meant *What could you want with me?*

'I have a favour to ask of you, Madam Karras.'

'What favour?'

'That you refrain, in the future, from shooting at the mayor. Please.'

'*What?*'

'You heard me. We know you did it, or hired somebody to do it, and if I can't be sure you'll never try it again, I'm going to have you arrested.'

'How *dare* you! What did you say your name was?'

'Zannis. Z-a-n-n-i-s.'

'You can't just —'

'I can,' he said, interrupting her. 'The detectives investigated the incident and they know how it came about and so, instead of taking you to jail, I'm telephoning you. It is a *courtesy*, Madam Karras. Please believe me.'

'Really? And where was *courtesy* when I needed it? Some people, I won't mention any names, need to be taught a *lesson*, in courtesy.'

'Madam Karras, I'm looking at your photograph.' He wasn't. 'And I can see that you're an extremely attractive woman. Surely men, many men, are drawn to you. But, Madam Karras, allow me to suggest that the path to romance will be smoother if you don't shoot your lover in the behind.'

Madam Karras cackled. 'Just tell me that bastard didn't have it coming.'

'I can't tell you that. All I can tell you is to leave him alone.'

'Well . . .'

'Please?'

'You're not a bad sort, Zannis. Are you married?'

'With five children. Will you take this call to heart?'

'I'll think about it.'

'No, dear, make a decision. The handcuffs are waiting.'

'Oh all *right*.'

'Thank you. It's the smart thing to do.'

Zannis hung up. Saltiel was laughing to himself, and shaking his head.

12 February. Berlin was glazed with ice that morning, perhaps the worst of the tricks winter played on the Prussian city. At Gestapo headquarters on the Prinz-Albrechtstrasse, Hauptsturmführer Albert Hauser was trying to figure out what to do about Emilia Krebs. His list of names was shrinking: some of the suspects had been arrested, success for Hauser, yet some had disappeared, failure for Hauser. That couldn't continue, or he really would wind up in Poland, the Hell of German security

cosmology. But he couldn't touch her. He worked, alas, for a moron, there was no other way to put it. The joke about Nazi racial theory said that the ideal superman of the master race would be as blond as Hitler, as lean as Göring and as tall as Goebbels. But the joke was only a joke, and his superior, an SS major, was there because he was truly blond, tall and lean. And a moron. He didn't think like a policeman, he thought like a Nazi: politics, ideology, was, to him, everything. And in that ideology rank meant power, and power ruled supreme.

Hauser had gone to see him, to discuss the Krebs case, but the meeting hadn't lasted long. 'This man Krebs is a Wehrmacht colonel!' he'd thundered. 'Do you wish to see me crushed?'

Hauser wished precisely that, but there was no hope any time soon. Still, brave fellow, he wondered if he might not have the most private, the most genial, the most *diffident* conversation with Emilia Krebs. Where? Certainly not in his office. Neutral ground? Not bad, but impossible. To the dinners and parties of her social circle, Hauser was not invited. And they did not yet have an agent inside her circle who could find a way to get him there. Down the hall, another Gestapo officer was working on the recruitment of a weak and venal member of the group – they were everywhere, but one had to fish them out – as an informant, but he wasn't yet theirs. So, no parties. That left the Krebs home, in Dahlem.

Alarm bells went off in Hauser's mind. 'Darling, the Gestapo came to see me today.' What? To my house? To my *home*? The home of the important Colonel Krebs? Of the Wehrmacht? An organization that didn't care for the Nazis and loathed the Gestapo. No, a simple telephone call from Krebs, going upward into the lofty heaven of the General Staff, and Hauser would be shooting Poles until they shot him. Those people were crazy, there was absolutely no dealing with them. So, better not to offend Colonel Krebs.

However . . .

. . . if the Krebs woman was involved with an escape operation, and Hauser pretty much knew she was, would the husband not be aware of it? And, Hauser reasoned, if he was, would his first instinct not be to protect her? How would he do that? By calling attention to the fact that the Gestapo considered her a 'person of interest'? Or, maybe, by hushing the whole thing up? And how would he do *that*? By telling her to end it. Stop what you're doing, or our whole lives will come crashing down around us.

Hauser, in the midst of speculation, usually looked out of the window, but that morning the glass was coated with frost and he found himself staring instead at the photograph of his father, the moustached Düsseldorf policeman, that stood on his desk. *So, Papa, what is the safest way for Albert?* Papa knew. *The list!* True. What mattered was the list. It couldn't keep shrinking because, if it did, so much for Hauser. Safer, in the long run, to have a chat with the Krebs woman.

Who should he be? He would dress a little for the country, a hand-knitted sweater under a jacket with leather buttons. A pipe? He'd never smoked a pipe in his life but how hard could it be to learn? *No, Albert!* A policeman with a Prussian haircut, sheared close on the sides – smoking a *pipe*? And then, clumsy with the thing, he'd probably burn a hole in the colonel's carpet.

And the colonel wouldn't like that. But, on the other hand, he couldn't dislike what he didn't know about. In fact, Hauser thought, if the meeting was properly managed there was at least a chance that she wouldn't tell him! Simply stop what she was doing in order to protect her husband. And oh how perfect that would be.

Therefore, no pipe.

But maybe spectacles.

Hauser walked down two flights of stairs to a department where objects of disguise were available. Not much used, this department. True men of the Gestapo did not deign to disguise themselves, they showed up in pairs or threes and hammered on the door. Here is the state!

But not always. The clerk who maintained the department

found him a pair of steel-framed spectacles with clear lenses. Hauser looked in the mirror: yes, here was a softer, more reflective version of himself. *Frau Krebs, I am Hauptsturmführer – no, I am Herr Hauser. Please pardon the intrusion. I won't keep you long.*

In Salonika, in the morning papers and on the radio, the news was like a drum, a marching drum, a war drum. On the tenth of February, Britain severed diplomatic ties with Roumania, because the government had allowed Germany to concentrate numerous divisions of the Wehrmacht, munitions and fuel, within its borders. And this, according to the British, constituted an expeditionary force.

Then, on the fifteenth of February, it was reported that Hitler met with certain Yugoslav heads of ministries at his alpine retreat in Berchtesgaden, known as the Eagle's Nest. Accompanied by a photograph, of course. Here was the eagle himself, surrounded by snowy peaks, shaking hands with a Yugoslav minister. Note the position of the minister's head – is he bowing? Or has he simply inclined his head? And what, please, was the difference? The ministers had been informed that their country would have to comply with certain provisions of the Axis pact, whether they signed it or not. To wit: increased economic cooperation with Germany – *sell us what we want, we'll name the price* – permission for the transit of German men and arms through Yugoslavia, and passivity in the event of a German occupation of Bulgaria.

What wasn't in the newspapers: BULGARIA CALLS FOR GENERAL MOBILIZATION! And what, on the sixteenth of February, was: BULGARIA SIGNS NON-AGGRESSION PACT WITH TURKEY! Over his morning coffee, Zannis read a quote from the agreement about the two countries' intention 'to continue their policy of confidence towards each other, which policy assures the security of peace and quiet in the Balkans in a most difficult moment, through mutual consideration of their security.' Which meant: When Bulgaria invades Greece, Turkey will not join the fighting. *If* Bulgaria invades Greece? The

Salonika journalist didn't think so. Neither did Zannis. And the phrase 'peace and quiet in the Balkans' did not originate with either Bulgarian or Turkish diplomats, it was Hitler's phrase.

So, now everybody knew.

Three days later, on the nineteenth of February, some time after ten in the evening, Costa Zannis lay stretched out on his bed, trying not to think about Demetria. A restless reader, he'd put Inspector Maigret aside in favour of a novel by the Greek writer Kostykas, a lurid tale of love and murder on one of the islands south of the coast. A yacht anchors off a fishing village, an English aristocrat falls in love with a local fisherman. So, who killed Lady Edwina? He didn't care. Staring blankly at the page, he returned to the night at the hotel, watching Demetria as she slept, the goddess at rest, sleep having returned her face to the composure he'd seen in the back seat of the Rolls-Royce. But she wasn't at all as he'd thought – now he knew her for an avid and eager lover, without any inhibitions whatsoever. In the past, he'd viewed fellatio as a kind of favour, performed when a woman liked a man to the extent that she would do it to please him. Hah! Not true. He had been simultaneously excited and astonished as he'd watched her, as she'd raised her eyes, pausing for an instant, to meet his. Such recollections were not conducive to reading, and he was about to put the book aside when the telephone rang. It was her!

'Hello,' he said, his voice reaching for tenderness in a single word.

'Costa . . . ?'

Not her. Some other woman.

'It's me, Roxanne.'

Roxanne? Why now? The ballet school, the love affair, the sudden departure on a small plane – it seemed a long time ago, and over forever, but apparently not. 'Why are you calling?'

'I must speak with you, Costa. Please don't hang up.'

'Where are you?'

'Nearby. I can be at your apartment in a few minutes.'

'Well . . .' How to say no?

'We can't talk on the telephone. What I have to say is, private.' She meant *secret*. 'See you right away,' she said, and hung up.

Now what? But, in a general way, he knew. The newspaper stories told the tale: when the political tides shifted, certain deep-water creatures swam to the surface.

A few minutes later he heard a car. A black sedan, he saw out of the window, which rolled to a stop in front of his building, there was barely room for it in Santaroza Lane. As the car's headlights went dark, a figure emerged from the passenger seat. Zannis headed for the stairs, Melissa watching him, to answer the knock at the street door.

Only a few months since he'd seen her, but she was not the same. Well dressed, as usual, with a horsewoman's lean body and weathered skin, but had there always been so many grey strands in her hair? And now her eyes were shadowed with fatigue. As they faced each other in the doorway, she offered him a forced smile and touched his arm with a gloved hand. Over her shoulder, he could see that the driver of the sedan had his face turned away.

In the apartment, she kept her raincoat on as they sat at the kitchen table. Zannis lit a cigarette and said, 'Would you like something to drink?'

'No, thanks. You're looking well.'

'So are you.'

'Forgive the sudden visit, will you?'

'Doesn't matter. I think I ought to let you know right away that I won't tell you any more about what went on in Paris than I told Escovil. I don't betray friends; it's that simple.'

'We don't care, not now we don't; you can keep your secrets. Have you been reading the newspapers?'

He nodded.

'The situation is worse than what's written. Bulgaria will sign the pact, some time in the next two weeks. They've asked

Moscow for help but, to turn the Bulgarian expression around, Uncle Ivan will *not* be coming up the river. Not this time, he won't. And, when that's done, Yugoslavia is next. The regent, Prince Paul, doesn't care; he stays in Florence and collects art. The real power is in the hands of the premier, Cvetkovic, who is sympathetic to the Nazis, and he will also sign. Then it's your turn.'

'Not much we can do about it,' Zannis said.

'Unless . . .'

'Unless?'

She hesitated, choosing her words carefully. 'There is some reason to hope there will be a coup d'état in Belgrade.'

Zannis was startled and he showed it – such a possibility had never occurred to him.

'A last chance to stop Hitler in the Balkans,' she said.

'Will it stop him?'

'He may not want to fight the Serbs – most of Croatia will side with Hitler, their way out of the Yugoslav state.'

Zannis wanted to believe it. 'The Serbs fight hard.'

'Yes. And Hitler knows it. In the Great War, German armies tore Serbia to pieces; people on the street in Belgrade were wearing window curtains, because the German soldiers stole *everything*. The Serbs remember – they remember who hurts them. So, for the Wehrmacht, it's a trap.'

'And Greece?'

'I don't know. But if Hitler doesn't want war in the Balkans, and the Greek army withdraws from Albania . . .'

From Zannis, a grim smile. 'You don't understand us.'

'We do try,' she said, very British in the way she put it. 'We understand this much, anyway, Greeks don't quit. Which is why I'm here, because the same spirit might lead you to help us, in Belgrade.'

'Us,' Zannis said. 'So then, *your* operation.'

She shook her head. 'It doesn't work like that, but we can help. And, if the Serbs mean to do it, we *must* help.'

'And I'm to be part of this?'

'Yes.'

Zannis crushed his cigarette out in the ashtray. 'Why me? How the hell did I ever become so ... desirable?'

'You were always desirable, dear.' She smiled briefly, a real one this time. Then it vanished. 'But you are desirable in other ways. You can be depended on, for one, and you have real courage, for another.'

'Why are *you* here, Roxanne? I mean you, and not Francis Escovil?'

'He does the best he can but he's an amateur. I'm a professional.'

'For a long time?'

'Yes. Forever, really.'

Zannis sighed. There was no way to refuse. 'Well then, since you're a professional, perhaps you could be more specific.'

'We know you have friends in the Yugoslav police, and we will need to control certain elements in the army General Staff, not for long, forty-eight hours, but they can't be allowed to get in our way.'

Zannis was puzzled. 'Isn't it always the army that stages the coup?'

'Air force.' She paused, then said, 'There are more particulars, names and so forth, but first make certain of your friends, then contact Escovil and you'll be told the rest. You won't know the exact day, so you'll have to move quickly when we're ready.' She looked at her watch, then, as she stood, she raised a small leather shoulder bag from her lap and Zannis saw that it sagged, as though it carried something heavy. What was in there? A gun? 'I have to say good night now,' she said. 'My evening continues.'

He walked her as far as the top of the stairway. 'Tell me one more thing,' he said. 'When you came to Salonika, was it me you were after? A target? A recruit? It doesn't matter now, you can tell me, I won't be angry.'

She stopped, two steps below him, and said, 'No, what I told you at the airfield was the truth – I was in Salonika for something else. Then I met you and what happened, happened.' She stayed where she was, and when at last she spoke her voice was barely audible and her eyes were cast down. 'I was in love with you.'

As she hurried down the stairs, Zannis returned to his kitchen and lit another cigarette. In the street below, an engine started, lights went on and the sedan drove away.

1 March. Zannis and Saltiel went to lunch at Smyrna Betrayed and ate the grilled octopus, which was particularly sweet and succulent that afternoon. Always, a radio played by the cash register at the bar, local music, bouzouki songs, an undercurrent to the noisy lunch crowd. Zannis hardly noticed the radio but then, as the waiter came to take away their plates, he did. Because – first at the bar, next at the nearby tables, finally everywhere in the room – people stopped talking. The restaurant was now dead silent, and the barman reached over and turned up the volume. It was a news broadcast. King Boris of Bulgaria had signed the Axis pact; German troops were moving across the Danube on pontoon bridges constructed during the last week in February. The Wehrmacht was not there as an occupying force, King Boris had stated, because Bulgaria was now an ally of Germany. They were there to assure stability 'elsewhere in the Balkans'. Then the radio station returned to playing music.

But the taverna was not as it had been. Conversation was subdued, and many of the customers signalled for a bill, paid and went out of the door. Some of them hadn't finished their lunch. 'Well, that's that,' Saltiel said.

'When are you leaving, Gabi? Are you, leaving?'

'My wife and I, yes,' Saltiel said. 'Is your offer, of Turkish visas, still possible?'

'It is. What about your kids?'

'My sons talked it over, got their money out of the bank and now they have Spanish citizenship. It was expensive, in the end I had to help, but they did it. So they can go and live in Spain, though they have no idea how they will support their families, or they can remain here, because they believe they'll be safe, as Spanish citizens, if the Germans show up.'

Zannis nodded – that he understood, not that he agreed – and started to speak, but Saltiel raised his hands and said, 'Don't bother, Costa. They've made their decision.'

'I'll go to the legation this afternoon,' Zannis said.

'What about your family?'

'That's next.'

'Let's get out of here,' Saltiel said.

They paid the bill and returned to the Via Egnatia. At the office, Zannis draped his jacket over his chair and prepared to work but then, recalling something he'd meant to do for a while, went back down the five flights of stairs. On the ground floor he passed beneath the staircase to a door that opened onto a small courtyard. Yes, it was as he remembered: six metal drums for the rubbish. Two of them had been in use for a long time and their sides had rusted through in places, so there would be a flow of air, just in case you wanted to burn something.

Late that afternoon, the bell on the teletype rang and, as Zannis, Saltiel and Sibylla turned to watch it, the keys clattered, the yellow paper unrolled and a message appeared. It was from Pavlic, in Zagreb. Zannis had been worrying about him over the last few days because he'd sent Pavlic a teletype – in their coded way requesting a meeting – the morning after Roxanne had said, 'Make sure of your friends,' but there had been no answer. Now Pavlic explained, saying he'd received the previous communication but had been unable to respond until their machine was repaired. However, as he put it:

PER YOUR REQUEST OF 23 FEBRUARY WILL ALERT LOCAL AUTHORITIES TO APPREHEND SUBJECT PANOS AT ARRIVAL NIS RAILWAY STATION 22.05 HOURS ON 4 MARCH

Zannis had only enquired if they could meet, but Pavlic had sensed the import of Zannis's query and set a time for the meeting. Nis was seven hours by rail from Zagreb and four hours from Salonika, but this business had to be done in person.

At six o'clock, on the evening of the first of March, Zannis joined the jostling crowd at a newspaper kiosk and eventually managed to buy an evening edition. In the five hours since he'd heard the report on the taverna radio, the situation had changed: armoured Wehrmacht divisions were said to be moving south, to take up positions on the Greek border. Well, as Saltiel had put it, that was that, and Zannis could no longer postpone telling his family they would have to leave Salonika. Newspaper in hand, he went looking for a taxi.

As the driver wound his way through the old Turkish quarter, past walled courtyards and ancient fountains, Zannis rehearsed what he would say, but there was no way to soften the blow. Still, in the event, it was not as bad as he'd feared. His mother insisted on feeding him, and then he explained what had to be done. The family must go to Alexandria, and go soon. There was a large Greek community in the city and he would give them enough money to secure an apartment in that quarter where, as he put it, 'there are Greek shops and Orthodox churches and our language is spoken everywhere.'

However, he would soon enough be fighting in the mountains of Macedonia, and he would not be able to send them any more money. He didn't say the word *charity* because, at that moment, he couldn't bear to. His mother, silent in the face of new and frightening difficulties, responded with a stoic nod, and Ari, who could not hide what he felt, was close to tears. But his grandmother, whose relatives had fought the Turks for decades, simply walked over to the table where she kept the sewing machine, removed its cloth cover and said, 'As long as we have this, my beloved Constantine, we shall not go hungry.' And then, moved by his grandmother's example, Ari said, 'I will find something, Costa. There's always something. Perhaps they have trams in Alexandria.' Zannis, swept by emotion, looked away and did not answer. When he'd steadied himself, he said, 'I will take you to the Egyptian legation tomorrow, so you will have the proper papers, and then I will buy the steamship tickets. After that, you should probably begin to pack.'

Back at Santaroza Lane, as he stroked Melissa's great, noble head, his voice was gentle. 'Well, my good girl, you will be going on a sea voyage.'

Melissa wagged her tail. *And I love you too.*

There was yet one more soul he cared for, but, once again that day, no letter in his mailbox, and the telephone, no matter how hard he stared at it, was silent.

4 March. Nis was an ancient city, a crossroads on the trade routes that went back to Roman times. A certain darkness in this place – as the Turks had built a White Tower to frighten their subjects in Salonika, here, in the nineteenth century, they had built a tower of skulls, employing as construction material the severed heads of Seribian rebels.

The station buffet was closed, an old woman on her knees was attempting, with brush and bucket, to remove the day's – the month's, the century's – grime from what had once been a floor of tiny white octagonal tiles. Zannis, his train an hour late getting in, found Pavlic sitting on a wooden bench, next to a couple guarding a burlap sack. Pavlic was wearing a suit and tie but was otherwise as Zannis remembered him: brush-cut, sand-coloured hair; sharp crow's-feet at the corners of narrow, watchful eyes. He looked up from his newspaper, then stood and said, 'Let's go somewhere else, I'm getting a little weary of this.' He nodded towards the burlap sack from which, as he gestured, there came a single emphatic cluck.

Seeking privacy, they walked out to the empty platform; no more trains were running that night, some of the people in the crowded station were waiting for the morning departures, others were there because they had nowhere else to go. On the platform, Zannis and Pavlic found a wooden handcart that would serve as a bench. They were, without saying much, pleased to see each other; the closer war came, the more conspiracy was a powerful form of friendship. They chatted for a time – the fugitive Jews coming from Berlin, the Germans in Bulgaria – then Zannis said, 'I've heard that if the Cvetkovic government signs the pact, it may be overthrown.'

'So they say. In every coffee house and bar. "Pretty soon we'll kick those bastards out!" They've been saying it for ten years, maybe more.'

'It's the British, saying it this time.'

Pavlic took a moment to think that over. There had to be a good reason Zannis put him on a train for seven hours, now here it was. 'You mean it might actually happen.'

'I do, and, when it does, if it does, they want me to work with them. And I'm asked to organize a group of police to help. Detectives, I would think,' Zannis said.

'Like me,' Pavlic said.

'Yes.'

'And like my friends in Belgrade.'

'Them too.'

'Which British are we talking about? Diplomats?'

'Spies.'

'I see,' Pavlic said.

Zannis shrugged. 'That's who showed up.'

Pavlic was quiet for a time, then he said, 'I might as well help out, if I can. No matter what I do, things won't stay the same here. If Cvetkovic signs, there's a good chance we'll have a guerrilla war in Serbia. Not in Croatia – the Ustashi have been taking money from Mussolini for years, because they want Croatia to be an independent state, an ally of Rome. But the Serbs won't be governed from Berlin. As soon as Hitler starts to push them around – tries to send the army into Greece, for example – they'll fight. It will start in the cities and spread to the villages. Assassination, bombing, the traditional Black Hand style.'

'And your friends in Belgrade?'

'They're Serbs. They're going to be caught up in whatever happens, but if we get rid of Cvetkovic and his cronies, we might get a few months of peace. What passes for it these days, anyhow – threats, ultimatums, the occasional murder. And, you know, Costa, with *time* anything can happen. America joins the war, Germany invades Russia, Hitler is assassinated, or who knows what. They'll take the gamble, my friends will, I think, but I've got to tell them what they're supposed to do.'

'Our job is to make sure that certain elements of the General Staff are kept quiet. Not for long, forty-eight hours.'

'Why would they resist?'

'Cvetkovic allies? Maybe reached by German money? You can't be sure, down here, about motives. And all it takes, like Sarajevo in nineteen-fourteen, is one determined man with a pistol.'

'How much time do I have?'

'It could happen any day now. In a way, it's up to Cvetkovic . . . he might decide not to sign.'

'He will, Costa. Under pressure, he'll give in.' Pavlic looked at his watch, got down from the cart and brushed off the seat of his trousers. 'I think we'd better find somewhere we can get rooms for the night, before they lock the hotels. We'll talk on the way.'

When he reached Salonika, the following afternoon, Zannis stopped by the Pension Bastasini and told Escovil that his friends in Belgrade would agree to join the operation. Escovil was clearly relieved; one of many things he had to do was now accomplished. Maybe too many things, Zannis thought – he could smell alcohol on Escovil's breath. 'We'll be in contact,' he told Zannis. What they had to do now was wait.

Back in his office, Zannis made a telephone call to Vangelis, then walked over to see him.

'You may as well close the door,' Vangelis said, a St Vangelis glint in his eye. He was very much a ruler of the civic kingdom that afternoon, in his splendid office with a view of the harbour: his shirt crisp and white, his tie made of gold silk, his suit perfectly tailored. 'Thank you for taking care of our esteemed mayor,' he said. 'And, by the way, the lovebirds are back together, all is forgiven.' This was accompanied by a mischievous flick of the eyebrows. 'So then, what's going on with you?'

'I will have to go away for a few days, Commissioner, some time soon, but I don't know exactly when.'

'Again,' Vangelis said.

Zannis nodded. 'Yes, sir,' he said, apology in his voice. 'Again.'

Vangelis frowned. 'Saltiel will take care of the office?'

'He will.'

'What are you doing, Costa? Does your escape line need tending?'

'No, sir, this time it's . . . a British operation.'

Vangelis shook his head: *what's the world coming to?* 'So now I've got a secret service running on the Via Egnatia, is that it?' But he was only acting his part, stern commissioner, and suddenly he tired of it – perhaps he slumped a little, behind his grand desk – because he knew precisely what the world was coming to. 'Oh fuck it all, Costa, you better do whatever you want, and you better do it quickly.'

'Thank you, sir.'

'It's probably what you should be doing, that sort of thing, though I don't like admitting it. What's the matter with me?'

'Nothing, sir.'

'I wish you were right, but you're not. Anyhow, you should probably go back to work, as long as you can, and I'll just say farewell.'

The word puzzled Zannis who, having been dismissed, rose slowly from his chair.

'What I mean to say, is, well, may God watch over you, Costa.'

'Over us all, sir.'

'Yes, of course,' Vangelis said.

Somebody was certainly watching over something. Zannis eagerly checked his mailbox when he got home, but what he was looking for wasn't there. Instead, an official letter from the Royal Hellenic Army, informing Lieutenant Zannis, Constantine, that he was as of this date relieved of active duty in the event of a call-up of reserve units, by reason of 'medical condition'. Signed by a colonel. What was this? Zannis read it again. Not, he thought, an error. Rather, it was as though he'd been moved a square on an invisible board by an unseen hand, because he had no medical condition. On the seventh of March, sixty-thousand British Commonwealth troops, mostly Australian and New Zealand divisions, disembarked from troop ships at various Greek ports. In Salonika, they were welcomed with flowers and cheers. Help had arrived. And, Zannis thought as the troops marched along the corniche, any nation that would do that might do all sorts of extraordinary things.

Finally, she telephoned.

The call came to the office, late in the afternoon. 'I'm at a friend's house, in Athens,' she said. To Zannis she sounded defeated, weary and sad.

'I was wondering,' Zannis said. 'What happened to you.'

'I was afraid of that. Maybe you thought I ... didn't care.'

'No. Well, not really.'

'I'm miserable,' she said.

'Demetria?'

'Yes?'

'Get on a train. Tonight. Call, and I'll be waiting at the station.'

'I *want* to ...'

'Well then?'

236

'I don't know what to do.' Now she was crying.

'I love you, Demetria. I think about you, I want you with me. Is there something you want me to say? Promise? *Anything.*'

'No! It's beautiful . . . what you say.'

'And so?'

Now she didn't speak.

'Please, don't cry.'

'I can't help it.' She snuffled. 'Forgive me.'

He paused – was there a worse time to say what now had to be said? 'There is something I have to tell you.'

'What?' He'd frightened her.

'I'll be going away, soon, I don't know when, and not for long. But I'll leave a key with the neighbour downstairs, I'll tell her to expect you.'

'Where are you going?'

'It's for work. A few days, only.'

For a time she was quiet, then she said, in a different voice. 'I understand, you can't say. But, what if you don't come back?'

'I will, don't worry about that.'

'Do you have a pencil?'

'Yes.'

'My friend's number is Athens, 34–412. Her name is Theodora. Telephone her when you return.'

'3, 4? 4, 1, 2?'

'Yes. You don't know when you're leaving?'

'Days, maybe a week, maybe more. It doesn't matter.'

'It doesn't? What if the war comes?'

Then you will be safe only with Vasilou. On his white ship. Finally, resignation in his voice, he said, 'I don't know.'

She sighed. 'Nobody knows. All they do is talk.' She regretted having asked him a question he couldn't answer, so now they would be strong together, not like the people who just talked.

'You won't come here now?'

'Telephone when you return,' she said firmly. 'Then I'll be ready. I'll be waiting.'

237

He said he would. He told her again that he loved her, and they hung up.

Zannis looked around the office, Saltiel and Sibylla had their heads down, engrossed in their work.

On 13 March, Hitler again demanded that Yugoslavia sign the Axis pact. They didn't say no, they said, *We're thinking about it*, the 'no' of diplomacy. Which might have worked, but for the weather. Spring, the war-fighting season in Europe, was just beginning: once the fields were planted, the men of the country-side would take up their weapons, as they had since the Middle Ages. The March chill receded, the rain in Central Europe and the Balkans was a light rain, a spring rain, a welcome rain. Winter was over, now it was time for action, no more speeches, no more negotiation – certain difficult matters had to be settled, once and for all. Hitler loved that phrase, 'once and for all', and so, on the nineteenth of March, he issued an ultimatum. Do what I say, or you will be bombed and invaded. Costa Zannis paced his bedroom, smoked too much, found it hard to sleep. Yes, he had papers and steamship tickets for his family, but the earliest sailing he'd been able to reserve was on 30 March. Eleven days in the future. Would Hitler wait?

On the afternoon of the twentieth, he stood on the railway platform where passengers were boarding the express to Istanbul and said goodbye to Gabi Saltiel and his wife. As the train rolled out of the station, Zannis watched it go by until the last carriage disappeared in the distance. He wasn't alone, there was a line of people, all up and down the platform, who waited until the train was gone.

24 March. Belgrade was quiet that night, people stayed at home, or spent long hours in the coffee houses. In the larger towns, special Serbian police had been assigned to ensure peace and quiet in the streets. The newspaper *Politika*, the most esteemed journal in the Balkans, and read by diplomats all across Europe,

had that morning been forced to print an editorial supporting Yugoslavia's signature on the Axis pact. Just before midnight, two armoured cars brought Premier Cvetkovic and his foreign minister to Topchidersko railway station so they could board a train to Vienna. There they would sign.

Costa Zannis had arrived in Belgrade that same evening, met by Pavlic and taken to the Hotel Majestic on the Knez Mihailova, the main shopping street in the city. As they drove down the avenue, Zannis saw a huge swastika flag hung from the balcony of a five-storey office building. 'What's *that*?' he said.

'The office of the German Travel Bureau,' Pavlic said. 'Getting an early start on the celebration.'

In the Majestic, Zannis stowed a small valise in his room and went downstairs to the hotel bar. There, Pavlic introduced him to a bulky pale-haired Serb called Vlatko – from the spread of his shoulders and neck, every inch a cop. 'He's from the homicide office,' Pavlic said, as the two men shook hands. 'And he speaks German.'

They ordered slivovitz, then Vlatko said, 'It's quiet here, but that's just on the surface. The people are in shock.'

'It won't last,' Pavlic said.

'No, big trouble tomorrow.' With this he grinned. He took, Zannis realized, great pleasure, a patriot's pleasure, from the anticipation of big trouble.

Both Pavlic and Vlatko, taking turns, told Zannis the news of the day: a terrific fist fight in the bar of Belgrade's best hotel, the Srbski Kralj, King of Serbia. Two American foreign correspondents and an Italian woman, their translator, on one side, five Wehrmacht officers – from the German legation – on the other. The Americans ordered whiskies, the Germans ordered schnapps; the Germans demanded to be served first, the barman hesitated. Next, savage insults, tables turned over, broken dishes. The Italian woman had thrown a drink in a German's face, he hit her on the head, then the *New York Times* reporter, a good-sized Texan, had fought two of the Germans. 'Knocked them down,' Vlatko said, ramming a huge fist into a meaty palm for emphasis. 'Out *cold*. On the floor.' Once again, he grinned.

'And broke his hand,' Pavlic said.

'Both hands, I heard.'

'One hand,' Pavlic said. 'I hope we can do without that.'

Vlatko shrugged. 'We shall see.'

From his inside pocket, Zannis brought out the sheet of paper Escovil had given him: a typed list of twenty-seven names. He laid it on the table and smoothed out the folds with his hands. 'Here it is,' he said. 'We have a day to find out the addresses.'

Pavlic and Vlatko put their heads together over the list. Vlatko said, 'Who are these people? Military, some of them, I can see that.'

'Not people who get their names in the newspapers,' Zannis said.

'Traitors,' Vlatko said.

'Possible troublemakers, anyhow,' Zannis answered.

'Well, we'll find them.'

'Tomorrow night,' Zannis said. 'When they're at home. We don't want to arrest them at staff headquarters, we don't want gun battles.'

'No, I guess not,' Vlatko said, bringing forward, with some effort, the sensible side of his nature. 'Pavlic and I have enlisted fifteen detectives, so we'll work in groups of three – that should be sufficient. Do these people,' he paused, then said, 'form a conspiracy?'

Zannis didn't think so. 'I doubt it,' he said. 'The wives won't warn their husbands' friends, if that's what you're thinking.'

'Would be best to start at seven – before people go out to restaurants or whatever it is they do.'

'They won't go out tomorrow night,' Pavlic said. 'They'll stay home with the radio on.'

'We can't all come here,' Zannis said. 'Vlatko, can you have them meet at six? You'll have to distribute the names this afternoon, so we'll divide up the names now and make new lists.'

'Where do we take them?'

'There's a holding cell,' Pavlic said, 'at the prefecture near the foreign legations, on Milosha Velikog. They're going to move their prisoners – to make room for ours.'

'Stack them one on the other,' Vlatko said. 'Who cares?'

'These people might be needed later,' Zannis said. 'We want them out of circulation for a day and a half – for them an anecdote, not a nightmare. We'd put them in a spa, if we could.'

Vlatko looked at him. 'You're very kind, in Salonika.'

'As long as it works, we are. If it doesn't, then we do it the other way.'

'Really? I guess we think differently, up here.'

A group of men came laughing into the bar, calling for slivovitz. They wore – Pavlic explained in an undertone – the black fur hats of the Chetniks, the ancient Serbian resistance movement, with skull and crossbones insignia on the front.

'They've come in from the villages,' Pavlic said. 'They're gathering.'

Back upstairs, Zannis was restless. The street below his window was deserted, the city quiet. No, not quiet, silent, and somehow sinister. Thousands of conversations in darkened rooms, he thought; they could not be heard but they could be felt, as though anger had its own special energy. And this, despite his better, too-well-learned instincts, he found exciting.

At seven the following morning, the telephone rang in his room, no name, no greeting, just an upper-class British voice, clipped and determined.

'Have you everything you need?'

'I do.'

'Tomorrow's the day. I know you'll do your best.'

'Count on it,' Zannis said, hoping his English was proper.

'That's the spirit.'

No way to go back to sleep. He dressed, holstered his Walther and went downstairs for coffee. When he returned, an envelope had been slid beneath his door: a local phone number, and a few words directing him to maintain contact, using street call boxes or telephones in bars, throughout the following day. Pavlic was going to pick him up at ten and drive him around the city. Until then, he didn't know what to do with himself, so he sat in a chair.

Outside, the people of the city began their day by breaking glass. Big plate-glass windows, from the sound of it, broken, then shattering on the pavement. Accompanied by a chant: *Bolje rat, nego pakt!* This much Serbo-Croatian he could understand: *Better war than the pact!* Outside, more glass came crashing down. He could see nothing from his room but, going out into the hall, he found a window at the end of the corridor. Down in the street, students were chanting and breaking shop windows. As cars drove by, the drivers honked furiously, waved and chanted along with the students: '*Bolje rat, nego pakt!*' One of them stopped long enough to tear up a copy of *Politika* and hurl it into the gutter.

At nine-fifty, Pavlic's car rolled to the kerb in front of the Majestic. Vlatko was sitting in the passenger seat so Zannis climbed in the back where, on the seat beside him, he discovered a pump shotgun with its barrel and stock sawn off to a few inches. As Pavlic drove away, a group of students ran past, waving a Serbian flag. 'Brewing up nicely, isn't it,' Pavlic said.

Vlatko was wearing a hat this morning, with the brim bent down over his eyes, and looked, to Zannis, like a movie gangster. He turned halfway round, rested his elbow on top of the seat and said, 'They're out on the streets, in towns all over Serbia and Montenegro, even Bosnia. We've had calls from the local police.'

'They're trying to stop it?'

From Vlatko, a wolf's smile. 'Are you kidding?'

'Rumours everywhere,' Pavlic said. 'Hermann Göring assassinated, mutinies in Bulgarian army units, even a ghost − a Serbian hero of the past appeared at Kalemegdan fortress.'

'True!' Vlatko shouted.

'Well I'll tell you what *is* true,' Pavlic said. 'At least I think it is. Prince Peter, Prince Paul's seventeen-year-old cousin, has supposedly returned from exile. Which means he'll be crowned as king, and the regency is over, which is what the royalists have wanted for years, and not just them.'

Zannis liked especially the ghost; whoever was spreading the rumours knew what he was doing. Ten minutes later, Vlatko said, disgust in his voice, 'Look at that, will you? Never seen *that* in Belgrade.' He meant two SS officers in their black uniforms, strolling up the street in the centre of the pavement. As Zannis watched, two men coming from the opposite direction had to swing wide to avoid them, because they weren't moving for anybody. Pavlic took his foot off the accelerator and the car slowed down as they all stared at the SS men, who decided not to notice them.

They drove around for an hour, locating the addresses that made up their share of the list. Two of the men lived in the same apartment building, two others had villas in the wealthy district north of the city, by the Danube – in Serbia called the Duna. Heading for the prefecture with the holding cell, they drove up the avenue past the foreign legations. The Italian, Bulgarian and Hungarian legations, in honour of the newly signed pact, were all flying the red-and-black swastika flag. 'Does that do to you what it does to me?' Pavlic said.

'It does,' Zannis said.

Vlatko stared out of the side window. 'Wait until tomorrow, you bastards.'

As they neared the prefecture, Zannis said, 'If Prince Peter becomes king, who will run the government?'

'Whoever he is,' Vlatko said, 'he'd better be a war leader.'

Zannis, hoping against hope, said, 'You don't think Hitler will accept a new government? A neutral government?'

Vlatko shook his head and said to Pavlic, 'A real dreamer, your friend from Salonika.'

At the prefecture, the detectives had been listening to the radio and told Vlatko and Pavlic the news.

'What's happened?' Zannis said.

'It's what hasn't happened that's got them excited,' Pavlic said. 'Cvetkovic was supposed to give a speech at ten, but it was delayed until noon. Now it's been delayed again. Until six this evening.'

'When it will be cancelled,' Vlatko said.

'Why do you think so?' Zannis said.

'I know. In my Serbian bones, I know it will be cancelled.'

And, at six that evening, it was.

7.22 p.m. A warm and breezy night, spring in the air. Pavlic pulled up in front of a villa; the lights were on, a well-polished Vauxhall sedan parked in the street. 'They're home,' Pavlic said.

'You don't want this, do you?' Zannis said, nodding towards the shotgun.

'No, leave it. It won't be necessary.'

There was no doorbell to be seen, so Vlatko knocked on the door. They waited, but nobody appeared, so he knocked again. Nothing. Now he hammered on the door and, twenty seconds later, it flew open.

To reveal one of the largest men Zannis had ever seen. He towered above them, broad and thick, a handsome man with blond hair gone grey and murder in his eye. He wore a silk dressing gown over pyjamas – perhaps hurriedly donned because half the collar was turned under – and his face was flushed pink. As he gazed down at them, a woman's voice, a very angry voice, yelled from upstairs. The giant ignored her and said, 'Who the hell are you?'

'General Kabyla?' Pavlic said.

'Yes. So?'

Again the voice from upstairs. Kabyla shouted something and the voice stopped.

'We have orders to take you to the prefecture,' Pavlic said.

Zannis didn't get all of it but followed as best he could.

'From who?'

'Orders.'

'Fuck you,' said the general. 'I'm busy.'

Vlatko drew an automatic pistol and held it at his side. 'Turn around,' he said, producing a pair of handcuffs from his jacket pocket.

'I'm under arrest? Me?'

'Call it what you like,' Pavlic said, no longer patient.

As the general turned around and extended his hands, he said, 'I hope you know what you're doing.'

In answer Vlatko snapped the handcuffs closed, took the general by the elbow and guided him towards the door. Where he stopped, then shouted over his shoulder so his voice would carry upstairs, 'Stay right there, my duckling, I'll be back in twenty minutes.'

At the prefecture, there were already three men behind bars. Two of them, disconsolate, sat slumped on a bench suspended from the wall by chains. A third was wearing most of a formal outfit – the white shirt, black bow tie, cummerbund and trousers with braces, but no jacket. He was a stiff, compact man with a pencil moustache and he stopped pacing the cell when a police-man slid the grilled door open. As Vlatko unshackled the general, the man in evening wear took a few steps towards them and said, 'We'll find out who you are, you know, and we will settle with you.'

Vlatko shoved the general into the cell, then took a step towards the man who'd threatened him but Pavlic grabbed his arm. 'Forget it,' he said.

The man in evening wear glowered at them. 'You can bet we won't.'

'Say another word and we'll throw you in the fucking river,' Vlatko said.

The man turned and walked away, joining the other two on the bench.

★

By ten-thirty they were sitting in the bar at the Majestic, having rounded up the other three men on their list, stowing all three in the back of the car, where one of them had to sit on another's lap to make room for Zannis. When the man complained, his dignity offended, Vlatko offered to put him in the boot and he shut up. On the way to the prefecture the overloaded car crawled along the Milosha Velikog, where Pavlic had to stop twice, tyres squealing, when armoured cars came roaring out of side streets and cut them off.

Throughout the next few hours, until well after midnight, detectives showed up at the bar to report on the evening's work, while Zannis and Pavlic kept score on the master list. Around one in the morning it was over, they had twenty-two of the twenty-seven men in the holding cell at the prefecture. Two of the named subjects didn't exist, according to the detectives – no trace in police or city records of their names. A third had escaped, having run out of a back door and, as the story was told, 'simply vanished, he's hiding out there somewhere but we hunted for an hour and couldn't find him.' A fourth was said, by a woman living at the house, to have been in Vienna for two years, and a search had revealed nothing – no men's clothing. The last wasn't at home. The detectives had broken into his apartment and looked for him, but he wasn't there. The neighbours shrugged, they didn't know anything. One of the detectives had remained, in case he came home, and would stay until the morning.

There had, of course, been a few problems. One of the subjects, having gone for a pistol in a desk drawer, had been knocked senseless. Several bribes had been offered, and there'd been a number of arguments and threats. One of the detectives had been bitten by a dog, another had been scratched on the face. 'By his woman,' the detective said, 'so we arrested her, and now she's in with the rest of them.' On two occasions, Pavlic was asked, 'What will become of these people?'

'According to the plan, they are to be released in a day or so,' Pavlic said, and left it at that.

Many of the detectives stayed at the bar; this was an important night in the national history and they wanted to savour their part in it. Zannis encouraged them to eat and drink whatever they liked – the hotel kitchen produced roast chickens, the slivovitz flowed freely – as the money provided for the operation would easily cover the bill. At two in the morning, while the celebration raged around him, Zannis used the telephone at the bar and called the number he'd been given. A woman's voice answered on the first ring. 'Yes? Who's speaking?' Her voice had a foreign accent but Zannis couldn't place it.

'This is Zannis. We have twenty-two of twenty-seven. Locked up in prefecture.'

'Names, please.'

Zannis worked his way down the list.

'Wait,' she broke in. 'You say Szemmer doesn't exist?'

'No record. He is Serbian?' Zannis had wondered about the name.

'A Slovene. And he does exist. He is very dangerous.'

'They couldn't find him. You know where to look, I'll go myself.'

'No. Captain Franko Szemmer, that's all we know.'

'Maybe, an office?'

'Where are you?'

'The bar, at the Hotel Majestic.'

'If I can find something, you'll be contacted.'

After the telephone call, Zannis decided to go outside for a time, have a smoke, look at the stars, try to calm down. The front door was locked but the bolt turned easily and Zannis stepped out onto the pavement.

Half a block away, up at the cross street, somebody else had the same idea, on a tense night in Belgrade, and Zannis saw the red dot of a cigarette. There *was* one difference, between Zannis and his fellow star-gazer, the latter was sitting on the turret of a tank, its long gun pointing down the Knez Mihailova.

Zannis finished his cigarette and returned to the bar. 'Maybe bad news,' he said. 'There's a tank out there.'

Pavlic swore, a nearby detective noticed the exchange and asked if something had gone wrong. Pavlic told him. 'It could be,' he said, 'that Cvetkovic has called out the army.'

Very quickly, the word spread. 'If that's true,' one of the detectives said, 'we're in for it.' He rose, went outside to see for himself, then came back looking more than worried. He spoke rapidly, Pavlic telling Zannis what he'd said. 'I think we'd better find the back door.' As most of the detectives left, a heavy engine went rumbling past the hotel and the floor trembled. Zannis went to the door, then said, 'Another one. Now they've got the street blocked off.'

Vlatko stood up, finished his drink and said, 'I'm going to find out what's going on.' A few minutes later he returned. 'They won't talk to me,' he said. 'Just told me not to ask questions.'

Zannis called the telephone number. When the woman answered, he said, 'There are tanks here, blocking Knez Mihailova.'

'I will see,' said the woman, took the telephone number, and hung up.

Out in the lobby of the hotel, by the overstuffed chairs and potted rubber trees, a large Philco radio stood on a table. Pavlic turned it on and searched for a station, but all he got was a low, buzzing drone.

Zannis stayed up until four-fifteen, waiting by the telephone, but it didn't ring. *The hell with it,* he thought, and decided to go to bed. The faithful Vlatko, the last of the Serbian detectives in the bar, wished him a good night, and headed for a kitchen door that led to a back alley.

★

248

26 March. 7.30 a.m. Zannis had taken off his shoes, set his glasses and Walther on the night table, and dozed. The roar of engines and rattle of tank treads woke him again and again, and finally he just gave up. He wouldn't desert his post, but if the army had been called out that was the end of the coup d'état, and he'd have to slip away somehow and make his way back to Salonika. Soon enough, somebody would discover the Cvetkovic loyalists at the prefecture and then, he hadn't a doubt in the world, they would enlist their own thugs and come looking for him. So, no trains. Perhaps, he thought, he could steal a car. He would, at least, propose the idea to Pavlic, whose problem was severely worse than his own; he might well have to leave the country. *Skata!* Well, they had tried, and now he would have company on the run. Where to go? East to Bulgaria was closer than south to Greece, but he well remembered the swastika flag flown by the Bulgarian legation. Would Lazareff help them? Maybe. Maybe not. Maybe, more than wouldn't, couldn't.

He walked down the corridor and knocked on Pavlic's door. Pavlic answered immediately, wearing only his underwear, and holding his own Walther PPK by his side. 'Oh, it's you,' he said. 'Well, good morning. Any news?'

'No. We'll have to run for it, I'm afraid. Marko, I—' He'd started to apologize, but Pavlic waved him off.

'Don't bother. I knew what I was getting into. Let's try to find out what's going on, at least, before we take off.'

He waited while Pavlic shaved – very much his own inclination at difficult moments. If you were going to face danger, even death, better to shave. After Pavlic got dressed, they went downstairs together and found the lobby deserted; no guests, no clerk, eerie silence. Pavlic unlocked the hotel door and they took a walk up the street. The tank crews were sitting on their machines, waiting for orders, content to relax while they had the opportunity.

Pavlic talked to the soldiers, his Serbo-Croatian much too fast for Zannis to follow. Brave sonofabitch, he really laid into them.

Finally the sergeant commander got tired of him, sauntered off and returned with an officer. Pavlic's tone now altered – serious and straightforward, as though saying, come now, we're fellow countrymen, you shouldn't keep me in the dark. But, no luck. The officer spoke briefly, then walked away, back towards a wall of sandbags stacked across a doorway – the barrel of a machine gun poking out of a space that left it room to traverse.

'Well, what did he say?'

Pavlic's face was alight. More than a smile – the cat had not only eaten the canary, he'd drunk up a jug of cream and got laid into the bargain. So, there was a joke all right, but Pavlic wasn't ready to share it. 'He didn't say much, only that it would all be cleared up as the day went on.'

Zannis was puzzled; one certain detail had provoked his curiosity. 'Tell me,' he said. 'Why was the officer wearing a blue uniform?'

Pavlic jerked his head back towards the hotel and, as they began to walk, he put an arm around Zannis's shoulders. 'He wore a blue uniform, my friend, because he is in the air force.'

As instructed, Zannis left as soon as he could – the first train out at midday. But they made slow progress; stopped for a herd of sheep crossing the track, stopped because of overheating after a climb up a long grade, slowed to a crawl in a sudden snowstorm, stopped for no apparent reason at a town on the river Morava, somewhere north of Nis, the name on the station not to be found on the timetable. It was the fault of the engineer, someone said; who had halted the train for a visit with his girlfriend. Late at night, Zannis arrived in Nis, where the train that was to take him south was long gone.

At two-thirty on the afternoon of 27 March, he was again under way, heading for Skoplje. On this train he discovered – wedged into a space beside the seat where it blocked a savage draught – a Greek newspaper, printed early that morning. A new government in Yugoslavia! A coup led by General Simovich and the officer corps of the air force, joined by an army tank brigade. Being a Greek newspaper, it spoke from the heart: the people of this proud Balkan nation were 'defiant', they had 'defied the Nazis', and would continue to 'defy' them – the journalist couldn't get enough of it! 'Hitler denied a victory', 'fury in Berlin', 'a defeat for Fascism', Yugoslav 'bravery', 'determination' and, here it came again, 'defiance'.

On the front page, a grainy photograph: a street packed with marching Serbs, their mouths open in song, some carrying flags and banners, others with pictures, taken down from walls and mantelpieces, of Prince Peter. Whose radio speech from the afternoon of the twenty-sixth was excerpted in a separate story on page two:

> Serbs, Croats, Slovenes! In this moment so grave for our people, I have decided to take the royal power into my own hands ... The Regents have resigned ... I have charged General Simovich with the formation of a new government ... The army and the navy are at my orders ...

The newspaper story carried supportive statements from American and British politicians. The Americans were passionate and blunt, while the British, as was their custom, were rather more reserved.

That same day, in Berlin, the newspapers wrote about Yugoslav 'criminals and opportunists', claiming that ethnic German minorities in northern Serbia and the Banat region were being attacked by Serbian bandits: their houses burned down, their shops looted, their women raped. This was handwriting on the wall. Because such falsehoods had by now become a kind of code: used first in Poland, then in Czechoslovakia, as pretexts for invasion. So the fate of Yugoslavia was that morning already in preparation, and stated openly, for all to see.

One of the people who saw it was Emilia Krebs. She had

done no more than skim the newspaper, being occupied with the departure of yet one more friend who had come to the attention of the Gestapo. This was a tall grey-haired woman of Polish descent, the eminent ethnologist and university professor known simply as Ostrova. *You know he studied with Ostrova. We went to a lecture by Ostrova.* But now, eminence had failed her, and her situation had become perilous. Thus, by eight-thirty, Emilia Krebs had served rolls and coffee, handed Ostrova a set of false documents and wished her safe journey. Certainly the news that morning was disquieting, and they'd talked it over. Yes, there would be war in the Balkans, but not yet. Maybe in a week, they thought. 'So I'd better leave today,' Ostrova said and, if the Hungarians had been forced to close the border, she would find a way through the countryside. The two women embraced, and a determined Ostrova set out for the train to Vienna.

Twenty minutes later, Emilia Krebs was having a second cup of coffee when she heard the chime of the doorbell. Now who could be calling at this hour? Likely one of her fellow conspirators, she guessed, properly afraid to trust the telephone.

However, when she opened the door she faced a man she knew she'd never seen before. Heavily built, with a Prussian haircut, he wore steel-rimmed spectacles and looked, she thought, something like a mathematics teacher at a military academy. But he wasn't that. He announced himself as 'Herr Albert Hauser', but, as it turned out, he wasn't that either, not quite. What he was, he revealed as he sat on her couch, was *Hauptsturmführer* Albert Hauser, of, as he put it, 'the Geheime Staatspolizei'. An official title, the secret state police, simply one more government organization. But in Germany it was common usage to abbreviate this title, which came out 'Gestapo'.

'Oh, that name, it's become so ...' he said, hunting for a polite word but not finding one, and instead finishing, '... you know what I mean, Frau Krebs.'

She did.

'I called because I was wondering if you could shed some

light on the whereabouts of a certain couple. Herr and Frau Gruen?'

Ah yes, she'd known them.

'Good friends of yours?'

Acquaintances.

'Well, it was reported to the local police that they'd disappeared, back in December this was, and when the detectives made no progress, it became my . . . concern.'

Not *case*, she thought. *Concern*. This Gestapo man seemed quite the gentle soul. Perhaps one could be, umm, *forthcoming* with him.

In a pig's eye.

Emilia's hands lay modestly folded in her lap, because she didn't want Hauser to see that they were trembling.

'Unfortunately,' Hauser said, 'I must consider the possibility that they met with foul play. They haven't been seen since then, and there's no record of their having – emigrated.'

They ran for their lives, you Nazi filth. No, she hadn't heard that they'd emigrated, but still, they might've done so. Could the records be at fault?

'Our records, Frau Krebs?'

'Yes, Hauptsturmführer. Yours.'

'I would doubt that.'

Very well. In that case, there was little she could add.

'Please, Frau Krebs, do not misunderstand the nature of this inquiry. We both know that the Gruens were . . . of the Jewish faith. But, even so, our security institutions are responsible for the protection of *all* our German citizens, no matter what people say.'

What people say. Do you mean that you are Jew murderers and should roast in hell for all eternity – that sort of thing? 'Yes, I'm aware of what people say, Herr Hauptsturmführer. Some people.'

'What can we do, *meine Frau*?'

You poor thing.

It went on, but not for long, and Hauser's exterior never

showed the slightest fissure – he was, certainly, beyond courteous. Still, there he was, in her living room, the coffee cup of the fugitive Ostrova sitting on the kitchen counter. He hadn't come in uniform, with three fellow officers, he hadn't kicked down the door, he hadn't smacked her face. Yet, nonetheless, there he was. And, as he prepared to leave, her hands shook so hard she had to clasp them behind her back.

'I wish you a good day, Frau Krebs. I hope I have not intruded.'

He closed the door behind him, it clicked shut, she called an office at the General Staff headquarters and Hugo was home twenty minutes later. It was the worst conversation they had ever had. Because they had to part. She was obviously a suspect, so obviously under surveillance but as long as he stayed where he was, she was safe, she could leave Germany. If they were to attempt to leave together, they would both be arrested.

She took the train to Frankfurt that afternoon. Was she watched? Impossible to know, but she assumed she was. At the grand house in which she'd been raised, she spoke with her grandfather, and together they made their plans. If, he said, it was time for her to leave, then it was also time for him. Since the rise of Hitler in 1933 he'd hoped for the sort of catastrophe that always, sooner or later, brought such people down, but it hadn't happened. Instead, triumph followed triumph. So now came the moment to abandon such folly, as Emilia's grandfather put it, 'and leave these people to their madness.' The next morning, with a single telephone call, he procured exit visas for a week-long vacation in Basel. He did not have to visit an office, he simply sent a clerk over for the papers. 'The general's aide asked that I convey the general's warmest wishes for a pleasant stay in Switzerland,' said the clerk, as he handed Adler a manila envelope. No more than expected, from this general, for Adler had made him a very wealthy general indeed.

★

It was a long drive, ten hours, from Frankfurt to the Swiss border, but Emilia Krebs and her grandfather were comfortable in the luxurious Mercedes motorcar. The cook, saddened because she suspected she would never see them again, had made up a large packet of sandwiches, smoked liverwurst and breast of chicken, and filled a large thermos with coffee. The cook knew what they knew: that even travelling in a chauffeur-driven Mercedes, and looking like powerful and protected people, it was better not to stop. There were Nazi luminaries everywhere along the way and when they drank, which was often, they were liable to forget their manners. The chauffeur drove steadily through the gusty March weather, Emilia Krebs and her grandfather watched the towns go by and, even though the glass partition assured them privacy, only conversed now and then.

'How many did you save, Emmi?' the elder Adler asked.

'I believe it was forty, at least that. We lost one man who was arrested at the Hungarian border, we never learned why, and a pair of sisters, the Rosenblum sisters, who simply vanished. They were librarians, older women; God only knows what happened to them. But that was in the early days, we managed better later on.'

'I am proud of you, Emmi, do you know that? Forty people.'

'We did our best,' she said.

And then, for a time, they did not speak, lost in their own thoughts. Emilia didn't cry, mostly she didn't, she held it in, and kept a handkerchief in her hand for the occasional lapse. Her grandfather was, in his way, also broken-hearted. Seven hundred years of family history in Germany, gone. Finally he said, some minutes later, 'It was the honourable thing to do.'

She nodded, in effect thanking him for kind words. *But we pay a price for honour*, she thought.

So now she paid, so did her husband, so did her grandfather and, for that matter, so would the Yugoslavs, and the Greeks. *Such a cruel price.* Was it always thus? Perhaps, it was something she couldn't calculate, life had somehow grown darker, at times it did. Perhaps that was what people meant by the phrase *the world is coming apart*. But mostly you couldn't question what they meant, because mostly they said it to themselves.

Hours later, they reached the Swiss border. The German customs officer glanced at their papers, put two fingers to the brim of his cap and waved them through. The Swiss officer, as the striped barrier bar was lowered behind them, did much the same. And then they drove on, a few minutes more, into the city of Basel.

29 March. There was little to do in the office – only Sibylla and Zannis there now, and Saltiel's bare desk, his photographs gone. The telephone rang now and then, the Salonika detective units continuing to work because they might as well, while they were waiting. Zannis read the newspaper as long as he could stand it, then threw it in the waste-paper basket. German troop forma-- tions moving south, diplomats said this and that; now it was only a matter of time.

'What will you do, Sibylla, when we close the office? Do you need help? With anything?'

'I've made my arrangements, chief.'

'Yes?'

'I have a job, as a bookkeeper, at the hotel where my husband works. Nice people, the couple that own the place.'

'And if the Germans question you?'

'Maybe they will, maybe they won't, but, if they should, I don't know anything, I was just a secretary. And there's a chance they'll never know I was here. The owners said they would backdate the employment records, if I wanted them to.'

'Will you do that?'

'Maybe. I haven't decided.' After a moment she said, 'I don't know what you have in mind, but, whatever that might be, if you need somebody to help out you only have to ask.'

'Thank you, Sibylla.'

Zannis sat out the day, then went up to see his family at six.

This he dreaded, and he found what he'd known he would: the chaos of departure. The open suitcases, piles of clothing that were never going to fit, a blackened pot that sat on the table, waiting for a miracle. In the middle of all this, his mother was cooking a lamb roast. 'We have a lot to give away,' she said.

'Why not just leave it here?'

'It will be stolen.'

'Oh, you can't be sure of that.'

His mother didn't answer.

'The *Naxos* sails at one-thirty,' he said. 'We'll go an hour early.'

'Well, we have packing to do in the morning. The bedding . . .'

Zannis found the retsina and poured himself a generous portion. 'One for me too, Constantine,' his grandmother said, staring at a ladle, then putting it aside.

The following morning, he telephoned Sibylla and told her he wouldn't be in the office until later, maybe two o'clock. Then he set out for the central market, Melissa rambling along with him, for the errand he couldn't face but now had to. After hunting through the goods in several stalls, he bought a khaki pouch with a shoulder strap, possibly meant for ammunition, from some army in the city's history. Returning home, he went to the kitchen, washed Melissa's dinner and water bowls, wrapped them in newspaper, settled them in the pouch and added her leash; she might just *have* to wear it. Then he went into the other room, but Melissa wasn't there.

The door to the apartment stood open. He only locked it at night, its latch hadn't worked for years, Melissa could push it open with her head. Oh *no*. Hoping against hope, he looked under the bed. No dog. 'Melissa? *Melissa!*'

She knew. Strange mountain beast, she knew what it meant – her only possessions packed up in a khaki pouch.

Zannis trotted down the stairs. He'd thought this through –

there was no possibility she could stay with him. Fighting in the mountain villages meant near starvation – crops burned, houses destroyed – and the animals, even beloved animals, didn't survive it. Out on Santaroza Lane, he called her name, again and again, but there was only morning silence.

He set out on her daily route, finding no help along the way because the street was deserted. He went as far as the corniche, then worked back towards the top of the lane, past the fountain, searching every alley and looking at his watch. By now, he was supposed to be with the family. Where had she gone? Finally he turned into the alley where a neighbour kept her chicken coop and, at the very end, there she was. Lying on her stomach, head resting on crossed paws, looking as miserably sad as any dog he'd ever seen. He squatted by her side and stroked her head. 'I'm sorry,' he said. 'You know you're going away, don't you. Well, good girl, it has to be. Now you have to take care of the family.' When he stood up, so did she, and walked back to the apartment, head carried low, close to his side. Facing the inevitable.

He arrived at the house in the Turkish quarter after eleven and shooed the family along in the last hectic stages of packing – God only knew what would be forgotten. He made sure that his mother put a packet of money in a safe place – the envelope pinned to the inside of her coat. Made Ari responsible for Melissa's travelling bag, looping the strap over his shoulder. Secured his grandmother's valise with a length of cord. And found a taxi.

By twelve-thirty they reached the dock; the *Naxos* already had steam up. Spreading out from the foot of the gangway, a great mob of people, some two hundred of them. And loud – babies wailing, people arguing and swearing, or shouting to friends. He manoeuvred the family towards the gangway, then settled in to wait until they would be permitted to board. The tickets! Frantically he patted his clothing, eventually discovering he'd moved them to a safer pocket. Now a few harassed customs officials appeared and tried to form the mob, hauling trunks and suitcases and bags, into a queue. But, clearly, that wasn't going to work.

Suddenly, gunfire.

The rhythmic thump of Bofors cannon. Amid screams, as people dived to the ground, Zannis searched the horizon. Far above the puffs of exploding shells in a blue sky, a small aircraft, perhaps a German reconnaissance plane. Some officer at the anti-aircraft battery down the bay had evidently spotted the insignia with his binoculars and given the order to fire. No chance of hitting it, not at that altitude. And the plane didn't evade, simply circled the city, then turned out to sea and disappeared into the haze. From the crowd, more than a few cheers. An old man, standing near Zannis, said, 'Where is our air force?'

The gunfire had certainly affected the passengers on the wharf. What had been an unruly mob now formed itself into a long queue, leading to a wooden table and two customs officers sitting on folding chairs. When it was the turn of the Zannis family, he hugged and kissed them all, knelt and embraced Melissa, now miraculously wearing her leash, and, taking his glasses off to wipe his eyes, watched their blurred forms wave goodbye as they climbed the gangway.

In the office, a telegram awaited him, sent from Basel.

HAD TO GO AWAY STOP BUSINESS CLOSED STOP MAY GOD WATCH OVER YOU STOP SIGNED FRIEND FROM BERLIN

'At least she's safe,' Sibylla said. 'And I suppose the operation couldn't go on forever.'

'No, I guess it couldn't. Maybe someone else might have taken over, but with war coming in Yugoslavia that won't be possible.'

'She did what she could,' Sibylla said.

'Yes,' Zannis said. 'She did.'

Next he went off to the Bank of Commerce and Deposit on Victoros Hougo Street. He'd paid for the family steamship tickets with his own money, but he wasn't going to abandon the secret fund – money was crucial to resistance. He was, however, not the only person in town that afternoon clearing his account. There were fourteen people in the queue ahead of him – all waiting for the bank officer who handled 'special accounts'.

The man was not holding up well; he seemed to Zannis pale and anxious. 'I regret, sir, there are no dollars, not any more. Maybe tomorrow, we might have some, but I wouldn't wait, if I were you.'

'No British money? Gold sovereigns?'

The man closed his eyes and shook his head. 'No, sir. Not for weeks. Gold is very desirable now.'

'What do you have left?'

'Drachmas, of course. Spanish pesetas and Swiss francs.'

'Swiss francs,' Zannis said.

The officer, having set the account's file card down before him, went into the vault and returned with a metal drawer that held packets of Swiss francs, a pin forced through the corner of each stack of one hundred. 'Do you have a briefcase, sir?'

Zannis produced it and, recalling the French king in the back of his royal motorcar, slid the packets into the case.

When he returned to the office, he found a message to telephone a detective in the second district. 'Costa Zannis,' he said. 'You telephoned?'

'Somebody threw a brick through the window of the German legation,' the detective said. 'Would that be something for your office?'

'Did you talk to them?'

'Yes. I went over there and wrote up a report. The consul was in a real fury.'

'He was, was he.'

'Oh yes. Red in the face, sputtering.'

Zannis laughed. 'First good news today.'

'I guess that means you don't care.'

'Well, I can't help him.'

'You should've seen it,' the detective said. 'It was really wonderful.'

Eventually, Zannis had to return to Santaroza Lane; he had nowhere else to go. Spring was heavy in the air that afternoon, and the two old women had their kitchen chairs out, gossiping in the last of the sunshine. As always they were pleased to see him. One of them said, 'By the way, your telephone's been ringing most of the afternoon.'

'It has?'

'Somebody's been trying to reach you.'

Zannis hurried upstairs. The apartment was very still without Melissa. He sat on the edge of the bed and waited, but the phone didn't ring for another forty minutes. 'Yes? Hello?'

'Finally! It's me, Costa.' Demetria, her voice strong and sweet.

'Where are you?' The connection was suspiciously clear.

'Not far. I'm in Salonika.'

'You've come home?' he said.

'No, that's finished.' She paused, then said, 'I'm at the Lux Palace, in 601, the suite on the top floor.'

'I'll be right there,' he said.

It turned out to be the same suite where he'd first met Emilia Krebs. When Demetria opened the door, they stared at each other for a long moment. *Well, now it's happened, I hope you meant it.* He rested his hands on her shoulders, wanting a good long look at her, his prize. She was wearing the bronze silk blouse and pearl necklace she'd had on the first time he'd seen her, in the back of the Rolls-Royce. Finally she raised her face, and he touched his lips to her smile.

'Well then,' she said. 'Maybe you should come inside.'

She gestured to the sofa, sat down at the other end, then

moved closer. For a time they didn't speak, their alliance settling on them amid the ambient sounds from the open window – seagulls, car horns, voices in the street. At last he said, 'Was it very bad?'

'Bad enough,' she said. 'I'm going to call down for something to drink, what would you like?'

'French wine? Champagne?'

As she went to the telephone, he watched her walk. Not that she overdid it, but she knew his eyes were following her. After she'd ordered champagne, she returned to the sofa. 'I suppose I could have done that while you were on the way but then I didn't know if you'd want a room service waiter . . . knocking on the door . . .'

'We have time,' he said. 'What a luxury that is.'

She looked into his eyes, excited to be with him, in love with him, and put a warm hand atop his. But she did this instead of responding to what he'd said. Because there wasn't very much time, she just didn't have the heart to say it. 'Yes,' she said. 'A luxury.'

His eye fell on an open suitcase that stood on a luggage rack. 'Is that all you brought?'

'Oh no, there's more in the baggage room. You should see what I brought. That's why I waited until we came back to Salonika. Then I told him.'

'How did he take it?'

'He was ice cold. He knew, I think. Either in his mean little heart, sensed I wasn't with him any more, or his spies told him what was going on.'

'It doesn't matter.'

'No, he's too busy settling his affairs before he leaves, to think about revenge.'

'He's going to America?'

She nodded. 'I would've liked to see it, but—'

A knock on the door. 'Room service.'

★

They drank the champagne, touching glasses in a silent toast. Zannis poured a second, then a third, and the effect was powerful. Darkness gathered outside the window, the last drifts of sunlit cloud low on the horizon. Demetria said it was beautiful, then she yawned. 'Oh God, forgive me – I couldn't help it.'

'You're tired, I'm not surprised, and the champagne ...'

'I'm exhausted.'

'Me too. A very difficult day, until you called.'

'Maybe we should sleep.'

'Why not? We'll stay here tonight, then—'

'Oh, we can stay as long as we like.'

'It's expensive, no?'

She shrugged. 'I don't think I'm rich, but I have a lot of money. He gave me money, I saved it. And there's more.'

'More?'

'I'll show you.' She went to her suitcase and returned with a slim elongated package – heavy oilcloth wound tight and secured with a waxed cord. 'A gift from Vasilou,' she said. 'He used to go up to the monasteries and buy things from the monks.' Carefully, she unwound the oilcloth, then burlap sacking, and held up a parchment scroll wrapped around a spindle. Very delicately, she extended the parchment. 'See? It's a royal decree, from Byzantium.'

The writing was strange; Zannis couldn't read it. At the bottom, a series of flourishes that glittered in the lamplight.

'The emperor's signature,' she said. 'Basil II. When the emperor signed a decree, it was sprinkled with gold dust and ground cinnabar, that's why it sparkles.'

Zannis peered at it. 'Well, if you're going to sign a decree ... Seems like we've lost something in the modern government service.'

She smiled, carefully rewrapping the scroll. 'Vasilou had a professor at the university read it. It orders a water system – for some city that no longer exists.'

As she returned the package to her suitcase, Zannis laid his head back against the sofa and, for a moment, closed his eyes. Then she said, 'Very well, that does it.'

She turned out the lamp and they undressed, she down to bra and panties while he, following her example, stayed in his underwear. She took his hand and led him to the bed, they crawled under the covers – exquisitely soft and fluffy in there – held each other, and fell asleep. For an hour. Then he woke, because she had unbuttoned the front of his underpants and was holding him in her hand.

Later, they really slept. And the next thing he knew she'd woken him by kissing him on the forehead. 'What time is it?' she said, urgency in her voice.

He reached a hand towards the night table, found his watch, put on his glasses and said, 'Eight minutes past six.'

'Something I want to see, so don't go back to sleep.'

They waited until six-thirty; then she led him to the window. From here – standing naked, side by side and holding hands – they could look out over the span of the harbour. Down at the dock, the white ship sounded its horn, two blasts, and moved slowly out into the Aegean. 'There it goes,' she said.

They put it off – a certain conversation, the inevitable conversation. Were very determined to leave it in the future, because they meant to have as much of this love affair as they could. So they made love in the late afternoon – first one kind of seduction, then another – decided to see every movie in Salonika, and ate everything in sight. A taverna he knew, one she knew, why hold back? Not now, they wouldn't, and money no longer mattered. They ate spiced whipped feta, they ate calamari stuffed with cheese, they ate grilled octopus and grilled aubergine and mussels with rice pilaf and creamy thick yogurt with honey. Zannis didn't go to the office on the first day, he just didn't, and then he did it again. They walked along the sea, over to the amusement park in the Beschinar Gardens and rode the Ferris wheel. Of course, being out in the streets, there were traps laid for them:

newspaper headlines in thick black print, posted on the kiosks. Reflexively, he started to comment on one of them but she put a finger to his lips and her eyes were fierce. So much warrior in Demetria, it surprised him. They weren't so different.

Finally, after two lost days, he went to the Via Egnatia on the third of April. No more than a raised eyebrow from Sibylla. 'A certain Englishman has been frantic to reach you,' she told him. 'He called and called and then, yesterday morning, he showed up here. Escovil, is that the name? Anyhow, he had a valise with him, and he left you an envelope. On your desk.'

Zannis sat in his chair and stared at it, an oversize yellow envelope, thick paper, you couldn't buy a more expensive envelope than that, he thought. Still, fancy as it was, only a paper envelope, and, with thumbs and forefingers, you could rip it in half. Sibylla was busy typing something, clackety-clack, what the hell had she found to do as the world came to an end? In his mind, he saw himself as he tore the envelope in two; then he opened it. A single sheet of notepaper, the message handwritten in Greek. 'This is for 5 April; you won't be able to travel after that.' No signature. And what was 'this'? *The hand of the gods*, Zannis said to himself. Because it was a steamship ticket for, of all ships, the *Bakir* out of Galata, Istanbul, the same tramp steamer that had brought a German spy to Salonika last October. A Turkish ship, the ship of a neutral nation, thus safe from German submarines and bound, at 2100 hours on 5 April, for Alexandria, Egypt.

So now they would have to have the conversation. Zannis, the ticket folded up in the inside pocket of his jacket, walked slowly, as slowly as he could, back to the Lux Palace. It just wasn't far enough away, not at that moment it wasn't, and, too soon, he rode the ancient grilled elevator to the sixth floor. At his knock, Demetria swept the door wide and gestured with the hand of a stage magician. Presto! Believe your eyes if you can! She had bought at least two dozen vases, no, more, and filled each of them with flowers, red and yellow, white and blue, anemones, roses, carnations, an entire flower stall it seemed. The air was dense with aroma. 'I took two hotel porters to the market,' she said. 'And I could have used another. We *staggered*.'

Enchanting. Well, it was. He touched a finger to the steamship ticket in his pocket, but he couldn't show it to her now – not when she'd done all this. Demetria circled around him and slid his jacket down his arms. 'Come and sit with me on the sofa,' she said. 'And behold! Demetria's garden.'

4 April. 7.20 a.m. Half awake, he reached out for her – he would stroke her awake, and he would do more than that. But he found only a warm place on her side of the bed, so opened one eye halfway. She was all business, getting dressed. 'Where are you going?'

'To St Cyril's, to the eight o'clock Mass.'

'Oh.'

Soon he watched her go out of the door, then fell back to a morning doze. But fifteen minutes later, she reappeared, looking grim and disappointed. 'What happened?' he said.

'Jammed. Packed solid. I couldn't even get in the door.'

Finally, at mid-morning, as they lazed around the suite, it was time. He'd let it go for a day, but now the moment had come; she would have only that day and the next – the *Bakir* was due to sail at nine in the evening – to prepare to leave. She was reading in an easy chair by the window – they'd found other uses for that chair – and he retrieved the ticket from his jacket and laid it on the table by her side.

'What's that, Costa?'

'Your steamship ticket.'

She was silent for a time, then said, 'When?'

'Tomorrow night.'

'What makes you think I'll use it?'

'You must, Demetria.'

'Oh? And you?'

'I have to stay.'

She stared at the ticket. 'I guess I knew it would be this way.'

'What did you intend to do, if the war came here?'

'Stay in Salonika. Even if we lose, and the Germans take the city, it won't be so bad. They say Paris isn't bad.'

'This isn't Paris. To the Germans, it's closer to Warsaw, and Warsaw is very bad. No food. No coal. But that isn't the worst of it. You are a very beautiful and desirable woman. When you walk down the street, every man turns his head, and such women are like ... like treasure, to an occupying army, and they *take* treasure.'

'I can dye my hair.'

From Zannis, a very rueful half-smile: *as though that would matter.*

She thought for a time, started to say something, thought better of it, then changed her mind again. 'I thought you would protect me.' *From Vasilou, from the world.*

'I would try, but ...' He left it there, then said, 'And they will come after me, they have a score to settle with me, and these people settle their scores. So I will work against them, but I believe I'll have to go up to one of the mountain villages and fight from there. Not right away, the war could go on for six months, maybe more. Look what we did with the Italians.'

'These are not Italians, Costa.'

'No, they're not. So ...' He nodded towards the ticket. 'It isn't forever. I'll find you, we'll be together again, no matter what it takes.'

'I love you, Costa, with all my heart I love you, but I am Greek, and I know what goes on when we fight in the mountains.' She reached out and gripped his hand. 'As God wills,' she said, 'but I can only *hope*, to see you again.' She looked away from him, out of the window, then down at the floor. Finally, her eyes turned back to his. 'I won't resist,' she said quietly. 'I'll go, go to' – she squinted at the ticket – 'to Alexandria. Not Istanbul?'

'The ship is going to Alexandria.'

'Won't I need a visa?'

'Too late. The Egyptians will give you one when you land; you'll have to pay for that but they'll do it.'

She nodded, then let go of him and covered her eyes with her hands, as though she were very tired. 'Just fuck this horrible world,' she said.

And then, it all came apart.

They decided that Demetria would repack for the voyage: take what was valuable, then bring the rest out to the house in Kalamaria and say goodbye to her mother. Meanwhile, Zannis had several things to do, and they agreed to meet back at the hotel at three.

Zannis went first to his apartment, to retrieve the Walther – better to carry it, now. The weather had turned to grey skies and drizzling rain, so the ladies were not out on their kitchen chairs, but one of them must have been watching at her window. Upstairs, he wandered around the apartment, coming slowly to understand that all was not as it should be. Had he been robbed? He didn't think so; he could find nothing missing. Still, the door to the armoire was ajar, had he left it like that? Usually he didn't. He tried to remember, but that night was a blur; he'd hurried away when Demetria called, so ... But then, a chair was pushed up close to the table – a neat and proper position for a chair, but not its usual place.

As he poked around, he heard a hesitant knock at the door. It was one of his neighbours. He asked her in, but she remained on the landing and said, 'I just wanted to tell you that some friends of yours came to see you yesterday.'

'They did?'

'Yes. Two men, well dressed; they didn't look like thieves. We saw them go into the house, and my friend on the ground floor wasn't home, so they must have been ... waiting for you. That's what we decided.'

'How long were they there?'

'An hour? Maybe a little less.'

'Any idea who they were?'

'No, not really. I don't think they were Greek, though.'

'You . . . overheard them speak?'

'It's not that, they didn't say anything, just . . . something about them. I'm probably wrong, perhaps they came from Athens.'

Zannis thanked her, then retrieved his Walther and ammunition and headed for the Via Egnatia. *They're already here*, he thought. *And I must be high on their list.*

At the office, he hung up his coat and left his umbrella open so it would dry. Then he said, 'I think today's the day, Sibylla. For getting rid of the files.'

She agreed. 'It's any time now, the Yugoslavs have mobilized.'

'I haven't seen the papers.'

'Well, all the news is bad. The German army is now at the border between Hungary and Yugoslavia. Though the Hungarians, according to the newspaper, have issued a protest.'

'To who?'

'I don't know, maybe just to the world, in general.' She started to go back to work, then stopped. 'Oh, before I forget, two men showed up here yesterday, asking for you.'

'Who were they?'

'Greek-speaking foreigners. Polite enough. Were you expecting them?'

'No.'

'What if they return?'

'You know nothing about me, get rid of them.'

It took, for Sibylla to understand, only a beat or two. Then she said, 'Germans? Already?'

Zannis nodded. 'It doesn't matter,' he said. 'And we have work to do.' He began to take his five-by-eight card files out of the desk drawer. 'We'll have to burn the dossiers as well,' he said.

'You read the name,' Sibylla said, 'and I'll pull them.'

He looked at the first card – *ABRAVIAN, Alexandre, General Manager, Shell Petroleum Refinery* – and said, 'Abravian.'

In time, they carried the first load down the stairs. Out in the tiny courtyard, enclosed by high walls, the sound of the rain pattering on the stone block had a strange depth to it, perhaps an echo. One of the rusty old barrels Zannis had chosen was half full, so he decided to use the other one. He crumpled up pages from Sibylla's newspaper and stuffed them in the bottom, knelt and used a rusted-through slit to start the fire. Burning papers, that ancient tradition of invaded cities, turned out to be something of an art – best to drop them in a few at a time so you didn't starve the fire of oxygen. A greyish-white smoke rose into the sky, along with blackened flakes of ash that floated back down into the puddles on the floor of the courtyard.

It took more than an hour, Sibylla working with mouth set in a grim line. She was very angry – this had been her work and she had done it with care and precision – and they didn't converse, beyond the few words necessary to people who are working together, because there was nothing to say.

When they were done, they returned to the office. Zannis stayed for a time, making sure there was nothing there for the Germans to exploit, then put on his coat. As he was doing up the buttons, the telephone rang and Sibylla answered. 'It's for you,' she said.

'Who is it?' He didn't want to be late getting back to the hotel.

'The commissioner's secretary. I think you'd better talk to her.'

Zannis took the phone and said, 'Yes?'

The voice on the other end was strained, and barely under control – somewhere between duty and sorrow. 'I'm afraid I have bad news for you. Commissioner Vangelis has died, by his own hand. At one-thirty this afternoon, he used his service revolver.'

She waited, but Zannis couldn't speak.

'He left' – she took a deep breath – 'several notes, there's one for you. You're welcome to come over here and pick it up, or I can read it to you now.'

'You can read it,' Zannis said.

'"Dear Costa: you have been a godson to me, and a good one. I have known, over the years, every sort of evil, but I do not choose to tolerate the evil that is coming to us now, so I am leaving before it arrives. As for you, you must go away, for this is not the time and not the place to give up your life." And he signs it, "Vangelis." Shall I keep the note for you?'

After a moment, Zannis said, 'Yes, I'll come by and pick it up. Tomorrow. What about the family?'

'They've been told.'

'I'm sorry,' he said. 'He was—'

She cut him off and said, 'There will be a service, we don't know where, but I'll let you know And now, I have other calls to make.'

'Yes, of course, I understand,' Zannis said and hung up the phone.

5 April. 8.20 p.m. The captain of the tramp steamer *Bakir* had six passengers for Alexandria and no empty cabins, so he showed them to the wardroom. At least they could share the battered couches for the two-day trip across the Mediterranean – it was the best he could do and he knew it really didn't matter. The other five passengers – an army officer, a naval officer and three civilians – had obtained passage, Zannis suspected, the same way he had: by means of the discreet yellow envelope. One of the civilians was prosperously fat, with a pencil-thin moustache, very much the Levantine, all he needed was a tarboosh. The second, thin and stooped, might have been a university professor – of some arcane discipline – while the third was not unlike Zannis; well-built, watchful and reserved. They spoke a little, the man knew who Zannis was and had worked, he said, for Spiraki. And where was Spiraki? Nobody knew. He said. And if they were surprised to find that a woman, a woman like Demetria, was

joining them, they did not show it. What the British did, they did, they had their reasons, and here we all are.

At twenty minutes to nine, the captain appeared in the ward-room. Zannis stood up – if the ship was about to sail, he had to get off. 'You can sit back down,' the captain said. 'We're not going anywhere. Not tonight we're not, problems in the engine room. We'll get it fixed by about eight, tomorrow morning, so, if you and your wife, or any of you, want to spend the night ashore, you may do that.'

Zannis and Demetria looked at each other, then Zannis ges-tured towards the passageway. He picked up Demetria's two suitcases, one of which was very heavy. 'Silver,' she'd told him when he asked. 'Something you can always sell.'

Back at the Lux Palace, Suite 601 had not been taken, so Zannis and Demetria rode back up in the elevator. The flowers were gone. 'Likely the maids took them home,' Demetria said. 'I hope so, anyhow.'

'Are you hungry?'

'No. The opposite.'

'Me too.'

'I was ready to leave,' she said. 'Now this.'

Zannis sat on the sofa. 'Well, a few more hours together,' he said. He certainly didn't regret it.

She managed a smile, weak, but a smile. Without saying anything, they agreed that the idea of making love one last time did not appeal to either of them, not at that moment it didn't. They talked for a while, and eventually undressed and tried to sleep, without much success, lying silent in the darkened room. And they were still awake at dawn, as early light turned the clouds to pearl grey, when the first bombs fell on Salonika.

The first one hit somewhere near the hotel – they could feel the explosion and the sound was deafening – and sent Zannis rolling onto the floor, pulling the blankets on top of him. He struggled to his knees and looking across the bed saw Demetria –

the same thing had happened to her – staring back at him. He got to his feet and headed for the window, which had cracked from corner to corner. She was immediately behind him, her arms wrapped around his chest, her body pressed against his back. Down on the waterfront he was able, after searching the line of docked ships, to find the *Bakir*. She was tilted awry, with a column of heavy black smoke rising from the foredeck. 'Can you see the *Bakir*?' he said.

She looked over his shoulder. 'Which one is it?'

'The one on fire. I mean, the second one on fire, in the middle.'

'What should we do?'

Towards the eastern end of the city, the smoke and thunder of an explosion; then, two seconds later, another one, closer, then, two seconds, another, each one marching towards them as bombs tumbled down from the clouds. Her arms tightened around him – all they could do was watch and, silently, count. Three blocks away, the roof of a building flashed and a wall fell into the street. One second, two. But there it stopped. From the far end of the corniche, long strings of orange tracer rounds floated upwards aimed at a dive-bomber heading directly at the battery. The gunners didn't stop, the pilot didn't pull up and the plane caught fire just before it crashed into the guns.

After that, silence. Well to the east, where the oil storage tanks were located, the rolling black smoke of burning oil had climbed high into the air. 'The railway station,' Zannis said. 'Our only chance.' They dressed quickly and took the stairs down to the ground floor, Zannis carrying Demetria's suitcases.

In the lobby, the hotel staff and a few guests were gathered around a radio. 'The Germans have set Belgrade on fire,' the head porter said, 'and they're attacking Fort Rupel with para-troops, but the fort still holds.'

The Rupel Pass, Zannis thought, fifty miles north of Salonika. He'd found photographs of the fort carried by a German spy in the Albala spice warehouse, back in October. Now, if the

Wehrmacht broke through, they'd be in the city in a few days. 'Is there a train this morning?' Zannis said. 'Heading east?'

The head porter looked at his watch. 'It left. Should have, twenty minutes ago but who knows, this morning. Still, if they can run they will, that's how it is with us.'

Zannis picked up Demetria's suitcases. As he did he saw Sami Pal, sitting in a chair in the corner, reading a newspaper, a cup of coffee by his side. Sami Pal? The Hungarian gangster? At the Lux Palace? But Sami seemed to be doing well, wore an expensive sky-blue overcoat, and, absorbed in his reading, apparently did not see Zannis.

Out in the street, a carpet of shattered glass sparkled in the early light. 'Off we go,' Zannis said. There were no taxis, no cars of any kind, though he could hear sirens in the distance. Demetria and Zannis moved at a fast trot, taking the corniche, coughing from the acrid smoke that hung in the air. 'Are you all right?' Zannis said.

Demetria nodded, breathing hard, a line of soot around her mouth and below her nostrils. 'We'll get there,' she said.

It took fifteen minutes. The station had been hit – a hole in the roof and a black crater in the floor of the platform – but there was a train. Perhaps it had been scheduled to leave but people were still trying to jam themselves into the carriages. A conductor stood by the door of one of the coaches. 'Where's it going?' Zannis said.

'It's the Athens–Alexandroupolis Express, one stop at Kavala, but it may go all the way to Turkey.'

'Why would it go to Turkey?' Demetria said.

'Because it's a Turkish train. Eventually it goes to Edirne, but, today . . .'

'Do we need tickets?' Zannis said.

The conductor laughed. 'We don't care this morning, try to get on if you can.'

The train was packed. At the far end, only four people were standing on the steps of the coach and there was room for one more. Demetria forced her way onto the first step, then put a foot on the second. Above her, a large angry man shoved her back. 'No room up here,' he said. His face – pitted skin, a well-trimmed beard – was knotted with rage.

'Make a space for the lady, sir,' Zannis said. He started to help Demetria up to the step, but this time the man pushed with both hands on her shoulders. Zannis led her back down onto the platform, then turned, climbed on the first step and hit the man in the throat. The man made a choking noise, a woman screamed, and Zannis hit him again, knuckles extended, between the ribs, in the heart, and he folded in two. The woman next to him had to grab him or he would have fallen. 'Now make room,' Zannis said. 'Or I will finish this.'

The man moved aside. Demetria stood with one of the suitcases upended between her legs. Zannis was wondering what to do with the other suitcase when Demetria reached down and grabbed him by the lapel. 'Please don't leave me here,' she said. Beside her, the bearded man was staring at her with pure hatred. Zannis climbed up on the first step and held on to the railing, straddling the second suitcase. He would, he thought, get off at Kavala. When the train jerked forward, Zannis stumbled, put one foot on the platform and, using the handrail, hauled himself back on. The train jerked again, the crowd on the platform was still trying to find a way to board. Somebody yelled, 'The roof! Get on the roof!' Slowly, the train picked up speed. One more man climbed on the bottom step, forcing Zannis against the railing. 'Beg pardon,' the man said.

'Can't be helped,' Zannis said.

An hour passed, then another. They crossed from Macedonia into the province of Thrace, the train chugged past flat farm fields, always twelve miles from the coast. The Turks had built this in the days of the Ottoman Empire and set the tracks inland so that military transport trains could not be bombarded by enemy naval vessels. Zannis hung on every time the train rounded a bend, the gravel by the track only inches from his feet, his hand freezing where it gripped the iron railing. They would soon be in Kavala, where he'd intended to leave the train, but he had two problems. The bearded ape above him, swaying next to Demetria, and the Turkish border post – if the train went that far. Demetria had no entry visa and Zannis well remembered what had happened to Emilia Krebs when she'd tried to bribe her way past the customs officials.

In the event, it was the train's enginer who made the decision. He did not slow down for Kavala, he speeded up. Zannis soon saw why. On the station platform, a huge mob of people yelled and waved as the train rumbled past them.

And then, another two hours on, at Alexandroupolis station, the same.

'Where's he taking us?' the man next to Zannis said.

'Edirne. Turkey.'

'Well, my wife is waiting for me in Alexandroupolis. She will be extremely annoyed.'

Zannis shrugged. 'We're at war,' he said.

Edirne. 3.50 p.m. Slowly, the passengers climbed down off the train and joined a long snake of a queue, maintained by Greek and Turkish gendarmes who tapped their palms with wooden batons by way of enforcing discipline. Rumours ran up and down the queue – some people had visas, and they were allowed to enter Turkey. Those who didn't were being sent back to Greece. This was apparently the case, since a crowd of passengers, looking weary and defeated, began to gather on the Greek side of the customs post.

'Will we get in?' Demetria said.

'We'll try.'

'Do you need money?'

'I have Swiss francs, more than enough.' *If they'll take them.* But they wouldn't.

When Zannis and Demetria approached the desk, the Turkish officer said, 'Passports and visas, please.'

276

'Here are the passports,' Zannis said. 'We have no visas.'

'You will return to Greece. *Next!*'

Zannis brought his hand from his pocket, holding a wad of Swiss francs. The officer met his eyes and began to tap a pencil on his table. 'If you dare—' he said.

'Excuse me.' This was reeled off in several languages: German, Spanish, French and English, by a man who had somehow appeared at the table. The officer stared at him – what did he want? Who was he? Bald, with a fringe of dark hair, spectacles and a sparse moustache, he wasn't much: a short, inconsequential little fellow in a tired suit, Mr Nobody from Nowhere. Now that he had their attention, he consulted a slip of paper in his hand and, speaking to Zannis in French, said, 'You are Strathos?'

'No, Zannis. Constantine Zannis.'

The man studied the paper. 'Oh, of course, my mistake, you're Zannis. Strathos is somebody else.' He turned to the officer, drew an envelope from the inside pocket of his jacket, slid out a letter typed in Turkish and showed it to the officer. Who stood, saluted Zannis and said, 'Forgive me, Captain Zannis, but I didn't realize ... You are not in uniform. The lady is with you?'

'She is.'

'Please,' he said, his hand extended, welcoming them to Turkey.

As the little man led them towards a dusty Renault, Zannis said, 'Captain Zannis?'

'That's right. You're an officer in the British army. Didn't you know?'

'I didn't,' Zannis said.

'Oh well,' said the little man. 'Always surprises, in this life.'

Once the suitcases had been put in the boot and they were under way, the little man got around to introducing himself. 'S. Kolb,' he said. 'That's what some people call me, though most don't call me anything at all. And, unfortunately, there are those who call me terrible names, but I try, when that happens, to be elsewhere.'

Zannis translated for Demetria, sitting in the back seat. Then said to Kolb, 'We're going south, not to Istanbul.'

'We're going to Smyrna. I mean, Izmir. I can never get used to that.'

He was a woeful driver, gripping the wheel as though he meant to choke it, squinting through the cloudy window, slow as a snail and impervious to the horns honking behind him. After battling his way around a gentle bend, he said, 'You'll work there, in Smyrna – ah, Izmir. Though I think they meant for you to be in Alexandria, to begin with. Meetings, you know, with the big brass.'

'We couldn't get to Alexandria, a bomb hit the ship at the dock.' Zannis wondered, briefly, how Kolb knew he'd come to Edirne by rail, then recalled Sami Pal, sitting in the lobby of the Lux Palace.

'The *Bakir*?'

'Yes.'

'Hmm, too bad, I liked the old *Bakir*. Anyway, a lot of Greeks are coming out of the country, and a few of them we'll send back. Resistance operations, spy missions, the usual, into occupied Greece. And we want you to run the Smyrna part of that – it's an important job. Ever been there?'

'I haven't.'

'Well, there's a big British expatriate community, and you'll find a way to get along with the Turks, no?'

'Of course,' Zannis said.

'You'll have to sign a few papers, but there's time for that.' Zannis turned halfway around in the seat, hung his arm over the back and told Demetria what Kolb had said. 'Smyrna, of all places,' was her only response, though she took his hand for a moment. A small gesture, for a couple who had indulged themselves in every possible intimacy, but it meant something, that late afternoon in Turkey, *we're safe for the moment, safe from a brutal world, and together*, something like that.

★

On 27 April 1941, Wehrmacht forces occupied Athens and, at 8.35 that morning, German motorcycle troops appeared at the Acropolis and raised the swastika flag. Some weeks later, at the end of May, two Athenian teenagers slipped past German sentries and took it down.

From the *Tulsa Star-Tribune*, 5 June 1942:

A new bookstore is coming to town. Two of our newer residents, the sisters Hedy and Frieda Rosenblum, will be opening The Bookmark tomorrow at 46 S. Cheyenne Ave. next to Corky's Downtown Café. The Rosenblum sisters, who've been working at the library, were brought to town under the sponsorship of Dr Harry Gutmann, a local dentist, from New York City. Before that, they managed to escape from Hitler's Nazis and are writing a book about their experiences. The Bookmark will carry all the latest bestsellers and will have a special section for children's books.

Not
The End

Go to channel4.com/tvbookclub for more great reads,
brought to you by Specsavers.

Enjoy a good read with